Diesel
ROSE

VANESSA LUISA

Remember I'm Yours & Diesel Rose
Cover Design: Lori Jackson
Editor: Ellie McLove, Emily A. Lawrence
Proofreader: Emily A. Lawrence, Gemma Woolley
Formatter: Stacey at Champagne Book Design

This book contains mature content.

AUTHOR'S NOTE

This edition includes the prequel, *REMEMBER I'M YOURS*. If you've already read it, you may skip to *DIESEL ROSE,* the full-length novel to Elijah & Rosalia's story.

Please Note: **Remember I'm Yours: Prequel to Diesel Rose** MUST be read first in order to understand the full-length book, *Diesel Rose.*

Happy reading! xo

Remember I'm Yours: A Prequel to Diesel Rose

From the moment I gazed into his melancholic onyx eyes, *I knew he would be mine.*

Elijah Diesel isn't just my gorgeous, older, mysterious obsession, he's also the lead vocalist of an up-and-coming alternative rock band due to take the world by storm.

He wanted nothing to do with me.
Yet he kept coming back.
And I let him.

And now, only one thing is certain.
This won't be the end of us…
Because it's only just our beginning.

NOTE: This is a 25,000-word prequel novella for DIESEL ROSE. The story concludes in DIESEL ROSE.

For all the monsters under the bed who end up saving lives
with their dark poetry...

And to Mamma, Nonna, and Nonno,
My love for you all is infinite.
<3

"Things are sweeter when they're lost."

F. SCOTT FITZGERALD, *THE BEAUTIFUL AND DAMNED*

"I said maybe
You're gonna be the one that saves me
And after all
You're my wonderwall."

OASIS, 'WONDERWALL'

Playlist

"Scary Love"—The Neighbourhood
"SUPERMODEL"—Måneskin
"Brooklyn Baby"—Lana Del Ray
"Tell Me The Truth"—Two Feet
"Wonderwall"—Oasis
"Beetlejuice chill"—Life After Youth
"Baby Came Home 2 / Valentines"—The Neighbourhood
"Enemy (with JD)"—Imagine Dragons, JID, Arcane, League of
Legends
"True Rocker"—Monster Truck, Dee Snider
"Triggered"—Chase Atlantic
"IN NOME DEL PADRE"—Måneskin
"Flawless"—The Neighbourhood
"Cherry"—Lana Del Ray
"Like A God"—Lia Marie Johnson
"Devil's Advocate"—The Neighbourhood
"Scary People"—Georgi Kay
"Love Become Law"—The Cherry Truck Band, Black Stone Cherry,
Monster Truck

Remember
I'M YOURS

A PREQUEL TO DIESEL ROSE

Chapter
ONE

Rosalia

I think I have a boy crush. Okay, let me rephrase that, I *do* have a boy crush.

One of my favorite things to do at a quarter to midnight whenever I can't sleep is scrapbook. My mom is a hairdresser downtown and always brings home old magazines clients flick through so I can cut out whatever I like. At first, it gave me the heebie-jeebies touching magazines a dozen other women (and possibly men too) had touched, but now I guess I'm over it.

Tonight was supposed to be like any other night. Flip through the magazines, cut out aesthetically pleasing vintage pieces with my pink diamanté scissors, and slap them in my scrapbook. Except, tonight *isn't* like any other night, it's different, because my mom didn't only bring home old editions of *Vogue* and *Harper's Bazaar* in a white plastic bag that's laced with holes. There's also something else.

Rolling Stone magazine.

And the good thing is, it's the latest edition.

May.

She's never brought a *Rolling Stone* magazine home for me before, and I wonder if she accidentally got it from the barber section at her work. I wasn't going to look through it, but I did, and *God,* how grateful I am that I did.

It's the first page I randomly opened on.

Page twelve.

And I haven't dared look away since.

Dark-gray eyes, the lightest shade of onyx stare back at me. They're the kind of eyes that are so cold, they should scare you. Instead, they have a sense of sugary thrill flooding my body. They're devilish. Wolfish. Everything my parents warned me about. *And everything I crave.*

My heart skips a beat because he's the most beautiful man I've seen, in a dark and edgy kind of way. A deadly piercing gaze. Perfectly high cheekbones. Thin full lips that remind me of James Dean's.

Everything about the black-and-white picture of this man leaning against a barbed-wire fence intrigues me. His punk-inspired leather jacket with silvery spikes around his shoulders and safety pins by the edges. The destroyed white tee underneath. His distressed black jeans. Those unlaced black Doc Martens with a single white broken love heart on the side of the left one, almost as if it's been stitched.

It feels like there's a story behind those white Band-Aids wrapped around some of his fingers that he has looped above his head in the wire. I'm fascinated by the ink on his hands, the ones more visible like the skull, serpent, and roman numerals, and I instantly wonder if he has more.

Why is he making my heart go so funny?

I like the way he's looking at the camera with furrowed brows, a mixture between broody and motionless, making it seem like he just doesn't give a damn. Like life has done a number on him.

I stare a little too long at the thin black eyeliner around his eyes. I always thought eyeliner was for girls, but seeing it on him, I know I've been wrong… *wow, it's really hot.*

I brush the pad of my finger over his face, almost intimidated at first, as I wonder if his eyes are really that dark or are instead a dark cocoa brown. Maybe it's just the dark ink of the page tricking me? Maybe.

Beneath his photo, a white cursive font reads:

The true hatesick up-and-coming sinner of Manhattan; Elijah Diesel.

Elijah.

"Elijah," I murmur to myself, wanting to get used to the name on my tongue. "Elijah Diesel."

He seems a few years older than me, okay, *a lot* older. Ten years my senior at the least, and although I so desperately want to read all of the little text surrounding the picture, I kind of want to make my own impression of the guy.

After chewing my bottom lip for the longest time, I cut out his picture, being careful to make it perfect, and stick it on a new page in my scrapbook.

Elijah Diesel

I write in permanent marker as a title on the page, and then I draw four little black hearts.

A little lower down, toward the bottom of my page, I write all my feelings out with my heart beating a million miles per second.

> *Right now I'm looking at you for the first time, and I think I'm going to get addicted to you. I want to know everything about you, Elijah. Or should I call you Diesel?*

Butterflies take over my stomach and I can't help just how deeply my cheeks burn. I roll over on my bed to my back and cover my mouth, softening my giddy giggles while New York's silvery moonlight merges with my warm yellow wall sconces.

"Stop being so foolish, Rosalia Philips," I whisper to myself. "He's just some hot rocker."

But I know he's much more than that.

He's the first person who's managed to make me crack a smile through my midnight blues.

The first man who makes me feel a funny type of way just staring at his picture.

The only one I think I'll get lost in forever, until he's staring right back at me.

Whoa.

I settle down and stare up at my ceiling, a seventeen-year-old girl trying to rebel from the world as she knows it, second by second.

Who are you, Elijah Diesel?

Exactly where can I find you?

And why does my heart beat so crazy for you?

It's been a month, and my mom hasn't brought home the next edition of *Rolling Stone* magazine for me.

I tried buying the latest edition before school this morning, but the damn newsagent had just sold out. I knew a couple more in the area, but I would have been late for the last day of eleventh grade before summer, so I promised myself I'd check out the other news-stands after school.

The anticipation has been killing me all day because as much as I know I can just search up Elijah Diesel on my phone, there's so much more thrill in turning a page and seeing him instead.

It's just after three o'clock when I step into the convenience store by my school.

The older guy behind the counter takes one look at my wavy blonde hair, my cropped white shirt, and pink-and-white plaid skirt and scoffs, "Kids these days."

With a clenched jaw, I ball my fists but continue walking to the section of the store I know all the hotshot magazines are, no matter how deeply the man's words hurt me.

I'm not even the worst of my generation. I swear, I'm not. First, I don't relate to my generation. At all. Second, I've never had a sip of alcohol. Never smoked. Done drugs in the bathroom. Hell, I've never even kissed a guy in my entire life.

I'm just a seventeen-year-old virgin who loves short plaid skirts and knee-high socks. I'm not hurting anybody, so to hell with this guy.

Why don't you fix your flickering lightbulbs, popcorn ceiling, and grossly stained carpet instead, dude?

I almost do a happy dance on the spot when the new edition of *Rolling Stone* stares back at me. It's the last one left. I grin and snatch it from the stand at record speed, then I actually start bouncing.

Yes. Yes. Yes.

Just as I begin flipping through it, wanting to see if I can see a glimpse of Elijah Diesel before I buy it, the man behind the counter clears his throat.

My breath slows and I don't like the glare he shoots my way. "Aye, blondie, this isn't a library. You want to read the magazine, you buy it and you get the hell out of my store."

Rude.

Narrowing my eyes, I slap a twenty-dollar bill on the counter and practically run out of the store, not caring about the change. My mom would kill me if she knew, but once won't make a difference, *right*?

Rushing down the street, I wait until I'm on the next block before I come to a slow by my bus stop. Even though I live in Brooklyn, I go to school in Manhattan. Don't ask me why, but my father—one of the most respected neurosurgeons in the city—wanted it that way. And that way it is.

Leaning against the bus shelter, I couldn't be more ecstatic as I slip my schoolbag between my feet and carefully turn each page of the magazine. New York's slightly warm breeze kisses my skin and blows my waves, giving me hope of a beautiful summer approaching.

But that hope slowly shrivels up when I go through the entire magazine, never seeing a photo of Elijah Diesel once.

My heart drops.

No.

No. No. No.

He has to be in here. *He's got to!*

I go over the magazine a second time, then a third, and by the fourth time I'm groaning. I seriously feel like slamming it right in the trash can, so devastated that I waited an entire month for nothing.

"It can't be." I sigh, shutting my eyes just as the bus pulls up. "How can he not be in it?"

It's just my luck. Something like this was bound to happen to me.

I just wasted twenty dollars. That idiot back in the store will probably wipe his mouth with it after devouring a greasy cheeseburger.

Ickkk.

For me, it isn't just false hope, it's giving in to the fantasy of Elijah Diesel slipping away from my very fingers. I so desperately craved another photo of him to put in my scrapbook. One I can stare at whenever I don't feel all right, just like I did for the past month, but now I feel like a fool for doing so.

You're the foolest of fools, Philips.

And yes, I'm hyperaware 'foolest' isn't even a word, but let's just pretend it is.

I flicker my eyes open, ready to take the bus all the way home with my head hung low, when something stops me. I don't know why, but my breath halts in my throat at the dark Doc Martens somebody stepping off the bus is wearing. I haven't glanced up yet, but those shoes look awfully familiar.

Doc Martens…

Unlaced…

A stitched white broken love heart on the side of the left one…

I swear I've seen them before but where?

Where? Where? Where?

And when it finally hits me, I internally gasp.

The picture! They were in that picture last month.

Wait, that would mean… No, no, it couldn't be. It can't.

As my gaze flickers higher, at the person descending the bus right in front of me, I slow by their studded leather jacket. And the moment those familiar melancholic onyx eyes bore into mine, I forget how to breathe.

Holy sweet Jesus, it's him.

Him.

Elijah Diesel.

And he's even more beautiful in person.

My mouth gets all dry and my hands become so sweaty holding *Rolling Stone* magazine that it slips from my grip. I cringe as it slides across the sidewalk like it's on skates. And I don't know if the timing could be any worse, but just as it slows, Elijah unintentionally stomps his feet right on the magazine.

Oops.

Almost on instinct, he picks up the magazine, stares at the cover, and then his eyes slowly flicker to the gap of sidewalk between us until they meet my pink platform sneakers.

Ever so slowly, his gaze rakes up my body with a sexily clenched jaw, and I'm happy to confirm his eyes are really that dark. It feels like a lifetime passes the way he's checking out my long, lean legs, my short skirt, and cropped white shirt with little floral-patterned peaches, some midriff exposed.

He stays there for a little while, and the longer his hot stare lingers, the more my chest heaves. My breaths are rushed and all frantic-like. I feel my nipples harden in arousal, stabbing through my lacy bra and outlining my shirt.

He does this to me.

He does this *all* to me.

And when those dreamy dark onyx eyes finally meet my face, my knees buckle.

The bus moves off behind him with a hiss, and it feels like we're in a slow-motion movie with the way his dark hair softly blows in the wind, the ends so wavy.

Arching a brow, Elijah gestures toward the magazine he's holding. "I think you dropped something, *Peaches*," he calls out to me, and *dear God*, his voice…

It's the perfect combination of a sexy raspiness and a murmur, as if he can disguise himself in them both, ready to pounce at any minute now.

Striding up to me, he extends the magazine out to me. Our fingers brush when I take it from him, and sizzling electricity shoots down my arm.

Gosh, this guy is a dream.

It feels so weird seeing Elijah up close after spending the past month looking at his picture all alone in my bedroom. *This is so much better.* I can't get over his musky, sandalwood scent with a hint of tobacco. It's a scent I've never smelled so up close before, and instantly I wish I could smell it forever.

Wow. He's so tall and I'm even wearing platform sneakers. He's easily six-two, six-three.

Wait a minute, did he just call me "Peaches?"

I nervously smile, an obvious blush crawling up my cheeks. "Umm, thank you."

Elijah nods, his broody gaze flickering between my eyes and my plump lips, which I can't help but softly bite.

He stares for a second longer, and just as his hot breath hits my lip, he steps back and begins walking away with such a swagger that his leather jacket sways from side to side.

Despite my fingers continuing to fizzle, a hollowness takes over my body and I don't know why. This was it, my chance to tell him whatever, and I just blew it. *Ugh!*

Chewing my lower lip, I watch as Elijah keeps on walking in the opposite direction of the convenience store. He must have lit up a cigarette in the seconds he walked away because now clouds of thick white smoke lace the air around him every so often.

He smokes.

Mama always tells me how bad smoking is. That neither me nor my older sister, Maya, should ever touch a cigarette. For the past years, I've believed her, thought it was such a dirty thing, but knowing *he* smokes changes everything.

He doesn't make it seem dirty as he looks both ways before jogging across the street, Elijah Diesel makes smoking look like it's heaven's cure to all the chaos here on earth. And perhaps it's that reason alone, (or the fact that I'm still astonished that he was right in front of me), but I do the unexpected.

Quickly stuffing the magazine in my schoolbag, I sling the backpack over my shoulder and wait for the lights before running across the Tribeca street.

Even though Elijah's several feet ahead of me, his studded leather jacket is still in view, and I use it as my guide while I weave through people, apologizing and jogging faster until I'm mere inches away.

The damn guy keeps on walking faster, and here I am treading along behind him, not even knowing what I'd say if he turns around. All I do know is that his scent makes me feel like home, and I could get used to the cigarette smoke hitting me from ahead.

"Hey, watch where you're going!" A lady pushing a stroller growls when I almost run into her as I turn a corner five feet behind Elijah.

I turn to her, mortified. "Oh my God, I'm so sorry, please forgive me, I'm just…"

She comes to a halt with a glare. "I don't care what you're '*just*' doing, be careful around corners!"

I feel bad right to my core, but she walks off with her stroller before I can say anything else.

Breathing out a strangled breath, I vow to forget it completely and focus on Elijah, but when I turn back around and there's no sign of him or any leather jacket, I begin to panic.

No. No. No.

I did not just lose him!

Where could he have gone?

He didn't cross the street again and there's no way he could have entered the cafés a little farther down unless he bolted, which is… highly unlikely.

Damn.

I glance around, frustrated with myself this too was all for nothing.

Stuff it, I'm going home.

Spinning on my heels, I'm adamant to call it a day when I unexpectedly slam into a solid chest and tumble back, almost losing my balance.

My schoolbag slips and falls to the ground with a thud.

What the hell…?

The second I crane my head up and glance at my victim, I'm pretty sure I'm about to piss my pants. It's Elijah, and unlike before, there's a deadly look in his steel-black-eyed stare.

"Are you following me?" Elijah growls ever so wickedly, stepping forward until we're only inches apart. "Because if you are, it ain't gonna be good for you, *Peaches*, believe me."

He continues to stare me down, awaiting my response, all while my mouth dries up and I wish I could just disappear. It doesn't matter how badly I've had a crush on him, right now if looks could kill… I'd be gone. Long gone.

Jerk.

I don't like the soullessness in his death glare or the way he clenches his jaw when I part my lips before closing them. I don't know this guy. At all. Which is why I do the only logical thing in my head during this current moment…

I take one last glance at my dark, edgy sinner, and then bolt in the other direction.

I run all the way home, (and yes, through the Brooklyn Bridge too) like I'm some sort of freak. It takes me over an hour, and by the end of it, I'm slow walking like I just won a marathon.

Or just came last.

But I keep on going until I lock myself in my bedroom, panting. And it's only then, as my breaths finally begin to stabilize, that I realize I no longer have my schoolbag. In fact, I don't think I ran home with it at all. It slipped from my shoulder when I slammed into Elijah's chest, and I never picked it up.

Oh. My. God.

He's with it. He has it.

And the worst part of all? I have a keyring on it with all of my information in case of an emergency.

My *name.*

My *number.*

My *home address.*

It's all at his fingertips.

Groaning, I dive onto my bed and bury my face into my silk pillow.

Ohhh no!

I'm so screwed.

Elijah Diesel is going to kill me!

Chapter
TWO

Elijah

If Hurricane Blondie thinks this is where our story ends, she's dead wrong.

Hurricane Blondie—that's exactly what she was the way she stormed into my life and left just as fucking fast. I mean, come on, it's one thing to drop your magazine; it's another to act like a complete psycho and stalk somebody down the street. It's exactly what Hurricane Blondie did to me; except she couldn't take the heat when I confronted her about it.

I've never seen a girl so scared in my entire life.

I'm used to the alternative rock, a little seductive goth, the kind of girls who wear fishnet stockings, quirky barrettes, and paint their nails the brightest neon colors. Those who don't give a shit. But Hurricane Blondie ain't like that at all.

I saw straight through her as fear laced her eyes after I asked if she was stalking me. Her emerald-green eyes widened so much, for a moment it was as if I was staring into a field of rolling green meadows, something you'd find in the South of France, with their bitter fucking excuse of sour grapes in exchange for the name champagne.

Fuck that shit. I'm not a champagne kind of guy.

I could never be.

I like the taste of liquor wrapped on my tongue like I like sex. Rough. Toxic. An overdose.

There's nothing fucking gentle about me. I mean, even my full name (it's real, by the way) alludes to something destructive. So, I get the fear in *Peaches's* eyes (*yes, that's what I'm calling her now*). I get her running away. I even get her not wanting to know a fuck about me. But what I don't get is why she left her damn schoolbag literally by my damn feet.

She couldn't have not noticed that she left it, and the fact that she still goes to high school… makes me wish I hadn't stared at those long, toned lean legs for *that* long as she ran.

She's got to be seventeen, or no more than eighteen, the perfect age to fuck up a life with peer pressure, tobacco, and narcotics.

Trust me, been there, fucking done that, although my personal hell began much younger.

And as I stare out at Manhattan through my loft's black steel casement windows hours later, her damn schoolbag shoved in the corner of the living room, (next to my lyric notebook, bass guitar, and rolled-up joints), I wonder if she—*Peaches*—has ever been involved in any of those three situations.

Peer pressure.

Tobacco.

Narcotics.

Hmmm.

She seems too smart of a girl to let people force her into situations she detests. And there's no way she's snorting coke in the bathroom at parties with the A+ paper literally hanging out of her schoolbag.

That only leaves one… *tobacco.*

I piece my eyes shut, letting the memories of her run through my fucked-up mind much longer than they should.

Nah, I don't see the narcotics either, not with those plump, candy-floss-colored lips that seemed so soft.

I wanted to sexily bite that lip down, all fucking primal, and discover if *Peaches* was the kind of girl to gasp or to moan.

But I'm not the kind of guy to kiss and tell.

In fact, I don't fucking tell at all.

My bandmates are a testament to that. I may as well be the coldest motherfucker in Manhattan. Some say I lack a heart; I say I wasn't ever born with one. So this *Peaches* girl, whoever she fucking is, better tread carefully because I'm not the kind of guy you fuck over and then expect I'll forgive.

I don't forgive.

I don't forget.

I fight. Hard. In the silence. Until I get what I want, and when I get it, I never want to let it go.

I treat my wants like black-winged butterflies with unique dots of yellow. Because although I have them trapped in my imaginary spray-painted brass vintage cage, I let them flutter free within the constraints.

And right now, all I want is *Peaches*.

I storm over to her schoolbag in my bedroom and flip over the keyring, all her information bringing a devilish smirk to my lips.

All I want is you, Rosalia Philips.

I wanna know every single thing about you.

Why you chose me. Why you didn't let me go. Why you keep on replaying in my head, like the lyrics of a sickly depressive melody disguised in the sweetest honeyed sin of voices. *Yours.*

And when I find you, Rosalia, you're going to wish you never ran away from the monster some call Elijah Diesel, but I call *"me."*

It takes barely five hours since Rosalia ran away from me for me to lose my self-control. The darkened ominous Manhattan clouds coat in midnight as I store her number in my phone.

Rosalia.

I decide I like her name.

I decide she suits it well.

I also decide she's a completely oblivious idiot for all of the information she leaves so freely on her schoolbag.

Fuck emergencies. If she loses it, somebody could stalk her ass and murder her. I hate people, I really fucking do, but the thought of such beauty vanishing makes me sick to my stomach.

So that's the first thing I'm going to tell her—to take this damn keyring off. The second? Well, you'll just have to see, won't you?

I'm not the kind of guy who texts or calls. I prefer seeing somebody's goddamn face, but for her, I'll make an exception… *just this once.*

Pulling out my phone from the pocket of my distressed jeans, I begin typing away and hit send.

> **ELIJAH:** Are you aware of what you left behind when you ran away from me?

I don't expect her response to come so suddenly.

> **ROSALIA:** Maybe.

Just maybe?

> **ELIJAH:** Do you want it back?

My phone buzzes in my grip.

> **ROSALIA:** Maybe.

My brows furrow. The fuck?

> **ELIJAH:** Is *maybe* all you're gonna say?

> **ROSALIA:** Maybe.

Fucking *maybe* again.

I grind my teeth because I don't know if she straight up doesn't know what else to say, or she's intentionally doing this to piss me off beyond repair. Either way, I don't like it.

Oh, is this how you wanna play it, huh? 'Cause I can fucking play, baby.

> **ELIJAH:** Make up your mind, Peaches, or else I'm gotta dump it.

Her response comes back in exactly three seconds, and finally it's more than just *maybe.*

> **ROSALIA:** Yes, I want it, please.

Please?

I almost scoff to myself.

Part of me likes how she didn't even ask who this number belonged to, she just assumed.

ELIJAH: Why did you run?

Those fucking bubbles do their dance, and then all of a sudden disappear. She leaves me on read. *Fucking read.* And if it's one thing in life I don't take, it's that.

My thumbs viciously throw daggers into my screen with every tap.

ELIJAH: Fine, continue keeping quiet, I'll be at your house in twenty minutes with your schoolbag.

That sure wakes her up.

ROSALIA: Oh, umm, I would prefer if you didn't come here. Can we meet somewhere public? Like a park? I know it's late but... I think a park is better.

ELIJAH: No. I'm coming to you so this time you won't run from me.

I sense the panic in her reply.

ROSALIA: The park would be better, please, Elijah.

ELIJAH: Not happening, Peaches.

And then I lock my phone, ignoring the following texts lighting up my screen—all from her. Because if it's something Rosalia should know about me, it's that I always win.

Always.

Just like I did right now.

And you better get used to it, Peaches, 'cause you just started a fucking war inside my mind.

Chapter
THREE

Rosalia

I wish I never bought that damn *Rolling Stone* magazine earlier today. *This is all my fault.*

As I glance over every fast car that passes, wondering which one will belong to Elijah, the light inside my chest dims. Truth is, my heart hasn't stopped beating in frantically wild pitter-patters ever since Elijah's text.

My entire body froze up at the unknown number, knowing exactly who it was even before I read it. Coldness rippled down my spine, the same one still present as I sit on the porch steps of my family's Brooklyn Heights brownstone.

He found me.

I can't stop nervously tracing the black wrought iron laced railing. My legs haven't stopped tingling from my madwoman run through New York to Brooklyn from earlier. My poor feet were already so blistered from ballet that the run made it even worse. I had to rest them in a salt bath the second I got home. Luckily, I was the only one home and didn't have to explain anything to my parents or my older sister about it or Elijah because *that* would have been awkward.

It's been twenty minutes since Elijah's last text, which means he's moments away.

If he sticks to his word, that is.

I didn't expect him to want to come to my house because as much as he intrigues me, it's too personal. And risky. But if there's anything I've learned about him in the past six hours, it's that he's persistent. Dominant.

It's why I've already dialed 911 and all I have to do is hit that tempting green circle. Can I really trust Elijah alone? I don't know. I mean, I don't know even *who this guy is.* Yes, he was in *Rolling Stone* magazine and that should mean he at least has some decency, but that doesn't mean he's *not* a serial killer. I mean, just look at Ted Bundy's tactics, *like, erm, helloooo!*

Okay, so maybe it isn't the whole stranger danger thing I'm freaking out about. I'm freaking out because my conservative parents are sound asleep inside. My father doesn't have a shift at the hospital tonight, but he's on call, and if there's an emergency and his pager goes off… yep, he's going to trip over me running down these stairs.

I'd probably be grounded for the entire summer, and who wants that? Certainly not me.

As I said, it's risky.

Too risky.

But I really need my schoolbag… *and I kinda want to see Elijah Diesel again.*

Wrapping my arms around my waist, I rock back and forth on the step, the slightly warm New York air doing nothing to calm me down. Even though it's the start of summer, the nights are still chilly, no matter how intense the dose of humidity is.

I wait.

And wait.

And wait some more, imagining which kind of car he'll pull up in front of my brownstone at almost one o'clock in the morning will be.

It may be all sleek and flashy like an Audi, or perhaps he'll show up in a vintage Mustang, a toothpick in his mouth and a smolder like it's some late '50s rock and roll film. All I know is that whatever he drives, I'm certain it's glossy and onyx, just like his eyes.

I've never done anything like this—waited outside with my house key between my pointer and middle finger, ready to attack, just in case. Although this is an elite area of Brooklyn with gorgeous historic homes and tree-lined streets, I'm still cautious. Of everybody. Including that rocker called Diesel who's now five minutes late.

Brooklyn's late-night buzz fills the air with rumbling cars and lively music in the distance.

I roll my eyes, wondering if he's been playing me all along and is actually not coming, but then I hear a deep rumble in the distance like the sweetest of rough purrs. The sound gets louder and louder until it's deafening, and a gasp escapes me when a Harley Davidson speeds up my street.

My eyes widen.

Could it be…?

Holy shit!

The Harley's roaring so loud, I'm pretty sure this guy just woke up the entire neighborhood, the five New York boroughs, *and* New Jersey!

The Harley, which is the sleekest one I've ever seen with a glossy onyx wrap and cool silver accents, comes to a slow right outside my brownstone.

The rider has a black helmet on, and the visor is down, preventing me from seeing anything under the warm glow of the art deco streetlight. But the moment my gaze moves to the spiky leather jacket, my heart jolts.

It's him.

He cuts the engine, kicks down the motorbike's kickstand, unclips his helmet, and hangs it on one of the handlebars in all less than three seconds. It tells me riding his Harley isn't just something he does, it's habitual. His livelihood. I'm sure he could ride the metal monster eyes closed.

When Elijah's hooded eyes finally meet mine, they darken, and all the air in my lungs is sucked out of me.

Oh my God.

Elijah doesn't drop his stare as he softly bites down on the tips of one of his tan leather gloves and winks before roughly yanking it off. He repeats the action with his other biker glove, and between that and his inky tattooed hands, it's the sexiest thing I've ever witnessed.

Too bad he could be a serial killer.

Elijah sets the gloves in his saddlebag and climbs off his Harley, raking a hand through his sexily tousled hair. Confidently striding up to me, Elijah slips his hands into his jean pockets, and he looks like heartbreak. A pure bad boy with the midnight moon cascading down his body, the silvery moonlight illuminates all the things that speak to me the most.

His deep Cupid's bow leading to those sinful, kissable lips.

His small gold hoop earring in his left ear with a detailed skull and angel wings hanging. Silver rings that beam in the light.

His wavy dark hair, which is wet and now slicked back, giving me the impression he just showered before he came here. A few strands hang low, some covering his eyes, and it instantly reminds me of Depp's *Cry Baby*.

In this moment, I'm kind of glad I didn't rip that picture of him in my scrapbook into a million tiny little pieces when I ran home. I want to stare at him forever, without him knowing. But that all ends when Elijah flicks his eyes to me.

"Hi," is the first thing that escapes my lips.

Obviously, it's a bad choice with the way his jaw ticks and he looks away. He continues climbing the porch steps, beyond the step I'm sitting on.

Huh?

Melancholic Sin literally walks past me until he's standing by my front door, his back to me.

"Um, excuse me?" I clear my throat; well aware I shouldn't get so lost in the lingering whiff of his musky sandalwood cologne. "Elijah, where are you going? I'm right here."

Elijah doesn't dare turn around, forcing me to stare at his broad shoulders and… I squint and twist my body around to see it better… *Is that F. Scott Fitzgerald's* The Beautiful and Damned *tucked in his back pocket?*

Yes, yes, it is, Rosalia.

How the heck did he ride here with that thing under his ass?

I'm confused because from just looking at Elijah, he doesn't seem like the kind of guy who would adore literature, especially the classics... *Because classics are what I like too.*

I wonder if he's read To Kill A Mockingbird, *the book I have safely tucked inside my school bag and constantly reread.*

And just like that, Elijah opens his mouth and ruins it all.

"I said I was coming *to your house*, not *to your porch*," he grumbles, like being here at one o'clock in the morning is the last place he wants to be. "You want your bag, I'm stepping in."

My jaw drops.

Is this guy serious?

I can just imagine my father coming down and seeing this eyeliner-wearing rocker with his seventeen-year-old daughter... Forget me being grounded for a summer, I'd be grounded for life.

"Well, no, you can't go inside." I laugh nervously because it's the only other thing I can do despite panicking. "So, you either give me my schoolbag here or I'll call the police for stolen property."

Glancing over his shoulder, Elijah eyes me for the longest time before scoffing. "Seriously? *Stolen property?* You're fucking lucky I brought the bag home with me to begin with."

"I *am* appreciative. Trust me, I am, but you can't come in. My parents are inside, and I..."

"You, *what?*"

"I'd prefer if we stayed out here."

Elijah gives me nothing as he shakes his head and faces the door with a shrug. "Well, I guess I'll just ring the doorbell then, won't I?"

Now it's my turn for the entire neighborhood, the five New York boroughs, *and* New Jersey to hear my shocked gasp. "You wouldn't..."

Elijah chuckles darkly.

"Oh, I totally would." He lingers his fingers inches from the glamorous oak and solid brass lion head doorbell. "Try me, *Peaches*. I'll press it so goddamn hard, you'll wish you just opened the door to begin wi—"

Standing up, I cut him off. "Would you please stop with all your ultimatums?"

"The world doesn't care for a *please*. I sure don't."

Ahhh!!!

I huff and give in, mounting the steps until I'm right beside him. It's there where I narrow my eyes, making sure he sees my deep, cruel glare. "You know, for a guy who was in *Rolling Stone* magazine, you act just like every other guy."

"Oh, how's that?"

"An asshole."

Elijah slowly smirks, and I hate that I find myself drooling. "*Oh*, you saw my article, did you? So you're not only a stalker, but you're also an ultra-stalker. I assume you were reading that new *Rolling Stone* magazine today to see if I was in that edition too, huh?"

Mind reader.

"No, not at all." Shaking my head, I jab my house key into the keyhole. "I have better things than staring at you all day, believe me."

You're such a liar, Rosalia Philips.

"Good. Now, do you want your damn bag or not?"

"Yes," I grit through my teeth, just as my front door clicks unlocked. I hold the knob close, keeping the door ajar.

Within seconds, Elijah's jogging down the porch steps and then back up again with my schoolbag. He had it in the big saddlebag at the back of his Harley.

When he's beside me again and I go to cheekily grab it from him, he slings it over his shoulder and glares down at me in his six-foot-three frame. "Nice try. As I said, I ain't afraid to buzz that doorbell, *Peaches*, so quit the good girl act."

"It isn't an act," I whisper and slowly step into my house with a finger pressed against my lips to signal silence. "Follow me, don't speak, and if it's anything you do, don't make a sound."

Elijah flicks his gaze beyond me, toward the house. "It's dark in there. I can't see shit."

I shoot him a death glare. "Well, you better figure it out, *amigo*, or else I'll kick you."

"Mmhmmm." Giving me a once-over, a smoldering smirk breaks out on his lips. "I'd like to see you try..."

I get lost in those eyes that swirl challenge.

I don't give in to him, no matter how badly I can feel my heartbeat lodged in my throat from how close we're standing.

When I finally look away, I suck in a breath and step to the side, so that Elijah can step in. His leather jacket brushes against my bare arm, like scorching fire attempting to unintentionally light me up. I let it go.

In the dark, Elijah follows me through my brownstone and up the two flights of stairs, until we're on the third level of my brownstone. I cringe at my parents' soft snores from the opposite side of the hall, highly aware there's an older man walking right behind me. Thank God my older sister is staying at her boyfriend's tonight because I swear that girl is nocturnal.

My plan sinks before I can victory dance when my bare foot hits that damn dodgy spot on the oak hardwood floor just outside my bedroom. It squeaks—*loudly*.

Oh no.

I freeze, but Elijah couldn't have known and blindly slams into me hard from behind with a big *oof*. Before I know it, we're stumbling forward, and I have just enough time to cover my face, bracing for impact.

Hands sink into my hips, slightly easing the velocity as I slam into my bedroom door, my face receiving the brunt of it.

Bang. Bang. Bang.

Oh shit.

Oh shit.

Oh shit.

Elijah stumbles with me, his body crashing into mine from behind, pressing up against the door. A low groan escapes his throat, and the warm breath tickles my neck, taunting me. My ass digs into him, and I don't know if I want to disappear or burst out laughing.

"What happened to making no noise?" Elijah whispers in my ear, the taunting smirk evident in his sexily raspy voice.

I thank God we're in the dark because I swear my cheeks are burning.

"Shut up. I think I just rearranged my face," I groan.

"You okay?"

Oh my God, is Mr. Mysterious concerned for me?

"I will be."

But my words mean nothing when I hear rustling from my parents' bedroom.

My father's snores have stopped.

Yikes!

Opening my bedroom door, I quickly shove Elijah inside and softly shut the door in his face, just as my father opens his bedroom door. The hall light flickers on, blinding me like I'm some type of vampire that hasn't seen the outside world for six long centuries.

My father narrows his gaze at me, shielding his eyes to look at me better. "Rosalia, everything okay?"

My heart is beating like crazy, knowing one slip-up could ruin this entire plan.

Yes, Dad, I'm okay, just have a Harley lover hiding in my bedroom, but it's all good, he's into Fitzgerald.

"Yeah, sorry." I smile. "I just went down to get some water and tripped up the stairs. I'm okay now."

"You sure? That sound woke me up." Concern is written all over his face. "Does anything hurt?"

I giggle, knowing his doctor side would come out. "I'm completely fine, Dad, I promise. I just got a fright, that's all."

My father goes to speak, but a yawn comes out instead. He chuckles, his light eyes warming as he nods toward his bedroom. "All right, if you say so, sweetheart. I'm heading back to bed. Good night."

I lean against my bedroom door as he flicks off the light. "Night, night."

I wait until my father's door shuts and then what feels like three minutes later until his soft snores fill the hall. When I step into the darkness that is the bedroom and blindly lock my door, I shut my eyes, wanting to kick myself for letting this go this far.

There's a grown man somewhere in my room.

A damn grown man who was in *Rolling Stone* magazine.

The same man I became obsessed with in less than a month, adamant to know everything about him, and look where it got me—frantically rushing around my room like a madwoman.

I can't remember where I placed my candles because turning

on the wall sconce lights at a time like this would be deadly with Elijah in here.

What if my dad wakes up again and sees the bright glow beneath my door?

What if he sees Elijah's shadow?

Hears his voice?

Nooope, the candles are far safer. Softer.

Only… *where the heck did I put them?*

Blindly reaching for my curtains, I pull them all the way up and let the soft silvery moonlight drown my bedroom. I almost jump when I see where Elijah is. He's sitting on the corner of my bed, simply waiting for me with a less than impressed glare.

My schoolbag is on the floor, on the edge of the bed. Home sweet home.

Maybe I don't need those candles after all…

"Soooo," I whisper, consciously wrapping my arms over my petite waist. "You're in my house, I have my schoolbag. This sneak upstairs was all for nothing, really. *Now* can you go?"

Completely ignoring me, Elijah's eyes drop to my chest and my body reacts. Heat rushes across my veins because I've never been looked at like this before. He looks at me as if I'm more than just Rosalia Philips—the organized, introverted, Brooklyn ballerina. He looks at me like I'm human. Like I'm worth something.

Glancing down, I subtly eye my tits and how obvious my hard nipples are outlined, even through my lacy pink bra. I know I should be ashamed of it, but for some outlandish reason, I'm not.

Elijah Diesel's a dark, twisted fantasy, the kind good girls like me shouldn't ever imagine.

I wonder what he would feel like. What hugging him would do to me. Wonder if I let him kiss me, if he'd recklessly use his tongue to devour me, and if he'd taste like musky tobacco or more like a fresh peppermint.

Eyes still on me, Elijah whispers in the low light, "How old are you, Rosalia?"

"Seventeen," I murmur back, rubbing my thumbs over the thin fabric of my top. "How old are you?"

"How old am I?"

"Mmhmmm."

"Why do you ask?"

I shrug.

"No, tell me…" He stands. "Why do you ask?"

"Conversation starter?" I say, but it comes out as more of a question if anything. *Darn me.*

Elijah clenches his cleanly shaven jaw. "I ain't trying to start a damn conversation, *Peaches*."

Okay, idiot, maybe I should have read your Rolling Stone *article after all. If I did, I would have known how much of a cold-hearted asshole you were in two-point-five seconds and would have never followed you.*

I get all worked up and actually start to hate him.

"You're in my bedroom at one o'clock in the morning. I think *you* owe *me* a *conversation*."

"All right, I'll give you something. Take that keyring off your bag. The one with all your information. You don't know the number of freaks you could attract with it on there."

"*Oh*," I scoff, the next words escaping before I can help it. "You mean *freaks* like *you*?"

My jaw instantly drops.

Oh.

My.

God.

I did not just say that.

I hate myself for it because I don't think he's a freak, *at all.* I was just angry, that's all.

Darkness takes over his eyes that I can only describe as completely emotionless. Pure carnage.

"Oh God." I slap a hand over my mouth with wide eyes. "I'm so sorry, I didn't mean t—"

"The fuck you didn't," Elijah growls through the skin of his teeth, probably doing his best to talk low, but I can hear the anger bubbling through. "If I'm just a fucking freak to you, then good, I guess in the end it's better this way."

"Elijah, please, I didn't mean it. I was just angry and—"

"Good night, *Peaches*."

And then without another word, Elijah storms out of my bedroom door, leaving golf-ball-sized guilt lodged in my throat.

I stand here, in the middle of my bedroom, lost.

I feel so bad.

I didn't mean to anger him. I just said those things in the heat of the moment. What hurts me the most was the glimmer of sadness that pooled in Elijah's eyes seconds before he left.

It kills me.

It was as if I had shot a silver bullet right into his chest, and that tough armor surrounding him began to fade away, stripping bare the real person Elijah Diesel truly is—a real sad boy.

The roar of his Harley has me rushing to turn around and glance outside my window, just making it in time as my gorgeous villain pulls out of my tree-lined street. And as he rides away, every echo of his metal beast ricochets into my sad heart.

It's only after I collapse on my bed with a frown that I realize something's digging into my pajama-covered thigh. I glance down, noticing the perfectly blue-bound classic book.

The Beautiful and Damned.

It's so ironically us, only there isn't an *us*. But if there were, I'd be the damned. After all, it's a story of tragedy, nonetheless. It must be.

I gasp because this is Elijah's book. *Elijah's.* It must have slipped from his pocket when he stood.

I caress the pad of my finger over the title, outlining it, wondering if I'll ever see him again. My vision turns glassy at the thought that I won't.

I continue to hate myself for tearing up over the guy. The guy who stole my breath since the first moment I saw him, and who even though is upfront and a little rude, had just enough kindness in his heart to bring me back my schoolbag.

Flicking through the first pages of the heavy book, I gasp when I see it's a first edition. I almost don't want to touch it anymore; too afraid I'll ruin it somehow. I'm just about to close it when I notice a message written on the title page in a thick black marker... and it confirms everything.

Oh my God.

My throat throbs, aching. I didn't expect this at all because I just ruined everything.

He wrote a personalized note... to me.

Peaches,

I saw in your backpack that you enjoy the classics, so I thought I should give you another.
Keep it, it's yours now.
I've reread it a million times.

Call me when you finish it, or whatever,
—E

Elijah Diesel didn't accidentally leave this F. Scott Fitzgerald bittersweet classic on my bed. He left it on purpose.
For me.
And that's when the first hot tear slips.

Chapter
FOUR

Rosalia

I read *The Beautiful and Damned* in an entire sitting the next day. *Tragic. Bittersweet. Beautiful. A literary classic wrapped in a dream.* And by the end, (well, even before the end), I so desperately wanted to tell him everything and anything about it.

I hesitated.

And hesitated more.

Then, I finally called Elijah.

The first call rang once, then it was obvious he ended it.

The second rang out for a damn century until I reached his voice mail.

The third rang straight to his voice mail; meaning he had switched off his phone.

None of this is his fault. I keep on trying to tell myself that.

It's *my* fault I was stupid enough to follow him around Tribeca.

It's *my* fault I let anger overrule and called him a freak when he's far from that.

It's *my* fault I was crazy enough to call him, even though

he had written that note before coming to my house, then later stormed out.

Now, it's been two months without Elijah, and I don't know what to do to fix it. I'm not saying we have to be best friends; I'm not saying we even have to see each other again if he really doesn't want to, all I want to do is apologize.

I hate fighting.

This is slowly becoming the worst summer of my life because I'm so tempted to search him up, but I don't want to. I want to know him for *him* through *him*.

I know he's probably some hotshot. I mean, if he's in *Rolling Stone* magazine, he kind of has to be, right? But there must be so much more to him than a single Google search can uncover, especially the person he is.

All I know is that I hate this.

I want to go back to before I made a fool out of myself.

You're not a freak, Elijah Diesel. I wish you could just believe me.

When I think of a perfect life, I can't see myself in it. I don't know why. I just think there are parts of me that are so disconnected from this wicked thing we call life, that at times I feel so numb.

I have good parents now.

I live on a good side of the city.

I have good grades, good friends, a good heart.

It's summer, for damn's sake, and yet I feel like my entire world is crumbling from the inside out.

Truth is, ever since I stumbled across Elijah months ago in that magazine, I've felt… different. No, I've *wanted* to feel different. I'm sick of the same old mundane life I've been conditioned to live. There's no thrill. No joy. It's the same thing on repeat, every single day.

I'm sure Elijah's life isn't like this.

There must be a little thrill in his.

Thrill.

Risk.

Challenge.

All those things excite me and have passion bubbling at the pit of my stomach.

I want to do something adventurous before this summer is over. *Even just one.* One thing that doesn't include my usual good girl act. I want to... I don't know. Trespass. Go to a party. Take one puff of a cigarette. Anything that makes me feel more alive.

I crave that adrenaline, the nervousness of getting caught, the palpitations in your chest you get before doing something crazy—like skydiving (which I'm going off second-degree excitement because I've never done it, but my best friend has).

Second-degree excitement? Godddd, that's so depressing.

Why can't I be that girl who jumps out of an airplane at fourteen-thousand feet? *Because with your luck, Rosalia Philips, you'll be the exception and somehow tumble to your death.*

I feel sick just thinking about it, but I've been playing life comfortable for too long. I want something more, and fortunately (or unfortunately), I know just where to find it.

Cue Naomi Ryder—my best friend, and the only person in the world who truly knows me inside out. Naomi and I have been best friends since we were six, when I stepped into ballet class for the very first time. We've been at each other's hips ever since. Through all the ups and downs. I love her to pieces.

She once fell in love with an English exchange student with a crazy soccer-style mid-fade. On their fifth date (*and yes, Naomi was counting*), he confessed that he was gay and only told her now because he felt bad and just went along with it.

Yup. For realsies, peeps. That happened.

It was safe to say that freshman year with him, her, and me in basically all the same classes was realllllly interesting. She was so brokenhearted for two weeks straight that I forced her (well, she was a willing participant) to watch (rewatch on my behalf) all of Matt Bomer's films with me, just so she could feel my pain that—he too—was gay.

Why are gay guys always the most beautiful?

Side note: She forgot about Brit boy *real* fast and grew an obsession with Matty B instead.

I let it go, but at the same time, fourteen-year-old me in my head said, *Um, rudeee, he's mine, thanks.* But Naomi's my best friend, and if this whole thing had to be a trio, so be it.

And as Naomi paces up and down my bedroom now, blabbing on about this cool restaurant that just opened up, I sink into my bed more with a frown.

I wish I were as gorgeous as her. She has the most perfectly silk brunette hair, always with those bouncy curls that are—wait for it— natural. If I wanted to get those curls, it'll take me over an hour and my mom is a HAIRDRESSER.

Brunette hair and piercing blue eyes, it's the rarest combination in my opinion, and yet Naomi is the exception. She's beautiful, beyond skin deep. I think Naomi is one of the kindest people alive, always with a pep in her step, *buttt* also has a little wild side within her that tonight I really need to feed off.

As I said, I want to do something a little crazy at least once this summer, and Naomi is my gal.

"Babe." She sighs, snapping her fingers in my face as she blindly coats her lips with even more gloss. "Are you even listening to me?"

I clear my throat. Oops.

"Yeah," I lie, rocking back and forth on my bed. "You were, like, talking about that wild restaurant that opened up downtown, right?"

Naomi doesn't seem the slightest bit amused. She's still depressed because her annual family vacation to France over the summer was canceled because her parents thought a getaway with just the two of them would be a great 'honeymoon revival.'

But it isn't all bad. She gets to spend the rest of the summer with me. Oh yes, that's right, this next month is going to be fun, and I'm not going to think of Elijah—at all.

Yeah, let's see how long that lasts.

But the whole Naomi-staying-over thing is rather fitting, really, seeing as my older sister, Maya, moved out only last week to Los Angeles for college. Naomi took over her room. I'm going to miss Maya a heck of a lot, but I think the number of times I've scarred myself tripping over one too many of her moving boxes in our hallway during the past week has made up for it.

"Yoooo, girl, are you tripping?" Naomi laughs, breaking me out of my haze for the second time tonight. It's only after she waves a hand in front of my face that a slow, mischievous smirk works up her lips. "Or are you really just thinking about him?"

"About whom?"

She gives me a 'no shit' look. "*Him.*"

I knew exactly who she meant from the start.

Elijah Diesel.

And it's precisely in this second that I half regret telling Naomi about Elijah, namely because she hasn't stopped teasing me about it, and second, she thinks he's a psychopath, (which he's not).

I laugh. *Laugh.* "No, not at all. I've already forgotten about him. I mean, who gives somebody a first edition and never answers their calls?"

"You called him a freak for a reason, Rosalia, because he *is* one."

There's a pang in my chest as my laughter flattens. "No, he isn't… Can you not remind me about that?"

"I'm sorry, but I just want to remind you that he doesn't deserve even thinking about. Besides, if he really was thinking about you too, he would have answered."

She isn't wrong regarding the calls. I mean, he really must hate me if he never called back.

"I know but… I can't stop thinking this is all my fault."

Softly smiling, Naomi sits on the bed beside me. "Babe, it isn't. This isn't on you."

I get all nervous, playing with my hands. "Then why do I feel like it is?"

Silence laces the space between us, and I hate it. I hate everything about this.

"You know what you need…" Naomi says after a little while.

I already know it's a bad idea the second her baby blue eyes sparkle. "Oh no, no, Naomi."

"You need a *distraction!*"

"No, I don't." I almost laugh. "The last time you said that, I had a damn vibrator arrive the next day."

Naomi wiggles her brows. "Well, hey, a vibrator is better than some seventeen-year-old heartbreak shit, but in saying that, I think this time you really need somebody to fuck all the anger out. Like, I don't know, a one-night stand or something."

My jaw drops.

Umm… what did she just say?

I look at her as if she's crazy. "And get emotional attachment issues for the rest of my life? Yeah, no, thanks, I'd rather die a virgin."

"Nooooo, Rosa, don't say that!" Naomi dramatically groans, falling on my bed and looking up at me as if I'm some heavenly angel. "It doesn't have to come with any emotional attachment. You just need to let go. That's all it is. The feeling… it's so *euphoric* and *real*. There's nothing like it, believe me."

Thump.

Thump.

Thump.

That's my heart, peeps, slowly going into overdrive.

I sigh because I get what my best friend is saying, I really do, but there's no way in hell I'll go there with a random stranger. I want my first time to mean something, not just throw it away to forget about another guy who probably doesn't even remember my name.

And then comes that damn devil on my shoulder that taunts me in ways it shouldn't…

Maybe Naomi is right. Maybe that crazy, wild thing you do this summer is break your forever dry spell, Rosalia Philips. Nowadays, everybody your age has already had sex anyway, including Naomi.

The smirk doesn't leave her lips. "Just think about it, Rosalia, okay?"

I nod with a small smile, even though I know I won't.

"Oh my God!" Naomi suddenly grins, standing up from my bed so fast, she has to readjust her short silver metallic dress after accidentally flashing me her tits. "I know what we can do tonight!"

"*Tonight*?" I screech, glancing over at my alarm clock. "Girl, it's ten thirty. The night's over."

Naomi dramatically groans. "Ugh! You're my best friend. You shouldn't be this introverted!"

"Sorry, not sorry." I grin with a wink. "Besides, aren't you tired? I am. We literally had intense ballet practice all day until six."

"Ballet ain't gonna stop me from partying my little heart out. Noah's party literally just started! We can get there in say… an hour? It'll be great for both of us. Come on, Rosalia! You know I'm really into Noah and if I play my cards right, something can happen before senior year begins in less than two weeks. Besides, think of all your hot options there!"

I glance down at what I'm wearing. Oh yeah, that's right—*my pajamas*—just like A NORMAL HUMAN WOULD BE WEARING after ten o'clock on a *Tuesday* night.

Ugh!

"Fine." I playfully roll my eyes but end up laughing when Naomi literally jumps on top of me on the bed and rolls us around in a hug.

"Oh my God! I love you! I love you! I love you!"

And then the real night begins. We spend the next half hour cross-legged on my bedroom floor, doing our hair and putting on makeup in front of my mirrored wardrobe doors.

This week my father's away on a medical conference in Seattle and took my mom with him, so I don't have to worry about coming up with an excuse for them. It's not that they don't trust me. They just don't trust the people at these parties and the possibility of me being exposed to liquor, drugs, or sex—*or all three.*

Drugs... a trigger.

It's just after eleven when best friend privileges begin to roll out. Naomi does my waterline, I do hers, she tells me I did a shit job, so I do it again. I tell her I literally have nothing to wear, and she sorts through my closet and pulls out a cherry-red satin crop top with thin lace straps and a real short denim pleated skirt for me to wear.

I don't even remember those being in my closet.

Naomi runs out of my room to the guest/her bedroom, and when she returns, she flings me a pair of her red stilettos.

"Don't wear a bra," she tells me, fluffing up her hair in the mirror. "Your huge tits will steal the show in that silk number."

"I don't know about *huge...*"

Naomi meets my gaze in the mirror and smirks. "Shut up, bitch, don't make me jealous. You're the greatest exception to ballet with those tits and are part of the zero-point-two percent that are going to make it in the industry based on your immense talent. You and I both know they're huge. Gah, it's honestly so unfair because you're so petite. Your modesty annoys me."

I snicker and get naked in front of her. Once I'm dressed, I walk over to my dresser and pull out a thin lacy white choker I bought weeks ago but haven't worn yet.

I run my finger over the detailed grooves of the lace, unsure as to why my breaths become labored over the fact the choker reminds me of Elijah. It's just something I can really see him liking on a girl.

I slip it on.

Light emerald eyes stare back at me when I glance at myself in my mirrored wardrobe. Naomi bumps her hip to mine. I smile, actually looking… decent. *Whoa.* The beach waves of my honey blonde hair make the fiery red of my soft eyeshadow, crop top, and stilettos really pop. I rub a glossy nude lipstick on my lips, and I'm done.

If it were up to me, I would have rocked up in a K.I.S.S. tee, jeans, and my hair in the messy bun it previously was. Aside from being such an introvert, it's why I never go out to parties without Naomi by my side.

I'm honestly her mom, *literally.*

Naomi does the drinking. I do the driving.

Naomi grinds on the hottest jocks at our high school. I daydream while sitting on a sticky couch with a full-on porno happening beside me.

Naomi glares down Noah Jacobs's girlfriend. I apologize to his girlfriend with a nervous smile because I'm pretty sure she could punch me in the face.

The same thing happens every single time, and to tell you the truth, I wouldn't want it any other way.

Just before I leave my bedroom behind Naomi, I glance over my shoulder and my gaze flickers to something catching my eye on the nightstand.

The Beautiful and Damned first edition.

The one *he* gave me.

Peaches,

I saw in your backpack that you enjoy the classics, so I thought I should give you another.

Keep it, it's yours now.

I've reread it a million times.

Call me when you finish it, or whatever,

—E

Gosh.

Sucking in a sharp breath, I flicker my bedroom light off and walk out the door without ever looking back.

Chapter
FIVE

Rosalia

The drive to Noah's penthouse in Manhattan is filled with off-key singing and talking about what we want to do before the end of August/summer in less than two weeks. So far Naomi has five million things on her list, and I have zero.

When we finally get there at eleven thirty, I manage to park my vintage mint green Fiat 500 around the corner, and we're walking to Noah's place with our arms looped in record time.

The tinge of humidity in the air outside is instantly demolished by the cooling inside Noah's lush penthouse apartment (well, his parents' anyway). Even though I've been here before, it seems so much bigger than last time.

Marble.

Marble.

Marble.

It's all I see.

Oh, and gazillion familiar faces of us upcoming twelfth-grade seniors.

The blasting doof-doof music and sweaty bodies grinding all up together give me major claustrophobia. *Seriously.* My throat starts to close up and I don't know where to move without accidentally bumping into some jock and them getting the wrong idea.

Part of me silently wishes I had just stayed in the comfort of my home, but then I remind myself of what I said earlier—that nothing good comes out of playing life too comfortable—so here I am at a high school party at almost midnight, but I'm here with Naomi, so that makes it better.

Naomi launches for the red Solo cups and downs the illegal liquor, then cheers at the top of her lungs when a group of three jocks swarms us. I, like always, don't let a drop of liquor fall on my tongue, and instead keep an eye on Naomi and the jocks, ensuring they don't get too handsy with her.

"Rosalia Philips," one of them I recognize as Cayden, the star quarterback, smirks, and not so subtly eyes my tits. "Fuck, you look so hot, baby. I didn't know you'd be here tonight."

I almost want to roll my eyes into the back of my head.

First, I'm not your baby.

Second, your tongue was practically down the cheer captain's throat a mere second ago. So, thanks, but no, thanks.

"Hi, Cayden." I softly smile, still trying to be respectful. "Yeah, it was a last-minute kind of thing. Naomi really wanted to come, and I guess it was a good idea for me to get out of the house, you know."

Cayden's smirk deepens as he hooks an arm around my waist and pulls me close.

His warm lips brush over my ear, so it's his voice I can hear above the music when he whispers, "Well, if you want to *get out of the house* more often and put that gorgeous mouth of yours to good use, all you've got to do is ask." He pulls away to glance between my eyes slowly. "Yeah?"

I cringe. *Actually* cringe.

"No, thanks. I, umm… I have a boyfriend."

Arching a brow, Cayden's smirk crumbles. "You have a boyfriend?"

I clear my throat and wish my voice didn't come out as squeaky as it does when I say, "Yeah, I do. Just ask Naomi."

When his head snaps my best friend's way, I curse. *I didn't think he ACTUALLY would.*

"Yo, Naomi, baby! Does your girl over here have a boyfriend?"

Naomi, who was giggling at something one of the two jocks beside her said seconds ago, snaps her attention to Cayden.

Her brows furrow. "You talking to me?"

"Yeah. Does Rosalia have a boyfriend or not? 'Cause she said she did, but I've never seen the guy."

Her baby blue gaze snaps to mine.

My eyes widen and I subtly nod. *Yes, say yes.*

Naomi turns back to Cayden with a Cheshire grin. "Oh yeah, she has a boyfriend, all right."

Ahhh, sweet relief.

As my breaths stabilize, I promise myself I'll love Naomi forever for saving my ass.

"From school? How come I never see him?"

Naomi casually shrugs. "Dunno why you don't see him, but he always picks her up. He's older, like fifteen years older, got a band and everything. A real hottie. Isn't that right, Rosa?"

You know what I said about my breaths five seconds ago? About them *stabilizing*? Yeah, forget I ever said it because the opposite happens.

Nerves ripple through my blood with every heavy thump in my chest.

Oh my God!

Did Naomi just reference who I think she just referenced?

In the same moment, their four heads snap my way. The glare in Cayden's eyes is deadly as I think on the spot.

Crap. Crap. Crap.

I can't even widen my eyes because they'll notice. What do I say?

Naomi wiggles her brows with a smirk, and I want to strangle her for teasing me like this.

"Yeah," I lie with the most genuine fake smile I can manage. "He's really into rock and roll."

And thereeee goes Cayden, roughly slamming his shoulder into me as he storms off into the partying crowd.

Naomi throws me a playful wink as she returns to talking to the two jocks. Well, not before I made her be witness to my pointer finger, which I use as a fake knife to slice across my throat.

Naomi - 1.

Rosalia - 0.

It feels like we've been at this party for five years, but as I glance at my phone, it's only been two hours. *Two.* One thirty a.m. brightly stares back at me, taunting me for all the times I *wished* my parents would allow me to stay up this late.

As I sink farther into Noah's leather couch, observing sixteen and seventeen-year-olds going crazy all around with girls leaned back with their mouths wide, giggling as guys pour vodka into their mouths and their friends shout, "*swallow, swallow, swallow,*" I wonder when exactly in my life I didn't get the memo.

The memo to be like them.

Free. Carefree. Without fear.

I wish I could be like them. Like Naomi. But I have a fear that nothing lasts forever, and it fucks me over, even when I try to escape it. I have my reasons to believe every single person in my life will one day disappear and abandon me, so I've tightened my circle so much so that when that day does come, the hurt will only come in four.

My father.

My mother.

My sister, Maya.

Naomi.

Nobody else can leave me because nobody else but those four people matter to me.

But as I eye Naomi dancing on the impromptu dance floor in the middle of the living room, slowly inching closer to Noah, who's laughing with his girlfriend, I wonder if that floating fifth person will fade before he ever was permanent.

Naomi—who for some reason isn't going as hard on the drinks tonight—waves me over to join her with a girly smile. But I've danced with her for the past two hours, and if I dance any more, I'm certain I'll be out of ballet tomorrow and that definitely won't be a good thing.

I signal I'll be there soon, and she playfully flips me off before she continues dancing.

Smiling, I glance back down at my phone, my blonde waves covering my eyes. There isn't a real-life porno happening beside me on the couch tonight (well, early morning), but there is a breakup, and suddenly I don't know what's worse.

The poor redhead I swear I had chemistry with last year can't stop sobbing, and it's those sobs that are the soundtrack to my mindless scrolling through my phone.

What to do...

The devil has me pressing on my messages, but it's my own curiosity that has me scrolling down to Elijah's name.

It's been over two months to the day since we last texted, or should I say since he told me he was coming to my house at midnight to return my schoolbag and I told him I'd prefer to meet somewhere else, and he just ignored the rest of my texts.

I'm so tempted to text Elijah.

To try one final time.

He ignored all my calls after I finished the F. Scott Fitzgerald classic, but he's got his text read receipts on, so I'll be able to see if he *intentionally* ignores my messages too and leaves me on read.

I know better than to message people at this hour, but seeing as he messaged me close to midnight the last time, I break all rules of common decency.

I bite my lower lip, drowning out the rumbling noise around and type away.

Should I really send it?

My thumb hovers over 'send.'

Stuff it.

I hit send.

Done.

Rosalia: If you don't reply to this, I'm deleting your number.

I don't expect 'delivered' to flicker to 'read' so fast, or for my heart to slow when it does.

Elijah: Don't.

Don't?

I haven't spoken to him in two months, and this is the first thing he says—*Don't.*

Ugh.

I blow out a sigh of frustration. The hell with this guy!

Rosalia: Then tell me where I can meet you because I refuse

to play this game any longer. We need to talk, Elijah. I think
we both owe each other an explanation. When can I see
you?

Elijah: You can't. Besides, you should be asleep. It's almost
two in the morning.

I snort and tap the little camera icon in the chat. Flipping it
around so I see my face, I angle my phone high and take a sultry
selfie of what I'm wearing. I make sure to cross my legs and cut the
picture halfway across my face, so he can only see my glossy bit lip.

I've never been one to play it sexy—intentionally, anyway—but
Elijah needs the push. He's not some seventeen-year-old you can just
bat your lashes at. Elijah's much more.

He's a man.

An extremely complicated, broody alpha male.

But a man nonetheless… one very much older than me.

So strangely enough, I have a feeling the picture I just sent him of
me on the couch with an eyeful of cleavage spilled and my skirt barely
covering my panties will do just that—push him a little.

Rosalia: Does this look like I'm sleeping to you? When can
we meet? Elijah… **Please**.

It takes Elijah exactly three minutes to reply, despite him seeing
the photo the second I sent it.

Elijah: Fuckkkk, don't send me things like that. Where are
you? I'll pick you up.

I smirk.

Checkmate.

Rosalia: You're not picking me up after avoiding me for TWO
months. Tell me where to meet you. I'll take a taxi so I can
leave my best friend my car.

Elijah: You ain't going in a fucking taxi wearing *that*. Tell me
where you are, **Peaches**.

Peaches.

My heart shouldn't swell this much, but I can't help it. Swallowing
thickly, I cast a glance in Naomi's direction as she grinds her ass
against Noah, his girlfriend nowhere in sight.

Well, it looks like somebody got what they came here for.

I turn back to my phone.

After sending Elijah the address, he tells me he isn't far and will be here in five.

Five minutes.

I disappear into the hall and after finding a bathroom that people aren't fucking each other in, go to the toilet and wash my hands. Warm emerald eyes stare back at me in the mirror as I push the strap of my purse farther up my shoulder.

The ball is in my court.

Elijah's going by my rules.

There's nothing to stress out about.

Except there is when I return to the living room. The first thing Naomi says when I hand her my Fiat's keys and tell her that I'm meeting up with Elijah is, "No, no, no, he could murder you, Rosalia! Please don't go out with him!"

Some teens around us snap their heads our way, but I'm just glad Cayden isn't within earshot.

Softly smiling at her concern, I reassuringly squeeze her shoulders. "He gave me a first edition. He's not going to murder me. I promise I'll be okay, okay? I'm just stressed about you driving home…"

"Don't be stressed. I literally only had one shot, but I'm worried about *you*…" Naomi slowly says, the light in her eyes dimming. "Are you sure this Elijah can be trusted? You didn't search him up, but I sure did. He's thirty-one Rosalia, *thirty-one* And guess what? He's going to be thirty-two this year! That's fifteen years older than us. Do you know how crazy that age gap is? And yes, he's in this upcoming alternative rock band, which okay, yes, it's pretty fucking cool, but *still*… I just love you, Rosa."

"I love you too, babe." I frown as I pull her into a tight embrace, her body sweaty from all the dancing, but I don't care. "I wouldn't be seeing him if I didn't trust him. Believe me, okay?"

Naomi sadly glances between my eyes until she finally gives in with a nod. "At least make me come out with you and see him, okay?"

I pull her into another embrace, my rosy scent merging with her patchouli one. "Okay."

We're out of Noah's penthouse in no time, glancing around for his sleek Harley, except there isn't one. Instead, double parked in front of a BMW is a glossy black vintage Chevrolet Camaro (I want to say late

'60s) that screams his name. And scream his name it does as Elijah steps out of the driver's seat and... *whoa.*

He looks different. *So different.* A good different.

He has dark stubble, and it makes him look sexier than ever.

His alluring gaze is darker, harder, like a real standoffish rock star.

And, perhaps the most shocking, there's no sign of his signature leather jacket. Instead, he wears a white T-shirt that hugs his broad chest and taut torso. It exposes his beautiful light olive skin, those big muscular biceps, and inky black tattoos that cascade across each arm.

Elijah's gray-eyed stare pierces straight through me, and electricity is all I feel light up my body. Sparks zoom across every inch of me at a million miles per hour.

He actually came.

But no matter how hard I want to smile; I keep my expression motionless.

"Holy shit, he's hot!" Naomi gasps under her breath, and before I know it, she's storming toward him in her five-inch heels.

"Hey! Asshole!" she grits, getting all up in his face, but he's so much taller that it's really in his chest. "I'm giving you the benefit of the doubt right now, but if you hurt my best friend, I will fuck you up, got it?"

Elijah slowly arches a brow. "Your friend was the one who wanted to see me, so you ask her."

"I don't care *who* said *what*!" Naomi's all serious as she wiggles a finger in his face. "You hurt her, I'll fuck you up! Understood?"

Manhattan's hustle and bustle rushes over their brief silence.

"Understood," Elijah growls. Taking a step closer to her on the sidewalk, he clenches his jaw. "But just so you know, I've never hurt a woman in my entire life, and I never *ever* will."

"You're fucking lucky I believe you." Naomi shoots him one final death glare before coming back to me.

She wraps her arms around my waist and kisses my cheeks, all while Elijah and I never take our eyes off each other. "You know what to do if he becomes difficult. Just call me, okay? I love you, girlfriend."

"I love you too, babe."

The second she walks back into the luxury apartment complex, it's just Elijah and me, and our stare-off. He steps back until he's by his vintage Camaro and pops open the passenger door, all while never taking his eyes off me. His hand steadies above the hood, leaning against it as his fingers begin to drum a rhythm that I feel plunges face-first into my heart.

He's waiting, waiting for me.

Cars that can't get past in the street because of him double parked begin honking, their extended deafening beeps doing nothing to Elijah, who stands composed, confident, and cocky.

Determined to prove to him that I too have changed since we last saw each other, I stride up to him like it's the catwalk of my life. My heels come to a halt just before I step into the passenger seat to glance up at Elijah with a glare of my own.

"If you piss me off…" I warn, fending off my nerves with clenched fists. "I *will* kick you in the balls, okay?"

Elijah stares.

And stares.

And stares.

Those gunmetal gray eyes send me to hell right here in the middle of Manhattan as the slightest half-smirk works up his lips.

"Nice seeing you too," he mockingly murmurs under his breath. "Nothing sweet about you these days, *Peaches*."

"Damn straight there isn't."

"Mmhmmm." Elijah nods, glancing into the distance before knocking on the car's roof twice.

Those wolfish gray eyes find mine and when they do, they darken as he gestures to his car.

"So, how is this gonna go, Rosalia Philips? Are you gonna get in, or do I gotta carry you in myself?"

Chapter
SIX

Rosalia

After slipping into Elijah's tan leather passenger seat, I slam the car door in his face. You'll be happy to know that I actually complied and got inside his car without him having to touch me (which, by the way, I *wouldn't* have been opposed to any other night but tonight).

I'm pissed off with Elijah Diesel. Actually, I'm livid. Nobody in their right mind ignores somebody for two months straight, no matter what goes down. It's deceitful. Disrespectful. And something his mother should have taught him better.

As I click on my seat belt and Elijah rounds the car, I hate how much the fight in my body begins to slip at this lingering scent. His car smells so good—exactly like him—and that musky, sandalwood blend with a hint of tobacco is everywhere.

I've never been in an upcoming rock star's car before, but Elijah has a habit of making me break all the rules, so I'm not surprised by this one.

Elijah's vintage Chevrolet Camaro is by far the most impressive thing I've ever seen. Everything is so neat. Organized. Perfect—like the restored original dash. There isn't any piled-up junk, wrappers, or thrown clothes anywhere. It's impeccable.

There isn't even an inch of dirt on the car mats.

Who even is this guy?

My body is highly aware of Elijah's presence when he pops his door open and slides into the driver's seat. He slams it shut with a clenched jaw, never looking at me once as he pulls out a cigarette.

I gawk at him for far more than I should as he lights his cigarette, lets out an appeased moan, and slips on his seat belt. In. That. Exact. Order. I think my ovaries just exploded at the sound of that gravelly moan, just saying.

Dear God.

I cross my legs, the growing heat between my thighs only intensifying the longer I watch him.

"Staring at me ain't gonna do shit to aid the gravity of this situation," Elijah mumbles under his breath, clouds of thick white smoke filling the air as he begins driving down the beautifully lit city streets.

I scrunch up my nose at the smoke. "I'm not staring."

"Oh, is that why I can feel your eyes still on me?"

I'm just staring at your beauty, jackass.

Why do boys always have the best long lashes?

And why does he look even hotter driving with one hand on the wheel? His other hand is pulled back, elbow leaning by the window as he slowly rubs a hand over his sexy dark stubble.

I scoff. "Are you always such a perpetual idiot, or is this performance just for me?"

And then something happens.

Something I never expected.

Elijah grins.

Grins.

And gah, where have those dimples been hiding all this time?

Elijah's pretty gray eyes flicker to mine just as he slows at a red light. We're first at the traffic light, and if I wasn't so fascinated by how the glowing red light cuts shapes into his perfectly structured face, I would have heard what he replied.

"Umm, sorry." I clear my throat. "What did you say?"

Elijah's grin extends to a full-blown smirk. "I said *perpetual* is a big word for a girl who just came out of pre-k."

Ugh!

I roll my eyes in frustration and stare out the window at absolutely nothing. "Can you stop teasing me about my age? I'm honestly only fifteen years younger. That's nothing."

"No, it's *everything*," he grits, and *hello, Mr. Cold as ice.* "It's everything when you're only fucking seventeen."

"You say it like it's a crime!"

"I say it like you shouldn't be in my car at this hour!"

"Seriously?" I spit, facing him just as the light turns green and he takes off. "Are you serious right now? *You're* the one who wanted to see me tonight. I was adamant in asking you for *a* date to meet, *not* for it to be *tonight.*"

I don't miss the way Elijah's fist clenches around the wheel, squeezing it so tight, his knuckles turn white.

"Jesus Christ, Rosalia," he growls, and this time I feel it cut into my ego. He continuously flickers his gaze between me and the road. "How the fuck did you expect me to react after the photo you sent me, huh? Of course I wanted to see you right away."

"Why?"

"Don't."

"Don't, *what*?"

"Don't question something after I say it."

I give him a royal salute. "Yes, daddy."

That is until I realize what I just said to him… *daddy.*

Oh. My. GOD.

Squeezing my eyes shut, I pray that I just disappear in *three… two… one.*

I open my eyes to Elijah's death glare.

Nope, still here.

I know I shouldn't be this turned on while he clenches his jaw twice. Slowly. Sexily. But I am.

"Unless I'm fucking buried deep inside you," Elijah begins with a growl, his glare only darkening. "In which *I'm not*, and *will not ever be*, then. Do. Not. Fucking. Call. Me. *That.* Again."

My jaw drops.

Ohmygod. Ohmygod. Ohmygod.

Elijah Diesel just said that.

I think it's fair to say that after the stare-off he has with me, the one that results in him looking even more broody and me even more flustered, the fact that we don't speak for the entire ride (to wherever the heck we're going) is justified.

His words replay in my mind, over and over again, until he pulls his car into park at West 36th Street in front of what looks like a studio… a music studio hangout?

Elijah kills the engine, but that's all that happens as we both continue staring out the windshield, the silent tension desperately needing to be cut with a knife.

He just keeps taking long drags of his cigarette, like this isn't affecting him at all.

"So, what's your band called?" I ask, attempting to deflect. "Do you have a manager? Record label? I think I should know before going in… yeah?"

His eyes find mine, almost shocked. "You really want to know?"

"Of course I do."

Elijah gazes away from me. His response only comes after he's taken a few more puffs of his cigarette, its amber tip our only light at this stage, aside from the silvery moonlight pouring through the windows.

"We're an upcoming band. That's why we were in *Rolling Stone* magazine. For exposure. We do have a manager, but right now until the right label comes along, we're enjoying the indie game. This is our own private studio where we practice, record, and just hang out. No one else occupies it. We own it," Elijah quietly explains. "What else did you ask?"

"What your band is called?"

"It used to be called *Odyssey*, but a month ago we came to a unanimous decision to change it."

"Oh, why's that?"

Elijah sighs, and it's a heavy one. Loaded. "Rebranding and shit, you know."

Something tells me it's more than that, but I let it go.

"So, what's your rock band called now?"

Elijah plays with a piece of loose string on his jeans, and when his dark eyes flicker to mine, pooling in something I can't quite explain, it's so intense, I gasp.

"*Diesel Rose*," he murmurs, looking at me for the longest time as if I'm supposed to understand something.

Diesel Rose.

Elijah *Diesel*.

Diesel.

And the 'Rose'?

Could it be that the greatest love of his life was or is called 'Rose'?

Think, Rosalia, think.

Wait… wait a minute.

Rosalia Philips.

Rosalia.

Rosa.

Rose.

Diesel *Rose.*

Diesel *Rose.*

My breath slows.

Could it be that…?

I internally shake my head to myself. No, there's no way. Ironic, maybe. But there's no way in the world that Elijah named his band after me.

He hates me, remember? Well, he certainly did a month ago, anyway.

Diesel Rose… It's the most beautiful, most tragically bittersweet band name I've ever heard. And I love it, for all the wrong reasons.

Deciding it's best to move on from this conversation, I deflect it the best I can.

"I didn't mean to…" I pause, gulping down my pride as I manage to come up with the right words. "What I meant to say earlier was in reference to the father kind of *daddy*, not *daddy* in the sexual kind of way. Sorry, I didn't mean to unlock your… I don't know… *kink*?"

Elijah practically slams his head against the headrest. "It's not a fucking kink, Rosalia," he hisses.

"The way you shut me down, it's obvious that it is."

"Should you be talking to a thirty-one-year-old man like that?"

Thirty-one.

"I don't know. Should you be staring at a seventeen-year-old's legs like that?"

I only said it to stir him up for catching him staring because there's nothing illegal about what he's doing. About what we're *both* doing. Whatever is going on between us, it's legal. The age of consent in New York is seventeen. If I really wanted to sleep with him, I could. It doesn't make it illegal, just forbidden. Very, very forbidden. *And risky.*

And yet, here, while two o'clock blankets the ominous New York Midtown skies through the windshield window, it's Elijah Diesel's hot stare on my legs that gives me a little life.

He notices what I said because the moment I say it, his eyes leave me and it almost makes me feel hollow inside.

I slowly turn to him, surprised his eyes are squeezed shut, almost as if it's killing him not to stare, but his pride is way too big to tell me.

I stare at his cigarette, how he lines it up to the center of his soft lips as he takes another hit.

"You can look at me if you want to," I find myself whispering. "I won't tell anybody."

"Looking at you ain't good for my sanity, *Peaches.*"

Peaches.

I chew on my lower lip. "Why?"

"Because I still haven't forgiven you for what you said to me two months ago. You think I don't remember, huh?" Elijah almost scoffs. "Because I remember it all right. I remember it well. No amount of those fucking sexy long legs of yours will make me forget."

And just like that, the walls come crumbling down. My lips part to nothingness and Elijah roughly opens his driver's door and steps out of the car, slamming it behind him.

I watch him confidently stride around the car, crush his cigarette under his Doc Martens, and not once acknowledging my existence beyond opening my door for me.

With a pang in my chest, I awkwardly thank him and step out of the car, placing a mental note in my mind that while he is an ass-hole, he does, oddly enough, have a slight chivalrous side. And I do mean *slight* because when he locks his car before unlocking the stu-dio door with a code, he strides in first and the door almost slams in my face before I jump inside.

He locks it shut after me.

There isn't much more I can say other than, "*whoa,*" when my eyes rake the space beyond Elijah. A long hallway with dark walls is what we're met with, cool vintage band posters aligning the wall with small lights above each poster like it's an art museum. It's as if those posters are inspiration for where Diesel Rose wants to be, and to be honest, I love it.

The warm lighting feeds into the atmosphere as I follow Elijah down the hall.

The Ramones.

Led Zeppelin.

K.I.S.S.

My favorite, *The Neighbourhood*.

This place is like heaven.

We come to the end of the hall and my feet slow by the dark oak hardwood floors. There are two options—left or right—and both are masked off with solid black doors.

I glance up at Elijah and he slightly glances over his shoulder at me. "Do you want to meet the boys first and then talk?"

I shrug, failing to ask him *what boys exactly* because I'm just so mesmerized by this space. I knew he was going to take me somewhere to talk. I just didn't expect it to be *here*—in his livelihood.

Elijah turns left and I follow him like a lost puppy. He knocks on the dark door twice, and when nothing happens, he lets out a curse word and presses his thumb against a security thing beside the door. A red light switches to green and the door automatically pops open.

Gritty bass guitar going wild, impressive drumming, and a low but passionate argument fill the room as Elijah steps into his throne of a studio room.

The first question pops into my head. "How did you expect any-body to open the door if it's supposed to be soundproof?"

"The door has sensors. A buzz rings inside this studio when somebody knocks twice, but these fuckers were probably too high to notice."

High?

He continues walking, but when he realizes I'm just standing here, turns around and presses a hand by my lower back, encourag-ing me in.

"You sure these guys won't kill me?" I whisper over to him with a side-eye, bouncing on my heels with both nerves and excitement.

Elijah dramatically rolls his eyes. "I'm in a rock band, Rosalia, not the damn mafia."

"What's the difference, big fella, huh? I've heard the saying sex, drugs, and rock and roll before… the mafia can't be too different. Well, I guess violence and live ammunition in exchange for rock and roll, but still! Hey, wait up! Where are you going?"

Elijah ignores me completely and keeps on walking.

Note taken.

I jump when the door dead bolts shut behind me and I run after him, feeding more into that lost puppy personification.

The vibes in here are honestly so damn cool. Epic exposed brick walls. Continued oak floors. Large angled Persian rugs. Everything feeds into the leather, steel, and pops of brass vibes I imagined for this place. Full-on rock and roll industrial in the best kind of way.

The studio is huge, like double the size of the first level of my brownstone with a main chill-out practice area, then farther along there's a soundproof glass recording studio. And a little farther down, a lounge area with brown leather buttoned couches and a black mini fridge.

The air is laced with tobacco, cologne, and whiskey. It's the most masculine combination I've ever smelled, which as three sets of eyes flicker my way, reminds me that I'm the only woman in this room.

The music comes to a slaughtering end and three guys who look like they just stepped out of MFWFR—Milan Fashion Week for Rockers (and yes, I did just make that up)—stare at me. Like a real-deep-into-my-soul-until-there's-complete-nothingness-left-inside-me stare.

I silently scream to myself.

Is this a bad time to admit that I don't do too well with meeting new people?

Elijah steps up beside me. "Guys, this is *Peaches*. You can call her Rosalia."

The drummer—who seems the most standoffish out of all of them—is the first one to slightly nod. He has a leather French type of beret on, but with spikes instead of bows. He's wearing full-on leather. Leather jeans. Leather shirt. Leather jacket. Did I forget to mention it's hardcore summer? I'm pretty sure if I could see his shoes behind the drums, they'd also be leather.

Everywhere I look, I get extra tough guy vibes from him; his gaze, the dark ink crawling up his neck, and his luscious long chestnut hair, which reaches his ribs with golden streaks, that my mother—if she saw—would admire for six hours straight.

"Nice to meet ya, Rosalia." He nods, spinning a drumstick in his grip.

"Hi." I give him a tight-lipped smile.

Not really knowing what else to do, I glance back at Elijah. He keeps his gaze on the drummer but is talking to me when he says, "That's Dave, as you can see, our drummer. He's been on tour with some of the greatest." A smirk crawls up his lips. "So, he's a fucking traitor, but now he's here to stay."

"Damn straight I am." Dave chuckles.

Elijah motions to a guy with perfect caramel skin to the left of Dave—the guitarist—who actually steps forth to take my hand.

"Yo, I'm Zander." He grins. He has the prettiest brown eyes with violet brush field spots I've ever seen, lined in heavy eyeliner. "Sick skirt."

I glance down at the short denim pleated skirt Naomi picked out for me and return my gaze to him, grinning. "Thanks, my best friend picked it out for me even though it was in my closet."

"Epiccc. Well then, I want to meet this friend of yours too now."

I find myself giggling because this wasn't what I was expecting Elijah's bandmates to be like at all. I thought they'd be all metal rock heads with death glares and flip me off whenever they got the chance. Instead, they're actually good guys, despite them all being tough rockers.

Okay, maybe these guys aren't murderers. Maybe it's just Elijah Diesel.

Speaking of… Elijah steps closer to me and his cologne floods my lungs, cuing all my damn butterflies as he clears his throat, slaughtering the laughter between Zander and me.

Zander awkwardly coughs and steps back, collecting his guitar from the Persian rug.

"Last guy…" Elijah mumbles, like he really hates doing this, and gestures toward a guy with a bass guitar strapped to his chest who's looking everywhere but me. "That's Knives."

Knives?

Just as I'm about to speak, Knives—who's smoking a rolled-up joint—pulls up his hoodie, covering his short dirty-blond locks. He grumbles something under his breath, and I only catch my name alongside a profanity before he continues typing away on his phone.

Well, two out of three ain't bad.

I turn to Elijah, perplexed. "Did you just say *Knives*? Is that his real name?"

"It's an acronym of the first three letters of his first name and the last three letters of his surname. *Kni*ght I*ves*. We just call him Knives."

"Whoa, that's actually cool, Elijah."

"The fuck?" Knives scoffs, his voice not as deep as I imagined. He flicks his light eyes to me, completely motionless. "Did you just fucking say *Elijah*?"

I stare at him with bile rushing up my throat. He's by far the scariest here and… maybe isn't a serial killer but could definitely be a psychopath for all I know. Especially when he starts chuckling.

I rock on the balls of my feet, my palms getting sweaty because suddenly four guys who are practically strangers are staring at me at two o'clock in the morning and I'm taking way too long at a simple question. It feels like I'm drowning in the waves of the Atlantic with no way out.

Is this guy playing with me, or did he just not hear?

"Yeah…" I say, finally finding my voice. "Why?"

He eyes Elijah and a smirk slowly crawls. "Thought you only went by Diesel, bro, no?"

Silence takes over the room.

I furrow my brows… *Am I missing something?*

I glance at Elijah, who is clenching his jaw at his bass guitarist with the devil in his eyes. "Shut the fuck up, Knives."

Knives simply shrugs and turns to me with a yawn before that smirk resurfaces from the apparent shadows of his dark heart. "Nice to meet you, Rosalia. You sing or something?"

"Umm, I dance ballet actually."

Dave and Zander glance at each other and snicker.

Shutting his phone, Knives lets out a hum and sizes me up. "Professionally and shit?"

"I would love to when I graduate, but my father would probably prefer me to do something in lieu of his profession."

Elijah—Diesel—or whatever the heck he wants me to call him,

crosses his arms over his broad chest and for the first time since we've entered this room, looks at me for more than two seconds. "Which is?"

"Medicine." I nervously smile. "My father's a neurosurgeon."

They're really beautiful guys, but Elijah—*gah*—there's just something extra about him. Maybe it's the mystery in his eyes, and how it comes with such sexiness, alongside the fact that he's the lead vocalist, but there's something really special about him.

It's crazy how we went from a tense argument in his late '60s vintage Chevrolet Camaro moments to him… introducing me to his bandmates. But I'm sure the convo Elijah and I need to have after this won't be as pretty.

"Oh, shit," Knives curses and he takes another drag of the joint, its toxic smoke lingering as he waves it up in the air. "Promise it's prescription."

"I'm sure it is."

"Soooo, how do you and Diesel know each other?"

My heart simmers into silence as I open and close my mouth like a fish. *Do I tell him the truth? That I was stalking Elijah/Diesel like a nutcase?* I'm lost for words because that doesn't give the greatest impression of myself, even though it is the truth.

Besides, it's not like Elijah and I are even friends… or lovers… So, what are we?

Does Knives genuinely not know how we met? Or did Elijah tell his bandmate about me, about how we met and is Knives now just testing me?

It would mean this introduction would be a lie.

Before I can make even more of a fool out of myself, Elijah Diesel simmers the silence with his raspy honeyed sin voice. "*Peaches* ain't answering, so it's question fucking skipped."

Elijah didn't tell them. At all.

"All right." Knives sighs, strumming a few notes on his bass, and it sounds so damn good. "Last question I have for right now. You know how you said you still wanted to dance when you graduate, but you probably should do something in more the medical fucking realm, yeah?"

"Yeah…"

"Well, what undergrad are you currently taking? And I warn you, answer carefully."

"Oh." I gasp and shake my head to clear the confusion. "I meant when I graduate *high school*, not *college*... I'm seventeen. I'll be starting my senior year when summer ends."

I knew my clarification would do some damage, but I didn't expect *this*...

"SEVENTEEN?!" Knives shouts, and not only do his eyes widen when he snaps his head to Elijah, but the others do too. "DIESEL, DUDE! What the FUCK? She hasn't even GRADUATED HIGH SCHOOL YET?"

His words echo in my mind, but all I hear is, *unworthy, unworthy, unworthy.*

"Shut your *fucking* mouth, Knives, before I shut it for you!" Elijah growls, shoving Knives's chest back when he steps forward. "*Peaches* and I are gonna have a little chat. In private. None of you find a way to sneak into the bar unless you want your balls severed."

"I like you, Rosalia, but I wouldn't sacrifice my balls for you," the drummer, Dave, mumbles under his breath as he hits his drumsticks together five times. "You're on your own."

And the drumming commences but does nothing to drown out my rapidly beating heart that rushes into overdrive. I don't like the way his bandmates are looking at me—Knives in particular—he's got a look in his eyes that tells me I don't belong here. With them. With Elijah.

Wordlessly, Elijah slips his hand in mine and we're out of the room in seconds. Any other time I'd be giddy, but after what just happened, I feel like curling up in a fetal position and never talking to any of these guys again.

Elijah doesn't let his tight grip on my hand go as we cross the hall to the only other door. It's only after the door clicks unlocked and we step in that our intertwined hands fall.

Holy... *wow, this place is so cool.*

This room is the exact size of the other but done up like a bar. The same exposed brick walls and oak floorboards, but for some reason, the ceilings seem taller. Frosted floor-to-ceiling black steel New York windows take over one wall, and I love the warm Edison pendant lights Elijah flicks on. There are so many of them and they cascade down on a thin metal rope, matching the industrial theme.

The bar's countertop is a soft charcoal marble, and instead of tables and chairs surrounding the room, brown leather studded couches, some buttoned like the one in the studio. It's the type of luxurious bar you would host a function, not have inside your studio, but I go for it.

Behind the counter is a lit-up wall filled with all kinds of liquor on brass shelves, and I really like how the two red neon signs above the bar glowing, **DIESEL ROSE**, and then lower down, **Sex, Drugs, and Rock and Roll**, gives the entire room a soft, devilish hue.

The second neon sign has me laughing inside. I said those exact words to Elijah when we entered this building, and I questioned the difference between his rock band and the underworld.

Feeling defeated, I watch as Elijah steps into the bar with tense shoulders. Although we never did start off in a good mood tonight, it feels like the air between us has become far worse.

So maybe it's the devil in me that makes me want to sin a little when Elijah spreads his hands firmly on the countertop, flicks his dark gaze to me, and not so calmly says, "You wanted to talk—*talk*."

But I invite it.

Livid, I don't stop giving him a piece of my mind from ten feet away. I tell him how much of a jerk he is for thinking he can act so nonchalant after ignoring me for two months. I tell him that if I could go back in time, I'd slap his face for even suggesting coming inside of my house, instead of simply giving me my schoolbag on the porch steps.

I tell him that I never meant to call him a *freak* and that it's been eating me up inside ever since.

That I finished *The Beautiful and Damned* weeks ago, and how rude it was to never return my calls. Then I question why he left me such a heartfelt book for a man so cruel.

I tell him everything.

Everything. Everything. Everything.

Including how frustrated I am that these things keep on happening to me. That people keep fucking up my emotions. Abandoning me—including him.

I tell him the thought of graduating next year makes me sick because I don't know what the hell I want to do with my life.

I tell him I'm sorry. I'm sorry for offending him and causing so much pain.

I tell him I never want to see him again, and then I tell him that

I do because for some reason I really like seeing him. Being around him makes me feel different... noticed... *seen*.

And then, when I'm on my last breath and am sure I'll either burst into a million pieces or pass out from all my lack of breathing, I give him an ultimatum—*to either stay in my life forever or to leave forever*—because there isn't an in-between for me.

Through all my shouts, Elijah doesn't move a muscle. He remains standing tall with all the space between us. Defiant. And while I'm here panting, trying to catch my breath, he. Freaking. Does. *Nothing*.

He just stares.

Stares.

Stares.

Until the onyx-gray coating his pretty eyes gleams in a reckless desire for neither life nor death. It's as if he has me hanging onto purgatory by a bare thread with the way his piercing gaze punctures me.

I have never—nor will I ever—meet a man as complicated as Elijah Diesel.

It has me ball up my fight. Grind my jaw. Stride up to him with my cherry-red stilettos and demand he tells me something. *Anything*.

I'm so fired up that when he eventually angles his body my way so we're both behind the counter, separated by a few inches, even more blood rumbles up my veins.

The stare-off doesn't end, not even when he begins to grind his teeth and blindly reaches for an open bottle of whiskey on the counter that I didn't notice before.

"I'm going to kill you for being so freaking cruel to me!" I grit, slamming my hand on the cold marble counter. "*Kill! You!* Elijah Diesel!"

He doesn't flinch, but I sure hurt my hand on the solid Italian stone.

Elijah does everything but give me a response as he arches a brow, his eyes darkening even deeper when he brings the whiskey bottle to his lips like a beast. He gulps down two fingers' worth, all without ever taking his gaze off me over the glass.

Like a true rocker, he doesn't even care to wipe his mouth after he slams the bottle back on the counter, making me flinch, alongside my heart.

And I hate it.

Hate *him*.

Hate him even more as my eyes settle on the remnants of the amber liquid coating his lips, enticed with the way it has his mouth glimmering in the low light. Between the warm hue of the Edison lights and the seductive glow of the red neons, Elijah Diesel, my gorgeous villain, becomes a wonderland I wish I could just wrap my body around and kiss. Devour. Love on until he tells me to stop.

It's one way to finally get him to speak to me.

It's one way to stop this silent cat-and-mouse game.

It's one way to know if the coldest melancholic-eyed rocker would kiss me back...

I've never been kissed before, and right now, as the air between us thickens, that same devil in me craves making Elijah Diesel my first. To let kissing him be that wild thing I do this summer.

I crave it.

I crave having his soft lips on mine. For him to kiss me back. Hard. Like he hates me.

I crave it like I do my next breath, which is why I lean forth and do exactly that...

I kiss the monster I've secretly prayed would crawl out from under my bed ever since he stormed out of my bedroom months ago. I kiss Elijah Diesel—the wicked devil—breathlessly.

Chapter
SEVEN

Rosalia

The second my lips crash against his, I know I'm a goner for all the wrong reasons.

I'm nervous. So damn nervous, I feel the trembles all up my spine as my heart kicks into overdrive, but it's that same adrenaline rush that propels me to hell's gates.

With my clammy hands awkwardly pressed against his chest, his hot breath tickles my cheek the second I slam my mouth against his. The sparks in my chest intensifying. Suddenly, I'm grateful for all the *Cosmopolitan* magazines Naomi and I used to read detailing how to give the most breathtaking kiss.

I'm not desperate. I'm a flustered seventeen-year-old melting against Elijah Diesel's soft lips. They're warm. *So warm.* Everything I wasn't expecting.

I kiss him slow, adamant, with everything that's in me, all while he remains motionless with what I sense is a vicious clenched jaw. He punishes me by not kissing me back.

I repeat…

Elijah. Diesel. Does. Not. Kiss. Me. Back.

He doesn't press me up against him.

He doesn't give me a sign that he wants this.

He doesn't part his lips, rejecting anything deeper.

Instead, he taunts me, like the cold-hearted beast he is, making me feel even smaller all while I rake my hand through his dark wavy hair, needing him closer.

My lips mold against his, sparks igniting my entire body because I've never been this daring before. Not with an older man I barely know. My heart slams against my ribcage so recklessly, panicking during this one-sided breathless kiss.

I kiss him hard. Endlessly. But it all amounts to nothing.

Shit. Shit. Shit.

I'm certain it can't get more awkward than this when I abruptly pull away.

Ohmygod, this is so embarrassing.

I just wasted my first kiss on a man who PURPOSELY didn't even MOVE A MUSCLE IN PROTEST just to show HE'S THE ONE WINNING this invisible game between us.

Because he's doing just that—*winning*—and it's only confirmed when I pull away with shameful eyes and Elijah's glare is indifferent. It's so obvious that he's the one who calls the shots.

He's so vain, he didn't even kiss me back.

God, I feel so pathetic.

It doesn't matter how blurry my gaze becomes. I hold back tears. There's no way I'm crying in front of him. *Because* of him. I won't. No matter how much of a painstaking reminder my smeared glossy lipstick on his lips is of my foolish action mere seconds ago.

Finally—FINALLY—after what feels like fifteen minutes since Elijah last spoke, he says a word. Well, he says more, but I suddenly wish he could have stopped at the one.

"*Peaches,*" Elijah rasps, and there's fury in his gaze, a deadly devilish fire, one I wish didn't just ignite right before my very eyes. "You shouldn't have kissed me."

Elijah takes a step toward me.

I take one back.

He takes another two steps forward.

I take two back.

He starts striding confidently, like a wolf wanting to claim what's his again.

Flustered, I rush backward and accidentally slam against the bar's exposed brick wall, chilling coldness trickling down my spine. A hiss escapes my lips at the force.

Ouch.

In a flash, Elijah has me properly pinned against the wall, his hips locking me in with nowhere to go. He towers over me, an entire foot of height difference. Frustrated, I attempt to shove him back, but his reflexes are so fast, he roughly grips my wrists with one hand before I make any contact with his chest.

A crazed growl escapes his lips and the grip on my wrists tightens as he slams them against the wall, above my head.

The action is hot. Demanding. *Dominant.* It's also the complete undoing for me because from this moment forth, I know I don't have the upper hand like I did earlier.

No, not anymore.

Not after I virtually smothered him in unreturned kisses and died from mortification.

Elijah's wicked glare slowly forms into a slow, sexy half-smirk, but a condescending one nonetheless.

"Rosalia, tell me something…" he begins softly, and then the smirk flickers to complete carnage with every staccato growl—a sickly reminder of how fast his mood can alter. "What. The. *Fuck.* Was. That?"

Hyperventilating inside, I stare back at him with wide eyes. My body is numb. My throat is dry. I have no words.

I'm so screwed.

"Ohhh, you're not going to speak now, huh? You think if you keep quiet, I won't talk?"

"I…" A staggered breath escapes me. "I, umm—"

"ANSWER ME!" Elijah yells, slamming his free hand against the exposed brick, missing my face by inches. "WHAT THE *FUCK* WERE YOU DOING *KISSING ME*?"

Shaking away some of my blonde waves that blew into my face when his fist hit the wall, I shut my eyes to the soundtrack of Elijah's heavy breaths.

This thing some people call a heart jolts—*just like it always does around him.* It scares me how much I'm still drawn to this even when he's like this. When he's pinning me up against the wall, bounding my wrists, and yelling in my face asking why I kissed him.

I have nothing but the truth—*my* truth—to give to him. Nothing else.

"I really hate the way I feel so nervous whenever I'm around you, the nervous that brings butterflies to my stomach… like right now," I whisper, barely hearing my own words myself as my eyes remain shut. "This adrenaline… I've been wanting to feel it for a long time, but now that I finally do, I don't know how to feel about it."

Elijah remains silent. His crazed breaths, lingering cologne, and warmth of his body pressed against mine remind me this isn't a tragic dream or bittersweet nightmare. He's here.

I continue, "At the start of summer, I made this stupid goal for myself to do something wild before August ends. I made the goal to prove I…" A lump forms at the back of my throat, drilling ache into my ocean of angst. "To prove I was worth it, and that I have what it takes to be free. I kissed you because I thought it would mean you would finally talk to me after everything I just said to you. I did it because kissing you is just about the wildest thing I could ever do."

The words that have been chained to my chest are finally out. I don't know how Elijah will take it, but all I do know is that there's nothing else I can say to explain myself. That was all of it.

I know kissing Elijah Diesel was foolish, but the way he reacted was as if I'd killed him.

I just want him to understand.

"*Fuck.*" Elijah sighs and shocks me with how intimately low his voice becomes. "You don't want that, *Peaches*, believe me. You don't want to be kissing me."

With my heartbeat in my throat, right beside that lump, I flicker my eyes open. I wasn't sure what I would be getting, but gazing up into Elijah's eyes now as he lowers his head so we're level, I see the change in them. The fury is gone, and in its place—nothing. Just wolfish onyx.

I want to lick my lipstick off his lips, bite his lip, and then slap him.

"I did," I confess with a frown. "I *do.*"

"You *don't,*" Elijah grits. "You're smart, Rosalia, so don't be this naïve. You're seventeen. I'm fifteen years older. What do you think will happen at the end of the summer, hmm? That you'd change me, we'd fall in love, and go running off into the sunset together?"

He cocks his head at my delayed response.

I shake my head. "I'm not saying that's going to happen, but—"

He cuts me off, "No *buts*. It ain't happening. Why? Because Elijah Diesel doesn't fall in love."

Elijah's grip tightens on my wrists, all while his other hand slowly comes down to give my lacy choker the gentlest of tugs.

Oh.

His gaze lowers to his finger, which squeezes beneath the tightest gap between the white lace and my throat, looping it, almost fascinated as he traces the detailing.

My breaths labor at just how close we're standing. I swear he can feel every pulse of my heart with his finger pressed up against me.

"I don't fall in love." Fixing his eyes back on me, he smolders and roughly inches me even closer with a tug of the choker that our noses brush. "Not even with self-acclaimed good girls who are actually bad girls wearing my weakness so fucking well."

I gasp.

I knew he'd like the choker.

His smolder deepens.

"And believe me," Elijah adds in a murmur. "I'm not saying this just to be all fucking broody. I'm saying it because you're seventeen and should know better than to be with me at this hour."

My jaw drops. *Is this guy for real? Does he seriously think he can spin this all around?*

Liar.

I don't believe his words for one second, and for the first time since he pinned me against this wall, I find my voice and tell him exactly how it is.

"Oh my God, will you stop being so hypocritical, Elijah?" I spit, narrowing my gaze with a frustrated scream. "*You* are the one who wanted to meet *me* at this hour!"

"Because you wouldn't fucking leave me alone!"

"Well, we both wouldn't be here if you didn't storm out of my bedroom like a darn hurricane."

"If you kept your insults to yourself, that wouldn't have happened."

"Oh my God, I get it, but I literally apologized to you!" I practically scream. "*Twice!*"

"Still doesn't change the fact you're only seventeen."

"For the love of God, will you stop with the age? I'm not dumb. I know what I'm doing. Besides, if you were to bend me over right this second and make love to me, which I wouldn't be opposed to, it would be legal. New York's age of consent is seventeen."

Bend me over. Make love to me. Wouldn't be opposed to.

I squeeze my eyes shut, mortified. *Oh. My. God.*

Yep. I just said that. Out loud. Not in my head.

You're such an idiot for speaking your mind, Rosalia.

Elijah's lips part to nothing, pause, and then violently shut closed.

Check-freaking-mate.

Silence laces the air, blanketing with a fizzled tension neither of us can avoid.

Desire. Hatred. Curiosity.

"Rosalia Philips." A slow, devilish darkness hangs on the edges of Elijah's lips. "Did you just say you want me to fuck you?"

Yes.

Time slows. I bite my lower lip and those onyx wonderlands flicker there.

Even through all this heated rage, am I still that obvious to him?

Well, I mean, you did just openly verbally admit it, Rosalia, so there's that.

I scoff to hide the blush crawling up my cheeks. "That's not what I meant."

Elijah arches a brow. "But you just admitted you want me, right?"

I look away, my answer evident from my silence… *Yes. Yes, I want you, asshole.*

Elijah Diesel—my melancholic addiction—growls. Like full-on sexily growls, almost on the verge of a moan. And just like that, the fury returns.

"*First,*" Elijah spits, his touch by my throat leaving to hold a finger up in front of my face. "I don't make love. I fuck. *Rough.*" He holds up another finger. "*Second*, I'm not going to fuck you, *Peaches*, so get that lust out of your eyes."

I can't look at him anymore. It hurts so much. It hurts to keep looking at somebody who makes your heart feel like it's going to burst out of your chest and him being so damn cold.

Elijah lets go of my wrists and I let them fall freely to my sides, not daring to move. Suddenly, those Edison pendant lights seem so important as I stare at them with blurry eyes like they're my cure.

"If you fucking try that again, try to kiss me, I will never speak to you again. Is that fucking understo—"

"No, it isn't, Diesel," I grit, cutting him off. "That's what you really prefer, isn't it—*Diesel*?"

His eyes flicker between mine. "Why are you doing this?"

"Doing *what*?"

"Fuckin' with my head. What the fuck do you want from me, little girl?"

"For you not to act like an ass after my epic fail of a first kiss."

Elijah laughs darkly in my face. "Oh, please, that wasn't your first kiss."

"It. Was. My. First. Kiss."

The laughter is slaughtered by a glare. "That's the most foolish thing I've ever heard."

"Wow, spoken like a true gentleman who reads F. Scott Fitzgerald. You're unbelievable, Elijah. I wish I had never kissed you, asshole!"

"Good. Because it was your first and last time kissing me."

"You're so confident you won't ever be in love with anybody, aren't you?" I hiss. "Well, I hope the girl of your dreams walks into your life, that you adore her with everything you've got, and then when you need her the most, she breaks your goddamn heart."

"That girl is you, *Peaches*, except you won't be the one to break my heart. Trust me."

"Fuck you!" I scream, and it gets harder to hold the tears when I shove his hard chest back.

Not expecting it, he stumbles back for a second, and the next thing I know, I'm being pinned up against the wall again with his hand roughly gripping my throat, and then… *he* kisses *me*.

Oh.

My.

God.

Elijah Diesel is kissing *me*. Hard. Recklessly. Far more breathlessly than I ever could.

I hate myself for wanting him.

I hate myself for caring.

I hate myself for kissing him back, letting him devour me in ways only devils know how.

My lips move in rhythm with his and my hands automatically return to weave through his hair and tug on the tips, while his free hand cups my face tight. Elijah Diesel's kiss is lethal, filthy—toxic, in the best kind of way. I can't get enough of the way our lips move so recklessly in sync.

Whoa.

His tongue caresses the center of my lips, in the gentlest of ways amid his recklessness. Our tongues collide like vicious fires, every single filthy stroke like heaven on earth with Lucifer.

A moan escapes my throat at how good it feels to be kissed by Elijah, and he must feel its loud vibration ricochet through my throat because his hold on it intensifies.

His grip is so dominating, so kinky, and something I'm really coming to love. Restraint. I can barely breathe in the sexualized chokehold, yet it's his passionate French kisses that revive me, again and again and again.

Elijah tastes like the sweetest peppermint and the darkest of whiskeys. There's also a hint of tobacco on his tongue, and it's all three of those things combined that has my warm sex continue to throb in arousal.

My poor excuse of a kiss minutes ago wasn't my first—*this* is my first kiss—and he knows it.

Elijah continues taking control, a moan vibrating through him too now as our tongues continue melting together, every hungered kiss turning even more desperate. Crazed. He consumes me. Completely. In ways I never knew existed.

It's so euphoric.

So addictive.

Bittersweet—because I know this will never happen again.

And it's only confirmed when Elijah abruptly ends our kiss,

coming back for more with two more final pecks. The last lingers, even after he sexily tugs down my lower lip, nibbling it softly like I'm his. Then, only after I moan out his name, he pulls away from me completely.

I instantly miss his touch. His heat. His kiss.

A darkened desire I know shouldn't be there is still so evident in his gaze when he stares down at me with heavy breaths, realizing what he just did. Our exhales merge together. He lets go of my throat and catching my breath has never felt more essential with the way my lungs burn in protest.

I ache for more. Ache for him. Ache for our tattered story.

Elijah Diesel was supposed to be a gorgeous rocker I admired in *Rolling Stone* magazine; he was never supposed to become a real-life fantasy that has changed my life in these months. He's all I think about, and I know it's wrong, but I really want to start fresh. I don't want him to be looking at me like he is right now, with so much… regret.

Then everything. Just. Softens. Down.

It gets quieter.

Intimate.

It feels as if we can look at each other without the world exploding in our faces.

"Rosalia…" Elijah murmurs softly. "Did you see the *Rolling Stone* magazine article I was in?"

I gulp down, suffering from a little whiplash because his question is so out of left field. "Yes."

"I know you asked me the name of my band, so that kind of answers it in itself, but did you read the article?"

"No."

"Have you ever… I don't know, looked me up?"

"No."

"Why?"

"I guess I wanted to deduce my own impression of you." I sadly sigh in all my truth. "I didn't and still don't want my thoughts on you to come from that *Rolling Stone* article, the world, or what an online source says. I want to hear it all from you, Elijah. The real you."

The air crackles between us, and I worry I said too much.

I try again. "I followed you that day not because I'm some crazy stalker or some lovesick girl. I followed you because I… I don't know why. You just felt like a risk, like the one person who didn't know me and therefore didn't have to see me for all my faults and sins."

"You don't have faults and sins, *Peaches*."

"I do." I sniffle, just as the first tear slips, cascading down my cheek to the corner of my lips. "So many, and I'm sorry for everything. I didn't mean for all of this to happen. For you to hate me. I just…"

"I get it. But I can't be your cure, Rosalia. It doesn't work that way." Resting his forehead against mine, Elijah softly shakes his head. "You ever try and kiss me again, I'll ruin your life."

"Please, I—"

"Shhh, *Peaches*," Elijah softly whispers, his thumb slowly brushing over my swollen lips. He's killing me slowly with his touch as he smooths over my soft skin, wiping the tear away. "So please don't cry for me because I can't be your cure. Not in the way you need."

"Why?"

I don't get his hot and cold.

How he can be so rough, then so sweet.

It's too much.

"Because I'll break your heart," Elijah whispers by my ear, his soft kisses down my neck leaving invisible scars. "And I'll leave without ever saying goodbye. So, to answer your ultimatum, I'm staying in your life, *Peaches*, whatever the fuck it means. Just don't fuck me over, don't take this for what it isn't, 'cause if you do, I'll just fuck you over right back."

The lump in my throat finally gives way and explodes in waves of vulnerability, dragging me down.

I'm losing him before our start.

Without ever looking at me again, Elijah pulls away, stumbling back until he's leaning over the bar countertop.

There's silence, and then…

"Rosalia… I didn't mean to hurt you, or for it to go this far either."

In the pain of losing him, a small smile works up my lips. "I forgive you... and I hope you find it in you to forgive me too. For everything."

Nodding, Elijah spreads his long legs out and downs some more whiskey before blindly throwing me his car keys from his back pocket.

I catch them, all skittish.

"Run, Rosalia," he whispers into the bottle of amber liquid, his head hung low. "Get in my car and drive the fuck home."

Confused, I shake my head, but he can't see me. "Elijah, I'm sorry. Can we please just work this out? I don't want to leave."

"You *need* to."

"But that doesn't—"

"*Please*," Elijah begs, emotion cutting in his voice as he shuts his eyes. "Please, just go. Because if I look at you again, I'll break every single promise I just made to you. Those of me ruining your life. If I look at you again even for a single second, I'll want you—just like you want me—and that, *Peaches*, that will fucking destroy us both."

And with an ache in my chest, I listen.

I run out of the bar, out of the building, and into his car.

His scent lingers in the lonely air, reminding me he shouldn't have ever meant this much to me. I don't know what comes after this. What this means for us. If I'll truly ever see Elijah again. All I do know is that when I'm with him, I feel better.

I come out of my shell.

I become the woman I want to be, without the fear of losing those I love.

Driving in his vintage Chevrolet Camaro feels odd without him. Tucking those keys underneath the doormat feels even worse. But what I hate the most as I tumble into bed, right beside a snoring Naomi, is that my heart feels bruised.

Tattered and bruised with Elijah Diesel's permanent mark.

Tattered and bruised with the taste of whiskey still on my tongue.

And if this is what it feels like with my melancholic rocker still wanting to be in my life, what would it have felt like if he said that tonight was the last time I'll ever see him again in my life?

Elijah Diesel, whatever happens next, always remember I'm yours...

Chapter
EIGHT

Elijah

*F*uckkk.

Rosalia Philips is a constant in my mind; long after she bolts out of the bar, my car's keys jiggling in her grip. It takes a solid ten minutes for me to get my shit together and finally glance up at the space she used to be—by the exposed brick wall.

Where she kissed me.

Where I kissed her ruthlessly.

Where I felt the last piece of my self-control slipping away.

Fuck. Fuck. Fuck.

I know I shouldn't have ever touched Rosalia. Should have never devoured her. But those gorgeous light green eyes were gazing into mine with so much desire, so much need, that I ached to be the monster to cure her nightmare of a first kiss.

Jealousy took over and I showed her what a real kiss felt like… *electrifying.*

Even though Rosalia left the bar a good ten minutes ago, her lips are still bruised on mine. I haven't stopped clenching my jaw and my grip around this damn whiskey bottle. I'm so fucking angry with myself that heated tension crawls up my spine, deepening my throbbing headache.

I don't like that my heart feels so funny.

I don't like that it *feels* at all.

I've never been the kind of man to notice my own heartbeats before in a bid to silence everything that I am, but ever since I first laid my eyes upon Rosalia tonight in front of some fancy fucking apartment, the pitter-patter in my chest have kicked into overdrive.

I've been obsessed with those glossy pink lips of hers, enticed by her fierceness, and my life has been hanging on the thread with borrowed air ever since.

And my cock, which is only settling down now, has been a hard, pulsing nightmare all night.

I know *Peaches* shouldn't affect me this way.

I know it's bad.

But the second she openly admitted she wanted me, *fuckkk*, I wanted to take that peachy seventeen-year-old ass of hers and spank it hard until her skin was flushed the darkest shade of scarlet blushes. I wanted to spank her until she took the words back. All of them.

I don't know how the fuck I kept it together when I was kissing her. How I had enough control not to piston my hips forward so that she didn't feel the aching erection she brought on.

Her.

Only *her.*

I've had a difficult life. A tragically depressing one. And I know *Peaches* should stay the hell away from me, but I can't seem to fucking let her go. It's not a good thing for a man like me, a man who's barely surviving by the air in his lungs. Who can't seem to get (nor want) the taste of sweet cherry off his tongue—*the taste of her.*

As I step out of the bar and into the studio, Dave, Zander, and Knives's instrumental melodies do shit all to ease my thoughts. These late night/early morning jam sessions aren't anything new for us. These lonely hours of the night seem to be when inspiration hits the most. When corrosive liquor, illegal joints, and Diesel Rose's melancholic alternative indie rock numbs my cold, cold heart.

"The fuck happened to you, man?" Knives smirks from where

he's lying down on the Persian rug, his fingers never too far from his bass guitar.

I grind my teeth.

Peaches happened.

Some confidence this guy has after all the shit he's put me through already.

Not having time for his taunts, I fucking ignore him and instead reach down to tug the rolled joint from his lips. He dramatically rolls his eyes and now I'm the one smirking.

Raking a hand through my hair, I take a drag off the joint, the instant hit bringing a little slice of bliss to the pain trapped deep inside my soul. Waves of calmness baptize my body in a way I can only describe as heaven.

I can feel all the guys' eyes on me, hot like fucking vultures just waiting for me to react. I love these guys. I really do. They're like brothers to me. We've been through hell and back together. Honestly. But right now, it's difficult. I don't feel like talking, and with my feeling obsolete anyway, they get the message without me having to say a single word.

I knew it was a fucking mistake bringing Rosalia Philips to the studio. Making her meet the band. *What the fuck was I thinking?* They'll just assume, and I don't want that. I don't want their thoughts. Not right now while I'm losing my goddamn mind.

I've never brought a girl to one of our late-night jams before, even though Rosalia didn't hear shit.

I've never introduced anybody (except my damn alter-ego) to the band before.

I've never given anybody a nickname before.

Yeah, *I'm in big fucking trouble*, and I ain't just saying it for shits and giggles.

"I don't want to talk about what you may or may not think," I say with a tense jaw, my gaze slowly stalking between the three of them while blowing out a thick, white cloud. "*Peaches* ain't my friend, lover, or acquaintance… she's simply *Peaches*. So I don't want to hear any of you motherfuckers telling me any different, 'cause you know me, I won't listen."

And then, without me waiting for them to agree, I take hold of the microphone and gold-plated stand I dropped to the floor the second I received Rosalia's text earlier tonight. It's easily my favorite stand laced in a detailed vintage snake and little rocker skulls.

I need to forget about Rosalia and what happened tonight.

I need to fucking forget it all before I deal with the consequences of giving her my prized possession to drive home—my vintage Chevrolet Camaro—something I've never allowed any soul to borrow, even for a split second, including the boys.

And that says everything in itself…

I've lost my fucking mind.

Because no matter how much I shouldn't, all I want is Peaches.

Diesel
ROSE

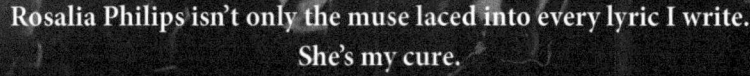

**Rosalia Philips isn't only the muse laced into every lyric I write.
She's my cure.**
The reason I'm still breathing.

Four years ago, I let her go. Now, I'd do anything to make her mine.
One night, while my famed alternative rock band is on a worldwide tour, our fate collides, and I become addicted to her.

I told her I'd ruin her life. That I wanted nothing to do with her.
I lied.

I'm the poetically tragic rock star.
She's the beautifully broken ballerina.
Together, we're the cruelest of enemies…and the messiest lovers.

Our attraction is chaotic like nineteenth-century Brontë.
Unpredictable like a psychopath's lullaby.
Diabolic like the Joker and his queen.

And yet, we won't stop till we unravel what we crave most…
to be loved.
Whatever that freaking means.

But just like every addiction, her love could be the very
thing that kills me…
And these are the reasons why…

**NOTE: This full-length book is a standalone and INCLUDES the
prequel, Remember I'm Yours.**

For all the monsters under the bed who end up saving lives with their dark poetry…

To Tash,
Fly high sweet angel.

And to Mamma, Nonna, and Nonno,
My love for you all is infinite.
<3

"I've been locked inside your
heart-shaped box
for weeks."

NIRVANA, 'HEART-SHAPED BOX'

I hope you live a life you're proud of, and if you find that you're not,
I hope you have the strength to start all over again…

F. Scott Fitzgerald

Playlist

"505" — Arctic Monkeys
"Belladonna (Adieu) — BLANCO
"Cherry Flavoured" — The Neigbourhood
"Smells Like Teen Spirit" — Nirvana
"Stargirl Interlude" — The Weeknd, Lana Del Rey
"A Little Death" — The Neigbourhood
"Dumb" — Nirvana
"Heart-Shaped Box" — Nirvana
"Baby Blue" — Luke Hemmings
"Cry Baby" — The Neighbourhood
"Knee Socks" — Arctic Monkeys
"Lithium" — Nirvana
"The Man Who Sold The World" — Nirvana
"Amour" — Izzamuzzic
"Lurk" — The Neigbourhood
"NEMESI (feat. BLANCO)" — Marracash, BLANCO
"BAD TALK" — Elvis Drew, Avivian
"California Down The Road." — Elvis Drew, Avivian
"You Know You're Right" — Nirvana
"$ting" — The Neigbourhood
"Come As You Are" — Nirvana
"Terrible Thing" — AG

Please Note: **Remember I'm Yours: Prequel to Diesel Rose** MUST be read first in order to understand the full-length book, **Diesel Rose**.

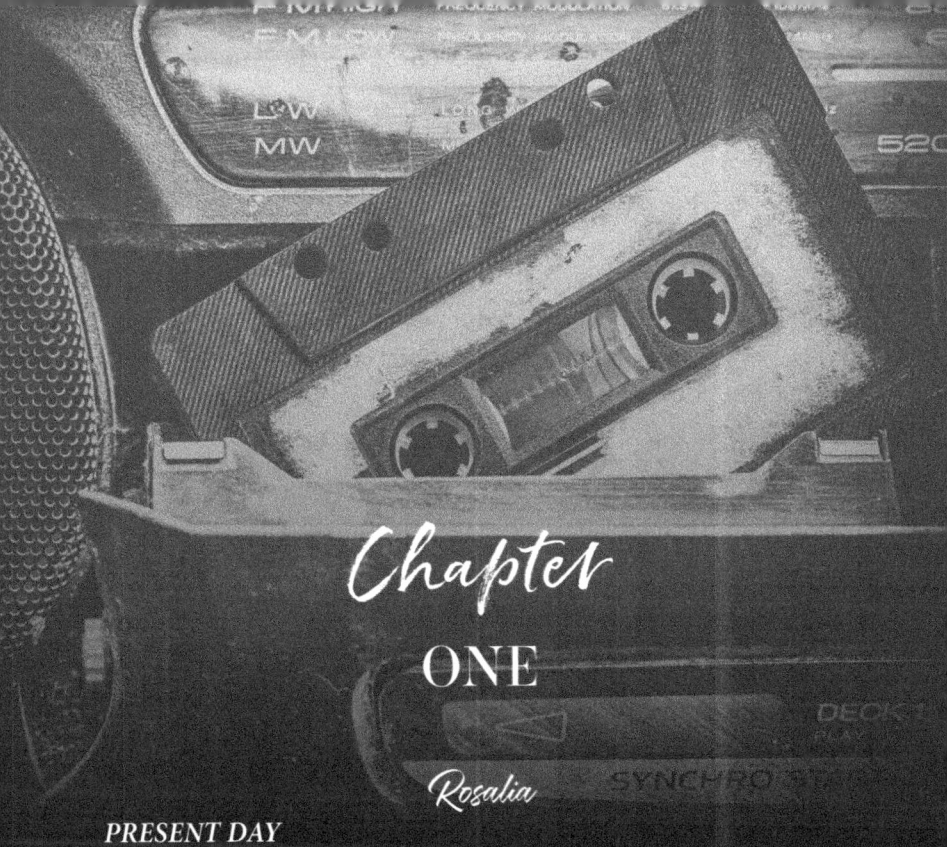

Chapter

ONE

Rosalia

PRESENT DAY
Three months prior…

When I think about the reasons I'm still breathing, it's because of The Neighbourhood, my favorite dusty pink ballerina shoes, and Elijah. *My bittersweet sinner Diesel.* And no, not the gasoline kind, even though he would argue he's equally corrosive…

I mean Elijah Diesel.

Complicated.

Toxic.

Devilishly beautiful in a rough yet gorgeous rock star kind of way.

Elijah Diesel.

He's a lovesick daydream, one that has my heart skipping a trillion beats per second. One I never knew existed before I first gazed into his soulless light onyx eyes. He always makes my heart skip; making it race like I'm boy crazy. And just to be clear, I'm not, boy crazy that is, I'm just crazy for one certain boy—*him.*

In actuality, he isn't a boy. Nobody six-foot-three with such a confident yet melancholic vibe could ever be called just a boy. In his own way, Elijah was a man, the rough and dominant bad boy alpha kind of man. One that was noticed by giddy teenage girls and their hot soccer moms. But Elijah has never been into those kinds of girls, no.

"Cross my heart hope to die, they ain't my kind of lovers, *Peaches*," he told me months ago when we were lying on the freshly mowed lawn of Central Park, staring up at the bright, blue sky.

I even remember how he was leaning up on his elbows and slowly brushed a strand of my hair away from my face when he said it. His calloused fingers were skittish, like he didn't know if his caress against my cheek would burn me or permanently mark my wildly beating heart. I decided it did both.

I never looked Elijah in the eyes when he said it, my cheeks heating up so quickly I was nervous he would mistake my blush for something that it wasn't. I mean, yes, my girly seventeen-year-old heart had a crush on Elijah Diesel (still does), but he couldn't know it. *Can't* know it. He would have never hung out with me if he did.

So, I kept it cool, always turning away when I felt a blush coming on and shutting my eyes whenever his stare pierced through my soul. *Peaches.*

He's called me that ever since I can remember. I'm not the type of girl to correct him, but I really wish he'd call me something more—like, *baby*. But we aren't even together, and Elijah's never been the type of person to give anybody nicknames—*anybody*—so I gladly take it.

Even after all this time, there isn't much I know about Elijah. He's a secretive mystery, but I've observed him. Observed him well. Good enough to know he only has three true loves in life.

I'll write them down for you...

1. His black leather jackets. One studded, the other plain. He literally wears them everywhere like his prized possession. He even has some safety pins threaded through the bottom of one, full-on rocker vibes. Last month, I noticed the leather jacket had split at the left sleeve, which was unusual seeing it's Italian leather. I offered to sew it up for him, told him I wasn't the best seamstress but for him, I'd search up all the YouTube videos to get it right. He declined with a look in his eyes that told me to never ask him again. From that point forth, I understood that his leather jackets symbolize his life, and nobody could touch them. Not even me. I accepted it, really, I did, no matter how big the golf-ball-sized throb remained lodged in my throat the entire bus ride home.

2. Elijah Diesel loves music. A specific kind. He likes alternative, rock, and heavy metal. He detests everything pop, jazz, and anything trap. His favorite bands are The Rolling Stones, Blink 182, Metallica, K.I.S.S, Nirvana, and Queen. I mean, he also has his own band, but that's a whole other story. A good story. One for later.

3. Elijah likes being alone, in any way he can, which is why I find it so strange that he also likes to hang out with me. I mean, he's never openly admitted that he likes it, and we never hug like normal friends do (I still don't know that we're really friends or whatever), but in his own strange Elijah Diesel way, I just know he does.

Elijah's three loves go hand in hand. Listening to Nirvana all alone at three in the morning in his iconic leather jacket. I don't know whether the vision is depression or inspiring, all I do know is that he's alone for too long.

He always finds a way to tangle himself in my life. But never by a text or a call (well, besides the first few months after we met). Elijah doesn't believe in those—text and calls, that is—and quite frankly, neither do I. You want to talk to somebody, you do it in their face (if, of course, you have the means to.)

But that's just it about Elijah; he's a complicated mess, one I wish I could stare into his gorgeous black eyes forever.

Everybody says he's a monster. The devil. Some depressing

antonymy of sin, but they don't know him like I know him. And I wouldn't want them to.

I like how only I know that he continuously rakes a hand through his dark wavy hair whenever he's nervous.

How only I know his first ever tattoo was one dedicated to his mother, and then the rest just followed.

How only I know *him*.

I feel like Elijah trusts me. Well, I hope he trusts me, or else this would all just be a tragedy waiting to happen. But that's the thing about him, you never truly know. He's rarely cracked a smile in my presence, belly laughed, touched even my skin, but then again, if he ever did, it was either for an unexpected moment, or it was a mistake.

We're not friends.

We're not enemies.

We're not lovers.

We're something in between; that gray area between reality and fiction. The area where all of the lines get blurred, and nothing is truly how it really seems. That's exactly what we are—scattered hearts— just two lonely, broken souls attempting to not drown in the waves that's called life.

Elijah Diesel was my everything. *Is* my everything. Which is why my heart still aches that he did what he did. How he left me with a genuine promise that I still don't know if he'll keep… *or break* when the clock strikes ten o'clock tonight.

Chapter

TWO

Elijah

It's early September, three weeks since her lips were last on mine, and I haven't recovered since. She's been so permanent in my mind, as if she's the only thing that fucking exists. It's been a crazy three weeks for Diesel Rose. For one, we've been playing gigs at bars like crazy, and have been receiving a heck of a lot more recognition.

The world is starting to notice us.

Starting to memorize *Diesel Rose* on their tongues.

Starting to hear our perfected alternative indie rock combined with elements of electronic, pop rock, and R&B. We're a rendition of Måneskin meets The Neighbourhood, with lyrics a little more bittersweet. Just four best friends trying to stay afloat in a world that constantly makes it feel like you're drowning. *Well, that's what it feels to me anyway.*

We're on the brink of releasing our second studio album, and part of me is ashamed to admit Rosalia Philips was my forbidden secret muse for it. The other part of me is fucking proud of it—considering I'm allergic to people except for five. It's those five I'll burn the entire world down for and save, even before I save myself.

Tragic, I know, but it's the truth.

I don't like people. I'm not a people person. It's why I prefer to drown myself in the shadows of the darkness. Disguise my smile in Japanese whiskey and use alcohol, tobacco, and sex as an escape to the madness running wild inside my head.

I'm grateful for my life. I'm grateful I'm breathing, but if it were up to me, I wouldn't even fucking be here. At all.

Songwriting makes me be myself.

Songwriting makes me come alive.

Songwriting makes me forget all else.

Ever since I was a little boy it has always been my escape. My parents were so concerned with how dark I painted the world in my music when I was just nine that my father had me see a therapist once a fucking week.

The day my heart turned cold was during my first therapy session. My therapist glanced over the songbook my parents confiscated and begged Dr. Squareface (yes, my nine-year-old mind was rather peculiar yet accurate) to both read and analyze it.

Dr. Squareface glanced at the black leather-bound cover where I had drawn skulls, knives, and smoking cigarettes in white-out, and shook his head. He read all the dreary lyrics, and with a sigh that I was adamant would blow my Bret Michaels-inspired bandana off, he slammed the book shut.

Unimpressed, Dr. Squareface's disturbed eyes met mine as he said, "*You*—Elijah Diesel—are going to make people like me very, *very* rich. Why? Because you're a natural-born psychopath and nothing will ever truly save you."

Those were his exact words. I remember them precisely because their echo never left me.

I stepped out of that session hating Dr. Squareface.

Hating anything that was bright, and happy, and filled with life.

Hating the normal, the ordinary, the conservative line, the heavens and all the angels.

Instead, I fell in love with the devil and his crimson red horns.

Craved the heat of hell and anything sinful, different, and dark that crossed the line.

Immersed myself so deeply with death that I had a fascination about it. I could feel its coldness. I could feel its bleakness. I could feel everything, yet I couldn't *feel* a thing.

Nothing affected me, not even all the blood and gore, and then I grew older, and something happened that changed my life. From that point forward it was either feed into fascination and drown in therapy bills or continue writing lyrics that resembled dark poetry.

I chose the latter.

I write to forget.

I write to feel numb.

I write so I don't go insane.

Each lyric is like a piece of my heart bleeding out cold. There's nothing more intimate than clutching an artist's raw work, like the first editions I collect like a Gothic-rock lovesick romantic. It's why I barely change the first lyric drafts. It's why whenever I co-write with my band, all our depression intertwines in a field of diesel roses.

It's also why whenever I'm all alone and the lyrics pour out, I recklessly write them down, letting them strip darkness from my tortured soul until there's nothing left.

Music consumes me. It's the only thing I want to be doing. It's my safe space.

And then a muse with silky blonde hair and the lightest green eyes entered my life, becoming the protagonist of my every thought and luring my mind into insanity, and I haven't recovered since.

Every lyric I wrote for this upcoming album was derived from *her*.

My gorgeous muse.

My inspiration.

My *Peaches*.

Rosalia will never know. I was adamant about it. But now September has come, alongside the chilly sweater weather and cocoa-filled nostalgia, and now all I want is to see her and make her listen to each track... like I'm singing them right now.

Diesel Rose is playing at a bar in Brooklyn Fields. Like. Right. Across. The. Fucking. Street. To. ROSALIA. PHILIPS. Brooklyn. Fields. If it wasn't so fucked up, it'd be ironic.

It's just after ten o'clock and the guys and I have just finished playing for the past couple hours. We did a little mix-up of our most popular hits, some exclusive sneak peek songs from the new album, and some covers the audience requested.

The atmosphere at this sold-out gig has been crazy wild. Adrenaline hasn't stopped rushing through my veins ever since I stepped on this raised stage with my band. It's been epic. Euphoric. Nothing comes close to singing out my truth disguised in poetic alternative rock lyrics while we collectively hit every single musical note.

Aside from just singing vocals, tonight, for some reason, I also played a little guitar alongside Zander.

The boys and I fist pump at the end of the last song, and I take the mic again with a darkened smile, "Thank you for coming out tonight, Brooklyn," I shout. "We had a blast. You were fucking phenomenal!"

The crowd screams back in cheers and whistles, clearly loving everything tonight was.

I glance over my shoulder at my band who step forward beside me, tonight the happiest I've ever seen them, but there isn't that same exhilarated smile on my lips.

It isn't because of them.

It isn't because of Diesel Rose—we were freaking incredible if I do say so myself.

It's because I've scanned my eyes across the crowd all night, searching and searching and searching for that little hope inside my chest that tells me that she was here. Watching on. But she isn't. There was no reason for her to be. No damn reason at all.

We haven't spoken since the night I gave her my car keys to drive home. The following day I collected the keys from under her doormat, got in my Camaro and left before I could overthink it. I thought it was the right thing to do. To create some distance between us.

But now three weeks has passed, and I don't know how to initiate anything.

I don't even know *what* I want, that's how fucking sad this is.

So then why am I so hellbent on stalking the crowd over and over?

Why, as the cheers for Diesel Rose get louder, do I feel like this room is caving in?

Why do I care my emerald-eyed muse with the most devilish kiss of death never came?

Chapter
THREE

Elijah

PAST

Devil's advocate must love me. It's a day after that Brooklyn Field's gig—*one*—and already my mind is trying to fuck me over.

Rubbing my stubbled jaw, I continue gazing in front of me.

It can't be her... can it?

I watch on as a blonde with the prettiest loose waves, rocks on her heels, staring at the bookshelf in front of her. Her back is to me.

Turn around. Let me see if it's you.

When I stepped into *Hayes' Bookshop*—this cozy Manhattan bookstore—a mere ten seconds ago, I had one thing and one thing only in mind—the classics. For as long as I can remember, I've always been drawn to books that drip toxic love and twisted poetry. *Or perhaps, they have always been drawn to me.*

Dave, Knives, and Zander always bully me for it in a playful kind of way, but it's just because they don't truly understand it. I get their perspective. I do. I'm not exactly the expected nor intended end user of classic romantic tragedies. But here the fuck I am—inked in tattoos, 90s rocker eyeliner darker than my soul, signature leather jacket and all.

Leaning on the adjacent bookshelf, I stare in amusement at the blonde who's been so heavily consumed with reading the blurbs of the several books she's holding that she hasn't even noticed my presence. Every time I cock my head to the side, attempting to catch a glimpse of her, her hair falls away over her face, preventing me from seeing shit.

Come on, Blondie.

Is it you?

As if it's some sort of telepathy, the blonde takes a few steps back and comes to a halt inches from slamming into my chest. A whiff of the sweetest cherry blossom has my entire body freezing up, and my hands—which are deeply hidden in my jean pockets—crave reaching out and holding her.

Don't ask me why, because I've never fucking held a woman in my life for more than a few moments, but knowing Rosalia Philips is standing *right* in front of me, my first reaction is I want to hold her—for a lifetime.

I know I keep on appearing and disappearing weeks at a time like a tainted ghost, I know it took fate for both of us to be in this low-lit Manhattan bookstore, but I haven't stopped thinking of her for the past twenty-two days.

This is my preferred vintage bookstore with an endless collection of classics. Walnut oak lines the floorboards and tall, wide shelves. The sage green trims and caged lights always gives me a late 40s, early 50s feel. And there's always this warm scent of freshly brewed coffee and baked muffins marking the air, just like it is now, lingering from the in-store coffee shop.

There's also a glassed-off quiet private study/reading area toward the back of the bookstore, or rather, what I like to call it; the *fuck-off-and-leave-me-alone* area.

"Ugh! Why am I so damn indecisive?" Rosalia grumbles under her breath to herself.

I break out of my haze and realize she only has two books in her hands now, but her back still to me. I glance over at her, at the limited edition covers of Brontë's *Jane Eyre* and Austin's *Pride and Prejudice* she's holding, and the smirk that crawls up my lips is priceless.

Gunmetal love...

Tragedy is loaded on her fingertips because whichever Rosalia does decide to choose is destined to end in just that way—tragedy— no matter if they're happily ever afters or not.

(*Which I happen to know, but anyway...*)

Rosalia steps forward and just as she's about to slip *Pride and Prejudice* back into the shelf, she comes to a halt, her fingers softly lingering against the walnut oak. Because the book is set up on a higher shelf, she's on her tippy-toes, and it causes the black gym shorts she has on to rise up, exposing the edges of her ass cheeks.

Dear God.

I suck in a breath and shift my gaze from her the moment heat rushes down to my hardening cock. It achingly stirs in the constraints of my jeans, and internally, I'm cursing.

She's seventeen, Diesel. Quit looking at her ass.

I shake my head, contemplating just walking away, but then the words she spoke after she first kissed me weeks ago echo in my mind...

If you were to bend me over right this second and make love to me, which I wouldn't be opposed to, it would be legal. New York's age of consent is seventeen.

Now the devil in me is the one shaking his head.

Fuckkk. You're gonna kill me, Peaches.

Rosalia's wearing ballet flats and a few inches of a sporty tight Lycra leotard is exposed, those gym shorts and a cropped denim jacket covering her up. Aside from the jacket and the shorts, everything else is the softest of dusty pinks, reminding me of the lightest shade of cotton candy or bubble gum.

It's evident by the gym bag she has slung over her shoulder that she's most likely just come out of some type of practice after twelfth grade. Something in my mind triggers and I'm reminded of how she mentioned she did ballet that night I brought her to the studio, and she met the boys.

Ballet.

That's what she must have come from... or, is going to?

I glance at my watch. 8:12 p.m. It's definitely not the latter then.

Just as Rosalia is about to slip *Pride and Prejudice* back on the bookshelf, she shakes her head and quickly puts Brontë's *Jane Eyre* back instead. Clutching Mr. Darcy to her chest, Rosalia spins on her heels, and I catch the slightest glimpse of her plump lips as she begins striding down the aisle toward the cash counter.

"Hmm, interesting choice." I smirk, crossing my arms over my broad chest as my eyes fall to her swaying ass. "I'm pretty sure Rochester will hate you for deserting him…. *Peaches.*"

Rosalia stops in her tracks, halting so fast the book almost flings from her grip.

Ever so slowly, she turns around and the second she sees me, a rosy glow spreads across her face. She's smiling, no, she's *grinning*, and my heart stops beating because of it. She's… *happy.*

God, she's so damn beautiful. Flawless.

Why the fuck am I so cruel to her at times?

Because it's in your fucking nature, Elijah Diesel.

There's a glint in her emerald eyes. It reminds me of the first time I saw her, when I stepped off that bus after hours of band practice and seeing her was like fresh air was knocked straight into my lungs.

Of course I'll never admit that, but yes, it was the first thing I *felt* when I first saw her—*the first thing I've ever felt in my entire life.*

I think that's why I love to hate Rosalia Philips. Because slowly, slowly, she's making me *feel* and I'm not used to that. I don't like that. I don't like feeling out of control. At all.

But as I said, the way Rosalia is gazing at me now transports me to the very beginning of summer when I handed her the *Rolling Stone* magazine she dropped, and she looked at me with so much anticipation.

Nervousness.

Yearning.

Now, a scarlet blush works up her cheeks in the low light, just like it did the very first day. And suddenly her eyes, which have always reminded me of spring, four-leaf clovers, and rolling meadows of lively Tuscan vineyards, become the most beautiful things I've ever seen.

And then just like that, all my thoughts intensify as a smirk breaks out on Rosalia's lips, "Well, well, well, look who it is. Elijah unknown-middle-name Diesel, are you following me?"

She's not upset it's been so long since we last saw each other, she's acting playful.

A slight chuckle rumbles up my throat, and *god,* how good it is to let go of a fucking breath and just laugh. "*Me*? Stalking *you*? Yeah, you wish."

Rosalia giggles as she steps my way like the pretty ballerina she is. Reaching the classics section, her eyes flicker down to her copy of *Pride and Prejudice* and she sighs.

"I guess you're right. Is Mr. Darcy really worth it? Maybe I should just go with *Jane Eyre*, yeah?"

My smirk simmers down to pierced lips. "Well, I think the real question you're asking is… *Is a tragedy really worth surviving in order to see the silver-lined beauty behind it*?"

Leaning against the bookshelf adjacent to me, Rosalia bends her foot to press against the oak and cutely chews on her lower lip. "Yeah, that's my question, I guess."

Thinking, I rub my stubbled chin, catching her gaze flickering to my vintage sterling silver rings which sink coldness into my skin as they brush against it. "I don't know, somehow I don't think I'm the type of guy to ask that question to."

"Oh, what type of guy are you then?" Rosalia arches a playful brow. "One that magically appears at weeks and months at a time?"

That smirk of mine resurfaces. "You're lucky I sensed the sarcasm in that, Philips."

"Oooo, so you're not going to slice my throat, *thanks*."

Studying her face, I step closer to her, towering over her five-foot-four frame in my six-foot-three stance. She's playful today. Happy. And for some strange reason, it allures me. I instantly prefer it over the hatred and sadness that spilled between us the last time we met.

But as I glance down at Rosalia, my eyes unable to pull away from those gorgeously plump lips of hers, her cherry-flavored tongue replays in my mind like crazy. When we kissed all those three weeks ago like scared wolves at war and I later told her that it'll never happen again, I meant it. But right now, the bookstore's lighting cascades down on us, highlighting her softly freckled cheeks and her glossy rosy lips gleam.

I can't help but want to feel the softness of them against mine again. She told me I was her first kiss—that I was a *first*—and fuck, my possession has never dominated me so hard than in that second. Heat rushes up my spine just thinking about it and knowing it'll never happen again.

A strand of hair falls over her face, and I so desperately want to brush it back, but I don't trust myself. I know the second her warm skin brushes against mine, all my control will backfire. And I'm not the kind of guy who likes to fuck over my control, 'cause that'll flick the switch of my insanity, and end with me locked in a fucked-up penitentiary.

Watercolor eyes. That's what she has.

The poetry pouring inside of me is killing me.

My muse is standing before me, looking at me like I'm a god when I'm the opposite.

Air crackles between us. It gets all serious with only the two of us in this aisle, soft instrumental blues that I only notice now filling in the space.

"*Peaches*?"

"Mmhmmm?"

"I really wanted to see you sooner, *Peaches*," I murmur, lowering my forehead to hers. "It's been intense with Diesel Rose, and we haven't slowed down. We're selling out gigs like crazy. I really wanted to see you like a fuck of a lot, but I'm not really into texting or calling, and I didn't know how to ask you without it sounding like a… date. 'Cause it won't be. I made that clear, yeah?"

"Yes." Rosalia gulps down before smiling softly. "Well, I'm here right now, and I don't have any other plans but an evening love affair with either Rochester or Mr. Darcy, so…"

Lazily smiling, I take the book from her grip and step away to find *Jane Eyre*. "Have you eaten dinner?"

"No, I just finished ballet and thought I should just head in here before taking the bus home. I'm not really that hungry actually."

Almost as if on demand, her stomach grumbles and she girlishly slaps a hand over her mouth in embarrassment.

"Okayyy." She nervously laughs. "Maybe *a little* hungry."

"Let me pay for these and we'll get something for dinner."

"Oh, thank you for offering but no, I'll pay for them."

I shoot her a deadpan stare. "Over my dead body, you will."

"Elijah—"

"You got this?" I ever so casually ask, pulling out Sylvia Plath's *Ariel*; the infamous collection of her iconic dark poetry. "'Cause it's pretty fucking rad, so if you haven't, I think you'll like it."

"Oh, no I don't actually. I've been meaning to, but my bank balance would literally pop out and kill me. I don't get paid until next Thursday."

Taking a hold of the three classics books, I start walking toward the cash register with Rosalia scurrying after me. She's adamant to pay but I ignore it all.

Mid-walk, I glance over my shoulder at her with my brows knit together. "You work? You never mentioned that."

Rosalia shoots me a playful glare. "Maybe because we've never had a proper conversation."

I roll my eyes with a chuckle. "Shut up, yes we have."

"I work just down the block at this café on the weekends, obviously with senior year."

"Would I know it?"

"It has bright pink floral wallpaper and is literally called *Tickled Pink*, so no, don't think you would."

I snicker. "You think you know me so well, hmmm?"

"Sure do."

The owner of the store, Mr. Hayes, tiredly smiles up at me from behind the counter. He's in his mid-seventies and always wears his lucky chestnut corduroy suits with a new fancy tie each day.

Remember those five people I mentioned earlier? Those ones I said are the only ones I truly care about in this world? Yeah, well, Mr. and Mrs. Hayes are those last two of them.

I scared the shit out of the poor guy the first time I entered the store years ago. He turned around and saw this tall, dark, mysterious tattooed beast and I swear to God I've never seen somebody's eyes widen that fast. Mr. Hayes was seconds away from hitting the panic button under the register counter when I paid for the books. But panic turned real for him when two guys entered the store with guns and ski masks, wanting to rob the place—well, more specifically the expensive first editions Mr. Hayes sold.

I made sure the poor guy (and his wife, who owns the café at the back of the store) didn't get hurt. I showed those attempted burglars who they were messing with then I knocked one of them out cold and performed a citizen's arrest on the other fucker. Safe to say Mr. Hayes has loved me ever since, no matter how fucked up it may be.

"Hey there, Eddie, what can I do for you today?"

Smiling (*yes, smiling, don't freak out on me now*), I set the three books on the counter. "Just these three for tonight, thanks, bud. I gotta friend with me and she couldn't choose between two... somehow we ended up with three."

His eyes warm when they move to Rosalia, who steps beside me. "Nice to meet you. Any friend of Eddie's is a friend of mine."

"Hi, I'm Rosalia." She softly waves at him, her cheery voice warm like a gun. "And yep, I'm that indecisive friend all right."

Friend.

Mr. Hayes chuckles as he scans the books. "Well, you're in good hands, sweetheart. Elijah's an expert in all things Brontë, Plath, and Fitzgerald. So, if there's anybody to get you out of a sticky situation, it's this guy. He's a good person behind all of those tattoos."

When both of their gazes move my way, my ears begin to burn as I pull out my wallet from the pocket of my leather jacket. I don't really take compliments well. I get all closed up and shit, and maybe it's all trauma from therapy, but it really paralyzes the rhythms of my heart.

Mr. Hayes announces the price and I once again decline Rosalia's relentless offers to pay while I slide the money across the counter, adding some extra bills like I always do for a tip for him and the missus. He's done so much for me, it's only right, no matter how many times he tells me it's not necessary.

Just before Mr. Hayes hands me the books in a brown paper bag, he glances between Rosalia and me with a mischievous smile. "Sooo, is she *really* just your friend, or are you actually going steady with her?"

Dun-dahhh.

Oh, what was that you ask?

That's my heart going... D. O. W. NNNNNNN.

"Fuck, oh my god, Mr. Hayes, no." I laugh like it's the most ridiculous thing all while I'm rubbing the back of my neck. "No. No, we're not together, we're... we just know each other."

If a body language expert were to step into this bookshop right this second, they'd hunt me down and use me as the prime example of a man in distress.

Mr. Hayes arches a 'I-don't-believe-you-for-shit' brow. "You just know *each other*, you say?"

"Mmhmmm."

Rosalia stays quiet beside me, but I don't dare look at her. *Hell no.*

"In all the years I've know you, Eddie, I've never seen you in here with anybody else."

"Wellll." I clear my throat, trying to think of any words other than the obvious; *Dude, you're ruining my reputation.* "There's a first for everything, right?"

"Wrong." Mr. Hayes smirks and glances at Rosalia. "So, when's the wedding?"

"I'm, uh, we're really just friends." She nervously smiles, and I notice just how much she's gripping the strap of her gym bag tight, like if she wasn't, they'd be trembling. "Promise."

"You sure about that?"

"Positive."

"She's seventeen," I murmur, cutting in the silence and Mr. Hayes fumbles with the paperback and it slams against the counter with a thud.

Well, that's one way to shut him up.

"Good heavens, seventeen? You helping her with a project in school or something?"

"Yep, that's it, for music." I nod, the lie slipping out of my mouth like nothing.

"Well, that makes much more sense now, I thought you two were… HAHAHA!"

Rosalia joins in the laughter and I dramatically roll my eyes. *Little devil.*

Mr. Hayes can't stop cackling and pushes up his glasses when they slip down his arrow nose. Finally, he settles down. "So, tell me, Rosalia, have you been to one of his gigs?"

A blush rushes up her cheeks. "I haven't actually. Elijah's never invited me to one."

"Well, I'll be damned!" he huffs, glancing at me with narrowed eyes. "Eddie, you must! Even I've been to one and *wow*, your music is so darn good!"

"I'm not taking her to a gig, Mr. Hayes, it's not—"

Mr. Hayes cuts me off with a stern finger pointed my way, "Listen here and listen sharp, Eddie! If you haven't invited her to one of your gigs by the next time you come here, I'll ban you for a week, no wait, a *whole month*! Got it, kid? A *month*! And don't you think I'm joking now!"

My jaw drops all while Rosalia and Mr. Hayes burst out in laughter.

"*Ohhh*, okay, I see how this is. Mhmm, I'm glad you two find this amusing, nice, nice."

When they've finally settled down and we've said our goodbyes, Rosalia and I walk out of the bookstore together. Manhattan's purplish-blue night sky blankets down on the nightlife of this city that truly never sleeps.

I slip the brown paper bag inside my leather jacket. *You know, chivalry and shit.*

Rosalia glances over at me with a knowing smile, all of her confidence exploding right in my face as she begins laughing out loud. "Seems like you're stuck with me now, Elijah Diesel. No more running away or else Mr. Hayes will honestly kick your ass and ban you—HAHA!"

"Ugh, fuck my life," I groan, walking down the street with Rosalia still losing it beside me. "A guy walks into a bookshop looking for one measly fucking book, he walks out with a damn laughing hyena."

Rosalia bows down in even more laughter, all while I internally slam my head against a wall. A few people walking down the street eye us, and two girls in particular rush over to me, asking for a photo. I nod and after the photos are over and they're down the street, Rosalia is STILL. FUCKING. LAUGHING.

God, I'll never understand women.

Ever.

It's only after she's wiped the tears from her eyes, her mascara slightly smudging, that she finally looks at me without the urge to laugh. "Oh my god, I'm sorry for laughing in your face."

"Well, I'm happy you found fulfillment from my possible misfortune, but it's okay."

We continue walking down the street, looking out for a place we want to dine in.

"Well, what do you like, Rosalia? French? Chinese? Indian?"

"I don't really have a preference. I'm happy with whatever you like best."

"French?"

"Uhmmm, on second thought, that sometimes gives me indigestion."

"Indian?"

"Oh, well, about that…" Rosalia nervously giggles. "I'm actually allergic to spices. Like honest to God, any spice. Cinnamon. Saffron. Chili. You name it, I'll flare up, and that's not pretty. Sad, I know, I literally cry about it in my sleep. Impossible? I don't know, but it happens to me."

This. Girl. Is. Literally. Going. To. Drive. Me. Insane.

"How about Chinese?"

"Hmm, maybe not tonight. Too much MSG."

I snap my head her way and narrow my eyes. "Rosalia, you're killing me slowly."

She apologetically smiles. "I'm sorry, it's not me, it's my body going against me."

"Nah, it's all good. I get it. Well, we're approaching Little Italy, so how about Italian?"

She grins mischievously. "When in Manhattan…"

"Rosalia Philips," I deadpan. "We literally both live in Manhattan."

"Um, boy, not necessary. I'm in Brooklyn, remember?"

Righttt. How could I forget?

"So Italian, yeah?"

"Yep, sounds good to me. Also, question! Why does Mr. Hayes call you Eddie?"

"I don't know." I shrug. "To be honest, I think he thinks that's my actual name."

"And you're not going to correct him?"

"And break his little *troublemaker* ass? Nope."

"Ahhh." Rosalia smiles as we come to a stop in front of a pizza place that I know is always buzzing with great reviews. "So you *do* have a little gold inside that cold, cold heart, hmm?"

Groaning, I hold the glass door of the restaurant open. "Shut the hell up, hyena."

Rosalia giggles and pokes out her tongue, and just as she's about to step in, I sprint in front of her.

"Cold hearts first, *Peaches*, sorry not sorry."

"Asshole," she grumbles behind me.

I grin devilishly. "That's better."

Chapter
FOUR

Rosalia

PAST

I think I'm in some twisted dream. Well, in reality, there's nothing *twisted* about it despite the fact I'm having dinner in Little Italy with the lead vocalist of Diesel Rose.

Prior to tonight, I was convinced he was born without the ability to genuinely smile or crack a joke, but right now I'm seeing so many aspects of him that are new. Different.

Like him buying me the three classics that are now tucked away in my gym bag.

He personally picked out the Plath for me, and I'm certain it'll be my favorite.

I couldn't stop grinning into my phone when I sent my parents a text saying I'm going to the movies and then having dinner with one of my other friends from ballet. My mom quickly replied, telling me to enjoy. My dad, who is supposed to be on shift, replied with a thumbs up.

I'm not one to fib, but the thrill that comes with executing one so well is… exhilarating. Exactly that adrenaline rush I was craving over the summer. The one only *he* brings out of me.

Elijah's wolfish eyes flicker to mine from across the table, above our menus, and I can just imagine what Naomi would say that I'm out to dinner with him. I'm certain it would go something like this…

"He said it isn't a date? Pffttt, as if. Girl, did you seriously wear a ballet leotard? A denim jacket and booty shorts aren't going to do shit to save you. Hold on a minute, just one minute while I have a panic attack."

Too bad Naomi's away for the week in California to attend her cousin's wedding. I'd hear her scream from Los Angeles if she knew about tonight, just like she started screaming like a madwoman when I told her weeks ago that Elijah and I had kissed. But when she realized it was my first kiss, she turned giddy in two-point-five seconds. When I proceeded to tell her that he kisses like the devil and it was the most beautiful thing I've ever partaken in, she just smirked, and then told me how much she was going to strangle Elijah.

It's safe to say it's all in the back of my head as my mind fizzles back to real time. To the gorgeous outdoor patio with detailed black cast iron seating, expensive beige paving, and four spread-out green olive trees that make me feel like I'm really in Italy.

To the fairy lights weaved above us, giving the perfect romantic glow to every table while the stars dazzle above.

To a gorgeous villain named Elijah Diesel who's sitting opposite me at a table with a red and white checkered tablecloth.

Here at *Sogni D'oro* there's a beautiful zesty scent in the air mixed with rustic Italian food. The entire restaurant, including the garden patio, is buzzing with lively laughter and enjoyment. Violinists are playing at the back corner of the patio, close to the brick wall surrounding us that's painted Italian colors.

It's breathtaking. A Roman oasis.

I love how this isn't a date, and yet it's the most romantic thing ever. It's the type of place a dream wedding reception would be in, not the place a guy in leather and a girl with half her ballet clothes on frequent at eight thirty at night. I probably should have worn sweatpants, but darn fate had to ruin it. I didn't know I'd be having dinner with Elijah tonight… *or ever.*

"Alright." Elijah clucks his tongue while setting down the menu. "What are you leaning toward?"

"Most likely the *spaghetti alla puttanesca*, but without the peppers and garlic because of my—"

"Crazy allergies, yep, I'll get that too. It sounds fucking amazing."

"It is. That's my specialty to make, and let me tell you, I drool over it."

Elijah seems impressed as he pours us both some water. "You said the name of the pasta dish with perfection, what does *alla puttanesca* mean?"

Oh, this should be interesting

A smirk crawls over my face. "You really want to know?"

Elijah chuckles and brings his glass to his lips, hovering them over the rim but never drinking. "Of course I want to know. Why? Is it some big secret?"

"No, it's just not something you'll expect."

"Spit it out, *Peaches.*"

I bite my lower lip.

He gulps down water.

I go for it. "It means spaghetti *in the style of a whore*, because the dish is… let's just say, spicy in more ways than one."

Without warning, Elijah chokes on his water and starts coughing uncontrollably, all while I slap a hand over my mouth, unable to mute my laughter. His eyes widen in pure shock and I'm sure other diners turn our way, but I can't look anywhere but at him as heat spreads across my cheeks.

"The fuck did you just say?" he gasps when we both finally settle down.

"You don't want me to repeat it."

He stares at me with even wider eyes. "And *that's* your favorite pasta dish to make?"

"Sure is."

"Really?"

"Mmhmmm."

Elijah keeps on staring until that heat in my cheeks deepens, and when it does, his eyes darken to the deepest shade of gray with speckles of onyx. He shoots me a slow, sexy half-smirk, and time… it just slows.

Instantly, I know I'm in trouble.

"*Oh…*" Leaning over the table, his sandalwood blend drifts to me as Elijah seductively murmurs, "So you like cooking like a pretty little fucking whore, hmm?"

He says that. All. While. Staring. Deep. Into. My. Eyes. *Without. Blinking.*

Yep. I think I'm choking on my breath. I had a feeling this would escalate, but ohmygod, why did that sound so hot?

I swallow thickly. *Is Elijah Diesel flirting with me?*

"I, uh…I-I like the…um, som—"

"Because I would say you kiss like one…" Elijah adds, cutting off my stumbling mess of a response ever so casually, like we're not in a busy restaurant right now. "But you don't."

My jaw hangs open. "I, uh… I don't kiss like a whore?"

"No, you don't kiss like a whore, Rosalia," he confirms and then shoots me that lazy hot grin of his. "You fucking kiss better."

The more I gaze at his lips, the more my butterflies flutter and nerves ripple because… *whoa.* That's how he makes me feel.

My lips feel like they're on fire. Electric. Sill surviving the consequence of this man from our kiss weeks ago. The one he so hungrily claimed like a starved wolf and then told me if we ever kiss again, he'll ruin me.

I think I'm addicted to a man that's going to break my heart without wanting.

Elijah leans back in his seat, and I'm glad he deflects because I would have made a fool out of myself. The grin has disappeared, but the darkness in his eyes remains. "I'm taking it you're Italian, yeah?"

"Half Italian, yeah. My… my father came here when he was six."

"*Philips?*"

I swallow the lump in my throat, praying to God that Elijah doesn't notice the vulnerability in my voice when I glance down at my menu and whisper, "That's not my real last name… It's a long story, but yeah."

A few seconds pass, before, "Are you fluent?"

Flicking my eyes to him, I nod.

"Can you order for us in Italian? I want to hear you."

"Why?" I laugh.

"'Cause I think speaking another language besides English is really fucking hot."

I make a mental note to have my parents enroll me in that Spanish school they've always forced me to.

"Okay, I'll order for us in Italian just for you," I say, just as he flags down a waiter.

I order our dishes in Italian, all while Elijah sits back in his seat and I feel his hot lingering stare on me. After the waiter collects our menus and leaves, I half expect Elijah to comment, but he doesn't.

I adjust myself better in my seat. "So, how about you? Do you speak another language?"

"French. I'm half French. My mom. Same kind of similar story with yours, only I was the one born in France."

"Aww, wow, that's so cool. What part of France?"

"Toulouse. It's in the south… it's the most stunning place. Truly breathtaking, Rosalia."

"Do you speak any French in your songs?"

"No, actually."

"Well, you should add some in," I suggest with a soft smile. "Even a few words here or there. I hear a lot of people are into songs featuring speckles of other languages. Gets the heart rate up, you know, *well*, it sure does for me anyway."

"I'll keep that in mind." Elijah smiles. *Actually smiles.* "Sooo… do you really want to come to one of my gigs?"

The thought alone makes me burst from the seams in happiness. I've never been to a concert or gig before, and the thought of Diesel Rose being my first does something to me I can't quite explain.

"I'd be really interested in it. I'm dying to hear you guys and soak in the lyrics… something tells me they're like dark poetry."

"Because they are. Tomorrow morning we're heading to Boston because we're playing at this well-known music venue at night. It's a three-and-a-half-hour drive. The boys are going to head up together because they're staying the weekend," Elijah explains, all while playing around with the leather and sterling silver chain bracelets around his left wrist. "But I'm riding solo as I've got a thing on Sunday night, so I'll be back here Sunday morning."

By the end of that all, he's looking back at me, almost studying me slow. His words echo in my mind, every single one an erupting fire.

I smile modestly, but inside I'm grinning like a devil. Why? Because everything's blurring into one. I'm so confused because *did Elijah just subtly ask me to come…?*

I know he's not the kind of guy that would outright invite me to one of his gigs, because I can imagine how intense they can be, especially with the pressure of somebody you know watching, but *heckkk!* Did I miss something?

I know I can just ask him, but it feels awkward. Mostly because I've *never had* dinner with an older, tattooed rocker before, so my pointer skills are at an all-time low.

"Boston sounds magical, I've never been. I'd love to come, but, um, maybe when you're next performing in New York would be better. My older sister lives in Los Angeles, and my kryptonite—my best friend—is also currently on the West Coast for a wedding… or else I could have used going on a road trip with either one of them as an excuse for my parents."

"Oh, you mean the one that promised to fuck me up if I hurt you?"

"Yep, that's the one, all right." I laugh. "*Naomi.* We've been best friends since forever. I'm sorry if she came off too strong that night. She's just protective of me. We're like sisters."

Elijah nods. "No, I get it. She doesn't want to see you hurt. I'm the same with my sister, and mind you, she's five years older."

A sister? Well, I wasn't expecting that. Somehow, I imagined him as an only child or having brothers.

"You have a sister?"

"Yeah, a nephew too, if you can believe I'm an uncle." He half chuckles to himself and pulls out his phone.

Tapping on the screen, he spins it around to show me his screen wallpaper. My heart squeezes from the cuteness overload of his nephew… *and dear God, who gave Elijah permission to look so smoking hot?*

It's a candid picture of him and his nephew. Elijah's sitting in what seems to be the dining room and it must have been somebody's birthday because there are streamers and red and blue balloons everywhere.

But what I focus on is the candid shot of a little boy with the most perfect curly hair in Elijah's lap. His hands are wrapped around his uncle's throat like a chokehold, mid-laughter. He's the cutest little boy, but what I love the most is how happy *Elijah* is.

Elijah's grin reaches his eyes, so deep that crow's feet sink by his eyes and his dimples carve through his stubbled cheeks. He's wearing a leather jacket with no studs, much like he is tonight, and his tattooed hands tightly wrap around the little boy's waist, holding him lovingly.

My rapid heartbeats match my breaths because I didn't expect this. I didn't expect to see an Elijah Diesel that's warm, vivacious, and adoring—yet here I am, staring right at it.

This is his phone's wallpaper.

His wallpaper.

Just so the people in the back hear better, I'll repeat. Elijah Diesel—the coldest, most gorgeously melancholic rocker I know—has a photo of himself with his nephew on his phone.

"His name is Clément," Elijah explains, and the screen turns off, but I reach out and tap it so that photo can refuel my lungs again. "They live in Seattle, so I don't get to see him as much as I want to, but when I do, it's special."

"I can imagine. Oh my god, he's got your eyes! Little heartbreaker."

"Hmmm, heartbreaker is right." Elijah chuckles. "My sister called this morning. He's been giving this one girl a flower every day, right, like every fucking day. During Show and Tell yesterday, that girl was all gloating, then all the other girls started crying because he *also* gave them flowers… every damn day as well."

I slap a hand to my mouth before I burst out laughing. "Oh my god, he's so cute!"

"Clément's cute, yeah, but he's also so equally stubborn. I had my sister put him on the phone after I spoke to her, just so I could try to explain that you can't be leading on all the girls like that, you know. We turned the call into a FaceTime and when I was finally done explaining it to him that he can't have all the girls in his class crying like that, you know what he did?"

"I can't even imagine!"

"He full-on did *this.*" Elijah crosses his arms over his broad chest, imitating his nephew with a glare. "And then he's just like, '*JahJah*', by the way, that's what he calls me, 'cause he knows how much I hate it. So, he's like, '*JahJah, I'm gonna tell you something and you ain't gonna like it…*'. And I said, '*Go on, blow my mind*'. This mischievous grin forms on his face and he full-on shouts, *'I AM THE KING OF THE JUNGLEEEEEEE, GOODBYE!'*, pokes out his tongue, and turns off the damn phone in my face."

I can't stop laughing. "Oh my god, that is such an Elijah Diesel move."

He shoots me a playful death glare. "My nephew *ended the damn FaceTime* when we were talking about *girls*. Talk about freaking deflection. Just like I said, that kid is stubborn."

"Oooo, I wonder where he got that from..."

"Smart-ass." Elijah grins, his dimples seeping in like slices of heaven as he shakes his head. "Don't be looking at me now, Rosalia, I can confirm I was an angel growing up. And yes, that may or may not be a fabricated lie."

I grin back.

He completely lights up talking about his nephew.

"How old is he?"

"Six. The reason why I can't be in Boston for that long this weekend is because he turns seven on Sunday, and I'm flying out to Seattle to see him. I'll be there for the next week."

My heart—I'm pretty sure it just melted.

"Seven, wow, that's so beautiful. I'm sure you'll love the time with him!"

"Yeah, and my sister too, I miss her a fuck of a lot... can't say the same for my brother-in-law though."

"Oh." I knit my brows together. "You guys don't get along?"

"No, we do, a crazy heck of a lot, but he's a cop and literally always confiscates my joints and cigarettes the second I step in the front door. Naturally, I would never smoke in front of Clément anyway, but he's like a fucking hound dog. Doesn't understand I need it to unwind."

"Well." I smile. "This next week will be an extremely interesting one for you."

"That it shall be."

Chapter
FIVE

Rosalia

We spend the time waiting for our dinner talking even more about our love for classics, *The Beautiful and Damned*, and his nephew, Clément. Elijah tells me how his nephew took up singing lessons at school because he wants to be just like his uncle. I ask him about France, and what age he moved to New York City. He tells me he was five and when he did move here, he didn't know a word of English. Kids at school used to bully him for it, but now his English is impeccable, flawless, with not a touch of an accent.

The *spaghetti alla puttanesca* arrives at our table and it looks divine. I drool just staring at it. With a shared smirk, Elijah and I dive into our dinner. We continue talking through it. He asks me what I love most about ballet, and I tell him—*the freedom*. I love how I can dance, and dance, and dance. How blank my mind is while I execute every pirouette, en pointe, and fouetté. How I don't need to think. How I love being in the moment—*feeling*—simply only needing the rhymes in my chest to feel alive.

Elijah stops chewing when I tell him that, and something in his eyes changes when he swallows down the pasta.

"Do you always feel that?" he whispers, his voice the lowest I've heard tonight.

"Feel, what?"

"Alive."

I nod, and despite his frown, I go on to tell him about how all of the entrusting long hours of training is worth it. How every advanced ballet dance step makes me come alive. I mention my favorite step— *Grand Jete*—and then I explain to him what it means. How it's the most challenging jump to perform because so much stretching and flexibility is involved. But every time I perform one, no matter if I fail or execute one, my coach always tells me to do it again.

To work at it harder.

Faster.

More poise.

And it's that reputation to obtain something until it's a fraction away from perfection is what makes me come alive. The thrill. The risk. The obsession that comes with that thirst to execute, and then do it all again—*that* makes me alive.

Elijah stays awfully quiet throughout that entire conversation, but at the end, when we've finished our pasta and he orders us a tiramisu to share for dessert, he asks me more. He asks if I want to go pro. If I've ever been to *Swan Lake*. If I'll say '*fuck it*' to pursuing something in the medical field like my dad hopes, and instead one day be a part of a touring company.

I respond with an evident blush crawling up my cheeks. I don't know if it's because Elijah believes I have the potential to strive for the stars, or if it's because nobody has ever shown so much interest in something I love so deeply, but I can't help but feel so flustered.

"Being a part of a ballet tour one day would be a dream, it's what I wake up for."

"Then live it, *Peaches*," Elijah tells me with a sparkle in his eyes. "Take the '*dream*' out of that sentence and make it a fucking reality. You've got the drive, so make it happen. It isn't just an idea. I see the passion pouring out of your words, it would be a shame to let it go."

My heart warms when I tell Elijah that I will pursue it. That I'll work hard for it. That I've never been to *Swan Lake* before as they always sell out crazy fast within seconds, but that it's my goal to enter the theater and watch every graceful move, imagining it's me.

I don't tell him I *want* it, I tell him I *need* this. I *need* ballet. I tell him that he's the person I'll owe it all to when my thirst for proving to everybody that I—Rosalia Philips—will make it, makes it. I tell him I'll "*fucking make it reality*", and when all of the anticipation brews inside me like a storm, Elijah Diesel looks at me as if he's the only person who can weather it.

Because maybe he is...

The tiramisu comes and we talk about his band. How he started songwriting when he was only nine years old. It's so impressive, seeing how almost twenty years of grit and determination has brought him to where he is today—an inch from worldwide victory. He doesn't tell me much about his personal life, only that his parents didn't really agree with him devoting everything to succeed.

But I think that there's something about a self-made man (or a self-made band in his case) that's super inspiring. That all of the blood, sweat, and tears is worth it in the end, because every single moment of success you gain is because of you.

I tell him all that, and he's modest about it. He doesn't want to make it seem like he's that close to the entire world knowing his name, but he is. I tell him I believe him, that *Diesel Rose* will be his legacy, that I respect him, even when he's being an asshole, and he sadly smiles as if it's the most depressing thing I've ever said.

But I don't care because even though I've never heard any of his songs (and god, how much my fingers have been itching to just search one up, alongside his band or simply *him*, but I haven't), I know that his voice will be music to my ears.

Therapy.

He tells me a little more about his band, about how sometimes aside from being the lead vocalist, he also plays some bass guitar because he loves it. *He's such a multi-talented man.*

We finish dessert and continue talking about everything and anything. All night.

"Can I ask you something?" I ask, my pending question burning my brain.

"Yeah."

"If we didn't meet by chance at the bookshop tonight, would you have contacted me?"

"Yes," Elijah responds in the same heartbeat, his eyes so poetically beautiful they almost sing their own song. "You know I would have, I just wanted to give us some space and didn't know what to say nor how to say it… for a songwriter, sometimes I'm pretty shit at words."

Just as I'm about to respond, our waiter comes by our table with a soft smile. "*Mi dispiace.* I'm very sorry to interrupt, but we're closing… well, not even clos*ing*, we're clos*ed*."

My jaw drops and that's when I glance around the patio and inside the restaurant and realize there is. Nobody. Else. Here. Not even the violists. Elijah and I are the last ones. We were so busy talking that we must have missed all the announcements of their closing time.

I glance at my phone which is face down on the table. I realize I haven't touched it the entire night while with Elijah. *He just makes me live. Like really live.* Flipping it over, my eyes bulge out of their sockets when I see the time—11:10 p.m. *Crap. They closed ten minutes ago.*

I apologize to the Italian waiter who can't stop apologizing *to me* that he interrupted the conversation. When we stand and I shake out my legs because I haven't gotten up in almost three hours, I offer to pay.

Elijah looks at me as if I'm insane as he slips *my* gym bag over *his* shoulder. "Thanks for offering, *Peaches*, but I've got it."

I like how the word 'Peaches' is coated in a little more tonight. It's like our chat has enhanced something. And although we're not friends, or lovers, or anything in between, for some reason, now my nickname slips off his lips coated in a little more sugar and less tension.

"Are you sure, Elijah? I honestly don't mind paying, you got me those books before."

"It's all good, really it is."

"But are you sure that you're sure?"

"Positive."

"Are you *sure* sure?"

Elijah rolls his eyes. "Yes, Rosalia, let's get the hell out of here before they lock us in."

He guides us through the restaurant with a hand on my lower back, and once we've paid, the chilly late-night air kisses our skin outside. We walk through New York in silence, with the stars winking down at us and my heart going wild, but never once do we discuss where we're going. We just keep walking and walking and walking.

Every so often I sneak a glance at Elijah, at his ever-so-masculine face carved by the silvery moonlight. I kind of like the way we always tend to see each other at night—aside from our first meet. Always seeing him in the late hours of the night makes this whole thing feel a whole lot more forbidden, taboo—whatever *this thing* may be.

Elijah Diesel is my very own secret. One that neither of us can seem to walk away from, no matter how desperately we both know we should.

Every so often, our hands innocently brush together, but the fiery sparks that ripple through me are anything but innocent. They're the realest things I've ever experienced, *well except for that time he pressed me against a wall with a hand around my throat and kissed me.*

It's.

All.

Just.

So.

Real.

With.

Him.

I'm just a seventeen-year-old blonde ballerina attempting to survive senior year, walking through Manhattan with a bad boy laced in everything my parents would label taboo with the strap of my gym bag slung over his shoulder. *Taboo.* And yet I do it anyway.

Somehow, without even wanting to, we end up on West 36th Street, right in front of Elijah's studio. It would have had to be an hour walk, and yet with Elijah, it felt like a breeze.

Elijah glances down at me and arches a brow in question. I never let go of his gaze, and I'm grateful that he sees it as a response in itself. Just like that, he walks up to the front door, punches in the code, and in seconds we're in that familiar warm room with the Persian rugs and smell of whiskey.

"I'm going to make myself a quick Jack and Coke in the bar, you want something?"

"Ummm… would you happen to have Cherry Coke?"

"Don't tell Knives, but it's his favorite." He laughs. "I'll get you one."

"I can open it, if you like."

Elijah chuckles by the door. "You don't trust me, Philips?"

"No, I do." I laugh. "It's just that, you know…"

He throws me a wink. "Got it."

After Elijah walks out of the room, I eye the microphone stand staring back at me in the practice section. My eyes widen. *Holy hell, it's gold!*

How did I not see this when I came here last?

Glancing over my shoulder to ensure Elijah isn't in sight, I walk up to his microphone stand, my fingers slowly tracing down the detailed snake that's so perfectly wrapped around the stand, like it's slithering. Its eyes are replaced with two glowing diamonds, and the skulls engraved on its skin is so Elijah.

It's the coolest punk rock thing I've ever seen.

Okay, so maybe I shouldn't say *'punk rock'* after Elijah shut down a little bit after I said the word *'punk'* back at the restaurant in reference to his band. He didn't give me a deep explanation for it, other than explaining that Diesel Rose is more of an alternative rock band, meaning they're not heavy metal or punk, and instead more of an alternative/indie/soft rock type of band, like The Neighbourhood.

I wonder what it feels like for Diesel to perform in front of all those people. What life must be like as an up-and-coming rock star. If it's euphoric like whenever I'm wrapped in my own little world being a ballerina, or if he ever feels lonely standing up on all those stages.

My eyes catch the drum kit not far behind, and it takes me back to Dave. The studio lights glimmer over the brass percussion as I find myself inching closer and closer to them. When I was a kid, I always wanted to be a drummer. Well, I also wanted to be a photographer, ballerina, vet, teacher, and wait for it… a tax attorney. Yep, I really did.

A smile shoots up my lips when I take hold of the drumsticks. There's no song in particular in my head as I start humming and pretend I'm playing the drums, never making a sound. I swing my head back and forth, pretending I'm at one of Diesel Rose's gigs with screaming fans. My wrists start burning from just how fast I'm going, but heck no if I'm stopping. This is the performance of my life. My hair is slapping my face from every head bang, and with my wildly beating heart echoing in my ears, I prepare for the epic crescendo.

"Oh, I wouldn't miss this for the fucking world."

"AHHHH! OH MY GOD!!" I scream in such fright that I uncontrollably throw the drumsticks in the air. *Ooops.*

They slam back on the drum kit, deafening the room in a loud *dun-dun-doooooooom.*

Oh. No.

Cringing to myself, I quickly pick up the drumsticks and put them back how I found them. When I turn around to the person that scared the shit out of me, I find my culprit leaning ever so confidently against the doorframe with a highball glass in one hand, and a glass bottle of cola in the other.

Elijah smirks, like full-on smirks, like he's the devil in disguise as he nods toward the drum kit. "Gee, Dave, you look different. Did you go blonde and shrink like six feet, huh?"

"Ha. Ha. Very funny." I glare at him and step forward, finding a secluded spot on the Persian rug to sit on. "I was living my best life over there, just so you know."

He sits down next to me and hands me my Cherry Coke. "Oh, I think that was evident with all the head banging."

"You don't say."

"Mmhmmm."

The coldness of the Cherry Coke glass bottle seeps into my skin, and I brush my thumb over the condensation, drawing a line. And then, just when my embarrassment dies down is when the real game begins. It's like life is straight-up laughing in my face as I fail opening the bottle. It's got one of those dodgy beer bottle caps that don't twist open.

The simplest solution would have been to just let Elijah take off the cap with a bottle opener back in their studio's bar, but my pride is too high from all those late-night murder episodes titled; '*STRANGLED AND SLAUGHTERED BECAUSE OF SPIKED DRINK!*'

Yeahhh, no thanks.

I've got nightmares from those episodes to last me a century, and then some.

Now just to be clear, I don't believe Elijah would ever—and I do mean *ever*—do that to me, but opening my own bottles and cans is just a little habit of mine that I've always had.

So here I am, just past midnight, struggling with all my life to open a damn Cherry Coke bottle. The pad of my thumb even starts reddening from the bottle cap's tiny steel grooves digging into my skin more and more.

"Would you happen to have a bottle cap opener in that bar of yours?"

"Nah." He smirks. "The boys and I don't need one."

Oh. My. God.

He's actually taking joy out of my misfortune.

Asshole. Okay, devilishly-handsome-*asshole.*

Elijah is all cocky taking a gulp of his Jack and Coke, and smoldering at me over the rim before he nods to my bottle. "You know all you need to do is ask, it ain't going to take your pride away. Would you like me to open it?"

"No thanks, I'll get it," I grit, half of my words inaudible as I try to take off the cap with my teeth. They always do it this way in those old classic western films with cowboys and shit.

I'm certain I spend another solid three minutes on it, groaning and moaning in frustration, all while Elijah calmly sips his liquor, even leaning back on his forearms to witness the disaster that is me even more comfortable.

"For the love of God, did you super glue this shit on?"

"I didn't, but at this point, I'm kind of wishing I did."

By my thirtieth attempt, I shove the bottle in his chest with a glare. "Just open the damn thing."

"Yes, ma'am."

And I watch in utter hatred (*okay, fascination*) as the asshole brings the bottle to his lips, and with his teeth, simply flings off the cap to the other side of the room *like it's nothing.*

Ugh, stuff him for being so perfect.

That was kind of hot.

Okay, a lot hot.

Elijah hands me back the bottle. "Anything else you'd like me to do? Teach you to walk? Guide you in riding a bike? Shine your already shined shoes?"

"How about you kick yourself in the ass for me?"

Elijah's smirk deepens. "How about you do it yourself?"

I move up and lie down on my stomach so that my face is right next to his.

"Yeah, you wish," I mumble under my breath, taking a sip of my drink and the moment the sweet blend of cherry cola hits my tongue, I'm moaning. "Mmhmmm, this is really freaking good. Oh, yeahhh!"

"Umm, can you *not* moan right in my face like you're giving head?"

Eyes wide, I choke on the cola, and it splutters everywhere.

Elijah throws his head back in laughter. "Got you back, *Peaches*. How does it feel?"

If I was the kind of girl to flip people off, it's exactly what I would have done to him.

"Evil, *JahJah,* you're evil."

"Don't you be calling me *JahJah* now."

"Whatever." I sip my Cherry Coke, enjoying my playful smile and the fact we've gotten closer tonight. "But in retrospect, I can call you whatever I like… *JahJah.*"

Elijah groans, but I know it's only to mock me as we stare at each other like there's nowhere else in the world we'd rather be. Because for me, there isn't.

I like it here.

With Elijah.

Just lying on his studio's Persian rug and chilling in the place he adores best.

"Question for you, Mr. Elijah Diesel…" I find myself murmuring as I press the cool bottle against my cheeks to ease just how hard I know I'm blushing. "What's the craziest thing you've ever done?"

"Oh, *Peaches*, you don't want to know."

"I do."

He laughs and shakes his head. "I can assure you, you don't."

Hmmm.

Staring at him as he leans even farther back, I bite my lip. "When did it happen?"

"Three, four years ago."

"And you really won't tell me?"

Elijah smirks. "Nope."

"Okay, *second* craziest thing you've ever done?"

His wolfish dark-gray onyx eyes bore into mine. "Probably right now, being here with you."

The air crackles between us, a sexual tension crawling that

I can't quite describe. All I know is that the longer Elijah stares at me like he is, the more the heat between my thighs intensifies. And then it dawns on me that I'm only wearing a fucking leotard, booty shorts, and a jean jacket.

Idiot. Idiot. Idiot.

All my breaths feel labored as Elijah's gaze flickers down to my lips and darkens. He takes a seductive gulp of his Jack and Coke, yet never takes his eyes off me. I think I'm getting drunk off him. Getting drunk off how hard his breaths are falling, and how I can feel the warmth of his touch from inches away, even though our bodies are not even brushing.

Is this how it's always going to be between us?

Sexual tension that we can do nothing else but stare to destroy?

"Rosalia Philips, you're up," Elijah sexily murmurs my name like its cotton candy, so sweet with the darkest touch of desire coated sin. "What's the craziest thing *you've* ever done?"

Easy.

"Kiss you, and then let you kiss me," I breathe softly, glancing down at my hands playing with the bottle's label. "Believe it or not, I'm actually really introverted, just ask Naomi. I'm not the girl that meets rock stars at midnight. I've never been on a date. Never been kissed aside from you. I've never…"

"Go on."

I suck in a breath. "I've never let anybody touch me, like let them fuck me or anything. You bring out this wild side to me that makes me… feel different. Real different. Really *good*." It gets quiet for a little bit before I add, "I don't know how else to quite describe it, really."

The pitter-patters in my chest explode because I've never been this intimately honest with anybody else but him. I know this isn't a date. I know there's no chance at anything conspiring between us. And yet, he's the one I'm sharing my dark, deep, and heavy truths with.

Three thuds come next.

Him setting his whiskey glass down beside him on the oak floors at the end of the rug.

He slips the Cherry Coke from my grip and also sets it down.

My heart going into overdrive, all because of him.

Elijah reaches out to me, his warm knuckles slipping under my chin to tilt my head up, and his sterling silver rings rousing my skin with their coldness—the slithering snake in particular. It forces me to glance up into his piercing eyes, to let my gaze stay there, and that's when I see he isn't smiling, or smirking, or laughing.

He's simply watching me.

Watching me watch him.

And I think he likes it.

Chapter

SIX

Rosalia

The soft pad of Elijah's thumb brushes over my lips, slowly carving each curve. His touch ripples through my skin and into my soul. There isn't a part of me that doesn't crave to be his. *All of me* wants to be his.

Circling his thumb around the center of my parted lips, those velvety gray eyes continue darkly gazing into mine as he slowly slips his thumb through the gap. It's erotic, the way my natural reaction is to lace my warm tongue around his skin, and I don't miss the moan that rumbles up his throat.

Oh.

My.

God.

Gripping my chin with his other fingers, he sensually dives his thumb deeper into my mouth until I'm seductively sucking on it. That's when the darkness in his eyes ripple into a lust I've only seen once—when he pulled back from kissing me breathlessly three weeks ago.

Elijah watches me.

Watches my plump lips.

Watches me suck his thumb.

"*Fuck*," Elijah whispers in that raspy kind of way I love. "Don't tell me those things, *Peaches*."

And that's when he slips his thumb even deeper, until it's almost touching the back of my throat. I almost gag, but he softly shakes his head in the silence, and I stabilize my breath, opening my mouth and giving him all of me. Our breaths fill the air, labored breaths of desire.

"Suck me harder, baby girl, that's it."

I submit and squeeze him tighter, circling my tongue around the tip of this thumb ever so slowly. It's enough to make Elijah shut his eyes for a moment, then inhale a sharp breath when those onyx eyes return to me and darken, no fragments of melancholy in them anymore.

Elijah pulls his thumb out from my mouth with a pop of my lips. And I know this isn't something that just happened by chance, he *wanted* to see me suck something of his. Hard.

His thumb glisters with me, and my mouth parts to a gasp when he runs his tongue over his thumb, so freaking slow it taunts me. I catch a glimpse of his skillful pink tongue gliding up and down it and I instantly wish that tongue was running along my skin, working me instead.

"*Fuckkk*," Elijah moans, finally letting go of his thumb. "You taste like cherries."

You can come taste me more if you like.

My entire body heats up because what I witnessed was the most erotic thing I've ever seen. I feel my nipples pebble and outline my leotard, brushing against the harsh fabric of my denim jacket, and part of me wants to take it off to let him see.

Elijah downs his entire glass of whiskey all in one go.

I look at him through my dark lashes. "Why don't you want me to tell you those things?"

His response, confident as ever, is instant.

"Because I'll want them," he admits in a frustrated growl. "*All. Of. Them.*"

Oh my...

I rub my thighs together, giving into that intensifying throb of my pussy and letting a little pleasure win. "What if I said I want that?"

"I'd say *no*." Elijah boyishly smirks. "So, this is me telling you *no*, Rosalia Philips."

I don't know why through it all I'm grinning like a psycho. This man just told me to my face that nothing can ever happen between us. He's reenforced it. And yet, I'm grinning.

Moments pass with our stare lingering.

Just him, and me, and the soundtracks of our hearts.

Elijah reaches over to an acoustic guitar set on the ground by the microphone stand and he begins strumming an untuned rhythm that awakens every beat of my heart.

"Tell me your favorite song," he says, without really asking.

"My favorite song?"

"Mmhmmm, you tell a lot from somebody from their favorite song."

I giggle. "Only the lead vocalist of a band would say that."

Elijah rolls his eyes for the millionth time tonight. "Shut up and answer the question."

Hmm. "I love The Neighbourhood, but I don't think I have a specific favorite."

"Oh, they're really fucking good. Met them last summer at a festival we were headlining, real nice guys."

"I'm so jealous."

"What's a song you keep coming back to?"

"*Wonderwall* by Oasis."

"Hmm…" Elijah half smirks and starts strumming the song. *It's incredible. He's incredible.* "There's the dark side of you coming out."

"Never said I didn't have that side."

"What's your deep, dark secret, Rosalia Philips?"

Oh.

A fog forms at the back of my throat, and no matter how many times I attempt to swallow it down, it remains. I glance down at my hands, and then at his and they so effortlessly play *Wonderwall.* My breaths all mingle into one. *Am I really going to say this to him?*

I've never been the type of girl to be so open, but as I said, Elijah changes that.

He changes everything.

As if he senses my response is going to be more loaded than first thought, his strum fades and he places the guitar back down. I don't expect him to move closer to me, for his hands to slip into mine, for his rings to caress my skin as he sits up, and yet he does.

The mood turns serious.

"You don't have to tell me if you don't want to, Ros—"

I cut him off, blurring out my truth before I lose the courage. "From when I was five to thirteen, I was in foster care. That changed four years ago when the people I today call my parents changed my life forever. They're the parents I never had. I can't thank them enough. I don't think I would have survived if I didn't have them... or Naomi. She never let me go through it all."

Elijah's eyes sadden as he gently squeezes my hand. "God, Rosalia, what happened?"

I gulp down, not missing the way my hands begin to tremble in my grip. I've never had to explain this to anybody before.

"My real parents... they loved me but were addicted to crack cocaine. Basically, any type of drug, my mom more. Looking back, I realize it was her kryptonite until it wasn't..."

I take a breath.

"When I-I was fi-five, I..." My gaze turns glassy, and it feels like his eyes are the only things keeping me from drowning. My entire body begins shutting down, ever so slowly, because this is the worst part. "Oh my god, I'm sorry."

"It's okay. Take all the time you need."

"I just don't want you to judge me."

"*Peaches*, I'm the last person to judge, especially somebody as beautiful as you. And trust me when I say I ain't just talkin' skin deep, I mean your heart, little girl, it's golden."

My throat closes up, and it feels like my body is strangling itself. That's when I start hyperventilating, because my entire chest tightens from the panic attack I feel coming on. The best way to describe it is that there's this big balloon in my mind, painted with tainted thoughts, and then all of a sudden, all the memories and nightmares become too much, and...

It.

All.

Just.

B.

U.

R.

S.

T.

S.

Bursts.

All my breaths become rapid, but I launch forward when I can't freaking swallow, Elijah is there to hold me. To tell me to forget about everything else and just focus on breathing. To walk us closer to one of the brick walls which we slide down. To tell me to count to twenty.

I count to twenty.

I shut my eyes.

I keep them open.

I try to do anything that help. But ultimately, the only thing that does work to stabilize my breaths is *him*.

"My family and I lived in the outskirts of Connecticut," I say shakily. "In a run-down house that was always rat-infested, and social security was paying the rent. It was the afternoon of my fifth birthday, and I stepped off the school bus but when I stepped inside, I... I..."

Elijah pulls my head to his chest, his fingers weaving through my blonde waves. The moment his warm lips brush against my forehead, my first hot tear falls, baptizing my cheek.

"Shh, it's okay, I got you," Elijah whispers. "You don't have to tell me, *Peaches*."

"But I want to, it's just... it's a lot to relive it."

"I can understand that. You're strong, *Peaches*, really fucking strong. Just believe it."

I nod, and when I summon the ability, I wipe away my tears and glance up at him, gazing between his eyes. "It was a murder-suicide," I sniffle. "My mom, she couldn't do it no more and..."

I don't need to finish. He knows. By the way, his stare turns tender, *he knows.*

Elijah squeezes his eyes shut. "Fuck, I'm so sorry, Rosalia... On your birthday, *fuck*."

"Yeah," I whisper into his chest, my vision all blurry. "Something like that happens and it changes you forever, you know? I try and keep a brave face on, I try and pretend I'm all good, but I'm not."

Silence lingers in the air for a little before I feel him nod. "The cruelness of life always eats away every inch of happiness you think you've kept hidden. Remember that, *Peaches*."

And there's something in his emotion-packed voice, a hint of vulnerability, that tells me he isn't just talking just to talk. He's speaking from reality. From truth. From experience.

"Fucking depressing is what it is."

"I know. Why do you think I sing?" Elijah sighs. "Yes, I enjoy the fuck out of it, but it's an escape. A huge escape for me. I mean, if one doesn't have an escape in their life, they're fucked. Life is too heavy to deal with twenty-four-seven. You got one? An escape aside from ballet, I mean."

I think for a little. "Photography, that's always been my escape too."

"Oh wow, let me see something."

Slipping away from him, I find my gym bag and rumble through it for my phone. When I return beside Elijah, I unlock it, not caring that he sees my password or half of my photos until I find those I'm most proud of. Those with all of the different chiaroscuro aspects I adore.

We sit with our knees up, and his denim thigh brushes against my bare one, and I'm not joking when I say goosebumps appear. It's hard to ignore what his touch does to me, as unintentional as it may be. Just like his hot breath hitting my cheek quickens my heartbeats as he glances down at my phone beside me.

"Whoa! That's epic stuff, *Peaches*," Elijah tells me with such genuine awe in his voice. It awakens my trampled mind. "They're so fucking cool, people would kill for that stuff."

I smile sadly through the pain. "That's really kind of you, Lijah. Thank you."

"There's no need to thank me, you're a naturally talented photographer, Rosalia." Elijah pauses to wipe away a tear that slips, his hand burning heat into my cheek that isn't just kinetic. "I'm sorry you had to go through so much at such a young age. You had to grow up fast. *Too* fast."

I nod slowly, not really knowing what else to say so I reach out

and run my fingers over his leather and sterling silver chained bracelets, feeling their braided grooves and he lets me.

Elijah's voice comes after a while. "You know what happened isn't
your fault, yeah?"

It was all my fault.

I nod again with a sniffle.

"Rosalia," he says my name softly in warning, in a way that tells
he doesn't believe me.

"I'm okay, really I am."

Elijah turns to face me properly, and it forces me to stare into
those pretty onyx eyes that right now are anything but wolfish. He
doesn't stare. He *gazes* at me, like I'm the only person in the world
that matters.

"*Peaches,*" he whispers, the warmest saddest smile breaking out
on his lips. "There's nothing you could have said or could have done
to make it have gone differently, okay? Sometimes, certain aspects of
life are already planned out for us, sometimes it's just all written in the
stars, and yes it fucking sucks, but sometimes there's nothing we can
do to change it. I know you're strong. I know you're trying to keep it
all in. I can see it in your eyes. But what I'm trying to say is don't let
the weight build up, because it'll kill you, *Peaches,* believe me."

With concern coated over his eyes, Elijah cups my face, and when
he does, my heart explodes because nobody has ever cared this much.
Nobody has ever cared enough to stay.

"You've *gotta believe me*, and I promise it gets better, *Peaches*. It
does, you've just got to believe it does and it will." Elijah presses his
forehead against mine, and instantly I feel calmer. "You've just gotta
let the pain out in any form you can. Let it flow out, baby girl."

Baby girl.

"I promise I will, I just… I just find it really hard to snap out of
sometimes."

"Because your real parents were stolen from you. And no matter
how much crack they snorted or fucking toxic shit they injected, at
the end of the day, they were your *parents.*"

"Exactly." I nod. *He understands me.* "That's what hurts the most. I
was too young to understand any of it, because if I did, I could have—"

"You were five, Rosalia, fucking *five.*" He shakes his head passionately. "Your job wasn't to figure it out. Your job was to drink hot cocoa

and I don't know, play with Barbies. It wasn't your job to save your parents from themselves, they were supposed to take care of *you*. They were supposed to be there for *you*. They were supposed *to be there*. But their addiction meant they weren't. Not *them*, their *addiction*. So, nothing you could have done could have saved them. *Nothing*."

I don't know where the hell Elijah pulls out a cigarette and lighter from, but he does. Tonight, the tobacco that laces the air feels like comfort, everything about this feels like a big warm hug in the solace of Elijah Diesel's presence as clouds of thick white smoke take over with every drag.

Leaning his head against the brick wall, his Adam's apple bobbles up and down in a thick swallow. Elijah glances over just slightly to look at me as he slips the cigarette out of his mouth just to say with a depressed half smile. "Rosalia Philips, you and I are more similar than I could have liked."

I rest my head against the wall too and glance at him, inches apart, and suddenly everything feels like it's going to be okay. I'll learn to heal this wound inside. I will.

I have to.

For myself.

For nobody else but myself.

Our thighs are still brushing as I shoot him a sad smile, and his only deepens. "Ditto."

Elijah reaches out to cup my opened palm, his thumb rubbing small comforting circles over each line. "Now can you see why I love coming in here? This studio is like a truth serum."

"Yeah, I honestly didn't expect to share so much."

"I'm grateful you did; it shows me you're real."

The moment his fingers crawl to my wrist, my heart drops when I attempt to pull away, but it's too late. He's already putting out his cigarette on the wall and blowing out the last of the misty smoke.

He's noticed.

He notices.

And all of the calm I felt seconds ago fizzles away. *No, Elijah. No. No. No.*

Elijah's brows slowly furrow, and I witness his jaw clench ever so slowly as he attempts to make sense of it all.

Overwhelmed with a stinging pain in my throat, I pull my hand closer to me, but he just reaches out to grip it again. His melancholic eyes return, pained this time as they flicker between me and the white scars on my wrist, his fingers caressing them slowly.

"Rosalia," he says in a strained whisper. "*Peaches*. Please don't tell me you tried to..."

And that's when I lose all control, and the sob that I thought I so perfectly could keep together begins to crumble. The ache in my chest intensifies as sobs escape me, heavy tears making it difficult to even see Elijah as he pulls me into the tightest embrace of my life.

Elijah Diesel holds me through every sob as I bury my head into his neck and grip on to his leather jacket like he's my savior. He's the one to comfort me in the middle of the night as all of the demons from my past rain down on me.

He's the one to press me deeper into the solace of his arms, his musky cologne consuming me as his heart beats a million miles per second, just like mine.

He's the one saving me from myself, all while he murmurs in my ear just how strong I am.

"*Peaches*," Elijah whispers with a strangled breath. "You're making it hard to hate you."

"Please," I beg through my cries, squeezing him tighter. "Please don't hate me, Elijah. I won't be able to take it. I won't."

Moments pass of us still wrapped in each other like we need this embrace to survive.

Elijah nods against my neck, his warm lips centering me when they brush against my neck. "Just please, *please*, promise me you won't get any crazy ideas or fall in love with me, Rosalia. Because I wasn't joking, I will break your heart."

The saddest smile all night traces my lips because this time I finally believe him.

Elijah Diesel will break my heart if I fall in love with him.

He'll shatter it into a trillion tiny irreparable pieces.

And the crazy thing is, after tonight, I'd let him...

"I promise, Lijah."

Come break my heart.

Chapter

SEVEN

Rosalia

PAST

From that late night in Elijah's studio where we spoke the heavy truths, I became *his*, even though he didn't have it in him to admit it. But I noticed it. I noticed it in the way he sent me photos of himself and Clément the entire week we were away in Seattle. How we spoke every day via text, even though he once mentioned he hated communication that way.

I noticed it on the grin on his lips when we met up on Monday after I had school. It was the first time I saw him in over a week and all I wanted to do was rush and embrace him, but I didn't. We're not at that level. Something tells me the warm embraces where he held me in the solace of his arms two weeks ago are a rarity for the lead vocalist of Diesel Rose. But the genuine grin that broke on his lips and dazzled his deep dimples was enough for me.

It felt like breathing in another life.

I noticed it in the way he would walk closer to me in Central Park, Manhattan shopping strips, and *Hayes' Bookshop* if a weirdo walked past or a guy eyed me for too long. Elijah's glare burned straight through them every single time, his very own superpower. And every time Elijah does walk closer to me in those instances, I always notice how he does it without ever brushing his fingers against mine, not even unintentionally, like my touch is illicit to him.

This past week with Elijah back in New York from Boston and Seattle feels magical. Although there were a few things I did when he was away that when I told him about it on Monday in Central Park, he chuckled, and suddenly I didn't feel so ashamed about doing it.

It was exactly two weeks ago today when I was working at Tickled Pink on my Saturday morning shift. It was a crazy morning with half of Manhattan wanting double macchiatos and avocado toast (trends these days, right? Ugh). I was minding my own business, working away with the clouded thoughts of the night before in my mind, the night that included Elijah, *spaghetti alla puttanesca*, and diving into my dark demons right in front of me, when something broke me from the thoughts.

The radio.

The radio in Tickled Pink was blasting a song that as soon as I heard it brought shivers down my spine. Not the scary kind, the kind you manifest your entire life to feel whenever something good is going to happen. Like your first kiss. Your first prom. The first time you do anything in life that comes with a little risk.

I didn't know the lyrics.

I didn't know the melody.

But I knew the voice. *Dear God*, how I knew it was him.

Him.

My melancholic onyx god.

Elijah freaking Diesel.

And his voice, as familiar as it was for me, was the most beautiful thing I've ever heard.

Raspy. Sexy. Dominant.

Elijah sang every lyric with meaning, like he was shooting a silver bullet down my body, expecting it to not hit my heart in the ruckus.

I felt chills all over, the heated kind that made me feel all funny. I so desperately wanted to absorb the song for what it was. For *everything* it was.

I wanted to listen to every lyric, every beat of the drums that I

knew belong to Dave, every moment of both varieties of guitars coming alive and creating an epic alternative rock masterpiece that bought
alive every single piece of me I thought was dead.

I wanted to sneak away and search up everything that was Diesel
Rose. And when my fifteen-minute break came, that's exactly what
I did. I downed a bottle of water at the back alleyway of the café and
got my detective on. I sat on top of a milk crate with repulsing dump-
sters only a few feet away and banana peels scattered on the ground
(literally *everywhere*) from our chef's signature banana bread, but I
didn't care.

I didn't mind the unpleasant hideaway. I just wanted to know
more about Elijah.

About Dave, and Knives, and Zander.

About Diesel Rose.

My breath was stolen with every song I managed to fit into that
fifteen-minute break, which was barely five, but for me, it was better than nothing. I spent the rest of the day waitressing with a goofy
smile on my face, the melody of the songs growing wild in my head
as I hummed along to the lyrics that were still all blurry to me, but
I loved them still.

I spent the entire bus ride back to my brownstone in Brooklyn
with my headphones in my ears and Diesel Rose on blast. I listened
to the songs while searching them up, hearing Elijah right in my ears
comforted me so much I felt like screaming and breaking out in a
happy dance, but that would probably have brought the heavily pregnant woman sitting next to me into pre-term labor.

And I was (still am) a wild lovesick band-obsessed seventeen-year-old, not an inexperienced midwife.

I adored every song and haven't stopped listening to their music
two weeks later. I listen to Diesel Rose *everywhere*. On runs. During
ballet warm-ups. At night when I can't sleep. That bus ride home
changed something for me.

It changed everything.

It showed me what heavy dedication, grit, and never giving up
does to you—success. When I first saw Elijah in that *Rolling Stone magazine* article months ago, I made a pledge to myself that I wasn't going
to ever search him up. That I didn't want to have any preconceived

ideas about him, and instead make up my own. But during that bus ride I couldn't do it anymore, said *"fuck it"*, and searched him up.

I also found out a lot about Diesel Rose. Elijah has been modest with me because what I found out about the true extent of their success—*wow*—they were going to make it big.

Because it wasn't just gigs that I found they've performed (and I mean *hundreds* of them), I also found they've done a lot of bigger music venues and headlined as the first act for several hot shot stars. That Boston gig Elijah told me about that night at the Italian restaurant wasn't in a little tiny bar, it was at Leader Bank Pavilion.

THE. DAMN. LEADER. BANK. PAVILION.

One of the most popular outdoor amphitheaters in Boston where artists like Billie Eilish have performed.

I recall my jaw dropping to the bus floor in that moment.

Diesel Rose is so much bigger than Elijah is leading it on to be.

It didn't surprise me that Elijah was the only band member to not post on his social media, namely Instagram, despite them already having quite a following.

I was silently laughing all of the bus trip home with the soundtrack of Diesel Rose in my ears as I went through their social media and all of the sarcasm that came from it. They were the type of guys that teased each other but would also cut their arms off for each other. Elijah told me they've been a band since they were sixteen. This year marked thirteen years. And it shows with how well they get along and how perfectly executed their music is. They love each other, to pieces. And their bond reminded me of Naomi and me.

It was the most hilarious thing going over their Instagrams. I found myself stopping on Knives a lot, since he had the most pictures with Elijah. There was one recent picture that I couldn't stop grinning at. Knives had posted a photo of Elijah who was sprawled out on the studio floor's Persian rug, fast asleep, a gray hoodie partiality covering his beautiful face.

The caption read;

> @knives.dieselrose: Never trust a guy who sleeps on the job… @elijahdiesel

The comments went like this…

@elijahdiesel: How about, never trust a guy who takes photos of the guy who sleeps on the job? @knives.dieselrose

@thatdieselrosedrummer: Where the fuck was I when this happened?

@zanderz: I'm so confused...

I'm pretty sure I drooled at the next photo of Knives and Elijah laying together at a beach with the location Florida. It's as if one of the other guys took the picture, because they're lying on beach towels and are both flipping off the camera, Elijah with sexy yet deadly smirk.

The reason I was drooling when I saw that picture is because Elijah's so damn ripped.

Oh.

My.

God.

Perfectly sculpted six-pack. Defined v-cut and mouthwatering trimmed short dark hair down the center of his v-cut, disappearing into black swim trunks. Those inky black tattoos that run down his muscular arms, and I also saw the slight indication that they sprawl across his back too. *And those weren't even all of the highlights.*

I had to zoom in on a certain aspect of the picture just to make sure I was seeing straight. I think the heavily pregnant woman on the bus next to me thought I was a full-on creep when I gasped at Elijah's nipple ring catching the light of the sunshine.

He has a nipple ring.

ELIJAH. HAS. A NIPPLE. RING.

As if that wasn't the hottest thing I've ever seen...

I think I died and went to heaven right on that bus.

Giddy, I remember quickly taking a screenshot and cropping the image so it was just of Elijah, because as mysteriously hot as Knives may be, Elijah Diesel is the man that makes my heart skip.

The caption read; Two psychopaths at work (yes, I'm talking about your split personality @elijahdiesel) ... tread lightly, rockers. Something is coming in the works! *rocker emoji* #it'sonthedlandbydIImeanDIESELROSEnotdownlow

@elijahdiesel: Look at this idiot... I'm going to pretend I never wasted the five fucking minutes I did trying to decode that hashtag. #letstalkaboutyoursplitpersonalitybro #notcool

@zanderz: On the DL, HAHAHA! Man, you kill me.

@thatdieselrosedrummer: Photographer credit, thanks, and fuck you guys too.

It was kind of a surreal experience in that moment when Elijah's name popped up at the top of my screen. A text. He sent me a picture of him holding a limited edition vinyl of Oasis' Wonderwall in Boston. *One of my favorite songs.* I kept on staring at his hand, at the prominent vein in his arm, at those leather bracelets I had been caressing that night, wondering how crazy it was that I knew *the* Elijah Diesel.

ELIJAH: Look what I found in my sister's collection! She's a sucker for vintage records. I saw this and thought of what you said. I'm playing the record for you, ***Peaches.***

My heart squeezed in my chest, and I can still think about that very moment now. The moment in which all of Elijah's songs flooded their way to that special spot of my favorites.

On Monday afternoon when we met up in Central Park, we gave into the Fall chill and laid down on the grass. It was a pretty odd sight for anybody looking in. A sexy, leather-wearing rock star and a blonde girl with a short tennis skirt and her school bag nearby.

There were a lot of teenage girls and their hot soccer moms walking through the parks, and even though some people had recognized Elijah and asked for a picture and autograph (which may I tell you, is one of the proudest things I've ever witnessed), but these women were staring. Like full-on gawking Elijah and kept making loops in the park to continuously walk past us. By the third time two of the soccer mom's daughters who had to be no more than thirteen began full-on staring me down.

"Don't worry about them," Elijah sighed when they finally disappeared. "I get that a lot, just the full-on staring, just smile and turn away, *Peaches.*"

"Doesn't it ever get uncomfortable? Like everywhere you go people know you?"

The way Elijah casually shrugged while looking out at the park will forever be loaded in my mind, especially because he was softly smiling while doing so. "It's a part of the job."

"That brunette-haired soccer mom seemed like she was really into you. When you're performing in Diesel Rose, do you ever look out at the crowd and pretend you're singing to somebody?"

"That's kind of fucking depressing, Rosalia."

"I know, but just answer the question."

"Nope. Never."

"How about to hot soccer moms who gradually show more and more of their cleavage with every loop around Central Park they do?"

The half-smirk burning up Elijah's lips when he looked at me exactly six days ago was everything to me. "Cross my heart hope to die, they ain't my kind of lovers, *Peaches*."

We returned to staring up at the bright, blue sky and I believed him. I believed every word.

They ain't my kind of lovers, Peaches.

I had a question for him in that moment, and it's been burning at the tip of my tongue ever since. Especially right now—*tonight.*

Who exactly is your kind of lover, Elijah Diesel?

But I couldn't ask him that afternoon while we were laying on the freshly mowed lawn of Central Park. I just didn't have it in me, because that's the type of question a boy-obsessed girl (which okay, I am, but still), asks that certain boy. It seemed too personal, and I vowed to Elijah that I wouldn't do anything stupid like go and fall in love with him, and so that question has been burning inside me all week.

That day in Central Park, I even remember how he was leaning up by his elbows and slowly brushed a strand of my hair away from my face. His calloused fingers were skittish, like he didn't know if his caress against my cheek would burn me or permanently mark my wildly beating heart. I decided it did both.

I never looked Diesel in the eyes when he spoke to me more, my cheeks heating up so quickly I was nervous he would mistake my blush for something that it wasn't. I mean, yes, my girly seventeen-year-old heart has a crush on Elijah Diesel, but he can't know it.

So, I kept it cool, always turning away when I felt a blush coming on and shutting my eyes whenever his stare pierced through my soul. And stare into my soul Elijah did, just like right now as I watch on from the VIP front row as Diesel Rose take Manhattan by storm.

This entire music arena is roaring, adoring everything that is Diesel Rose. I'm so obsessed and can't get enough of how thrilling this live performance is. I thought listening to their music on repeat on my phone was something, but *this, whoa,* it's something else.

Their music is therapy, and Elijah's voice is sinfully sweet like honey made by the devil himself. I want him to coat that honey all over me, make me drown in an ocean of Diesel Rose and die right here in his arms. It's addictive. Lethal. Tragic.

Diesel Rose is officially my favorite alternative rock band. (Okay, my fave band EVER.)

It's an adrenaline rush seeing just how much the crowd—which is in the thousands—loves them. They sing along, can't stop cheering and banging their heads as the red and blue lights go crazy wild, flashing, moving, and slowing in lieu of the music. Red flares light up the side edges of the stage, giving it a seductive smoky look that is so on brand with them.

Elijah's words are dark poetry. Trauma. Heartache. Desperation. It's all in the lyrics, giving air to my lungs with astonishing solo bass sections, powerful drums, and *his* honeyed sin voice that brings chills down my arms. Each lyric the heavy truths that rip at your heart.

Elijah has barely taken his eyes off me all night, despite the fact he only smiled twice in the past hour (yes, I counted). When Elijah asked me if I wanted to come to this gig of his, I answered in milliseconds. I had Naomi, who's currently screaming her heart out next to me, tag along. He gave me the two VIP front row passes yesterday when we met at Central Park again and he helped with algebra. I noticed the sleeve of his Italian leather jacket was ripped which was odd and offered to sew it up. He declines with a look in his eyes that told me to never ask him again. So then, between him and Naomi's fake IDs, everything was set.

Except the more I stare into his wolfish onyx eyes, the more I feel my promise begin to fade away. *The promise of not falling.* I've never been in love, so I don't know what it's supposed to feel like, but what I do know is that it's that tear in your chest when you think you won't be able to spend the rest of your life with that person. Those sparks electrifying your heart with each beat. The intensity of every single second with them. And I feel that all with Elijah.

I feel every single thing.

It's why staring at the masterpiece that is Diesel Rose absolutely killing it on stage with the best alternative rock hits is so bittersweet. Elijah, Knives, Dave, and Zander are all bittersweet. Because I can't help but fear that tomorrow I'll wake up and it'll all be a dream. I know what Elijah and I have—whatever it may be—can't last forever.

The reality is that he's a rock star. A rock star fifteen years older than me. I don't know what the hell I want to do with my life, and here he is, his career blossoming with every single lyric he sings. He's thriving and progressing with every performance, because this was exactly what he was born to do—*Succeed in being a true rocker.*

He's not going to become ultra-famous in a couple of years or even a year, I feel it coming much sooner. Months. Weeks. Days. And I hate that it scares me. But it does. *Because what happens then?*

Every drumbeat echoes in my chest, taunting just how fast my heart is beating. I feel the music within me, caged inside. And as Naomi and I dance to the music, perspiration lacing my skin as the leather jacket I'm wearing licks my skin, I feel his hot stare on me.

All night.

And that's when I realize I'm the girl he's zoned out in the crowd and am singing too.

I'm that blonde girl he keeps on mentioning in the lyrics—the beautiful to his damned.

I'm the one who's going to be brokenhearted by the end of this, all while Elijah Diesel will prevail in stealing the hearts of millions with his flawlessly raspy melancholic voice.

But right now—tonight—he's staring at *me* while he starts singing a *Wonderwall* cover. And it's much more than just a song, or my favorite song, he's singing the lyrics *to me.*

> *There are many things that I would like to say to you, but I don't know how*
> *Because maybe, you're gonna be the one that saves me*
> *And after all, you're my wonderwall.*

Tonight, Elijah Diesel is *my* flawlessly raspy melancholic rock star. We share a soft grin and the pitter-patters of my heart explode. *And that's all that matters.*

Chapter
EIGHT

Elijah

PAST

This day is never going to fucking end…

Knives smirks over at me from the passenger seat of my Camaro, his hoodie half over his face. "So, we're not going to talk about it at all?"

"Talk about what?"

"The fact that we're parked in front of a ballet school 'cause your girl asked if you could pick her up."

I turn away from his burning stare and instead focus on the glass doors of the damn ballet school that haven't fucking opened in the twenty minutes we've been here.

My jaw involuntarily clenches. "Rosalia's not my girl."

"*Oh*, is that why she's always in the studio with us guys?"

This asshole.

Groaning, I roll my head against the headrest until my narrowed gaze meets him. "Just because she's the only girl I've felt comfortable enough to bring to the studio, it doesn't mean we're…"

"You're, *what…?*"

"Together, you idiot," I grit under my breath, hating how much amusement he's getting out of this. "We're not *together.*"

Ever since Knives and I first met when we were sixteen before forming our band, he's always busted my balls. We're like brothers, and although I respect him, I hate him for knowing me more than I do myself.

Knives isn't stupid. He knows I'm not the guy to do this shit.

I'm not the type of guy to bring a girl to hang out at our private studio.

I'm not the type of guy to invite a girl to an arena I'm playing at with Diesel Rose.

I'm not the type of guy to alter our damn schedule mid-way and sing *her* favorite song.

I'm not that guy. Not at fucking all. *And yet, I did every single one of those things.*

For her.

For Rosalia Philips.

God, I hate myself. I really fucking do.

Knives turns away from me to continue scrolling through his phone. "Does she know that though?"

"I've made it clear, yes…. I don't even know why we're talking about this; *I* was the one who offered to pick her up anyway. Her car is in the garage because some fucker backed into her, and I don't want her to take the bus home in practically only a fucking leotard."

Knives shuts his phone but never puts it away. Tense silence simmers between us as his light eyes stare out through my windshield. "The fuck did you just say?"

Shaking my head, I turn back to gaze at the ballet school door. "I'm not fucking repeating what I said, man, because I know exactly what you're thinking."

"Oh, what am I thinking, mind reader?"

"That I'm in love with her or some shit when I'm not."

I feel him turn my way, his voice genuine as he says, "Dude, I'm not saying you're falling for her, I'm saying you don't do this shit. This isn't you! Rosalia has got you wrapped around her damn finger and you're so blind you don't even see it! You don't see what she's trying to do here!"

"She's seventeen, Knives. She ain't trying to do anything."

"Yes, she is! She's so fucking into you, Diesel!" he practically shouts. "Can't you see?"

Rosalia's into me?

Over my dead body she is.

Yes, we share stolen glances for way too long, and we've kissed once (which I still haven't told the boys about), but I made it clear to Rosalia what this is. We're not friends. We're not lovers. I don't know what the fuck we are, but if I want to keep her in my life, this—whatever *this* may be—is how it needs to stay.

Maybe it's that, or maybe it's the fact today has just been so freaking off to me, but I turn to Knives with a look of death that tells him to shut the hell up. "She's not into me."

And do you know what Knives does?

He. Fucking. Laughs. In. My. Face.

"Yo, dude." Knives shakes his head, mocking me with his laughter. "I don't know if you're high or some shit, but last time she was in the studio with us, she was checking you out for a full-on hour while we practiced."

I grind my jaw and find a cigarette to light before I light up this car. "No, she wasn't."

Knives cockily nods, a half-smirk on his lips. "Yes, she fucking was, Diesel, I know because I was looking at *her*. You just don't wanna hear it, bro."

I continue staring at him with a tense jaw, all while I take drag after drag after drag of my cigarette, wishing the white clouds could just rise up and consume me all.

There's no way Rosalia Philips is falling for me.

It's impossible.

Ludicrous.

"She's not in love with me, Knives, so get that thought out of your head. I—" My words get caught in my throat at the sight of Rosalia stepping out of the ballet school. A five-foot-four blood wrapped in a white leotard that accentuates her every curve and that petite waist of hers. One look at her, at the way her eyes warm when she spots my car and starts jogging, and I'm a fucking goner. Because I instantly forget what to say with all this lack of air in my lungs.

Knives is cursing under his breath, telling me that *this* is exactly what he means, but I ignore it all because I'm that stubborn. Instead, I nudge his side, without ever once taking my eyes off the golden ballerina with the most beautiful of smiles.

Dead. That's what she's going to make me end up.

I've never seen a woman as beautiful as her before, with eyes so piercingly green I forget my damn name. There's nothing but warning signs going off in my head the closer she approaches the car, signs that tell me those emerald-greens have the devil in them, because every time I look at her, I feel consumed by the heat of hell.

"Get in the back seat," I order Knives, nudging him even harder when he stays still.

"What the hell? The back? Dude, I was here first."

"I ain't letting her sit in the back seat like she's in a freaking taxi. Get in the back."

Knives groans and unbuckles himself with a curse. He throws his phone in the back seat and climbs over the console to the back seat in the most fucking dramatic way he can. He almost freaking kicks me in the face with his fancy fucking spiked boots that *totally* go with his sweatpants and hoodie.

"You owe me for this, chickenshit," Knives warns, flinging himself in the back seat so hard that the entire car shakes, my fucking balls with it. "I won't forget you demoting me like this."

"Shut up." I smirk, a chuckle finally coming through when I glance at him in the back seat and he's pouting. "Be on your best behavior, okay? I ain't trying to scare her away."

The most diabolic grin works up Knives's lips. "Don't you worry about me, Diesel."

The click of the passenger side door has my gaze flicker there, just in time for Rosalia to slip inside with a graceful smile. She hasn't even been in the car for a second yet, and already I'm flooded with that coconut and cherry blossom blend of hers that keeps me up at night, tossing and turning.

It's freaking biblical the way she stares at me, comfortability, her gaze darkening with something I don't quite understand. Rosalia is an angel, a dark angel, one that comes with the devil's eyes and his sin. I've said it before, I'll say it again—*my Peaches is going to kill me.*

Wait… Wait a minute.

Did I just say '*my*'?

Fuck.

"Hi, Elijah." Rosalia smiles, like the way she rolled my name off her tongue like it's the sweetest thing didn't just go to my dick. "Thank you for picking me up, I appreciate it."

"Anytime." I nod and glance away from her with a clenched jaw, knowing that if I stare at her for a second longer, I'll be a goner.

I pull out of the car park and start driving.

In my peripheral vision, I feel her set her gym bag by her feet before glancing behind her shoulder. "Hi, Knives."

"Hey there, blondie. How was ballet practice?"

I shoot Knives a death glare in the rearview mirror. *That was supposed to be my line, asshole.* My best friend catches my eyes and flips me off with a knowing smirk. *Fucker.*

"It was good. Tedious. We have a competition coming up just before the end of the month, so training has been even more excruciating, but worth it. My best friend, Naomi, would tell you differently. She skipped tonight's practice to meet up with this guy she's really been eyeing for a while."

I chuckle as I turn to her. "That Noah guy?"

Rosalia's eyes light up as if she's impressed I even remember the guy's name from all of the things she's told me about. But I do. I remember every single thing she's ever said.

"Yeah." She laughs, almost to herself. "That's him alright, he just broke up with his girlfriend and Naomi took two-point-five seconds to slide into his life. Tonight will be interesting for her. She'll probably call me as soon as she gets home tonight."

"You'll have to tell me all about it."

Rosalia shoots me a slow, seductive smile. "Of course."

I come to a slow at the damn red lights and my gaze never drops from her. She keeps on staring, and *fuckkk*, I swear to God if she bites that lower lip for a second longer, I'll kiss her.

What the hell am I saying?

My hardening dick, which has been against me this entire drive, jolts against the constraints of my jeans. I do nothing but ignore it. Ignore how much it aches.

I really need to get fucking laid and forget all about the mind games and Rosalia.

And of course, it's Knives that not so subtly clears his throat, breaking our intense stare. The lights flicker green, and I hit my foot on the gas, zooming down these Manhattan streets.

"So, blondie," Knives says, and I'm already shaking my head. "*You* got a boyfriend?"

My brows knit together as I flicker my gaze to the rearview mirror, but Knives isn't looking back at me, he's staring right at the back of Rosalia's head.

My breaths heave. *The hell is he trying to do?*

"Um, no," Rosalia softly replies. "I don't."

"Why's that?"

I clench my jaw. "Because she just said she fucking doesn't."

Knives ignores me completely, and I know exactly what he's trying to do. He's trying to fish for any evidence that can be used against me. Knight Ives may look like the tragic Diesel Rose bassist that was a love child between two gorgeous porn stars (*which he was, by the way*) with either the look of death in his eyes or a cunning smirk, but he's one intelligent guy.

He figures you out without you ever realizing he's doing it.

Sly. Complicated. *And* my cherry-cola-addicted best friend.

Go figure...

Knives tries again. "Is there a guy at school that likes you?"

"Cayden Montgomery," Rosalia says after a little while, so low we could have missed it. My ears instantly perk up because she's never mentioned the guy. "The jock of the school."

Ah, right.

I already hate the fucker.

I inhale a sharp breath, not knowing why my head feels all funny knowing there's a guy at her school that wants to kiss those damn sweet, fairy floss lips. *Those that I devoured first.*

"Cayden Montgomery," Knives ponders. "Sounds like an ass, but why don't you like him?"

"Wellll," Rosalia sighs. "Do you want the short or the long version?"

"I'm too fucking sober to hear that long version, give it to me short, blondie."

"At a party I went to during summer, he practically whispered in my ear that whenever I wanted to get out of the house to *put that gorgeous mouth* of mine *to good use*, these are his words by the way, then *all I got to do is ask*. So no, I'm not into guys who throw their dicks in my face when they *literally* just had their tongues down another girl's throat seconds before."

My eyes widen and I almost veer into the freaking sidewalk.

I want to kill this Cayden Montgomery. Right. Now.

Knives chuckles as he leans his crossed arms over the back of Rosalia's headrest, all while I'm bursting at the seams. Fuming. I think my jaw has clenched thirty or forty times.

"Interesting..." my best friend comments. "What about guys who don't play like that?"

Rosalia glances over her shoulder at him, well, not before catching my eyes for a moment, "What do you mean, Knives?"

"I mean, if you're not into *boys* like that, how about *men* like Diesel? Are you into him?"

Wherever the fuck my heart is, it drops.

Rosalia stares at him for what feels like forever and tries to act all cool, but I see beyond it. I see how her eyes widen a fraction, and that scarlet blush I love begins to crawl up her neck and plaster on her soft cheeks. "What? You..." She clears her throat. "You think I'm into Elijah?"

"Until you tell me *no*, yeah, I fucking do."

Oh mon dieu.

Raking a hand through my hair, I squeeze my eyes shut for a split second before I drive into traffic. *Of course he had to go there.*

Silence laces the air, and it's nothing like the silence when it's just her and I, this one is awkward. Tense. Pointed. Knives asked her a direct question about me, and she knows it.

Rosalia turns back around, so she's facing the windscreen, a breath escaping her. "Guys my age don't know how to treat me, that doesn't mean I fall in love with every older man I meet, Knives."

"*Oh*, and do you meet many?"

Fuck. Me.

Slowing in front of our studio, I glance at my best friend. "Would you shut the hell up before we get a new bassist?"

"Yeah, new bassist, my ass, you guys would be fucked without me." Knives smirks, not getting the memo that this is where his ride ends as he turns back to her. "Are you into *Elijah*?"

"Oh my god, no." Rosalia blushes. "No, we're just really good friends."

"*Friends?*"

"Mmhmm, yeah."

"Okay." Knives clicks his tongue with a slight chuckle, and if there's anything I know about my best friend it's what that '*okay*' really meant was, '*Don't believe you, but okay.*'

His gaze flickers to mine as he slaps my shoulder. "Alright, man, guess this is my drop off." He glances back at Rosalia, and I can see in his eyes that nothing's really changed since the first day he met her. He still doesn't trust her, and I don't like it one bit. "Ciao, blondie."

The second Knives steps out of my car, I'm driving en route to Brooklyn Heights. *Well, this twenty-minute drive to her house is going to be interesting, to say the least.*

I rake a hand through my hair, just like I always do when I'm a little anxious. "Don't worry about Knives, he just likes to bust my ass."

Rosalia's fretted eyes find mine. I don't miss the nervousness in her smile. "It's okay."

But it's not. And it's evident in the silence brewing between us, the one that remains for twenty minutes straight until I park in front of her brownstone, wanting to kill Knives for causing this apparent fracture between us. For the past few weeks, everything between us has been so real. The laughter. The banter. The emotion. It's. All. So. Fucking. Real.

So why don't I know what to freaking say right now? Why am I staring out the damn driver's window, out at her front door with a hand repeatedly raking through my hair in distress?

"Would you like to come in? My parents are at work."

Motionlessly, I nod, and within moments, we're in her bedroom. The first and only time I was here it was after midnight in early June when she sneaked me in after I returned her school bag. Now it's Fall. Late September. And it makes me feel a kind of way glancing outside of her bedroom window at the orange-brown leaves which hang on to her tree-lined street for dear life, a soft breeze working through them.

It's just before seven thirty p.m. and the night sky is just beginning to blanket over the darkening orange glow, giving her bedroom a golden radiance.

I hear Rosalia move around behind me, but I keep my hands pressed against her windowsill, staring forth. I can't stop the clenching in my jaw, no matter how damn hard I try.

"Whatever you're thinking…" Rosalia softly murmurs. "*Stop.*"

"*Peaches*, you have no idea what I'm thinking."

"I do. You think what Knives said affected me. You think what he said is going to scare me away. Guess what, Elijah? It won't, so let it go. He was just curious to know, that's all."

Moments pass before I turn around, glancing down at my blonde angel with the most devilish of eyes. She's smiling at me—warmly— and right now I don't know if I'm at the gates of purgatory or if this is all a fucking dream.

All I know is that when I wrap my arms around her waist and pull her close, heat rushing across my torso, it's like she's all I'll ever need.

Fuck.

Blowing out a sigh, I press my head against hers and hold her tighter.

"*Peaches…*"

Rosalia wraps her arms around my neck, our noses brushing. "Just stop thinking."

"I can't."

"Elijah, please."

"What the fuck are we, Rosalia?" I whisper against her lips, my heart running wild because I hate the way I ache to taste her cherry lips one more time. "Tell me."

Her hot breath tickles my lips. "I don't know."

"Tell me, *Peaches.*"

"I—"

Before Rosalia can respond, a thud ricochets throughout the entire room, and it takes me a second to realize what's happening before vicious shouts fill the room.

Rosalia's bedroom door bursts open, slamming against her wall, and a man wearing navy scrubs who I presume is her foster father stands by the doorframe.

Oh fuck.

The man's face reddens, a bulging nerve appearing down his forehead the moment his wide eyes meet mine.

And.

Everything.

Just.

Slows.

This isn't good. At all.

"Dad!" Rosalia screams, rushing out of my arms like I'm poison. "What are you doing home?"

"What am *I* doing *home*?" her father growls. There's so much disappointment in his eyes when he looks at Rosalia and it kills me.

It kills me because I know how much she's been through and how much she loves him.

Needs him.

I'm the problem in all of this.

"WHO THE FUCK ARE YOU, HUH?" Mr. Philips roars, eyes flicking to me with a fiery I can only describe as hell. "Hey! I'm talking to you! WHO THE FUCK ARE YOU? GET OUT! GET THE FUCK OUT OF MY HOUSE BEFORE I CALL THE POLICE!"

Within seconds he's charging right at me and while everything within me says to run, to get out of this fucking house and never see her again, my heart—which I've never *ever* aligned with before—tells me to not move an inch. And so, I don't. I stand tall, defiant with a clenched jaw because I know exactly what this means...

Everything that ever conspired between Rosalia and me is over.

It's over before it even fucking started.

He isn't even giving me a chance.

"Dad, stop! Please!" Rosalia pleas, rushing in front of me seconds before her father storms me. What's worst is that her warmth—which I should ignore—gives me air again.

"If I ever see you around my daughter again..." Mr. Philips stops dead in his tracks, and with darkening eyes, points a finger in my face. "I *will* fucking ruin you. Understood, Punk?"

Punk.

My throat closes up.

"What the fuck did you just call me?" I grit, staring her foster father down, not caring who the hell he is right now. Not after what he just said. "Oh, come on now." I chuckle darkly in a mock. "Don't get all shy now."

Mr. Philips grinds his jaw, all while Rosalia is trying to play referee between us.

"Is this the way you speak to Rosalia, huh? Who the hell are you and what are you doing with my daughter? She's *seventeen* and you look double her age! I. Said. Get. Out." Pausing, Mr. Philips cocks his head to the side and taunts me with an arrogant smirk, "*Punk.*"

Clenching my jaw, my eyes widen in fury.

That fucking does it.

Anger boils my blood and before I think it through, I launch forward toward him, only for Rosalia to push me back with a squeal. That's when her father tries to take a swing at me, but I grip his wrist before he can make a hit, not fucking caring if it's his surgery hand or not.

Mr. Philips doesn't know what he's doing to me. What he's doing to my mind that's spiraling at the word he spat.

"Dad, please stop, can you just let me explain—"

"He's right, *Peaches*," I murmur, cutting her off while eyeing her father down. "After all, I'm nothing. The only thing I am in this world is just a fucking *punk*, right?"

"Elijah, you know that's not—"

"Don't," I grit, flicking my gaze down at Rosalia, witnessing the sadness pooling in her emerald-greens. "Don't even try to make things better, I think your father said enough."

That's when I notice just how heavily I'm breathing. How my chest feels like it's about to explode from all of the adrenaline and malice lacing my body. I can taste blood in my mouth. Metal. It tells me everything I need to know; I need to get the fuck out of here before everything comes crashing down.

And that's exactly what I do, I don't run—I sprint—out of this damn brownstone, because perhaps escaping is the only thing I've ever been good with in life.

When I'm finally in my Camaro and speeding through Brooklyn Heights to God knows where, nothing feels the same.

My knuckles whiten gripping the wheel so tightly, and I hate myself for being so foolish. Rosalia Philips is too good for me. Too good for a tragic *punk*.

"FUCK!" I yell, slamming a fist against the wheel, the swell in my throat throbbing.

Knives was right.

I've been blind.

So fucking blind.

Because Rosalia Philips could never be mine.

Chapter

NINE

Rosalia

I have never been grounded in my entire life… *until tonight*. Nothing compared to the disappointment in my father's eyes when he burst through my bedroom door in scrubs and saw Elijah.

I've never seen my foster father so angry before, so livid at me. He's the cool dad. The calm dad. The kind I always wished to have. And ever since I was blessed to have him and his wife as foster parents (and my foster sister), I've respected them. Adored them. Loved them.

I've been a good girl.

With good grades.

And a good heart.

All I wanted was to impress them, to let them love me enough so that they wouldn't leave, but tonight, it just all blew up in my face.

I can't begin to imagine what my father thought when he stepped into my room, and I was embracing a man that mirrors the definition of sin to him—everything he and Mom warned me about.

The tattoos.

The bad boy alpha.

The darkened smile of a devil's paradise.

When Elijah stormed out of my bedroom, it felt like a dagger being lodged in my chest. I didn't know whether to run after him or to face my father. *I did the latter.*

But he just kept staring down at me, disgust written all over his face before uttering five simple words, "No ballet for a month."

The reality of things began to set in fast.

A month.

Ballet means everything to me. *Everything.* And it was all just taken from me.

I have a competition in less than a month, it means I'll miss it, but the only person I'm angry at is myself. Me, myself, and I.

My father didn't speak to me all night, and I didn't dare want to face them, so I stayed in my bedroom. My mom came in once, brought my dinner plate, sat at the edge of my bed when I had already dived under the covers, and asked me to tell her everything.

I told her everything about Elijah, including the kiss. By the end of it she stared at me with the saddest blue eyes I almost wanted to cry right there, but I didn't.

The softest of smiles outlined her lips, and she didn't say anything else all while she kissed my forehead, just like she does every night, and then walked out of my bedroom without ever looking back.

There's been this great emptiness in my chest ever since. I hate that this happened. I hate that my father called Elijah a word that's so obviously triggering for him. I hate that this all exploded in my face before it even began.

I've been tossing and turning all night, never getting more than a few minutes of shut-eye before a jolt rushes up my body and I sit up in the bed, panting.

It's just after midnight now and I can't get rid of this sick feeling in my stomach. There's rumbling in the kitchen that's on the other side of the wall and inaudible murmuring turns into louder, culpable words.

"A fucking rock band, Jessie? Is that what she said? That he's in a fucking *rock band*?" My father's agitated voice vibrates against my headboard.

I squeeze my eyes shut. *Oh my god.*

My mom's response is lower, inaudible.

It's silent for a few minutes before his shout makes my nervous heart jump. He isn't shouting at my mom; he's shouting at the situation.

"Jesus Christ! He's going to be thirty-two, he's *fifteen years older*! What the fuck were they thinking? Rosalia isn't in love, she's seventeen. *Seventeen*. Fuck. Me."

I know they're protective and only want the best for me, but I can't take it anymore. It's why I dive under my bedsheets with my phone pressed to my chest, the heat of each breath killing me from the inside out.

I squint at the brightness of my phone illuminating the silk sheets as I scroll through my contacts with a knot in my throat.

Sniffling, I land on Elijah, desperate to fix this. I don't know how he'll take this, but I've finally summoned the courage to text and that's a step within itself.

ROSALIA: Please don't hate me.

Delivered instantly flickers to read, but Elijah doesn't reply for seventeen minutes.

Seventeen.

I wonder what he's doing. Is he at the studio? Rolling in his sheets with some stunning rock chick? At home? *Home.* What does home look like for Elijah Diesel?

I'll never know.

I shake away the thought and attempt to remain optimistic no matter how deeply my lungs are burning when his reply lights up my screen.

ELIJAH: Why would I hate you?

I blow out a shaky breath, not knowing what this means.

ROSALIA: For what my father said. How he reacted when he saw you. I'm really sorry that all happened. I feel so bad, so sick to my stomach, I barely touched my dinner.

ELIJAH: You shouldn't be speaking to me, Rosalia. I think it's best for both of us if this all stops.

I read over the last past of his message twice, none of it feeling real as my heartstrings tug in pain.

I'm shaking my head to myself because this is the worst possible outcome.

No. No. No.

ROSALIA: I don't want this to stop, please, Elijah, you can be my secret. I miss you.

ELIJAH: I'm sorry for any of the trouble I caused, but it does all need to stop. What's the damage, **Peaches**?

ROSALIA: I'm grounded from ballet for a month.

ELIJAH: Oh, fuck.

ROSALIA: Yeah, I'm going to be missing my competition…

ELIJAH: Rosalia.

ROSALIA: Yes?

Hope fills me.

ELIJAH: Delete my number. Block me. We can't see each other again, not after tonight.

And just like that, everything comes crashing down. Including my own sanity.

ROSALIA: But when will I see you again?

ELIJAH: If you're lucky, **never**. This was a mistake, Rosalia. We both know it. I should have never let it get this far. You're getting punished for something that never even happened.

ROSALIA: It's the consequences, Elijah.

ELIJAH: There wouldn't have been any consequences if I just stayed the fuck away from you. This is the end, Rosalia.

ROSALIA: Please don't say that. I need you. I'll do anything, Elijah, anything at all.

ELIJAH: Delete my number.

Desperate, I hit call as tears blur my vision, but I don't dare blink hard enough for them to fall.

Elijah ends every single one of the calls.

ELIJAH: Stop calling me, I'm not answering.

ROSALIA: I just need to hear your voice, please.

ELIJAH: I can't.

ROSALIA: Are you with somebody?

ELIJAH: That doesn't matter, I said I can't. It's not healthy, Rosalia, you deserve somebody who'll really be there for you. Somebody who can tell you who the hell you are to them. A guy your age. A guy like Cayden.

ROSALIA: Seriously? Don't you dare, Elijah, don't you dare do this to me.

ELIJAH: We need space. You and I both know that.

ROSALIA: Please. I just need to see you, please, Elijah, just give me this.

ELIJAH: I can't.

ROSALIA: Just one more time, *please.*

Three little gray bubbles taunt me, his reply not coming until a couple minutes later.

ELIJAH: One month. I'll meet you in front of my studio on Halloween. 10 p.m.

ROSALIA: Okay, I'll be there. Promise me you'll be there too.

ELIJAH: I promise.

ROSALIA: This hurts so much, Lijah.

ELIJAH: Peaches?

Peaches.

ROSALIA: Yeah?

ELIJAH: Don't you dare try and find me before Halloween, I'll run. Good night.

And just like that, it's all over. Every single inch of us shatters like glass all over my tarnished body.

He's breaking it.

He's breaking my heart—*just like he vowed*—and it bleeds out all over me.

It hurts so much. Hurts to breathe.

Hurts that his coldness is back.

Hurts that I was stupid enough to ever care about him this deeply.

But what hurts the most, above everything, is knowing that we'll never be the people we were when he wrapped me in the solace of his arms weeks ago on his studio's floor.

When he told me "*I got you*", and never let me go.

When he—Elijah Diesel—protected me from the dark monsters that right now crawl out from under my bed, destroying me slowly.

Chapter

TEN

Rosalia

One month Later...
PRESENT DAY

It's been a month. An entire thirty-one days without Elijah Diesel. Without ballet. *Without feeling like myself.* Albert Einstein once said insanity is constantly doing the same thing over and over again and expecting a different result. Tonight, his proverb runs deep, because insane is all I've ever felt lately.

I went from an introverted boy-obsessed (well, one *man* in particular) girl, to one riddled in darkness, because nothing feels the same anymore. It isn't that I think I've lost Elijah, it's that I've lost that spark within myself. Those moments of confidence. Of thrill.

My father didn't catch Elijah and me kissing.

My father didn't catch Elijah and me fucking.

My father caught us intimately hugging. *Hugging.* That's what upsets me the most.

It was innocent. Chaste. Something *normal.* But to my parents, there's nothing normal about an older six-foot-three man in my bedroom—hugging me. The crazy thing is… *I get it.* I understand their point of view, but October has been torturous. I mean, Naomi almost died when I told her it all, and I don't blame her. This whole thing was pretty messy.

And yet here I am, minutes after ten o'clock, sitting up against the exterior brick wall of Elijah's studio, waiting for him like I promised. It's Halloween, and I can't even count how many Draculas, devils and angels, and sexy nurses (what the hell is even up with that costume? I mean, it has nothing to do with HALLOWEEN!) have passed me.

The ominous dark clouds blanket over Manhattan, and it feels like it's going to rain any second now, but as I press my legs farther into my chest, I tell myself I don't care. I don't care if it rains. I don't care if these dressed-up ghouls think I'm a loner. I don't care how deeply my heart will hurt me the moment I see *him*. All I care about is that Elijah shows up.

He can't stand me up.

He can't.

We haven't spoken in this entire month of Halloween, just like he wanted, but that doesn't mean I haven't been itching to call, to text, hell, to do anything.

I always pass *Hayes' Bookstore* when I go to work on the weekends, and it kills me. There's been so many times where I've hurried my steps, or better yet, crossed the street so I don't have to compress the nostalgia that laces even seeing the storefront.

Other times, when I'm in a '*I don't give a shit, let the entire world burn down*' mood, I slowly walk past the bookstore, strangling all the memories that hold me captive. Those are the weekends when I stare into the glass windows, searching for a peek of leather, with zero plans of knowing what to do if I were to see Elijah inside.

But I haven't seen him.

Not a glimpse.

Not an inch.

Not a scare.

Did Elijah ever think about me during this month?

The question gets lodged in my throat as the late-night chill kisses my skin. I glance up and down the street. Up and down. But there's no sign of Elijah. I know he's not inside the studio because neither his Harley nor Camara is parked out front.

Maybe he won't come.

Maybe this was all a stitch up.

I shake my head, adamant to prove myself wrong, but as I glance at my phone and I see it's ten after ten, I'm not so sure. It's the night in which the sweet scent of candy laces the air. The same cold air monsters inhale and terrifyingly roam the city, dressed in death.

Death.

I can't stop shivering in the cold, my teeth clanging from just how cold it is. Or it could be the nerves. Or a combination. *A combination sounds better.* But whichever way, it's all the same…

Elijah Diesel… please don't break your promise to me.

I told my parents I'm staying over at Naomi's for the night because in the history of excuses, there was no excuse I could use to cover up meeting with Elijah. My punishment is *just* wearing off come midnight, and with Naomi being the only person I do trust, it worked.

All I can say is thank God her parents are away on another work trip, because my mother would have called her mother an average of fifteen times to ensure I was *actually* there… *which I'm not.*

A man dressed as a vampire who's holding hands with a sexy nurse passes me, and I roll my eyes. *At least add some fake blood and be Dracula's sexy nurse or something. Jesus.*

I groan as ten thirty nears, and I'm just about to stand up and walk away when I hear it. The rumble of a familiar metal monster devilishly approaching. A Harley.

And instantly I know it's him.

Him.

Elijah.

"Oh my…" I whisper into the night while shutting my eyes. "Oh my god."

My heart jolts in anticipation because I don't know what tonight means for us both. If it'll break us more or bring us closer.

The Harley's loud purrs intensify, and it sounds as if it's right in front of me before the engine cuts off.

After counting to ten, I blow out a sigh, opening my eyes to confront the night that is. And there he is, looking as wolfishly beautiful as ever, staring back at me. Elijah Diesel takes my breath away—endlessly—even when I don't want him to.

Those melancholic onyx eyes stare deep into my soul as he slips off his helmet and shakes out his dark wavy hair that's grown a little longer since I last saw him. The ends almost kissing his leather-covered shoulders, softly blowing in the wind as he locks down his kickstand. His spikey biker boots hit the ground firmly, but he's still positioned on his bike, straddling it.

My heart skips a beat, then and another, and another. *I'm still so crazy about him.*

The gap between me sitting on the sidewalk and him parked feels like bare inches apart because he's looking at me so intensely it consumes me.

Elijah gestures behind him. "You comin' on or what?"

My eyes wide. *Umm, WHAT?*

Standing, I slowly approach him, trying not to admire how beautiful the soft glow of the art deco lampposts caress his face. "I'm, uh, I'm not getting on that thing. I thought you wanted to meet here and then go inside the studio, no?"

There's a lot I've missed about Elijah in this past month. His heart. His wisdom. Just his presence alone. But right now, as a slow, half-smirk crawls up his lips, I think that it's his happiness that I missed the most.

"No."

I arch a brow. "No?"

Elijah's smirk vanishes as quick as it appeared, and *hello Mr. Motionless.* "Riding makes me clear my mind, and it was exactly what I needed to do before seeing you tonight. So, I can either get the fuck out of here—alone, *or* you could hop on, and we could go to my place."

His place.

Gulping down, I eye his shiny black Harley. *It's stunning, yes,* but I'm not looking to die tonight—*especially on Halloween.* They already say this night is cursed, so I don't need any more bad luck.

"Are you sure it's… safe?"

Elijah does everything but laugh in my face. "I've been ridin' since I was sixteen, Rosalia, that's sixteen years now without killing myself, so I don't know, you tell me."

"Smart-ass," I mumble under my breath, taking his dark helmet when he hands it to me.

It takes seconds for Elijah to put the helmet on me, and strap it on so if he decides to go a gazillion miles per hour and I fling off, at least my head will survive while the rest of me dies.

I shudder. *Goddamn. I'm risking my life for you, Elijah Diesel. Be nice to me.*

I don't even question if Elijah has another helmet as time slows when he gazes at me, his fingers getting lost in my blonde waves while flinging it behind my shoulders. Thank God he doesn't see the blush crawling up my cheeks with my helmet on, and when he flicks down the helmet's visor, so the city lights soften around me, my heart thumps because I don't want this to be the last night I see him.

Elijah helps me straddle the Harley behind him, no biker gloves on him tonight when his hands slip over mine and guide my hands around his waist, tight, so I'm safe. Butterflies, it's all butterflies I feel as I press my helmet against his back and shut my eyes, wanting this nightmare to all go away.

I care about Elijah. I care about him dearly, and I hate how the word my father so viciously screamed in his face last month echoes in my mind as Elijah zooms through Manhattan at exasperating speeds.

Whoa.

This is the rush I was talking about during the summer. The thrill. The risk. *Euphoria.*

My heart flies to my throat with every corner he turns and new speed he reaches as we zoom out of traffic.

It's just me. It's just him. It's just *us*—an imminent rock star and his ballerina.

My hair is blowing in the wind as I hug him tighter, not because I'm scared of the adrenaline rushing through me, I hug him tighter because there are tears in my eyes. All the city lights turn all blurry as the hot tears begin to glide down my cheeks.

I don't know how much time has passed before Elijah slows in front of an industrial Manhattan apartment complex, unclips my helmet, helps me off his Harley, and wordlessly guides me into his penthouse, but it doesn't feel like long.

Elijah flicks on the lights, kicks off his biker boots, and a gasp escapes my lips at the beauty of his penthouse loft apartment. *It's so him.* Exposed brick walls. Tall ceilings with huge black steel framed windows overlooking a dazzling skyline. An open plan at its finest with an industrial kitchen, brown buttoned leather couches in the living room, and farther away, strategically hidden with a makeshift wall of hanging white macramé, his bed.

There are vintage band posters on the wall, and warmth ripples through my body at the Diesel Rose one I stand under. I love the speckles of Elijah replicated through his apartment; like the whiskey, the hanging bass guitars, and the tall vintage bookshelf opposite his bed.

It smells so much of him in here, of that alluring musky sandalwood cologne of his mixed with a little tobacco. The apartment is spotless. Nothing is out of place, except for the three pieces of luggage by his king-size bed. He must have had a gig out of the city and still didn't unpack his bags yet.

I'm about to comment on the awe of this place when his voice floods the silence between us. I glance back at him, my hair slapping over my shoulder when I do, to find that Elijah has switched on his fifty-inch wall-mounted television. The classic 1996 *Scream* is playing on one of the channels. I notice it instantly because it's one of my Halloween favorites.

A young Skeet Ulrich fills the screen with that iconic white T-shirt, those dark soulless eyes, and sexy strands of hair hanging over his eyes like a true bad boy, and I can't help but see the slight resemblance between him and the rebellious man standing before me.

Especially when that said man strides to the wet bar section of his kitchen, pours himself a glass of whiskey, and glances at me through his lashes, his tempting eyes hooded.

Holy. Shit.

Why haven't I ever seen the slight resemblance before?

With his eyes never leaving mine, Elijah strolls back to his fridge and pulls out a… *Cherry Coke.* He takes off the cap with his teeth like the savage he is and slides it across the counter.

I step closer with a nervous smile, thanking him, and that's when I notice the card resting on his dark countertop.

A birthday card.

"What's this?" I murmur, tracing the adorable drawing of what seems to be of a guy with a big, black jacket holding a little boy with curly hair's hand. *Elijah and… Clément.*

"My sister and nephew sent it to me." Elijah's silent for a moment, before his voice comes out in a raspy barely whisper, "It's… my birthday today."

I feel my heart physically drop.

What?

My jaw drops when I look up at him with wide eyes.

"It's your *birthday?*" Groaning, I shake my head because I feel so bad. I didn't know. "Oh, Elijah, why didn't you tell me it was your birthday?"

"We didn't talk for a month, Rosalia."

"I meant earlier tonight."

Elijah shrugs and walks toward the couches. "Didn't think it was important."

"Of course it's *important*," I sigh, taking a sip of that cherry bombshell while following him. I take a seat on the couch beside him. "Every birthday is important, Elijah."

He simply stares at the television with a furrow in his brows, his jaw contently clenching and unclenching as he gulps down his whiskey. "I beg to differ."

"Don't be like that," I whisper, craving wrapping him in an embrace. "You're alive."

Elijah flares his nostrils and continues watching the film, but he isn't actually *watching*, he's just staring. It's a distraction. A distraction from what?

From you, Rosalia.

I blindly set my glass bottle on the coffee table. "Elijah, I—"

"What did you tell your parents about me?"

Taking off my Doc Martens, I bring my knees up to my chest on his couch. "What?"

"You heard me, Rosalia."

Poison.

My name is like poison on his tongue.

It's as if we did a complete reverse, and just like that, we're right at the start again.

I swallow thickly. "I told them the truth. Everything."

"Fuck," Elijah grumbles above the rim of his whiskey before sipping without ever glancing my way. "What did they really think of me? Well, your father in particular?"

I'm cautious, because the last time he and my father were in a room, it wasn't exactly ideal. I'm convinced that if I wasn't there a full-on brawl would have started.

Not knowing how to answer, I flicked my gaze to the television. "Look at Billy go…"

I feel Elijah's hot eyes burning straight through me. "Rosalia."

"You know, I've always wondered if Billy had just—"

"*Peaches*," Elijah cuts me off, bringing a hand over my fishnet stocking-covered knee. He gently cups it like I'm going to disappear right in front of his eyes. "Don't ignore me."

Peaches.

My heart squeezes… this is the first time he's called me it all night.

"Baby girl, look at me," Elijah murmurs, and it's the softest heavenly sound, the kind lullabies are made from. "Tell me what he said to you. I want to know."

And that's when my crush on Diesel Rose's lead vocalist merges into something more.

I turn to him, hurting inside, because his warmth by my knee is scorching. "You're not going to like it, Lijah."

"Didn't think I would."

"My father thinks we've been intimate. That the only reason you're hanging around a seventeen-year-old girl is because you thought I was…" I make quotation marks, using my dad's exact words. "*Naive*. An *easy target*. He thinks I'm in love with you. That I'm blind. That the only reason you kept coming back was to *take advantage of me*, and that I *let you*."

"Jesus fucking Christ."

"I know. I told him *I* was the one that wanted to know *you*. That I'm not in love with you. That we're not, nor have we even been, in a relationship, but he doesn't believe me."

"And your mom?"

"The same."

"Fuck, Rosalia," Elijah grits, almost to himself. He tugs at his hair, those pretty dark-gray eyes dimming. "They think I'm *fucking you*? That I'm *blinding you*? That you're *naïve*? You're the most intelligent, wisest woman I've ever met. You've been through a lot and that has matured you. You're not naïve, not an inch. How dare they fucking take that from you?!"

Staring down at my hands, I nod, because his stare is too intense.

I know he's upset. Upset at my father first for the word his used, and then at them both for viewing me as incapable. I know because it hurts me too. I wish my parents could just believe me. Trust me.

"I told him it wasn't true, but he... you know how fathers are."

"That's fucked up, Rosalia. I know he doesn't get it, but he should believe you when you're stating the truth."

"He doesn't see it like that. He saw you in my room, assumed the worst, and freaked."

Silence.

There is nothing but silence aside from the film's murmurs and my rapidly beating heart that I can feel all throughout my body. My ears. My throat. The pads of my fingertips.

Elijah's pointer finger reaches out to lift my chin, and for the first time since I met him, his touch is as cold as ice. The birthday boy urges me to stare into his war-torn eyes. It's as if there's a battle in there with fiery ammunition and teargas. Like the only things that will save him from the gloominess of those grays and toxicity of those speckles of the darkest of onyx is... *me*.

I don't know what we're doing. I don't know what *this* is. But *here* is all I want to be.

Elijah gulps down desolately and just keeps staring.

What is he pondering so deeply?

And then I find out exactly.

"Rosalia..." he whispers. "Am I taking advantage of you?"

My eyes almost pop out of my head. "Oh my god, Elijah, no, of course not. You haven't even touched me, no."

"I'm not talking sexually, I'm talking emotionally... mentally. Is—*was*—it hard for you to navigate me? The push and pull? I'm complicated. I'm messy. Being a part of my life is so fucking chaotic, I know it is, it's just all... depressing. I know I'm not the easiest guy..."

"Of course not."

Elijah shakes his head. "I want you to be honest."

"I am."

"You're not."

A shaky breath escapes me as I prepare to tell him my truth. "Okay, mentally it can get a bit tough. This past month without you, I've felt so... lonely. The loneliest I've ever felt. I feel like I don't have that person to talk about the things we used to... Brontë, life, *anything*.

I miss it." I smile at him sadly, my voice failing me as it breaks. "I miss *you*. I just feel so stuck, and it…"

I melt at the way Elijah scoots closer to me, all of those promises he made to me via text a month ago seeming to fizzle away as an agony crosses his eyes. We're so close our knees brush, and I feel my sweater dress rise the more I inch closer to him.

Elijah cups my cheeks and I lean into his hand, shutting my eyes for a moment because this is all getting too much. Too deep. I don't like the way my heart is beating so skittishly.

"I don't want to make you feel trapped, *Peaches*," Elijah whispers against my lips.

Please don't call me Peaches.

Not now, Elijah Diesel.

Because I'm falling.

"I don't feel trapped," I admit.

"Just lonely in your thoughts about me, hmm?"

When I don't reply, he exhales a breath and shakes his forehead against mine. "*Peaches*."

I slip my hands over his on my cheeks, warming them. "Why did you plan to see me tonight—on your *birthday*?"

"I…" Elijah avoids my question completely. "Maybe your parents are right, Rosalia, maybe you should run away from me while you have the chance."

My heart, which I've noticed all night more than ever, is aching. "Don't say that."

"It's true. We both know it is."

I swallow thickly. "Lijah…?"

"Mmhmm."

"You're not a punk. For whatever reason, I know that word hurts you, triggers you. I'm sorry my father pushed you that far all those weeks ago, I'm sorry he made the pain sting."

Emotion laces his voice in a way I've never heard. "Don't fight your father's battles."

"I want to."

The air crackles between us.

"I don't want you to feel lonely…" Elijah whispers. "Not when I'm right *here*."

And just like that, his touch slips as he rises from the couch, and I miss it already.

I miss *him*.

Elijah is already lying down on his bed when I sink onto his soft bedsheets. There's a world of him I want to uncover when he glances over me, his eyes blanketed in something I can't quite understand, before reaching out his hand to me. His fingers thread through mine, and I smile through the sadness, just as screams pierce through the television.

We ignore it.

We ignore everything else but our tempting dark stare.

My warmth heating them up when I bring our intertwined hands to my lips and kiss his every tattooed knuckle. Slowly. Like I want to make this last a lifetime. *Because I do.*

I want to ask him about every single one of these tattoos.

I want to lie down on this bed with him forever.

I want to be his.

"Happy birthday, birthday boy."

Elijah slowly smiles back, but it doesn't quite meet his eyes. He smoothly tugs on my hand, and I lay down beside him, loving the way his first reaction is to thread his fingers through my hair and hold me close. Because this doesn't feel like him letting go of me. At all.

His hold is so tender it would make angels cry.

"There's something I need to tell you." He gulps down. "It's been eating me up inside."

"Yeah?"

Elijah studies me, glancing between my eyes. "Diesel Rose signed with a major label a month ago. Business-wise, it's been going fucking amazing since then. We were recently approached and asked to be the support act of a major band's tour. The original support act had to pull out due to scheduling conflicts. The arenas… I'm talking twenty-thousand people a night attending. It's currently still on the down low, our manager wants it to be a surprise for fans."

"WOW! OH MY GOD, ELIJAH!" I gasp with a full-blown grin. "That's epic news! I'm so happy for you! When do you and the guys have to give your official decision to them?"

"We already did." An almost shy smile works up the corners of his lips, blanketed in melancholy. "Knives, Zander, Dave, and I accepted. Three weeks ago."

Three weeks ago.

This is amazing news—life changing news—so then why does it feel so bittersweet?

"Whoa! I'm so proud of you, like genuinely, so freaking proud! When does the tour begin?"

Elijah's smile fades as he clears his throat. A hand slithers down, his thumb ever so slowly tracing over my plump lips, gazing into them before eventually looking up at me through his long, onyx lashes.

"Tomorrow," he whispers. "Our flight is tomorrow morning. London."

All the air escapes my lungs as I stare at him with wide eyes. "What? *Tomorrow?*"

"I know it's hard to wrap your head around, but yes… I'm leaving tomorrow. As I said, the original support act pulled out at the last minute, so we haven't had long to digest it either."

"How long will you be away for?"

"Well, it's a worldwide tour. The tour begins in London, we do the rest of the United Kingdom, and then go right through Europe, Asia… Australia, New Zealand, then the Canadian and US tour commences. It's sold out, so high-demand that new shows may be added duri—"

I cut him off, "How long, Diesel?"

Diesel.

I just called him Diesel.

"Ten months, *Peaches.*"

My heart capsizes in the fateful waters inside my chest. *Ten months.*

Ten.

That's… *September next year. I'll be in college, that's how long it'll be.*

Oh my god.

Oh my god.

Oh my god.

I roll out of his grip, staring up at the tall ceiling with my hands over my mouth as my head continues to spiral.

It's all starting to make sense.

The luggage by his bed.

The reason he's been looking at me like that all night.

Him wanting to see me tonight—the night before he leaves to be the support act in a famous worldwide tour.

I'm losing him...

"Rosalia, fuck," Elijah sighs in agitation beside me, and I feel him lean on his forearm to face me. "Please say something."

"I'm happy for you, I really am, it's just... wow, it's just all happening so fast."

"I know." He nods when I finally glance up at him. He has that look in his piercing gray eyes again. The one of complete and utter agony. "Which is why we can't see each other beyond tonight."

The ache at the back of my throat... it explodes.

Don't break it, Elijah.

Don't break my heart.

"No, you can't do this to me, Elijah." Shaking my head, I hold back tears and reach out to cup his stubbled jaw. "Not on your birthday, *please.*"

"I'm sorry, *Peaches,*" Elijah lowly murmurs, his tender kiss on my forehead lingering. "Please, I told you, don't make this harder."

The first tears uncontrollably gush out and I can't do anything but embrace them. My lips are pinched so tightly, because I fear if I were to open my mouth, only sobs would escape.

All of my demons resurface. The abandonment. The walking away. My real parents. It all comes back in waves deeper than the Atlantic, drowning every single therapy session.

"Rosalia, if I were another man, I would be selfish and tell you to wait for me, to come with me, but you have your entire life ahead of you and I'll never be the person you need me to be."

"What if I told you I was in love with you, would that change anything?"

There's a battle within his gaze as he glances between my eyes. Guilt. Desire. Anger.

"No," Elijah replies, sucking in a breath. "No, it wouldn't. It'll only break our promise."

"But I... I think I'm..." I sniffle, realizing I don't have a single thing to lose when my hand that's cupping his cheek begins trembling. "I'm in love with you, Elijah Diesel."

Elijah's breaths quicken and I'll never forget the way pure sadness coats his face when he rasps, "This isn't love, Rosalia Philips, this is me saying goodbye. Please remember that."

And then his lips baptize mine in the most devilish of kisses.

It's passionate.

Aggressive.

Fiery.

So much more desperate than the last. I kiss Elijah back like he's all I have, because in retrospect, he is. My heart can't take the warm darkness pulsing through as his body pins against me, and I wrap my legs around his waist, tears still gliding down my cheeks.

I'm in love with Elijah Diesel.

I'm in love with Elijah Diesel as our tongues dance and I moan into his mouth, wanting this to last forever.

My lips are going to bruise from just how hard we're kissing, but I don't care. It's so consuming, so heavenly as his hands roam my entire body, awakening every inch with sparks.

It's as if Elijah wants to savor me. Wants to give in to the forbiddenness of us. Wants to remember the taste of the cherry cola on my tongue and the whiskey on his. Wants to drive me crazy, one last time, just before he leaves forever.

We're both panting when we pull away and he pulls the sheets above us, not caring we're both still clothed. My legs are still wrapped around Elijah when my head hits his pillow and look up at him with even more tears in my eyes.

We share the kind of sad smiles lovers do before the tragic third act. It's torturous.

Elijah Diesel is my poetic tragedy.

My throat burns and my lungs feel as if they've been pierced with a dagger during that kiss, because there's no way I can let go of him now. He's the only thing that makes sense in my life. The only thing I've ever adored by playing life with all of the risks involved.

Elijah kisses away all of my fallen tears, his lips so soft against my cheeks it hurts.

"Hate me," Elijah quietly begs against my swollen lips. "Don't love me, hate me."

"I can't."

"You will." His mouth finds mine again, this time so much slower, only breaking the sensual kiss to sexily moan, "Hate me, *Peaches.*"

I don't know how long we stay like this, simply wrapped in each other's arms, kissing like it's our last breath. *Because it may as well be.* But just before my heavy eyelids defeat me, I glance up at those melancholic onyx-gray eyes belonging to the only man I'll ever truly love.

I make him promise me he'll wake me up in the morning before he leaves.

I make him promise me he won't leave without telling me goodbye.

I make him promise me he means it.

He promises, and with every oath kisses my lips until it's a temporary remedy to all of the pain. All of our hurt. And all of my trauma resurfacing.

I let Elijah Diesel—my melancholic-eyed leather rock star— kiss me until sleep blankets me with the rhythm of his heart pressed against mine.

It swallows us both in a magnitude of dark poetry that can only be revived by the melody of his iconic raspy voice that I will never hear whisper, "*Peaches*" again, not after tomorrow.

The morning sunlight peering through Elijah's windows is blinding. I want to rush out, shut his sheer blinds, and then rush inside the bed again, but I'm too comfortable. Too comfortable in his bed. Warmth licks my entire body, despite New York's chill brushing against my face.

The events of last night feel like a nightmare, but they can't be any more real.

Elijah is leaving for London in a few hours. He's leaving to become a true rock star, and I couldn't be more thrilled for him, but this ache in my chest… I don't think it'll ever ease.

I only have a few hours with him.

Hours.

Through all of the tears I've cried, I find myself softly smiling as I brush my fingers over my lips. They're swollen from last night. Swollen from kissing Elijah Diesel all night. There were so many times when I wanted more, but it would only complicate things.

Elijah's cologne lingers in the air, along with my coconut rose perfume, and the mixture of them together makes me feel the most alive I've ever felt. It creates an *us*—right here in his king-size bed.

Yawning, I rub my puffy eyes. We only had a few hours of sleep.

The television is still softly blaring in the background because we didn't switch it off last night. And as I glance over my shoulder, prepared to swallow my pride, and face the devastation that comes with having to say goodbye to him, my heart drops.

My breaths slow.

Everything. Just. Stops.

Elijah… *he's not in the bed.*

No.

I call out his name, I shout out again, I check inside the bathroom—the only room with a door—*nothing.*

Anger laces my veins when I rush back to the bed, only to slow in my tracks.

The luggage… *it's gone.*

His phone isn't on the nightstand.

There's no trace of him everywhere.

No, Elijah, please don't tell me you…

Something catches my eye on the dark kitchen countertop. Something that's replaced Clément's birthday card, because it wasn't there last night… *a sheet of paper.*

No. No. No.

I feel sick. Sick to my stomach because I thought he was better than this.

He promised me.

He broke the promise.

He left without saying goodbye.

My fingers tremble holding the letter, his dark cursive handwriting burning me slow.

Peaches,

I'm sorry. This is the only way I can leave without destroying myself in the process. I know you'll hate me for it. Good. Hate me. Hate me until you forget my name. Please don't call or text,

I won't answer. It's best this way. For the both of us. Especially you. You don't need me. I promise you, baby, you don't.

Thank you for being the most beautiful and realest thing in my entire life. I've never felt anything in my life before, and then I met you, and fuck, you made me feel everything. Intensely. And the more I hated myself for it, the more you taught me to feel. Please understand this isn't me breaking your heart, Peaches, this is me setting you free.

You're sleeping so fucking peacefully in my bed right now, I hope you can forgive me for the final kiss I stole from you. I couldn't resist it; you were too beautiful. It almost convinced me not to leave. That's what your kiss does to me. It consumes me. It makes me feel. It's a fucking kiss of death, Rosalia, one I never want to quit. And that's why—exactly why—you deserve more than I could ever give.

After all, I truly was The Damned. In fact, with you, I was crazy to believe I wouldn't be. So even though you may hate me right now, know that I did this to save you from myself.

Wherever life will take you, with every wave you survive, just know in your heart I'm there with you. And most of all, my darlin' Rose, remember I'm yours. Forever. Yours. Even though I shouldn't be, which is why I need to let you go.

Forgive me, Peaches,
Elijah Diesel

The aching knot at the back of my throat has it impossible to breathe as the tears I've so strongly held back reading the entire letter viciously begin to fall. This is the worst thing that could have ever happened.

The absolute worse.

And here I am, left to shatter into a million pieces, knowing a part of me will never recover from the gaping hole Elijah Diesel just ripped out of my heart.

I flip the letter to its back, and those final strokes of onyx fuel me with lovesick hate.

PS: And yes, I named Diesel Rose after you, Peaches, so you could stay with me forever, even if it's in another form.

Oh my god, Elijah.

There's more, and his handwriting... the words... *everything...* it all destroys me.

* PPS:

For what it's worth: it's never too late or,
in my case, too early to be whoever you want to be.
There's no time limit, stop whenever you want.
You can change or stay the same,
there are no rules to this thing.
We can make the best or the worst of it.

I hope you make the best of it.
I hope you see things that startle you.
I hope you feel things you never felt before.
I hope you meet people with a different point of view.

I hope you live a life you're proud of,
And if you find that you're not,
I hope you have the strength
to start all over again.

—F. Scott Fitzgerald

Just like that, everything hits me at once. Sobs take over, drowning me in waters deeper than the Atlantic as I scrunch up the letter—the last piece I'll *ever* have of him—into my palm.

Elijah is breaking my heart, just like he promised, and I hate him for it.

I'll hate him forever.

But most of all, I hate myself for ever falling for the devilish rocker.

Because something tells me this isn't the end... *that it's only just our beginning.*

And if that be true, Elijah Diesel won't ever be one of those reasons I'm still breathing.

Not again.

FOUR YEARS LATER...

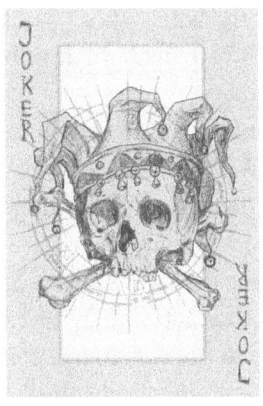

Chapter
ELEVEN

Elijah

Almost Four Years Later.
Rosalia is 21. Elijah Diesel is 35.

R oaring fans echo around the packed stadium, every scream a rippling bullet being shot into my fucking chest.

This is what it feels like to be alive, Elijah Diesel.

When my alternative rock band, Diesel Rose, broke out into the spotlight four years ago, I don't think any of us could have imaged the intensity of our success.

Four studio albums with our current record label and another two that we indie produced. Three world tours, not including five separate US tours. Thirty-eight platinums and golds combined. Consecutive Grammy awards—nine, to be exact.

We've broken Billboard records.

Had over 100 million records sold worldwide.

Tickets to concerts being sold out in 0.2 seconds, a record. And I'm talking arenas and fucking stadiums that hold over 45,000 fans. Legendary places like Citi Field, MetLife Stadium, Madison Square Garden, and Crypto Arena.

And that isn't even the half of it.

Grateful. That's what I am, with a side of fucked-up. *Okay, maybe a little bit more than a side.*

We're playing at Yankee Stadium right now, and if this place had a roof, it would have blown off. The fans haven't stopped cheering all night. All 54,000 of them. Every single one of them gives me life. *Purpose.*

Their love hits me like my favorite drug. So corrosively sweet that I've gotten used to the buzz that rings in my ears hours after a performance. I've gotten used to the demand. Our crazily hectic schedule. The magazine front covers, autographs, and pictures (which I always have to pretend to look fucking sober in).

What I haven't gotten used to is this numb feeling. I still can't seem to shake it.

Diesel Rose wins a Grammy.

Numb.

We play in the biggest venues in the world.

Numb.

I return to my hotel room and the melancholic thoughts begin, crawling inside my veins like a monster's ache.

Numb. Numb. Fucking numb.

Being a cutthroat rock star definitely comes with its perks. Like seeing the beauty of the world with my three best friends. Giving back to fans. Letting music fuel my soul.

It also comes with its cons...

1. Lack of privacy (and I really do mean that's a big one, especially for a guy like me).

2. Highly unlikely chance of fucking up and the world NOT noticing.

3. Loneliness. And I'm not talking missing this person, and missing that person, can't do shit with a FaceTime *loneliness.* I mean soul-sucking, brain-shattering, heart-aching *loneliness.*

Because lonely is all I ever feel. Even when I'm surrounded by 54,000 other souls. Even with my band right beside me on stage, like right now as Knives finishes his epic bass solo and I continue singing our new smash hit, "Fragments of You".

The gravelly rasp in my voice is a disguise for all the nights I've been through hell.

Dave's drumming intensities, and that's when Knives and Zander go wild with the bass and guitar, lighting up a fire in me with every world I sing. Devilish flames shoot up from the edges of the stage, electrifying the crowd that grows crazier and giving into the hell we've created here with the sexy lightening, a soft red hue, coating the stage.

Everything is melodic with us. Everything works together. I couldn't do anything without my true rockers.

Knives.

Zander.

Dave.

These boys are my kryptonite. The only people who have seen the behind the scenes of the real shit that goes on. The grueling grit to always up-level. Always outlast. I'm so fucking stubborn that our sound checks run for double the time, just because I'm a perfection-ist and want to go over everything twice. And these fuckers, they lis-ten, because they get me.

They get me.

Not many people in this world can admit that. Fuck, I can't even say it and I'm talking about myself. It's because deep down, in my heart of cold fucking hearts, I don't know who the hell I am either.

I know I'm a tortured soul.

Troubled by temptation in the form of liquor, tobacco, and shit.

Slowly losing myself to the vicious waves day by day.

Still singing, my gaze flickers across the stadium, glancing over every single face in the first few rows in the mosh pit. It's the most I can see before faces get blurry. There are women in lacey bras and leather. Some are even topless with *Diesel Rose* and more explicit things written across their bouncing bare tits. Those chicks have all kinds of boldly colored hair, standing out with either red, hot pink, or violet. Or midnight blue.

There are men too with leather jackets and piercings, some with hair a little too long. It's as if we're back in the '80s when rock truly ruled.

Rock *still* rules.

Rock 'n' roll will never fucking die.

The success of Diesel Rose will outlast us all.

Since I was a kid, music has always been my therapy. It's my oasis away from the cruel, dark world as I know it. A reckless musician is the only fucking thing I have going for me. I never wanted to be anything else because that would mean being somebody else.

Every poetically tragic song I write relates to scars surrounding my heart. (And yes, I do freaking have one, a heart, you smart-ass).

I'd like to say it also heals those scars, but I don't know if I can go as far as that. All I know is that I can't stop scanning the first few rows. Scan them for *her*. I know it's diabolic. I know she's not here. *She can't be*, and yet I still do it.

Four years ago, I walked out on her and told her to forget about me.

Four years ago, I told that certain honey-blonde girl I never search for somebody in the crowd and pretend I'm singing to them the entire performance.

Four years ago, I was her first kiss, devouring those cherry-flavored lips, and quite truthfully, I haven't recovered since.

Rosalia.

Rosalia Philips.

She used to be my reason for breathing, and now without her, I'm fucking dying. In fact, my tangled heartstrings feel like they've been frozen this entire time.

It's been four years. Four years without her in my life. And yet, every single concert, I search the front row for her, hopelessly hoping.

I know I shouldn't. I shouldn't because I forced her away. Made her hate me. Made her break. I hate her too. I hate her for making me feel. For making me crave her. For... *Fuck*. I blame Rosalia Philips for being my undoing.

But tonight, as my band kills it, my nostalgia wins. It does every fucking time. I'm losing my mind. *Dear God, I am*. I'm at the point of breaking. The complete brink.

Everything is just too much.

If one more tragic thing happens in my life, I'm done. My body will go into shock. It'll break down. I know it will. I'll break into a trillion little unsalvageable pieces.

Rosalia Philips used to be my lifeline.

My green-eyed edgy ballerina.

My forbidden secret.

And I need her.

Just one more hit of her.

Just need to overdose on her once again.

She'll never know. She'll never know how much I need this.

Because Rosalia isn't only a woman who hates my guts, she's my muse, but four years ago I lost her. Lost her to my own selfishness. Lost her to my sociopath mind.

All I want is one final breath. I promise. I just need *Peaches* to give me one final breath, and then I don't care if I wake up in heaven, in hell, or in purgatory…

Or better yet, *dead*.

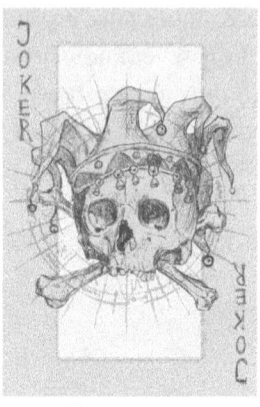

Chapter
TWELVE

Elijah

I think I've lost my fucking mind.

As I sit deeper into the comfortable red ballet theater chairs, I wonder if I've upgraded to a complete sociopath or full-on Joe Goldberg mode with all these tendencies.

This was never supposed to happen.

I was never supposed to be in Lincoln Center.

I was never supposed to be sitting on the balcony level.

I should be in my Manhattan hotel room, resting for the second half of the US leg of Diesel Rose's world-wide *Killing Me Slowly* tour that commences tomorrow night.

I shouldn't be *here*.

My bandmates would kill me if they found out.

So, what went wrong? I'll tell you what went wrong—my nostalgia—that's fucking what. And the memories of her cherry-flavored tongue laced around mine while we made out all damn night.

I told Rosalia Philips to hate me.

I told her to run.

I told her I wasn't breaking her heart, just setting her free.

I lied.

I wanted Rosalia. *Still* want her. But I wasn't selfish enough to make her wait for me while I knew it was a turning point in my career. One I had to sink my teeth into and claim.

Ever since my alternative rock band and I headlined for renowned heavy metal rock band *Devil's Advocate and The Fiery Halos*, Diesel Rose has become legendary in the world of rock and roll.

Within these four years, within every show, *she's* the person clouding my mind… *Still.* I often wonder what Rosalia Philips is doing now. It's merged from late-night thoughts to constant reminders of her.

Cherry Cola. Ballet. Classic romances. Nothing is the same.

Does she still hate me?

Probably.

What do you mean, 'probably'? Of course she does still hate you, chickenshit.

I literally give myself an eye roll.

I mean, yes, I was a dick and chose not to confront my problems and instead run away from them that fateful November morning when I decided to leave without ever saying goodbye, breaking our promise, but I have reasons.

I—Elijah Diesel—am not the type of man anybody could ever truly fall in love with, including Rosalia. I'm too old for her. Too forbidden. Most importantly, I don't fall in love.

Rosalia.

Rubbing a hand over my stubbled jaw, I scan my surroundings. Expensive golden accents. Onyx, velvet red, and brass are all a see. A fully packed ballet theater with a thrilled audience. It's art deco, a ballet lover's dream. This entire place feels like a grand golden palace that you'd find in the heart of Italy or France.

Tall ceilings. Detailing. An architect's heaven.

It's so left field from my usual leather, whiskey, and rolled-up joints. But for tonight, just for tonight, I'll have to adjust to this elegance to let my late-night cravings win. I mean, I even have a (slightly unbuttoned) white dress shirt, black slacks, and shiny Italian leather Oxford shoes to play the part.

Fucking Oxfords.

Side note: My jaw is clenching from the small smirk I felt creep up your lips. Not. Cool.

I still have my ionic leather jacket on with the spikes and safety pins, but this entire thing of looking 'socially acceptable' is pathetic. *Torturous, if you ask me.*

I'm a damn rock star, not Tinkerbell, for God's sake.

It's officially fall. The second last Tuesday in September, *Swan Lake*'s opening night, and Rosalia Philips is set to steal the stoplight. It's been a lifetime since I last saw her/we last spoke, so *how* do I know she's set to rule the world, you ask? *Well*, a few weeks ago I lost my damn self-control onstage while singing our hit single, "Fragments of You".

(*P.s Yes, that song is about exactly who you're thinking of...you fucker.*)

Anyway, as I was saying...where was I up to? Oh, yes, righttttt. Guy tells girl to forget about him, almost four years pass, guy gets fucking nostalgic on stage, searches her up in the comfort of his hotel room hours later, and *bingo*, he finds a gold mine.

As it seems, Rosalia has been thriving without me, and I do mean *thriving*. There are endless articles outlining the early success of stoic ballerina Rosalia Philips. One stood out...

Talented corps de ballet *dancer, Rosalia Philips, set to be one of the youngest triumphs at the prestigious ballet company, New York City Ballet, at only nineteen.*

That was dated three years ago. The articles dated this year, even during these past few months, categorize Rosalia Philips as a living legend. A professional dance genius. The *prima ballerina* at the company—the best of the best with agility, remarkable accomplishments, and skill—at only twenty-one.

For some fucked up reason, I couldn't stop smiling at my phone as its brightness lit up my darkly ominous hotel room after that tour concert at Yankee Stadium three weeks ago. Since then, our band has toured Orlando, Ft. Lauderdale, and Tampa in Florida, North Carolina, and Pennsylvania. We're back in Manhattan now and will be doing our eighth show in a row in New York City tomorrow night before moving to Cleveland, Ohio. In all that time, Rosalia Philips has still been on my mind.

New York City Ballet.

Yes, that fancy, elite ballet company that only recruited about ten ballerinas after their one-year apprenticeship dancing. Of course Rosalia was one of the lucky ones.

Totally didn't research the shit out of that.

That's when I stumbled on tonight's performance. It was the only one that coincided with my tour schedule seeing as tomorrow night I'll be performing at Madison Square Garden before leaving for Ohio on Thursday.

I've never been to ballet before in my life. Never been fucking interested. And then Rosalia stepped into my life, and all I wanted was to unleash the devil within.

I bought the tickets in seconds. *Seconds.* Not even knowing what it meant for me. But some strange comfort in the fact that for the first time in years, Rosalia and I would be in the same room, even if she'll never know.

Some articles defined Rosalia Philips as the next Ana Pavlova with her beauty and grace on the stage with every single movement of modern ballet. I always knew Rosalia would be a star. I saw the passion, grit, and determination in her eyes that night we had dinner at that Italian restaurant and she told me about her dream—becoming a professional ballerina.

And now that's exactly what she is.

I remember her telling me how she couldn't breathe without ballet, how it makes her come alive, how it's all she ever really feels. I knew from that moment, when Rosalia Philips was sitting across from me like a goddamn angel eating spaghetti (in the style of a whore), that she would be something great.

Which is why I let her go.

I didn't want her to be strapped to me.

I wanted her to thrive in what she loves doing, and she couldn't do that with me.

I wanted to let her find those wings and fly. And fly she fucking did. Right into one of the most famous ballet theaters in the entire world.

It's Rosalia's seventh official ballet season tonight. Her opening performance. And as the minutes count down before it all commences, I'm still trying to process that I'm actually here.

Rosalia will never know.

Never know I'll be right here witnessing the masterpiece that is her, *coming to life.*

Warm lights fill the ballet theater, giving a moody, bright glow. I can see the orchestra down on the ground section, men and women in black and white suits with their hands covered in sleek white gloves that from all the way up here seem like silk.

I glance down at my program book of New York City Ballet's *Swan Lake* (yeah, I bought one, stop judging me), my heart pumping into overdrive at the stunning photo of Rosalia and some idiot (who I later learned is some dancer named Chad) on the cover.

Rosalia is in a flawless extended pose, standing on pointe, and his hands are wrapped around her in dance from behind. They're in costume. I can't stop staring at her white leotard, sheer tights, glittery tiara, and feathered tutu. They're all so damn striking.

I get lost in her elegance. *She's a cure…*a Cherry Cola addicted ballerina.

Rosalia Philips is so beautiful.

So damn beautiful.

I can't take my eyes off her expressive face, her thrilled doe eyes, and those plump lips painted the most seductive shade of red. It taunts me beyond words… *I've kissed those lips.*

Kissed them all night.

I even remember their softness and how she moaned my name.

That's right—not that Chad's name—mine. Hmmm.

Blowing out a sigh, I know I need to distract myself from her beauty and instead flip to the first page. A description of Swan Lake reads:

Swan Lake, a story of bittersweet love, manipulation, and tragedy begins with Princess Odette (portrayed by prima ballerina, Rosalia Philips), the embodiment of beauty and pure perfection. Odette encounters Baron von Rothbart (portrayed by Trent Daniels), an evil sorcerer who transforms himself into a charming man.

Enticed by him, their dance of life ends with her being captured by him, bewitched, and imprisoned in the body of a striking white swan. Powerless, the lake becomes her only means of surviving.

Years later, Prince Siegfried (portrayed by Chad Butler), who is troubled by a royal obligation, seeks solace in the woods. There, he discovers Odette, now the queen of the swans. With her damned to suffer from Von Rothbart's spell forever, Siegfried promises his allegiance and eternal love to her...only then will this curse be broken.

Damn curses. Just like Devil's advocate one on me tonight.

Shoving the program under my thigh, I rake a hand through my dark wavy hair and kick myself that I'm actually kinda tense to see her again in real life, even if it's not face-to-face. I bought the tickets and had my bodyguard/driver discreetly drive me here without thinking it through too much. *What will I do when I see Rosalia Philips again?*

I exhale a shaky breath.

I don't fucking know.

And just like that...*I learn.*

The lights softly dim. Only after two fancy-ass people step out from the sides of the curtain-covered stage and give a preface into Swan Lake by saying...well, I don't really know as I kind of zone out after they explain Swan Lake is "*a story about love and the capacity for forgiveness*," does the real show begin.

By the orchestra, the conductor emerges and the loud claps blare through the theater as the entire orchestra stands. The conductor nods with a smile. I find myself clapping along and glancing around in awe, wondering what kind of cult this is. That's when I feel eyes burning into the side of my head...

I ever so causally glance to my left at a posh older woman sitting beside me. She studies me, her eyes widening in horror at my metal spiked leather jacket.

Um, okay...weird.

I glance to my right at a blond guy who seems to be in his mid-twenties dressed in a pin-striped suit. His gaze flickers to me, and his clapping slows.

Smiling, he subtly gives me a rock 'n' roll hand signal and leans over.

"Yo, dude!" he not-so-quietly whispers, "I may look like this, but I'm a huge fan!"

I smirk softly and lean back in my seat. "Thanks, man, appreciate it."

"Diesel Rose is my kryptonite, especially that new song, *wow!* Man, you're really fucking good. It's an honor sitting next to you, Diesel. I think I—"

"Shh!" The older woman sitting to my left hisses, her narrowed eyes flickering between both of us. "We have come here to watch a *ballet performance.* You want to talk about…I don't know, drugs and guns, you do it outside."

Seriously?

The blond man gulps down, flashes me an apologetic smile, and then turns to the stage below. And the woman beside me? Oh, she full-on stares me down like I'm the devil reincarnated. I give her my darkest, devilish glare and she literally squeals before turning away.

Fuck. The hell is this place?

If it wasn't for Rosalia Philips, I would probably throw myself off this damn balcony right about now. I hate this place, and the feeling only intensifies when the orchestra commences, drowning the ballet theater into a utopia of melodic violins, trombones, and symbols.

Ugh!

I cringe, remembering exactly why I also despise classical music.

Tall, velvet curtains tinged in the darkest shade of sunflower yellow part to an icy blue stage with gloomy woods and a lake for the background. The orchestra intensifies into a crescendo and then the instruments soften to complete nothingness, synchronized with the stage darkening for a split second.

The softest light streaks through the stage, illuminated by the moonlit lake, and just like that, with the march of soft cellos, emerges the angel herself.

My angel.

Peaches.

Oh. My. God.

And then the craziest thing happens as I watch Rosalia Philips flawlessly dance into the center of the stage…my heart explodes. I can feel its pieces all around me, surrounding me into a pit of utter doom.

All my beats feel flawed, like I'm the monster destined to steal her shine.

She's here.

Right fucking here.

And it hurts to breathe.

I watch on as the only woman who's ever stayed long enough to care dances her heart out, so poised and confident. Demanding the stage in her dance, her ballet pointe shoes twist a knife inside my chest. It aches.

She must have been the happiest she's ever felt strapping them on tonight.

Rosalia comes alive in the light, grinning, her eyes the most vivid emeralds I've ever seen. Just like in the program, her lips are a bold red, complimentary to the fiery woman underneath all of that white.

She isn't wearing a tutu like in the program. Instead, she's wearing a sheer white ballerina style dress complimenting her every petite curve. The V-cut neckline so low it has me staring. Rosalia's hair is down, those honey-blonde waves of hers so effortlessly styled, part of me wonders if her foster mom—being a hairdresser—did it for her.

The orchestra shifts to a darkened pitch as the evil sorcerer, Baron von Rothbart, appears from the depth of the woods, lurking as he watches Odette (Rosalia). Without her ever noticing, he disappears for a split second before reemerging on the stage dressed all defiantly charming now.

Is it wrong that boiling jealously rushes through my veins when she twirls around, her hair gliding against her bare back in the spin, and their eyes meet for the very first time?

Rosalia isn't mine.

I let her go.

And yet my heartbeat is in my throat as I watch on intrigued as Von Rothbart slowly bows, and she curtsies before he approaches with sensual darkness.

Rosalia seems comfortable with his touch despite the hesitance, and it makes me wonder if she's close to the male dancer outside of ballet. I mean, yes, they would have a crazy training schedule and it's a career that requires closeness and intimacy, but could it mean that…

Their hands slip together, and he kisses her knuckles while I'm here clenching mine.

How does it feel to torture yourself, Diesel?

To voluntarily watch on as another man presses his lips on her skin?

I softly growl, edging forward in my seat to watch them even closer.

Shut. The. Hell. Up. It. Is. Just. Ballet.

The devil on my shoulder scoffs. *Yeah, a ballet performance that runs for the next six weeks. That asshole will be kissing her knuckles almost every night. Imagine what goes on backstage…*

Backstage.

Does Rosalia have a boyfriend?

Is this guy—Trent Daniels—her boyfriend?

Fuccck.

At this point, I'm starting to regret my decision to even come here, because…*why did I even come? Why did I want to see her? Why do I even care what Rosalia is doing with her life?*

Why?

Why?

Why?

Because you're a jealous sociopath of an edgy rock star, Elijah Diesel, that's why.

Their stare lingers as he stands to his full form, gazing at her with intensity. The orchestra's angelic violins intensify and burst the orchestra with a violent clash of a symbol as Von Rothbart suddenly lifts Rosalia up. The instruments continue to build with clashes and beats, a deadly taunt as the two dance a reckless ballet, her gracefully attempting to escape his capture with long, lean legs and such expression that it ricochets across my entire body in emotive passion.

Okay, so maybe ballet isn't that bad…with Rosalia, that is.

There's no escaping for Rosalia as Von Rothbart forces her into the woods, the instruments simmering to mallet percussion beating in anticipation.

Three.

Two.

One.

That percussion grows when Rosalia surfaces from the darkened shadows of the woods, so evidently the Swan Princess now. He's put her under a spell, and fuck, Rosalia looks so gorgeous in this strapless jeweled white leotard and feathered tutu. Her hair is now slicked back in a bun, and she wears the prettiest diamond tiara that dazzles in the somber stage light.

Her hands rush toward the audience, pleading in distress. Von Rothbart is right behind her, except now he's dressed as a monster in dark greens and onyx.

He's the symbol of darkness and death, while she's the symbol of light and life.

Soft violins pave the way to complete ominous as they partake in a riveting ballet dance. The story is telling itself without any words and it's so damn captivating. His arms lace around her waist, rendering her powerless. There's a moment where she breaks free, and he lets her.

Rosalia Philips is the damned swan and allows the entire ballet theater to feel her agony (myself included—the guy who doesn't feel). I don't know much about ballet, but I'm pretty sure what she's doing are some twirling pirouettes then some even more complex with her hands controllably kissing the air. She moves on the tips of her tippy toes like she was born for this, and it's so evident she was.

She's a sensation.

Powerfully professional.

Honestly, a natural-born talent.

My wild heartbeat drums in my ears and I literally stop breathing as she breaks out into a solo dance because I see beyond it, even after the stage dims to complete darkness and opens on Price Siegfried.

I see beyond her flowing movements.

Beyond the bold makeup.

Beyond the white swan.

I see *Rosalia Philips*—the girl who once told me she was in love with me.

Rosalia Philips—the pro ballerina selling out Lincoln Theater and taking the world by storm.

Rosalia Philips—the woman who I left sleeping in my bed almost four years ago and walked away without saying goodbye to pursue my rock and roll career and a life without her.

I see how ballet is therapy for her. Therapeutic.

This is the performance of her life.

Nostalgia digs in my veins, but it doesn't matter because there's nothing I could ever say or do to fix all our broken pieces.

The next two hours of Swan Lake pass so quickly. I don't want it to end, don't want to stop holding onto this piece of her.

I don't want to lose her again.

Not as the performance ends in complete tragedy. Not as all the dancers reemerge, rushing farther up the stage, bowing together in a line. Their smiles widen as the theater erupts in cheers, claps, and whistles.

I don't even know when I stood up, only that I'm applauding Rosalia Philips as if my life depends on it. Applauding her like I didn't walk away from us. Applauding her because *this*—I promise—will be the last time I ever see her in my life.

I just needed another dose of her. *Just another one again after almost four years.* Now I've got it, and it's enough to refuel my aching lungs… *Almost.*

The bright grin stretched across Rosalia's face hurts me.

She looks happy. Joyous. And I fucking hate it.

Rosalia will never know I'm here—that I watched her first performance this fall—ever.

And in a strange twist of fate…that suddenly makes me happy.

Happy she pursued ballet professionally as an escape from all her demons.

Happy she'll believe I never came back for her and will hate me more for it.

Happy she forgot about the melancholic, onyx-eyed rocker named Elijah Diesel.

Chapter
THIRTEEN

Rosalia

I barely recognize the woman staring back at me in my dressing room mirror.

Bold Rudy red lipstick.

Dramatic glittery eyeshadow in the shape of a swan.

A sparkling tiara, feathered tutu, and sheer leotard with hundreds of hand-sewn dazzling Swarovski crystals.

Swan Lake.

The euphoria rushing through my veins is unlike anything else I've ever experienced before because I've just finished my first ever performance of this season, *and I aced it, baby.*

I strip out of my clothes and pointe ballet shoes but keep on my sheer G-string (which may I add, I don't always wear panties during performances or training). Yeah, don't get all shocked on me for going commando, considering it's the not-so-hidden ballet secret that our tights allow enough coverage and comfort).

Neatly hanging up my consume on my clothes rail so wardrobe can store it away with ease, I slip on my black silk robe and return to my cool down stretches. These stretches are a necessity after any sort of training or rehearsals, especially after an extensive two-hour performance.

I did it.

I grin to myself, feeling everything explode inside my chest.

Thrill.

Accomplishment.

Feeling alive.

I actually freaking did it!

This is the second official year of preforming as a professional dancer here at New York City Ballet (well, *third* if you include my apprentice year), but it's my first with the new title of *prima ballerina—* first ballerina. It's a rare title, those only given to the most elitist and most ruthless of ballerinas, and all my blood, sweat, and tears led me down the path of becoming a highly respected dancer.

Exclusive competitions, extensive ten-hours training a day, acting every performance—it's all needed, but they're only the bones of what makes a ballerina the best. There's so much more involved.

The, at times, selfish grit.

Learning from failure and getting back up again to perfect it.

The dedication and perseverance to sacrifice the things you lost to become *more.*

That's what makes you the best in this industry.

I mean, don't get me wrong, I'm still that fiery, cherry-addicted girl who loves everything pink and ballet, but I've grown into a woman who doesn't give a shit about the things that don't matter.

Like jealous competition.

Like mundane toxicity.

Like Elijah Diesel.

Ever since that onyx-eyed melancholic god savagely walked out of my life without even saying goodbye, my life has excelled, and there's got to be some irony in that.

And yes, there's still a small part of my heart that belongs to him and jolts every single time something Diesel Rose catches my eye, like…

1) *His songs blaring everywhere. Yeah, I wish I were joking. I guess that happens when you're a super popular edgy rock star.*

2) *Their faces plastered all over Manhattan because right now they're on a world tour.*

3) *Whenever I need to get fucking gas (depressing, I know).*

But I've learned to just embrace the heavy waves that come with once being in love with that eyeliner wearing rocker, Elijah Diesel.

So yes, I've been forgetting him, one beat at a time.

My dressing room 'roommate', if you will, is Portia Evans and she hates my guts. Yeah, I wish I were lying. I mean, she was really friendly when I first stepped into New York City Ballet all those years ago. She was one of the ballerinas I was auditioning with that day.

We were even close at some point, but ever since I became *prima ballerina*, I swear she has some sort of vendetta over me. I always catch her eye rolls and the way she taunts me behind my back. I'm a ballerina at this prestigious New York City company because dance is my livelihood, not because of the damn bitching.

But that's Portia. And my rival. I swear to God she curses my every performance, praying I fall and break a leg so that she can take over my place.

Sorry, sis, not happening.

I glance over at her chair and sigh, grateful she's nowhere to be seen.

And yet, the dressing room is still my safe place. It's huge, big enough to practice a few complex leaps and endless pirouettes. Tall ceilings. Posters of the most legendary and inspirational ballerinas of all time. White exposed brick walls, aside from the one mirrored wall above the large white marble countertop that we use to put on our makeup and perfect our hair. *Welcome to my safe place.*

Warm Hollywood style lightbulbs align each section of the wall, and right now, as I take said makeup off with a face wipe, I pinch myself that I'm living my dream, even though the monsters still manage to crawl in, drowning my deep.

Now, only the important things matter to me.

My reputation matters.

My happiness matters.

My foster parents matter. My foster sister, Maya, who now lives in Seattle, matters. My best friend, Naomi, matters as she bursts through my dressing room door like a damn hurricane. Even though she isn't supposed to be in here.

I catch her eyes through the mirror, doing the last of my cool down stretches, my muscles burning.

Yeah, I'm going to need a good soak in an Epsom salt bath as soon as I get home.

"Oh my gosh, girl!" Naomi squeals, her pearly whites shining mid-grin. "You freaking legend! You were incredible out there!"

Aww.

Smiling, I spin around on my toes, and before I can say anything, she crushes me into the tightest embrace of my life. I squeeze back, harder, laughing while desperately trying not to ruin her little white dress with my makeup.

"You're going to give me a big head with all these compliments, babe." I wink.

Still grinning, Naomi playfully rolls those baby-blue eyes of hers. "Shh, please, you're a superstar and we all know it, Miss *Swan Lake.*"

Have I mentioned how much I adore my best friend? Well, I do.

Yep, Naomi with the gorgeously curled hair and recklessness at a hundred on a scale of one to ten. A lot has changed in these past four years, but one thing that hasn't is just how strong our friendship is. We're still going strong, always there for each other. Four years ago, she and Noah officially became an item (who ended up being a real jerk, by the way), but stole her away from the things she loved the most, until she was kicked out of The School of American Ballet for lack of a steady attendance, leaving me all on my own and her heart broken.

After graduating senior year, we moved in together in this shoe-box-sized apartment in Manhattan. But we didn't care. It was the thrill of moving from Brooklyn Heights to NYC and simplified life seeing as at that stage Naomi was set to attend Colombia University studying journalism, while I had just gotten into a one-year apprentice at The School of American Ballet.

We've since upgraded to a much chicer brownstone in the heart of Manhattan.

Naomi was there when I sobbed in my pillow for a solid month after Elijah walked away from me. I had never been through a breakup before, but the ache I felt spread across my entire body. Aside from school, work, and ballet training, I didn't move from my bed without a wave of nausea, which resulted in more sobbing. It was an endless roll of Seinfeld reruns, painkillers, and Ben and Jerry ice scream to make up for all I'd missed out on since the beginning of time.

Side note: Elijah Diesel had created such a huge gap in my chest that I forced myself to forget him. Seriously, that guy caused me so much damage, I wish I could have just strangled him when I had the chance.

Possibly the night I was on cloud nine when we went to that Italian restaurant.

Or that Halloween night when we couldn't stop making out in his king-sized bed until my lips were possessively claimed by him. Swollen. *Marked.* The night before he left, ruining us.

Ever since I was a little girl, becoming a professional ballerina was my greatest dream throughout all the tragedy I endured. Ballerina was (and still is) the only thing that when I'm executing, I don't want to do anything else. Every single graceful movement fills my heart with glee and floods my lungs with purpose.

Ballet saved me.

It continues to save me.

It's the only thing that makes me feel my true authentic self.

I loved (and still do love) everything about ballet.

The cheering audience.

The gorgeous Royal-like theaters we would perform in.

The success in seeing hard work being paid off in every show.

And that, ladies and gentlemen, is how Elijah Diesel fucked up my life and triggered all my trust issues and abandonment problems to flare up and eat me alive. Seriously. I didn't eat a proper meal for the entire month of November, only surviving on Cherry Cola and thinly sliced apples.

(Another side note: Halloween will always be ruined for me. I hate it. *Sorry, Skeet.*)

My parents were so worried all those four years ago that I was slowly turning into dust, so I put on some Jerry Springer, drowned myself in the longest shower in the world, shaved, and after a three-hour pep talk with Naomi (who convinced me my life WASN'T over), started breathing again.

And yet, right now, almost four years later, I hate that I'm thinking about Elijah…*still.*

"Rosalia." Naomi smiles, breaking me from my haze. Taking my hands, she squeezes them softly with a softness rimming her eyes. One of such tenderness and warmth. "I'm honestly so damn proud of you. Of everything you've become, and I'm so grateful to say I got to see it all happen."

Happy tears brim my vision and I pull her into another tight hug, breathing in that sweet coconut blend of hers.

"I love you, girl. Seriously. I wouldn't know where I'd be without you."

Just as Naomi's about to respond, there's a soft knock on my dressing room door. It creaks open, revealing the owner of those dreamy dark brown eyes and my heart goes all crazy.

Oh, helloooo there.

Trent Daniels, Swan Lake's evil dancing sorcerer but *my* beautiful boy, slowly grins the second our eyes lock. Naomi practically shoves me to him, and his soft chuckle echoes straight through me when I jump into his arms.

"Hey there, gorgeous," Trent murmurs against my lips. His hands snake around my waist and he presses us up against the door with darkened eyes. "You were a fucking dream out there."

"Ugh, says you, *superstar.*" I smile, trailing my fingers over his bare chest and that birthmark right by the junction of his collarbone and base of this throat that I love. "I just wanted to kiss you when you emerged from the woods like my very own monster."

"Mmhmm, okay, mind reader. Well, we're not on stage now, so…"

"*So* kiss me, stupid." I laugh, shutting my eyes the instant Trent leans forth and does just that. He kisses me wildly, like I'm the only thing that matters.

His peppermint-coated tongue rolls around mine as we make out like two teenagers in love. His hands rush under my silk robe, which has fallen away from my thighs, to cup my ass and squeeze it tight. It has me groaning against the kiss and grinding up against his workout shorts.

I thread my fingers through his blond locks, which are still so firm with all the hairspray. Within his warm hold, I can't help but smile through the exhilarating kiss.

Trent makes me feel so safe.

Worth it.

Seen.

I know he would never go behind my back. I trust him. Enough to know he'll never leave me without having the balls to simply be honest, look me in the eye, and say goodbye.

Trent, who I've been dating for the past three months, is exactly five years older than me. No, *literally*, we have the same birthdays. March 23. *Crazy, right?* Aside from being my Aries twin, it also means that his level of elite is much more stoic than mine regarding dance experience, but he always likes to beg to differ.

After all, a relationship wasn't something I was eyeing with my crazy ballet schedule and lack of balance, and then my friendship with Trent merged into something more one night when he ever so casually leaned over and kissed me while we were having a '90s rom-com marathon on his couch. (Don't judge, I'm sure he secretly likes all the swoon too. Those moves are like catnip.) And there you have it, the history of us in a tiny little bottle wrapped in a tight bow.

And yes, we're still just dating at three months. So technically, he's not my boyfriend, but I often like to playfully call him that just to rile him up. I like the heat in his eyes whenever I do. He's not much into labels (or fucking me hard against his steel-framed Central Park penthouse windows), but with him, I'm willing to compromise the entire world. Even an earth-shattering orgasm.

Three years.

It's been three years since I got any action, and yes, I do mean *any*. Yep, depressingly enough, when Elijah walked out of my life, I became *that girl*. The one who runs off impulse. Like almost losing my virginity at eighteen to Cayden Montgomery in the bathroom of his penthouse.

I know, judge me, I would too.

It was at another one of those crazy wild parties Naomi forced me to. And yes, we're talking about the same egotistical jock who once prepositioned me into giving him a blow job whenever I *wanted-to-get-out-of-the-house* Cayden Montgomery.

I know, I knowww what you're thinking.

How could you do that, Rosalia?

How dare you almost reduce yourself to him?

And why in the bathroom of his fancy penthouse?

Well, here's the answer in short. And first, remember I did say— *almost* lost my V-card.

I was a little lonely, somewhat desperate, and a hell of a lot horny.

Because while Cayden may have been cocky and I did shut down the sex, his tongue was *incredible*. I let him do things to me up against his marble vanity (without ever actually having sex) that I've only ever dreamed about. We quickly became a thing, but with my strict ballet schedule and his crazy high school football one, the spark burned out real fast.

The more we went on dates (which always ended up being a group date at diners and the movies with all of his friends and their new flings), the more I knew things were headed south. And then I did that...*thing*.

I caught myself comparing...*to no other than the devil with the prettiest onyx eyes*.

(Spoiler alert: Yes, *him*.)

1. Cayden drove a new Audi, but I missed the thrill of a Harley's purr.

2. Cayden didn't read, *at all*. He literally *watched* all the literature we were required to read at school. I'm talking the books that were required for our finals that would contribute to our GPAs, which would contribute to our LIFE. Nope, Cayden didn't care.

3. He wasn't a man; he was a boy pretending to be a man. I mean, Elijah Diesel was stubble at all. Cayden could barely grow a mustache. I think all the testosterone went to his head.

Cayden and I went out for a solid five weeks, and what I mean by *went out* is—go to the mall, make out in his car before either of our practice, and watch movies, which always resulted in him sweet talking me into fingering me or dry humping like the teenagers we were, or both.

A month and one week was our limit before he broke up with me the morning of the family dinner where he was set to meet my parents. Turns out, he was cheating with another girl right behind my back—*that damn cheerleader*.

Talk about being a jerk.

Safe to say my parents and Naomi hated him for it. I did too but let it go after a while because despite him cheating (which I keyed his car for), in reality, I knew Cayden wasn't going to last. It was to fill the void. A distraction from Elijah.

From what happened.

Being with Cayden made me feel like I was rebelling against Elijah in my own very way. Making him jealous without him even knowing. Privately rubbing it in his face for being such an asshole and choosing the easy way out…

To leave without saying goodbye.

Without facing responsibility.

Making me forever hate him.

Just thinking about him while I'm kissing my (anti) boyfriend makes me see red. Adamant to get him out of my mind, I kiss Trent with everything I have. I kiss him hard all while knowing my lips, which still have a lingering tinge of red from my lipstick, will be swollen all night from the way he likes to suck on them.

"Oh my God, guys, stopppp, you two are like the cutest!" Naomi squeals from the other side of the room, and I pull back from Trent, so lovesick off his kiss that I totally forgot she was still in here. "Gah, you guys are making the Tinder date I have after this seem like freaking Paw Patrol."

Trent gives me one final peck before glancing over his shoulder at her. My gaze drops to his cleanly shaven chiseled jaw, loving how he still has some smeared dark face paint on the edges from the role he plays in Swan Lake. I lick my thumb and gently wipe the stubborn paint off his face.

"Sorry, not sorry." Trent smiles over at her. "Just wanted to show my girl how much of a superstar I think she is."

Naomi beams in the middle of my dressing room, and it's safe to say Trent isn't the type of guy she wants to strangle, unlike Elijah. Trent is caring, considerate, and if it makes any difference, my parents actually really like him too. He's a good guy. An honest guy. *My* guy.

There's nothing forbidden about us. Nothing risky. Nothing out of place. It's simply *us.*

I glance between Trent and my best friend. "You two are giving me way too much credit. It was a group performance."

"I don't know about that…" he murmurs. "You're pretty much the entire show, *superstar.*"

"Stop being so nice." I grin, feeling my cheeks heat as I playfully wave a finger in his face.

Smirking, Trent softly bites down on it. "Never, Rosalia."

Seeing him so happy has my heart singing.

This is what it feels like not to give up.

Because as I said, a lot has changed in these almost four years, and the best of those sugary changes is standing right in front of me. He's my unexpected lover. My gorgeous Trent Daniels.

Which is why I need to do one final thing to rid myself of everything Elijah Diesel...*forever*.

Chapter

FOURTEEN

Rosalia

Mr. Rubin Tommy (or HotLips for short) isn't happy with me. My two-year-old velvety gray bunny stares at me with big expressive dark eyes, his cute little mouth munching away on juicy leaves of lettuce while its nose twitches away.

"I'm sorry, baby," I whisper, his fur a soft cloud beneath my fingertips as I softly ruffle his forehead. "I'm sorry Mommy had to be at work all day. I'll make it up to you. I promise."

Mr. HotLips shuts his eyes in glee, gracefully accepting my apology for such a long ballet day in exchange for food and affection.

"Gah, you're so freaking cute!"

HotLips chews away on his food in complete happiness.

My best friend, Naomi, always wanted a pet, but after being allergic to the entire world, I suggested a bunny. We couldn't decide on a name, so we wrote a list down. We went for *Rubin* because that seems like a cute little bunny name you can call out in a cute pet voice, right?

Rubin Tommy!

RuRu!

RUBIN!

The *Tommy* was after our mutual love for Tom Hardy. (Hi, Tom!) And as for the *HotLips*, well, if you've seen Hardy's full lips, you'll know. Spoiler alert: They're sensational. (Not that I've personally kissed him or whatever, but you know, a girl can dream.)

Pressing a kiss on HotLip's head, I grin and waltz back into the kitchen, heating up my chicken and rice dinner that I pre-cooked at the start of the week. With my hectic schedule, I sacrifice a lot, so meal prep is my only option because I ain't cooking a meal from scratch at 11:00 p.m.

My parents saw my performance on opening night, and my foster sister was able to come down from California too. She had to leave this morning, but we talk close to every day, so in a way, it's like she never left.

After everything that happened four years ago with Elijah Diesel, it took a lot of time to build that trust back with my parents. My father especially. But now that he knows I've moved on, he feels better about it.

It's Saturday night after an extensive Swan Lake matinée *and* evening performance. All I want to do is elevate my feet, watch *Fifty Shades Darker* for the millionth time, and then pass out in my cozy bed after taking three Advil and magnesium pills. It's exactly what I do after I take a warm Epsom salt bath and then warm my ankles with heating pads during dinner.

And Naomi, well, she's out on that Tinder date. I can't wait to hear tonight's story. She ends up in the most peculiar of stories.

Speaking of the devil… I've chucked on a lacy bra, white tee, booty shorts, fluffy high ankle socks, and am halfway through the sexiness that is Christian and Ana when my phone buzzes on the coffee table.

I chuckle.

NAOMI: Okay, get this. An hour ago, Joe Manganiello's doppelgänger and I left the restaurant to head to his place, and…this guy owns a Jaguar. A fucking *Jaguar*! I stepped into the car, right, and there's a baby seat in the back. A. Damn. Baby. Seat. He said he's a single dad, I called bullshit. You know these married cheating bastards.

ROSALIA: Oh my God, Naomi!

NAOMI: I know, I know. Anyway, he drives me to his house. There's a nanny, sleeping little kid, and then shows me the divorce papers. I mean…can you make fake divorce papers? The law firm matches up.

ROSALIA: Shit. Why do these things always happen to you? You can do everything these days, so yeah, I think divorce papers could be falsified. But if he didn't bother to hide the car seat, openly admitted to being divorced, and showed you the evidence…why would he lie? You know. Like on what scope?

NAOMI: See? This is why you're my best friend because that's EXACTLY what I thought too. I was really excited about the prospect of him, but then after all that, I got all icky.

ROSALIA: Ohhh no, that's not good, babe. Do you feel anything for him worthy of another date? What happened next?

NAOMI: Well, one thing led to another, and I was sucking him off in his bedroom (the size of the fucking Yankee Stadium, his bedroom, not his cock). He's moaning, telling me how good it feels but, in my mind, I'm just thinking; '*y**eah, okay, just come already because I swear to God there's flee powder in this carpet and my knees are toast*.' Then… and I'm telling you this gets creepy… He starts murmuring the ABCs. The *ABCs*, Rosalia! The fucking kiddie song! He comes, right, then looks me directly in the eyes and says in this chillingly low voice, '*Fuck, yeah baby, now you know your ABCs*.'

My jaw drops in complete horror.

What the…hell?

Snatching my one-liter bottle of water, I hover it against my lips but don't sip yet and instead furiously fly my thumbs across the keyboard.

ROSALIA: OH. MY GOD! Naomi, get out of there! He's a damn creep!

Anxiously awaiting her reply, I take a long and refreshing sip of water.

> **NAOMI:** Bitch, I did, I got my ass out of his penthouse so fast right after that. I'm at some midtown Manhattan club now and specifically requesting for no 'singing the ABC**s** while you're orgasming down my throat' applications. Girl, I think I'm scarred for life. I mean, was he serious? What does this guy start singing when he's fucking a girl doggy style*? Who let the dogs out?*

I burst out in laughter, choking on the water I've yet to swallow, and it splutters everywhere. And I do mean *everywhere.* I glance down at myself, observing my drenched chest and how my white tee is all transparent now, revealing my lacy bra and pebbling nipples.

Oh shit.

Glancing back at my best friend's hilarious text, I laugh even harder while I continue to choke.

Who Let The Dogs Out! HAHA!

Finally settling down after I slip from the couch to the floor, giving Mr. HotLips a fright, I grin while wiping happy tears from my eyes like I'm some sort of blonde nut.

> **ROSALIA:** God, I love you so much, Naomi. I literally just spilled my water all over my tits!

> **NAOMI:** Yes girl, we all loveee that look for you.

I playfully roll my eyes.

> **ROSALIA:** Shut up. But on a side note, I'm happy you're okay now and not with that ass. Block his number and unmatch him on Tinder. ASAP. Come home safe, call if you need me, all right?

> **NAOMI:** Of course, girl, kisses and sleep tight. Oh, and kiss Mr. HotLips for me! It's starting to look like he's the only man I'll ever love.

> **ROSALIA:** Love you and Mr. HotLips kisses you right back, *chica.*

Setting my phone on the coffee table, I stand, peeling my shirt off my body. It's so soaked that it's like I've partially just run a marathon with the way it's clinging to my skin. *Well, nose-dived into the pool tits first.*

Mr. HotLips slows on chewing his lettuce and side-eyes me from the corner of the open plan living room. He's got a white natural cotton teepee bed with Pom Pom details, but he seems way interested in me instead.

Smirking, I playfully cover my cleavage, my tits spilling from my bra, and give Mr. HotLips the stink eye. "Hmm, just like any other man, aren't you? Tsk. Tsk. Tsk."

Mr. HotLips responds by abandoning his dinner and cutely hopping his way to me. I forget all about my shirt as I scoop him up in my arms, his fluffiness against my skin like heaven. I actually start laughing and rocking him around like he's my own little baby when his nose twitches by my drenched tits and he begins to lick the water right between my cleavage.

My laughter turns hysterical as I slowly pick up my phone, take a selfie of my current situation, and send it to Trent, alongside…

> **ROSALIA:** Hmm, look what you're missing out on, seems like somebody beat you to the job.

Trent's response is instant, despite him going out to a bar tonight after our performance with some of his friends. I just wanted a quiet night, so he'll probably come over tomorrow night.

> **TRENT:** Wow, I don't know whether to be jealous or…turned on?
>
> **ROSALIA:** You can say both.
>
> **TRENT:** Jesus Christ, Rosalia, you're impeccable. Wish I were there.

I half expected him to say he'll call it a night with his friends and come over to spend some time with me considering Naomi's out and we rarely spend a lot of time together outside work. But I know better. I knew the conditions surrounding us when we first got together. Ballet is our everything, so that's what we excel at best.

Still, it gives me major red flags at times because aside from kissing, he's never initiated anything else. *Maybe Trent just wants to play the good guy card. Maybe he wants you to take the lead, Rosalia.*

I shrug to myself and master the courage to smile as I type away with Mr. HotLips still in my arms.

ROSALIA: Whatever you're drinking at the bar, you could come here and pour it all over my tits, then lick it off…

The heat between my thighs intensifies just thinking about it.

I wait, and wait, and wait for a response, but it never comes.

ROSALIA: Sorry… Too much?

TRENT: Are you watching that crap again? Fifty shades?

My heart plummets to my feet at his response.

ROSALIA: It's not crap. Yes, I'm watching it, you know I love it, why?

TRENT: It just seems like an unrealistic representation of sex.

ROSALIA: Hmm, I disagree. I mean, sure you don't have to be a sadist or tie me up BDSM style, but restraint is something a lot of women find real sexy. Empowering. A fantasy.

TRENT: Yeah, nah.

Yeah, nah?

What the hell is that supposed to mean?

I don't know why this newfound anger spills through my veins. Probably because Christian and Ana just ripped each other's clothes off and another sex scene begins, while I'm here with a bunny licking my tits.

This sex scene is even more sizzling hot than the last. I'm not only angry, I'm pissed off at Trent because I shouldn't be this turned on when I'm texting with my (anti) boyfriend and he's not taking any of my cues, nor did he react to the tit pic I sent him with Mr. HotLips.

Ugh.

ROSALIA: Okay…

TRENT: Yeah, sorry I've got to go. Boys want to move on to another bar. Night. See you tomorrow.

Is it just me, or did that sound brief as hell?

Groaning, I practically throw my phone across the room to the soundtrack of Anastasia's intensifying moans and his grunts. I slow for a second by the TV, checking out Jamie Dornan's toned ass for the millionth time.

It just seems like an unrealistic representation of sex.

I scoff at Trent's words. If only he knew all the dark and twisted fantasies I have. Those including having my hair pulled and my pussy fucked so rough and senseless that sex becomes a drug.

I've used my trusty vibrator one too many nights just thinking about them, thinking about Trent. But right now, as arousal pulls my panties at the intensity of the sex on my screen, all I wish was that he were here instead, not at some bar getting drunk before our night performance tomorrow.

Trent Daniels is a good guy. He's educated, kind, and comes from money, not that I cared about the latter. Big money. His father is one of the most renowned dentists in not only NYC, but America. His mother is a famous Austrian opera singer currently touring the world.

What first attracted me to Trent beyond friendship was that again, he was such a nice guy. After the ache Elijah left behind (and Cayden to a certain extent) I wanted nothing more to do with the bad boys. They could all go to hell if it were up to me. So there was something refreshing about being with a professional dancer who had no time to run away without a goodbye or in Cayden's case, secretly pursue another woman.

Trent doesn't know anything about my past with Elijah. It just doesn't feel right to relive the past, not right now. Besides, there was no relevance to it. Elijah Diesel is out of my life. Forever. And I couldn't be happier.

With just my sheer lacy bra on, I'm about to set Mr. HotLips down on the light oak hardwood floors and slip into bed myself when a buzz ripples through the entire brownstone.

It takes a full half a minute and another deafening buzz to realize it's the doorbell. I'm so used to being out of the house for ten hours at a time that I rarely hear it since I'm always home at this time. Midnight.

Shit.

Who is it?

Is Naomi on the other side, too drunk to find her key?

Or is it Trent…? Was he lying about still being at the bar and is here instead?

Going with the probability of the latter, it's slowly starting to make sense to me. Perhaps Trent's briefness was to throw me off and instead, he was surprising me.

Maybe you're not going crazy after all, Rosalia.

Mentally deciding it's Trent, I skip putting on a new top and instead jog toward the mint-colored front door with just a suggestive lace bra, booty shorts, and Mr. HotLips in my arms.

I grin, my heart slipping a million miles per hour as I unlock the door and open it wide, expecting those wintery hazel delights staring back at me. Instead...

Oh.

My.

God.

My jaw drops.

What the...

Gasping, my wildly beating heart pumps into overdrive. I stand frozen, forgetting how to breathe. It's as if all the oxygen has been sucked out of my lungs. My sanity becomes a tangled nostalgic mess, and I hate myself for it.

Familiar eyes I once labeled the most beautiful shade of melancholic onyx with the darkest speckles of gray stare back at me.

It's been almost four years.

Four years since I last saw *him.*

Elijah.

Elijah Diesel is at my door at midnight, and for the first time in years, I feel numb.

Chapter

FIFTEEN

Rosalia

Gazing at me like a rebellious daydream, Elijah's ever so casually smoking a cigarette, clouds of thick white smoke destined to circle my soul and drag me into the depths of my personal hell.

What is he doing here?

I catch myself staring at his short dark beard and perfectly chiseled jaw, the way his jet-black hair is slicked back, yet a few strands sexily cascade down his face. The man who broke my heart and ran over the shattered pieces.

We stare at each other wordlessly. Elijah's eyes darken, recklessness lacing them as they drop down to my long, toned legs. I'm standing here, my mouth all dry as I watch Elijah slowly check me out. His gaze rises to my belly button piercing and ballerina abs, confusing written all over his face at the sight of Mr. HotLips in my arms. But it quickly fades as he rasps a low "*fuck*" before inhaling sharply the second he sees my tits.

Clenching his jaw twice, all the control in Elijah's eyes explodes.

I swallow thickly, wanting to pinch myself because this doesn't feel real. At all.

That *Fifty Shades Darker* sex scene continues blaring behind me, moans the soundtrack to Diesel Rose's front man, Elijah Diesel, checking out my breasts. My heart drops. *Freaking hell, Christian Gray, couldn't one of your kinks have been sexily covering your hand over her mouth?*

My breasts are anything but covered in my lacy bra. It's sheer lace, meaning he can see my light olive skin beneath and my dark pink nipples. *Oh my God.* Manhattan's cold chill kisses my skin and I blame it for the reason my nipples pebble, stabbing through the lace.

Mr. HotLips snuggles deeper into me while the questions taking over my mind keep spiraling, swirling together until it's all a jumbled mess. When Elijah's gaze drifts to mine, his wolfish onyx eyes heat to that place between heaven and hell.

The one I seem to know so well.

Purgatory.

The way he's looking at me makes me want to forget how he walked out on us, even for a second. But I'm stronger than that.

That's when I notice the four books he's holding. Four *very* familiar classic romances.

Plath.

Brontë.

Austen.

Fitzgerald.

And. Then. Everything. Just. Slows.

Oh my God! The books I donated to Hayes's Bookshop! How did he get them?

I donated them the other day in a bid to forget Elijah for good. I want nothing else to do with them. With him. I even refused to get any money for them from Mr. Hayes. But apparently, the devil is making it a habit to come bite my ass because here stands Elijah Diesel right in front of me, looking all broody and pissed off as fuck with the four books I donated in his hands.

Elijah practically growls. "Do you always open the door dressed like this?"

My jaw ticks.

Is he SERIOUS?

It's been almost *four years* since I last saw this jerk, and THESE are his first words. I have so much anger for this man, so much resentment, and this comment just tops the cake!

"I can dress however I like, thank you very much," I grit. "Besides, it's none of your business, jerk."

It's devilish the way he slips the cigarette between his fingers and steps closer. Sandalwood with a tense hit of tobacco becomes my air. That's when the slow, sexy half smirk crawls up his lips. I hate a part of me feeds into nostalgia. *And gah, he still smells so good…*

"Wow, did you just call me a *jerk*?" Elijah scoffs. "Is that all you've got for me? Hmm?"

Oh, are we just going to ignore all the heartbreak you caused me? I don't think so!

Before I can respond, Elijah hands me the four books, well, more like slams them in my chest, missing Mr. HotLips by inches. "Didn't your biological parents ever tell you that you don't throw away gifts, little girl?"

Thump.

Thump.

Thump.

My chest heaves, all my heartstrings tightening in agony. Elijah's words leave scars because *he knows* my parents died of a murder suicide. *He knows* how much it kills me. But he's decided to come in hot and heavy, rubbing salt into my already heavily bleeding wounds.

But I'm not giving in. I'm not letting him win.

My jaw tightens and I shove the books in his chest the hardest I can. "I didn't throw them away, Elijah, I *donated* them!"

"I bought them for *you*, not some random fucking stranger looking for a classic."

"Well, Elijah Diesel, you can't win them all!"

"These. Are. Yours. Rosalia."

"How did you find my address?"

"Quit deflecting."

I glare up at him defiantly. I forgot how tall he is. Just how much he towers over me at six-foot-three. "If you don't answer my question, I will slam this door in your face, not that I'm *not* planning to do so anyway."

"Mr. Hayes and I are really tight."

My jaw drops because it only means one thing…Mr. Hayes shared my *personal* details that I had to write down to file the paperwork on *The Beautiful and Damned* first edition. The one Elijah left on my bed with a note on the title page all those years ago.

"But it's *confidential information!*" I practically scream and poor Mr. HotLips jumps in my arms. I scratch behind his fluffy gray ears to calm him down. "Mr. Hayes can't share it."

Elijah smiles smugly like the cocky bastard he is. "Well, I guess I'm the exception."

I roll my eyes. *Of course you are. Let me know when ego isn't up your ass anymore.*

He hands the pile of books back to me, but I refuse to take them. "I said I don't want them! When are you going to get that through your thick head?"

"*Fuccck.*" Elijah's fuming. The side of his throat sports an inky rose tattoo with thorns, and it begins burning up, the scarlet flush rushing up to his face. "I thought you adored the classics…"

Raising my chin, I step closer and almost on instinct, Elijah cranes his head lower so that our hot breath merges in a fiery uproar.

"I *did*, but now I can't turn a page without thinking of you and I hate it! I *hate you!*" I seethe in disgust. "Just like you told me to hate you four years ago, remember? Right before you kissed me all night."

I stare and stare into those onyx wonderlands until his eyes darken to pure carnage, and that's when I smirk darkly.

Ah-ha.

I think I hurt the monster's feelings…and I like it.

Elijah ticks his jaw, his nostrils flaring with no defense. Rage is all I see and it's all I need to confirm my suspicion. *He hates that he hates that I hate him.* And just like that, a psychopathic coldness glazes his eyes as a smirk stretches his lips.

"Ohhh, *right.*" He chuckles, mocking me, and then continues to slaughter me slowly with a glare. "That was around the time you said you were in love with me, isn't that right, hmm?" he grits, sucking in a breath. "*In love,* yeah? So, what the hell are you trying to prove, Rosalia?"

Rosalia.

My heart stammers at the way he says my name. So slow and rich, yet filled with angst. Nobody else has ever said my name like that before. So attached with desire. Not even Trent.

Fuck.

You.

Elijah.

Diesel.

Carelessly, Elijah takes a final drag of his cigarette before tossing it to the porch. He crushes it with the heel of his black worn-out leathered Dr. Martens. The ones with the white broken heart on the left boot. *The ones he wore in that Rolling Stone article and on the day we first met.*

Anger bubbles through me so intensely that I set Mr. HotLips behind me, and he hops over to his bed.

Perfect.

I go to slam the door right in Elijah's face, but he's too fast and slips through the gap seconds before the door slams shut. *Shit.* Without ever losing my gaze, he throws the classic books on my kitchen countertop, then blindly locks the front door behind him. And then, it's just us in the warmth of my house with the lights dimmed low and *Fifty Shades* blaring in the background.

I rush over and shut the damn television off because right now erotica can go fuck itself. *Literally.* I storm back to him at record speed, almost slipping on the floorboard with my socks.

"I want you out of my house right now. You're not welcome!" I hiss, roughly shoving his chest, but he doesn't stumble. "I SAID GET OUT OF MY FUCKING HOUSE, ELIJAH!"

Elijah just stares with those wolfish dark gray eyes, and it kills me inside.

"You were fucking in love with me," he continues, rounding me until I pin myself against the closed front door, its coldness chilling me down my spine.

Elijah stalks closer to me, a wolf starving for his prey, and when he gets to me with recklessness in his stride, he ensures our bodies brush. I'm pretty sure he can feel just how rapidly my heart beats.

I despise how he invades my personal space when his arms reach out on either side of my head, pressing against the oak and caging me between it and him. My breaths tangle into one, adamant to break free any chance I get.

"You were fucking in love with me," Elijah repeats, but now in a much softer, bare whisper. "Your words exactly, so I highly suggest you get your story straight because you were just a seventeen-year-old girl aching to be kissed. We both know I didn't start what we had."

Cruel.

He's so damn cruel.

I scoff. "Bullshit. You wanted me."

"I never told you I was in love with you, did I?"

Side note: I want to strangle this guy.

I stare at his Adam's apple as it bops up and down. I refuse to look him in the eye because they're too heated, too laced in the history of us. He must notice because he lowers his face to mine and our noses brush. His tattooed fingers find my ponytail holder, tugging it loose and letting it fall on the floor. My voluminous blonde waves fall down, covering my breasts and the way my heart stops.

Elijah Diesel looks at me as if I'm the only thing that exists, with eyes so expressively anguished it only ruins me more because *he* was the one who left without a goodbye. *He* is the one who broke my heart. *He* is the one who deserves the worst. So why is he staring as if it's me?

"Elijah," I whisper. "Please go."

"No."

"Elijah—"

"Look at me."

I can't. *I won't.*

Sighing sharply, his hot breath tickles my lips, taking me back to that very Halloween night when we made out all night. Until our lips were swollen, drunk off each other. My heart aches just thinking about it. I've moved on from Elijah. Moved on from his betrayal. But the homesick mark he created has left a permanent scar.

I can't do anything without thinking of an aspect of my life with him.

Like music.

Like Cherry Cola.

Like Halloween night.

I feel Elijah's glare deepen. "You can't even look at me, huh?"

"This isn't the time, Elijah."

"*Oh*, then when is the time?"

And that, ladies and gents, is when I absolutely lose it.

"ARE YOU FORGETTING *YOU* LEFT *ME*!" I scream, snapping

my eyes to him with clenches fists. "All you are is a coward, Elijah Diesel! There's nothing to talk about, so *leave!*"

Panting, we're left staring at each other. The air thickens as he clenches his stubbled jaw. And I meant it when I said Elijah Diesel has sociopathic or psychopathic tendencies because there's no other way to describe how callous it is when his glare softens to a sad smile without ever recognizing my fury.

"You looked beautiful on opening night, *Peaches*," Elijah murmurs against my lips, his eyes shutting in time to miss the shock rippling through mine.

My lips part to nothingness.

What… What did he just say?

Tension snakes around my entire body, beginning at my knees, swirling through my stomach before landing right through my chest like a silver bullet. And my heart? Well, it's in my throat.

You looked beautiful on opening night, Peaches.

I don't know if it's the fact that I just heard Elijah Diesel call me *Peaches* after so many years, or the fact that he just admitted he watched me perform Swan Lake in Lincoln Center, but I feel sick to my stomach.

"I was there," Elijah continues, and when he reopens his eyes, there's so much depth in them. "You were in that pretty feathered tutu and all, dancing ballet around the stage like you were fucking born for it, because you are."

For the first time all night, he looks real sad. Depressed even.

He finishes whispering, "I'm just so proud of you, *Pea—*"

"Seriously? Did you just say you are proud of me?" I spit, shoving his chest, and this time he stumbles back a little. "Oh my God, you are unbelievable! Don't you dare suck up to me and pretend like you didn't ruin me! You are acting LIKE NOTHING HAPPENED!"

Oooo, and hello Mr. Hyde.

Venom returns on his tongue, in his eyes, and plunges deep into his ice-cold heart.

"If you think that, then you're fucking blind, Rosalia!"

"Oh, thank you, yep, now I'm blind too. Okay, so, what is that now." Pissed off, I hold up three fingers. "I'm *ungrateful for gifts*, a former *seventeen-year-old aching to be kissed*, and *blind*. Thank you *so much*."

Elijah groans, pinching the bridge of his nose. "Come on, Rosalia, you know I didn't mean it like that."

"I don't care how the hell you meant it. I have nothing to say to you, so please just *go*."

Something close to guilt ripples across his face.

"I'm not leaving," he whispers, as sweet as honey. "*Peaches*, I—"

"Don't," I hiss, my voice on the verge of breaking as tears rim my eyes. "Don't you dare call me that or try to fix this. I'm fine. Really, I'm fine. I'm working at my dream ballet company. I'm happier than ever. I have a boyfriend who loves me. I do not need you, Elijah."

The air crackles between us for a solid minute. I know because I count.

Complete silence, and then…

"Boyfriend?"

Well, Trent doesn't want any labels, so technically he's not my 'boyfriend', but the hell with it.

"Yes, I have a *boyfriend*."

Elijah doesn't seem the slightest bit happy. "How long have you been together?"

"It doesn't matter."

"How. Long. Have. You. Been. Together?"

"I've been with my *boyfriend* for a few months."

"Define a *few months*."

I look at him as if he's crazy. "Sheesh, what are you? My father?"

Elijah clenches his jaw, like ten times in a row, and I hate how alluring I find it. "I believe the correct term you once used for me was *daddy*, so just answer the damn question instead."

"I don't owe you anything, Elijah."

"Except freaking hearing aids… How long have you been with that fucker?"

"A *few* months."

He sighs. "Six months?"

"More like three."

"*Three*?"

"Would you like those hearing aids now? With my Amazon Prime subscription, they'll probably come by morning, so I can drop them off at your holding cell before ballet training."

Elijah deadpans me, totally unimpressed, *and if looks could kill…*

"Does he treat you right?"

Jealous much?

"You know what? *Yes.* Yes, he does treat me right. Better than you ever could."

Elijah darkly narrows his gaze. "Who is he? That fucking evil sorcerer guy? *Tent Daniels*?"

My eyes widen. "How…how did you know?"

"Swan Lake's damn program book. I saw the way he was looking at you all night."

Taunting him, I scrunch up my nose. "The way he was *looking at me*? And how's that?"

He grinds his jaw, and suddenly everything just seems to slow, just like it does at times whenever I'm with him. The intensity of our conversation hovers over us, lending me incapable of stopping from digging deeper into his rock-hard armor.

Elijah glances between my eyes, his voice soft velvet when he says, "Your *boyfriend* was looking at you the same way *I* used to look at you."

Used to.

His words are scorching fire to my already ignited heart.

"Don't play that card with me, Elijah." I almost laugh because this entire thing is crazy. "You're toying with my mind. You were never in love with me and you know it, so back the fuck off before I call the police."

"The police? Really? Who the fuck do you think you are, Rosalia Philips?"

"A woman who's taken too much shit in her life to take any more! *Move.*"

He doesn't. "Why don't you call that boyfriend of yours instead? Or is he only good for stopping circulation and compressing his balls in those tight fucking stockings of his?"

"THEY'RE CALLED TIGHTS!"

"The fuck if I care! I don't trust guys in pants so tight you can see the outline of—"

"What the hell is your problem with my boyfriend? You saw him for, what, two hours?"

Elijah dramatically nods, continuously. "Trust me, two hours was enough to scar me for life. He looks like the kind of guy who'll give you a card with chocolate, roses, and a little fucking teddy bear to constantly celebrate one-week anniversaries."

I simply glare at him.

Elijah must have some type of telepathy…

How the hell does he always guess it right?

Okay, so I'm totally acting like I didn't scream out at the world yesterday when the huge pile on the top shelf of my wardrobe (containing all stuffed teddy bears and chocolate Trent has given me) fell on my head when I was attempting to sort it all out.

But I'm no longer a foolish seventeen-year-old obsessed with both the sin and forbiddance only Elijah Diesel, the lead singer of an alternative rock band, embodies. I'm a changed twenty-one-year-old woman. A happy one. One with a grudge.

"Well, is he that kind of guy or not?"

"Not that you even deserve to know…" I grumble under my breath, not knowing why I'm even admitting it. "But yes, he is."

"So. Fucking. Predictable." Elijah shakes his head. "*Wow*, Rosalia Philips, I really thought you were edgier than that. A girl who preferred the eclectic and imperfect over bandwagon and predictable shit."

"Well, I guess you just don't know me anymore."

He glances down, eyeing my diamond navel piercing. "I beg to differ," he mumbles, almost to himself, his eyes then holding mine. "All I know is that if I see Trent again, it won't be pretty."

"Oh my God! How can you be so disrespectful after YOU are the one who left? You fucked up, Elijah Diesel, you *fucked up*!"

"I thought leaving was the only way to make you understand I wasn't a forever guy."

"No, don't even try to make it seem like you did this for my benefit. You didn't." I stab my pointer finger against his white T-shirt, between his open leather jacket. "You did it for *you*! I'm so happy you're a star, that the world knows your name. Really, I am, but you wanna know something? They'll never know how much of a pathetic dick you are for not having the balls to be a man and tell me goodbye to my face, not in a damn letter!"

"Don't be so fucking hypocritical." Elijah's eyes narrow. "You told me you were in love with me just to make me stay, but you didn't really feel it."

"I *did!*" I scream in his face, thumping my finger against his chest again.

"You *didn't*, Rosalia," he spits, his hips pinning me against the door when I attempt to run. He stares me down until my soul feels bruised. "It was all fucking *puppy love* for you."

"You do not get to tell me how to feel!"

"Okay," he scoffs. "Says the girl who acted so desperate in wanting to make me stay."

"DESPERATE?" I gasp. "Are you out of your goddamn mind?"

"No, but you are, and so is that fucking boyfriend of yours."

"Trent has nothing to do with this!"

"Is Trent's mother the owner of the ballet company or something?" Elijah leans in closer, our lips almost touching as he whispers darkly, "Are you only fucking him because of that? Hmm, Rosalia? Is that how you got the pleasure of being *prima ballerina* at only twenty-one, because you're fucking a mommy's boy?"

"Are you CRAZY?" I gasp. All the air sucks out of me. "Did you really just say that?"

That cocky smirk of his reappears. "What are you gonna do about it?"

Oh, that freaking does it!

My hand is inches from colliding with his ridiculously gorgeous face, but this guy has killer instincts. He grips my wrist before my palm collides, restricting it. It leaves only one of his hands remaining pressed against the door, beside my head.

Darn it!

I want to scream.

Elijah's grip on my wrist tightens, his sterling silvery sings that I remember so well kissing coldness against my skin, freezing me deep with memories. He arches a brow as if to say, *see what happens when you're a bad girl*, and it makes me raise my left hand to slap his other cheek, but *THIS MOTHERFUCKER!* He sees it coming and grips the wrist with his free hand, constraining me *again*.

A gasp escapes my lips when he eventually slams both my wrists above my head and binds them together with his hands.

It's so controlled.

So darn dominant.

So Elijah Diesel at his absolute finest.

AHHHHHHHHHHHH!

(That was me screaming inside of my head. Just excuse my melt down, thanks.)

The position of my hands lends my breasts to naturally pop out more, having my hair fall away to the sides of my lacy bra and my tits pressed right against his leather jacket. My nipples, which are still stabbing through the sheer material, softly brush over the cold zipper and the sensation it brings... *God.*

I feel it all over.

I can't help the electricity rushing through me at the friction between the lace and zipper, its coldness making my nipples even harder. It takes over. I bite down my lower lip to hide my soft moan and how Elijah triggered the warmth between my thighs without trying.

This is so unfair.

I have a 'boyfriend.'

I despise Elijah with a passion.

So why am I feeling this type of way?

Elijah scans my wrists and then my eyes, something brewing in his that I can't explain.

In all my rage, I fight Elijah's grip and somehow manage to break out of his hold. My feet slap against the hardwood floors and into the kitchen, craving an escape.

The first thing I do when he follows me is the unthinkable. The loud slap echoes around the kitchen, replaying in my head like a golden record. I slap his face so hard he's probably seeing stars. At the hit, Elijah's face falls to the side and he shuts his eyes, those long onyx lashes taunting me as his face tenses, all while a blush-colored handprint gradually paints his cheek.

My handprint.

The second thing I do is grip his white T-shirt, bunching it with so much force it'll be creased forever. I rise on my tippy toes—the move so natural to me—until my lips brush across his dark stubble and then higher to his diamond stud earring and other piercings. Finally, I reach his ear, feeling like the most powerful girl in the world as my heart begins to settle.

Elijah's breaths labor, so I clench my fist tighter around his shirt, bringing him so close his sexily tousled hair tickles my nose. I don't give a damn about it. I'm ready to ruin him and serve him sweet revenge on a shiny silver platter, just like he did to me nearly four years ago.

"Take that back," I hiss in his ear, a wicked smirk crawling up my lips. "*Punk.*"

Elijah steps back, creating distance, but it also means I'm the witness to the reckless rage brewing in his gaze. It's as if he's the devil reincarnated looking at me, and the thing is, I'm not scared. Not of him. Not of how he may react. Not of how I just called him something that I know is a trigger to him. *Punk.* I've pushed him, far into the deep end because of *karma.*

Before he broke my heart, I used to daydream of the woman I'd be now.

If she would be weak or strong.

If she would become a doctor like her foster father wanted or a professional dancer.

If she would one day marry Elijah Diesel or if they were just a fleeting moment of fate.

I never knew the answer, but right now, staring into the onyx-eyed monster who used to own my heart like an unhealthy obsession, I'm grateful I chose the latter to all those things.

"You want to say that again, *Peaches*?" Elijah grits through his teeth, cocking his head to the side like I've just crossed an unforgivable line.

There's no turning back from this. I mean, he can't even apologize, own his shit, or be accountable.

My chest tightens because he's messing with the wrong girl.

"I. Said. Take. That. Back. You. Freaking. *Punk.*"

Every one of my staccato words burns a hole in Elijah's ego. I witness it happen.

"Is that a threat, Rosalia Philips?"

"No, it's a *promise.*"

"Oh yeah?"

"Oh yeah."

He glances between my eyes. "Prove it."

"Pretty sure I just did."

Without warning, Elijah grips my throat, just like he did when we first kissed, and I gasp with wide eyes. *Oh my God.* It's such an erotic yet aggressive move that my head spirals.

His chokehold tightens, and yet, it still has a level of gentleness to it.

Now it's his turn to brush his lips against my ear, a soft moan escaping my lips when he blows soft air all up my neck, electrifying the doomed sparks.

"You like playing dirty, huh, babygirl?" he sexily growls, my heart-beat throbbing against his fingers.

He pulls back, watching the hot flush crawling up my cheeks. I'm ashamed of it.

"'Cause I'll show you fucking dirty, *Peaches*." Elijah grins, knowing exactly what he's doing when he slowly inches forward until our noses brush. "I'll show you it so fucking good."

His touch becomes passionate as he teases me by edging forward like he's going to kiss me, and then at the last second, when a breath escapes me, he pulls back. He never kissed me once, but the anticipation has my body on fire, sizzling, even after he steps away.

Dripping in dominance, Elijah lets go of my throat.

Fresh air fills my lungs. I feel dirty for missing his touch. *I used to like it when he gripped my throat...is it bad that I still do? That I like it?*

Gulping down, I step away from him until my back hits the refrigerator. I don't like that Elijah makes me feel like this. That he can just come back into my life years later and deep down, in my heart of hearts, I still get the thrill that comes with him looking at me like this.

I can't help but think. *This is us. This*—as we pant, and our stare intensifies into chaos—is precisely us. Elijah Diesel and me together... we're destructive. Aggressive. Explosive.

We're fire and water, unforgiving yet passionate in our own reckless way.

Filthy.

Messy.

Bad for each other.

But the truth is, there's a tainted part of me that misses it—*misses him.*

Tense tension doesn't simmer between Elijah and me, not even through silence. We're both catching our breaths, staring at each other from across the kitchen like two lost souls.

"I said I have a boyfriend," I whisper, rolling my head across the cold fridge, exhausted.

"Does it look like I fucking care, Rosalia?"

Air crackles between us.

"Well, *I* care, and I would like you to leave. *Pronto.*"

Leaning against the kitchen counter with his long legs spread out, Elijah shakes his head. He locks his ankles and guilt lodges in my throat when I catch myself staring at the bulge in his arms through his leather jacket as he crosses them over his broad chest.

It's guilt for myself but also Trent because I know he wouldn't like this. He doesn't know anything about Elijah. I didn't think it was relevant to tell him. But if he did know, I'm certain he'd be here in a heartbeat, telling Elijah where to go. *Not that Elijah would listen…*

There aren't any lights on in my modern kitchen, but silvery moonlight trickles through the window, highlighting Elijah's ever flawless feature. Despite the chaos of moments ago, somehow right now everything seems calmer. For a minute, all the anger subsides in his eyes and gazing into those onyx-grays feels so pure. Clouds of raw emotion.

"Does Trent know all the things I know about you?" Elijah begins in a whisper. "Does he know all your little quirks? What happened to your biological parents?"

"Don't."

"Don't *what*, Rosa?" He arches a brow, his voice so chillingly calm. "Don't be *truthful*?"

"Please don't dig up things I told you in confidence."

But it doesn't seem to matter to Elijah as he strides my way until he's standing right in front of me, his sandalwood tobacco scent intoxicating.

"Does he see your pain? How grief laces your eyes?"

"Elijah, please stop."

He ignores me to pick up my left wrist, my entire body on the verge of trembling when his callous thumb ever so gently rolls across the very beginning of my wrist. I know what he feels. *Exactly what he feels.* And it's for that reason—while Elijah softly rolls his thumb over my faded white scars, some not so faded—tears form in my eyes.

In the silence, Elijah and I share such intimacy. We're looking at each other as my heart aches. *Vulnerable.* It's a vulnerability we've ever only skimmed the lines of before.

And then, as my heart continues burning up, something shifts between us.

Elijah's expressive eyes darken, but not in anger, in *pain*. "Does he see the scars on your wrist, huh?" He sucks in a breath, and when he does, the first hot tear baptizes my cheek. "Does he notice those things, Rosalia?"

"Elij—"

"Does Trent Daniels *really* care enough to notice the things I've noticed in minutes?"

I remain quiet, the knot at the back of my throat too painful to speak.

Elijah knows my answer. He knows it without me saying anything.

"WELL, DOES HE?" Elijah screams, slamming his fist on the fridge in frustration. I flinch, him missing me by inches. "Does he know you've tried to fuckin' kill yourself, HUH?"

And then, right in front of me, Elijah Diesel crumbles into the most emotionally contorted man I've ever seen. Bringing my wrists to his lips, he softly kisses over my every scar, making my heart beat like crazy.

Through my blurry vision, I gaze at the man who was once my everything, wondering why everything inside me hurts so bad. Elijah stares back at me like he's drowning. His eyes are glossy when he buries his head into my neck, his warmth like a breath of fresh air.

He wraps me in the solace of his arms, leather and all, and the sensation is so new.

"Because *I* do," Elijah whispers, piercing my already bleeding heart. "I see your pain. How grief laces your eyes. I see the gashes. The scars." He sucks in a breath. "I notice these things because I care— *too much*. I don't know how deep the devil haunts you, or if the cuts are small doses of relief or something more damaging, but whatever the fuck it is, it kills me inside. It did that night I first saw them four years ago, and it kills me now. Do you understand?"

So overwhelmed, I can't master the strength to reply.

"I don't want to…" Tears brim his eyes as he hugs me harder, his voice breaking. "I don't want to read about somebody finding you in a fucking blood bath, *Peaches. Fuck.* Trent doesn't love you. If he did, he would see your pain. He'd want to kiss it better, babygirl."

And that's when I break, sobs escaping me in waves.

This is too much. This is too much at once.

My throat is so scraped and what I hate the most is what I love the most. Anxiety sets through, and when it feels like I can't breathe from all the weight of the world, Elijah Diesel is there to wipe my tears away. To rest his forehead against mine. To ease my panic attack.

I'm trembling as Elijah softly cups my face like I'm made of porcelain. "Just like I do."

"This isn't fair." I sniffle, my voice a terrible mess. "You can't just come into my life after this long and expect… You made me believe you were always going to be there. That you had my back, and then you just left."

"I didn't want publicity to go wild."

"So you were thinking about yourself?"

"No, I just…I thought it was the right thing to do. The only thing to do. I know I'm all fucked up, but I…" Elijah's hands return around my waist. "*Fuck.*"

"You left, Elijah, you left me when I needed you the most."

"I know, babygirl." He nods, rests his forehead against mine, and the saddest smile ever traces his lips. "And I've regretted it every single day since, believe me."

My fingers rush under his jacket, slowing over his cotton shirt and prominent muscle. His heart beats wildly against mine as I lean my head against his chest, our height difference making him softly rest his chin on my head. Moments ago, we were fighting, and now…*this.*

This is our first embrace, our first ever form of physical contact aside from the kisses and hand holding, and I don't know what any of this means for us.

I can tell Elijah isn't used to this. Isn't used to an intimacy that's slow and not crazed.

Through all my hate, through all my tears, through all the reasons why I shouldn't, I hold Elijah tight, and he squeezes back—*tighter.* The scariest part is after everything he's done, I think there'll always be a part of my heart that will be his. *Always his.*

"Sorry if me leaving contributed in any way, but you were seventeen, Rosalia," Elijah whispers, the smoothest melody to our angst. "*Seventeen.* I was only trying to protect you."

"I wasn't a kid. I knew my limits. I didn't need protecting. If I wanted protection, I would have asked for it. You were selfish, forgot about me, and solely thought of your career."

"No, that isn't it at all."

"Then tell me I'm wrong."

Silence.

Elijah sighs after a while. "I never told you I was looking for a relationship."

"I get it. Heck, how I do, but we still could've *spoken*. You didn't have to shut me out."

Silence paves the way to the beginning of the end for us.

His voice cuts into the white noise. "What would the world have said, Rosalia? My bandmates? Your parents? A seventeen-year-old girl with a thirty-one-year-old man?"

"It was legal!"

Elijah shakes his head against my hair. "It was taboo, and you know it."

"You…" I shut my eyes, getting lost in his warmth until it all gets too much. "Should go."

His body tenses but as soon as it appears, it vanishes.

Elijah shouldn't be here, hugging me, not when I'm yet to forgive him for all the pain.

I hate that I instantly miss his touch.

I hate that I try to savor his presence before his thumping footsteps become distant.

I hate that I don't have the courage to reopen my eyes until I hear my front door slam shut.

But most of all, I hate that when my gaze lands on the kitchen counter, the classic books are gone, along with the final piece of our history threading us together.

They're gone.

All except for one.

The Beautiful and Dammed first edition.

That's when I slide down the fridge and the tears begin flowing—uncontrollably. Because etched in that tragic Fitzgerald romantic classic, somewhere, there's *us*…

A melancholic rocker and fated ballerina, destined to burn in the flames of this depressing world.

Forever.

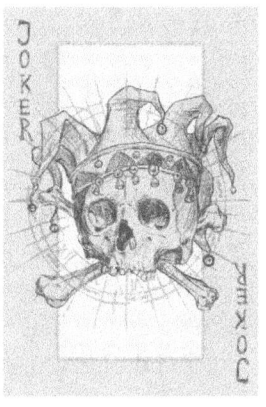

Chapter

SIXTEEN

Elijah

K^{*nock.*}
        Knock.
Knock.

"Open the damn door, you motherfucker!" Knives shouts in the murky distance. "I swear to God, Diesel, you're filing the skin off my hand."

Groaning, I push the linen bed sheets over my head, my best friend's shouts outside my hotel suite deafening. His continuous shouts mixed with the fucking annoying knocking explode inside my already pounding head.

I'm not in a good mood. At all. The last thing I need is all this racket. Last night, I saw Rosalia Philips for the first time in four years, and I think I just made everything worse.

Rosalia looked so beautiful, so happy without me, it hurt. The moment she opened the front door to me, she took my breath away, just like she always does. I know I'm the lead singer of the famous rock band Diesel Rose, but whenever I'm with her, I never seem to thread words right. She's my undoing, my complete undoing, and I hate myself for it.

I didn't exactly have a plan when I showed up at her door unannounced, but I didn't expect our conversation to be so heated. Intense. That's what every second feels like with her—*a bittersweet hurricane.*

Unable to deal with the demons that tainted my mind when I stormed out of her brownstone, I stepped into the first bar I saw and drank my sorrows away. At the time, the liquor on my tongue made the pain subside, allowed the thought of never seeing Rosalia again to fade. But now I'm hungover, and the crippling depression plays devil's advocate while my mouth feels like the fucking Sahara.

"DIESEL!" Knives tries again, this time screaming at the top of his lungs like we're in Madison Square Garden. I curse, rolling over on the king-sized bed, my back to the door as the shouts continue. "DUDE! YOU ALIVE IN THERE?"

"I wish I fucking weren't…" I half shout back.

"What? I can't hear you if you mumble."

Mumble?

My eyes shut. I smirk at my best friend through my pounding headache. "FUCK OFF!"

"Yeah, I heard that one all right, asshole."

I roll my eyes and after inhaling a sharp breath that I've felt deprived of all night, I strip the sheets off my body. Manhattan's coldness ripples over my skin. It feels like somebody is planting chilling kisses all down my spine.

Aside from my black Armani boxer briefs, I'm naked. I always sleep completely naked, but last night I crashed onto my bed face first—drunk, depressed, and definitely couldn't be bothered flinging the cotton fabric to the other side of the luxurious suite.

"Holy shit," I grumble, rubbing a hand over my eyes when I open them too fast, and not only is the world still spinning, but the bright sunlight blinds me through the sheer curtains.

Sheer… I know what else was sheer last night.

My heart does a double back flip just thinking about the blonde goddess that is Rosalia Philips in that sensual sheer lace bra and tiny booty shorts. *God.* All I wanted to do was apologize with my tongue, beg for mercy between her toned thighs, tell her I'm a jealous man, and that Trent doesn't deserve her, but I couldn't. I couldn't do any of it.

I was losing my mind just watching her, pretending I didn't notice her carved out beauty and the way I was rock-hard almost throughout the entire conversation. I once said this woman was going to be the death of me. I wasn't wrong.

My chest is so tight it might just burst.

Fuck. Why is my life so depressing?

Sighing, I step out of bed to Knives's knocking, which is not merged into a melodic drum beat to the rhythm of our hit song, "Fragments of You". I shake my head, unable to help the snicker that escapes me.

This guy...

He's not even our damn drummer.

The moment I open the door, Knives leans against the doorframe with his arms crossed over his chest. Shaking his head, he slowly rakes his gaze down my body and rolls his eyes. He's wearing baby blue jeans and a hoodie, the hood over his head, a few strands of his dirty-blond loose curls peeking out.

"Dude..." he says slowly, studying my eyes, which I'm sure are still glazed in whiskey, and *oh*, also some gin. "What the hell happened to you?"

"Nothing."

"Bullshit." Knives arches a suspicious brow. "You're literally still swaying, and I don't like it 'cause we've got a private jet to catch in, like, three hours."

I internally groan.

Ohio.

That's right.

How did I forget about that?

We're performing at Rocket Mortgage FieldHouse on Monday night...which is tomorrow. Thank God our team over at our sleek black private jet don't give a shit if we're drunk, high, or if there's a threesome mid-flight with two chicks you definitely won't call again after landing.

The thrill of filling my six-foot-three body with liquor sounded like *the* perfect alternative to being numb a good five hours ago. Now? Not so much.

Giving up on me like the lost cause I am, Knives sighs and pushes past me. He steps into my suite, which features my cigarette, a half empty whiskey bottle, and those damn three classic romance books scattered around the two teal velvet chairs by the floor-to-ceiling windows, overlooking Manhattan's skyline.

It took a while for Knight and me to get back on the same page after everything went down four years ago. He was a large contributing factor to the tension Rosalia and I developed when he questioned her intentions. He made me realize how blind I was, how we could never work, but also, he ruined me.

Barefoot, Knives slows by the books and freezes, only glancing over his shoulder at me when I sink onto the edge of the bed. "What the hell is this? Did you go to that bookstore or something?"

"Not exactly."

"They yours?"

"Not exactly."

Knives fully turns to me, confused as fuck. "That all you gotta say this morning? *Not exactly*?"

Clearing my throat, I pinch the bridge if my nose, not believing I'm about to have this conversation this early. But I need to tell someone before I break. I couldn't have exactly spilled my pain to the bartender last night. She would have told the entire world, I'd be making headlines, my PR team would've killed me, and my manager would have probably forced me into therapy for a month. *Yeah, that's a big 'no, thanks' to the ripple effect.*

I scratch the back of my neck. "It's…complicated."

"You wanna talk about it?"

I shrug.

Knives shoots me a death glare. "Well, then pack your shit. We gotta be in Ohio soon. I'm the fucking bassist, not our group therapist. *Literally*." He holds up three fingers and wiggles them. "Zander is in freaking midtown shopping for his girls. Dave's been on a sex-fest all night. Seriously, they're still going at it like she's his fucking drum kit. And here *I* am knocking on *your* damn door for twenty minutes straight because I thought you…"

My heart pangs from the depths of his words and something shifts. Something I don't like that makes me nauseous, and it's not the hangover.

Clenching my jaw, I shake my head while playing with my rings. "I'm okay. You know I'm not into…*that* shit anyway."

Concern lacing his eyes, Knives gives me a serious look that says, '*don't speak so fast, Elijah.*'

"*Anymore…*" I add lowly because this is leading to a deep conversation I don't want to have this early. *Or at all.*

The mood between us gets tense, and I can't even bare to look him in the eyes. My throat gets foggy, and I stare down at my silver snake ring, feeling all its detailed grooves and edges to temporarily ignore the ache surrounding my chest.

These past four years have been about success and rock 'n' roll.

They've been about becoming known worldwide.

Rolling Stone magazine naming us the most iconic alternative rock band of this century.

Fans going crazy and loving our music.

But…these four years have also been filled with so much more, *for me anyway.*

Depression.

Addiction.

Rehab.

It's not something I'm proud of, at all. But that's what happens when the devil keeps taunting you, keeps on whispering in your ear until all you crave is the numbness only certain drugs and death can give. I'm not suicidal. I just hate this world sometimes. *Most times.* But I'm getting better. Yeah, I'm…trying to crawl out of this, masking the pain in tobacco, euphoric orgasms, and rolled joints instead.

I can't go back to how I used to be. It destroyed me, but that feeling of being completely and utterly distorted felt better than the grief that continuously flares up until it hurts to breathe.

I can't fix my name in the tabloids.

I can't fix my worldwide bad boy reputation.

I can't fix how badly I wish I could have overdosed on Rosalia instead.

But I can change my tomorrow.

I can change my future.

And my *right now.*

"Look, man." Knives sighs, breaking me out of my haze. The bed dips when he sits down beside me, his hands squeezing my shoulders.

"You know I'm heartless and shit, but I *do* care." He pauses for a moment to suck in a breath, and I know exactly what's resurfacing in his mind. Me. All the shit I put not only him but the entire band through. "You've scared the shit out of me, Diesel, one too many times. Times we thought we were going to lose you. You can understand my pain."

"I know."

"So, whatever this is that's bothering you, spill it out. Tension is crawling in your eyes. I know you're going to explode if you don't tell me. So, *tell me.*"

Knives isn't wrong.

Clearing my throat, I don't expect my voice to be so sad and raspy when I say, "I went to see her last night…"

"Who?"

"*Her*… Rosalia."

"*Rosalia?*"

I nod. My body reacts to her name, my heart frantic.

Instantly, Knives's eyes widen, just like I presumed. "Dude, what the fuck?"

"I know, I know. In hindsight, I shouldn't have. But I was feeling all fired up after that call with Mr. Hayes. I couldn't stand looking at those books a second longer. They belonged to her. Not me."

"Jesus, and how did she react?"

"Badly, as expected. The second Rosalia opened the door, it was like she saw a ghost. She was only wearing a bra and booty shorts. Sheerest fucking bra I've ever seen. Then I looked down, and I thought I was fucking high or lapsing on some LSD or some shit."

"Why?"

"She was holding a fucking bunny."

Knives's jaw drops. "A *bunny*? Dude, that's some crazy shit."

"Yeah, I was really fucking confused. Anyway, it was a shit show. She was shouting for me to get out, that I was a coward for leaving the way I did. She even threatened to call the police…"

"Damn, is she married or something?"

The thought alone makes me want to finish off that half a bottle of expensive amber liquid. "No, not fucking married, *thank God.* But she's got a boyfriend. Three months. They've been together for three fucking months. He's a fucking ballet dancer."

Knives looks at me with wide eyes, as if he's losing his mind. "A ballet dancer?"

I grind my jaw. "Yeah."

"So, she went from a rock star to a balle—"

"Shut up," I grit, anger fueling my veins just thinking about it. "Don't want to talk about him."

"Jealous or something?"

I flip him off and he starts chuckling like the psycho he is.

"She's a ballet dancer…a *prima ballerina*."

Knives leans back on the bed. "The fuck is that shit?"

Side note: I definitely didn't tell Knives (or a single soul) that I went to Swan Lake to see Rosalia.

I roll my eyes. "It basically means she's the best of the elite. She works at New York City Ballet, one of the most prestigious and renowned ballet company in the entire world."

Knives slowly nods, glancing off into the distance before his eyes zone back on mine, and a slow smirk rises. "So, basically, you left her without even saying a proper goodbye and now she's ruling the ballet world? Hmm, there's some irony in that, no, brother?"

And then the fucker snickers in my face.

I give him my most unimpressed blank face. "Not helping."

Knives's snickers slowly settle, but the smirk remains. "Okay, so go on. You opened the door, she looked hot as fuck, you started talking, and it turned into a nightmare, *then* what happened?"

"Well, then…things really changed, and it got really…quiet. I was trying my best not to look at her lips." My voice lowers to a murmur, and I look at my best friend genuinely. "I really wanted to fucking kiss her, Knives. I wanted to tell her I'm sorry for all of the pain, but the more she looked at me, the more my presence was killing her. She told me to leave, so I did."

"And then you got drunk? To forget her?"

"Somewhat."

"*Fuck*!" Knives spits, shaking his head in disapproval. "That wasn't our fuckin' deal."

"I know, I just…" I let out a shaky breath. "I just really needed to take the edge off."

"Whiskey?"

"Yeah."

"Just whiskey."

I clear my throat. "Always."

Knives studies me slowly. "Seems like it didn't help."

"Nope, not one fucking bit." I laugh in frustration, glancing at the sheer shades. "Because then fucking 'Wonderwall', her favorite song, started playing at the bar and I almost broke my damn glass."

"So, what are you gonna do now?"

My heavy heart can't take it remembering the one key moment I intentionally didn't tell Knives about. Where I saw Rosalia's scars, questioned if her boyfriend noticed the things that I did, and then kissed every single scar with emotion in my throat.

I don't know if Rosalia understands the extent of just how deeply they affect me. Some were fading scars, but others not so much. She's hiding from the world. Masking her pain. But she can't from me.

"I don't know." My eyes dim when I turn to Knives, and suddenly everything gets real quiet as I whisper my truth, "I really fucking miss her, Knight."

The smirk drops in a flash of a second.

"Oh no, no, you don't," Knives warms, shaking his head like the cold bastard he is. "No, no, you don't miss her. You miss the *idea* of her, but she's happy, Diesel. You said she's a dancer. She's got a boyfriend. She's forgotten about you. You can't destroy her more than you already have. Forget her."

His words tear me down because it's the truth.

"I can't get her out of my mind." I sigh, running a hand through my disheveled hair. "Four years. I've been like this for *four* fucking years."

"And where has it got you? Tell me. Getting fucked up in the head, losing inspiration to write 'cause she's your muse, her telling you to leave with books thrust back to you, *huh*?"

We share a deadly stare. I hate that he's right.

"Look, listen to me," Knives says after a while, standing from the bed. "We're headed to Ohio and have got another day before our arena show. We'll check out Cleveland, do some practice, and *then* I'm making it my personal mission to find you a hot distraction."

I grumble, just thinking.

All I want is Peaches.

Nobody else.

"I don't need a distraction."

Diesel Rose's bassist gives me a pointed look. "Okay, maybe *you* don't, but *your dick* does. Because while I'm your friend and would do anything for you, sucking your cock isn't one of them."

Rolling my eyes, I flip him off and we burst out laughing.

God, it feels good to laugh again.

To be free.

When Knives is about to head to the door and pauses by the classic books again, I speak up, "I left her one…"

He points at the best stack of books. "These?"

"Yeah."

"Which one?"

I hate that one night, years ago, I got too high and depressed and told Knives *everything*. He knows more than anybody about the history between Rosalia and me. So, when I tell him it's *The Beautiful and Damned* first edition that I left her, he groans so damn loudly.

It really fucking hurts she attempted to donate all the books, at Hayes's of all places.

"NO!" Knives stares at me with a narrowed gaze, trying to figure me out. "Oh no, what the hell did you leave in the book?"

I tense up. *Fuck.*

"Nothing." I shrug.

Totally wasn't nothing…

The idiot knows me too well and glares me down, making it hard for me to lie.

"Spit. It. Out. Elijah. Diesel."

"It was nothing, really…"

"Fucking hell, my balls are sweating. *Spill it.*"

"My new number."

Knives's jaw drops. "Dude, no, what the fuck? She said she has a boyfriend!"

"I wrote it down before I went to her house. How was I supposed to know she had a fucking boyfriend?"

"That's exactly my point! You *shouldn't* have written your number to begin with! She ain't calling you, trust me. Come on, bro, this girl is ruining you." His eyes soften. "You *need* to forget her."

With all the weight on my shoulders, I nod because I believe him.

God, how badly I do.

But the second Knives leaves my suite and I lie down on the bed, staring at myself in the mirror above my bed, I crumble. I barely even recognize myself with the gloom clouding my face.

Redness laces my eyes. I rub my stubbled jaw, needing to shave, but I couldn't care less.

Nothing matters.

Nothing but *her*.

My muse.

But now I need to forget all about Rosalia Philips.

Forget that I was my happiest when I was around her.

Forget there was once a time when my lips were on hers.

Forget how her warm smile has the ability to light up an entire stadium.

I have to forget her for my own damn sanity. *Which is easier said than done…*

I just knew Knives's idea of *a distraction for Elijah Diesel* would result in utter disaster.

My best friend is smirking darkly, staring at me across the booth of this rowdy downtown club, his fiery angel right beside him, seductively kissing his neck. Don't ask me how the coldest motherfucker scored a girl crazy enough to love him, but he did. I mean, sure, their story started with hate, and they go back and forth, but they're made for each other in their own reckless way.

Some days Knives and his girlfriend, River, have screaming matches. Other days they have sex-fests that last for fucking hours. I wish I were joking (…*or not*). I swear I've walked in on my eccentric bassist and his lilac-haired girl one too many times. But my point is, he should be in his hotel room fucking her, not babysitting me at some grind-up-on-everybody-and-have-a-groupie-with-some-strangers club.

I don't even want to be here, in this club. I want to be in my hotel room, but Knives is stubborn, and so is our drummer, Dave, and guitarist, Zander, who just joined the bandwagon. They're all in this black leather booth, doing what friends do, trying to pick out a girl in here who'll make me forget all about my green-eyed wonderland, Rosalia Philips. *Pathetic, I know.*

We're in Cleveland, Ohio, now. City of vibrant art, musical history, and culture. Freaking parklands and sandstone everywhere. Of course, in the twelve hours we've been here, we've been around downtown, checked out Rocket Mortgage FieldHouse arena (where we'll be performing in front of just over 19,400 fans), and then also The Rock and Roll Hall of Fame on East 9th Street.

It wasn't our first time at The Rock and Roll Hall of Fame, but whenever we're in Cleveland, we like visiting 'cause it repumps our fuel and keeps us grounded.

Now, it's almost eleven o'clock at night, and all I want to do is rest ahead of our intense schedule tomorrow. It's going to be a killer day and will go something like this...

Wake up. Gym with our traveling personal trainers. Breakfast. Call my sister and talk to my nephew, Clément. A full run through practice until we're bleeding out cold. Annoy the shit out of my bandmates and then kiss their asses. *Smoke.*

Three exclusive interviews.

Smoke.

Feature on a high-ranking radio station. *Hella—fucking—hello.*

Smoke.

Thank fans for all their loving support.

Smoke.

Impromptu new tattoo.

Smoke.

Think I'm done? *I haven't even reached the fucking afternoon yet.*

Rehearses. Rehearsals again. Lunch. Even more rehearsals. Me probably perfecting the shit out of everything with our stage director and roadies, ensuring everything is ready to go. Gym again. My manager calls, and I email my publicists, who pray I'm being good.

Sound check.

THE ACUTAL TWO-HOUR CONCERT.

Meet and greet time, babyyy.

Dinner. Whiskey, thanks. More whiskey. Even more fucking whiskey. Read. Sleep. Can't sleep. Turn around. Try sleep. Still can't. Count rock stars. Curse. Song write. Finally sleep.

Oh, 'breathe' also goes in there somewhere.

But I can't rest. Not right now. I hate that my Diesel Rose band-mates know me more than myself. I won't breathe straight the entire tour if I don't get the crippling anxiety out.

I wonder if she loves him.

I wonder if she wants to marry him.

I wonder if they want to move in. Have ballet kids. Live a happily ever after fairy tale.

Swallowing thickly, I roam my gaze from our private security guards standing outside our booth, and then to the glistering bodies dancing and grinding on the low-lit dance floor, red and blue lights flashing everywhere.

Does Rosalia want to be Mrs. Daniels?

The entire thing makes me sick and has my stomach swirling and everything in it (namely whiskey, but still). Twenty-four hours ago, I was in Manhattan psyching myself up to see her. *Now* I'm in some fancy club in the middle of Cleveland, trying to forget her with somebody else's taste.

"Dude, we gotta be here all night?" Dave shouts from beside me, and yes, it's loud as heck in here, but he's *right next to me.* The poor guy is probably deaf from the intensity of his drumming. The roots of Diesel Rose. "Can't you just, I don't know, forget her with whiskey?"

"Stop busting his balls," Knives grumbles. "Can't you see he's still recovering from getting shit-faced all on his own like some loner?"

"True. Look, brother." Dave chuckles. "I don't know about you, but I wanna get some sleep before we put on our game face tomorrow."

Says the guy who just came off an all-night sex marathon…

I roll my eyes and laugh. "Shut up, man, we all know what went down last night."

Smirking darkly, Dave flips me off.

Introducing Jaxen Davidson, *ladies and gents.* He hates Jaxen, so we just call him Dave instead. He looks like the kind of guy you won't easily forget. Fully inked, including up his neck. Long chestnut hair with golden streaks. Leather everything. He's slightly taller than me and I'm six-three. He's a few years older than us, but his experience working in a few other bands before sticking with Diesel Rose is gold.

He also looks like he'll murder your entire family, including the plants, but if you get to know him, like really *get to know him, you'll see he's a real rad guy.*

Loyal.

Dedicated.

Effortlessly talented.

The effortless mediator.

Dear God, how many fights he's simmered down between us all. I mean, we're not a dysfunctional band, not in the slightest—I love these guys. Would cut off both arms for these guys—but living with them six to eight months at a time on tour sometimes is a nightmare waiting to happen.

I'm a very private guy. Like to keep to myself. Be alone with my whiskey, literature, rock classics, my inner demons, and all my trauma. It's why I write and am a renowned lyricist—because I crave escaping my flaws and I do it with dark poetry I lace into hit songs.

Then there's Knives, similar to me, *minus the literature.* My stand-offish best friend either sits in the corner of rooms, glaring at everybody with the devil in his eyes and that signature pulled up hoodie, or tries to talk and talk and talk to somebody to try and cleverly figure them out. Kind of like how he scared Rosalia away by always being so intense with her.

Ugh.

Then there's Zander, our charismatic guitarist with perfectly caramel skin, iconic brown eyes with violet brushfield speckles. He LOVES the heavy eyeliner, and while we all pride ourselves on being the scariest motherfuckers in the rock 'n' roll world, deep down Zander's a real softie. It's probably why he's the only one with a fiancée. *Also* why he's the only one of us who has a kid. Two-year-old Lola. She's the cutest damn thing. Has his eyes too. His girlfriend and Lola used to join some legs of our tours, but now that she's getting older, and we've really blown up, it's harder to do.

I know Zander constantly misses them. It's why right now he's going between typing on his phone with a smile, and then returning to true rocker mode the second he sets it down and glances my way, a smirk burning his lips. "So, you gotta forget about Rosalia or not?"

"I don't really know when this became everybody else's problem, but okay."

"Since I ratted you out because your depressed vibe affects the band," Knives offers.

Traitor.

Shrugging, I sigh. "I don't know, man, everything seems just so farfetched now…"

Knives's girl, River, moves her lips from his neck at my response. Slipping onto his lap, she gazes at me with a little sadness in her baby blue eyes and a small pout. I like to give her a lot of shit for dealing with my best friend, but we really formed a bond fast.

Surprising, I know. I hate people, remember?

But River's a fantastic, quirky woman who knows how to tame Knives's reckless heart. She's a little younger than us, a little rocker at heart too, and most of all, she understands the intensity and importance of Diesel Rose.

The grit.

The sacrifice.

The fact that Knives and she aren't always together.

And yet, they make it work through the bittersweet, the tabloids, and all the oceans.

"Diesel, do you really want to forget her?" River asks, her question still echoing in my head moments later, despite the hardcore rap with a heavy kick drum booming in the club.

Everybody's eyes flicker to me like I'm the main event.

Knives arches a brow behind River, telling me his girlfriend is wrong and *he* is right.

Do I really want to forget Rosalia?

The words are out before I know it. "Yes, I want to forget everything about Rosalia."

Liar.

Knives nods.

River frowns.

That's basically the perfect description of their relationship, by the way.

"I don't think that's really what you want to do." She sighs, adjusting her silver minidress, which glimmers in the dim light. "There was a part of your life that was consumed with her, yeah?"

"I wouldn't say *consumed*…"

Zander arches a cocky brow. "Man, should we roll back the tape four years back and show you the proof? She was always at band practice with us. You two used to stay in the studio late doing God knows what."

I glare at him. "Nothing. Happened."

He shrugs and gestures to River. "Okay, don't listen to me, but listen to her."

"Thanks." She grins. "Anyway, I say if you really want her, you need to prove it. Redemption after heartbreak is huge for us girls. You can't only tell her, you need to *show* her."

"She'll just tell me to leave…*again*."

"*Showing* her that you've changed doesn't need to cross a line, you can do it subtly."

"How?"

River shrugs, looking around the boys for help, but when they stare at her blankly, she turns back to me with a small smile. "Well, firstly…what are some things that she likes?"

Thinking, I scratch the scuff on my chin. "Ballet."

"Yeah, that's a given. What else?"

"Poetry and classic romances."

Knives scoffs. "Nauseating."

"No, it's not." River nudges his side and continues. "Cool, tell me more, what else?"

"Ummm." I drum my fingers against the sticky oak table. "I think…she likes hares."

Glancing up from his phone, Zander chokes on his vodka shot and turns to me with wide eyes. "The hell? *Hairs*? She likes hair*s*? What is she, a wig expert or something?"

Dave throws his head back in laughter.

I groan at Zander. "No, you fucker, not like that. I said *hares*, like rabbits and shit."

"*Bunnies*," Knives corrects, all serious, referring to what I told him this morning.

Remind me to kill him later.

"Okay, okay." River nods with her pearly white grin, cutting into our chaos. "So how about you find a way to make her forgive you via one of those avenues?"

"Like…" I rake a hand over my hair, clueless. "Buy her another first edition classic?"

"GOD NO!" Knives practically screams and bangs his head against the leather booth. "*That* is *exactly* what GOT YOU IN THIS MESS to begin with! NO MORE BOOKS!"

Our personal security guards snap their heads my way.

Dave gives them a head shake to signal we're all good, just some passionate talks.

"Okay, then what? What can I possibly do to win back her trust? God, I'm so fucking bad at this."

River smiles sympathetically and reaches her hand over the table. When I do nothing but stare at it, Dave sighs beside me and physically raises my hand to lace through hers.

Can you tell I'm not used to all this touchy-feely shit?

"Sometimes it's not about planning it to perfection, Diesel." She smiles softly. "Sometimes, it's about those heat of the moment gestures. You'll figure out what works for her, you will. You just need to be yourself because that's what Rosalia fell for. So do it."

With a heavy heart and even heavier breath, I nod, meaning every word. "I plan to."

"Sooo, does that mean no distraction?"

"Never wanted one, but yeah, no distraction. Let's get the hell outta here."

Grinning, River squeezes my hand tighter. "Plus, she sounds really cool and I'm in need of some more estrogen."

"But, babe." Knives sighs. His hands glide around her waist, and God, it's so weird seeing him the slightest bit affectionate. "It's clear that Rosalia doesn't want Diesel. She's long forgotten him. He hasn't."

I gesture to myself. "Yo, bro, can you not talk to me like I'm not just sitting here?"

"Shhh." He rolls his eyes. "I'm talking to my girl. Do you look like *my girl* to you?"

River cranes her neck to look at her boyfriend. "My gosh, you're the least romantic guy I've ever met! Just because you claim she's forgotten him doesn't mean she *really* has."

Knives arches a brow, almost taken aback. "And how would you know that, hmm?"

"Because I'm a woman."

"*Shocker.*" Dave snickers, gulping down his Jack and Coke. "Jerry Springer anyone?"

Knives glares him down. "Shut it, big fella."

"Big fella, huh?"

"Yeah, you're broad as fuck, ripped as hell, and tall as shit."

"Knight Ives!" River snaps, "*Skittles*, can you say one sentence without swearing?"

Silence trickles between all of us, and I can hardly keep it together as Knives looks at his girlfriend like she just told him she's hired a hitman to take him out. Wide eyes. Gaped mouth. A scarlet blush rushing up his neck and tip of his ears, mortified, and we all know why.

I can't suppress my amusement anymore and burst out laughing. "*Skittles*?"

Everybody erupts in rumbling laugher. It becomes a melodic sound…and then there's Knives, who has the look of death painting his face. He doesn't seem the slightest bit happy.

"Do you want to get murdered tonight, Diesel?" he grits.

It only has me chuckling more.

I flash River my widest smirk all night. "River, baby, so do you really call him *Skittles*?"

"Hmmm…" She wiggles her brows and turns to Knight, all giddy. Wrapping her arms around his neck, she purrs, "Do you want to answer that for me, or shall I, *Skittles*?"

And by the look in his eyes, Knight Ives wants to kill the entire room, a rocker in love.

I want that.

I want their happiness. I crave it. I just don't know how to give it. I don't know how to love and love back. *But I want it.*

Fuck, how I madly want to learn how with Rosalia Philips.

Chapter

SEVENTEEN

Rosalia

The following morning after *the night of*, Naomi definitely knew something was wrong. It wasn't anything I said in particular as I hand her a freshly brewed, warm cup of coffee across our kitchen counter, but it's the way she looks at me. *Even in her hungover state.*

"Girl." Naomi snaps her fingers. "I swear if you don't spill your little secret, I *will* go into full detective mode and find out."

I grin, loving not being able to control the way a laugh escapes me at just how amusing she looks right now. Her dark hair is up in a messy bun with that just-got-fucked look attached to it, and the mascara from last night is still smeared around her eyes like a full-on rock chick.

Rock.

My heart plummets.

I'm glad one of us got some action last night, well, *action* that didn't include bawling your eyes out over a guy who isn't exactly an ex but has the same sentiments in your heart to be exactly that.

Don't even think about that asshole, Rosalia.

I shrug, my smile small as I bring the coffee cup to my lips and take a small gulp.

Mmhmmm coffee. I'll forever love the Brazilians for this.

"Nothing's wrong." I shrug, *again*. There's a weight in my shoulders and it doesn't let go. "I'm just really tired from everything to do with Swan Lake and all the training, you know."

Naomi's eyes narrow. "So, this isn't about the fact that Trent didn't give a shit about you last night and chose his bros over his hoe?"

I can't help but laugh for what feels like the first time in forever.

"No, I'm totally fine with that. Trent and I aren't the kind of couple who do everything together. We need our space. He can have his freedom. I can have mine. I'm totally fine with that."

My best friend playfully rolls her eyes, then not so subtly says under her breath, "Aside from when you want that guy to fuck you, but he still hasn't because he's a damn celibate…"

Oh. My. God.

I almost choke on my coffee. "Trent is not a celibate. He's just… waiting."

"*Waiting*?"

"Yep."

"For what? Tom Hardy to come along and sweep you off your feet instead of his dic—"

"For the right *moment*. That's what he's said to me in the past."

Naomi's jaw drops. "Shit, he's a virgin?"

Groaning, I dramatically roll my eyes into the back of my brain. "Girl, so am I. What's wrong with that?"

"No, nothing, I'm all for it. I just…" Naomi screws up her brows. "Personally, I've just never been with a guy who's never fucked, that's all."

I stare at her blankly. "Naomi, you either find your guys in grind-on-me-all-night clubs or online where they end up being real-life daddies, so of course they aren't virgins."

Naomi groans, covering her eyes. "Oh God, don't remind me of that guy last night…"

"Just did." I wink, but the giddiness ripples out of me the second I reach for the refrigerator to grab a bottle of Aloe water before my excruciating eight hours of training, rehearsals, as well as my matinee and evening performances. I freeze, inches from the handle.

Elijah.

I pressed up against the damn refrigerator last night with Elijah.

I'm bursting to tell Naomi about last night to get her intake on all of this. My mind's still spiraling about everything that is *his* leather, edgy rocker presence. Elijah left me with so many questions last night. He left me with so many heartstrings snapped, ones I don't know if they'll ever be fixed and seamlessly put together again, like they were before he knocked on my door.

Last night, after Elijah left, I felt so numb. Like every single part of me was rocking me deep inside, like an internal hurricane. Each wave, each beat, each violent shaking sensation ricocheted in my heart, the same heart Elijah Diesel promised he would break four years ago.

The same heart I foolishly yearn for him to pull into the solace of his arms.

The same heart he stole and ripped out, leaving oozing crimson bloodstains all over.

With a heavy breath, I force Elijah to fizzle out of my mind and instead turn around to Naomi, offering her a small smile.

It takes a second for me to round the kitchen counter to her and lace her fingers through mine. "Okay, I've got to confess something, but you have to promise not to tell anybody…"

"Girl, we literally only hang around each other, but okay."

It's now or never, Rosalia.

"I saw Elijah Diesel last night," I blurt out.

"WHAT?" With widening eyes, Naomi's jaw drops at record speed. "Rosalia!"

Okay, well, that didn't go as smoothly as I would have liked.

"I know, I know. Elijah literally showed up at the front door last night. Remember those classic books that he gave me that I donated to a bookstore?"

"Yeah?"

"Well, he showed up with them. All four of them. Including *that* first edition."

She sighs but nods. "Well, go on, what did the asshole want?"

I go on, telling her everything about last night.

"OH MY GOD!" Naomi gasps when I finish. Her eyes soften as she brings her lips to my wrists, kissing my every scar like a silent tender lullaby to me. "*Babe…* Are you going to tell Trent?"

"That's the thing, I…I don't know."

"What are you going to do about Elijah?"

"I don't want to see him again."

Naomi's arches a knowing brow. "As much as I hate the guy, and I mean *really* hate that rock star, I know you're lying."

Dammit.

"I'm not."

"Girl, I know you. Tell me the truth."

"Okay." I sigh and squeeze her hand tighter, my voice softening to a whisper. "I didn't expect my heart to clench as much as it did last night. Seeing Elijah… I really missed him."

"Noooo," she groans, shaking her head. "You miss the *idea* of him, not *him.*"

Silence trickles between us, white noise, and my scattered heartbeats.

"But what if it isn't just an idea, Naomi, what if it's more?"

My best friend shakes her head confidently. "Babe, it's not. You just haven't given yourself time to really reflect on it all. It just happened last night. I promise that in time, you'll see Elijah just isn't for you. You two together…it's toxic, and not the good kind either."

I slowly nod, desperately wanting to change conversations and return to the one we were having about Trent. Because right now, it just seems safer.

"And, babe, I know it's so damn frustrating about Trent," I say. "But if roles were reversed and I was the alpha guy with gorgeous muscles and sparkle in my eye, and my girl told me she wanted to wait, I would wait, which is what I'm doing. *Waiting.* Plus, a relationship is much more than just sex. We're just…much more emotional than we are physical, I guess."

Pouting softly, Naomi nods. "I know, I know, but what I'm saying is; are you neglecting something because of him?"

"I'm going to give Mr. HotLips some breakfast…"

"Don't you dare move your fine ass." She laughs, pulling me closer, concern pooling in her eyes. "Does it get to you, Rosa?"

"Sometimes."

"So, tell him."

"I have."

"No," she says sternly, shaking her head. "You sit his ass down and you *tell him.*"

"I'm not trying to scare him away."

"You won't…" Naomi looks at me suspiciously, rocking on a wooden bar stool like it's just going to fly into outer space at any given second. "Okay, there's nothing wrong with *waiting,* but it's a red flag if he's telling you that he's waiting *for the right girl.*"

"He hasn't said that."

"Maybe not directly, but perhaps indirectly, yes."

"Look," I say, blowing out a sigh because it's way too early to talk about this. Especially when I'm still recovering from everything that is Elijah Diesel. "I totally get that, but Trent hasn't shown me any signs of anything wrong. I mean, he's so supportive and he's always there for me, and my parents love him—

"Aside from the fact he actually hasn't met your parents yet because of *schedules clash.* Yeah, because that was totally what you were saying last week when he canceled plans last minute to meet with your parents. Because he had a *thing* on."

"It was his mother's birthday in Vienna."

"And he didn't want you coming with him?"

"Maybe he wasn't comfortable with us meeting this early on."

"Or maybe he's fucking some bimbo in his dressing room."

My eyes widen. "Naomi!"

"Sorry, I don't know what came over me." She sighs, shaking her head. "Look, I'm all for Trent. I adore him. I think you guys are the greatest couple. But, you know, I'm the wisest, hungover girl, and my pounding head has a suspicion that this guy needs to prove himself a little better. You've been hurt before. So many times. I just don't want you to get hurt again."

My heart is pounding out of my chest as I stare into her glassy eyes. I know exactly what Naomi means. I feel it deep inside my core. I'm not stupid. I get what she's saying. Fuck, I've even *thought* about what she's saying so many times before. But Trent, I feel in my gut… is *different.*

He's not one of those guys who'll leave me hanging—he genuinely cares.

I see it in his eyes.

I see it in his actions.

I see it in his graceful words.

In all those small moments he thinks I don't even notice, *yet I do.*

Trent Daniels is my kryptonite. He really is. And nobody can change that.

My dressing room 'roommate', Portia Evans, *still* hates my guts. There's nothing quite like having a rival staring you down during excruciating hours of training, conditioning, daily company class with our ballet mistress, rehearsals, and even more rehearsals on top of that. *Then* to rupture the already grueling tension between me and her. It's seriously the last thing I needed today after the whirlwind that has been these last twelve hours.

I seriously still don't know how *everything* happens to me. I feel like it does, even though I know, deep down, it's just fate. *Well, maybe fate fucking with my mind constantly.*

The hatred isn't only embodied in the glares she gives me every time our shoulders brush in the corridor. All the way I always hear her talking behind my back to the other ballerinas in our team.

I want to say that I'm a social person, that I talk to everyone and everybody, but truth is, I like keeping to myself. But I guess in this dance industry, keeping to yourself can only get us to a certain place. Yes, with solitary beings roaming around the dance floor with our pointe ballerina shoes, extended positions, and all that jazz, but ballet is a community…

Just like everything else.

And yes, there are winners and losers. And there's nobody who can tell you you're a bigger loser than the owner of New York City Ballet and other high-class people like the head director of HR, Madame Eléa, but for the most part, it's a grueling, social sport. We need to rely on each other. Make sure we stand united and don't fall. *Literally.*

There's so much grit and trust that we have to put in everybody else. We all understand the sacrifices. The endless hours. The blistered feet, aching muscles, and scattered breaths. The reasons why we miss certain things like birthdays, parties, *life.* And yet, I find myself to be my best self when I'm alone.

I adore those quiet hours. Those where I book private dance rooms and dance all by myself, perfecting each move. Those where it's only the music, my wildly beating heart, and the own reflection of my every movement in the tall, mirrored walls.

I already knew today *wasn't* going to be like any other day. Not after Elijah. Now after Naomi, and resurfacing troubled waters in my relationship with Trent. It's got me on edge, and of course Portia has the fuel to the fire, because, well, of course she would.

Ever since I was appointed *prima ballerina*, Portia's had it in for me. Backstabbing. Lying. Bitching me to all the other dancers about how *ludicrous* that I, Rosalia Philips, at the prime age of twenty-one, am already that elite.

I'm not scared to prove my point because I've put in all the fucking work to get where I am. I've put in the grit. The determination. The long hours. And I know while everyone else has to have gone the extra mile and *I am not afraid to say it.*

I know my worth. I know my desires in life, and I'm not letting *anybody*—including Elijah Diesel, who alluded to fucking my way to the top—destroy me.

Portia's glare doesn't waver as I brush past her on the way to the private rehearsal rooms. She's in a group with four of her ballerina friends, on the floor stretching with their knee-high leg warmers and perfectly slicked back hair. Our matinee performance of Swan Lake isn't until another two hours and yet they already have their heads so perfectly slicked back.

Those crazed eyes narrowed down on me as I catch the end of what one of the other ballerinas says to Portia with her stuck-up smile.

"I still don't get how *she* is the *prima ballerina*," the ballerina gossips. "I mean, you came here before her, right?"

Portia keeps her eyes on me as she murmurs back loud enough for me to hear. "Sometimes favoritism wins all battles."

Seriously?

I can't help myself. I arch a brow because I am not taking this shit. Especially not today.

I slow in my stride, my heels planted on the white Italian marble floors. "If there's something you want to say, Portia, you better say it to my face. I've got better things to do today than pull knives out of my back."

The group of five girls simultaneously roll their eyes at me like they've practiced it. Like *this* is the performance of their lives.

Portia practically scoffs in my face. *Well, technically not in my face as she's still sitting on the floor.*

"Everything I've ever thought of you, I've said to your face, Rosalia."

Fire fuels inside me because, *is she serious?* Why can't we just all be happy for each other and supportive? Why does there always have to be this competition? And jealousy? It's honestly like this is some ballet version of *The Real Housewives of Manhattan*, except… we're not housewives.

"I don't know, you tell me, Portia," I hiss. "Seems like you've got a lot to say about me today."

"Oh, yeah?" Portia taunts. "And how would you know about that?"

"Your passive-aggressive tone."

"I don't have a passive-aggressive tone." She arches a cocky brow and full-on glares at me with that deep, mocking smolder. "Maybe *you* should check yourself out, Rosalia. I didn't know…it would be unfortunate if something were to happen during this season. Something that could shatter your whole career. So, I'd watch my back if I were you."

I glance around, aimlessly looking for a candid camera or something like that.

Did Portia seriously just threaten me?

I want to laugh like some psycho. I really do. But I'm way much more cultured than to stoop down to her level.

"If you think threatening me with a little bit of voodoo is going to do something in terms of the black magic you always seem to practice in our dressing room," I say, motioning my hand toward her and her posse, "then go right ahead, baby. But just be warned…" I pause for a second, solidifying my point with a cold hiss. "I am not, nor will I ever be, afraid of you."

And just like that, I storm off, my shoulders all tense and my mind spiraling with anger. It fuels my lungs every step away from them. I can hear their soft murmurs, cackling and belittling me even more, but I don't care.

I am Rosalie Philips—the *prima ballerina*—and I proved my shit to get here.

I ripped my own heart out of my chest, smeared my crimson blood all over the mirrored walls, until it was a beautiful yet tragic, poetic canvas of my life.

Torment.

Torment.

Torment.

And now, finally, through all the darkened clouds, I have emerged, the kind of girl I want to be. The kind of girl I always dreamed to be. The kind of girl who isn't taking shit anymore.

Not again.

Not after today.

Not from anybody.

Chapter

EIGHTEEN

Rosalia

Madame Eléa is my first pit stop before heading inside my dressing room. She's the head director of Human Resources and Organizational Development here at New York City Ballet. Any problems any dancers have, she is the person to speak with her and only her.

When I stepped into Lincoln Center just over three years ago, my heart literally ricocheted out of my chest. I was so built up with nerves that I felt as if I was having a nervous breakdown right there surrounded by the grand and luxury that faultless ballet at its finest. But then, after my numerous auditions and acceptance, I met with Madame Eléa, who congratulated me, and quite honestly, she isn't as scary as what everyone else perceives her to be…

You just have to be on a good side.

And '*being on her good side*' means being the absolute best you can be.

There isn't any room for failure here. I've learned that all from experience.

Madame Eléa's office is filled with everything that you could ever imagine that screams Parisian and Roman luxury intertwined into one. Golden accents. Velvet handcrafted furniture that possibly costs more than everything combined in Buckingham Palace.

I'm not even joking.

And of course, for the sweet *piece de resistance*, her entire tall ceiling is filled with gorgeous hand-painted masterpiece that embodies the Renascence and Michelangelo's 16th chapel at its best.

It's basically heaven in here…*or hell if she hates you.*

I softly knock on the edge of her open door and her light eyes flicker from typing away on her Mac behind her desk. The second Madame Eléa sees it's me, she shoots me a soft smile and motions with her head to come inside.

The views of Manhattan are crazy beautiful from her floor-to-ceiling windows. Seriously, I've never seen anything like it. The city is lively with the afternoon rush. I've been in this office a few times as night falls with the dazzling lights from Empire State Building to Brooklyn Heights, where I used to live.

It's beyond phenomenal. Something out of a movie.

Dreamy.

Incredible.

Hers for the taking.

Madame Eléa is a skilled and former experienced ballet dancer from Paris. She began dancing at the age of two and now that it's only a hobby, hasn't stopped yet. She's won numerous competitions, being the best of the best, and beating me by being *prima ballerina* of her Parisian company at the age of nineteen.

She's been dancing for the past forty years as an elite, and now she coaches one of the best if not the greatest ballet companies right here in New York City, baby.

"Rosalia Philips." She smiles broadly, her French accent thick as her perfectly red lips glowing in the warm Manhattan sun trickling through the room. "What can I do for you?"

I sit down, almost laughing because she was basically screaming her head off this morning after one of the ballerinas failed to tell her that she couldn't make the matinee dance.

Yeah, that was a nightmare waiting to happen.

"Madam." I smile back, raking a hand through my honey blonde hair when I see her blonde bombshell waves stab daggers into mine.

"I was wondering if there were any updates regarding the dressing room discussion that I brought up with you last week?"

Ah, that dreaded dressing room discussion.

Last week, I finally grew the balls to speak to her and subtly explain the whole situation between Portia and me. I mean, I never once mentioned anything to do with Portia or threw her under the bus, but I simply requested if I could have another dressing room. And I didn't care if it was with another ballerina, or with Trent, or by myself. I simply wasn't and *still* am not comfortable being around Portia's personal vendettas in a professional setting.

"Mmhmmm." Madame Eléa nods softly, a hum escaping her throat as she drums her perfectly manicured nails on her oak desk. They're the softest of dusty pinks, the same shade on my nails. "The board hasn't contacted me with an update as of date. However, I can request a follow-up via email."

And yes, peeps—*there's a board.* There's literally a board for everything. Any problem you have, anything at all, well, there are people who decide your fate before you plummet into said fate.

"No, that's okay." I smile, standing. "Don't disturb them. I just wanted to see if there were any updates—"

Madame Eléa holds up her hand, silently telling me to freeze with her eyes locked on her Mac, as her fingernails continually click away on her keyboard. "No, Rosalia, don't leave. You're here right now, so before I get my hands on any other task, I'll do this one right here."

Oh.

She blindly motions to the seat I just stood up from. "*Sit.*"

To the soundtrack of her erratic typing, I submit, sinking into the velvet chair with a tall, poised posture, my legs crossed and toes pointed.

With a few more clicks, she must hit send because this big swoosh echoes throughout her grand office.

Madame Eléa turns to me with a smile that doesn't quite meet her eyes, but then again, none of her smiles do. She's a reserved woman. Elegant. Private. Talented.

And rose perfume obsessed, but who am I to judge? That shit is probably Chanel or Dior.

"Is there anything else I could do for you, Rosalia, while you're here?" She glances down at her thin gold Rolex. "There's only an hour

and fifty-four minutes before your matinee show. You shouldn't be…
well, here."

"I know. I'm sorry. I just wanted to request any updates. So, you'll
let me know?"

She nods. "Definitely. As soon as they email me a response, I can
assure you that you will be sitting back down in that seat, looking into
my eyes with a sparkly new dressing room."

I nod back, and suddenly the tension begins to stiffen as things
get a little…awkward. I mean, there's nothing else I want to say to her,
but she's still staring back at me with authority, judgment circling her
light eyes. And although her smile is still there, it weakens in curiosity.

"While you're here, Rosalia, there's actually something I want to
talk to you about."

I keep on staring at her blankly.

"It will only take a few seconds," she adds.

"Of course, Madame."

"Well…" The glorious Madame Eléa leans back in her seat, her
satin rose gold pant suit glowing in the sunlight as that huge yellow
diamond rock on her wedding finger catches my eye. It's her third
one I've seen.

Yes, three marriages in the three different years I've been here.

I'm not judging. I'm just wondering what she does with all the
money aside from vacations to the Himalayas, charity work, and pulling into work with different cars every day.

Madame Eléa clears her throat (elegantly, may I add, not like a
dying chicken like me) and it snaps my attention back to her eyes.

"I've had a few concerned…*members* of our ballet company approach me lately about you, Rosalia," she begins. "More specifically
at the commencement of *this* Swan Lake season."

It takes all of me to control widening my eyes.

My breath stills…*what? What is she talking about?*

Concerned members? About me?

"Regarding…?" I trail off.

My fingers subtly wrap around the other wrist, cautiously tracing
my scars, out of view. I've never been more conscious of them than
last night when Elijah kissed them. The entire thing has me in knots.
I do so well to hide them and the demons away at work.

Did somebody…?

"*You,*" Madame Eléa repeats, ever so casually. Like I'm not here hyperventilating in front of one of the most renowned and prolific ballerinas turned HR aficionado to ever exist.

"*Me?*" I question, unsure how this all fits into place. "Concerned about *me?*"

She blows out an impatient sigh. "Yes, Rosalia, there is nobody else in the room."

"I, um—"

"It has come to several people's attention that perhaps your relationship with Trent Daniels isn't... How do I say..." Madame Eléa motions her wrist around in a small little wave as she thinks. "*N'est pas platonique.* Isn't professional. Innocent. *Professional.*"

Okay, someone come and kill me now.

While there isn't any exact policy, company policies surrounding in-house relationships, it's highly unadvised.

I get it. Professional lives can blur with personal lives and sometimes when there's tension that's left behind because of an ill-will lover, it's not exactly the greatest thing if you have to continue *working* with said dancer for the rest of a ballet season. Let alone having to have the entire company in on your turbulent relationship.

It's why Trent is so cautious about giving us any labels, and I get it. I really do. But it's not like Trent and I have banged our brains out in the communal kitchen when nobody is around. We're platonic as platonic can be when at work. *Well, aside from some makeout sessions after performances in either of our dressing rooms.*

My brows knit together in confusion. "I don't understand, Madame, is there a problem?"

"There *could* be," Madame Eléa warns, cocking her head to the side, all while lacing her fingers together and setting them dominantly over her crossed knees. "But I highly doubt that it's something the board would issue an inquiry on *if* nothing unfitting has happened between you both..."

She arches a stern brow. "Because *nothing has* happened in Lincoln Center, *oui?*"

"Correct."

"And you do not intend on anything *unfitting* happening here in Lincoln Center?"

Before I can answer, she's at me again. "To confirm, Rosalia, this relation that you have with Trent Daniels is beyond just professional, correct?"

"Yes, we've…been in a relationship for the past three months," I say, but when all she does is stare, that's when adrenaline kicks in, dopamine in my veins. *A thrill of risking it all…just like I felt whenever I was with Elijah Diesel.* "I didn't think it went against any of the rules—"

"Correct, it *doesn't*," Madame Eléa snaps, her eyes narrowing and *uh-oh*, looks like I'm slipping into her bad books. "However, can you confirm to me while looking in my eyes, Rosalia Philips, that *you*, a highly respected *prima ballerina* at New York City Ballet, may I add, are not engaging in any unsolicited sexual contact with Trent Daniels during working hours while representing one of the most, if not *the* most, prestigious and renowned ballet company, yes?"

With battered breaths, I nod softly. "Yes, Madame Eléa, at work, it is all platonic."

And in the bedroom too, but hey…

"Perfect. If that were to change, I want you to understand, Rosalia, that you will be hindering your reputation and position here at this company, as would Trent." Her gaze flickers to her Mac, uninterested in me as she huffs. "With that all said, you may leave now."

All the confidence I felt strolling into this office has deflated. I don't know at what point my conversation with her took a turn for the worst, but as I stand from my seat and bid her goodbye without her even noticing me, I know it has everything to do with my anti-boyfriend.

Her Mac pings a notification, and I take that as my cue to get the hell outta here.

I'm at her office door, seconds from stepping out, when Madame Eléa calls me back. "Oh, Rosalia, the board just replied with a confirmation on the success of your inquiry. You will be relocating to a dressing room of my choosing effective imminently… *Trent Daniels*."

Oh.

My.

God.

I'm thankful I'm still facing the door because my jaw literally drops.

And just like that, Madame Eléa is testing me...*just like every-thing else in this world.*

Dio Mio.

Trent hasn't stopped smoldering since I told him we're sharing a dressing room. I'm pretty sure Portia put some type of voodoo on me to trip and fall during our two Swan Lake performances today, but I didn't, so there's that.

Swan Lake. It's been one of my favorite stories ever since I was a little girl. So bittersweet. Poetic. I feel every emotion with every dance, every electric thrill and rapid heartbeat. Ballet has always been therapy for all the monsters clawing their way inside.

It's my livelihood.

Preforming in front of thousands isn't just rewarding, it's euphoric, and I get to do it all with *him.*

Trent.

Trent Daniels is all that matters as I snuggle into his warm arms with a content grin on my lips. He's staying over at mine tonight for the first time in forever. We're only a week into our first season, and already we're feeling the brunt of it. But I wouldn't have it any other way.

We're not like other couples. I've said this from the beginning. We exchange date nights for intense ballet rehearsals, and romantic spa days for soaking in Epsom salt baths with muscle aches and bunions. Yeahhh, I wish I were kidding. But right now, as the clock trickles past midnight and we zone into *Saturday Night Fever* playing on my TV across the room, it's just me, Trent, and the entire world at our fingertips.

It's all I think about as our fingers lace together over my bed sheets. His lips haven't stopped grazing over my bare shoulder the entire film and it has me smiling as I sink deeper into my silk pillow.

We may not be having mind-blowing sex, but all these little affectionate moments make up for it.

"So, I'm finally going to have a dressing room buddy, hmmm?" Trent chuckles.

I playfully roll my eyes. "Yeah, so no more staring at yourself in your mirror when you think nobody is watching."

Trent dramatically gasps and I giggle as I zone into his warm eyes. "Rosalia Philips, I would never."

"Prove it."

Trent keeps on staring at me in the low light, the TV's flickering reflection our only light. He studies me so intensely, his gaze ever so slowly moving from my eyes to my parted lips.

Kiss me, Trent, I want to murmur. *Kiss me, hug me, do anything.* But he doesn't.

"No." He simply flashes me that million-dollar smile and then rolls back to his side of the bed, his arms folded behind his head as he watches John Travolta and '70s disco at its finest. But I can't. I can't do anything but watch Trent with a soft frown tracing my lips. *Trent, do something.*

When we met, we instantly hit it off as friends, so it only makes sense that our friendship is still so tight. Movie nights. Mentoring. Being comfortable in each other's presence. It all comes naturally. It's our whole *relationship* that confuses me beyond words. I don't get how sometimes we slip back to simply being…

I want to feel those butterflies in my stomach. I want to feel them flutter like crazy and make me go insane, but truth is, ever since I saw Elijah Diesel last night…things have felt *different.* I've realized that the intensity of my feelings for Trent isn't as strong as everything I used to feel with Elijah. And while that's not a bad thing, it concerns me that we're in bed on a Monday night watching *Saturday Night Fever* for the millionth time instead of just *talking.*

But then I remember Trent was there at my worst. When I was in my blues, when the nerves became too much, whenever I thought I wouldn't be able to make it in this ballet career, Trent Daniels was *there.*

He isn't a rock star.

He isn't a literature lover.

He isn't a Harley obsessed leather kind of guy.

And that is *okay.*

Trent Daniels is a good guy, but I don't want to be just a convenience for him.

"Okay, so I haven't said anything…" Trent says with a slight chuckle, slipping one hand from behind his back to gesture toward the TV. "But that fucking book has been obstructing my view for the past forty minutes."

My eyes flicker to what exactly he's pointing to and...*oh*. My heart jumps up to my throat, swirling with nerves. *The Beautiful and Damned*. The one Elijah gave me. I left it there last night before diving straight into my bed, detesting the reminder of him.

"Oh, it's a hardback. Sorry, I'll move it."

"Don't worry, babe." Trent smiles over at me, and relief floods over me...that is until he practically jumps out of bed like we haven't been pushing our bodies all day. "I'll do it."

I don't make it in time to rush to Trent before he grips the hardback. I don't know why it bruises my soul so deeply as his fingers brush over the detailed cover and all the way down the book's spine. Maybe because there's still part of me that's nostalgic over the fact this was Elijah's, and he gave it to me. *Me.*

"Shit," Trent murmurs, flickering through the book while I'm here shifting from foot to foot because he's getting so close to destruction. I don't want to explain it all. Not tonight.

A kaleidoscope of '70s violet, pink, and red flashes across Trent's face as his brows furrow, stopping at a page. The title page. I don't need to look at Elijah's onyx cursive yet ever so masculine writing to know what my *boyfriend* is staring at. I already know. I just feel it.

But there's something new on the page. Something a little farther down what Trent read and Elijah's number. *There's another number.* My breaths slow as I try to make sense of it all. *Did Elijah...write down another number last night? Is that why he left this book behind?*

"Damn, Rosalia, is this a first edition?"

"Mmhmmm."

"You bought this?"

"Not exactly..."

Trent brings the page closer to the TV so he can see better. He mouths the words in silence, all while music blares from the speakers right beside us. After reading the words over twice, his eyes slowly roam up to meet mine. "Who the hell is *E*?"

I go to speak, but my dried mouth betrays me.

Trent glances down at the book, reading out the words I know so well I could recite them in reverse and have them written on my skin like a tattoo. "*Peaches*, I saw in your backpack that you enjoy the classics, so I thought I should give you another. Keep it, it's yours now. I've reread it a million times. Call me when you finish it, or whatever, E."

I shut my eyes, hating my palpitating heart.

I didn't need this reminder. At all.

"Is he a past lover boy or something?"

"Something like that…"

Silence fills the space between Trent and me, and when I reopen my eyes, there's a storm brewing in his. "Can you respond back without giving me half-ass answers?" He sneers, his jaw ticking, and for the first time since I've meet him, anger ripples across him. "Who the fuck is E?"

My jaw drops. "Trent—"

"Answer the damn question."

"He's no one. Just a guy I used to know when I was seventeen."

"A guy who just randomly goes around giving out first editions?"

"No, he gave that to me because he knew I loved classics." I sigh, shaking my head that it's come down to this. "He was in a band. A rock band."

Trent arches a cocky brow. "And he reads this shit?"

"Seriously? It's not *shit*."

"It's outdated."

You're outdated, thanks.

Glaring him down, I clench my jaw, taking in his true colors after dark. "It's *iconic* literature."

Trent can't even look at me for a full second before scoffing. "Sure, whatever." He practically slams *The Beautiful and Damned* in my hands and storms away. "I'm going to bed."

"Oh my God, Trent, what the hell?"

"It's fine, Rosalia, let it simmer," he grumbles, never daring to look at me once as he slides under the sheets, turning his back to face the wall.

My heart stings because…*what just happened*?

"Trent, listen to me, there's absolutely nothing you should be worried or jealous about." I try again, my feet still planted in the same exact spot, shocked. "He's nothing to me."

Trent doesn't even bother turning to face me, instead grumbles toward the wall, "Is that why you can't even tell me his fucking name?"

"What difference will it make, huh? Sounds to me like you don't trust me."

"Okay, fine, whatever, good night."

"Can we have a proper conversation? You're jumping to conclusions!"

"*Me*?" he screeches, launching from the bed. The second he eyes me as I tightly grip the hardback to my chest, he *scoffs*. "I'm not jumping to anything. You're the one acting all…"

"Acting all *what*?"

"Secretive."

My jaw drops.

Oh, fuck this shit for a joke.

We have a stare off, poison lacing my veins with every moment that passes.

"Okay, fine," I roar, waving my hands around, the book still in my grip. "His name is Elijah. Is that what you want? Huh? Elijah. *ELIJAH*! That's his fucking name and we were never together, so there is nothing to be jealous about. Maybe if you had an orgasm or two, you wouldn't be this freaking uptight!"

Yep. I just said that.

"Are you fucking serious, Rosalia?" He gapes. "So *that* is really what this is about, huh? The fact that we don't fuck?"

"It has nothing to do with that and everything to do with you not showing me you care!"

Trent scoffs again, all arrogant and snarky. "Oh, so I don't *care* now? Okay, okay."

"Not when you get all defensive when this should be a simple conversation!"

"Why can't you just let it be?"

"Because I want to know you're serious about us, that this isn't all a convenience for you!" I scream, grateful Naomi is out tonight because my pitch would have woken her up. "I mean, come on, give us a damn label! You're my *boyfriend*, what's so bad about that?"

"WHAT HAVE I SAID?" he grits, flinging the covers off him, exposing his iconic silk pajamas. "I said I don't want any labels!"

My brows rise.

Nah-ah, boy.

I'm like a damn hurricane with the velocity I stomp to Trent, just as he sits up in bed. I'm left glaring up at him, so pissed that our first fight has to be about *him*.

"Firstly," I hiss, snapping a finger in his face. "Don't you *ever* dare talk to me like I'm a minority in this damn relationship. We're equal, Trent Daniels. You want to scream at me again? You get out of my house and scream at my front door instead, got it? Secondly, news flash, buddy, there are two people in this relationship, so this is a *conversation*."

Trent can't stop shaking his head as he bores his eyes into mine. "You want a label?"

"Yes."

"Rip out that page with that guy's number and we'll have a freaking label."

"You don't trust me?"

"I don't trust *him*, whoever the hell he is."

"That just means you don't trust *me*," I screech, so sick of all of this. "I'm not ripping the page of a first edition out. I don't want to go to hell. I don't even talk to the guy, *at all*."

Trent steps closer. I've never seen him like this—so demanding. "Rip. Out. That. Page."

"Get. The. Hell. Out. Of. My. Face."

Trent does, but it barely makes a difference. His breaths heave into one as he whispers, "I care about you, Rosalia, a whole lot, and for you to question me is revolting. Good night."

And then he dives into bed, faces the other way, and pulls the sheets up over his face.

Is he serious?

Groaning, I switch off my TV and fall into the blanketing darkness with the fated *The Beautiful and Damned* hardback still in my grip. I can't believe this. *At all.*

Thanks, Elijah. So. Much.

When I slip back into my bed, Trent's warmth taunting me, the monsters crawl back in.

Again.

Chapter
NINETEEN

Rosalia

PAST.
Four Years Ago…

I used to believe in devilish monsters, but that stopped the day I met Elijah Diesel.

I was five when tragedy made its mark on my unsteady life.

Five when the first of the darkened monsters seeped into my skin.

Five with only my favorite rock chick Barbie with ratty hair and worn-out ballet slippers to my name.

I remember hugging them to my chest so tight when the two policewomen escorted me out of my childhood house that reeked of carnage. The house that was a crime scene. One I vowed to forever hate as they rubbed small circles on my back and helped me into their police cars.

They tried to distract me.

They put on the radio to some kid station.

They wanted to make me smile so brightly.

But nothing worked, and the ache in my heart let the monsters in.

I still remember the sympathetic look on the blonde police officer's face when we arrived at the police station, and she brought me into a room with red-colored bean bags and a coffee-stained oak table with colored paper and crayons. Looking back now, I understand why it wasn't a caged metal room with a tape recorder on the table that they brought me into.

They asked me questions about my mommy and daddy. Asked me what it was like to live with them. If they made me happy or sad. If they ever fought or shout. If Mommy would ever hit Daddy or vice versa. I remember constantly looking at my hands, which were all bloodied with the final thing I'll ever have of my parents.

I tried to wake them up.

Tried to shake them.

But their coldness transfixed me, and through my screams, that's when the first jolt of numbness in my heart unlocked its way to tears. Uncontrollable tears that turned into sobs as the pretty blond officer tried explaining, in the best way she knew how, that Mommy and Daddy were never coming back. That they had fluttered up into the bright blue sky and settled into a cloudy wonderland some like to call heaven.

I was five years old and a half when I entered my first foster home.

I was nine and a half years old when I entered my sixth.

Nobody knew how to handle me.

The girl who barely spoke a word, lacked stability, and barely looked people in the eye because death had haunted her heart. I had nobody during those years. Nobody to hold on to and squeeze tight. All I had was my Barbie and those ballet slippers, which at this point moths had eaten their way into the soles of my slippers and my Barbie was missing her head because some mean kid named Ryan snapped it off when I brought it into PE one day.

All of his friends laughed, and I spent the entire lunchtime with tears brimming my eyes, locked inside a cubical, adamant to reattach her head.

After the millionth cry, I slammed her head against the bathroom door, and then I did something in the heat of the moment that looking back, I don't know if I'd regret too much. I stormed right up to Ryan with my diamanté covered scissors and stabbed him right in his arm.

I was only seven, peeps.

Seven.

And I was already learning the ways to be a natural-born killer.

Oh, what was that you say? Ryan deserved it? Why yes, he really fucking did.

But it still didn't erase the fact that he ended up in ER with eight stitches, me with a one-week school suspension, and the police showing up at my former foster parents' house, and my Barbie *still* fucking decapitated.

"She's going to be trouble!" My former stepfather growled by my door at his wife that night when they thought I was asleep. "We can't keep her. We can't. She's going to end up on The First 48."

I was out of their house at the end of the month and thrust into the arms of another foster family soon after. And then another. I was eleven at this stage and I think that's when grief really hit. When the severity of everything that really happened to my life and trauma *really* started to sink in and make sense.

Eleven was a big year for me. It was the year of starting middle school. The year my former foster parents enrolled me in tennis and track, even though ballet was what I really loved. The first time getting my period and I literally thought I was bleeding to death.

Eleven was the year I began walking home from school or taking the bus. When I began noticing the not so nice side of New York and witnessed people shoot up cocaine, drinking a lot of alcohol, and popping pills, sometimes kids not much older than me.

Eleven was the year I learned what syringes were. What drugs were. How they could paralyze your life from the inside out, really fuck you over until it hurts to breathe.

It was also the year I learned the truth about my parents' deaths. That it was a murder suicide. That my mother shot my father in the heart with his own pistol, spraying blood everywhere and then she overdosed.

Eleven was the year I started skipping meals.

When I learned that life was a bleak, cruel mess.

Where I got into the dance team at school, and ballet fueled my lungs again.

It was also the year that changed me the most but destroyed me the absolute worst.

Grief became too much, so I started to rebel in the only way I knew how...speaking up. I got into one too many fights with my former foster parents that I know I shouldn't have. I told them that they couldn't control me. That I wasn't nor could I ever be their true daughter.

My foster mom was cool about it and would always try to empathize with me.

My former foster father, who was the kindest man I knew at that stage, was always calm, but that night he lost it. He slammed up against my bedroom wall, gripped my chin, and full-on shouted in my face, "WOULD YOU RATHER BE BACK WITH YOUR CRACKHEAD PARENTS? HUH? WELL, IT'S TOO FUCKING LATE FOR THAT, ROSALIA. THEY'RE DEAD. ALL BECAUSE THEY COULDN'T LOVE YOU."

And then he hit me so hard in the face that I saw stars. It was so vicious that when I went to protect my throbbing cheek, he hit me again, but this time his wedding band seeped across my skin so viciously that it created a cut between my hand. It wouldn't stop bleeding and he couldn't stop apologizing.

I forgave him.

I did because I didn't want to adjust to another family.

I was already hurting. I didn't want to go over it all again.

But it was too late.

A neighbor heard all the commotion and called the police. CPS took me away that same night and... That's when the abandonment issues began branding themselves. When the monsters crawled in and stayed with me every lonely night as the bats fluttered like crazy outside my bedroom window, a new scar running down my hand, forever reminding me of pain.

And then my current foster parents came through and it changed *everything.*

They loved me.

Accepted me for me.

Let me get out of my skin.

They made me see a therapist, which did shit all, but still, I appreciate the gesture. With them, I feel seen, and I just want to make them proud.

It's crazy how life works sometimes. All the silver linings that come out of the bittersweet. Like how when my foster mom found those dusty ballet shoes of mine and surprised me with new ones *and* allowed me to take ballet classes before organizing for me to audition at The School of American Ballet, the most renowned ballet academy in the world, right here in New York.

My heart has beat to a different rhythm ever since.

One with love. And warmth. And hope.

I aced the summer program, which led me to excel and be accepted as a ballet student year-round. Four years later, and now at seventeen, I owe all my success in being an advanced ballerina to my foster mom and dad. They don't try to treat me like anything I'm not. They simply treat me as me.

And yet, still, most nights those monsters still crawl through. Taunting my dreams and hindering my breaths. Flashes of my parents, so lifeless. It's tortuous. It ruins me slowly, and yet the moment I set eyes on my edgy onyx-eyed rock star, Elijah Diesel, with his iconic studded leather jacket and soft black eyeliner, all the fear began to melt.

Being around Elijah makes me want to embrace those monsters. Makes me want to face them and show them I'm no longer that frightened five-year-old girl. I'm a seventeen-year-old girl with a forbidden boy crush, and I'm ready to kick ass.

I try and let that be my mantra right now as I sink deeper into the plush bus seat.

Smiling softly, I can't help but stare out the window at Manhattan's blinding lights that rush past me in fast motion. It's a few hours since Elijah and I had dinner at *Sogni D'oro*. Less than forty minutes since Elijah closed up the studio where we spilled out dark, heavy truths and offered to hail me a taxi home.

I told him I preferred to take the bus, and when I said that he went into full-on alpha mode. Elijah Diesel may have a heart as hard as steel, but underneath all that armor, I know he really does care. Which is why he suggested (okay, more like demanded) he take the bus home with me to make sure I got home safe. My dried tear-stained cheeks were replaced with a crawling, big, goofy grin when he said it.

Now we're seconds away from reaching the bus stop right around the corner from my house, and as I glance over at Elijah, I find he's already looking my way. I've had such a good time tonight. We've come a huge way and I don't want any of that to end.

Not now.

I like how real Elijah makes me feel.

I like just how much of my true self I can be around him.

What I admitted to him tonight, about my real parents, was a big thing for me. I've never been so honest with anybody before, nobody aside from my best friend, Naomi, who is literally going to die when I tell her that this hot, broody rocker rode the bus with me just to ensure I made it home all right.

"Rosalia? You good?"

I clear my throat, snapping out of my trance and getting lost in his eyes instead. "Yeah, why wouldn't I be?"

"You zoned out for the past ten minutes."

"Huh?"

"You were staring out the window so intensely, and I tried calling your name, but I couldn't snap you outta it."

There's a pang in my chest as I swallow my pride. "Oh, sorry, I've just been thinking…about my parents a lot."

"Your biological parents?"

I nod.

Elijah flickers his gaze back and forth between my eyes, his stare intense and hot like a gun. Slowly, he furrows his brows, as if he wants to understand something. "Do you think about them often?"

"Often enough."

"Do you…" Elijah pauses for a moment and lets out a long breath. "Do you want to talk about it more?"

"Not really."

Nodding, he rakes a hand through his dark hair with the waviest ends, a habit I've noticed he does whenever he's a little stressed or anxious.

"Okay, but, uh." Elijah leans forward in the bus seat, his elbows by his jeans-covered knees as he rubs his stubbled jaw. "You know you can…"

His eyes shut for what feels like a century, strained, as deep crow's feet appear. When his gaze finally lands on me, there's a depth within it that takes my breath away. It's so different, raw, and *beautiful.*

Real emotion.

This is real emotion I'm getting from the guy who once busted into my house at midnight to give me back my schoolbag.

"You do know," Elijah begins, almost seeming a little nervous, like it's killing him to say this. "If you ever wanted to talk about it, even if you just want to have a rant session to feel fucking better, I'm…*here.* You can call or text me whenever."

Oh. My. God.

Did Elijah Diesel really just say that?

And remember, we're talking about the man who DETESTS calling or texting!

My heart squeezes even though I know this means nothing to Elijah. Not in the way I would have hoped. He's made it clear that what we have here, whatever we may have, needs to remain platonic.

"That's really kind, Elijah." I smile softly, leaning my head against his shoulder. "I may just take you up on that."

I love how I can feel his heartbeat grow wild against my ear, his scorching skin beneath his shirt. He took off his leather jacket the second we got in here, and it's just been neatly resting in his lap, alongside the paper bag the three romantic classics he bought me are in, the entire bus ride.

Elijah doesn't reply, but by the way his breaths labor, I know he understands how much just him being here means to me. I'm seventeen. He's almost thirty-two. He shouldn't be the one I'm with in the middle of the night, and yet, for some reason, I always am.

The bus comes to a slow, and I glance out the window, noticing it's my stop. It's just after 2:00 a.m. and the streets are coated in darkness aside from the warm glow of Art Deco streetlights every few houses.

If I didn't see Elijah tonight at the bookstore, I would have been home a good five hours ago, but I prefer it this way. Elijah's making me live. The very thought of stepping out of this bus alone and encountering a night crawler makes my skin do just that…crawl.

It's as if my melancholic God reads my mind completely when he says, "I'm walking you home, *Peaches.*"

I would break out into dance if there weren't four men scattered around the bus practically eye fucking me.

Jerks.

I'm not blind to the stare off Elijah gives every single one of them as he slips his hand on my lower back and walks off the bus with me.

The bus driver literally speeds off the second our feet hit the sidewalk.

We walk around the corner side by side, in a silence that's probably the most comfortable it's ever been. I like how relaxed my body is around him. Which made no sense at all, and yet, in some strange fucked up way, it did.

I want this feeling to last forever.

Sadness ripples through my entire body when we come to a slow in front of my Brooklyn Height's brownstone. The one with the mint-green-colored frontage, iron casting rail, and golden lion head for a doorbell.

I turn to Elijah, and he glances down at me in his six-foot-three stance.

"Well, I guess this is"—I clear my throat, letting the unfinished sentence fizzle in the air for a second—"where we say good night."

"I guess." Elijah shrugs as if it's nothing, but I can tell through my Spidey sense he's just trying to play it cool.

I don't know if I've ever seen Elijah so awkward before as he rocks on his heels, his eyes everywhere but me. He blindly hands me my books, but there's a clench in his jaw that I don't quite understand.

What are you thinking, Elijah Diesel?

Are you thinking the same thing as me?

"Thank you for tonight, Elijah, I really mean it."

He nods, his eyes still not quite meeting mine.

"And thanks for the books."

Another nod.

"Oh, um, and thanks for dinner too. You know, I could have paid for it…"

A half smirk crawls his lips when he eventually finds my eyes. "We've been over that, *Peaches*."

I guess we have.

I stand there, wrapping my arms around the books against my chest for dear life, wanting to stall as much as I can. I don't want this night to end. I want to stay like this with him forever.

Our stare intensifies, so much emotion laced inside all of our forbiddance.

"Thank you for—"

"Jesus Christ, Rosalia." Elijah laughs, and when he does it's a beautiful one, his dimples seeping through his dark beard. "Didn't think I did enough for you to thank me like I'm some god."

I girlishly grin because all I can think is, *You are some god, Elijah Diesel. My god.*

"I was just going to say…" That damn knot at the back of my throat begins trickling through, reappearing. "Thank you for allowing me to speak my dark and heavy truths. They've been weighting down on me for so long, and even though it's not everything, it's something."

Elijah looks at me with so much genuine care, I almost cry.

"You never, *ever*, need to thank me for that, *Peaches*," he whispers, all low and raspy. "Promise me."

"Well." I suck in a breath, summoning the courage to say the next words even though they bring hurricanes to the pit of my stomach. "I should head inside now."

"Mmhmmm." He nods, and simply slips his hands into his jean pockets. "Yeah, you should."

With my thumb, I motion to my brownstone behind me. "Well, uh, good night."

"Night." Elijah dips his head, doused in the moonlight, tobacco, and sin.

When the heat in his stare gets too much, I spin on my heels and rush up my porch steps like a fool. *Why didn't you hug him? Kiss his cheek? Shake his hand? I don't know, anything.*

I internally groan.

Ugh. You're such a loser, Rosalia Philips.

The second I unlock the front door with my key, I shut my eyes and count to three. When I glance over my shoulder, a soft bite in my lower lip, Elijah Diesel is standing there like my midnight protector, simply waiting for me to enter safely.

"*Sogni d'oro*," I murmur into the darkness. "It means *sweet dreams*, like the name of the restaurant we went to."

The warm chuckle that escapes this man is so cold it'll forever haunt me for all the right reasons. "*Beaux rêves*. French. Means the same thing, angel."

Angel.

God, hearing him speak French does something to me…something wild.

The moment I'm inside my brownstone and I click the door locked, I waste no time rushing to the formal living room that overlooks the street view. Like a damn detective, I slowly part the shades, adamant to get one final look of my guardian devil dressed in leather.

But like a walking ghost, *Elijah's already gone.*

And that's when the monsters crawl in, eating out my heart, leaving me empty inside.

Chapter

TWENTY

Elijah

That plan I have to win Rosalia Philips back, well...it isn't exactly going smoothly. Last night after our Connecticut show, I felt sorry for myself and did something a grown-ass man pushing thirty-six should never do.

Yep. I did it.

I did the inevitable.

Searched up Rosalia online at a quarter to two in my Uncasville hotel room, and what did I find? Disappointment and a whole lot of fucking depression on top of it.

Hurricane blonde (as I once referred to her) has all of her social media set on private. And unless I grow this magical ability to erase the past four years and how we left things, my chances of doing a little digging into her life are at an all-time low.

But, oh, I landed a goldmine with that fucker she's *dating*. Turns out Mr. Trenton Daniels—shortened to Trent because he's one of *those* guys—is a dance mastermind. Lover of all things vegan, partying, and himself. I would have guessed he's one of those assholes who post pictures of themselves with their first ever fish catch, but then I scrolled down his feed to the depths of hell and found that exact picture.

There were photos of him.

Photos of traveling the world, late-night ballet rehearsals, his lively team of dancers.

Photos of them.

I swear to God, with every photo, Rosalia stole my breath away. She told me they've been together for three months, but there were photos of them from before that, so it must have been some friends-to-lovers shit.

I hate seeing them together.

Hate their kisses in front of a huge Swan Lake sign, the dazzling lights illuminating her flawlessness.

Hate how perfectly synced they are to each other and how they just make sense.

She's a ballerina.

So is he.

He's all prim and proper.

So is she.

He wears dress shirts, slacks, ties.

She wears cocktail dresses, blazers, stilettos.

Trent is changing her. Changing her for the worst. Some of the things I adored about Rosalia were the chokers, the fishnet stockings, the rebellion fluttering in her eyes…*she doesn't have that with him.*

That asshole isn't a fucking rock star.

He isn't the man who trampled over Rosalia.

He isn't a product of a psychedelic nightmare laced with anxiety, poetry, and mommy issues.

He's Trent Daniels, Rosalia's boyfriend, and my personal demise.

And I won't stop until he gets his hands off what's mine.

Fuccck.

I mark a thick line through the mammoth of lyrics, throwing my leather journal to the floor with so much intensity its slap ricochets throughout our silent private studio.

"Dude, the fuck?" Knives jolts, practically slamming his hand against his bass guitar, his rings smacking against the rosewood. "What the hell happened to our quiet time?"

Our drummer, Dave, arching a brow as he glances at us from the couch he's lying on. The visual is uncanny. A five-foot-five giant on a couch that was intended for…*well*, not guys built like him.

"*Quiet time*?" He chuckles. "What are we in? Fucking kindergarten, man?"

"Can you guys just shut up?" Zander roars from the other side of the room, pacing up and down with his phone still pressed to his ear like a magnet. He covers the speaker and glares at every one of us. "I'm trying to talk to my *fiancée* and there's no privacy. This place is like a fucking dungeon."

Seriously?

Now it's my time to arch a brow at our guitarist. "Am I the only one who cares about this deadline? We have a *new single to record and produce* in the month after this tour ends. We seriously only have a few weeks to perfect writing it and everything else that comes with it. We signed a contract with Emmett. I mean, what the fuck were we thinking, huh?"

Knives groans from where he's standing, swirling a glass cola bottle in his grip. And the more I focus on that bottle, on the condensation lathering on every side, I see exactly the kind of color it is. And my heart, well, it plunges into depths of hell.

Cherry.

Cherry Cola.

That was *her* favorite *too*.

The memories of her sweetened tongue laced with mine and the desire that it brought fires a sensation across my chest that I've never felt before. *A sensation I'm pretty sure I'll never feel again.*

Fuck. Why is she a constant in my mind?

Raking a frustrated hand through my hair, I stand up, kicking the trash can with overflowing pieces of cursed papers. Crumbled papers. Torn-out papers of lyrics and lyrics and lyrics that don't sit right.

When I write songs, it's like fuel. An endless amount of word vomit. I black out to a space of no return. It's like a gray area. A purgatory. When I write what's deep inside my soul, I zone out. And I don't expect anyone else to interrupt me until the words pour out like liquid gold.

But that isn't the case today. Shit, it hasn't been the case on the tour.

Emmett, our trusted record producer, has been on our backs to get this new single released shortly after the end of the tour. We've already released six albums in total, the last just before commencing this world tour, but the fans want more, and quite frankly, so do we.

But my muse is dead. *And so am I.*

Okay, Rosalia Philips isn't dead. She's very much alive. But she's taunting my mind. It's been two weeks. Exactly two weeks since I showed up at her door and yet, nothing.

No calls.

No texts.

Nothing.

It's clear that she's blatantly ignoring me...or meant it when she told me to leave. Maybe it's true. Maybe she wants nothing to do with me. But the look in Rosalia's eyes—that swelling pit of emotion, that lust roaming up those green irises when I held her tight after seeing those faded scars and she squeezed me back like it was the end of the world—isn't a girl trying to forget a guy.

It's a girl adamant, and in her head, is telling her heart to forget me.

I'm not being selfish. I'm not an ass. I'm not crazy. *Okay, maybe.* But the truth of the matter is, if Rosalie Philips truly wanted me out of her life, I would step away.

Undoubtedly.

A hand to my icy cold heart, I would.

But when I looked in Rosalia Philips's eyes two weeks ago, they were begging me to stay, even though the rest of her was telling me to *get fucked.*

So yeahhhhhh, the lyrics aren't exactly fucking flowing.

My mind isn't exactly the seamless place it should be.

And my muse—well, as I said—*fucking dead.*

It's why I give my bandmates a death glare, glaring around the claustrophobic private studio that we've hired for the remaining weekend while we're playing here in Connecticut. It's one of the cities that we're staying in the longest. Four days, to be exact. And after a killer concert last night, today, even though my ears are ringing (something I'll never quite get used to), we're working on this single instead of resting. 'Cause resting's for the wicked, right?

I want to get the new song right. *I want to get this single, so fucking right.*

I want people to feel the emotion.

I want the rock to ricochet through their brains.

I want the lyrics to emote something. Let them be all waxy and poetic. Let them be as purple prose as they can be. I want something that speaks to the mind. That fuels us and the entire world with it. That makes Diesel Rose even more iconic than what we already are. That makes me feel like Rosalia Philips is *right here.*

A heavy breath escapes my lungs, licking the air laced with tobacco and rock 'n' roll.

I want her to hear these lyrics.

I want these lyrics to be *for her.*

I don't care if the song is encrypted.

I don't care if it brings controversial publicity and my manager and publicist blast my emails and my phone with calls because I've alluded to a woman and now fans want to know everything. *I've already had that problem. Numerous times. Namely, for "Fragments of You".*

I don't care if my bandmates give me shit because I'm a perfectionist lyricist at heart.

I don't care if the diabolic part of me causes so much carnage until I can barely breathe.

I. Want. To. Get. These. Lyrics. Dead-on.

"So, if you wouldn't mind," I grit, violently slamming my Sharpie against the wall with so much aggression, I don't care if I've punctured a hole in it or not. "I'm trying to do something over here."

All guys snap their heads my way. Dave gets up on the couch to look at me as if I've just told him I'm on a suicide mission.

"Calm down, Diesel, ain't nobody brought fuel to your fire," he says slowly—*the mediator*—his eyes darker than what I remember. "We're *all* in Diesel Rose. It ain't just you."

"I'm the damn lyricist. If hell comes burnin' up on us, it's all on me!"

Knives keeps on staring, while Zander, after murmuring something into his phone, presses it to his chest.

"Well, luckily, you're not a solo act," he spits, and just like that our guitarist storms out of the studio.

Knives arrogantly murmurs something under his breath.

I arch a brow, my blood already boiling and not because of him. But right now, these guys are the only people in view. The only ones I can take out my angry on, as much as I shouldn't.

"The hell did you say, hmm?" I snap, cocking my head to the side. "You trying to say something? Because then I think you should fucking say it, Knight Ives, if you've got something on your mind."

"Calm your fucking nipple rings, Diesel." Knives's jaw ticks, forever glaring me down.

Dave stands up and rolls back his shoulders, his notes slipping from his lap to the couch.

"Come on, dude." Dave sighs while tying up his long hair into the meanest man bun, his dark nail polish glimmering against the bright recessed lights. "Stop killing yourself over this. Your definition of perfect is unattainable. It's only going to lead to burnout, and we can't have that, man. You're the bones of Diesel Rose."

He picks up one of my leather journals and flickers through my scattered lyrics, his eyes lighting up when he does. "Yo, you dick, are you blind or some shit? Look at this! Look. At. This. *This is all* motherfucking gold. I'm telling you. You're Elijah Diesel. Anything you write is pure gold. It's magic. Our fans will love it, like they always so, so don't be a pussy."

I grind my sexily defined jaw. "I'm not being a fucking pussy about it."

The idiot has the audacity to crack a soft smirk. "You are, but sure…"

"I can't get the lyrics to flow. Nothing makes sense."

"I'm looking at them and I'm telling you they are."

"They. *Aren't.* I want something that blows my freaking mind. What I have isn't it."

"It could be."

"It doesn't work that way," I growl, bunching up my fist because it's the only thing that brings me solace. "If we don't have it right, we're fucked. Emerson and Emmett are expecting this to be perfect. Hell, the entire whole world is."

"Perfection isn't everything," Knife snaps.

I almost laugh in irritation. "But it's *something*."

Knives rolls his eyes, running his fingers across his bass. Each deep chord reverberates inside my chest, beating slower with every fleeting second.

A boyfriend.

She has a fucking boyfriend in tights.

Jesus.

The room simmers without me saying another word, and just like that, psychopath Elijah Diesel is back from the pits of hell. Obsessive. Catastrophic. Motionless. It's the type of man I become when the world becomes so dark, I can barely breathe. It's a constant—the darkness. It's been buried in my soul since the day I was born.

Dark, dark, darkness…it's all I'll ever see. It's all I'll ever be.

And.

That.

Fucking.

Scares.

Me.

Yeah, that's right, I'm *scared* of myself.

Of what I may do if I don't get this song right.

Of what I may do if I don't see Rosalia Philips again.

Of what I may do if I just don't feel like breathing anymore.

It's why those faded white scars on her wrist (and some not so faded) affected me so much, because I've been there. I've been to that level of not wanting to be alive. And right now, it doesn't matter that I'm rich. It doesn't matter that I'm a rock star.

It doesn't matter that people know my face. My voice. My name.

All that matters is that my heart doesn't feel right. It feels lost. Super lonely. Swimming in an endless ocean of nothingness. And I know I deserve it. I'm a bad guy. It doesn't matter how much I pay my publicist to prove I'm not. *I. Am. A. Bad. Guy.*

Maybe Rosalia deserves a good guy. Maybe she deserves Trent Daniels after all. But…

I need *my* muse.

And I *need her now.*

Before I fuck this up for all of us.

She texted.

I think I may have a nervous breakdown right here in the middle of my hotel room as I grip my phone tighter, reading the text from the *unknown* number three times.

> **UNKNOWN:** If you don't collect *The Beautiful and Damned,* I'm shredding it.

Slowly, I smirk.

Oh, hello there, Peaches…

I quickly save her new number on my phone after deleting it four years ago.

> **ELIJAH:** You wouldn't dare…

> **ROSALIA:** Try me.

Another text vibrates my phone.

> **ROSALIA:** Can I leave it at Hayes's Bookstore for you?

> ELIJAH: No, I'm in Connecticut until tomorrow morning, then the boys and I are flying out to Boston. Tonight was our last show here in Connecticut.

> **ROSALIA:** When will you be back in NYC?

> **ELIJAH:** I won't. Not until the end of next month. October 29th. I'm on tour.

> **ROSALIA:** So… I shred it?

> **ELIJAH:** Fuck no. I'll meet you somewhere tonight.

> **ROSALIA:** Tonig*ht*?

> **ELIJAH:** Did I stutter?

ROSALIA: Ha. Ha… Didn't you say you're in CT? How can you meet me?

ELIJAH: Easy. I'll drive to NYC.

ROSALIA: It's almost midnight.

ELIJAH: And? You're the one who messaged me at this hour.

ROSALIA: I just got off work.

A moment passes where I get lost in the thought of her.

ELIJAH: Rosalia?

ROSALIA: Elijah?

ELIJAH: Meet me at Tipi's Laundromat on 9th Ave in NYC at 2a.m.

ROSALIA: 2.a.m? What the hell? And did you just say a laundromat?

I chuckle.

Rosalia, Rosalia, Rosalia, you've never met anybody like me…

ELIJAH: It's a quiet, twenty-four-hour place. Don't stand me up.

My heart is in my throat when I shut my phone with a sharp breath. *Yes, Elijah Diesel, you chickenshit, this isn't a dream. You're actually fucking doing this.*

I'm going to see Rosalia Philips, for the first time in weeks, in a damn *laundromat.*

The small smile I didn't even know I had smeared over my lips drops.

Wait… why did I suggest a laundromat?

Oh.

My.

Rock 'n' Roll God.

I. Need. Fucking. Therapy.

When my bodyguard/driver slows in front of Tipi's laundromat in rainy New York City, all the words I want to say to Rosalia are all jumbled up inside. There are so many things I *could* say. So many things I *should* say. And yet, every thought seems like broken pieces of poetry.

Just like those lyrics I can't seem to find...

"Mr. Diesel," Maverick announces, flickering his gaze to me in the rearview mirror. "We've arrived."

I roll my head across the leather headrest with a slight nod, my eyes burning from all my missed sleep. But I don't care. I'm not missing this occasion to see Rosalia Philips. She thinks I'm here because I so desperately want the book—I don't. I'm here because I want to smooth things between us, and that means owning my shit.

Maverick isn't only my driver. He's also my personal bodyguard. This guy travels with me everywhere. Tours. International awards. Walking down Sunset. You name it, he's there. Except for right now. It's just before 2:00 a.m and heavy rain cascades across Manhattan, violently beating down.

I've missed this city.

It's nostalgia.

The reflection of warm red hue store lights in puddles, the murky, darkened navy vibes.

"Don't wait for me here. Don't know how long I'll be. I'll text you when I need you."

"You sure you don't want any eyes on you?"

A boyish half smirk works up my lips. "Cross my heart, brother, go around."

The moment I step out, that familiar Manhattan air fuels me. God, it's been so long since I've called Manhattan home. After the craziness of being the opening act for *Devil's Advocate and The Fiery Halos*, and Diesel Rose exploding, the boys and I have traveled to so many cities, immersed ourselves in so many cultures. But I still call that industrial loft apartment in Lexington Avenue home.

There's just something about New York City that I can't detach myself from... *Her.*

If I could have it my way, I would have kept everything how I left it that night...

The bedsheets kissed with her scent.

My lips on hers all night long.

Scream blaring from the TV.

But I can't, and I'm reminded of it with every cleaning invoice.

Rain pelts down on my studded leather jacket, slithering down like a dozen snakes before dripping to my tattered hands. The rain doesn't bother me. The way it seeps across my face and ripples down my neck when I run my fingers through my hair, sticking it back.

With a honk of the horn, Maverick pulls away from the sidewalk and I watch with bated breath as the black BMW becomes smaller and smaller. There are not too many cars going around tonight. It's strange. This feels like the calm before the storm, and I don't like the eerie feeling.

I'll make it back to Connecticut before dawn. Before Knight, Dave, or Zander question my absence. *Because that would be a nightmare.*

Ugh, I've got to make it better with them too.

I didn't mean to snap. I just…I hate how at times they don't see the lyrics like I do. They don't understand that it's the shit holding the whole band together. Without the lyrics, we have no true purpose, and the fact that they're not flowing out of me…it worries me.

So fucking problematic.

But perhaps, seeing Rosalia will change all that…

Squaring my shoulders, I step inside Tipi's laundromat, its fresh linen and lavender detergent settling my violent mind. There's nobody else in here. *Good.* It's a huge laundromat, the modern kind with sleek white marble floors, low rock music, and industrial washing machines aligning the back wall, alongside the maze of washers, dryers, and vending machines.

It's an escape. A flashback to my old life. One that didn't include being mobbed whenever I went. I like it here. In the quiet. During the quiet hours with the slightly dimmed lights, giving a little bit of a softer hue across the laundromat.

I check my watch for a thousand times, and when it hits 2:00 a.m. and Rosalia still isn't here, I begin walking around the neat washing machines and dryer setup.

The walking turns into pacing.

Pacing into crippling anxiety.

Crippling anxiety into cursing.

Cursing into sitting on top of one of the benches on top of the machine and lying down, wondering if perhaps Rosalia Philips will never show.

And then I hear it, the chime attached to the door ringing straight into my soul.

She's here.

Rosalia Philips is *here.*

And suddenly I don't feel so alone.

One peek at her and she's my personal ecstasy. There isn't a word in the English or French dictionary combined to explain the way my lungs fill with the freshest gulps of air.

Staring at me is my blonde angel.

My Hurricane Blondie.

Peaches.

Everything I've ever categorized this woman as floods into one, resurfacing with only three words that will forever shake my core…

Cherry Viper Eyes.

That's what I feel looking into her gaze. It could kill a thousand warriors, and yet be so soft and sweet like cherry. It's her favorite drink, sweetness that's so sickening that it's desired.

Lyrics begin to flow through me.

> *They say not to adore sin,*
> *But she's my cure*
> *A ballerina in a green-eyed disguise*

Oh my God.

What. The. Hell.

It's been months. *Months.* Since I've been able to brew any lyrics worth my time, but those…they feel so raw. So poetic. Everything Diesel Rose stands for.

Lust rushes up my spine. A heat that I've never felt this intensely before as I sit up, my worn-out leather boots kissing the ground even though I'm propped up on top of the washing machine bench.

I've got nothing to say.

No defense.

I'm just mesmerized. Lost. Floating in those captivating green meadow eyes.

Jesus. Oh, here we go…

> *I'm not just a saint to be so cruel*
> *Baby, you've got the melancholy in your eyes*

Rosalia is frozen by the laundromat door, her plump lips parted, glossy with a tinge of pink. The same pink that crawls up her cheeks as she stares at me, without blinking, without speaking, just *staring*.

She looks gorgeous. She always does. But tonight, or this early morning, however the fuck you want to categorize it, she looks different. A *good* different. There's no anger simmering in her eyes. There's no tension in her shoulders. There's no fight.

It's just her and me.

A broken rocker and a faultless ballerina, fractions of the people who we were four years ago, and yet I still see glimmers of us.

> *Cherry viper, I'd like to meet you, againnn*
> *Again*
> *Cherry viper eyes, ah ah*
> *Cherrrry viper, mmm-hmmm*

Rosalia steps forward, a soft thud echoing round the spacious laundromat, and when I flicker my gaze down, I don't know why my heart warms at the white Dr. Martens she's wearing.

Not stilettos.

Not ballerina flats.

Not fancy dress shoes.

Dr. Martens.

Rebel. Heartbreaker. Lawless leathers.

She's wearing my kind of style.

Not *his.*

Not *Trent's.*

Mine. And I fucking love it.

Fluffy white wool coat with metal spikes over the shoulders and a tie-up belt accentuating her tiny waist. A peek of her faded charcoal Metallica band tee below, half a skull on show with roses for eyes. Iconic mom jeans, each rip exposing white fishnet stockings underneath.

Rosalia's thick, onyx lashes lift a little higher as she takes five steps forward until she's directly in front of me. It's here that I can see just how deep her scarlet blush is. That hue. And I want to know if it's for me, or if it's because that Trent drove her here…is he waiting outside? I want to know if they fucked, and that's why she's in a flustered haze

I don't stare at *The Beautiful and Damned* first edition for even two seconds when she slips it out of a coat pocket. As I said, I didn't come here for that. I came here for *her*.

"Here." Rosalia offers me the book, her voice soft and tranquil, yet I know her better. I know this is affecting her like it is me. "This is yours, four years overdue."

Always the smart-ass.

I swallow thickly. "When I gave it to you, I didn't intend on you returning it to me."

A slow, sexy smile breaks out on her lips, and even though it's a mocking one—*dear God*—it captivates me even more.

"Well, no, Elijah Diesel, I didn't take you as a personal library, but everything must come to an end…"

Rosalia brushes her knuckles over the thick hardback before knocking it. Twice.

"And *this*," she adds, lifts her darkening eyes to me, and they tell me everything and nothing at the same time, "is where our story ends."

Fucking hell.

She's adamant, but I see through it. I'm not seeing Rosalia Philips for the last time at a damn laundromat at two o'clock while I'm on tour.

I need time.

So much more time with her.

"Did you think I would drive all the way to Manhattan just for you to break my heart?"

"Break *your heart*?" Rosalia scoffs, that sexy, smug smirk deepening. "Last time I checked, you didn't have a heart."

"Never said I did either."

And just like that our stare off begins, all while that familiar coconut and vanilla scent merges with the lavender, killing me slowly. When it gets too much, Rosalia slips a book into my hands and our fingers brush for a split second, but it's enough to make me feel, and God, I haven't *felt* for four years.

I hate how she makes me *feel* alive.

I hate that she makes me simply *feel*.

Yet right now, I crave it. More than anything.

A heaved breath escapes Rosalia as she quickly jolts her hands back, leaving me with the hardback. Her eyes never meet mine again, those wet blonde strands sticking to her face, framing it as she spins on her heels and B-lines directly toward the laundromat glass door.

She's leaving...

I'm still trying to comprehend everything when I jump off the washing machine, shoving the book behind me on the counter and jogging up to her.

The second Rosalia reaches for the door handle, I press my hands on both sides of the glass door beside her head, trapping her. My chest is inches away from being pressed against her back.

The slight reflection in the door has me witnessing the moment she slowly shuts her eyes, and another strangled breath escapes her.

"Elijah," she whispers slowly, piercing me to the core because she's one of the only people who call me by my first name. Still. "I… I really need to go back home."

My jaw ticks. "Why?"

"Because it's two a.m., and you have your book now, and I don't want to see you."

"Is that fucker outside?"

"It doesn't matter if Trent is out there or not, Elijah."

I scoff, his name poison. "What, so he's not out there?"

"I never said that."

Air crackles between us.

I can't help myself or my cocky half smirk.

"Does he know about me?" I murmur.

That's when the gasp escapes her lips and Rosalia twirls around in a fiery glow, her nose practically brushing against mine when I lower my head, so that we're eye level.

"There is nothing for Trent to know about *you*," she grits, and I don't miss the way her eyes narrow. "We were *never* anything."

"*Oh yeah*?" I grind my jaw, pissed. "Is that why you're still giving me four years of history back tonight? Is that why you're looking at me like that?"

"I'm not looking at you in any kind of way, Elijah Diesel, so stop getting it twisted and get your face out of mine."

I arch a brow. "You really mean that, huh?"

Silence trickles between us.

God, those eyes.

Lyrics. Lyrics. Lyrics.

Shaking away the words only my muse can pull out of me, I try again, this time with a growl, "Tell me that you mean it and I'll walk away."

Rosalia's glossy lips part, and just as she's about to speak, they slam shut.

Hmmm.

Rosalia can't look at me.

She can't hold my gaze.

She's staring at my earring, the sterling silver one with a little feather attached. She just keeps on staring and staring, as if it's got to come alive and flutter away. As if it even matters.

A slow, sexy smirk burns up my lips as I study her. The tension between us brewing.

"You don't really want to leave, do you?" I whisper softly.

When she still doesn't look at me, I lean forward, my lips brushing against her ear. I can't resist the way my tongue roams around her earlobe, erotically rolling around her diamond stud and seductively sucking it slowly.

"You just don't want to admit it to my face."

"Yes, I can." She snaps back fast—*too fast*—her warm breath tickling my neck.

I let out a devilish chuckle, something the Joker would admire.

"No, *Peaches*," I rasp. "You want to stay here. You want to see me. You just don't want to say it. Isn't that right, hmm? The only reason you would agree to meet me at a fucking laundromat at two o'clock in the morning, after a long day being a flawless ballerina, is because you wanted to see me."

Silence.

Absolute silence.

My stubbled jaw clenches. "If what I'm saying isn't true, if not a glimmer of what I think you truly feel is true, and you *don't* want an apol—" The word gets tangled on my tongue, taking all my strength. "An *apology* from me, then walk out the door. *But* if you do walk out, just know, you're walking away for good, Rosalia Philips."

I push off the door and without glancing at Rosalia, spin around, turning back to my spot above the washing machine, that F. Scott Fitzgerald classic that's become our doomed fate right beside me.

Staring ahead into nothingness, I wait, half expecting that chime above the door to forever haunt my mind, and yet it doesn't.

There's a footstep.

And then another one.

Followed by a few rushed more.

"This apology better be *golden*, Elijah Diesel, or I'm walking out that door. *For. Good.*"

When I feel the warmth of her presence sitting on a washing machine bench directly adjacent to me, I know Rosalia Philips never truly forgot about me, as I have never forgotten her.

Chapter

TWENTY-ONE

Rosalia

I know I shouldn't have come here. I shouldn't be here with Elijah Diesel at past 2:00 a.m., days from the fourth week of my Swan Lake season. Three weeks are down, three weeks are to go. The exhaustion and aching muscles fuel my body, but the glitter wrapped around my heart makes it all worth it.

I should be in bed sleeping, with a clear and conscious mind. Instead, a part of me caved thinking about *that* first edition. I wanted tonight (this morning) to be the final time I see Elijah Diesel.

This has to end. This game of cat and mouse. This damn first edition. It's Elijah's now. *His.* And after I hear his explanation, I'm ready to let go of Elijah forever.

That same Elijah Diesel with that iconic spiky leather jacket filled with tattoos, piercings, and jewelry. The same Elijah Diesel with the damp jet-black hair that's ever so perfectly slicked back, a few loose strands to sexily cover his face. It reminds me of Skeet Ulrich's *Scream*. God, I can never look at that movie the same after that time. It's too close for comfort.

It has to be a good five minutes since my Dr. Martens sealed my faith and walked back over to the washing machine sitting directly opposite him. I've been waiting for Elijah. Waiting for a glimmer of his apology to come to light.

Quite honestly, I didn't expect him to even offer an apology, but right now, I'm kind of getting my hopes up with the way that he hasn't moved a fraction for those five minutes straight.

He just keeps on staring at everything but me. The marble floors. The vacant industrial dryers. Anything really, *but me.*

With my fingers settled underneath my thighs. My rings uncontrollably jittering together and scraping against the bench one too many times because I'm *that* nervous, I don't fail to notice the tension crawling across Elijah's every muscle, ricocheting as if he can't stand the wait, yet he's the very one I'm waiting on.

Elijah leans farther back against the bench. His long, toned, jean-clad legs and worn-out biker boots so readily iconic for the man.

The legend.

The rock star.

Elijah Diesel.

I haven't been able to change radio stations for four years without hearing that melancholic voice. That deep, raspy, sinful voice that right now is a bittersweet dream to me. *Sweet* because that's what Elijah used to be to my seventeen-year-old heart. *Bitter* because, well, look at how we've ended up.

But what I stare at most, second to his Metallica T-shirt underneath the leather that matches mine, is just how much older he looks since those four years ago. He's still gorgeous. Still that broody mystery. But he's *older.* I can see the faded crow's feet. The way his stubble is a little bit thicker. The way his eyes are tired and laced with a redness one can only get from too much adrenaline, sleep apnea, and liquor or joints.

Eventually, Elijah pulls a cigarette from his pocket, lights it up, and blows a few puffs, the thick white smoke clouding his face, totally ignoring the no smoking sign on the back wall. *That's Elijah, peeps, the one man who knows how to break the rules and break them well.*

"Elijah," I call out, not expecting the wave of rainbows lighting up inside me when his piercing eyes eventually snap my way. Gosh, I don't remember them being so alluring. Actually, I do, but they're deeper now, those gray-onyx eyes mixed with…desire?

Regret?

I didn't know.

A mix of both, I think.

"Elijah," I repeat, my voice a little softer, but still with that same toughness I pride myself on. "I'm not waiting here all morning. I literally have to be up in less than four hours."

"Thought you didn't perform on Mondays…"

I chose to ignore the fact that I never told him that information. That he must have looked up the Swan Lake performance schedule.

"I still have training. Yes, it's a rest day, but I have…plans."

Elijah's brows perk up at that. "Plans?"

"Yeah, plans."

Like a normal person…

He doesn't even offer me a slight chuckle, or that mocking half smirk. He's simply motionless, like he's pondering his own faded death in my eyes.

"You going on a date with Tre—"

I don't let him finish. "No, I'm seeing my parents."

"Ahh." Elijah coldly chuckles. And here it is, ladies and gents, that infamous half smile that still has my heart skipping a beat. Even after all these years. Even after everything he's done to *us*. "How's your foster parents going? Your father, the neurosurgeon? Still going around calling people names that are so fucking insensitive?"

It takes all of me not to roll my eyes to Mars.

"He's great." I cockily grin. "Last night he completed one of the most renowned procedures in the world. He's doing *great*."

Elijah nods, but it's at a distance. "Your mom? She all right?"

"As good as can be."

Cocking his head to the side, his eyes bore deeper into my soul. "And you, Rosalia Philips? You doin' just *great* too?"

I slap my mouth shut, staring back at a man that right now I can barely recognize. It's as if he's the famous rocker and the Joker all at once. So cold yet fierce. Such sinful yet charismatic. So possessive, yet carefree. He's toxic to my blood, and yet, I'm *here*.

"Don't ask me that, Elijah."

"Don't ask you what?"

"Stop deflecting."

"What am I deflecting from?"

"The apology."

"*The apology*," he repeats *slowly*, like he wants it to sink in.

Like he likes the way it sounds on his tongue.

Like it's one of the first few times he's muttered the words out loud.

I've never taken Elijah Diesel as the apologetic kind of guy. I kind of think he creates carnage and damn hurricanes wherever he goes without glancing back. So, the fact that he's apologizing to me, or aims to, means one thing only—he wants to slither back into my life—and *that* is not happening. Not again.

Elijah rakes a hand through his hair, tugging on the ends a little too roughly before gliding his fingers back down to his lips and blowing a long drag.

Smoke.

Everywhere.

When he looks at me now, I see just how tired he seems, like this tour is killing him. I have no idea of the intensity of how a worldwide tour would both thrill and exhaust a rocker, but I know with my six-to-eight-week ballet seasons that the pain is excruciating, endless, but it's all worth it for those who watch and become captivated by it.

"There's a lot I want to say." Elijah's voice softens yet again to a husky murmur that's almost unrecognizable. "I didn't mean to… well"—he blows out a sigh—"I guess the first thing I want to say is…I, I never meant to allude that Trent—"

He squeezes his eyes shut for a moment, not bearing the name slipping his tongue.

"I didn't mean to allude that Trent Daniels got you the position as *prima ballerina*. I know you did it with grit, determination, and because you are Rosalia Philips and can achieve the whole freaking world with your flawless talent, so I take that back."

I continue staring, giving him nothing, wanting to know how far this goes.

"I, uh…" Endlessly blowing puff after puff, he grips his hair again with his free hand. The tobacco ripples through me, and in some strange twist of fate, I didn't know why it brings me so much solace.

Elijah is the only smoker I've been around, and something about it just makes me nostalgic of the people we once were.

Sucking in a breath, he continues, "I was angry and hearing Trent's name that night made me feel obsessive, possessive and…"

"And?"

Elijah's jaw ticks in frustration.

"*Jealous.*" He grits, his eyes devilish flames. "I was fucking jealous."

"There was nothing for you to be jealous of. We were never together."

He shrugs as if it's nothing, but I know it is. "I know, but I..." He rubs his perfectly stubbled chin. "*Fuccck*, I'm so bad at this."

I chew on my bottom lip. "What? Are you telling me you've never apologized before?"

I know I shouldn't be mocking him or trying to put him down while he's trying to apologize, but I can't help it. I've been through so much with him that I'm just...so tired of it.

"There's never been a *need* for me to apologize before."

What?

Elijah's confession has my brows rising.

"*Really?*" I scoff. "Because let me tell you something. You're not exactly the clean-cut kinda guy. I mean, I'm not the perfect human, nobody is, but at least I own my shit."

Elijah doesn't like that. "I'm trying to own my shit too, Rosalia. This is big for me."

"Wow, sorry, yep. This is your moment. I get it. Go on."

Asshole.

His eyes narrow, unimpressed. "This is hard for me, okay?"

"Why? Because you never did anything wrong before? I didn't think so, Elijah."

He involuntarily grinds his jaw. "Because I didn't think anyone has ever deserved or merited an apology before you."

"That's so—"

"You know what?" Elijah scoffs, shaking his head and jumping off the washing machine, gripping the first edition to his chest like it's the only thing he's surviving on. "If you're just going to be like this and not give me an opportunity to apologize, then I'm going. We're done. Fuck this shit, whatever."

My former Melancholic God begins walking and my jaw drops so fast, I don't even know how I managed to shout the next words.

"Elijah Diesel, turn the hell around and apologize to me!"

The cocky bastard keeps on walking.

"Elijah!"

Nothing.
He.
Keeps.
On.
Walking.

"Jesus Christ, you're like a psychological sadist or something. You can't even apologize? Seriously?" I practically scream, losing it. "You've never had to apologize in your life? Is this how your parents brought you up? To walk away from every single problem that flies your way? Because it's all that you've done. I'm sure your mother would be *so fucking proud* of you."

That does it.

Elijah snaps his head my way, and when he does, the cloud of white smoke frames his face so cruelly sexy, it's as if I'm staring at a GQ front cover. He gestures his cigarette directly at me, anger in his scrunched-up face. *Have I hit a nerve?*

His eyes aren't wonderlands, they're a real-life inferno. I've never seen his jaw so tense. His broad shoulders so boxed in. The way he's standing so tall and defiant, a cover-up to all the flaws I see weaving in.

"Don't you dare talk about my mother," Elijah growls, but it's low, so low I barely hear it.

My heart slows. I *have* hit a nerve.

"Okay." I swallow thickly, only because as much as I hate him right now, I respect what he just said. I don't want to be talking about my parents either. It's so much shit for another day. "But you want to apologize to me? You do it properly."

Elijah storms my way, his stride a confident masterpiece, flickering the cigarette to the ground without barely putting it out. That sandalwood and tobacco mixed with lavender, adding my own coconut body wash, making a whole new aroma, making all of my butterflies reappear.

I shouldn't feel this way.

It's really bad I'm feeling this way.

Gosh. It's so forbidden. But I can't stop it.

Elijah's right in front of me now, his hips brushing against my knees, burning kinetic energy. He's not happy, not with the storm brewing in his eyes as he slowly grinds his jaw.

Without warning, Elijah dominantly spreads my thighs and steps closer, so that I'm practically wrapped around him. *Oh?* My heart pumps into overdrive, becoming reckless when he roughly grips my chin with a devilish look, his hold alluringly enraging.

Just when I think my heart can't race any faster, Elijah leans forward, lowering his head so that we're inches apart. In the danger zone.

"I *want* to apologize, little girl," he snarls seductively. "But you won't like *how* I do it."

Little girl.

"Try me," I spit.

Elijah's grip tightens as a dark, sexy smirk works up his lips. It brings a wicked smirk to mine too, distorted in his hold. The intensity of his stare is beyond anything I've ever felt.

Elijah tugs off his leather jacket and recklessly throws it behind him, landing on the floor with a soft thud. A loud gasp rushes up my throat when he grips my hand, bringing it to meet the waistband of his jeans and skim over the sharp spikes of his leather studded belt.

Ohhh, okay.

Elijah guides my hand slightly higher, tugging up his T-shirt. His hot bare skin beneath my fingertips is scorching fire. All I can think about is Trent and my own moral code when my fingers glide over his perfectly tanned olive skin, over his taut washboard abs and prominent vaunted V-cut muscle that would make a sculptor cry.

He's all toned muscles with those edgy rocker tattoos. Every ridge, groove, and divot of him is unreal.

My gaze flickers from his darkening eyes to those toned bulges in his biceps, his narrow waist, and inky tattoos down his arms and across his exposed narrow waist and along his V-line, inches from me. It makes me feel a type of way.

God, why does he have to be so gorgeous?

The butterflies rush down, settling between my thighs, arousal pooling in my panties at the way he's looking at me with so much need.

With his warm hand still covering mine, he gently folds all my fingers away until it's only my pointer finger remaining.

"Elijah..."

"Shhh."

He guides my hand down the right side of his waist and hips, lower, past the gorgeous V-cut muscle, to a tattoo positioned dangerously close to his dark happy trail that disappears beneath his waistband. So close to the edge of his boxers that I can make out the dark waistband's label. *Emporio Armani.*

All the air sucks out of me when Elijah stops my finger on the tattoo. It's not just any tattoo…

Oh.

My.

God.

Shit, somebody help, I don't how to breathe anymore. Everything just gets lost in my lungs. Because right here, staring back at me in thin black cursive writing, is a word that means everything.

Peaches

Wow.

If it were anybody else, it would be so freaking corny, but this is Elijah Diesel we're talking about.

ELIJAH DIESEL!

The guy who doesn't feel a fucking thing.

Who probably only has one-night stands.

Who doesn't know how to keep a good thing when he has it.

The private, secretive mystery who has fans screaming his name and *millions* of them all over the world adoring his music.

The Elijah-freaking-Diesel TATTOOED MY NICKNAME ON HIS BODY.

OH MY GOD.

"You're crazy," I whisper, tracing his tattoo ever so gently, even after his hand disappears from mine. "When did you get this?"

I'm so mesmerized by the tattoo and the pang lodged deep inside my chest that when Elijah begins speaking and I look up at him through my long lashes, it's all a haze.

"In London. Four years ago."

The first city of his opening tour when he left all those years ago, leaving me in his bed.

"Why would you…" The words get lost on my tongue, unable to concentrate right with my hand trailing his warm skin, so I pull away, no matter how desperately I don't want to in my heart of hearts. "Get this?"

In the silence, Elijah softly cups my cheeks with both hands. The most tender he's touched me all night as he gazed back and forth between my eyes. "Do you think I forgot you? For a moment? For a second?"

"You—"

"I *didn't*," he rasps, rocking his hips forward, his obvious thick erection grazing against my jeans. "No, *Peaches*, you were right *here*."

My lips part to nothingness, warmth rushing down my spine at his hard-on inches away. There's something about the way Elijah grazes a hand down his taut body until he reaches that tattoo that drives me crazy for all the wrong reasons.

Trent.

Ever since our blow-up last week, we haven't really been speaking, which is REALLY awkward seeing as we're dressing room buddies. Tonight isn't helping. Not at all.

"The truth is, I hate that I left. Left you. But I…" Elijah's gaze settles back on mine, and when it does it's laced with desire, guilt, and messy broodiness. "You created this fire in me and I didn't know how to stop it. Affection and sensual moments have never been my thing, but the way we were holding each other that night, the way we were kissing until our lips were all bruised and swollen, it was…" He lets out a breath. "*Different*. A good different. And I didn't know how to handle it."

"By *staying*."

Elijah shakes his head softly, his thumbs rubbing small circles across my cheeks, pushing back the strands of hair still sticking to my face because of the rain.

"I don't know how to stay," Elijah whispers, so close to my lips I can feel his heat. "Because nobody in my life has ever done that before—*stayed*."

My heart's beating so fast, I'm certain he can feel it. If that's bad, I'm pretty sure the heat of my flustered cheeks is transferring through his touch.

"I left because I knew I could never be enough for you. I'm not the type of guy to love, Rosalia. I was…I was scared you were falling in love with the idea or the illusion of me. I wanted to set you free, let you roam wild like a fateful butterfly. But now, I can't stay away from you…"

Swallowing thickly, his hands on my cheeks slip, and instead, he replaces his warmth with our brushing foreheads. We shut our eyes simultaneously, our hot breathes merging into one.

"I'm incapable of letting you go, Rosalia," Elijah whispers, emotion etched in his voice. "I don't want to be your destroyer, and if I had kept in contact all these years, I would have done just that. Destroyed you."

"You don't know that would have happened."

"I do. I suffer from... I've been to rehab a lot of fucking times. I've been trying to stay clean."

My heart aches. In fact, my entire world stops.

Suddenly, I don't feel so good.

"You were trying to stay *clean*?"

Elijah blows out a sigh, guilt lodged in his waning gaze. "Yes. And when I'm not clean, and even at times when I'm withdrawing, I...can get problematic. Dependent. *Super jealous*."

I slowly nod, wanting to give him the opportunity to continue because I know this is big for him. Apologizing like this, in his own way.

"I'm certain my publicist secretly fucking hates me for the number of times she's saved my ass."

"Saved your ass from what?"

"Fuck," he murmurs under his breath before shaking his head. "Things I'm not proud of."

I flicker my eyes open, surprised to find those piercing wolfish onyx eyes already studying me. "Elijah, you can tell me."

"I'm a..." His breaths speed up, not quite finding my eyes until he says so low I barely catch it. "Rosalia, I'm... I *was* an addict."

Boom.

That's my heart, cascading down.

Coldness ripples over every inch of my body, shaking me to the core as I stare up at Elijah, frozen, my mouth totally gaped.

An addict?

My biological parents float in my mind and everything I endured. "What...what type of addict?"

"Alcohol." He sucks in a heavy breath. "I was an alcoholic."

I freeze up. "How long have you battled with it?"

Without blinking, sadness pools in Elijah's eyes when he answers me straight away with a thick gulp. "It started in small doses since I was ten. Intensified when I hit seventeen."

The world feels like it's spinning as my jaw drops. "*Ten?*" I whisper. "Elijah, no."

My heart aches for him. Aches at the way he's looking at me right now, full of dark anxiety.

Elijah glances down at his hands, playing around with his rings as if he doesn't know what else to say. Like there's a war brewing in his mind. Some type of hell simmering through his bones.

"One of my mom's boyfriends…he hated me, just like I hated him. He wasn't good for my mom, but my mom only gave a fuck about herself. So, she kept him around." Elijah inhales a sharp breath, breaking him. "He was violent with me. The alcoholic my mother adored. He would hold a knife to my throat, call me a *punk*, beat me up real fucking bad."

Punk. That's why it hurts so much for him. It brings him back to a place of hell. Trauma.

"Shit." I place a hand on my breaking heart, all the cracks slowly beginning to make sense. "I'm so sorry, Elijah."

"Yeah." Elijah glances up from his hands, and for once, I can understand his emotionless expression. *He's conditioned himself not to feel.* "Me too."

Pain spills from his words.

"One night, when my mom passed out from her high, he put a knife to my throat and forced me to try some liquor. Told me I'd be nothing but my mother's son. I went to fight him, but it got messy. So, I tried it. Forcefully."

"What did you feel?"

"Numb to the world. It was like a psychedelic dream…a nightmare. As I got older, I fed off that escapism, learned how to hide it, how to manipulate people into believing there wasn't a void inside me."

Instinctively, I reach my hands up, cupping his stubbled, chiseled jaw. The way this man, fifteen years my senior, leans his head into my hold, as if it's the only thing keeping him afloat, makes my heart hurt even more.

Elijah Diesel might be an asshole, but he has a story, and that… that means something.

"Those months I spent with you were the cleanest I've ever been— sober wise. My mind was still a fucking mess. I was drinking *responsibly*…but I…I felt the craving come on, the dependency to reach that euphoric place I only knew could exist in…in my mind. I couldn't drag you with me, Rosalia. I didn't want you to see me like that. The opening act in the United Kingdom…it ruined me."

"What happened?"

"Can't really avoid liquor in this rock 'n' roll world. I was exposed to excessive amounts for the first time in years. I was sad, lonely, and depressed. I took it, then a little more, then a little more. Until it became an addiction. The tour, up until we reached Spain, was basically me living off several bottles of that deadly poison like they were my life support."

"Did you seek any help?"

"Not personally, not at first. But then… Knives, my friend, he walked into my hotel bathroom one night and saw me…" Elijah shakes his head, pinching his eyes shut for a second. "Not in a good state. I was rushed to the hospital and when I came to, I couldn't stop the panic attack. It was as if my lungs were closing in. I felt like death. The doctor gave me liquid Valium to calm me the fuck down."

Valium.

A burning knot tangles up at the back of my throat.

"I've been on that before too…"

"Fucking crazy, right?" Elijah frowns.

"Deadly."

He nods and continues, "The doctor gave me Valium, and everything began to fade. The angst. The bruises. The grief. All I felt was numbness. No emotions. No feelings."

"And then?"

"I relapsed. Once again, I became addicted to narcotics, any kind, not healthy, Rosalia. An excess of that shit will kill you. Doctor looked me straight in the eye and told me there wouldn't be another time. That it'll kill me alive. Know what I said?"

I shake my head softly, hands still cupping his face. "What?"

Elijah chuckles coldly. "I told him my life had ended a long time ago, when I let go of *Peaches*. He looked at me like I was insane, as he should've, but I haven't been the same."

That hurts me, so much so that my vision becomes glassy because I didn't know Elijah was in all this pain. That he left because he didn't want me to witness all of it.

"Do you talk to your band about it?"

"No," Elijah says. "I mean, we silently talk about it… A look in the eye is enough."

"You need a support system, Elijah."

"Yeah, that ship sank the day I was born." He cups his hands over mine, bringing my hands down his broad chest, right over his heart.

My own heart slows with every one of his vicious heartbeats. I smile softly, hopefully, and Elijah smiles back, so melancholy small.

"I'm trying to get better, Rosalia. Really, I am. But I've got so much shit locked up, it's hard to trust. It's hard for me to love and show I care because I've never had that. People may love the rock star, but they don't *know me* to truly love me," Elijah confesses, his voice breaking a little. "But I… Rosalia?"

"Yes."

"All the goodbyes that I've ever gotten in my life were laced with death, so I don't…I don't take them well. It feels like I'm losing something, and I didn't want to lose you. I'm really sorry, I…"

"I forgive you, Elijah."

"Really?" Elijah's eyes widen a fraction, and to be honest, the words that just slipped my lips surprise me too.

I nod through my glassy vision, that knot in my throat burning as I sadly smile. "I understand why now, and even though it bruised me, you left to save me from you."

I'll never forget his beautifully shy smile.

"I made you something on the way here," he whispers, almost bashfully, which is so unlike him. "It's nothing really, the boys gave me shit for it, but I…I wanted to make something by hand to show you how sorry I really am."

Slipping his hands free, he dives inside his pocket, pulling out a leather bracelet with silver charms that look handmade.

Elijah slowly cups my hand before folding the bracelet into my grip. Our warm fingers brush for a full four seconds. I know because I count, just like I always do.

I glance down at the bracelet, feeling its smooth braided leather grooves, my eyes slowing on the three charms attached.

A lusciously round peach.

A perfectly detailed ballerina pointe shoe.

A tall bottle that looks a whole lot like a vintage cola bottle.

Elijah Diesel made this for me?

Air gets lodged in my throat, reminding me there's a part of me that will forever still beat for Elijah.

This nervousness settles in the pit of my stomach when I flicker my gaze to those onyx-grays that leave me breathless.

Speechless.

Elijah gazes down at me, a glimmer of hope flickering across his eyes as he wordlessly takes the bracelet and rolls it on my left wrist. "There you go, *Peaches*. For you."

I stare at him all while he stares at the bracelet, working aimlessly to make it perfect on my wrist. His fingers linger for longer than they should, all while I can't stop studying his face and lower, to those fated full lips.

This is Elijah's way of apologizing and I need to respect that. I need to let it go.

"Wow." I softly grin at how the bracelet fits my wrist so perfectly. It's truly stunning and unlike anything I own, which makes it that much more special. "It's so beautiful, Elijah. Thank you."

He nods, getting what I mean.

"I'm also sorry for the word I called you." I squeeze his hand, tight. "Really, really sorry. Now I understand the gravity of them and how deeply they hurt you... Can we just move forward?"

Elijah nods, that soft melancholic smile still on his lips when he steps back and collects his leather jacket. He slips it on, all while staring at his bike boots. "Well, that's all. I guess I'll go..."

Wait, what?

It gives me whiplash the way Elijah collects that first edition and turns to walk out of the laundromat, his head hung low.

"Elijah."

He slows but never turns around.

"Don't go," I whisper, nostalgic over him.

"I ain't going anywhere, babygirl."

Elijah doesn't walk back, he runs, and so do I after hopping off the bench. Jumping right into his open arms, my legs wrap around his narrow waist. He spins us around in circles, while I bury my face into his neck, gripping onto him for dear life because... *I miss him.*

Elijah Diesel once meant so much to me, and right now in his warm embrace, sinking deeper into the solace of his arms, I *still* feel the same. The butterflies. The blushes. The sparks.

But now, everything is different.

I'm seeing another guy.

Elijah is a famous star.

We're not the same.

But in this moment, all I care about is how his arms feel like home. *My* home. Away from the monsters.

When Elijah sets me down, he's got this look in his hooded eyes, a twisted lullaby. The one of the broken monster and the ballerina angel. The one of *us*. And I melt.

But when Elijah's phone begins blaring and he answers it, he mutters a few words before rubbing the back of his neck.

He ends the call and turns to me. "That was my driver on standby. I better get going."

Elijah came here from Connecticut.

Before I can say anything, he presses a tender kiss on my forehead, and it lingers. "Call me when you finish your ballet season, and I'll fly you out to the city I'm touring in, okay?"

Elijah stares into my eyes just long enough to witness them sparkle.

"Okay."

And then, just like that, he's gone, leaving me with a heavy heart, his lingering effect, and braided leather bounding us back together again.

Chapter
TWENTY-TWO

Rosalia

"**W**here have you been, Miss I've-got-a-secret-admirer?" Naomi's voice floods my ears the second I step into our Manhattan brownstone just after 3:00 a.m.

Ahh shit.

Dramatically groaning, I lock the front door at record speed and lean against it with a coy smile. It doesn't seem to wipe off my lips, no matter how hard I try to act normal. "Out."

Naomi, who's literally only wearing panties, arches an I'm-not-buying-your-shit brow. "Girl, I get your ballerina schedule is hectic as fuck, but I know you. You're not a party girl, meaning you weren't *out*. So, where were you?"

Shrugging, I kick off my Dr. Martens and strip off my coat in our open plan living room, flinging the woolen Manhattan staple on the couch. Mr. HotLips is cutely sleeping in his cotton teepee bed, and there's only one lamp on in the living room, its warm glow my flushed cheeks' personal demise.

"Rosalia Philips, you nut, I know something's up!"

"Nothing's up."

"Who did you see? Trent?"

I cringe just hearing his name. *Yeah, Trent and I haven't exactly spoken ever since our blow-up about that damn first edition while Travolta danced around in the background. For the past week, we've been sharing a dressing room and it has been nothing but AWKWARD.*

"Not Trent. I haven't spoken to him since he sneaked out in the middle of the night."

"So, who did you see?"

I feel Naomi sneak up right behind me.

She will KILL me if I mention Elijah.

I roll my shoulders back, easing up some tightness. "Nobody. I just went out."

"Yeah, *right.*" Even though my back is to her, I can hear the smolder in her voice. "Is that why you can't even look me in the eye, hmmm, girlfriend?"

I muster the courage to turn around, all my pride hidden underneath as I bite back the damn stupid smirk threatening to rise up my cheeks. I don't know why I feel so giddy about seeing Elijah tonight (ahem, early morning). Maybe because it brings me back to the time I craved to do something thrilling. Exciting. Out of bounds.

Okay, I still crave it, but now I've got rent to pay and a prestigious ballet company to keep happy, so bye-bye rebel with-or-without a damn cause.

The second her light-eyed gaze flickers to my chest, Naomi's jaw drops. "GIRL, NO!"

"What?"

"You saw Elijah, didn't you?"

I glance down at myself. I'm wearing a vintage Metallica *band* T-shirt... *Oh. My. Dear. God.*

How the hell is she guessing based on that? I. Need. A. New. Friend.

"How the fuck...?"

"I notice this shit," Naomi says and then gives me the evil eye before crossing her arms over her bare tits ever so casually. I've literally been more naked around her than around any guy I've ever tried anything with. Plus, we have matching diamond nipple piercings.

"Okay..." I let out a breath I didn't even know I was holding. "I saw Elijah."

"ROSA! NO!" She practically squeals, deafening me. "Ugh, what did he want?"

"*I* texted him. I wanted to give him his first edition and be done with everything."

"Oh. My. God. I literally go out to a fancy-ass dinner, and you go bat-shit crazy? Rosa!"

Laughing, I roll my eyes. "I survived. I'm a big girl, thanks, don't need hand holding."

"Aside from the fact you wanted to give him back that damn book…"

"It's a first edition," I try to argue.

Naomi doesn't bat an eyelash. "So?"

"*So*, it belongs to its rightful owner."

"What did he say?"

"He apologized…and I kind of, umm, forgave him."

Breathing out the biggest sigh, she pauses for a moment, frowning. "Why?"

I plop on the couch and glance up at her, spreading my feet out. "He opened up a little. Okay, not a little, but said something about his past. His mother not really being there, her boyfriend really fucking him over. I'm talking being violent with him. Calling him a punk."

I refrain from telling her anything about the alcoholism because it's personal and I kind of feel like it's Elijah's story to tell, not mine. I want to respect him and his past.

Sadness laces Naomi's eyes. "Ouch."

"Yeah, that's why he hates being called it now. It's traumatic. Rubs salt in the wound."

"So, you're just going to forgive him?"

"I feel freer and, honestly, I don't want to be holding onto stress. I'm stressed enough."

"So then what happened?"

"Well, Elijah was really nervous when he apologized. I've never seen anything like it."

Naomi groans, sitting down next to me. "Why didn't you just kick him in the balls?"

I literally burst out laughing, the warmth feeling so nice lodged inside my chest. "He…also got a *Peaches* tattoo."

"Holy mother of cow! *What*?" Naomi gasps, leaning closer to me. "Where?"

I take my best friend's hand and mimic how Elijah guided me to his V-cut. When her fingers brush over the same spot on me, I say, "Right *here*. It's cursive and all pretty, and my heart fluttered when I saw it, but now...I don't know how to feel."

"I don't blame you."

"Yeah. I mean, I tested him at one point when I was questioning the fact that he said he doesn't apologize. So, he just walks up to me, grips my throat in that sexy kind of way, and growls, '*I want to apologize, little girl, but you won't like how I do it.*' And in my head, I was just like—"

"*Take me now, asshole.*"

"Precisely."

Naomi begins fanning herself. "Okay, I still hate Elijah, but *damn*, that was hot, Rosa."

"It was." And just like that, guilt sets in and I frown. "But I couldn't stop thinking of Trent."

My best friend sighs and takes my hand into hers. "I get it, Rosa, you're in this strange middle ground now. But look at it this way. At least you don't have to see him ever again now."

Yeah, about that...

I smile nervously and hold out my wrist, showing her the braided leather bracelet Elijah made me. "Well, he kind of also made me this and said to call him when I finish ballet season."

Naomi gasps so loud that poor Mr. HotLips wakes up and starts hopping around. I scoop him into my arms, kissing his fluffy head, and rock him around like he's a little baby and it currently isn't just after 3:00 a.m.

"You're not actually going to call him, are yo—"

"Babe? What are ya doing outta bed?" a husky Australian accent calls out of nowhere, and I scream. My freaking heart jumps out of my chest because I was not expecting it at all.

Naomi throws back her head in hysterical laughter while I glance over my shoulder at a guy with chiseled abs and the most golden skin staring right back at me at the beginning of the hallway.

He looks to be in his late twenties and just out of some Magic

Mike stripper tour from down under. And he's naked, may I add. Like *full-on naked* and sporting a very, *very* eager hard-on.

He flashes me an apologetic grin and awkwardly covers himself up with his hand. "Whoops, sorry, my bad. I thought Naomi was watching some reality show shit all alone."

"Hi, it's okay." I smile back with a wave and then turn to my best friend with a *what-the-hell* arched brow. "Well, well, well, I didn't know we had company, Naomi Ryder."

"He's new and…*really good*," she whispers to me, never breaking her grin when she glances up at her Australian bae. "Hey, I'll be there in a minute. Just trying to help a girl out."

"I *really* need the help too, Naomi baby." His eyes darken in front of me. "Right. Now."

The sexual tension between them is sizzling so hot that I'm almost the one getting all hot and bothered. I mean, it also doesn't help that they're both practically fully naked and I'm just here looking like I'm ready to go to a rock concert.

"Don't you have to leave and get ready for work already?" Naomi teases in a purr, standing up, completely forgetting how she wanted to kick Elijah in the balls a moment ago.

The hot Aussie's grin deepens. "I've got two hours to spare."

"Oh really?"

"Mmhmmm."

"Early riser, huh?"

"Something like that," he smolders, wrapping his arms around her waist when she nears. He whispers something in her ear that makes her laugh, and then, he goes to work kissing and nipping her neck with hickeys.

I haven't seen her this happy since…well, *forever*.

"Shut up." Naomi giggles, and let me tell you, my fiery best friend *never giggles*.

I love how she finds the common courtesy to glance over her shoulder during this real-life porno.

"Hey, this is my best friend and roommate, Rosalia. Rosalia, this is…Brad."

He pulls away with a slight chuckle. "Uh, it's Chad."

"Right, sorry." Naomi *giggles again*. "It's been a long night."

"And it's about to be even longer…"

"All right." I stand, not helping my laughter as Mr. HotLips rushes out of my arms and back into his bed. *Yeah, good choice, bud. Hide.* "Well, I know when I'm interrupting a real good fuck when I see it. I'm going to head to sleep, so…" I motion down the hall. "Yep."

"It's nice to meet you, Rosalia." Chad flashes me his pearly whites, all while squeezing my best friend's ass. "I'd like to say your friend has told me a lot about you, but she hasn't."

Naomi playfully rolls her eyes. "We literally just met."

"Don't I know it, babe."

Grinning as I near them, I mouth to Naomi, "Who is he?"

She grins. "My best victim yet…the CEO."

My jaw drops, all while she wiggles her brows. *She went to dinner with the new team at the job she's starting next week… Chad is the CEO?* Ah, fuck it, they look so good together.

"Naomi Ryder, you are my inspiration," I whisper in her ear before rushing down the hall, in time to witness her wink and shout at the top of her lungs.

"The one and only, babyyy."

And just like that, the fifth week of my Swan Lake season is complete as the audiences' applauses seep deep inside my veins. I grin with each curtsy, the blinding lights illuminating the grand theater that is Lincoln Center, capturing my every rapid heartbeat.

With my team of dancers beside me, the yellow curtains finally drop, and we make our way backstage. I try not to let the presence of Trent walking directly behind me get to me. We've barely spoken in three weeks, and quite frankly, the tension couldn't be thicker.

I slow the second I open our shared dressing room, my hands rushing up to my mouth to cover my gasp at the holistic aroma flooding through.

Oh.

My.

God.

There are vivid black and cherry brandy salmon-pink roses *everywhere.* I've never seen the two combinations before, but there's just something so dark, goth, and edgy about it that I love. Delicate petals cascading all over the ground, romantically leading to the makeup stations.

"Oh my God, Trent," I murmur without looking back, aware of just how pressed up he is against me. "Wow."

Silence.

Silence.

Silence.

And then…

"Rosalia…I didn't do this."

Everything stops.

My eyes bulge. "*What?*"

Rushing forward, I pick up the frilly note beneath my Hollywood mirror and read it.

Peaches,

Because I'm so fucking proud of you for living your dream. I never meant to dim your light with the words I said. I hope you believe that now.

You're my rock star.

One week.

Whatever the hell you're supposed to write here,
Elijah

Butterflies. The good kind. The bad kind. They're all I feel.

My heart warms with every single word and *his* perfectly cursive handwriting.

How did he get this all in here?

But then…

"Trent…"

"Don't," he spits directly behind me. "Don't even try to fix this."

I spin around, a victim of those judgmental narrowed eyes. "This isn't what it looks like. Elijah and I…we're not together."

Trent scoffs like he doesn't believe me. With his dark stage eye makeup and that darkish green and charcoal costume still on, he begins pacing up and down the dressing room, kicking away the roses to clear his path.

He shuts his eyes, as if he's pondering everything and nothing at the same time. The second I shut the door, so we have a little more privacy, he explodes.

"What the fuck, Rosalia?"

"I didn't know he was going to do this!"

"Don't you see anything wrong in that freaking sentence? Huh?" Trent growls, rushing up to me until we're inches away. There's so much sadness rippling in his eyes and for some stupid reason, my heart hurts because of it. His voice softens. "Who the fuck is Elijah?"

"I told you, somebody I used to know."

"In some band?"

"A rock band, yes."

"You guys together or some shit?"

"No." I shake my head. "I'm not cheating on you. I would never do that."

Trent grinds his jaw. "Then what the hell is going on?"

I say absolutely nothing.

There's nothing to be said.

Trent Daniels and I are slipping.

Cursing under his breath, Trent opens his drawer beneath the makeup desk and pulls out his phone. "What's his name? I want to know what this guy looks like."

"Trent," I warn, not liking where this is going. "Please don't do this."

"What. Is. His. Name."

My throat aches.

"Elijah Diesel."

Trent's mouth gapes open. "As in Dies—"

"Diesel Rose? Yes."

Trent taps a few things on his phone and spends the next chilling moments scrolling through his phone, all while his heaving breaths trickle coldness down my spine. I don't know what Trent sees, but at a certain point he slowly flickers his gaze to me, then back to his phone, and then right back to me without a word. *Judgment.* Just so much judgment.

"What's the story, Rosalia?"

"As I told you, I met him when I was seventeen and we...had a thing."

"A *thing*?"

"Yeah." I nod, my cheeks burning. "Before he broke my heart."

"*And now*?"

"A few weeks ago, I saw him again after four years and...there's still something there."

"You mean, you still feel something for him? More than you do with me?"

I don't glance down at my hands. I don't distract myself with the flowers. I look Trent Daniels in the eye and without a bit of hesitation, speak the words proudly, "Yes, immensely."

Trent scoffs, "Well, I hope you find luck with the fucker because, no offense, but he doesn't look like the type of guy who knows how to handle a *woman like you*."

"What do you mean *a woman like me*?"

"One who isn't into sex, drugs, and rock 'n' roll."

"Or maybe, you just don't know me at all, Trent Daniels, so you and I are *done*."

"Good!"

The thud ricochets around my heart when Trent walks out the door, slamming it shut, leaving me with dozens of blossomed roses, laced with the only man who makes my heart race.

Elijah.

That is until my phone buzzes and all my thoughts drown.

NAOMI: Don't forget about our double date tonight. Chad and I are already here, we found a spot in a booth at the back. See you soon xo

Oh no.

Oh no. Oh no. Oh no.

I totally forgot about my double date...with *Trent.*

Oh, fuck my life. *Sidewards.*

Talk about the awkwardest double date in the world...

Somehow Naomi thought it was a great idea if Trent and I broke the ice with a double date. But we've been at this sushi restaurant for the past thirty minutes, and we haven't spoken a word. The taxi ride here together was even worse. As for Chad and Naomi, well, they haven't stopped flirting all night, as they should.

We're tucked away in the corner of this low-lit restaurant, in a toffee-colored leather booth with a golden bamboo feature wall, and all I want is to escape and dive into my bedsheets.

"Guys." Naomi grins, snapping her attention back to us, her hand slowly inching lower and lower down Chad's dress shirt. "Did you know that Chad was born here in New York but moved with his parents to Melbourne, Australia, when he was two? He's a Brooklyn baby!"

"Wow, that's"—a soft smile touches my lips—"amazing."

"Melbourne." Trent nods beside me, slowly chewing on the pickled shredded carrots and cucumbers like it's the last thing he wants to do. "That's where the Opera House is, yeah?"

"Nah, that's in Sydney, mate." Chad chuckles, his gaze flickering to me. "Your boyfriend's a funny guy, huh?"

Boyfriend.

"Mmhmmm." I smile politely. "*Real* funny."

I feel Trent's hot gaze zone into the side of my head, but I ignore it.

I force a smile as Chad continues talking about his upbringing and how he ventured back to New York. If it were any other night, I'd be happily listening on, but tonight isn't one of those nights. I feel off. I have ever since what happened between Trent and me earlier tonight.

As Chad continues talking, I don't notice the way I'm playing with the leather bracelet Elijah made me until I feel Trent lean closer to me and whisper in my ear, "You got to ignore me all night and play with that thing instead?"

"I'm not ignoring you."

"You haven't batted an eyelash my way."

"Because we're in *company*."

Trent sighs and returns back to eating his damn pickled vegetables, while I devour the rest of my sushi. Avocado and salmon California rolls. Naomi and Chad hold the conversation the entire night, and when it comes to saying goodbye, I'm about to get in Naomi's taxi, but Trent steps forward.

"Do you think you could possibly stay over at mine tonight?"

I look at him as if he's insane. "Why would I do that?"

"So we can actually *talk* this through. I hate how we left things…"

"That's not the best idea, Trent. I think it's clear where we stand now. It's been a long day, and I really want to go home."

Sighing, Trent eventually nods, slipping his hands into his slack pockets while Manhattan grows wild around us.

I'm inside the taxi with Naomi before he can say anything else. *Thank God.* I feel his stare on me linger outside on the sidewalk as the taxi pulls away from the curb.

Naomi notices instantly because that's her sixth scent. "Babe, what was up with you two? You barely spoke to each other all night. Trouble in paradise?"

"You mean hell." I sigh, lean against the headrest, and shut my eyes. "We broke up."

"Oh my God, Rosalia, really? What happened?"

"Elijah happened."

When silence fills the air between us, I open one eye.

My best friend is staring at me awfully confused. I don't know whether to laugh or cry. "Elijah? What? How…?"

I pull out my phone from my purse and show her the pictures I took. She gasps.

The roses. The same roses I had to have delivered to my brownstone.

I fish out the note Elijah wrote me and hand it to Naomi. She studies it for the longest time before letting out an exasperated groan and sliding down the leather taxi seat. "Ugh, why is the rock star psychopath so perfect in the worst way?"

"Don't know," I groan, certain I'm going to hell for this. "But I'll let you know when I do."

"Do you want to talk about it?"

"Not really."

Naomi flashes me a sympathetic smile. "Don't you worry, girl, you're onto bigger and greater things. I promise. You deserve somebody who will scream from the top of the Empire State Building that you're his. You really do."

I find myself genuinely smiling for the first time all day. "I love you."

"Love you more, girl."

Naomi rests her head against my shoulder for the rest of the trip, and it isn't until we're only a few minutes from home that I feel her doze off. I laugh to myself while I pull out my phone, knowing I need to message a certain someone.

> **ROSALIA:** I think my heart fluttered out of my chest when I saw the flowers. How did you know cherry brandy orange is my favorite color? Thank you, Elijah.

His response is instant, only five words, and yet, it has the ability to fuel my lips with a burning smile all the way home.

> **ELIJAH:** A psychopath's intuition, I guess.

> **ROSALIA:** Omg. You're not a psychopath.

> **ELIJAH:** That's right, babygirl, I'm worse.

I grin, refraining from telling him anything about Trent. It doesn't feel like the right thing to say now. I'll tell him in a week when I see him in LA, where he's finishing his tour.

I don't know what any of this means.

I don't even know where we stand.

We're not lovers. We're not friends. We've veering past enemies.

So, what are we?

I don't know.

But for Elijah Diesel, I'd fly all the way to the moon if it means seeing the broken rock star I used to adore.

Okay, *still* adore.

Chapter
TWENTY-THREE

Rosalia

As the applauses intensify for my final ever show of Swan Lake this season, this bittersweet sensation forms in the pit of my stomach. It's Saturday night, marking the end of six intense weeks.

I adore this production, everything about every classic dance, the dazzling costumes, and the family that has formed with all the dancers, but it all ends right now as we rush off backstage.

It's down one of the corridors where we all huddle together and give a massive group hug, which is virtually impossible.

Portia even offers me a half smile, which I think is nice…but slightly odd.

Oh well, maybe she put on her big girl panties and realized this industry is also about supporting each other.

Trent is somehow already inside our dressing room when I step in. Long gone are the scattered roses of a week ago, and instead tension laces the air. He slows at wiping the makeup off his face when our eyes lock in the lit-up Hollywood style mirror, and for a split second guilt lodges in my throat before it simmers to a pit of nothingness.

I have nothing to be guilty about.

I didn't cheat on Trent with Elijah.

Nothing. Happened.

We just fell out of touch.

I ignore him for the rest of my time in the dressing room, stripping off behind the five-panel divider dressing screens and slipping on my silk bathrobe. Awkward doesn't even define the moment I slip into my seat, elevating my legs as I too work on getting off all my dramatic Swan Lake makeup.

I've got a flight to catch in less than three hours, so I need to move fast.

"Rosalia… I'm moving to Vienna tomorrow… Austria."

The soft makeup wipe slows by my cheek as I turn to Trent, my eyes widening a fraction. "Vienna? Wow! When did this happen?"

"A few weeks ago. Months ago, before we…were a thing, remember how I auditioned for that prestigious ballet company in Vienna?"

"Yeah?"

"Well, I was accepted. I didn't give them a definite response until a couple weeks ago. I wanted to talk it over with you, but…we parted ways and then there was no reason to."

A warm smile rises up my lips, and it couldn't be more genuine. *I'm so proud of him.*

"This is amazing news, Trent! It's what you've always wanted, no?"

Trent gives me a half nod, his eyes hot on mine, pleading for me to tell him something. *Anything.* He's got this look in his eyes, one full of guilt that almost begs me to tell him to stay.

But our story finished before it even began.

I'm happy for Trent. Happy he's moving on.

It brings me peace, and quite honestly, that's all I ever want.

I reach out my hand, and with hesitation at first, he slips his fingers through mine and squeezes. We stare at each other, once so close that it almost hurts. Almost because this doesn't have to signify the end of our friendship, it's just the end of anything more.

"You deserve this so much," I murmur. "You're a good guy, Trent. Austria will change your life. I believe it. One day you'll be happily married to a beautiful wife who loves you and little kids running everywhere. I'm really sorry for the shit I told you. It wasn't fair for me to speak to you like that—"

"It's okay, Rosalia."

"It's not." I gulp down. "I just want you to know that even though we didn't work out, it doesn't mean life is over for us. It's just the beginning, and Vienna will show you that."

With his Evil Sorcerer makeup smeared all over his eyes, Trent offers me a weak smile that only gets sadder when he leans over and kisses my forehead. Softly.

"I wish you just the same, Rosalia," he whispers, and the emotion laced in each word is so evident. "You're the most talented *prima ballerina* I've ever seen. The most beautiful. I'm sorry for everything. I hope you find happiness. I truly hope you do, and if it's with *him*, then so be it, but I hope he treats you right."

When he pulls away, I notice just how glassy Trent's eyes have become, and it rushes my own wave of emotion through me. My heart aches because I'm losing a solid friendship.

I feel sick to my stomach about it, but as I sniffle away impending tears, I know this is the right thing to do.

I squeeze his hand tighter.

"I hope so too, Trent Daniels."

"I hope you know what you're doing." Naomi frowns, kissing my cheek just as she's about to head out the front door with Chad. She waves a hand toward my suitcase. "If Elijah breaks your heart in La-La land, just know I'll break his neck."

Laughing, I can't help but roll my eyes. "Promise he won't do that. Besides, I don't even know what this trip will be about."

"All right, but promise to call me, every day."

"I'm literally only staying for the weekend…" I furrow my brows. "I *think*."

Well, to be fair I don't really know how long I'm going to California for…

In an email last week, Elijah sent me a one-way ticket to sunny Los Angeles. It's where he's currently touring. Tomorrow is the last show of Diesel Rose's *Killing Me Slowly* tour.

"Call me!" Naomi grins, blowing me a final kiss before rushing out with Chad, who throws me a wink just before shutting the door.

And just like that, I'm alone in my brownstone, a nervous wreck as I urge myself to head out the door. I've already said goodbye to Mr. HotLips, checked over my suitcases three times, and stressed even more. I need to leave, or I'll miss my flight.

But first, there's something I need to do…

Thump.

Thump.

Thump.

Elijah answers within the first three rings.

"Hey there, Rosalia."

Wait a second… that's not him.

"Um…hi?"

"It's Dave. The drummer." A deep voice chuckles. "The asshole is having a heated email thread with his publicist."

"Ohhh? Is everything okay?"

"Yeah, nothing Elijah can't handle. Okay, he's glaring me down now. Here he is."

There's shuffling, some murmuring, before a soft door closes and Elijah's hot voice floods the line. "*Peaches.*"

Hearing his voice is heaven.

With Elijah hating everything that is calling or texting, we haven't spoken since we met at the laundromat. Well, aside from when I texted to thank him for the flowers, and last week when he asked for my email so he could send me the plane ticket.

"Hey there." I foolishly grin to myself, twirling a finger around my hair. "How are you doing, stranger?"

"Stressed, but when am I not?"

"Is everything okay? Dave mentioned something about you and your…publicist?"

"Yeah, she doesn't think it's the smartest thing for you to come to California, but quite frankly I don't care. I want you here."

My heartstrings tug.

Awww.

"You do?"

"Mmhmmm. How did tonight go?"

"Sensational. I think we all shed a tear."

"I'm proud of you. Even though I wasn't there, I know you freaking killed it."

"Thank you. Oh, I got your email the other day, by the way, with all the details of my flight to Los Angeles. *First class*? Elijah, you didn't have to do that."

"I wanted to."

"What's gotten into you tonight?"

"What do you mean?"

"You seem…happy."

His warm chuckle seeps into my chest. "'Cause I'm talking to you."

Elijah.

I'm grinning so hard my cheeks are aching.

"Ah, fuck," Elijah groans. "My publicist is calling me, probably busting my ass because I stopped replying to her emails. I better get this. Have a safe trip, okay? My driver, Maverik, will be waiting for you at LAX holding a sign with your name on it. You won't miss him."

"Elijah?"

"Yeah?"

"*Thank you.*"

"You don't need to thank me, Rosalia, at all."

"I do, and you know it. It means a lot that you want me there."

I feel him smirk when he mumbles, "You can find other ways to thank me when you're here."

And then he hangs up.

Oh. My. God.

This devil.

Peaches

A giddy grin rolls up my lips at the sign staring back at me, and then at the tough-looking man holding it. He's tall, with a rough buzz cut, navy custom-made suit, and bulging muscles. *This must be Elijah's personal bodyguard, Maverick.*

"Hi." I smile, approaching him with a slight wave, while my other hand grips my suitcase holder tighter. "Nice to meet you."

"Good morning, I'm Maverick." He softly smiles and dips his head. "It's nice to meet you too, Ms. Peaches."

Ms. Peaches?

My grin extends.

Oh my God, Elijah, what have you done?

"Oh, you can call me Rosalia."

"Are you sure?"

"Positive."

With another nod, Maverick takes my suitcase and carry-on bag and leads the way through the LAX airport. It's as if I'm on some secret service mission with all these luxurious upgrades.

Elijah must be waiting for me at the hotel.

I've never been to Los Angeles before, and right now as the 3:00 a.m. (thank God for time zones, I just gained three hours) darkened skies blanket the sky, I smile at the sultry breeze. A warm tinge hits my skin as we step outside. Even though it's early October and fall, it's not wrong what people say about LA weather—always perfect.

Maverick slows at a large, sleek black SUV parked near the shuttle buses. The Volvo screams attention, *importance*, with those huge-ass wheels and windows tinted black that I can't see a damn thing inside.

This thing is probably also bulletproof.

And belongs in Transformers.

I stand awkwardly by the pavement, wrapping a hand around my waist as Maverick rounds the Volvo and attentively packs my luggage into the trunk. Loud rock music booms from inside the car, even though I can't see in from where I'm standing.

Soundproof too.

Maverick is by my side in no time, opening the back seat door with a smile. "Rosalia."

I thank him, that familiar rock anthem riveting up my heartstrings. The same heartstrings that tug and burst into a million butterflies at the gray-onyx eyes staring back at me in the spacious back seat.

Elijah.

My heart pumps into overdrive.

Why did I think he wouldn't be here?

Elijah Diesel gazes at me happily, a fire in his eyes that I've never seen before. It's been three weeks. I still feel the same way I felt that early morning in the laundromat—*sparks.*

I quickly climb into the dark leather seats, my knees brushing against his as I do, and *God*, I swear he must feel the electricity too.

Maverick shuts the door behind me, and when it just becomes us, I practically jump my seventeen-year-old crush.

Literally.

I've never seen a smile so beautiful silk over Elijah's lips, to the point his dimples sink into his stubbled cheeks as I wrap my arms around his neck and embrace him tight. It feels like heaven the way Elijah chuckles hotly in my ear. His strong arms wrap around me dominantly, scooping me into his lap. It leaves me straddling his waist. *Home. He feels like home to me.*

I'm not ashamed of the soft whimper that escapes my throat.

Of how I bury my head into his warm neck, his familiar erotic cologne doing something wild to me—heating between my thighs.

Of cupping his spiky beard, resting my forehead against his, and in the low light, whispering inches from his lips, "I missed you, Lijah."

Chapter
TWENTY-FOUR

Rosalia

E lijah doesn't respond.

He doesn't say a single word.

He just leans back and rests his sexily tousled hair against the headrest so he can study me better with desire in his gaze. *Like he's never been missed before.*

Elijah flickers between my pleading eyes, flushed cheeks, and slows by my eagerly parted lips. So. Achingly. Slow.

What are you thinking?

My heart feels funny from the intensity he's watching me like he wants to do it forever.

Those wolfish eyes linger on my lips.

Kiss me, Elijah, please…right now.

My sex is aching, throbbing at the mere thought of him. At the mere thought of *us*—together. It's frustrating. Agonizing. The way I want him so badly. The way I *need him*, as my breaths begin to thicken.

"You missed me?" Elijah murmurs, his voice a raspy wonderland.

"Mmhmmm."

I'll never forget the way that slow, sexy half-smirk carves up his lips. His hands, which are positioned by my hips, snake up my body, feeling every single curve as arousal pools further.

I'm pretty sure it's obvious the way my heart is beating so fast for him. The way it *always* beats so fast *for him*, even when I was trying to deny it.

Elijah's right hand settles by my neck, brushing up ever so slowly before wrapping around the back of it. His fingers weave into my blonde waves, wrapping around my ponytail before tugging it back slightly.

Ohhh.

I like that.

The gasp that escapes my lips is like no other. I'm so lost in his pretty dark gray eyes that the sound of Maverick slamming the driver's door shut and the car beginning to move doesn't even faze me.

It's just Elijah and me in this car.

And Elijah makes it obvious when his free hand disappears somewhere behind me, and there's a rolling sound. It softens the blaring Led Zeppelin rock music.

Elijah must have closed the dividing window between his driver and us, giving us privacy.

"Guess what, *Peaches*?" he whispers, teasing me as he leans forward like he's going to kiss me, but at the last second, pulls back.

He does it again, slightly cocking his head to the side, and just before our lips collide, he pulls back, his infamous smirk deepening.

I groan in frustration, and all he does is smolder.

He's enjoying this torture.

Elijah Diesel knows how to play this game.

He knows how to play *well*.

He knows exactly what turns me on and exactly what makes me want him even more.

Elijah's right hand continues getting lost in my hair, the other smoothly caressing up my thigh. His fingers roam wild, brushing every gap of my fishnet stockings until his hands disappear beneath my white tennis skirt, stopping inches from my panties, where I need him the most.

He can probably feel the heat of my pussy. In fact, I know he does, given how his eyes darken even deeper.

"I fucking missed you too," Elijah growls, and then his lips are on mine, ravishing me selfishly, as if this is our first kiss.

Yesss.

My gorgeous addiction kisses me with so much intensity, my head spins. I'm sure my lips will bruise before dawn. *And I love it.*

I feel him everywhere, pulling me closer, and I moan into the kiss. My hands wander through his beard and then to his sexily tousled hair, tugging the wavy ends until he's also moaning. His sounds vibrate down my throat, making me borderline delirious.

Whoa.

I can't keep up with the way he's kissing me, with so much recklessness it almost hurts.

Elijah's lips are so smooth. Our tongues dance and I taste creamy whiskey, sin, and everything that is Elijah Diesel—lead vocalist and lyricist of an epic rock band taking the world by storm.

Every moment of the kiss is like poison.

An addiction roaring in my blood.

A drug that cures me slowly.

We don't come up for air. We don't stop. We continue kissing, recklessly, until we can't no more. My lungs are burning as he kisses me breathlessly, a silent plea of just how much he's missed me too.

With my tits pressed against his sweater, I break the kiss to catch my breath. Elijah's got the devil in his eyes, lust so evident in the way he's caressing my skin and holding me tight.

Elijah seems so crazed with his dark hair all tousled like that and my cherry red gloss smeared all over his swollen lips.

It's the hottest thing I've ever seen.

I think I die and go straight to heaven when Elijah rubs the gloss off with his thumb and licks it off, liking my cherry (and no, not *that* one…*yet*.)

"You like that, Princess?" Elijah groans, and that smirk returns. His fingers trail over my cheeks, tracing over my light freckles. "Look how freaking pretty you are, blushing for me."

Grinning, I bite my lower lip, causing him to rock his hips forward. *Dear God.* My heart almost pumps into overdrive at the sensation of his hardening cock grinding against my panties.

The friction of the lace, stockings, and his black jeans is so thrilling. I buck my hips forward, rolling my head back with a moan at the long-awaited pleasure shooting all over my sensitive clit to my entire body.

"God," I whimper, my hands pressing against his solid, broad chest. "Elijah..."

I haven't dry humped a guy since I was a teenager in senior year, but this...*this feels so much different.* It isn't with a boy, it's with a man fifteen years older than me, and my panties are soaking wet.

Continuously grinding on him in a rhythm, I grin through my desire when Elijah's hands meet my circling hips. I witness the exact moment his eyes glaze over, hungry like a wolf staring at his prey.

Mmhmmm, I'm Elijah Diesel's prey, and I freaking love it.

"Fuckkk, Rosalia." His hips meet my every grind, our sexes so close I can feel his warmth, and the way his hardening cock stirs for me with every move. "You're gonna kill me."

"Good."

It comes so naturally the way I roll my shoulders back, push my breasts out, and seductively move my body around. I dance for him, while Maverick, his bodyguard/driver, is on the other side of the car divider.

The thought alone turns me on even more.

I rush my fingers through my hair, slipping off my velvet red hair ribbon holding my ponytail together, and playfully throw it at him. The devil seamlessly catches it with his teeth, rolling his head into the leather headrest like my own diabolic prize.

Mmhmmm.

Elijah watches me with hooded eyes while I fluff up my voluminous hair, knowing just how much he loves it like this.

For a moment, I imagine what it would be like if we weren't in his moving SUV. If we were in his hotel room, naked, no friction in the way. I'm so wet that gliding my pussy over his jean-covered erection becomes so smooth and vigorous, and I can't help myself. It transfers to his jeans, creating a mess filled with my arousal.

My hardened nipples stab through my crop top and I almost go over the edge when he squeezes my tits, my piercing so obvious through the thin fabric of both the crop top and my lacy bra.

I can't get enough of this warmth surrounding my heart, the nervousness, and the thrill capsizing inside me all at once.

Our eyes lock.

Elijah smirks, flickering my sensitive nipples with his thumbs. And then…

"Ohhh, yeah!" I moan, and without warning, warmth rushes up my spine. "Yes, yes, yes."

I explode, my mouth forming an O shape. I was so damn sensitive, I just knew I wasn't going to last.

This feels incredible.

He hasn't even touched me yet.

This is so embarrassing, but I don't care.

My orgasm takes over, and with every throb of my pussy, Elijah grinds me even more erratically over him, prolonging the desire rippling throughout my entire body.

"Yes," he groans. "Just like that, babygirl, come for me just like that."

Elijah's grip on my hips turns deadly, and just like that, I'm erratically bouncing. My ample breasts jitter, and his tongue sucks on my nipples through my crop top so seductively rough, it causes my breaths to thicken even more, all because of him.

I can barely keep my heavy eyes open.

It's impossible, no matter how much Elijah tells me to.

My arousal seeps through both my panties and stockings to his jeans, leaving more wet patches. I don't stop grinding, giving into pleasure.

"You're such a good girl. I want you to do that again for me." Elijah smolders, praising me. "But not until I allow you to."

Wrapping the velvet ribbon around my neck, he tugs me close with it, diving his tongue into my cleavage. His mouth growing wild over my silk-covered nipples. "Hmmm, so good."

Jesus, oh, wow.

His tongue ravishes me, circling and sexily nibbling on my nipples before focusing on my left one, sucking on it, while his tongue flickers my piercing around.

It. Feels. So. Good.

I press him closer into my tits, losing my rhythm dry humping him because the way my body is responding to him is fucking with my head. Nobody has ever played around with my nipple piercing like he is right now.

"You feel so fucking good, baby, I need more."

"Me too, Elijah. *Ohmigod.*"

"Use your words, *Peaches.*"

"I can't…I—*OH*," I moan, mind blown away with just how good his tongue feels, all the while his thick cock brings me closer and closer to complete bliss. "Elijah, I need you to…"

"To *what?*" He breathes, his voice all rough and teeth gritted, trying to control himself.

My heart can't stop racing.

"You know…"

"Spill it out, Rosa."

Before I know it, he unclips my tennis skirt and throws it behind me, leaving me with only my fishnet stockings and panties. I love the way he roams his hands over my flat stomach, slowing by my navel piercing. *He likes it.*

With his every rock, he moves my hips faster against his cock, and my words fail me yet again.

Dear God.

This is too good.

My clit continuously hits the button of his jeans, and it lets go of that part of me that needs to be professional, sophisticated, and controlled in my everyday life. Elijah brings the freak out of me, the girl craving a taste of hell right here willingly grinding on the devil's cock.

It's too much.

So much.

My crazed breaths flood into one, his sandalwood blend all I breathe.

"I'm so close again, Elijah."

"Tell me what you want."

"Touch me. Feel me. Choke me," I whisper lowly, gawking at him through my lashes, conscious his bodyguard can still hear us as muffled rock music fills the air. "Whatever you want."

We're dry humping so erratically that my tits are bouncing like crazy beneath my top again.

"My pretty little slut," Elijah pants, eyes shutting with a growl in desire. "I fucking love the way you feel against me."

I grin his signature devilish grin. *He wants this too.*

Craves me.

Elijah's moaning so loudly, chasing exactly what I'm chasing too, that the sounds of my slippery pussy and his denim loudly gliding against lace makes me feel that thrill I've always wanted.

Pressing my hands against his broad chest, my rocks fasten.

Hmmmm.

When he frantically slams a hand above him, the car rocks and a bright light shines down on us. We glance up simultaneously at the car light he blindly switched on, and laughter follows.

His cheeks are flustered, a tinge of red that works so beautifully with that stubble I'm aching to feel graze my inner thighs, alongside his dangling silver feather earring.

I want this man to destroy me, and I want it now.

How could I have ever hated a man so gorgeous?

"Fuck," Elijah hisses, ravishing his lips along my neck, devouring it with kisses and crazed bites. "You're treading a very dangerous line fucking my mind up like this, Philips."

"Maybe I want to go there."

"Trent would love that."

My eyes meet his.

I never told him.

"Trent and I broke up."

A fire brews in his gaze as he growls, "And you're only fucking telling me now?"

"I didn't think it was important…"

"Stop teasing."

I giggle.

"If you didn't break up with him, I would have killed him. I'm not joking, Rosalia."

"Hmm." I smile, brushing my lips over his. "Well, you're the only man who can *touch me* now, aren't you?"

"I would shut that pretty little mouth of yours before I fuck it."

My mouth hangs open.

Speechless.

My pussy is aching, desperate to be touched by him, so much so that in my fluster, I rush a hand lower, between my thighs. *Yes.* I only get to brush my fingers over my clit, circling it twice before Elijah slaps my hand away.

"*Mine,*" Elijah growls, and before I know it, he roughly throws me across the spacious leather seats, laying me down.

He wastes no time climbing over me, and I smirk when his hand naturally wraps around my throat, his kink getting the better of him.

Desire drips from his eyes. "Only I get to touch this pretty pussy of yours."

Rippp.

I gasp at the echoing tear he just made in the crotch of my stockings, giving him perfect access to me. "Elijah! These are the only fishnet stockings I brought with me to LA!"

"So, I'll buy you another pair."

Just as I'm about to protest, Elijah rips my lace panties and all my words form into a series of loud moans the moment he leans down and presses a kiss on my throbbing, bare pussy.

Oh my God.

It's never felt like this before.

I glance down at him, my breaths all tangled, and he stares up at me between my thighs, a true rocker.

I'm bare to him.

Completely bare.

It surprises me that I don't feel the least bit conscious when Elijah rakes his eyes over my sex, studying it slowly with that smirk of his. "God, you're so beautiful, I can't wait to taste you."

His words prompt even more arousal to drip and I lean up on the leather seats with my forearms, my ass involuntarily grinding against the seats, waiting for him.

I suck in a breath as Elijah kisses up my thighs, blowing hot air, and licking up the clear arousal gliding down them. Slowly.

I desperately need to orgasm again.

I know dying right here with Elijah Diesel between my thighs would be heaven, but freaking breathe, Rosalia.

Feeling my cheeks blush, I bashfully smile. "Elijah, *please.*"

"You want this, *Peaches*?"

"Yes, so much."

"Want me to fuck you hard with my tongue?"

"Mmhmmm."

"Do you always get this wet?"

Because we didn't switch off that car light above him, I notice how his lips glisten and he hasn't even started.

Chewing my lip, I shake my head. "I only get this wet for you."

Without breaking his dark stare, Elijah slaps my pussy downward, hitting my clit first. I gasp, the tingling pain filled with immense pleasure having me squeeze my legs around him.

But he dominantly grips my thighs, spreading them so wide over the leather seats, like I'm doing a mid-air split jump (thank you ballerina perks), and spanks me again. Again. And agai—*fuckkk.*

My head tips back on the seats. Wet echoes have me moaning louder, my entire body convulsing.

"*Oh*! Please touch me, or I'm going to…"

"Patience, my desperate little slut."

I grin. "What if Maverick hears me?"

Elijah boyishly grins back. "Let him hear, babygirl, let him hear me claim what's mine."

The second his warm tongue glides up my sex, I know it won't be long until I come undone. Moaning, I slam a hand against the window, its coldness rippling across my skin, fading in his heat.

Elijah's grip around my throat tightens, his other hands molding my tits as he recklessly works my pussy with his gifted tongue. He rolls it ever so achingly slowly around my swollen clit, circling it, teasing me cruelly until he darkly chuckles. The vibrations make me lose my mind, and he turns into a savage beast.

His tongue is wild with each swirl, suck, and rub. Diagonally. Up and down. Swirling round and round as my arousal laces the air. He doesn't come up for a breath, instead eats me out like a madman.

"Fuck. That feels so good, Elijah baby."

"Mmhmmm."

"I want to feel like this forever."

If this is hell, I want to stay here forever.

I feel the waves of desire rippling through me, so close to the edge that my legs begin to tremble.

"Don't you dare come," Elijah growls against my pussy. "I'm nowhere near done with you."

"I…oh my God, I can't help it."

"Rosalia," he warns, choking me harder when my only response is screaming out his name, but my heaving breaths only make my clit throb faster.

I writhe, desperately wanting to hold on. But when he erotically bites down on my clit, I lose it, feeling like I'm on my final breath when I moan out his name, abs tense as my body squirms around.

Oh my.

My legs tremble around him, tightening by his broad shoulders with a blurred vision. Elijah continues eating me out, all while I orgasm around his tongue.

He turns even more vicious when his chokehold slips. *Fuck, he's not going to stop until he punishes me for coming.*

He's moaning against my pulsating pussy, his face fully submerged in me. I rock my hips, grinding on his face with my legs now wrapped around his neck.

I can't help myself.

My self-control is out the window, the pulses intensifying at Elijah's sounds alone.

"You're such a bad girl disobeying me like that."

"What are you going to do about it?"

"Punish you. But not right now."

Elijah circles his tongue lower, and the moment he pushes it inside me without warning, I scream out his name, my fingers rushing to tug his wavy hair and dive him deeper into me. It works.

I'm not going to survive this.

He lifts my hips off the car seats, elevating my body with his hands squeezing my ass. The new angle hits differently as I ride his face, abs still clenched. I can feel just how wet I am, how it's seeping down my thighs and into his stubble that grazes my inner thighs, sparks shooting alive.

The roughness of his beard becomes more intense as every second goes by, his jaw working tirelessly between my thighs.

My eyes roll back at the warm bliss.

"Please don't stop," I beg.

"Baby, that isn't even a freaking option."

I'm so sensitive that when Elijah roughly spreads my thighs wider again so he can work me deeper, I almost tell him to stop. But I don't want him to. I want him to ruin me and ruin me good.

My continuous moans lace with the heavy sounds of him eating me out and his own groans. Setting me back down on the leather, his fingers slip into me without warning, pumping me fast with two fingers before slipping in a third.

"Elijah!"

"Breathe, baby."

Elijah turns up the pace to lightning speed, and I feel incredible, like the luckiest girl alive. I'm so flustered that when he sinks a fourth finger in and out of me, finger fucking me so deep, my mouth gapes from the intensity and just how tight I am.

Oh.

My.

GOD.

But it doesn't matter to Elijah, whose tongue moves to my glistening clit, not breaking our heated stare once with every fast, reckless flicker. *Mhmmm. I'm gonna come again, all over his face.*

I expect it to hurt more, but as he stretches me deeper, rocking into me so viciously that happy tears stream down my cheeks, I feel nothing but immense satisfaction.

Satisfaction while he fills my pussy with him, never stopping as he rocks his fingers beyond knuckle-deep, my body tensing up.

"Tell me, has anybody ever fucked you like this before?"

I shake my head, spent. "Never. You're the first."

"You like this, baby, hmm? You like it when I fuck your pussy with my fingers like this?"

I can't stop nodding. "Yes, so much."

"You're taking it so well. I can only imagine how it would feel with my cock pumping inside you instead, then in that pretty ass of yours."

Oh?

"I want that."

Elijah savagely grins. "With time, *mon ange.*"

My angel.

I slam my head against the leather car seat, perspiration gliding all down my body. My uncontrollable moans intensify as Elijah sucks on my clit, so filthily hot, and sounds so erotic, my toes curl up. The double penetration is…*whoa.*

Quivering, I lose my mind when Elijah smirks, sexily spits on my clit, rubs it in, and then goes back to devouring me. I'm turned on even more by it and the passion that I squeeze my large breasts, rolling around my pink piercing with my thumb, just like Elijah did.

"It's too much," I squeal, gasping louder when he pumps me even harder, gauging a reaction. My heartbeat is in my pussy, pulsing as fast as the beat in my chest. "I'm going to come!"

"No, you're not, not until I tell you to." Elijah shakes his head, my arousal glistening all over his lips. "Not unless you ask nicely."

"Please."

He softly shakes his head again, his fingers growing even wilder fucking in and out of me, so much so that he's pushing me higher up the seats I'm lying on.

I bat my lashes, our pants fueling the air. "*Please*, Elijah."

"*Ask*, Rosalia, don't *beg*."

"But I like begging."

"I'm sure you do." Elijah devilishly smirks, abruptly slipping four fingers from my pussy.

They're coated in me as he hooks his fingers in my mouth, silencing me, and I submit, tasting myself.

Hmmm.

So good.

He continues doing that, slipping his fingers from my pussy into my mouth, making me taste myself. Over again. It's such an erotic exchange.

"Look at you, Rosalia, so wild and flustered over your own taste. Have you ever tasted yourself before?"

With my cheeks burning up, I shake my head.

Elijah's gray-onyx eyes darken to no return. "*Suck*."

Submitting, I suggestively suck on Elijah's fingers, coating my tongue with my sweetness, the first time I've ever tasted myself in my life.

Hmmm, so erotic.

"You like it, hmm, don't you?" Elijah growls, almost fascinated. His free hand cups my face, all while I grind on his jeans, needing him. "You like tasting your cum on my fingers. I see it in your eyes. I bet you'd like sucking your orgasm off my thick cock someday too. You'll do it so well, Princess, I know you will."

His fingers hooked inside my mouth render me incapable of speaking, so I nod instead, licking off the sweetness of myself with a slight grin. I feel so filthy given how badly I like the taste of myself but love the admiration in Elijah's eyes when I do, merged with the sounds we both make.

"I really want to come all over your face," I murmur when his fingers slip out of me with a pop. "Please."

"Say it like you mean it, Princess."

"I'll be a good girl if you let me come." Moaning, I brush my lips against his and ever so achingly whisper, "*Please, daddy.*"

Elijah pauses for a moment, pure lust between us before he dives back between my thighs. Everything gets even crazier. He fingers me so fast, I see starts. Like literal fucking stars. A galaxy.

With his raspy voice telling me to come, I let go of every angelic piece of me and give myself to the devil for the third time in minutes.

"Oh fuck, yeah, that's it, be a good girl and come for me, *Peaches.*"

I'm *there.*

I'm right freaking *there.*

Oh my dear God!

I come undone violently with Elijah taunting me, slapping my pussy so good that pleasure explodes and I tense my abs, uncontrollably beginning to squirt. With every slap, I gush, my eyes widening in awe.

Oh my…wow.

It gets even more messy when he slides his fingers deep inside me, then vigorously pulls out, my squirting cum spraying *everywhere.*

I can't control my convulsing body.

How desperately I want this to last forever.

How badly I just want to kiss Elijah Diesel every time I press my thighs together to intensify my pussy's throbs, yet he dominantly slams them spread and spanks me even harder, drowning in me.

This is so unreal.

Holy shit. Earth-shattering is what it is.

I can't get over this feeling…complete bliss.

With my stomach clenching and body quivering, I scream out his name until my throat aches from my intense orgasm. I've never squirted in front of a man before, only a damn vibrator. But Elijah changes that.

He changes everything.

My heart is erratically beating, unchanged. I can't stop gushing, my abs all tensed up as I squirt all over his stubble, face, and tongue.

Elijah widens his mouth more with every spray, and I feel so dirty in the best way. He's enjoying it. Enjoying our sinful attraction.

"You're such a good girl. Look at you. I'm so proud of you." He grins, rubbing my swollen pink pussy and swallowing every single drop of me. "Hmmm, you taste so good. I can't get enough."

The more he fingers me, the more I come gushing. He makes it a rhythm, adding his tongue too, fucking me deep with everything he's got, all while my legs uncontrollably shake, coming right down his throat.

His tongue laps around my pussy and clit, riling me on until my intense orgasm settles down to soft pulses, reminders of him. I'm breathless and completely spent, my limbs numb off euphoria.

Fucck, he's so good.

I grin up at him, all dreamy. "I think you destroyed me, Elijah Diesel."

Elijah glances back and forth between my eyes, smiling. "As I should, *Peaches*."

"Mhmmm."

"How do you feel?"

"Ecstatic. Like I'm floating."

Elijah's lips find mine and the taste of myself on his tongue makes me wish this had happened between us sooner.

Cupping his drenched stubbled jaw, the passionate kiss is by far the most aggressive one we've ever had. It's so hot, filthy, and loud, that when he pulls away, he erotically bites my lip, tugging it to him, and I can't help but grin.

I rub my tongue over his wet stubble, and that only makes him hold me in the solace of his arms tighter. It confirms everything.

I'm addicted to Elijah Diesel—the edgy, melancholic rocker—and by the flutters in my chest, I know I always will.

A loud buzz like an intercom interrupts our make-out session. Maverick's voice floods through what seems to be a speaker. "Mr. Diesel, we have arrived at the hotel…um, like fifteen minutes ago."

Elijah and I share a look.

Oops.

"Shit, he probably thinks I'm some…I don't know, a hoe."

Elijah rolls his eyes, helping me slip on my tennis skirt. "No, he doesn't, Rosalia."

"He will! And look at the car! We can't leave it like this!" I panic, my cheeks still flustered. "Trust me when I say Maverick won't even look me in the eye. He probably heard everything."

Elijah cups my jaw for a second, planting a kiss at the corner of my lips. "Said I wanted him to fucking hear. I wasn't lying. Stop stressing, Princess." He chuckles. "He's gotta get used to it with you around me."

Okay, I have definitely died and gone to heaven.

I nod, my gaze then falling to his jeans, and just how painfully hard he is. "Um…"

Elijah follows my eyes, and when he glances back up at me, his eyes are full onyx. He doesn't say a word, yet his smug smirk doesn't fall off his lips all while he slips my panties into his jean pocket, and I do my best to make myself presentable and fix up my stockings.

This is going to be a total disaster.

"Rosalia?"

"Yeah?"

"When you step out of the SUV, just brace yourself."

I look at Elijah like he's crazy. "Brace myself for what?"

He flashes me his infamous smirk, nodding toward the car window. "You'll see…"

I whip my head around to glance out the tinted windows, and the second I do… "Holy shit."

There are fans camping outside of the hotel with red velvet gold barriers and security guards holding them back. And I'm talking *hundreds*. They're jumping, mouths gaped open, probably screaming, but I can't hear shit because this Volvo is soundproof. There are camera flashes everywhere and just like that, my heart sinks.

What if they throw invisible rocks at me?

Elijah must sense my worry because he offers me a soft smile. "Don't worry. This is just normal. Just stay with me while I walk through, okay?"

I nod because my mouth is the definition of dried up Sahara style.

The moment Elijah opens the car door for me, blaring screams and joyful shouts drum my ears. My gaze catches a girl with her tits out and '***Marry Me Elijah Diesel***' written over them, even being inventive enough for having the two *i*'s in his name align with her nipples. She also looks straight out of the '80s and is as high as a kite while smoking a joint, so there's that. She's being pushed back by one of the security guards, and I kind of have to smile.

Rock and roll at its finest.

I stand out of the Volvo and Maverick is there, holding my luggage. By the way he's looking everywhere else but at me, I know he totally heard Elijah bringing me to complete ecstasy. Three times.

Shit.

I feel Elijah's warmth as he steps out behind me, much-needed fresh air kissing my skin. I'm certain my cheeks are beet red.

The screams intensify at Elijah Diesel's presence, the fans held back on either side of the red-carpet runway leading to the hotel simultaneously rushing forth. But the guards are on top them, shoving them back so there's a clear path again. The thundery flashes of cameras from all angles go crazy, brightening up Los Angeles at 3:30 a.m. *This is Elijah's everyday life.*

Wow.

I'm kind of in awe when Elijah waves at his fans and signs a few autographs, takes a few selfies while actually *smiling* because there as so many sides to him. I know the Elijah who literally hates everybody, and the Elijah who adores his fans. He has a dark, lonely heart, but every once in a while, a sun shower passes through, leaving rainbows and permanent marks of hope.

I'm quick to get all my luggage while Elijah returns to my side and he and his bodyguard exchange a few words. Not wanting to make this any more awkward than it already is, I shift my gaze to the hotel in front of us and *whoa.*

It is STUNNING!

Blue-tinged glass, a gazillion levels, and LA luxury at its finest.

Before I know it, Elijah takes my luggage and slips his hand into mine as he guides me inside the hotel with one final goodbye to the dedicated fans.

PSA: He literally just casually glided his fingers through mine, okay. I'm like hyperventilating over here, guys.

I know better than to question him because this is just another example of his possessiveness at its elite.

"Wow, that was intense!"

"Welcome to my life." Elijah slightly chuckles when it's just us. "It's…a constant."

"You mean they camp out at your hotel all the time?"

"Every city at every hour, yep."

My eyes widen. "That's what I call dedicated."

"Yeah, they're pretty hardcore."

The hotel is even more grand inside the lobby with ceilings so tall, my neck hurts just looking up at the dazzling chandelier. I expect to slow at the lobby desk, but when Elijah nods at the front desk clerk and concierge and then just continues walking, I arch a brow at him.

"Um… Don't I have to check in?"

"I'm already checked in," Elijah says ever so causally, walking up to the brass elevators.

"I know, but I just presumed I was staying here too…"

"You are. I'm in the presidential suite."

My jaw drops. "*What*? I'm in the…?"

"You're staying with me." Elijah smirks as the doors ding open and we step into the elevator car. "In the presidential."

He presses the *69—presidential suite* button and I almost want to roll my eyes because of course that everything has to seem so sexual now.

Wait.

Did he just allude we're sleeping in the same bed?

My eyes widen as I stare up at him, not really registering what he said because *God,* I'm still trying to recover and catch my breath from the three orgasms he wildly stole from me.

"I…huh?"

His smirk deepens. "The presidential suite features two separate bedrooms, Rosalia."

"Oh, righttt." I smile, feeling stupid that part of me thought… *one bed.*

Before I know it, the doors ding open and wow, I didn't know this was a private elevator. Staring back at me is something out of *Sex and the city*. It's our very own Manhattan loft style presidential suite, right here in California.

Floor-to-ceiling windows of Los Angeles dazzling lights.

Italian charcoal marble floors with thin gold veins.

Expensive leather furniture that I'm almost too scared to touch.

Elijah guides me down a hall leading to two rooms. He takes the right, nudging the door open, revealing a gorgeous bedroom dipped in a silvery blue hue because of the moonlight. It's three times the size of my bedroom at home.

Elijah sets my luggage at the edge of my bed, his erection so damn obvious as he strides back to me with a lingering smile. Cupping my jaw, he traces my lips. *Happy. He seems happy.*

"I suggest you get some sleep, just like I'm going to," he says, his voice low. "This is your bedroom. Your private en suite is beyond your walk-in closet. If you need me for anything, I'm in the bedroom directly opposite this one."

If you need me for anything.

I nod, still trying to comprehend that I'm in Los Angeles with a man I used to fantasize about at seventeen, and now… all those fantasies with this fated rocker are coming to life.

"Yep, think so. En suite's beyond the walk-in closet and I'm right across the hall, okay. Got it. Thank you for this, by the way."

"It's okay. Well, I'm going to head to…" He nods, the air crackling between us in a sexualized silence as he gestures behind him. *His bedroom.* "Bed."

"We need to talk, Elijah. About all of"—I loosely motion a hand between us—"*this.*"

"It's late. We'll talk in the morning."

"Sounds good. Well, good night." I smile softly, my heart beating like crazy in my chest.

"Night." Elijah swallows thickly, his smile simmering to…*just him.* He doesn't move. He doesn't leave. *He stays.*

Something shifts, it becomes quitter, so quiet I can hear my every breath. And the way Elijah's looking at me…as if he's still devouring between my thighs.

Hunger. So much hunger.

Need.

Attraction.

And I'm talking emotionally too. Mentally. *Deeper.* He's looking at me with such solace in his glossy eyes like I'm the only one who understands him and his crazy.

"Elijah…is everything okay?"

The air crackles between us, and what comes next shocks me.

"I don't know how the fuck this is gonna work, but, Rosalia Philips, I wanna be yours."

And then, without ever looking at me again, he's gone.

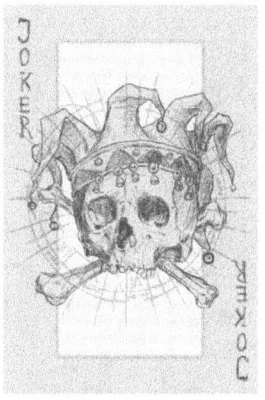

Chapter
TWENTY-FIVE

Elijah

I*'m so fucked.* Actually, I'm beyond it. Everything I've ever done in my life has been to avoid *feeling*—a coping mechanism for all my trauma—but Rosalia Philips wrecks me every single time.

I just told her I wanted her.

I do.

Of course I freaking do, but God, why did I have to vocalize it?

Why couldn't my mouth have pit stopped two seconds at my head?

Silvery moonlight cascades across my presidential suite bedroom, rippling over me. It's been seconds since I walked out of Rosalia's bedroom. *Seconds.* What's worse is that I can't do anything without thinking of her.

Guilt sets in as I kick off my biker boots and pace my luxurious suite, my head all fuzzy.

Is it wrong that Rosalia Philips can't stop invading my mind?

That I flew her out to LA without even telling her the reasons why?

That she trusted me enough to fly to me without a proper explanation?

It's so wrong.

So fucking wrong.

I keep on forgetting how young she is. Twenty-one. But that's only because her wisdom and fieriness are golden. I may be fifteen years older than her; we may hate each other some days, but there are just some things that really click for us.

Like emotional trauma.

Like classic literature.

Like *orgasms*.

Ahh, fuccck.

I rake a hand through my hair, taking a seat at the edge of my bed with a million thoughts, none that truly make sense.

Should I go over to her room and talk to her?

No, no, she could be asleep.

She just finished six weeks of intense ballet performances, Elijah, she needs to sleep.

Well, then what the hell do I do with myself now?

It's almost 4:00 a.m.

I can't sleep.

It's Diesel Rose's last Californian show in the *Killing Me Slowly* tour in exactly sixteen hours. I'm going to look like shit, but I don't care. I'm going to feel like even more shit if I don't sort this out.

Rosalia.

Rosalia.

Rosalia.

What have you done to me?

The more I devoured her in the Volvo tonight, the more lyrics filled my lungs. Words coated with truth, coated with us, coated with those viper eyes.

The melodies wouldn't stop, the riffs and beating rhythms matching my heartbeat.

But now I'm all alone.

Again. Without her.

And I hate it.

Rosalia Philips a constant in my mind.

A drug I crave overdosing on.

My muse.

The same muse behind all the provocative thoughts chaining my mind when I sink into my king-sized bed with an achingly hard cock. As much as I know I shouldn't, I can't help myself, cupping my constrained erection through the denim of my jeans. *Dear Satan, save me.*

My breath slows at the taunting scrap of lace hanging out of my pocket. *Her panties.* The same blue panties I ripped off her earlier, still coated with her orgasm. It's forbidden as sin. I know it is. But as I said, *I can't control myself.*

I feel like a psychopath for slipping them out and feeling their wetness before taking a whiff of her panties, smirking darkly against them as I do.

Jesus Christ.

My eyes flutter shut, my cold heart defrosting because *fuckkk,* they smell of her.

Rosalia Philips, what have you done?

My thick cock begins to throb, every single pulse so fucking visible through my pants. I need a release from the sexual tension, and I know just how to reach that euphoric level of complete ecstasy, followed by complete numbness.

No feelings.

No troubles.

Just pleasure.

I strip off my clothes in seconds, flinging them on the other side of my suite with no care in the world. Only her ripped panties remain. My hard cock slaps against my abs like a greedy beast, and it takes all of me not to waltz into Rosalia's room and demand she gets on her knees for me. I saw the way she was gawking my cock earlier, how she wanted it. *I did too.*

My usual rosy, pink head is now even darker, a borderline tinged red from just how sensitive I've gotten from dry humping and witnessing Rosalia orgasm three times.

You're killing me, Peaches.

I waste no time slowly descending a hand down my taut abs and defined V-cut, the sensation electrifying when I grip the base of my dick, roughly stroking my thick shaft. I groan, heat strangling my breaths as I wrap her rippled panties around my cock, her warm arousal coating my length like it's her tongue doing this to me. Destroying me.

I wrap the lace around my head, edging it down my shaft with each fury-filled stroke.

Oh God.

Oh God.

Oh God.

Fuckkk yes.

I shut my eyes, imagining that pretty pussy, the way she screamed my name and came for me. The way her cunt spasmed for me, soft as velvet, burning a fire deep inside me. The way she squirted on me like a goddamn queen... *As if I need the fucking reminder right now.*

A hiss turned moan escaped my throat at just how badly I'm turned on.

This is all Rosalia's fault.

All Rosalia's fault as I recklessly fuck myself, squeezing myself tighter, especially at my crown, making my abs tense up. I let the fantasy of her spur me on, my entire body desperate with just how fast I'm working myself.

Sandalwood coated arousal in the air and her lingering taste on my tongue drives me wild. I love that I can still taste her. That her orgasms are still smeared over my face.

I didn't lock my bedroom door.

The mere thought of me getting caught jerking myself off to Rosalia has me circling the head of my throbbing cock with my thumb, the thin silvery metal rolling around my skin, edging me on more, until pre-cum leaks out of my swollen head.

I'm so into it that I coat it over my shaft, using it as lube, alongside her orgasm filled panties.

"Ohhh," I pant, thrusting my hips from the bed, ass tense, meeting every rough stroke. "*Fuckkk.*"

My heart jolts at the loud knock on the door. So does my cock.

Ohhh shit.

"Elijah?" Rosalia calls out, genuine concern laced in her voice. "Is everything okay?"

What does she think I'm doing in here? Killing myself?

I don't say a word.

Not a single word.

I don't trust my mouth enough not to growl for her to come in.

I'm so close.

I'm so damn close and there's nothing I can do to stop it, not even when my bedroom clicks open. I don't let myself register it, too caught up in a fluster, and simply keep going.

My eyes flicker across the room, and…

Hell.

I stroke my cock even more erratically, a slow smirk burning up my lips at her gasp.

"Oh my God!"

Amused green eyes meet my gaze, tired from ballet and the flight, sparkling in a desire I've never seen before.

Here Rosalia Philips is, in my presidential suite, watching me fuck myself with a tan oversized sweater and the tightest leggings on. The moonlight falls ever so perfectly over her, illuminating her messy bun, and the way she hasn't moved a single fraction from her position by the doorframe.

Yeah, baby, come touch me and watch me come undone for you.

I rub her lace panties slowly around my thickness and then throw them to her. She catches them with a wicked smirk and drops them to the floor by her feet, far more interested in me.

Good.

I rock my hips faster, edging my dick on, loving how Rosalia seductively bites her lip, how she squeezes her thighs together and helps herself, her wide eyes wandering to my hard cock, staring.

"Oh my God," Rosalia gasps for the second time, her hungry gaze growing wild. "You're so…*wow!*"

My rhythm intensifies and I cup my heavy balls with my left hand, squeezing them softly. All I think about is her. *God.* I crave kissing her with both our orgasms on my tongue.

Cursing in French with just how much I need this, I keep going, over and over, leaning my head back into the silk pillowcase, my eyes still locked on her.

I turn into a starved wolf, my gaze darkening.

"I know you want it, *Peaches*," I growl. "Come fucking get me."

In a heartbeat, Rosalia rushes to me, but I halt her mid-way.

"Not *here.*"

I rise up from the bed and stride right past her to the floor-to-ceiling windows, early morning Los Angeles staring back at us with dark skies, twinkling stars, and skylines.

Leaning my shoulder blades against the cold glass, I pivot my hips forward so my ass isn't pressed against the window. With my shoulders slumped and eyes hooded as I gaze at my twenty-one-year-old muse, my bittersweet venom, my babygirl.

"*Here,*" I clarify in a seductive breath. "If you want to suck my thick cock like a good girl, you do it on your knees, right *here.*"

Rosalia's jaw hangs open. "But…but half of Los Angeles can see you!"

I shoot her a smoldering half-smirk. "Exactly."

Desire fueling my veins, I'm not thinking straight, but I don't care. I'm horny as fuck, and I want this. *Want her.*

I don't stop working myself, massaging my balls, and grinding my cock in the air as she strides to me, eager. Her fingers skim over the trim of her oversized sweater, wanting to strip, but I stop her.

"No, don't take it off." I shake my head with a growl. "I'm a starvin' man, *Peaches,* a selfish, starvin' man wanting you to come blow my mind and cure my aching cock."

Coming to a halt inches from me, Rosalia's gaze drops *there* and… her jaw drops.

That's when the slow, sexy smirk burns up my lips.

Mmhmmm.

She just saw it.

Rosalia does a double take at my cock numerous times, her mouth falling even wider, and not to be all smug and stuff, but I can practically see her salivating.

"Holy shit, Elijah!" Her longing eyes flicker to mine in amused shock. "You're…"

"I'm *pierced,*" I finish off her words with a rasp. We simultaneously glance down at my cock piercing on the tip of my head as it glimmers with my precum, skimming the moonlight. I fist myself rougher, coating the thin metal ring with a fixed small centered metal ball in more of my leaking pre-cum. "Fuck, yeah, I am."

An uncontrolled moan escapes Rosalia.

"What are you thinking?" I whisper lowly.

"Everything. I'm just so…fascinated. *Wow.*"

"Yeah?"

"Yeah." Rosalia nods, her smile so dirty with speckles of bashfulness. "Did it hurt?"

"Not as much as my cock is aching right now."

Rosalia beautifully smiles as I circle her so that she's the one with her back against the floor-to-ceiling windows. I leave a gap, cautious, because I know it won't take long to explode with a single touch by her. I've been edged on badly enough; I need the real thing. *Right. Now.*

"What should I do about that, Mr. Diesel?" Rosalia purrs, teasing me.

I can't help cupping her cheeks and the aggressive peck I place on her lips. If I kiss her any longer, it'll consume me. I need to get lost overdosing on her. I don't want to *feel*.

I pull back, seeing just how much she's enjoying this.

"On. Your. Knees. Rosalia." I growl, my voice softening to a moan as I add, "*Please*."

Rosalia nods but takes a detour first. She gazes into my eyes, almost asking for permission with those heart-shaped lips of hers parted in pure delight before they're on my hot nipple piercings.

I instantly fist her hair, unable to believe just how good it feels with her tongue driving me wild like that. Rolling them around with her tongue, devouring me, and then sucking on my nipples hard.

I throw my head back, my Adam's apple bobbing up and down. "*Ohhh fuck.*"

She keeps going, obsessed with my nipple piercings, all while I continue stroking my cock, slower, desperate to have her ruin me before I explode.

Rosalia does just that, planting open-mouth kisses down the center of my abs, adding her swirling tongue the lower she descends down my body, seductively nibbling on my abs.

With eyes locked on me, she falls to her knees, her lips inches from where I need her.

My smirk deepens.

Yes.

For a fraction of a second, something close to panic flashes in her eyes. "I, um, I've never… I've never really done this before."

I arch a brow. "Never done *what* exactly?"

Silence trickles in the space between us for a moment.

"I've never done *anything* to satisfy a man before."

My heart slows. "You're a virgin?"

Rosalia's cheeks heat, all flustered. "Yes."

That smirk of mine grows even wilder as I trail my pointer finger across her jaw. "That Trent idiot never fucked you?"

"No."

"Never made you come?"

"Elijah!"

Fire swirls in my eyes. "Just. Tell. Me."

Rosalia shakes her head softly. "We were never really intimate, not as much as I would have liked anyway. We were waiting for a right time."

"There's always a right time, Rosalia, not with you. Your beauty outruns any *Wuthering Heights* rose garden, Austen's *Persuasion*, or dripping poetry of Plath's."

Her entire face lights up. "That's so beautiful."

"It's the truth. Didn't that asshole see the light in your eyes? The desire?"

"Yeah, well…no. I'm a virgin."

"So?" I whisper. "Is that supposed to change anything between us?"

"Well, you…I thought maybe you'd prefer somebody more experienced. So if I'm…lacking, I—"

I squeeze my pierced hard-on for emphasis. "You gave me an erection, are making me lose my mind, and I can still taste you on my tongue, Rosalia, so trust me, you're not lacking. Besides, I want to be your first one of these days, pop that needy cherry."

The warmest smile rushes up her lips. "Okay."

"I'll help you, babygirl. Teach you," I whisper, slipping my hand away from my prized possession. "I promise."

She nods.

I let out a groan as she detours from my aching cock, and instead roams her mouth over my happy trail of short dark hair, and then my vaunted V-cut, right over the **Peaches** tattoo I got inked years ago.

For her.

"Just so you know, nobody else can touch you," Rosalia whispers, using my words from earlier this morning as she kisses over the tattoo a trillionth time, sucking on the warm skin above until I'm moaning at the hickey she makes. "You're *mine*, Lijah."

I love the possessiveness in her eyes as she creates another reddish hickey, then another.

Jesus.

"'*But it happens that I want you, and so I just haven't room for'…*" Rosalia breathes, quoting Fitzgerald's *The Beautiful and Damned*, all while seductively glancing up at me through her onyx lashes, the devil in her eyes. "'*Any other desires.*'"

And with my heart lodged in my throat, Rosalia's fingertips are fire as they wrap around the base of my thick cock and my eyes almost roll back from the pleasure she gives.

I'm so big that her fingertips don't meet with one hand alone, so she works me with two hands, stroking me slowly at first, and I think I'm dying.

She just recited a line from The Beautiful and Damned *for me.*

Our book. That's our fucking book.

The first edition that laced us together.

"Yes, baby, that's it." My grip around her hair tightens so fast, it almost jolts her head back. "You don't need my permission to go harder. Don't be scared. Promise I won't bite."

"Always a smart-ass, huh?" she muffles back under her breath, but her grin is golden.

Throwing her a wink, I grin through the groans she prompts when she works me harder, twisting her grip and squeezing me fast like the dirty girl she is.

I place a hand over hers, gliding it up my cock and slowing by my sensitive head. "Tighten your grip whenever you come up here, yeah?"

Rosalia nods and when I slip my hand away, gives it a try. "*Oh, like this?*"

"*Tighter.*"

She does it again, this time tightening her grip by the crown in a smooth motion, rougher with every twisted stroke, exactly how I meant. "This?"

"Holy fuck, yesss." My eyes roll back, and that's when I slip another hand through her hair, readily aware I can't hold back much longer.

Her hands grow wild around my cock, the pumps fasten, so reckless in speed that I can't even breathe. It's just pants and groans and uncontrollable noises escaping my throat at the sound of arousal gliding on my cock with every jerk.

At this point, I don't even care how loud I'm being.

Rosalia's warm lips baptize my darkened head, and I swear to

God my heart is going to blast out of my chest at her moan. The same chest that's heaving, rising up and down violently.

Her tongue explores my cock piercing, never losing my gaze with that devilish smirk. She circles her tongue around my slit, right by my piercing, and then teasingly pulls back.

My entire body is hot. Glistening. Throbbing.

I need her more than ever.

Pre-cum shoots from my cock, coating her lips in a pearly gloss with every stroke. Rosalia rolls her tongue over her pink plump lips, tasting my arousal, and we moan at the same time.

"Daddy's little girl is doing so fucking well, hmmm?"

"Yes, I love the way you taste," Rosalia breathlessly purrs. "I had a Cherry Cola before knocking, so you taste like cherries to me. Like pickled cherries—tartly sweet, a little briny."

My heart pangs.

I stocked the refrigerator with them for her.

"Give me a taste." Curious, I softly brush my thumb across Rosalia's glistering lips, my cock jolting in her grip when she sucks on my hand. That's when I bring it up to my own lips, licking my pre-cum merged with a distant Cherry Cola taste. *Hmm.* "You're right, it tastes really fucking good."

Rosalia grins, pressing my dick up against my taut stomach so she can rub me firmer from my full balls, all the way up to my slit. I can't stop moving, going crazy in her grip.

"Touch yourself, Rosa. I want to see you be naughty."

Eagerly nodding, it's almost as if she's been waiting for me to give her permission as she slides a hand under her oversized sweater, fingers vigorously crawling to the waistband of her leggings.

"No." I click my tongue. "Take everything off except your panties, I wanna see you touch yourself like a whore."

Rosalia sultry nibbles on her lower lip, then whispers, "I'm not wearing any panties, Elijah."

Jesus fucking Christ.

"Then you better do what I tell you before I fuck you face down on the bed with your pretty ass up, little girl."

Complying, Rosalia pulls away from my dick for a second as she strips off her oversized sweater. I scan her defined ballerina abs and return the shy smile on her lips as she stands, motioning to her bra.

My erratic breathing does nothing but intensity the second my fingers skim over the blue lace of her sheer bra.

Unclipping her bra, I watch as it falls to the floor and she slowly spins around, her ample breasts springing free, looking so soft yet naturally firm.

My frantic hands cup her naked tits for the first time since we've met, our gaze darkening in the same exact second. I'll never forget the beautiful smile that spreads across Rosalia's lips when I instinctively kiss the junction of her neck, my lips erratic in open-mouth kisses. I can't stop sucking on her sweet coconut skin, sexily biting it, swirling my tongue, making hickeys, listening to her groan.

I think I count four smile lines on either side of her lips—no, five, and *gah*, how it captivates my tainted soul.

She slides her ponytail holder off. Her loose waves cascade down her chest, framing her breasts. Her light rosy nipples taunt me. That pink diamond piercing sparkles in the light, setting me on fire.

I want to suck on those tits, slowly, all night.

And I do the exact opposite, lowering my head and recklessly mauling them with my erratic tongue. Squeezing her ample tits with my big hands, I suck on her peddled velvet nipples. Hard. Giving them both the attention they need with my flickering tongue, making her crazy.

Rosalia's got a pretty beauty spot right by her nipple piercing that I ravish, sucking her so hard that if she were lactating, it would spray across the bedroom.

"Elijah," she moans, her hands sloppy against my dick, too concentrated on her own intense pleasure. "Fuck."

I pull away from her nipples with a pop, too selfish of a man right now than to hear those moans anywhere else but pressed up against my cock leaking pre-cum.

There's a tattoo beneath Rosalia's breasts. A thin outline of diamond scissors is in white ink, wrapped in a shaded soft gray ribbon, and exploding from the side are outlines of blooming flowers in the darkest of reds. The entire tattoo is small but big enough to grasp and get lost in.

I know Rosalia Philips too well.

There's a story in that tattoo.

There has to be.

Rosalia and I don't share a word as she strips off her leggings, almost shyly, the crotch completely soaked as it lands beside us in a heavy thud. *Fuckkk, that bare pussy.*

"God, you're so fucking hot. Turn around for me, baby," I muse, softly stroking my hot cock. "Do it slowly."

Rosalia does exactly that, her gorgeous naked body and the sight of her bare ass screams for me to make marks until it's no longer a creamy tan, but tinged in red like a devil. And patches of white in the shape of my handprint.

I want to kiss it, caress it, fuck it, never forget it.

"Bend over. I want to see that pretty pussy of yours."

Rosalia does, the ends of her blonde waves kissing the floor as she takes it one step further when she wraps her hands around her ankles, giving me a full view.

"*Fuckkk*, Rosalia, look at that pretty pink pussy begging to be fucked. You want me to fuck it, baby?"

My baby is so wet, just like in the Volvo earlier. She's so wet her entire pussy glistens in desire, pooling at her needy entrance and coating her inner thighs.

Fuck me.

I can't help but abandon my cock to squeeze that peachy ass of hers as she involuntarily rubs her thighs together, all while I keep pulsing hands-free. *I need her grip and tongue back on my cock.*

With my heart going crazy, my thumb glides to her tight, pink asshole, spreading her clear arousal around.

Rosalia's entire body quivers.

"Elijah!" She gasps, sounding shocked I'm touching her *there*. "I...I, oh my God, that feel *so good*."

I arrogantly smirk, wanting to plunge said thumb inside her, but she's so tight, I keep rubbing instead. "I can't wait to eat this ass, lick it slowly, and then fuck it with my weeping cock until you're fucking cryin' my name."

"Elijah!"

"*Cryin'*. Tell me you want that."

"I do," Rosalia breathes hotly. "I want it so bad."

Unable to control myself, I roughly spank her ass three times in a row with a growl, and it's so loud that its echoes remain in my mind.

The chains of hell come undone.

The more Rosalia gasps and moans, the wetter she becomes, the more I spank her harder until her ass is a beautiful slight tinge of flushed red, my hand imprinted on it like a tattoo.

"Oh my!" Rosalia pants, shooting her ass closer to me. "Elijah, *please*, I really want you to fuck me."

"Ditto, baby." I spank her again with a growl. Never been this aroused before in my entire life, but this time I make sure my fingers collide over her sensitive pussy with the slap, involuntarily pushing into her entrance. "This is what you get for coming undone earlier in the Volvo when I told you no."

I spank her like that again until her legs are shaking, her entire body grinding back against me in desire.

Rosalia *screams*.

Screams out my fucking name.

"Such a bad girl. I'm going to mark you for days. That way every time you sit down, you'll recall your decision to cum before I told you to, babygirl."

And it only edges the adrenaline more as she attempts to stand, but I push her back down and wrap a hand around her hair and yank it down, keeping her bent. With my jaw clenched, I spank her over and over and over again, until her ass is the perfect shades of scattered scarlet, ruby, and vermillion, all while she's panting out.

I keep going, spanking her until she almost comes.

Until I lose my damn religion teaching her a lesson.

Until she tells me to stop and collapses onto the bed, attempting to roll over, but hisses because of her sore ass.

Rosalia's eyes meet mine, filled with pure lust, a few tears scattered down her cheeks. Her mouth remains gaped wide as she lies sprawled on the bed. She's breathing so hard that the cords in her neck tighten and carve out against her neck with each heavy inhale.

I shoot her a slow, sexy smile, loving how frantically she's breathing, imagining her furious heart and the way her chest is rising up down, her tits softly bouncing, causing that pretty pink piercing to sparkle in my eyes.

Finding the strength, Rosalia slides to the edge of the bed and crosses her legs. Her eyes almost roll back, and I can imagine it's the way her pussy is throbbing, edged.

"You took that so well, *Peaches*."

And when that beautiful, confident smile crawls over Rosalia's lips, I know I'm a goner. "I really liked that."

"It was supposed to be punishment, *Peaches*."

"I know, so why did I like it?"

"Because you're my girl, so you're a little freaky like me." I growl the next words so aroused, it's painful. "Now get back on your knees and make this grown man go fucking wild. Make me cum for you while you touch yourself."

With flustered cheeks, Rosalia crawls over the bed before her feet skim the marble floor and once again she falls to her knees, and the moment her lips meet the crown of my cock, I fist my fingers into her hair tightly.

"Just like that, baby, fuck yeah." I grin, watching as my baby rubs her tongue over my pre-cum-coated length.

Rosalia's left hand wanders between her thighs, her breath a hot mess against my cock between satisfying me and fingering herself, the sound of her wetness music to my ears.

Spanking her made me insane, but watching her fuck herself while she's staring up at me, licking my cock, *ohhh fuckkk, I want to learn to love and then love on her all night.*

I softly cup Rosalia's face as she continuously blows my mind away with her touch. There's no doubt in my mind that we both know what's gonna happen after this.

My hips uncontrollably grind against her, rocking into her face, letting the entire Los Angles watch us through the large floor-to-ceiling windows overlooking nearby apartments, some with lights on. In fact, I can even see a shadow in one.

My bandmates and publicity will kill me, but I adore Rosalia so much.

I want this exact moment to be a breaking TV headline. First page news. Porn inspo.

Elijah Diesel—Diesel Rose frontman—dead by Rosalia Philips— legendary young ballerina—caught with her tongue wrapped around the rocker's pierced cock, jerking him off.

I smolder. *Ohhh yeah, I love the sound of that.*

"I really want to punish you again," I whisper, playfully slapping her cheek. "Wanna fuck you hard until you say I'm yours." I inhale sharply, shutting my eyes for a moment to control myself from coming. *So damn close.* "I want to fuck this pretty little throat of yours till you're gagging and there isn't a drop of cum left in my cock."

Rosalia slowly nods, fingering herself faster, but I see nervousness rippling across her body at my words.

Jesus Christ, Elijah, she's never done this before.

Maybe she's anxious about it? Worried?

Go slow.

"I meant someday, not now," I add, reassuring her. "We have all the time, *Peaches.*"

"Thank you." Rosalia smiles up at me bashfully, and yet, in the same breath leans forth and brushes the underside of my cock with her lips, the tip of her tongue swirling all over my sensitive skin.

Her hand slips from her pussy and moves back to my dick, jerking me off just like I told her earlier. *So good.*

"Look at you working a cock belonging to a thirty-five-year-old man like a dirty little devil."

More pearls of liquid pool at the center of my abs as she jacks the base of me, her lips still taunting my underside. Another hiss escapes my throat at the slight twist in her grip every time she reaches my velvety crown, but now, she slows.

Rosalia concentrates on my tip, rolling my piercing around like my own little sinner.

For a former handjob virgin, she's *incredible.*

Ohhhh fuck.

"You feel so fucking good. I can't hold on any longer."

"So don't."

"I won't," I pant. "I can't decide if I want to cum on those perfect tits of yours or coat your pretty face."

Heat rushes up my dick, and the moment it does, I know I'm seconds away from bliss.

Rosalia keeps going and going until my muscles are quivering and my abs clench tightly.

"Ohhh, fuck, Rosalia, your tongue feels so good, I'm gonna come. I'm gonna come. I'm g—*OHHH!*"

My moans echo throughout the bedroom at the inferno inside me, my heart beating so damn crazy.

I squeeze my eyes shut, heated lust rushing across every inch of my body, my cock heavy and pulsing in her grip. Rosalia rushes a hand up, and with a pinch of my pierced nipples, I make it just in time to tug her hair back and fist my cock in my own hand before exploding.

Oh.

My.

Fucking.

God.

The orgasm hits me in intense waves and I come violently, pumping my crown, fuckin' roaring out her name. Breathlessly, I shoot long thick ropes of hot cum all over her lips, face, neck, and tits. "*Fuckkk.*"

Rosalia's giddy grin and sounds of pleasure work me up even more. "Yesss, baby. Give it to me, all of you."

My dick doesn't stop throbbing as I jack myself rougher, my orgasm painting every inch of her, my hips thrusting into her face with every jolt. Frenzied.

I press myself so close to her that she stumbles back, and before she can catch herself, I sexily tug her hair and slam her back against the floor-to-ceiling windows, the urge unreal as I finish milking my cock all over her face, Los Angeles staring right back at us.

There's even a point where I spank my cock over her cheeks, and she likes it, so I do it again.

And when my body releases, all the tension rushing out and instead pants fuel the air between us, I step back, observing her as she remains there, on her knees for me.

Rosalia Philips is an angel.

My pretty little angel, grinning, coated in my creamy, white cum. *Just how I like it.*

I can't catch my breath, no matter how desperately I try. It leaves me to watch her with hooded eyes, and then she does something that blows my mind. In the low light, with her eyes on mine and all flustered, she licks my orgasm off her lips, her moans never subsiding.

Rosalia even reaches up, collecting some of my arousal from her face, and sucks it off her fingers, letting them slip out with a *pop*, but there's too much cum.

Something shifts inside my chest when I drop to my knees and she sexily crawls up to me, some of my arousal dripping from her chin to the marble floors like sweetened honey. But it all comes secondary to the way my heart slows because we're staring at each other with such tender desire.

Raw sensuality.

Vivid emotion.

Emotion is clouded in Rosalia's eyes as she glances up at me, panting. She's looking at me like she needs me, and I'm not talking only sexually. I'm saying she *needs me*. Like I'm her cure. Her everything. And I don't know what to do with that. I've never… I'm not used to this.

Fuck.

Rosalia's beautiful.

In every single way.

In the shallows, in the depths, she's *beautiful*.

In the silence, in the loud, she's *beautiful*.

In the beautiful, in the damned, *flawless*.

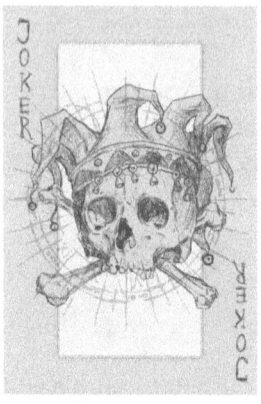

Chapter
TWENTY-SIX

Elijah

Dear Lord, what did I do to deserve her?

And then, with my heart beatin' outta my chest, Rosalia slowly slides a hand down my rippled abs, slowly wrapping around my sensitive crown again. *Fuck.* Her touch shoots up my entire body, my aching cock hardening again, stretchin' thick in her grip like I didn't just explode.

"You're playing with fire, little one…" I tell her, my stubbled jaw rubbing against the softness of her cheeks. "And you and I both know it's the devil's home."

With my orgasm smeared all over, Rosalia looks at me confidently, her eyes dipped in the darkest shade of desire. "I want you so badly."

"How badly?"

"*Bad. Please*," she begs, squeezing me tighter, practically having me hiss in the best kind of painful pleasure. "I've been waiting four years for you to be inside me."

God.

"Thought you were a good girl, *Peaches*, the kind that get down on their knees and pray to heaven. Good girls don't beg like that."

Slipping her hand from my dick, Rosalia clasps my hand and slowly drags it over her face, collecting my warm cum with my fingers. Without another word, she swirls her tongue over my orgasm, sucking my fingers so deep my rings graze her plump lips. It's hot as fuck watching as my girl does it again, over and over again, until there isn't an inch of me left on her.

And then, she crashes her lips on mine, our tongues merging together like wicked flames.

Hungry for her, I cup her face, my wet fingers getting lost in her blonde waves as I taste my salty orgasm that she's yet to swallow rushing wild between us during the savage kiss. It swirls between our tongues and we both swallow it down while my cock slips over her dripping cunt, grinding against it slowly, but never entering.

Fuck. Fuck. Fuck.

She's so goddamn dripping wet.

So ready for me to destroy her good.

I've never been so fucking turned on before. She's letting me taste myself on her tongue during our groans and rushed breaths, proving which side of sin she's on.

My cock is so hard it desperately needs me to fuck her. Part of me is concerned Rosalia's tired between the flight and ballet, but she ain't letting it on and I'm not gentleman enough to ask.

She's teasing me the best way she knows how through the taunting kiss that I end to growl, "I need your virgin pussy, *Peaches.* Need you to be a good girl and let me fuck you hard like an antidote against melancholy."

Rosalia rushes to catch her breath, licking her ruby red lips, all swollen because of me with her eyes all sparklin' like stars. "I'm all yours for the taking, Elijah Diesel."

Without another word, I slam my mouth against hers and lift her up, her legs automatically wrapping around mine. I throw her on the bed, and without warning, spin her to her stomach so that my hips piston against her ass.

Caressing her red-tinged toned ass, I spread her cheeks farther apart, obsessed with the beauty of Rosalia's rosy pussy staring back at me. "Bend over on all fours with your ass up and hands spread out over the bed. Yes, just like that, baby. Rub yourself against my cock like that."

I tip my head back for a sec, giving in to her grinding her dancer body on me. It feels so good with my cock piercing adding another level of pleasure. "*Fuckkk.*"

She's mine again, all mine and in my submission when I tug on her long blonde hair, a cry escaping her when I do. I wrap her hair around my fist and roughly yank it toward me. Her head tips back while she's bent over, doggy style, her hands spread out over the sheets.

"I'm so fucking obsessed with you," I whisper, leaning down to butterfly kiss down her spine tenderly. "Trust me when I say I am, *Peaches.*"

"I'm obsessed with you too."

"No, you don't understand, I'm fucking Joker obsessed, baby." I stroke my cock with my free hand, rubbing the tip against her hot, velvet pussy. I focus on my metal cock piercing rolling over her sensitive clit and how it makes her drip arousal. "Even if I don't always show it, baby, I am."

Rosalia can't stop wriggling in pleasure. "Do you have a condom?"

Shit.

"Fuck. No, don't have one on me."

"Oh, because I, umm, I'm not on the pill."

"Should we… Should we stop?"

"No, God, no. I don't want to stop. I feel safe with you. I'm just… not on the pill."

The desire in her eyes burns deep. *She wants this. So bad. Just as much as I fucking do.*

Flustered, I'm not even thinking straight through the sexual tension when I smirk. "It's okay. I'm clean. I'll just pull out."

"Promise you'll pull out?" Rosalia's voice is nothing but innocent as she glances over her shoulder at me, but I know deep down how much she must be freaking out.

So, I cup her small face, studying all her beautifully faded freckles. "I promise with all my soul, *Peaches*. I wouldn't lie about something like that."

"I know you wouldn't, but I…" Her cheeks heat. "I just wanted to be sure, you know."

"Of course."

A second passes with just my wildly beating heartbeat piercing my ears and the soft hustle and bustle of LA's nightlife, when she softly rasps out, "Elijah?"

"Hmmm?"

"I want you to know something…" Those pretty green meadow eyes are lustful delights filled with nostalgia, and her slow, warm smile lights me up inside. "I never stopped falling for you, even when I should've. Even if you're sin. I was always yours."

With her intoxicating gaze still locked on mine, I let go of my demons and let my gorgeous twenty-one-year-old muse take over instead as I recklessly thrust into her warm, greedy pussy.

A moan escapes our lips at the same time, followed by a groan due to her tightness. Rosalia's eyes widen before she drops her head to the sheets, her legs spreading farther.

"You okay, *Peaches?*"

"Yes." She nods. "Keep going."

I grip the junction between her hips and ass, using it as momentum with every slow rock until I'm fully stretched in her, and then, I grow wild.

Beasts, that's what we are as I pound into her hard, my breaths cutting short, but I don't give a damn. The intensity in which I am fucking her is so ferocious it feels as if the entire room is spinning.

"That's it, *Peaches*, glide on my cock, ohhh yeah," I say, eyes heavy with need. "I can't fucking resist you."

"You don't have to." Rosalia slams down against the bed, over and over. "I'm you—"

"*MINE*," I growl, gripping her ass before slapping it. "You're fucking mine." Slipping around her waist, my hand rushes low between her thighs, rubbing her swollen clit. "Nobody can ever fucking touch you again after this."

"Oh my God…*Elijah*," she breathes, bucking her hips backward to meet my every vicious thrust. "Fuck."

"Is that understood?"

"Yes," she moans.

"Say my name with it."

"Yes, Elijah."

"Babygirl, I wanna hear you whisper it."

She does.

"Now louder."

Rosalia's too lost in her bliss to listen to me.

Grunting, I pull her hair tighter, the other hand on her clit, fucking her deeper with every thrust. "*Louder.*"

I'll never forget the way Rosalia screams my name, the giggles and muffled moans as she bites down on the pillow. Desire hasn't stopped heating up my spine, sparking through my veins as I fuck her virgin pussy like the good girl she is.

"I want to spend the rest of my life fucking every inch of you, baby." The next words escape in staccato, alongside every breath. "Every. Single. Inch."

My cock grows crazy, throbbing, and arousal pools at the tip inside her, making her bleed a little, but I can't stop. She can't stop. *We* can't stop this addictive feeling.

I lean forth, my vaunted V-cut slapping against her ass as I drive her wild, my cock gliding in and out of her so fucking flawlessly with only her wetness as lube.

There comes a point where my lips meet her glistering neck in bites and kisses, leaving a grid of hickeys. My hips tip forth, having my cock fuck her from a new angle, ruining her deep with the way my piercing hits her right where she needs it most.

"Gosh, your piercing…too good." Rosalia quivers underneath me, her sex squeezing my dick in a chokehold. "It feels like heaven, Elijah."

"Fuck, baby, breathe." I moan in her ear, desperate to take in every second of this. "Stay with me, come on."

Rosalia nods, the left side of her face pressed against the bed, making me see the rosy hue in her cheek. We share a smile and something inside me shifts when the hand gripping her hair slips and instead, I pin her wrists behind her back, causing her shoulders to dive deeper on the bed and ass higher up against me.

She looks so fuckin' pretty bent over like a sinner for me, wearing nothing but the charm bracelet I made her. The one wrapped in leather that dazzles three reminders of us.

In my restraint, I fuck Rosalia like I've been starved of her. *Because I have.* I fuck her like a goddamn sinner, breaking out from the riddled chains. I fuck her like she's the only thing that matters to me because she is.

Her silky blonde hair sticks to her face the sweatier we become.

I let one hand go to trail down her perfectly round ass that teases me with the marks I've left.

My other hand keeps both of her hands restrained behind her back, her fingers finding a way to lace through mine.

My fingers weave in hers.

Her hips grind in rhythm with mine.

Our hearts, I'm sure, are beating in time.

Fuck. I need more.

"*God*," I groan, slipping my cock out to run my tongue over the reddish hues of her smooth yet taut ass. "I want to fucking taste you so badly, baby, taste this pretty ass of yours."

"Elijah!" She gasps, stunned with a nervous breath. "You want to…"

"Mmhmmm."

Even though Rosalia can't see me, I'm smirking smugly when I lower my head, spreading out her ass with my hands. *My God. She's beautiful.* My tongue drags over her throbbing clit, swirling across her dripping pussy and slowly running upward her slit from behind.

I don't stop at her entrance. I pause, getting lost in her sweet scent as her legs begin to tremble.

My smirk deepens against her pussy. "I'll let go of one hand, but you've got to promise to listen to daddy and do what he asks, okay?"

"I promise," Rosalia practically moans, catching her breath in anticipation of what I'm about to do to her.

I let go of her right hand, keeping the left held behind her back. "Slip those fingers into your pussy for me and fuck yourself in the same exact way I'm going to fuck your ass with my tongue."

"What?"

I bite her ass in frustration. "Concentrate, Rosalia."

"I am, it just… my heart is going to explode in a minute. I've never felt like this before."

I rush both of her hands behind her back. "Keep them both there. If any of your hands move, I'll stop and fuck you so mercifully with my cock, you won't be able to walk straight for the entirety of our time in California."

"E-Elijah… I…" Rosalia's words transform the second my fingers dive into her pussy without warning, *four* of them, and fuck her vigorously, prepping her for the thickness of my cock again soon. "*Oh, yes. Yes. Yes.*"

With my other pointer and middle finger, I slip them on either side of her light pink asshole, spreading her wider. And that's when I plunge my tongue wide over it, circling slowly.

"*Oh, FUCK YES.*" Rosalia gets lost in the sensation on both ends of her as my fingers, tongue, and jaw work tirelessly as she becomes breathless. "I'm going to…I'm going to come, Elijah."

"No, you're not," I warn darkly, my eyes shutting with a groan at her sweetness. "You know what happens if you come too soon, Princess, I get to paint your ass red."

"*Please.*"

Rosalia spasms, rocking her hips back and forward, her pussy and ass grinding against my face in a bid to tempt me. I know it won't be long…long until we're both coming. I'm seconds away myself with the way I'm thrusting my hips against the mattress, her arousal still coated around me like honey.

"*Once.* Princess, you can come once, but then you're coming again with me."

Rosalia screams something inaudible into the silk pillow, and with her pussy quivering around my fingers and asshole throbbing against my tongue, my speed quickens.

"Come on, that's it, baby, come with my tongue in your ass."

Her screams intensify as she comes undone, losing control, squirting all down my fingers. She grinds against me so intensely that my tongue slips from her ass as her legs quiver around me. I don't stop mauling her pussy, swallowing down her sweetness, watching as it sprays all over me, on the bedsheets, and across the room.

What a fucking show.

Her orgasm is flooded from the cum she sprays all over my face instead, riding her clit on my stubbled chin, groaning more at the friction.

My girl's a squirter and I fucking love it.

When Rosalia finally collapses to her stomach, I realize she never pulled her hands away from behind her back, just like I told her. I want to reward her for being good.

Flipping her over by the hips, Rosalia grins up at me, her face as red as her ass and tits even fuller than before. I give them some love, sucking and nipping them, all while her hands get lost in my hair.

When I lower my body on top of Rosalia's, keeping the weight off her with my forearms, I push her legs up so that they're above my shoulders and spread wide like the ballerina she is.

"You took that so well, *Peaches*." I smile against her lips, kissing her slowly, loving how all of our tastes merge into one. "You like my tongue in your ass, hmm?"

Rosalia can't stop nodding, her arms wrapping around my neck, those gorgeous green eyes flooding with something close to adoration. "I like everything about you."

When I slip my cock back inside of her pussy, her orgasm is still throbbing in waves, gripping my dick with every single thrust. I bury my head in her neck, kissing the hickeys I made earlier that are bruising a dark purple.

Rosalia's biting my shoulder, moaning into my skin as I fuck her aggressively in possession, in need of her reaching that high again, this time with me.

"You're so beautiful," I whisper in her ear, loving her warmth wrapped around me, my ass tense as I dive deeper into her, feeling my heavy balls begin to tingle. "Save me from myself, and I'll save you."

I feel like I'm drowning and being revived every minute we're fucking. I feel so much, intensely, and for the first time in my life, I embrace it. Completely.

I can't stop touching Rosalia; trailing kisses down her body, stealing passionate kisses from her swollen lips because of our previous vicious kisses.

Running a hand along the dimpled muscles of her abs, emotion coats my throat. There's literally sweat coating my washboard abs and we're fucking like animals, grunting in pleasure, and yet, *emotion.*

"*Pourquoi me fais-tu sentir comme ça?*" I murmur softly to Rosalia in French, gazing into her eyes, my cock drilling into her. "*Pourquoi tu t'en soucies? Pourquoi est-ce que je veux te voir toujours, ma chérie?*"

As much as I loved fucking her from behind, there's something just so raw and intimate about the way we're fucking right now, as we lose ourselves with our gazes locked and hot breaths melting together.

Rosalia's face lights up even further. "I understand some French, Lijah."

"Where did you learn? High school *three* years ago?" I smirk.

Rolling her eyes, she playfully shoves my chest. "Yes, I actually did, so shut up!"

"Tell me what I just said."

"You said, *why do you make me feel like this?*" She slows, recalling the rest. "*Why do you care? Why do I want to see you forever, my darling?*"

"*Je ne me suis jamais senti comme ça avant pour quelqu'un.*"

"*I've never felt this way before…*" She pauses for a second, reciting my words back to me with a smile. "*About anyone.*"

"*Dis-moi comment faire pour que ça s'arrête.*"

"*Tell me how to make it stop.*"

Swallowing thickly, I flicker back and forth between her eyes. "*Ressens-tu cela aussi?*"

"*Oui, je ressens ça aussi,*" Rosalia whispers, answering my question like it's a cure.

I asked her if she feels the same way too.

She said yes.

My heart is fluttering, fucking *fluttering*, like full-on butterflies. I have never in my life felt this from sex, from caressing a woman. This is my first. And I know it's the last.

Rosalia Philips is my girl. My muse. The lyrics flooding in my veins. And the closer we get to complete ecstasy, my grip on her ass tightening with every thrust, the more I know these moments are going to change everything.

I don't stop, not even when she tightens around me and begins to quiver again. Don't stop when her long nails scratch down my back, urging me on. Don't stop as sweat coats our skin, my abs clenching, desperate to let go.

Instead, I show Rosalia what it's like to taunt the beast while she cries out my name with happy tears streaming down her face when she loses it and comes gushing out her fifth orgasm of the early morning. Her legs tighten around my shoulders and it's a beautiful mess, so intense my cock slips out as she sprays her cum over my thighs, aching balls, and dick.

I don't know who kisses who, but it's so hot and filthy, desperate, and just in time to soften my loud moans as heat rushes down my spine. *Oh fuckkk.*

But Rosalia's not on the pill and I'm not using a condom, so in the numbing bliss that takes over me, I somehow manage to think straight.

Knowing I'm seconds away, I break the kiss to pull out of her and move my hips up higher. Fisting my cock in my hand, with our sweaty foreheads pressed together, we both watch in pants.

Fuckkkk.

Groaning, I orgasm hard, my hot cum shooting all over Rosalia's abs, tits, and neck. I can't stop. There's too much. All I want to do is fall into heaven with her and never recover.

Desire rushes straight through me, intensifying in waves when Rosalia palms my crown while I stroke my base.

I grind my hips into the air, letting her take over. And she works me fast, squeezing out the last of my cum.

Knowing that she's covering herself in me for the second time in an hour…

"Fuckkkkk, *Peaches*, I think you just killed me."

We can't stop panting, and I collapse on top of her, my muscles a weak mess, and Rosalia's beautiful spent smile making me even weaker.

Fuck.

I think I…

I think I want her forever.

And I don't know how to stop it.

Rosalia's legs slip off my shoulders and as we lie here together, covered in our mixed orgasms. I don't know what to make of us. All I know is that looking into anybody else's eyes and sharing a tender smile has never felt *this* euphoric except with her. I *feel*. And it saves me.

The mood shifts between us, but not to something less of…*it's something more.*

Rosalia's falling for me. I see it in the way she looks at me.

In the way when I take her wrists and gently kiss her scars, the thin leather bracelet I gave her that's still on as her green eyes turn glassy.

In the way she slowly cups my chiseled stubbled jaw before resting her head against the crook of my neck.

Her warmth against mine is foreign sin, and yet I crave holding her close. I'm shit at affection within little moments, but for some reason she makes me want to be better at it.

I'm the only person I can't run from, and yet, Rosalia Philips always runs back to me.

I don't care that she makes my orgasm stick to my body, that's it's messily chaotic—*just like us.*

I don't care that people will talk because I'm a big rock star and she's a prolific ballerina.

Because I'm pushing thirty-six at the end of the month, while she's only twenty-one.

Because according to logic, guys like me aren't supposed to be with girls like her.

Quite frankly, I don't care about any of that shit.

All I really care about is the fact that Rosalia wraps her arms around me and squeezes me tightly like I'm about to disappear right before her eyes. Like the entire world will drown, and we'll be all that's left, drifting apart, not anchors. Like this, whatever *this* is, could be the end—*our* end.

This rush of coldness comes over me, and it gets harder to breathe.

Yes, this could very much be the end.

The end of the melancholic rock god and his muse.

I mean, we haven't even spoken anything through, and we really need to.

But… For whatever it may mean, I don't want this to be the end. *The end of us.*

Four years ago, I told Rosalia Philips to stay away from me or I'd break her heart. Now, I'm telling myself those exact same words instead. *Peaches, come break my heart, if you dare.*

"What's wrong, Rosalia?"

"Nothing. I'm just really happy I'm here with you," she whispers. "I missed you so much."

"I feel like there's more on your mind, cherry viper."

Rosalia sniffles in my hold. "*Cherry viper?*"

"Yeah."

"You've never called me that before."

Because I think I'm growing crazy for you. You and all the lyrics attached to you.

"Well, I guess a nickname has to begin someplace, yeah?"

I feel her lips rush up into a slight smile at the junction of my neck. "Yeah. I like it."

My heartstrings come alive.

I like you, Peaches.

"*Cherry viper,*" Rosalia whispers, testing it out on her tongue again. "How did you come up with that?"

"Long story."

"I've got time."

If such sadness didn't lace the air around us, I think I would have chuckled. Here it is again. All of our hot and cold. How we move in waves, crashing to the shore, then back again. With Rosalia, nothing and everything seems certain, yet we keep running back to each other.

Even through our hate.

Our vulnerability.

Our desire.

We. Run. Back.

I don't know why the melody of "Fragments of You" runs wild in my mind, the lyrics on repeat, over and over again, as I scoop Rosalia into the solace of my arms.

So many other things in mind
And my heart is falling in two
Plummeting into the water
Laced. With. You

The clock strikes 4:30 a.m.

I carry Rosalia in my arms into the main presidential bathroom. It's gorgeous in here, charcoal, brass, and gray-toned marble everything, and yet, it isn't as gorgeous as *her.*

Rosalia and I don't share a word as I take her hand. Not a single fucking thing as we step into the shower, which literally takes up the entire wall with a massive rainfall shower head. But you know what? We don't need to exchange a damn thing because our gazes say everything within themselves.

We—Rosalia and I—we're changing.

We're falling into each other. And I don't think either of us wants to stop it.

Understand it.

Dissect it.

And yet, it could all end tomorrow…

I toggle the shower on, warm water rippling over our naked bodies, creating misty steam. It surrounds Rosalia, like ballet surrounds her, illuminating her every flaw and hiding her imperfections.

I think she's perfect.

Faultless.

Flawless.

But she's told me to my face there are parts of her she hates, those scars on her wrists, and I want to fix her. Cure her. Let her heal through me.

Here we are, in the middle of the night, two broken souls held together by the poetry of life. We're such opposites, from different worlds, and yet…*there's just something 'bout her.*

My hands, still nervously trembling, find their way around her hips, brushing her ass, and I pull her close. I like the way we work so naturally together, how while the warm water baptizes our skin, the sensation of her taut ballerina body that's perfectly etched with all of her wounds, battles, and successes, pressed against mine.

I blindly reach for the body wash and scrub it all over her skin, wiping away my orgasm off her first. We take turns rubbing each other's bodies with my sandalwood scent until we're standing here, all lathered up, the rainfall shower head rippling down, replenishing our skin, just her and me and Los Angeles.

And then, we return to embracing each other in the solace of my arms. Rosalia's so much shorter that her head rests by my chest, but it's okay because I can still tenderly cup her jaw and lean down, kissing her softly like I do now.

More lyrics of Diesel Rose's smash hit flow during the kiss, the ones I wrote for her…

> *And it's killing me softly*
> *And it's killing me with time*
> *The chemicals are corrosive, fueling up my mind*

Rosalia moans into the kiss, but it's different than earlier on when she was driving me to a mind-blowing orgasm. It's much softer, rawer, and filled with a need beyond just lust.

Her lips are so smooth, so tender, that part of me wants to stay like this forever.

> *My only wonder*
> *My only cure*
> *Is. You.*

We pull away, gently smiling, and it feels so weird to have no stress, just acceptance.

If Rosalia is exhausted about the fact she not only had the closing night of Swan Lake tonight but also an almost six-hour flight, she doesn't show it. Under her eyes is light, and there isn't a fraction or indication that she's going to pass out in my arms at any given minute.

One minute we're in the shower, the next we're brushing our teeth and in a fresh set of clothes. Oh, and I'm slipping inside her bed. We didn't discuss it, but I'm not leaving her alone. I want to sleep beside her.

I've never, *ever*, in my life slept beside a woman before, so this is a first for me.

"I like that we're like this," Rosalia whispers in the low light. Her hands loop around my neck, keeping my lips near hers. "I like this quiet. That we can say everything and nothing."

"Mmhmmm."

"It kind of reminds me of some moments back in your Manhattan studio years ago. Does Diesel Rose still own that?"

I nod softly against the silk pillow, my arms around her waist as my forehead brushes against hers. "Yeah, I mean we have a record producer, so we use his provided studio now, but we still have the old studio too that we own. Well, now *I* own it… I get nostalgic about things. Can't let them go."

Sadness pools in her eyes. "Nostalgia can kill, Elijah."

A beat passes. Our stare extends.

Rosalia's so damn beautiful.

Fuck.

Why is my heart hurting? That cold little thing never hurts.

"You must miss your old studio, though, hmm?"

"Immensely."

A few moments pass of Rosalia staring up at the ceiling, and then she whispers, "I miss it too. During these past four years, whenever I was struggling, I silently wished I could just escape to that studio. Be with you. That Persian rug. That damn Cherry Cola bottle that wouldn't open. There was a stage of my life where I would have done everything to step in there with you, one last time…just *one*."

And that's when Rosalia's first tear slips, gliding down the side of her face to her neck. Sniffling, she covers her face, hiding her vulnerability from the world. "I'm sorry. I don't know why I'm crying."

"What's going on, Rosalia?"

"I'm okay."

"You're not. I sensed something was wrong earlier, when you were looking at me like I was just going to disappear."

White noise crackles between us.

One.

Two.

Three.

"Believe it or not," Rosalia begins, turning to face me properly, her fingers laced in mine, spread out between us on the sheets, "I have a lot of trust issues, abandonment issues with certain people. Sometimes I don't allow myself to *trust*, in the fear of getting hurt, so I don't allow myself to get fully invested. It's kind of like a defense mechanism."

My throat closes up.

Fuck, it's like I'm staring into a mirror.

"I found myself doing it with Trent, a lot. In consequence, I wasn't really present."

I ignore the reference to that fucker. "Why do you do it?"

"To protect myself..." Rosalia sighs. "But with you, I've always been myself, trusted you even when my heart said no. I'm just scared you could walk away any second and I'd still want you."

Our cheeks press against the silk pillows as we stare at each other for the longest time, until it feels like I'm gazing into another galaxy. One solely filled with rock music, leather, and her.

Rosalia's eyes swell up. Early morning truths are hitting us hard. I squeeze our intertwined hands.

"The world can be a scary place, *Peaches*," I whisper, my heart of hearts exposed. "When you let that little voice inside your head dictate your emotions and thoughts, it can be corrosive."

"I know."

"It's scary." I can't quite meet her eyes when I trace her hand. "How did it start?"

"The murder suicide. My biological parents."

I nod, getting it, a huge weight rippling my shoulder because I know what she's about to say holds depth for her. Hurts her. *Haunts* her. And that in return, haunts me too.

Her parents left this earth. Left her.

How the fuck does one get over that? They don't. They. Fucking. Don't.

Rosalia craves escaping the world, avoiding any more trauma, and I understand it.

"I'm scared that somebody will rip my heart out of my chest… Elijah, the world feels so dim sometimes." Slowly, she lifts up her wrist, bravely showing me her scars. The moonlight just barely kissing over them. "On the night before my fifteen birthday, I decided I didn't want to be alive anymore. Didn't want to breathe anymore."

Rosalia exhales a deep sigh, pausing as her voice cracks and becomes all shaky. And for the first time ever, I feel sad. So fucking sad that this happened to her.

I just want to wrap her in my arms. Tell her that everything is going to be okay. That nothing can hurt her anymore. *But life isn't always that considerate.*

She's trying to keep it together, trying to be strong, but I wish she knew she didn't have to be.

"I locked myself in the bathroom, and I…" Rosalia whispers, more tears burning down her cheeks. "My foster father found me in the bathtub. I was admitted to the hospital for a week because I kept on slipping. There was a forty-eight percent chance I wouldn't make it from just how much blood I had lost. I was fixated on that number, Elijah, trying to do anything I could to raise it. Anxiety toxified my lungs, every single second of every single minute. That's when the doctor gave me Valium."

"Shit."

"Yeah…but the panic attacks never really faded. Slicing my skin just a little bit relieved me of that weight, that sting…it was the only thing keeping me alive."

Rosalia's words leave a sting at the back of my throat because they've come with so much depth. She's sharing so many truths, opening up so much.

I hold her closer.

"I'm so sorry, *Peaches.*" I frown, wiping away her tears ever so gently, my heart skipping a beat because I'm readily aware that I've *never* said those words in my adult life. "I wish I had known you back then to prove to you just how beautiful you are, how talented."

Rosalia gives me the biggest sad smile. "Sometimes I don't think it's enough."

"This is me telling you that you're enough. And you're worthy. And you're beautiful."

Sniffling, Rosalia reaches out to brush the outline of my warm lips, her breaths merging with mine. "You really think I'm beautiful?"

"Yes. You're more beautiful than any other woman I've set my eyes on." I swallow. "And I fucking mean it," I add, pressing my lips to her forehead. "When was the last time you cut?"

Rosalia seems almost ashamed to answer, staling for a minute. "Four years ago, the day before I saw you in the *Rolling Stone* magazine. I think you saved my life, Elijah Diesel."

I softly smile, seconds away from replying, but then I don't…

I think you're saving mine, Rosalia Philips.

"Lijah?"

"Yeah?"

"I have a question."

"Hit me."

"Why did you fly me to Los Angeles?"

And just like that, the mood shifts again, but I don't forget the rawness behind what she just shared.

"Because I can't stand the idea of not seeing you, and as much as the thought scares me, it's the only thing I think of."

Rosalia softly smiles in the moonlight. "I need to have stability, Elijah."

Stability.

Moments pass between us.

She wants stability. What does that mean?

I swallow thickly. "What are…you saying?"

"That I need a definition for what *this* is."

Silence, and then… "Stay with me a little longer than the weekend and we'll find one."

Yep. I just said that. Meant it too, ladies and gents.

A deeper smile carves up her lips, as if she didn't expect me to say that. "What do you mean?"

"Well, I know it's hectic with ballet, but I, uh…umm…." I clear my throat because I've never said these words before and don't know why my insides are shaking all of a sudden. "How long is your off-season?"

"Three weeks, but I've got training in between. Normal gym routines, though, not rehearsal." Yawning, Rosalia's eyes sparkle. "But I'm expected to be training at the ballet company on that third week, so really, my off-season is two weeks. Why?"

Perfect.

An idea forms in my mind. A crazy fucking idea, but hey, it's us.

Swallowing thickly, I brush strands of her towel-dried hair away from her face. "Stay with me."

Her eyes almost bulge out. "*What?*"

"Join Diesel Rose's tour with me." I shyly smile. "It ends in exactly two weeks. We only have tomorrow night's show here in California, then it's just Portland and Seattle to go. I know you need a gym to train, but us guys have touring trainers with us, so that could work."

Plus, my birthday's in two weeks...

Rosalia gazes back and forth between my eyes for a moment. "Wait, you're serious?"

"Never been more serious in my life, *Peaches.*"

It's probably why my heart is palpitating, beating so viciously out of my chest, just like it always does when she's around me.

"But what will the other guys think?"

"That I've lost my mind, and maybe I have, but it feels right."

She blinks twice, her grin big as ever. "Are you sure they'll be okay with this?"

"Yeah, they'll be cool about it." Nervousness is all I feel, and I do a shit job trying to get the next words out. "I...I, umm, I want you to stay with me for the rest of the tour, so yeah, I kind of—"

I don't expect Rosalia's lips to crash on mine, for her to kiss me ever so tenderly, like a soldier before heading to war.

Our tongues collide in the softest of battles, and fuck, I just want to protect her from the world.

The more we ravish each other, the more her smile grows during the kiss. It becomes impossible to kiss her straight, but I don't mind, 'cause I'm smiling too.

"Let's do it." She grins all girly when we pull away, like a little kid in a candy store. "We should make some ground rules, though."

I nod, my heart fucking singing.

Eventually, we come up with three...

1. No breaking any hearts.

2. No bringing up the past, except if it's positive.

3. No going crazy or turning into a full-on psychopath, please and thank you.

"I'm not going fucking crazy, baby," I murmur against her lips. "I already *am* crazy."

"Well, it just so happens I like crazy, and rock music."

"*Beaux rêves.* Sweet dreams, *Peaches.*"

She snuggles into my chest deeper, glancing up at me with swirling nostalgia in her eyes. "You've said that to me before, remember?"

I remember.

When I took the bus with her home four years ago, after going to that Italian restaurant and then the studio. The night we really opened up to each other. *The night I caved.*

I kiss Rosalia's forehead, my lips lingering. "Mmhmmm, I remember. In fact, I never forgot it."

And when Rosalia falls asleep in my arms with the biggest grin on my face, I want to set fire to the world around us if it means we're the only ones left thriving.

I've been trying to dismiss this feeling in my chest all night, but I can't no more. It's nostalgia, mixed with all the sentiments I have for her.

The fact that she makes me feel like life is worth it. Like *I'm* worth it. And maybe, just maybe, all my breaths do amount to something.

The melody of "Fragments of You" continues to run wild in my mind, never escaping with her in my arms.

It's *my* song.

Our song.

The one I wrote about *her*—my muse—the only person who makes me stay up all night with my own thoughts, my crawling anxiety drowning at the very sight of her.

"Fragments of You".

Diesel Rose's greatest hit. The melody fans scream the loudest for whenever I've performed it during this current *Killing Me Slowly* tour.

Eight months.

That's how long I've been away on this worldwide tour.

Diesel Rose's third worldwide tour in the last four years.

I've been carrying the lyrics in my chest, burdening my heart and piercing every last bit of my sanity.

I wrote this song on the flight to London four years ago. When I left her, alone in my bed. Tonight will be our last show of our tour, and God, if the torture of eight months singing our fated travesty all adds up to this moment, with her being right *here* dosing in my arms, then *fuck*, it's worth it.

Every single struggle.

Every single strained breath.

Every single dagger in my heart and rolling depression *is. Worth. It.*

Worth it because it led me to this moment right here, wrapped in her, in bed.

I'm obsessed with her, obsessed with *Peaches* when I shouldn't be.

She's forbidden.

Her father hates me.

I'm fifteen years older.

She's supposed to be this prolific ballerina. She's supposed to be free, roam, like a butterfly, not being trapped by the cages that come with being with a rock 'n' roll lover. With a Harley Davidson crazed man. With a troubled, anxiety crippling psychopath.

Because that's what I am.

Sociopath.

Psychopath.

It's all the fucking same to me.

These next two weeks, they could be my demise.

Guess I was born evil. I'll always seep in my blood. And yet, whatever I'm with Rosalia, I want the penitentiary to give me their hand and I want to kiss it. Slowly. Then lick it. I want to have everything to be the good guy. But I can't.

I won't ever be that good guy.

Ever.

But that doesn't stop me from trying.

Just like she makes me want to be better.

Just like I *need* to, in order to survive this life.

Just like the devil slaughters me inside as I whisper into the hopeful darkness, "Sleep tight, my darlin' *Peaches*, for I ain't going anywhere."

And this time, I promise I mean it.

Chapter
TWENTY-SEVEN

BREAKING NOW:
Diesel Rose's secret blonde
bombshell ballerina

By Beatrix Helfrich, ROCK 'N' ROLL PRESS
October 18, 2022

Diesel Rose's broody front man, Elijah Diesel, was spotted in the early hours of this morning accompanying professional dancer, Rosalia Philips, into the luxurious The Saxton hotel in Los Angeles.

Fans described the couple as intimate and iconic as Elijah, approaching 36, locked hands with the 21-year-old ballerina. Despite their taboo fifteen-year age gap, it seems that something is brewing in their dazzling punk paradise. Perhaps this blonde bombshell can conquer the heart of the notorious, raspy-voiced, bad boy rocker who is taking the world by storm.

Sources say this could be the beginning of something new for Elijah, who in recent years has battled demons in and out of the limelight. Diesel Rose is currently staying at the hotel during the Californian leg of their worldwide Killing Me Slowly tour, with only Portland and Seattle left to perform in before the end of the tour on October 29th.

Rosalia Philips, who just completed six intense weeks of headlining this season's Swan Lake at New York City Ballet, made the desperate dash to Los Angeles less than eight hours after being on Lincoln Center's stage for the closing performance.

In recent hours, Elijah Diesel's rep denied any claims, stating Diesel and Philips are simply mutual friends. However, it's certain that true rockers and fans all over the world are watching these two after their not-to-secret 3:30 a.m. rendezvous…

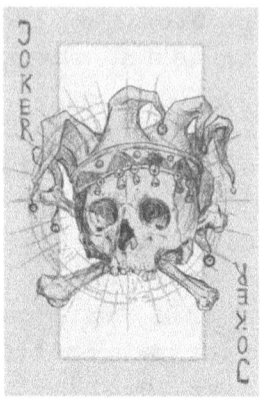

Chapter

TWENTY-EIGHT

Elijah

"Do you understand what time it is?" I grumble into my phone, keeping my voice hushed because Rosalia is still asleep beside me as the early morning sunrise beams through the floor-to-ceiling windows, blinding me shitless.

"It's almost seven a.m., not *three thirty a.m.*, Elijah, and what I would call a public relations emergency," Lydia Fitz, my publicist and personal pain in my ass, hisses into the phone. "Therefore, I can call whatever time I see fit."

I almost smirk.

She's so done with my shit.

Imagine having to deal with me and keep me in line every day. *Yeahhh, poor thing.*

Wait.

It's almost 7:00 a.m.?

Shit, I was set to be in the gym training with my P.T…forty-five minutes ago.

"What did I do this time?" I softly sigh, my fingertips skimming across Rosalia's soft skin. She's got her face pressed into my neck, and her silky blonde waves and body practically sprawled all over me, but I don't mind it. *Actually, I really fucking like it.*

"Perhaps it's about what you *didn't* do."

"Look"—I rub a hand over my eyes, clearing their blurriness—"I don't have time for a headache, so, either you spill what you're trying to allude or I'm going back to slee—"

"You *deceived* me."

Huh?

"Lydia, darling, with all due respect, I may be an asshole, but I do *listen* to you."

If only that were the truth.

"I specifically told you to cancel Rosalia Philips's flight. This is not the image you want to present yourself because I know you, Elijah, this is only going to end in chaos. I have worked tirelessly to rebuild your image after the numerous troubling headlines and rehab, when you were on the brink of death. Do you understand?"

My jaw ticks, hating how much she's pressing me. "I remember, Lydia, *trust me.*"

"Oh really? Because I think you need a reminder—"

"*Don't,*" I sneer, cutting her off as my grip tightens around my phone, almost breaking it to pieces. "Don't you dare do that, Fitz."

"I almost lost my job because of the level of dedication I give to you! You're not my only client, Elijah, and I know we've had meetings regarding this before, but you leave fires burning so intensely in the media, one day it's bound to become an inferno I can't control."

"It's your job to do that, Lydia. It doesn't matter what shit I do."

Frustrated, my publicist huffs through the phone. "Are you even hearing yourself?"

"Got anything else to say? Because I'm about to hang up *and* fire you."

"Yes," Lydia hisses. "Without me, Elijah Diesel, you'd be nothing."

That fucking does it.

"Oh, I'm *something*, baby." Strategically slipping out of the bed in a way that doesn't wake Rosalia, I stride into the private en suite, shutting the door behind me. "If you think for a minute that I can't make one phone call and destroy your reputation, then think again. You do not get to call me regarding some fucking *public relation emergency* and then character assassinate me like I'm some fucking criminal for going to damn *rehab.*"

The line falls silent to the point where I pull my phone away from my ear to check if we're still connected. We are. I've just reversed my publicist into a dead-end with no return.

And that's when Lydia's exaggerated sigh comes into play, alongside that damn ticking. It's her ballpoint pen against her marble desk back in Manhattan. I know it is. Whenever we've Skyped or we've had to have face-to-face meetings, I noticed it's a habit of hers whenever she's a little apprehensive.

"Elijah," she starts off, softer this time than her last attacks. "I'm not trying to allude to or degrade you in any way for going to rehab. I think it equals bravery and strength. What I *am* concerned about is your reputation. Your brand. *You.*"

"I get that, but—"

"I'm rebuilding you, and you let it crumble. I cannot control your every single move, including the breaking news of you and Rosalia Philips entering that hotel room in the early hours of this morning. That is solely up to you."

Breaking news?

"Respectfully, Lydia Fitz, my love life is none of your business."

"Elijah, you have no connotations to that one-syllable word."

My blood begins to bubble. "Rosalia Philips is *important* to me."

"Do you have any idea of the severity of this? Rosalia is an elite ballerina, young. Younger. *Significantly.* If you cause an uproar and it will equal slander. New York City Ballet does not play around. It is a prestigious company that, if you become reckless enough, will destroy you. *This* is the specific reason why I highly suggested you didn't fly her out to LA. You want the world's eyes on Diesel Rose. On music. On the tour. On Dave. Zander. Knight. Not a short-lived fling. So, I would proceed with caution."

Am I hearing this straight?

A short-lived fling?

Usually, my publicist is more tactful with her words, but we've been having a feud in these past few days that's been brewing for the past four years. Yes, I trust her. Yes, she constantly saves my ass. Yes, I'll most likely forgive her for this. But this is so out of line.

"*Short-lived fling?*" I growl through the phone, meeting my eyes in the vanity mirror and witnessing the fire rushing up them, licking my irises. "What Rosalia Philips and I have is much more than a *short-lived fling*, thank you very much. Besides, we've known each other for four years."

"*Oh*, so you've known her since she was…what? Seventeen? Wow, I'm sure the tabloids would love that."

"I swear to God, Lydia, you're really pissing me off."

In my rage, I hang up and refrain from slamming my phone into the vanity mirror when another argument reforms in my mind and I redial her number.

Come on, pick up.

She picks up on the third dial, and I don't even give her a chance to speak before roaring, "And what the hell do you mean to proceed with caution? What is that even supposed to fucking mean?"

"It means whatever you have with Ms. Philips, it needs to end if you want to save yourself."

I smirk. "Nah, thanks, I think I'm a little too comfortable in the pits of hell."

"Elijah Diesel. Do you have any idea of the gravity of the headlines?"

"What headlines?"

"Rock 'N' Roll Press. This morning. *Blond bombshell. 3:30 a.m. rendezvous. Fans described the couple as intimate.* My team is working readily to get rid of these articles, namely because they are distracting momentum from the tour."

"Okay, I'll be more careful."

"It's not about practicing this, Elijah. We've had so many excessive meetings these past few years. You need to be on top of this, all right?"

"Okay, I'll be more subtle."

"I don't believe you."

"Trust me then."

More silence, and then.

"I've shut down what I can. Your agent is currently representing you, stating Philips is a mutual friend. That is what you stick with."

"Lydia," I groan, rushing a hand through my tousled hair, playing around with the wavy ends. "Come on, Lids, don't be like this, you're acting like I killed somebody."

My publicist completely ignores me. "I have a press meeting in two seconds, but I'll be in contact. Rest assured I will extinguish all and any spitfires. However, you must hold your weight too, Elijah, or else *me* representing *you* is not going to work. At. All. This is your last and only warning."

And then Lydia simply hangs up, leaving me swimming in an ocean of frayed thoughts.

And I don't like it one bit.

With my back pressed against the en suite door, I type up my name and scroll through the endless articles, halting at the specific one my publicist mentioned in the jaded call.

Rock 'N' Roll Press. It's all info dump to me.

Fans described the couple as intimate and iconic.

Despite their taboo fifteen-year age gap, it seems that something is brewing in their dazzling punk paradise.

This could be the beginning of something new for Elijah, who in recent years has battled demons in and out of the limelight.

Ah shit.

Punk. The word twists my soul.

My messages, missed calls, and emails are flooded with people I need to get back to. My manager. My agent. *Emmett, Diesel Rose's record producer, pushing updates on the new single.* It's as if the world is ending, but I know better than to brush this off, so maybe it is.

I'm not a good guy. Rosalia is gonna be dragged in the mud 'cause of me, and I hate it.

And yet, I can't let her go... Not now.

TWENTY-NINE

Rosalia

"**W**hat the fuck do you mean by *SHE'S JOINING US* for *THE REST* of *THE TOUR?*"

Launching up from the king-sized bed at the distant shout that broke my sleep, I slap a hand to my chest, easing my rapidly beating heart. *Huh?*

It isn't Elijah talking.

Umm, what the hell was that?

I'm still half asleep as the bright Los Angeles sunlight spills through the lush floor-to-ceiling presidential suite windows, blinding me dirty. Elijah isn't in bed beside me, but when I slither a hand across the soft bedsheets, his side is still warm.

He must have just gotten out not too long ago.

My muscles (and ass) are aching from ballet and *sex*. I catch myself grinning like a fool. God, it was so intoxicating. *Elijah Diesel* is so intoxicating, and I can't get enough of him.

The way he knows how to pleasure my body.

Spoke to me in French.

Said our dark truths.

"Could you not scream so fucking loud that the entirety of California hears you?" It's Elijah speaking now, a hiss in his tone, but by no means as loud as the other voice. It sounds like he's down the hallway. Like in the kitchen or something.

Gah.

His gorgeous voice electrifies my veins, reminders of last flooding through, and how much we uncovered. I think I could listen to his voice all day. I could do it forever.

I think I'm falling for Elijah Diesel.

A lingering giddy smile traces my lips as I wrap myself in the bedsheets, breathing in his lingering scent. I can't stop imagining what the next two weeks joining along with Elijah's touring rock band will be like. The thought alone fuels my lungs with hope. Hope that perhaps Elijah is my ticket out of all the dark and crazy thoughts spiraling in my mind.

Oh my God! Wait until I tell Naomi. She is going to kill me.

Aside from Naomi, I've never been so open like last night about my scars. *Only him.*

"Tell me this is some fucking joke, Diesel? Come on, man, she ain't good for you."

Wellll, that's one way to kill a smile.

Adamant to uncover this mysterious source and Dr. Who this shit (and also defend my ass against this *Anti-Rosalia* guy), I rush out of bed with an oversized Nirvana sweater. It takes me two point five seconds to exit the bedroom and skid down the sleek hallway in my fluffy wool socks until I'm in the suite's lavish great room and big open-plan kitchen.

There my edgy rocker is, sporting only low-rise gray sweatpants. Eye candy. I'm serious. Beautifully defined vaunted V-cut lines. Washboard abs so hard you could grate *parmigiano* and then lick them. Nipple piercings catching the light of the bright sunshine and dazzling in it—yep, Elijah Diesel wants me drooling.

(AND, MY GOD, *HIS STUNNING COCK PIERCING*, I ALMOST DIED OF AWE!)

Elijah still hasn't seen me yet, his eyes shooting straight ahead instead while chewing colorful cereal with a *fork* in what looks to be a *highballer whiskey glass*. And…*wait a second.* My jaw drops in horror. *Dear God, are those fruity pebbles? He's eating kid cereal with a fork.*

This rock 'n' roll lover *is* crazy.

"Will you just shut the fuck up?" Elijah grumbles at the guy sitting on the bar stool with his head in his hands. "Rosalia and I aren't killing anyone…we're just spending time together."

I instantly recognize the other guy as Knight Ives aka *Knives.* Diesel Rose's bassist, hard-core rough rocker, iconic leader of the *what-the-hell-do-you-mean-you're-only-seventeen* movement, national winner of the iciest eyes championship, and overall, not a sweet as candy kinda guy.

I mean, *yeah*, I get it, it kind of makes sense that Elijah's friends with all of the crazy guys, but come onnnn, why is Knives still so up-tight about me? I didn't do anything to him.

Ugh!

Give a girl a chance, man.

"I'm not shutting the fuck up about this," Knives grits, clenching his coffee mug, and I swear he must have some sixth scent when he snaps his head my way, glaring me down with these icy light eyes, even though I didn't even move. "Well, well, well, speak of the devil…"

Gasping, I narrow my eyes back at him. "I think you should take a look in the mirror."

"I do. Every morning. Love what I see," Knives grits. "*Thanks.*"

Scoffing, I motion a hand toward the asshole and lock my eyes with an amused Elijah. "Does your friend still have a petition over me?"

Before Elijah can speak, his best friend cuts me off. "You want to talk about me, you look me in the eye, and you *talk* to *me.*"

Is this guy serious?

Five strides later and I'm standing right in front of Knives, sizing him up with a clenched jaw and not giving a shit when he stands tall to his full six-foot-one height while I literally am as tall as a rock.

"What is your damn problem, Knight Ives?" I spit, staring him down. "You don't even know me!"

"I don't need to"—Knives arrogantly makes inverted commas—"*know you* to have a problem *with you.*"

"Is that so?"

"Mmhmmm."

Elijah cuts into the tension, his voice the sternest I've ever heard.

"You talk to her like that again, you and I are gonna start having problems."

Knives scoffs, his pointed gaze shifting to his best friend. "Looks like we've been having problems ever since this chick entered your life and there's only one way to stop it."

"Oh, and how's that?" I cut in, holding my ground with a snarl. "Get me to leave?"

Knives stares at me blankly. "No, I call Ghostbust—*OF COURSE* it's to get you to leave."

If I thought Knives was a douche before, he's even more of a douche-bag now.

"Listen here, buddy—"

"I ain't your *buddy*, blondie, so back up."

"Listen. Here. *Buddy*," I grit, snapping my nails together with each staccato word, the weight of the world being lifted from my shoulder with every rushed breath I take staring into Knives's chilling eyes. "I'm staying a part of your life for as long as Elijah and I are riding whatever freaking wave it is we're riding. If you grow to like me, then *namaste*, if not, kindly look the other way whenever I'm near and shut your trap."

Before Knives can say another word, I flip up his hood, pull down the strings of his hoodie, scrunching it around his face like he's Kenny from South Park, and then when he's on the brink of steam rushing out of his head, I steal his hot coffee mug with the most wicked grin.

Ha!

Rounding the oversized kitchen counter, I devour the delectably brewed coffee, cup Elijah's face, and with that growing smirk on his lips, say fuck it and kiss him possessively.

Desperately.

All mine.

I don't care that I can feel the heat of Knives's stare blast through me, and neither does Elijah by the way he's mauling my lips, just as reckless as last night's passionate moments.

Elijah's warm arms wrap around me in the solace of his embrace, and my smile is so dreamy mid-kiss, I think I may explode. *Butterflies.* It's all I feel whenever he's near. Especially after last night. It all felt like a dream, the best kind, one I don't want to wake up from. I know we've got so much to speak about, but right now, it all comes second to this kiss.

Something's changed between us. Something so intense it almost hurts. And I love it.

"Morning, Lijah" I whisper against Elijah's lips with the biggest grin, setting the mug on the counter to wrap my arms around his neck. "I can't stop thinking about last night."

"Ditto, babygirl," he murmurs, and when he does, all I want is to be alone with him.

The private elevator's loud ding brings us back to reality and we watch as a gorgeous woman with blue hair and bold lilac eyeshadow waltzes through wearing an off-the-shoulder white sweater with a studded butterfly on it, tight leather jeans, and biker boots that match the rest of the Diesel Rose attire.

The gorgeous blue-haired woman sighs when she sees Knives, straight away slapping both hands by her hips. "Ugh, what are you doing here, Knight? Told you to leave the guy alone."

Oh. My. God.

Knight actually *smiles*, like full-on genuinely *smiles*. "I'm incapable of listening, baby."

Who is this chick? His girlfriend?

Pretty sure my jaw is on the floor.

"I can vouch for that." The stunner jokingly flips him off before rushing right up to Elijah, kissing his cheek softly, and my blood pressure rises. "Morning, Mr. Man of the Hour."

Elijah playfully rolls his eyes. "Flattery is dead, Riv."

Grinning, she bops his nose, dread filling his face. I like her already. "Maybe for you."

"Ha. Ha."

Her eyes meet mine before widening a fraction. "Holy shit!"

"Hi, um, I'm—"

"*Rosalia.*" She grins, her pearly whites all I see before she swarms me into the tightest embrace of my life, flooding me in her enticing flowery perfume. "I'm River, Knives's girl. I've heard a lot about you!"

"Oh?" I arch a brow as we pull away, my gaze not so subtly shifting to Elijah. "You have?"

The blue-haired beauty can't stop grinning, all while Elijah looks everywhere but me. And oh my God, are his cheeks blushing a tinge of pink or are my eyes deceiving me? No, I'm not going blind, Elijah freaking Diesel is getting *flustered* over being caught.

"I hope Elijah has only said nice things about me."

"Girl, he's crazy about you."

Welllll, that sure gets his attention.

Elijah's head snaps between us so fast I think it may fly right off. "Riv!" he half hisses, half groans, never daring to look at me. "I'm not crazy about *anything.*"

River rolls her eyes, her grin deepening. "Bull-freaking-shit. Okay, sure, deny it all."

Elijah. Is. Not. Happy.

I can't help smirking.

Cute.

"Okay." Knives clears his throat, breaking the tension. "Well, I don't know about you, babycakes, but Diesel and I have rehearsals until the afternoon. Meet you back here, yeah?"

Instead of replaying, she jumps in his arms and plants a big ol' kiss on the idiot's lips. "See you later, *Skittles.* Kill it out there, yeah?"

"I always do for you, babes."

They proceed to snog their faces off, and I don't miss the way Knives doesn't shut his eyes, and instead glares me down, giving me back some of my karma for no apparent reason.

Wait a second... *Skittles?*

I almost choke on my saliva on just how funny it is.

I turn to Elijah, completely amused. "Did she just call him...?"

"Yep."

Our stare ends in five seconds when we both burst out laughing, pissing off Knives beyond repair and confusing River, but it doesn't matter. It just feels good to laugh with Elijah, to not fight and instead figure out a way in which we can both exist, happily, together.

Whilst River and Knives continue saying their goodbye by the private elevator doors, Elijah takes my hand and guides me down the hallway, back inside his hotel bedroom. Somewhere during that route, he abandons the whiskey glass with the cereal contraption and when he catches my eyes, I just shake my head with a smile.

The wild, familiar, chaotic Elijah is back the second he pins me against the bedroom floor-to-ceiling windows. Flashbacks of early this morning flood my mind. His hips piston over my stomach, and when they do, I can feel just how hard he's becoming. It's short-lived, though, because I know he needs to go to rehearsals for tonight's show, no matter how badly I want him to stay.

Elijah's fingers brush my jaw. "Proud of you for defending yourself, *Peaches*. For not letting the monsters crawl in."

His touch sparks reminders of last night; his lips scattered all over my body.

"I'll always defend what I believe to be true."

"A livin' prodigy." His voice is all breathy as he adds, "It's what I like about you most."

Ka-boom.

My heart, dear God, it's melting.

I grin because I don't want to look like a full-on psycho for breaking out into a happy dance and shake my ass while this longing heat crawls up my body.

"How are you feeling after last night, well, early this morning?" Elijah asks, moving off me to get ready for rehearsals. "I can't stop thinking about it, babygirl, thinking about you."

I play it cool while this gorgeous rock star fifteen years older than me strips off his sweatpants, his perfectly toned ass staring me down as he sorts through the wardrobe until he throws a pair of white boxer briefs on the bed, alongside dark Levi jeans.

I admit I'm a full liability for the way I'm checking out his toned tattooed back muscles, and the way his dimples of Venus are the perfect dips. A weight tugs my heart at the deep white scar along his spine that runs deep, the same one I first saw four years ago, the one I know nothing about but want to.

"Rosalia?"

Snapping my eyes to his, I realize he's all dressed now, finished off with a charcoal hoodie of Diesel Rose. It's stunning in the most Elijah way with a white half skull wrapped in an onyx snake with scattered rose petals. Diesel Rose is written in their iconic logo font, and when he turns around to slip on his Dr. Martens, I see all the tour dates written on the back.

I want it.

Stepping away from the door, I pretend like I wasn't full-on gawking him and my pussy doesn't miss the way he brought me to five orgasms in the early hours of this morning. *Five.* "Uh, yeah? Sorry."

"Everything good?"

"Yeah, why?"

Elijah disappears into the en suite, and I hear water gushing from the tap. When he's back, his dark hair is slicked back in wet waves, and his breath smells of fresh peppermint.

"You zoned out after I asked you that."

"Asked me what?"

Slowly smirking, Elijah pauses lacing his ties. "I asked how you're feeling after last night."

"Electrifying." I smile. "Really, *really*, good."

"Are you sore?"

"Just a little. Okay, a lot, but I can handle it."

Elijah's eyes darken mid-smirk. "Want me to kiss that pretty pink pussy of yours better, baby?"

Always with that dirty mouth…

I blush. "If you weren't busy this morning, I'd say yes."

"It was only practice. I was taking care of you because I knew how tired you must have been after ballet and the six-hour flight."

Only practice?

Holy shit, does this guy remember how crazy he made me? My legs were shaking. *SHAKING!* That's never ever happened before to me whenever I make myself come or Cayden and I were foolin'.

I bite my lower lip. "So, you want more too?"

A devilish smirk flashes across Elijah's face as he strides up to me slowly. "Fuck yeah, baby doll, I ain't done with you."

"I hope you're never with me."

"You into the forever shit?"

I nod.

Elijah smiles. "If only the Brontës could see you now, *Peaches*, and those watercolor eyes that enchant thee, for they shall vex me forever."

And with a final perfect kiss that lingers, he's gone. I almost want to cry from the beauty of the words he left me with, his own words and feelings reimagined into old, slammed poetry.

It doesn't take long for my dreamy heart eyes to dissolve when River leans against the doorframe with the biggest smile. "Well, well, well, if it isn't Miss Rosalia Philips caught in an Elijah Diesel sized daydream."

"If this is a daydream"—I grin—"never wake me up, girl."

If I thought I was caught in a daydream before, hours later at Elijah's sound check, I'm on cloud nine. Hearing Elijah speak about his passion and going to one of his gigs years ago when he was up-and-coming is one thing, but actually seeing the grand scale of Diesel Rose ensuring everything is prepared for their last night on tour at SoFi Stadium, damn, it's inspiring.

In a couple hours, there are going to be over 90,000 people filling these currently empty seats and mosh pit. Apparently, the capacity is 100,000 seats. However, some seats are unavailable due to large screens positioned behind the stage, bringing it to just over 90,000.

Which all sold out in seconds.

Unreal.

I spent the last morning and afternoon exploring LA with River. Despite Knives being a grizzly bear, she's the definition of a cute puppy…with fangs. In other words, she's extremely sweet but isn't afraid to bite if you fuck her over. Just like me. I think it's one of the reasons we got along so well.

She's originally from Washington State and her story with Knives is a complicated one, but right now they're really solid.

I swear we went to every single store on Rodeo Drive. *I love how we shopped until we dropped,* sans the actual buying part. We were in West Hollywood, and River was helping me pick out some new clothes seeing as I was staying abroad longer than expected, when Naomi called. It's safe to say she freaked when I told her the news that I'd be staying on tour with Elijah for the rest of the two weeks.

There was this pause before a squeal took over as she told me she didn't know whether she wanted me to marry the guy or slap the guy for her. I rolled my eyes either way with a smile. "He's different, Omi," I told her.

"How *different*?" My best friend sighed, miles away.

"I don't know how to quite describe it, but when I look at Elijah, I can't see myself anywhere else but with him."

"Aww, babe. Does he feel the same way?"

"I really think he does. You should have seen the way he was so nervous to ask me on tour. I've never seen him like that before. So shy." I remember biting my lower lip, watching River from a distance as she continued to shop away, all while my best friend was waiting through the phone. "And, umm, there's also something else…"

"Rosa! Why did it sound like you're blushing when you said that? You sound all giddy and shit."

"Because maybe I am." I grinned, nervous about how she'll take this. "I've got news…big fucking news."

"STOP KILLING ME, GIRL!"

"Elijah and I fucked last night, and it was *magical*…then he asked me to stay with him for these final two weeks of tour, and I said yes."

"Oh my God, babe! YOU DID *WHAT*? Fuck yes!"

We spoke for a little while longer, well, the best I could while standing in the corner of the store and whispering while people flooded my space. I was the one to hang up, promising to call her from Portland and for her to give my love to our bunny, Mr. HotLips, who I missed immensely, but apparently, he didn't miss me too much given the pictures Naomi sent me of HotLips on Chad's bare chest in bed.

Traitor.

But I was only kidding. I was stoked that he was a good guy. She deserved it after all of the shitty men and even shitter lies.

River and I were both excused by lunch that we stopped for some much-needed caffeine, açai bowls, and serious girl talk.

When we headed back to the hotel before arriving at SoFi Stadium with our VIP 'with-the-band/crew' passes (I know, guys, I'm literally going to frame the special lanyard I'm wearing around my neck), we caught the last half hour of Diesel Rose's rehearsals. Watching Elijah now is like watching him four years ago…*magical.*

And just like that, in an echoing stadium filled with roadies, sound technicians, and some other fancy people like that, Elijah's microphone screeches, making my ears bleed.

I cringe.

Ouch.

"Because that's what we want on the last days on tour, yeah," Elijah grumbles to himself as a crew of six people with black clothes and caps scramble in all directions to resolve the issue.

The microphone returns back to normal in a few seconds, thanks to some busty blonde. Elijah, Knives, Dave, and Zander continue the sound check, and *wow*, Elijah's voice, I think I could get lost in it forever…that is until his mic is cut completely.

"For fuck's sake!" Elijah grumbles, slamming the microphone on the stage and beginning to pace instead. "WHAT IS THIS?"

The crew returns.

Shutting his eyes, Elijah can't stop cupping the back of his head. Pacing. Pacing. Pacing. *Why is he reacting like this?*

This isn't like him at all. He can't just be frustrated about this. There must be more.

When the issue is taking far longer than expected, Elijah storms right past me, backstage, without ever once turning back.

Oh.

"Shit," I whisper, glancing behind me toward River, who's sitting cross-legged on the stage. "Is he always like this in sound check?"

She shakes her head with a pout. "Never."

I stand up from sitting on the edge of the stage and jog toward a concerned Zander. "Hey, should I check on him?"

The rocker with the brushfield eyes offers me a jaded smile. "Whenever Elijah gets like this it's just better to give him some space, but hey, you could change that."

"He'll listen to you," Dave adds, setting his drumsticks aside, all while Knives does his best to ignore my existence. "Find him, Rosa."

It doesn't take long. One of the stage managers is kind enough to guide me to where his dressing room is, and that's exactly where I find my melancholic rocker, sitting in the fancy leather chair, a thin cigarette to his lips. He puffs on it, over and over, and it's only when I get close enough that I realize it's a joint.

"The boys want you back, Lijah."

Elijah physically tenses even though my reflection in the mirror is so evident, the one he's staring at himself in, but his gaze is too far gone.

"Elijah?"

"They can wait."

Silence.

When I meet his eyes in the mirror, the normal glimmer isn't there. Instead, they're coated in a murky concern, having me frown.

My heartbeats soften. "Hey, everything okay?"

"Yeah, everything's fine, why wouldn't it be?"

"Just wondering."

A slow smile curves on his face, but it's laced with something melancholic when he spins in his chair, facing me with every drag.

"No need to wonder," Elijah murmurs.

But it's more than that for me. I'm skeptical.

I flicker back and forward between his eyes, not believing him. "You sure?"

"Mmhmmm."

"*Elijah*," I warn, frowning because I instantly think the worst. "What is it?"

Please don't let it be anything bad.

What if he regrets early this morning?

Or if he regrets flying me out to see him?

Groaning, Elijah falls back into the seat, gazing at me with his fingers rushing through his wavy hair. "Rosalia, there's seriously nothing for you to worry about."

That's when the panic sets in. Nobody says those iconic lines when they truly mean it.

I can't stop staring, studying his face. "Are you sure? You seem worried."

"I'm never worried."

Okay, Mr. Perfect.

I can't help rolling my eyes. "I'm serious. You know you can tell me *anything*."

"I know, but it's—"

"It's?" I arch a brow. "Bad?"

He finally sighs, the light in his eyes further dimming. "It's just that since this morning…we're trending."

Trending?

Oh. My. God.

My stare widens a fraction. "*What*?"

"Well, you remember how we walked into the hotel earlier this morning and there were those fans and all that flashing light?"

"Yeah."

"Well, apparently they weren't all just fans taking pictures there…"

Paparazzi floods in my mind.

I part my lips to speak, but Elijah nods without me having to say a word.

"Show me."

"Are you sure?"

"Positive."

Sighing, Elijah reaches for his phone on the industrial dressing table and does just that.

I slip his phone into my grip, my eyes roaming over the articles. I read every single one of them, my breaths slowing. My face is posted *everywhere* with Elijah's in photos attached.

Photos of my Swan Lake production.

Photos New York City Ballet have posted on their social media of me during rehearsals,

Photos of Elijah on tour, onstage, walking around. *Those with his three band members.*

Photos of us together, our zoomed in hands as we stepped into The Saxton. Elijah—holding my luggage with my lace panties slightly edging out of his jean pocket, and yet nobody noticed anything—and me with my flustered cheeks, voluminously messy hair, bruised lips.

It's so obvious.

So evident.

To the naked eye, we would look like a perfect couple, but that isn't what's happening.

Shit, if only the world knew I'm not wearing any panties in that picture.

I can't risk *this*. This exposure, and I know Elijah can't either. New York City Ballet would slaughter me. Madame Eléa would kill me if she saw this. I'm still supposed to be training. I mean, yes, it's my off-season, but I should be training and chasing increasing success in preparation for upcoming rehearsals for the next ballet season. *Not chasing distractions.*

This was supposed to be a little secret hideaway, but now the entire world knows.

But… What if this is a good thing, Rosalia?

I mean, what did you expect? He's a rock star.

Maybe the articles are a blessing in disguise?

By the way Elijah is looking at me with those stormy onyx eyes that brew a wild madness filled with angst, I know it's not.

It's the complete opposite. This. Is. Not. Good. *For either of us.*

"So what do we do about it?" I ask.

Elijah ponders my question for a moment. "Lydia Fitz, my publicist, who I had a volatile call with this morning, suggests we stick to the cover that we're mutual friends."

"*Mutual friends?*" I almost laugh. "Who do we know in common?"

I appreciate Elijah's warm chuckle in a moment like this. "I don't fucking know, but obviously somebody's stringing us together. She most likely meant friends of River's."

"So I'm her...*friend*? That's what your publicist wants? Why can't we just, I don't know, say the truth?"

"I know." Elijah sighs, leaning closer to me. "Lydia thinks it will taint my image."

My heart falls to the pit of my stomach.

"*Taint your image?*"

"Yeah, she thinks I'm going to fuck you over and in return your ballet company will be on my back and reputations will be shattered. But I...I don't believe that." Elijah pauses for a moment. "I mean, we haven't even discussed...*things.*"

"As in *what we are?*" I question, thinking out loud, even though part of me is hurting from the fact that his publicist thinks being with me will destroy him and his reputation.

"As in *what we are*, yes," he confirms with a nod that tells me it's a little more complex than that.

Because, to be honest, it's true. It *is* complex. *What exactly are Elijah Diesel and I?* We've had this walk before, this dance, this long waltz of questioning our label, and it brings me back to four years ago when I was wondering *who the hell this guy is to me?*

Because he ain't my friend. He ain't my enemy. And yes, let's say it all together. *He ain't my lover either.* I've said this for so long it's become a chant, a rhythm, a tune. Hell, it could be an entire cheer performed at the Super Bowl.

But it's true.

What the hell are we?

That's what I would love to know.

"So what do we do from here?"

Elijah sets his phone back down, and when he does, I don't expect him to move closer to me. To stand and voluntarily wrap me into the warmth of his arms like it isn't one of the few times he's showing me affection, and then look deep into the depths of my soul.

"I don't know what fucking happens from here," Elijah whispers so low it's almost chilling. But all of his heart is in those words, all of his soul, I just feel it. "But…"

My heart plummets.

No.

"But…?"

"But what I do know is that I'm not scared of those fucking articles," he continues dominantly. "I don't care what my publicist says. You're staying with me in Los Angeles."

I swallow thickly because while these are the words I wanted to hear from Elijah, and fuck, how my heart's in rainbows right now, I'm hyper aware of the bigger picture.

Those articles were a huge wake-up call. Elijah Diesel isn't just a man I used to know years ago. He's an iconic rock star, and his every move is traceable, documented, inhabited. *Seen.*

"What if…" I begin, quicker than I would like. "What if Lydia is right, though?"

"She's not."

"You don't know that."

Elijah's jaw ticks. "Yes, I freaking do," he practically growls, that possession shining in his eyes. "You're *mine*, Rosalia. I'm not fucking letting you walk away now, not unless you want to. I want to have time with you. I want to take you…"

With my heart pounding a trillion miles per hour, Elijah's face crumbles as he mutters a soft curse word before squeezing his eyes shut. That's when his arms slip away from me and he turns around. But I saw enough.

I saw the vulnerability in his gaze.

The slight glassiness in his eyes.

And right now, as I rush a hand under his hoodie, across his tattooed back, my fingers roaming against the work of art, he's trembling.

What's going on?

Sadness pools across me because Elijah isn't like this. He wouldn't just…break down like this.

"Elijah, is everythi—"

"Yes."

"It doesn't seem that way."

He's quiet for a moment.

"I just get like this sometimes."

My brows furrow. "Like what?"

Elijah shakes his head. "I'm fine."

Even more silence trickles between us, but I know better to press him. Maybe he just needs some time. It's the only logical thought that keeps my sanity alive while I rub tender circles against his scorching skin.

It takes three minutes.

Maybe four.

But when Elijah speaks again, the words ricochet in my chest so beautifully tragic that I can't even breathe straight.

"I want to take you out, *Peaches*, on all these fancy freaking dates. I want to be the man you deserve and ask you to be my girlfriend, but I…I don't know how to. I've never…done it." A few seconds pass before he adds in a mere whisper, his voice shattering in pain. "I've never really been good with perfect. All I ever do is break things."

With all my strength I nudge him back, and when Elijah hesitantly turns around, those onyx eyes so watery staring back at me, my heart breaks even more.

"I just feel you're so fucking young, and I don't want to hold you back from anything because of it—"

"You won't."

"Yes, I will, Rosalia. What, you think you can just tell your parents about me? That they'll be happy? How about the articles that are already out? What do you think they'll say?"

I part my lips, but no words escape.

No.

No.

No.

Sighing, Elijah squeezes his eyes shut, pain written all over his face. "I want *this*, so fucking badly, but our age gap will evidently hold us back in the end. It's the reality. I'm too fucking old for you. Too complicated. Too much. *But*…at the same time, I don't give a fuck."

"Elijah," I murmur, falling into his arms while cupping his defined stubbled jaw. "Listen to me."

I hate how sad he looks, like he's been conditioned to believe he's the destroyer and therefore, he lives by it.

It hurts me so much because he doesn't deserve to feel this way about himself. *Who told him these things? Who told me that he wasn't good enough?*

"I don't want perfect, Elijah Diesel. I don't want fancy, or the ordinary, or guys my age." I sniffle with all my heart, just as the first tear burns down my cheek. "I just want *you*, Lijah. I want it all, all you're willing to give. The quirky. The rebel. The rock obsessed."

For a second, actual hope fuels his eyes.

"But you'll get sick of me," he whispers, redness dimming his eyes, like it's an expectation. "You'll leave me."

"I won't."

"You can't promise that."

"No, no, I can't." I nod, intensifying the raging fire inside my lungs. "But I promise not to run because that would only be breaking myself too."

Elijah swallows thickly, rushing his hands up to cup my cheeks, and pulls me closer until our foreheads brush. I lean forward, my hair falling over the edges of our faces, trapping us into our own wonderland filled with roaming lips, fastened breaths, and blonde blinkers.

Elijah can't stop kissing away my tears, can't stop tenderly touching me, holding me tight against him like I'll disappear if he doesn't.

"Don't cry, *Peaches*, not for me."

"I can't help it." I gulp down, the back of my throat an aching mess. I wander back and forth between his eyes. "I hate that you feel this way about yourself. That you think you're incapable, that you'll fuck this up when it's only our start."

"Because I know myself."

"Then let go of what you know," I whisper. "And let's start from zero instead. *Together.*"

Smiling sadly, Elijah's fingers weave through my hair, cupping the back of my head. "Just so you know, no one has ever cared for me as much as you do."

"That's what girlfriends are for."

Elijah's eyes light up, a sad boy in the shell of his broad, beautiful superstar body.

"You're my girlfriend, *Peaches*," he tests the words on his tongue, creating sparks all over me. "And I fucking adore the way it sounds."

I adore you.

Elijah Diesel kisses me wildly, backing us up until I'm pinned against one of the dressing room walls. It's fast. Desperate. Hot. As if the world is about to self-destruct any second now. And his tongue, damn, it's magical and always knows how to drive me wild with every swirl.

But this kiss is much more.

We can't stop touching each other, exploring each other with our hands, as if this may all just end tomorrow. It won't. I know it won't. But there's so much emotion poured into this kiss, so much vulnerably, and those are words I never thought I would correlate with Elijah.

Elijah kisses all the crazy, the complicated, and the imperfects that we are. Our love is going to be messy, scary, and raw, but fuck, how much it makes me feel already.

And I will never get sick of that.

"You're perfectly imperfect, Lijah." I smile once we pull away, meaning every word. "That's what I like about you most. It makes you real, and it makes you *you.*"

We gaze at each other for the longest time, grazing foreheads and rubbing noses in Eskimo kisses. *Our love is intense, just like hurricanes.*

The most beautiful smile breaks out on Elijah's lips, meeting his eyes, and it's the most happiness I've seen in him. Yes, some sadness is still there, but now it's replaced with smile lines, dimples, and *hope.*

Smiling deeper, he buries his head into my neck, trailing slow peppered kissing up it until he reaches my ear. "*S'il te plait ne m'abandonne jamais.*"

My heart warms at the French, exploding in fireworks at every single word.

"*Peaches,*" Elijah seductively whispers while I slowly weave my fingers through his wavy hair. "Please don't ever give up on me."

Never.

Chapter
THIRTY

Rosalia

Elijah said he wanted some time to sort out the shit in his head and it's exactly what I plan to tell his bandmates when I step outside of his dressing room. What I don't expect is Dave to be strolling my way backstage before I can twist my words together.

"Hey there, Rosa." Dave half-smiles, readjusting his man bun that's a little shorter than the last time I saw him, but still dark with those angelic caramel highlights. "Any luck finding him?"

I gesture toward the corridor I just came from. "Yeah, dressing room. He just needs some time. He's a little stressed out today."

"Did he tell you why? Diesel doesn't really share that shit with us. I mean, he does, but about a century after the fact."

I don't know why that brings a smile to my lips. "I think it's just a combination of everything, especially with his publicist."

Dave hums. "All right, if the tough guy wants some breathing time, let's give him some."

On our walk through the polished concrete corridor with stage people with headsets floating around everywhere, I grip my VIP Diesel Rose lanyard anxiously, feeling its sudden weight.

Why couldn't Elijah tell me about the tabloids earlier this morning at the hotel?

Is he scared what his publicist is saying is true?

But if he is, why would he declare that he wants me?

"I can see your mind ticking." Dave clicks his tongue, his smile wafting to a tender smile. "But I'm telling you, there's no need."

I slow in my step. "Why? Has he ever…told you boys anything about me?"

"Diesel's mentioned you in these years, really brief, like he used to get all quiet whenever Knives used to drink a Cherry Cola, or whenever his birthday came around, but ever since you reentered his life, there's a glow to him."

"*A glow?*"

"Sounds fucking crazy, right? But it's true, my boy has a glow."

A giggle rumbles up my throat. "How so?"

We commence walking again, and when this eyeliner addicted giant wraps an arm around my shoulders, breaking the ice, I feel better about this entire conversation.

"Well, Diesel's just been…*different* with you in the picture. For one, we have a single that we have locked in with our record producer. It needs to be written, recorded, and produced by the end of November, right? Well, Diesel's been suffering from the biggest writing block, but the moment you two rehashed things at that laundromat, his lyrics have been flowing, man, like honey."

Aww.

My heart clenches. "He told you about the laundromat thing?"

"I mean, I only had to force him about it and almost broke his balls, but yeah, he did."

"Elijah never told me about that single."

Dave boyishly smirks, and when he does, everything feels like it's going to be okay. "Probably 'cause he's writing that song about you, Rosa. You know you're his muse, yeah?"

What?

All the air is sucked out of me as I stare at one of the closest men to Elijah, my eyes wide.

No.

No way.

There is no way.

Diesel Rose's drummer is playing with me.

I can't seem to breathe straight anymore, not even when we reach the side stage and stop there for a moment so our conversation isn't out in the open.

I'm Elijah Diesel's muse?

He's writing a song about me?

All my thrill swelters into nerves. The good kind. Those that make you lovesick and can't sleep over all the adrenaline pumping.

"Honest to God?" I ask.

Dave does the sign of the cross, twice. "Promise to the Father, o' Jesus, or else the devil can fuck my soul. Elijah's crazy about you. He may just have a funny way of showing it. Like, I don't know, has he made any plans for tonight?"

I shake my head. "He mentioned how you guys were going out for drinks. Did you mean just us two?"

"Mmhmmm."

"Well then, no, he hasn't spoken of plans."

"Do you want to go out with Diesel?"

My cheeks begin to burn at the intensity of this conversation and the intrigue in his eyes. "Yes, he's really special to me. I'd like to take this further."

Dave groans, rubbing his forehead. "Ah, goddamn, he's so unbelievable. What the hell is he doing? He flies you out to LA and he's too chickenshit to ask you out on a date?"

Okay, now my cheeks are burning because Dave's really freaking nice. I like this guy.

"Simplicity isn't really his thing." I smirk.

"I'd say." He winks. "Listen up, Rosa, let me tell you a trade secret when it comes to Elijah Diesel."

"Mmhmmm?"

"Despite being a cocky bastard and having full-on Joker vibes, at times, he can get really shy, like when he's nervous or uncomfortable about a certain topic. So you don't shy away from it, ask him those scary questions. He's never really had support and affection growing up. It's molded him a lot, not for the better. Feed into it, and I promise, he'll never want to let you go."

I nod, Dave's words absorbing in my mind, and just before he leaves to join his bandmates, he turns back to me with a smoldering grin as his lips brush against my ear. "Oh, and by the way, 'Fragments of You' is about you too. He's just too shy to admit it."

And that, ladies and gents, is when my knees buckle. All these years, whenever I heard a Diesel Rose song, I always skipped it, muted it, or hum over it with another song to blur the lyrics. I didn't want to know.

I wanted to forget Elijah, every single part of him, including his prized possession—his music. Yes, I always listened long enough to catch a glimpse of his voice and then the anger would resurface again, but now that's going to change.

I'm here, tonight, about to watch Diesel Rose perform at the peak of their career.

I'm going to be right *here* in a busy stadium listening to every single song, beat, lyric.

I'm going to be side stage with VIP access, watching on, my lips bruised by his.

And it's going to change everything...

I've become *that* girl. That Elijah Diesel obsessed twenty-one-year-old girl who second by second is falling deeper for him.

The one who wears faded black cut-out jeans with a clipped chain and safety pins attached, an exclusive Diesel Rose *CREW* T-shirt I cropped, and stilettos as red as Satan's kiss.

The one with burnt orange velvet ribbons in her hair, sparkly pink eyeshadow, and glossy fiery red lips.

The one who was gripped by the throat by the edgy rocker, kissed sensuously before he emerged on stage in the darkness with his rock band after the opening act, and then, with a loud riff of Knives's bass, seductive red lights went wild. Striking fire emerged from the edges of the stage as the packed SoFi Stadium roared screams back at Diesel Rose.

It's been almost two hours and is nearing the end, signalizing the end of their fourth consecutive night touring LA, with two more to go following tomorrow's rest day. Watching Elijah's passion unfold right before my very eyes is something beyond ordinary because with every song, every lyric, every beat, there's so much passion, sadness, and depth.

I was right when I once said I imagined Diesel Rose's songs like dripping poetry, because they are, only they're in the form of rock.

I can't get over Elijah's sexy, raspy voice. Hell, I don't think the entire audience can either with the way they shout back every single lyric. There are so many times, with River by my side at side stage, that I find myself staring out at the hardcore fans. All ninety thousand of them, and it leaves me speechless.

There are so many of them who chant along the lyrics, who pump their fists, having a rad time. *And to think this isn't even a fraction of Diesel Rose's global love… it's insane.*

Millions.

Elijah has a million lovers.

The boys have been on tour for eight months, all over the world. Tonight's show is unreal. Glowing fire with every intense song, fans putting on their phone flashlights and swaying with the slower ones, like a beautiful storm of glowing fireflies.

I can't help but stare at the four men living their dreams, being a witness to just how far they've come. From practicing in their private studio in Manhattan with no guidelines, rules, to label record but their own, to *this*.

Dave killing it on the drums, his hair swaying like crazy wild, dressed in all leather.

Zander on the guitar, the most reserved out of them four, but he's so in his element, enjoying every second.

Knives, who is still an asshole, *but* I have to give credit for the way his notes and riffs perfectly etch into every single song.

Elijah looks the happiest he's ever been with those dimpled cheeks and effortless raspy voice that brings chills down my spine, electrifying the entire stadium.

I love everything about tonight. From the huge screen behind them with a mash-up of lyrics, cuts from their music videos, and also exclusive content that make me swoon, no matter how hardcore they are. To the way Elijah's wearing that leather jacket with the spikes on the shoulder and the tear on his left sleeve that he still hasn't fixed. To those gray-onyx eyes that have barely left mine all night, lined in light eyeliner, always glancing over toward the side stage. Especially when he sang a cover of Oasis's "Wonderwall", my favorite song, just like old times.

His smile extended every time I waved.

An antidote.

That's what Elijah is to all the pain crawling inside. All the anxiety and stress that comes with being Rosalia Philips melts. It *all* just melts away, until there's only him.

"You're looking gorgeous, LA!" Elijah shouts into the microphone, a few strands of his hair falling into his eyes from all the moving around the stage, but he doesn't seem to mind. "Make some noise, babyyy!"

The blaring screams have my grin deepening.

"This is our last song for the night. I know, I know, it's depressing as hell, but we love you guys and can't thank you enough. We'll be back here soon. I promise. Anyway… This next one's a song I wrote almost four years to the day. It's about…" Elijah's eyes flicker to mine and my heart flips. "Someone real fucking special to me."

Oh my God.

I gasp, slapping my hands to my mouth, just as his grin transforms into a darkened smirk. "It's about leaving her when I shouldn't have, and then suffering from the agony of getting lost in the fragments of her."

"Fragments of You".

It must be the next song.

Mamma mia.

Dave wasn't kidding when he told me Elijah wrote it about me. That I was his muse.

I flicker my gaze to Dave to find him already staring. Throwing me a wink, he points and motions for me to come on stage, all while Knives rolls his eyes.

What?

My eyes widen.

Oh, hell no!

"ROSALIA!" Dave shouts with a smile, calling me over, but I shake my head and motion a knife slicing across my throat.

There is no way in hell I'm getting up on that stage. *No wayyy, José.*

"Come on, girl, I'm going too!" River beams, getting the okay from security with a nod.

"No, River, don't you leave me."

Laughing, she blows me a kiss before rushing into Knives's arms, candid riffs of his bass guitar blasting through the stadium.

And that's when those familiar gunmetal-colored eyes meet mine and I know I'm fighting an inevitable battle. Especially when he steps away from the mic, the show pausing for a second as he pulls out one of his earpieces. Sandalwood floods my air as he nears with a tender smile I've never seen before.

It's like he needs me. Needs me right here as he snakes an arm around my waist, his lips brushing my ear as he rasps through all the noise, "Come on, Princess. For me."

"But your publicist?"

"I couldn't care less."

I shake my head, frowning, anxiety flooding my lungs. It's one thing to be a professional ballerina and thrive on dancing onstage in your element. It's another when you're propelled into a brand-new world. "Nooo, I don't want to reenact some *A Star is Born* moment. I'm no Lady Gaga."

"Pretty sure Bradley would have dragged her ass out by now."

"He's a gentleman."

"And I am not." Elijah smirks with a wolfish growl. "I'm no Heathcliff either, baby."

The air crackles between us as a soft blue hue flickers across his face because of the lights. We spend a lifetime gazing into each other's eyes, his hands slowly wrapping around mine, his warmth transfixing me as he tugs me toward the stage, all while fans chant his name.

What's the worst that could happen, Rosalia?

You could be forever hated, that's what.

"No, I can't, Lijah."

He sighs, disappointed. "Tell me a good reason why."

"Because I will… I'll…" I practically blur out the rest. "I will literally piss my pants! Do you want that? I don't want that, Elijah, please!"

"*Well*"—he softly chuckles, slightly amused by my choice of *elegant* words—"you'll be doing it in front of over ninety thousand people, so either way, you'll go viral."

"Elijah! Shut up!"

"*Please*," Elijah whispers, a plea in his gaze I've never seen before because I've rarely heard him utter those words. "You want me, Rosalia?"

One beat.

Two beats.

Three beats.

"Yes, so much so."

I want you so much I think I may explode.

I want you so much I want to scrapbook again solely about you.

I want you so much, Elijah Diesel, that I may just walk onto this stage with you.

Elijah nods toward the crowd. "Then this is my *life*. My every day. And I want the world to know about it."

That's when it hits me. That this is about so much more than my willingness to face thousands of people. It's about the courage in supporting what he loves in a way nobody else has before. It's living his reality. *Tonight.*

"But what if…what if something happens between us and then… this is all just…?"

Elijah arches a brow. "A moment in time?"

My heart hurts when I nod. "Yeah."

"Then I'll always remember us this way."

An invigorating ball of fire takes over me, his words sinking in without any barriers.

This is how I prove to him I want this.

"You owe me dinner." I shyly smile, planting a kiss on his cheek. "Fuck it, let's do this!"

Elijah's wide grin, with those smile lines sinking through, will forever be burnt in me.

The crowd goes crazy as Elijah squeezes my hand and leads me on stage, my cheeks burning up to a trillion Fahrenheit as he does.

Holy cow.

I can't believe I'm doing this.

I can't believe I'm doing this.

I SAID I CAN'T BELIEVE I'M DOING THIS. MY FEET ARE LIKE JELLY.

"My girl's got a little stage fright." Elijah smirks into the microphone, never leaving my side. "How about we all make her feel welcome, hmm?"

More cheers.

I'm amazed by the intensity of the electrifying screams that bolt straight through me, of how they look like thousands of millions of dots everywhere. I don't know how Elijah can still hear. Watching the crowd is so overwhelming, incredible, and yet…*freeing.*

"I want us all to say *we got you, Peaches,* in the count of three, okay? One… Two… Three…" His eyes shift to mine, just as he and over ninety thousand more fans scream, "WE GOT YOU, PEACHES!"

"Holy shit." I smile, my entire body laughing up.

Elijah always makes me feel so special.

Some crew guy rushes from backstage with a set of earpieces and a small black clip-in monitor. Elijah takes it from him and slips the earpieces in and clips the black monitor thingy that they're attached to into the back of my jeans. The crowd instantly softens in my ears, and it becomes just Diesel Rose.

"Get her off, booo!" Knives shouts into his mic.

The stadium bursts into laughter, which erupts even louder when I flip him off.

As the boys get ready for their next song, Elijah wants me by the mic as he blindly pulls off one of his rings. "Wear this one for me."

"You've got a lucky ring or something?"

"Maybe."

I rush my fingers over the ridges and edges of the ring, the detailing almost tickling my skin. I can't get over the beauty of the snake ring, diamantes shining back at me. It makes me so happy Elijah is like this. I really adore how in touch he is with jewelry. Eyeliner. Black nail polish. It makes him seem authentic. Alive. Define his own reality.

I slip the ring on my right thumb. *Honored.*

"This song is for you, *Peaches,* and it's also a fuck you to being just mutual friends."

The music begins and instantly I know this song's a little slower than the others, but still with the same intensity. The camera flashlights return, blanketing the entire stadium in swaying fireflies, but all I really see is *him.*

And when Elijah Diesel turns to me, our gazes never break as guitar riffs and tempo drums grow wild and he begins singing. Not even when our hands slip so he can grip the microphone better, his warmth remaining.

So many other things in mind
And my heart is… falling in two
Plummeting into the water
Laced. With. You

And it's killing me slowly
And it's killing with time
The chemicals are corrosive, and fueling up my mind
My only wonder
My only cure
Is. You.

Oh. My. God. I'm already breathless.
Elijah Diesel has the voice of an angel in the devil's disguise.

I feel the waves
Rippling through
My head
And I've never been so tireddd
What a bittersweet lieee
If only I knew…

His words touch me. Ruin me. Build me back together, but most of all, they leave me wild, craving him. The rawness in the way he sings from a place of poetic tragedy *kills me.*

And then the chorus hits, all the instruments and his voice molded together are bliss.

You were killing me slowly
I would have gone away
Away somewhere so lonely, where the hurricanes stay
But I left you so low
I knew you since May
And now I know, I'm just a fragment of you

A fragment of…
You

Mmmm-hmmm

Don't miss this getting lonely
All my tears have run dry
Never knew I'd be holding to the solace in your eyes, I—
I
Keep
On
Figh-ting
For what's left

With every single lyric, Dave going crazy on the drums, the melody intense, just as Elijah reclasps his hand in mine and faces me. The crowd grows wild, as he sings *to me*, like I'm the only girl to ever exist.

'Cause there's a cure in my head, and it keeps going round
and round
Never knowing when depression will lace with suicide
But
I
Keep
My head up high, now

If I knew you were killing me slowly
Or softly inside
Would have given you the motions of my only heart
I've. Been. So. Low. Without you hereee
It's killin' me slowly

Oh-ohhh
Oh-ohhh

A fragment of you, that's all that's left
You riddled me slowly, oh, you did it your best
Your words
Your love
Your flaws are still here, undressed
But I'm not loving, no-thing else but…
These fragments of… (You)

Oh my God.

Wow.

A crescendo builds, Zander's and Knives's guitar riffs going crazy in a breathtaking duet, alongside Dave's intense drumming. And then, just like that, the stadium flickers red as Elijah blesses us more, just as the rest of the music fades, giving him an acoustic section. The next words are sung with the audience joining in and clapping in beat for every last lyric in the line.

> *And it's killing me slowly*
> *Fucking up my mind*
> *Never knew how lonely*
> *I left you that night*

The music returns, all while the growing lump in my throat doesn't let go. I'm tainted by it and just how blurry my vision becomes because he wrote this song *for me*. About *us*. I thought Elijah forgot about me all those years ago. I thought he didn't crave me like his very own antidote, and yet he did.

> *It comes in waves, and I don't know what to say, but I know*
> *you're hereee*
> *Inside*
> *My mind*
>
> *In a small little place, where,*
> *I keep all the no-stal-gia*
> *And fragment of…*
> *You*
>
> *Mmmm-hmm-mmhmmm*
>
> *Fragments of you, hey*
> *Mmmm-hmm-mmhmmm*
> *The fragments of…*
> *Mmmm-hmm-mmhmmm*
>
> *Fragments de toi*

Mmmm-hmm-mmhmmm

Elijah steps away from his gold snake vintage microphone, looking at me in a way he never has before. Maybe because witnessing what he loves makes me so proud. Maybe because there are hot happy tears baptizing my cheeks. Maybe because there's emotion clouding his own eyes too—glassy—like this is a first for him, his heavy breaths cathartic.

The guitars play a series of contained chords, all while Dave's crazily rhythmic drumming builds up more and more, until it's so beautifully loud it mimics the rapid speed of my heart.

All I see is Elijah.

We can't stop staring at each other, his pants fueling my need.

And then, in all the wildness, the music all slows before there's one final crash-out, coming together on one final chord before the music stops and the crowd cheers back with even more screams, whistles, and claps.

Glowing amber fire rushes up from the edges of the stage, signifying the end of the Californian leg of Diesel Rose's tour, with only Portland and Seattle to go.

"You're killing me softly, *Peaches*," Elijah whispers, and then he's kissing me roughly with that intoxicating tongue, in front of thousands of screaming Diesel Rose fans.

I can't stop. Stop wanting him. This kiss replenishes me in ways I never knew existed. I really like kissing Elijah, the roughness that he's laced in, but right now, it slows right down.

Sensual.

So sensual as my tears glide down, coating our ravishing lips.

He wrote that song about me. For me. And he wanted to sing it to *me.*

Tonight, another part of us is unlocked, the part with no barriers in the way anymore.

It only confirms even deeper what I believe to be true in my heart of hearts…

I'm falling for Elijah Diesel, *and I don't ever want to stop.*

Chapter
THIRTY-ONE

BREAKING NOW:
Fragments of the poetically tragic rock star
and his muse...

By Beatrix Helfrich, ROCK 'N' ROLL PRESS
October 18, 2022

Elijah Diesel has stunned fans with an impromptu serenade on stage in Los Angeles after his rep shutting down rumors of a brewing romance with his blond bombshell ballerina.

The 35-year-old rock star locked lips onstage with Rosalia Philips, prima ballerina at New York City Ballet, during the final Californian show of his rock band's Killing Me Slowly tour.

This comes amid rumors the two are an item following their 3:30 a.m. rendezvous walking into The Saxton hotel hand-in-hand.

Before performing their last song, Diesel Rose drummer, Jaxen Davidson (Dave), 39 years old, was seen encouraging Philips, 21, up on stage with a broad smile. The Diesel Rose lead singer then walked toward the side stage to Philips before they walked out on stage together.

Diesel sported his iconic studded black leather jacket with safety pins. His luscious dark hair was slicked back, the ends left in a wet curl. The beauty cut an ultra rock chic figure in a cropped Diesel Rose tee and red Valentinos. Her honey-blonde hair flowed down her chest in loose, voluminous waves, laced with apricot-colored velvet ribbons.

'My girl's a little stage fright' the hunk singer smirked into his vintage microphone with a detailed snake. Before encouraging the sold-out SoFi Stadium holding over 90,000 fans to make her feel welcomed.

Sources described their chemistry as electrifying as Diesel handed Philips a nostalgic vintage snake ring before serenading her with an intimate performance of "Fragments of You".

Moments prior to the serenade, the twice crowned Sexiest Man of The Year earlier went into detail about Diesel Rose's record-breaking and Grammy's winning single, "Fragments of You". Diesel stated he wrote the song four years ago, alluding to a connection between that time period and Philips with the sizzling stolen glance they shared.

Over 90,000 fans roared back at Diesel and Philips after they stole a passionate kiss at the end of the performance, leaving the world to wonder who exactly Rosalia Philips is to one of the most talented legends of rock 'n' roll history…

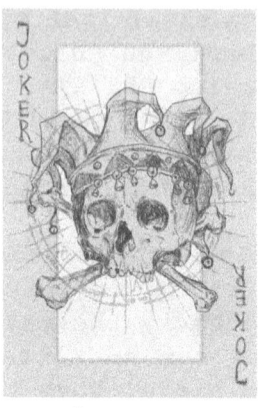

Chapter

THIRTY-TWO

Elijah

The devil's been holding me captive for too long. Now it's my time to run free. The last Californian meet-and-greet on this tour couldn't go faster. I couldn't stop wandering my gaze over to Rosalia despite the continuous line of fans. She's like my very own drug, intoxicating with the sweetest, sinful taste.

Truthfully, ever since we had sex last night, my mind's been a fucked-up place. I don't know the first thing about affection, and yet last night, for the first time in my life, I fell asleep beside another beating heart. I never saw the novelty in it before. Never thought it was me. And then I wrapped my arms around her twenty-one-year-old waist and pulled her tight, and her warmth kept me alive.

I don't know what it is I'm feeling, only that I want to explore more of it with Rosalia before I decide if it'll be my healing or my undoing. I don't trust myself to keep a good thing glowin', but fuck, how pretty the fire in her smile is… I want to play with it, play with fire, let the amber flames lick the tips of my fingers, the chains padlocking my chest, and the lyrics flooding my lungs.

"Don't fuck this up with her," Dave whispers in my ear when the boys and I almost finish the meet and greet, flipping a Sharpie in his grip in lieu of his drumsticks. "She cares."

Cares.

That word lunged inside of me like a silver bullet.

I've never been cared for before.

Not in the way I wanted.

I was always an afterthought.

Could it be that…*Rosalia does care?*

When I flicker my piercing gaze to Rosalia's, who is across the room talking to River, I study her slowly, watching as she laughs beautifully at something they're talking about. Gah, those smile lines, they ruin me slowly, suck out my breath. *Get me lost in the fragments of us.*

As if it's some kind of telepathy, like she feels somebody watching her, mid-laughter, Rosalia's eyes scan the room, the smile slipping when she sees me.

Dun-da.

My fucking heart, guys, I think I may die.

Time slows between us. Everything is in slow motion as cameras flash while I'm beside Dave and some redhead, Zander, and Knives on the other side of her, but it's all a blur to me. I'm not looking into the lens. I'm looking into *her* lens. *My peaches.*

It feels like slow motion with my heartbeat growing wild in my ears. I don't know what this means, not at fucking all, but as the warmest smile slowly carves up Rosalia's lips, and I replicate it, timidly giving her a soft nod, knowing this feeling will soon end up destroying me.

The feeling of finally being seen.

Of being cared about.

Of being validated.

But most of all, the feeling of simply *feeling*, and I think that's what hurts the most.

I wrote a song about her.

I performed it in front of thousands of fans.

I gave her an open letter explaining everything spiraling in my mind.

And she didn't run away.

Rosalia…she *stayed.*

Right *here.*

With.

Me.

Rosalia's jaw hits the ground the second I walk here into my favorite little LA hideaway as the clock strikes midnight, D.A.R.K. "Oh my God, Lijah! This is…*whoa!*"

Insane is the word she's after, because she's right, this place is the definition of ecstasy.

D.A.R.K. is one of my favorite three-Michelin star restaurants/ bars that doubles as a vintage lover's paradise. D.A.R.K.'s entire theme is vintage photography inspired, modeled to look like a dark room used to develop film photographs.

Fucking cool, right? The low lights with a sexy soft tinge of red have got to be one of the best parts of this place, alongside the hanging rolls of vintage film and candid polaroids aligning the walls. And every night they have a different black-and-white Golden Age of Hollywood projecting from the sky-high ceiling. Tonight, Hitchcock's *Psycho* is playing.

D.A.R.K. isn't open for walk-ins and has an extensive six-month waiting list, but the owner and guys at the door know me, so I always get in.

That familiar vanilla bean smell laces the air, and some diners glance my way, but I ignore them all, keeping my eyes on the only woman in here who I serenaded on stage tonight.

Rosalia can't stop glancing around the joint in awe, even after the owner personally welcomes us in and gives us the best seat in the entire place—the table for two with the gorgeous floor-to-ceiling windows overlooking the Los Angeles dazzling skyline, the Hollywood Sign visible if it were day.

"Look at these!" She grins, pointing up at the rolls of vintage film reels hanging from the ceiling when I push in her chair, because *spoiler*, I'm playing some big gentleman cards tonight. "What's the story behind all the polaroids on the wall?"

"Basically, there comes a time during your stay where the owner, Dean, steps out and takes a candid snap of his guests. It can be a candid emotional moment or a joyous one, basically anything that screams *living*. Then he keeps the polaroid and it becomes a memory wall, keeps this place feeling alive."

"Wow! I think I adore this place even more now. It's a dream!"

"I thought you would like it here because I remember you once told me that photography was one of your passions. So I figured, if you like photography, you'd like this."

Gasping, her eyes widen and meet mine as if I just told her we're driving to Vegas after this to get married by an Elvis impersonator. "Elijah!"

"Rosalia…" I slowly say back, slipping into the seat adjacent to her, setting down the velvet box I brought with me on the edge of the glass table.

Her eyes, *fuck*, they pool in glassy emotion in the erotic low light. "Oh my gosh…you remember me saying that?"

"How could I forget? This is our last night in California. I wanted it to be special for you and take you somewhere I know you'd—"

I don't even have time to finish my sentence before Rosalia is bolting out of her chair and into my arms. She embraces me so tightly, so tenderly, that at first it takes me off guard. I'm not used to the way it feels so natural to hug her back, lean into her warmth, and chuckle as she says *thank you* a million times.

"Sooo, Elijah Diesel…" Rosalia smirks over at me once she's back sitting across the restaurant/bar/I-don't-fucking-know-how-to-describe-it glass table. Her flirtatious grin the deepest I've seen. She gulps down some water. "How long is this going to take for you to admit this is a date?"

I smugly wink back at the tiny devil, conscious she's goddamn right. "Okay, it's a date."

"Geez, and you're only telling me now?" she teases, motioning to what she's wearing. "I would have dressed up in something more, I don't know, *eloquent*."

My darkened gaze roams down her body in this low-lit restaurant with a sexy red tinge and beautifully exposed brick. I slow over her Diesel Rose self-cropped CREW T-shirt, faded jeans with chains and safety pins, and those killer red stilettos that haven't stopped roaming up my thigh from the second we got here moments ago. It doesn't take long before I'm gawking at her sparkly eyeshadow, those pretty velvet ribbons in her hair, and the way I begin to imagine those painted red lips creating stains all down my body, smeared over my cock.

Between the way Rosalia is looking at me, that crawling stiletto, and my wild imagination, I feel my cock begin to stir, stretchin' in the constraint of my jeans because the devil likes me tonight.

"I don't think there's anything wrong with what you're wearing. *In fact*"—I hover the rim of my glass of water over my lips but don't drink yet to half-smirk—"I'd prefer less."

Rosalia's cheeks light up. "*Oh?*"

"Mmhmmm."

Our sizzling stare lingers, loaded with sexual tension.

A full-blown smirk completes my lips at just how flustered my babygirl already looks.

The waiter appears, breaking us out of our trance, and when he does, Rosalia gets me to order, seeing as I know the place. I order a little bit of everything, but of course request no spices or anything else that could kill her.

The waiter leaves with our fancy fabric-laced menus, promising the wait won't be long.

"I've been meaning to ask you something..." Rosalia smiles.

"Yeah?"

"How are your sister and nephew, Clément, doing? Have they seen one of your shows?"

She remembers.

"Yeah, they're well. Little guy just started sixth grade a couple months ago...*hates* it."

"Oh my God, why does he just make me think of what you would have been like at eleven? Is he still the class flirt?" Rosalia laughs, raising her brows. "Or does he ghost girls too now?"

"Shut up." I chuckle and jokingly roll my eyes. "Happy to report he's not giving out flowers like it's his lifeline anymore. Well, that's a lie. I flew him and my sister down to New York when I was performing here weeks ago, and the first thing Clément did was give Knives's girl, River, a bunch of violets...it's her last name. River *Violet*."

Rosalia slaps a hand over her mouth, riddled in laughter. "He's something else."

"Yeah, wait until he meets you. *God*," I groan just thinking about it. "He'll literally beg my sister to buy him a peach to give to you."

I expect her to continue laughing, but instead, it settles as she looks at me fondly. "You want me to meet Clément one day?"

"Yeah, of course I do. You're my girlfriend. Why wouldn't you meet him?"

"I don't know. I just thought…"

"You thought, *what*?" I half-smirk. "That just 'cause I don't know half the shit one is supposed to do in a relationship, I'm gonna skip the *meet the family* stage, huh, little one?"

Her cheeks tinge a deep scarlet, even redder with the moody restaurant lights. "Maybe."

"Then you thought wrong because I want you to meet them. They're the only family I have left." Feeling this conversation's getting too deep for a date, I deflect. Nudging the flat velvet box across the table, I nod to it. "Anyway, I bought you a little something earlier…"

"Oh, you didn't have to do that, Elijah."

Oh, baby, if only you knew…

I bite my lip. "Wanted to. Open it."

"But you already gave me the greatest gift tonight!"

"What was that?"

"Baby, you dedicated a song to me in front of all your fans."

"Oh, *that*." I grin. "Just wrote down everything you made me feel, *Peaches*."

"It was really special, so thank you, and for giving me the courage to stand beside you."

"The entire world's gonna know now."

"My parents are going to kill me."

I chuckle. "Should have listened to them when they said not to be with a rock star, huh?"

"Yeah, something like that." Rosalia grins. "They'll probably call me in the morning."

Oh, that's gonna be interesting. Her dad already made it clear how much he hates me…

Going back to my gift, Rosalia takes the longest time attempting to untie the delicately tied red velvet bow on top. *Yeah, I may have gone a little overboard and knotted it one too many times 'cause I'm me.*

She finally gets it undone, and that's when I notice her black nail polish and the little love hearts she has painted in the centers in white. She's so edgy and quirky, just like me.

Rosalia opens the lid but pauses at the sheets of black tissue paper to arch a suggestive brow at me. "This tissue paper says *Deseo*…"

"Mmmm."

"Well, isn't *Deseo* that luxurious Spanish lingerie label?"

"Mmhmmm."

"But…there isn't anything scandalous in here that you'd give me at a *restaurant*, right?"

I shrug, failing at a straight face.

Definitely something scandalous.

Anticipating her reaction, I gulp down my water and trace the pads of my fingers over the rim when I set it down. She pushes out the black tissue paper and my breath halts at the first sight of the delicate light orange lace she runs her fingers across, the same color of peaches.

"Oh my…" Rosalia slaps a hand over her mouth, her voice a soft melody. "They're *beautiful*."

A slow, sexy smile rushes up my lips. "Hold them up to me. Nobody's watching."

Her eyes widen. "Ahem, yes, they *are*, you're Elijah freaking Diesel!"

"And?" I shrug. "I'm just a guy who likes leather, rock and roll, and tobacco."

"Oh no, you don't." She playfully deadpans. "Don't try and play me the modesty card when you just got off stage with nearly ninety thousand people watching you."

"What I'm tryin' to say, *Peaches*, is that I don't notice anybody else but you."

A breath escapes her.

"So," I add, folding my forearms against the table and leaning forward. "Open it."

Timidly, Rosalia does just that, a bright smile that transforms into giggles as she glances around the restaurant before holding the gorgeous peach G-string panties up to me, her fingers still fascinated with rubbing over the lace. "Jesus Christ, Elijah, these are the tiniest things I've ever seen!"

"I had to replace the ones I ripped."

"I love them. Thank you."

Next, Rosalia pulls out the matching bra, and she can't stop grinning once I show her the inside of the left cup. In the soft padding,

Elijah is written in fancy stitching, right where her nipple piercing would rest. I like the way she can't seem to take her eyes off me after that, how she keeps on bashfully smiling after she sets both pieces of lingerie inside the velvet box.

"Got something else for you." I slide her the velvet pouch that's been burning up inside the pocket of my leather jacket all night. "It's nothing, really, just something to remember me by."

Rosalia looks panicked for a second. "Why? Where you going?"

"Nowhere." I wink. "Said it just in case you get sick of me."

"I could never."

The giddiness slips off my face because she could be wrong. *In fact, I know she will.*

Rosalia gasps so loud when she opens the pouch and the silver swan charm slips into her palm, I think she may cry when she studies it slowly before looking at me with those glassy green eyes.

"*Lijah*, you gave me a swan," she whispers, but it's not a question, it's the devil's prayer. "Wow, it's stunning. Where did you get this?"

"I made it."

"Did you make all of mine?"

I nod, unsure as to why my fingers are trembling and my body burns in intense waves of tender carnage. "I'm really proud of you for acing your season and I wish…I were there for the closing night."

Her emotional smile reaches her eyes. "It's okay. I'm happy you were at least there for the opening, unbeknownst to me, though."

I smile weakly, not really wanting to touch on just how far I'd go to find her again.

To the end of the fuckin' world, that's what I'm afraid to tell you, Peaches.

Not caring about how jiggered her breaths have become when she outstretches her hand, Rosalia silently asking me to thread the charm onto the bracelet I made her. Rolling it off, I put on the new charm with unsteady hands.

I do it without looking at her.

Without saying a single word.

Without breathing straight because if I do, the sudden pull in my chest will intensify.

Fuck. I'm not used to this.

Not used to these tender moments. Any of this.

Yet I crave it with her, more than I do my very own existence.

When the silver swam is perfectly attached and I put the bracelet back on her, I go to slip my fingers away, but Rosalia catches my hand tightly with a light in her eyes. "My heart is singing right now, Elijah. I want you to know that. It's racing so fast. *This*"—she jerks her wrist, her charms shaking around—"is the sweetest, most thoughtful gift anybody has ever given me. Know why?"

Don't look at me like that, Rosalia, you're killing the cold-hearted man I thought I was.

I softly shake my head. "No."

"Because I once was a little girl who walked out of a house of chaos without a single thing. Only dirty pointe ballet shoes and depressed Barbie doll, but looking into your eyes right now, I feel like I've got everything I've ever dreamed of. I feel like I can trust you, Lijah. Like you would never leave me again. I have gone through my entire life with trust and abandonment written all over my face, but you make me want to break the stigma. Want to fall into life with open arms." With a crumbled smile, her voice breaks at the next words, and the first hot tear slips, but she wipes it away just as fast. "It's why I can't help falling in love with you, Elijah Diesel."

Oh.

Oh. My. Fuck.

If gazing into Rosalia's cherry viper eyes emits rolling meadows, then my heart is a battlefield.

Guns and roses sprawl all over my caged chest, shooting at the lock until it melts a slow death. I feel butterflies and life. A rendition of my heartstrings tugging to the beat of "Fragments of You". Until they become fragments of us, fragments of me, fragments of *her.*

Staring into her eyes, after she just told me she's in love with me, I can do nothing else but allow this numbness to take over me, and then, just like that, bring a sledgehammer to it, so I, Elijah Diesel, am not numb anymore.

I hear Rosalia's words.

I *feel* them.

Felt it deep in my chest, let it play with my head, because nobody has ever told me that *L* word before. Not my mother. Not my father. Not my sister. Not my band members. Nobody has said *love* to me in a way only a woman crazy enough to want me too would know how.

"Babyboy," Rosalia murmurs, leaning forth over the table so that our warm foreheads are brushing. The shockwaves of her smile carving into a smile vex me with need. "You don't have to say it back, you don't even have to feel it yet, but I just want you to know I mean it."

Her words… They shake me to my core and give me life again.

Fuck, I think I wanna give this girl my heart.

I wanna be her goddamn lifeline.

Where she goes to hide away.

A white flash blankets the space between us, and Rosalia and I glance over at the owner of D.A.R.K., Dean, grinning over at us with a Polaroid camera in hand. My heartbeat is in my throat, palpitating, and the look I give him lets him know he's interrupting something special.

"I'm not going to say anything…" The idiot flashes me a cocky smile, setting down the candid polaroid he took on the table before nodding over at my girl. "Except that whatever it is you told him, it seems like it just changed his life. Keep this polaroid. I think you'd want it."

Dean leaves and I can't stop shaking the polaroid with my free hand, Rosalia's fingers still laced in the other, my vintage silver snake ring that I gave her on stage glimmering in the flashlight. I'm a warm and beautiful disaster, a nervous mess, a troubled mind.

She comes around to my side, her chin nestled on my shoulder from behind as we watch as the picture of us appears through the darkness. Our heaving breaths are the same, and I can feel her heartbeat growing wild against me. *Rosalia and I emerge in the polaroid and…fuck.*

It's beautiful.

We're seated at this table, hands clasped together. Dean has captured the utter affection in Rosalia's eyes, the tenderness in her smile, while I'm there completely and utterly vulnerable to her. In the polaroid, there's an intensity in my stare, in the way I'm holding on to her, like I may wake up tomorrow and it's all a dream.

I'm no longer oblivious to the world.

I don't think I can be after we found each other again.

Because I'm obsessed with Rosalia Philips, and she—forever and now—is my *world*.

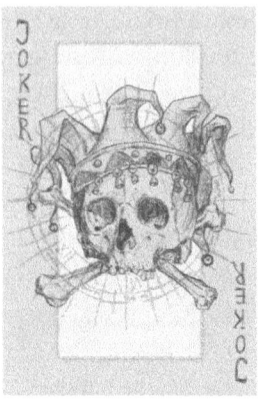

Chapter
THIRTY-THREE

Elijah

R osalia hasn't stopped staring up at me as we share late-night Sicilian cannoli on the king-sized hotel bed, her damp hair stuck against my chest as she snuggles closer to me under the covers. We decided to bring the dessert from D.A.R.K. home instead, and now, after washing away the day, we're here in bed, watching reruns of *Seinfeld* on the drop TV.

I've got Plath's poetry open on the edge of the bed for later when I wanna read some to her.

This is better than anything else could ever be, just having Rosalia close, being so intimate, caressing her petite waist, hearing her giddy laughter whenever George Costanza breaks out into one of those iconic lines.

This is where *nostalgia* is born from.

Yeah, there I go again with the nostalgia.

But it's evident, written in my veins, maybe because I've been deprived of it for so long. Maybe because my childhood was wrapped with complete agony, but looking down at Rosalia Philips now as I continuously thread my fingers through her hair, I smile at the way she's goofily grinning at the TV, knowing I could never truly let her go.

"Is this your favorite show?" I ask.

"*Seinfeld*?"

"Mmhmmm."

"Yeah, I love it. I just think the writing of this show is iconic, and the characters, I mean, just look at Kramer!" Rosalia bursts out in laughter, pointing at the TV. "HAHA! Look!"

I can't. I'm too lost watching her, wondering if she's real, and what I deserved to let all the guardian angels guide her back home into my arms.

I love that she likes *Seinfeld*. I remember watching it back in the '90s…*when she wasn't even born yet.*

God.

"What's your favorite show?"

"I don't think I have a clear favorite." I smile, taking the final bite of Rosalia's cannoli when she brings hers to my mouth, finishing them all. "*Sons of Anarchy. Westworld. Corpse Bride* is my favorite film."

"So basically, anything gritty, dark, and a little scary, just like you?"

"Basically. Oh, and I like *Peaky Blinders* too."

"Tom Hardy in *Peaky Blinders*, *gahhh*." She grins. "Did you know Naomi and I named our bunny after him?"

"Seriously?"

"Yup. Wanna hear HotLips's full name?" She beams without ever batting an eyelash.

I throw my head against the bedrest in laughter. "Fuck no, that's not his name, is it?"

"It sure is. Wanna hear it?"

"Go for it."

Rosalia dramatically clears her throat. "Mr. Rubin Tommy HotLips."

I stare at her as if she's crazy because heck, she is. "I'm not even going to ask…"

"Sure, don't ask, but just know I chose you instead of him for two precious weeks."

"Well, well, well." I smirk down at her. "Aren't I just the luckiest man in the world?"

Caressing my stubbled jaw, she cracks a terrible British accent. *"Simply divine, darling."*

We can't stop staring as I continue raking my fingers over her damp hair, mesmerized.

"I totally fucked this up, didn't I?" I chuckle, rubbing a timid hand over my face because, yeah, I really feel bad that this night is ending like this. "I really wanted to take you out on a date somewhere special, and instead..."

"There's no '*instead*', it *was* spectacular. Besides, I'm here with you, aren't I?" Rosalia's eyes glimmer in the moonlight cascading through the windows. "And that's all I wanted."

Fuck.

Staring into her eyes rushes dopamine through my body that I can't just describe.

"You didn't want to go somewhere else after dining at D.A.R.K.?"

Switching off the television, Rosalia shakes her head against my chest. "Nope."

"You just wanted to be here?"

"Yeah."

"With me?"

"With *you*."

"*Why?*" I shake my head, almost scoffing when my gaze narrows slightly. "I'm nothing special. I'm just some poetically tragic rock star who"—I suck in a breath, my next words escaping in a frayed whisper I'm not proud of—"is really freaking lonely inside without you."

"Then I'm...just a sad ballerina who's really lonely inside without you too."

"You're more than that, *Peaches*."

Rosalia weakly smiles. "Then so are you."

Because this is our spark.

Our endless traumas lacing together.

The thing that connects us both—*loneliness*.

It's etched in our core. The crust of the shells of the broken souls that we are. In this raw moment, I hate the way my throat starts to suffocate inside, like I can't look at Rosalia straight without wanting to let a tear slip.

I haven't cried in...

I don't know.

But with her, I want to let it all out.

It's why when Rosalia sits up and straddles my waist, I let myself feel everything.

When she trails tender open-mouth kisses down my neck, I feel everything.

When she rocks her sex slowly against my cock, I feel everything.

When she leans forward and murmurs against my lips, "Baby, I want to thank you for singing to me in front of all those people tonight. Can I?" and I nod, I let myself. Feel. *Everything.*

My fingers bunch up under the Diesel Rose hoodie she's wearing that's actually mine, but she finishes slipping the hoodie off, spilling out those creamy ample tits that enthrall me. *Gorgeous.* The second I go to flicker my tongue over her taunting pink nipple piercing, Rosalia grips my wrists and roughly slams them over my head, jolting my body against the bedrest.

Even though the air between us is laced with emotion, we share the dirtiest smirk.

I like where this is going.

I'm a pawn in Rosalia's ever-growing game of Russian roulette as I watch her with intrigue as she slips off the bed, only a raunchy pair of red panties on. I don't know what the hell she's looking for as she searches the floor, but the moment her eyes light up, I know she's got it.

Rosalia slowly holds up my studded leather belt. The same one I threw before stepping into the shower with her, and while we solely had a shower, now I wish we were still in there.

Bashfully smiling, she throws it to me, and it brushes against my taut chest, each spiked metal emitting coldness in my lust. "Keep your hands against the headrest. I'll be back, okay?"

I'm left to just gawk at her pretty little body, a starved man with his hands up above my head, just as the blonde angel asked.

Rosalia rushes out of the bedroom, leaving me a hot mess with the way my thick cock is pulsing and stretchin' against my black Armani boxer briefs.

God, help me.

I tip my head against the headrest, shutting my eyes with a groan. *Where the hell did she go?*

It doesn't take long for that question to be answered by the loud slapping against the marble floors. The second I lay eyes on my hurricane blondie, I think I may have just died and gone to heaven.

Rosalia Philips is my fucking undoing.

There she is, looking sultry as hell in the middle of our bedroom in the tiny peach lacy G-sting panties I bought her and the matching bra, her damp blonde locks cascading down and framing her tits.

Fuck.

My cock jolts in my boxer briefs.

Dear devilish God, this is too freaking hot.

"Look at you, babygirl, you're beautiful." I groan, loving the way the soft peach of her lingerie compliments her sun-kissed skin so well. "Turn around for me. Let me see that ass."

All the ballet has made her body a toned wonderland, with her abs cutting through and as she spins around for me, the firm smoothness of her peachy ass. I'm happy to find said ass still has a red hue from all my spanking, and *holy shit*, my handprint bruises her ass, marking her with me.

Just how I want it to be.

I can't stop staring at the thin scrap lace of her panties, how they rush down her hips before disappearing between her ass cheeks. Rosalia spins, and I eye-fuck her more with a heavy gaze. Her breasts spill out of the bra I gifted her tonight ever so perfectly, her cleavage a nirvana. *For my eyes only.* And knowing my name is engraved in the fabric right over her nipple piercing pumps life into me.

And then I see those devil red stilettos she has on, the same ones she keeps on as she seductively *crawls* up on the bed, those green eyes dipped in a lust we both can't escape. I almost break her rule to create even more marks on that ass.

"Hands behind your back like you're being cuffed, Lijah."

"Baby, let me do it to you instead."

"Hands. Behind. Your. Back."

Soldering, I submit.

That sultry grin doesn't slip off Rosalia's lips when she reaches for my wrists behind my back and quickly bounds them together with my own studded belt around them, all while her cleavage is propelled in my face.

I'm so eager to devour her that I run my tongue over her pretty tattoo and then higher to her exposed tits while she's tightening my restraints.

"Mmhmmm."

Loving her coconut taste, I slowly curve and nip her skin, losing my breath over the love bites scattered down her neck from last night. The ones faintly covered up with concealer.

Wait, what?

"I want to fucking spank you again for covering my marks," I growl, all sexually frustrated and horny. "How dare you, Rosalia Philips. How dare you cover what I desire most?"

"I was scared people would talk if they saw them at the concert."

"*Scared people would talk?*"

"Yes."

"Let them fucking talk, Princess."

Finished buckling my hands up behind my back, she pulls back, a devilish smile on those lips I set to destroy soon. "My God… You're so possessive."

"Of course I am. I want men to know you're mine. So don't fucking hide them again."

Rosalia leans down like she's about to kiss me, and as our heads turn, we play a dance of kissing foreplay, almost kissing. Just as she's about to crash her lips on mine, she pulls back with a cunning smirk, ruining me. "But what if I do? Hide your marks, that is?"

"Then I'll bruise your taunting lips so hard and let's see how you handle it." I'm fast to shut her up by grinding my hard cock against her panties, a hiss escaping my lips at the way her hips glide with mine, her wetness seeping through the lace to my boxers. "Can't hide them."

"I'd like to see you try kis—"

Like a ravished beast, I jerk forward and slam my lips against Rosalia's with a growl. I don't wait for her approval as a satisfied whimper gets lost down her throat.

Yeah, cry, little girl.

Cry for your daddy.

I kiss her roughly, like it's my last night on earth. I kiss the woman fifteen years younger than me with so much spiraling chemistry and intensity that my hands jerk against the belt binding them together, desperate to touch her, but I can't.

Luckily for me, I can improvise.

Lifting my knees so they graze over her back, I tug her forward, causing Rosalia to slide closer to me. It's there, with a hand threading through my long hair, tugging on the ends, while another rushes through my spikey beard, steadying the reckless kiss, that I show her what it really feels like to corrupt me into caring.

I go between softly gliding my tongue against hers in open kisses, to pulling back and sucking on her plump lips, sexily nipping their softness before biting down so hard, my teeth pierce her skin.

She gasps through the kiss, liquid trickling against my own lips. *I don't care.*

I kiss her through it like the psychopath I am, swirling my tongue over her blood-coated lips, feeding off the metal taste and cherry tinge mixed with luscious Italian custard and powdered sugar from the cannoli.

Addicted.

Addicted.

I'm so damn addicted.

I let Rosalia get flustered—*desperate*—let her do all the touching that I can't. She roams her hot hands all over me, at one stage caressing my cock through the cotton of my boxers, edging out my pre-cum.

I do everything in my power to kiss her breathlessly sans hands. I mean every fucking second as we get lost in synced moans and groans.

Wanting to prove my point, I suck on her bleeding lips a little longer, deliberately, so it'll leave marks of me for days. Then I go back to kissing her slowly yet aggressively, the sound of our wet kisses in the middle of the night tranquilizing my soul.

Mid-kiss, Rosalia's fingers teasingly slither over my waistband. Slowly. The sound that I make when she pushes my boxers down and my dick springs free in her grip is like no other. She strokes my throbbing shaft hard and fast, making the warmth of my pre-cum coat me all over, jerking me with ease.

Oh fuckkk.

Her covered pussy grinds all over my cock, getting wetter and transferring her arousal onto me too. The lace drives me insane, sparks friction made in heaven.

My hands are struggling against my restraints as she works my cock, the durable leather burning my wrists, desperate to flip her over and have my way with her...

But.

Rosalia.

Tied me up.

That alone drives me insane, heat rushing down to the base of my spine. She's a good girl, remembering just how rough I like to be jerked, tightening her grip by my crown with a slight twist. The thrill is too good, pleasure swelling inside me, edging me on, and on, and on.

Pulling away from the kiss with my eyes still shut, our breaths heaving into one—panting—and we inhale at the exact same time. My cock piercing clashes against her charm bracelet, and the euphoric tremors of the metal clanging have my hips thrusting, franticly fucking her hand while she's straddling me.

"You wrote me a song," Rosalia murmurs. "About the fragments of me lost in you."

"Mmhmmm. Baby, I'd write a million more if it equals this."

"I'm your…muse?"

"Yes."

"*Whoa…*" she breathes against my lips. "You don't know how much that means to me."

"You'll always be my muse, *Peaches*," I promise in a whisper, and then I kiss her more.

Rosalia's hands slow by my cock, and the next thing I know, her smooth, bare pussy is gliding up and down my length, but never entering yet. *And if I thought I was in heaven before… Fuck.*

Fuck.

Fuckkk.

I feel myself throb every single time she glides over me, gripping my cock and rubbing it between her folds. My heart, which I haven't felt beating since we kissed, jars back to life, and I get lost in rapid waves of pleasure from her wet warmth dripping all over me.

Rosalia's panties must be pushed to one side by the way she grinds herself over my glistening length. I feel her hips tip forth and I don't know how much longer I can last with her pulsing clit constantly hitting my pierced head in hurried succession. She stays there for a while, using me in gratification until she's making sexy noises through the kiss that ricochet through me, her orgasm wild.

Feeling her sexy pussy spasm against me, her thighs squeezing around my narrow waist, ruins me. So when she lines my aching cock with her entry, ready for me to slip inside her as she calms from her high, I have to fist the bedsheets to control myself from taking over.

I break the kiss, yearning to witness her go bad.

Our eyes flutter open in the low light and meet in a dripping, dark desire.

That sensual mouth of hers… Jesus. I want to take pictures and stare at it forever.

Rosalia's lips are the darkest shade of scarlet, all swollen and bruised from the erotic kiss we couldn't control. She swipes her tongue over blood-stained lips, spreading it around like Joker, tasting herself, and the moment an outlandish smirk burns up her lips, I know she's my girl.

She likes getting wild.

Freaky.

Filthy.

Just like me.

Pseudo Harley Quinn's lips are marked by me, and I hope, now, she learned her lesson.

Just like I imagined, the panties that I bought Rosalia are pushed to the side. *Mmmm.*

"Look at yourself, *Peaches*, so desperate for me." I praise, my lips grazing her erotically bloody ones. "You want to be daddy's little slut, Rosalia? Want to ride my cock like one?"

With flushed cheeks and her eyes almost rolling back in pleasure, she nods. "I want to show you just how grateful I am after how special you made me feel tonight, and every single day."

"Then show me, princess, show me how bad you are for me."

"Yes."

Unable to control myself, I do what we silently both want and viciously thrust my hips upward, causing me to break through her tightness and slip into her, balls deep. "*Fuckkk.*"

Not expecting it, she screams with wide eyes, her nails scraping my chest. "ELIJAH!"

"Take over."

Rosalia begins to rock her hips slowly, squeezin' me good. For every time she grinds herself against my cock, my hands ache to grip the side of her hips and guide her up and down. But she quickly catches a sensual rhythm that turns senseless, meeting my every frazzled thrust.

But I want more...

And she feels it too.

With her hands pressed on my chest, nails digging into me, Rosalia rides me hard, her tits vigorously bouncing in that bra, shaking the bed.

I'm a caged beast, letting her fuck me into oblivion, our skin slapping so fast I fall back onto the bed, my hands bound behind me.

"So good." I moan. "Yeah, baby, like that."

My head rolls into the silk pillow as she thanks me with her sexy pussy destroying me.

"*Ohhh, fuck.* Rosalia, just marry me already."

Her sweet giggles have me grinning as I look down at her through my onyx lashes while she fucks me like a god.

"Shut up."

"Your loss." I wink, failing to catch my breaths with how my body begins tensing up.

Rosalia takes every single one of my thrusts so well, smiling as she leans down to press kisses down my body mid-fuck. She leaves small trails of blood from her lip, but when she looks up at me, seductively licks them away, the devil in her eyes.

We're such a frazzled mess, all sweaty and desperate, that when she rushes a hand behind her, slowly massaging my heavy balls, I can't do this no more. I need to touch her, feel her.

My lips part in time with hers, moaning out as she clenches around me.

"Please, baby, please undo my hands."

Rosalia shakes her head and keeps on riding me fast.

My abs clench in need, holding onto this orgasm for dear life.

"Rosalia, *please*," I beg, feeling her purposely fucking over my mind with the way she constantly grips her pussy around my cock, squeezing me in rapid motions inside her warmth.

"No."

"Please, I need to touch you so bad before I lose it."

Squeezing her breasts through her bra, she ignores me completely.

My jaw tenses up in desire because at the rate she's fucking me,

I'm going to come inside her any second. Without a condom. Without birth control. With all bids of carelessness.

Rushing to sit up on the bed, with Rosalia smirking against my lips, her bra grazes against my chest, the soft lace bouncing against me, taunting me. She grips my cock tighter with her pussy as it begins to quiver and *fuck, fuck, fuck, I can't hold back any longer.*

Growling, I savagely pull my hands apart with all of my force, and the five-hundred-dollar European leather belt snaps in two like it's melted butter, setting me free from its trap.

To the soundtrack of her shocked gasps, I roughly throw Rosalia on the bed, pinning her face down. The first thing I do is pull off her panties, throwing them behind us, and the second thing, as she wriggles beneath me with her thighs slick in arousal, is spread her legs wide.

"*Peaches.*" I smirk darkly, wrapping my hand around her hair before tugging back. *Hard.* "I'll always find a way to fuck you like I crave, even when you're playing games."

And then I thrust into her, my pulsing cock obliterating her, conscious I don't have long.

"Always remember it."

Rosalia's screaming into the pillow, telling me *yes*, biting down on her clenched fists.

"I'll always fuck you just like you need." Tipping my head back, my tense abs stretch as I fuck her balls deep, three times the intensity she was doing me before. "*Always.*"

Our rapid breaths go crazy, to the point my head feels all dizzy, but I don't care.

"I need *this*," I hiss loudly. "I need to make you cum for being so fucking good to me."

Leaning forward, I press my V-cut against her ass, my chest against her back. I can't help but shut my eyes, overpowered by need as I bury my head into her neck. That's when I pull her hair in a way that she moves her face to the side. *That smile.*

"I like that you allow me to be so rough with you." I kiss the corner of her bruised lips, my rough stubble grazing her cheek, sparking even more light in her eyes. "I love that you trust me."

Love.

"I love that I want you," I growl, tightening my grip around her hair so firmly that as I fuck her now, she's bouncing on the mattress, her face slamming against her pillow with each thrust. "I love that you want me."

Rosalia whimpers in response, the honeyed sin sounds consuming me.

Sex laces the air.

Relentlessness fills our every move.

And the bedsheets, *fuck*, they're all in ruins.

My free hand can't stop touching her, disappearing in the places she needs me the most. I manage to crawl it between the bed and her core, my fingers stiff before I graze over her clit. It's so swollen, pulsing with every second of my pounding.

"Touch me," Rosalia begs against my lips. "Make me feel like I ain't breathing."

I do just that, roughly circling her clit before rubbing it steadily back and forth in the way I know makes her crazy.

And crazy it makes her as her hips buck even faster against mine. Even more so when I spank it.

"*Lijah!*"

She's a hot, sweaty mess with a sinner's smile, while I'm here, kissing her body slowly.

"I want to come with you, but I don't think I can hold on anymore, so I…" She manages to choke out, the rest of the words lost.

"It's okay, baby, come when you want."

Coming back onto my knees, my hands move to her hips, slamming them hard against my dick to the point where I feel the metal piercing on the crown reach a depth I've never felt before.

She's so tight and I know she'll hurt in the morning, but she's taking my length so well.

Rosalia slightly turns around, twisting her body around to see me better, glancing over her shoulder as I squeeze her peachy ass selfishly. I adore how she watches on in amusement, especially when I spread her cheeks wider to trace my thumb over her pink asshole, obsessed with it.

"One of these days…" I pant, spanking her ass again and again until she gasps. "I want a diamond pink plug in here. Need to stretch you out and get ready for me to take your ass."

Lust blooming in her eyes, she nods.

"I love that you like all of this." I lean forward again, my cock slipping deeper in her when I wrap a hand around her throat. Tight. So tight her skin already begins to blemish. "That you let me choke you."

"Mmhmmm." Rosalia grins like the dirty girl she is. "*Tighter.*"

My fingers sink deeper into her throat, just how she likes. A hint of darkness glazes over her eyes.

Her breaths fastening, and I can feel her pulse fluttering against my fingers like butterflies. Wild butterflies that have me sinking into her deeper, without aversion.

"I like that you're crazy, baby," I whisper lowly, a killer's confession. "*Crazy like me.*"

Rosalia's breaths become mine.

All mine.

I slip out of her pussy entirely and then wait a second before hotly slamming right back into her. The dirty words she whispers to me have me doing it again, and again, and again until I'm fucking her normally, back into oblivion.

It has her fisting the sheets, her knuckles whitening, all while my grip around her throat intensifies.

"Give it to me, baby."

My lips are inches from hers when she lets out the loudest moan all night and just like that, she's falling, coming undone all over my pulsing cock.

"That's it, let go, babygirl. I'm so fucking proud of you."

Her earth-shattering orgasm has her entire body convulsing, but I don't stop fucking her. *I can't.*

My urge to release tingles all over me in hot blushes, my balls tensing up with every second Rosalia's clenching my cock.

It all comes undone when I slip my hand from her throat and see just how red-tinged her skin has become from my hand. My marks stimulating something inside me beyond anything I've ever felt before.

I fuck her like I'm selling my soul to the devil.

Rosalia orgasms again, this time attempting to press up on her hands, but I continue thrusting into her so hard that she falls flat on the bed, her face a deep crimson now.

She's smiling through her desire, her blond waves sprawled all over like splattered ink.

The aftershocks of her orgasms are intense around me that, *ohhh*, I fucking lose it too.

Getting lost in wanting to devour her until the very last second, the first cumshots almost shoot inside her as I'm pulling out, but I quickly manage to let them hit her inner thighs instead.

Fuck. Too close.

Stroking my cock with a devilish moan, I unload my hot, thick cum all over Rosalia's toned back, spine, and pushed up ass as she quivers, obviously new to the sensation.

"I wanna frame this moment, *ma chérie*, and fucking look at you sprawled here, all beautiful and spent, forever."

Rosalia grinds her ass against my balls, all while long streaks of my white cum paint her skin, and she whimpers with every single one until the last of my milked orgasm laces my hand. That's when I rub my cum into her skin, spreading it around until it sinks into her, all sticky, creamy, and screaming out that she's mine.

Mine.

She's all mine.

And I crave more.

When Rosalia spins around, I don't think twice before giving into her all over again. I know she wants it too by the stoic smile that stretches her lips the second I push my aching cock back inside her warmth. I'm still hard, my stamina on a high, just like it always is.

It feels like velvet the way we collide.

I can't stop fucking her at an intensity that has me lose my mind.

Gripping her toned legs, I wrap them tight around me and squeeze her thighs against my narrow waist. It has me pound into her deeper. Harder. Faster. We're both sweaty, sensual messes, the thrill of sex too fuckin' good as we consume ourselves in an erotic makeout session, mid-thrusting. It convinces me that breathing is secondary to the sensations Rosalia gives me.

The feeling of her heartbeat pressed up against mine is pure ecstasy. I've never heard something so beautiful. Never knew I needed something so tangible. But I do. *Fuck*, how I do.

"*Pour toujours…c'est reel*," I murmur against her heart-shaped lips, then kiss her.

Forever… It's real.

We come undone together, getting lost in each other, our gaze never falling. She's an angel. An angel beneath me. One fluttering out of heaven. So trapped in those gorgeous green eyes, this time I'm not that careful when I pull out as we glance down, witnessing my throbbing cock wildly pulsing out my warm cum all over her bare pubic bone and swollen clit. It then continues to erotically drip lower. Milky white coats her pinkness in ways I'll never forget.

It's beautiful.

She's beautiful.

We're beautiful. *Together.*

When we finally settle down, I lower beside her and kiss her sweaty forehead. She's quick to caress my wrists, rubbing them over with her soft hands before kissing over the reddened tinges.

Through my pants, I slowly smile, and she wraps herself in my arms, smiling back.

"Wow, that was some... thank you..." I trail on.

My sweet girl giggles, beautiful smile lines cutting through.

We remain like this, gazing into each other's warming eyes, catching our breaths, for what feels like forever.

I hope Portland is like this too for us...

Rosalia in the solace of my arms has my heart skipping a beat. There's just something so calming and intimate in the way our fingers rush up and lace together in the night air.

Staring up, my long fingers run through hers before I bring them down, kissing over the silver vintage snake ring on her thumb. The one I gave her during the concert tonight.

My gaze becomes locked on hers. "It's yours now, baby. I want you to have it."

"Wow, thank you." Emotion clouds her light eyes. "You really know how to make a girl feel special, Elijah Diesel."

"Not any girl, just you, *Peaches.*"

Smiling deeper, Rosalia snuggles closer to me.

And I can't get enough of her.

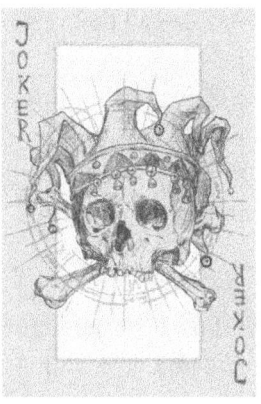

Chapter
THIRTY-FOUR

Elijah

O ur sex is a damn drug.
High.

That's what she gets me. *High all the time.*

I get lost in a high I never wanna recover from.

The same high so strong that I must doze off, 'cause when I open my eyes again, we're under the covers. Rosalia's back in my hoodie, curled up on my side, smiling up at me like an angel's prayer. She smells of sweet peaches and tangerine bodywash, and her hair is wetter.

"Did I fall asleep?"

"Mmhmmm."

"Shit. How long was I out for?"

"Not long, only a few minutes. Ten at the most." A grin stretches across her beautiful face. "You must have blacked out from the mind-blowing sex."

I smirk. "Yeah, must've."

"Mmhmmm."

Comfortable silence. That's all that remains, spiked with a new-found zest for breathing.

"You know…" Rosalia begins, her fingers trailing down to the center of my defined, sweaty abs.

Her gaze flickers to mine and it's not about just attraction this time, it's depth, it's her and me.

It's *this*.

"When we first met," she adds. "Or rather, when I stalked your ass after you stepped off that bus, I got the impression that you enjoyed being in solitude… I don't know, it was almost as if you wanted to be a rock star, but you didn't want any eyes on you."

I nod, remembering feeling that exact way.

Because guess what?

I still feel it.

"Well, how did you overcome that? I know I'm a ballerina and per-form in front of people too, but not to that extent, and when I dance, I don't need to lock eyes with anybody else but the dancers. How do you deal with being watched like that? I'm not just talking on tour, I'm talking constantly, your day-to-day. How do you…live with that?"

"You want the truth?"

"Mmhmmm."

"I don't."

A line forms between her eyes. "What do you mean?"

"All that confidence when I'm on stage, it isn't me. Every time I lock eyes with a fan, I feel like I'm drowning. It's not that I'm un-grateful. I just…I just wish I could make music without the world watching me."

"Why?"

"Because music is my therapy."

Rosalia stares at me for a long moment, indifferent.

"From the…" she whispers lowly, refraining herself from saying it, scared it may rush out and stab my melting heart to death. "Do you feel like being famous invades that therapy?"

"Little one," I breathe, brushing my lips against her forehead. "It's okay, you can say it."

"Is music your therapy for the alcoholism?"

Nodding, I blink slowly, not believing I'm admitting this to her.

"I want to ask you something, Elijah, to understand it better, but it may sound stupid."

"Ask."

"You know how you said you're sober, trying to be better?"

"I drink in moderation, but yes?"

"Do you have any triggers? Like…does seeing others drink trigger you?"

"No, seeing people happy triggers me." The words I've been holding onto for so long are finally out, and when they are, anxiety rushes out of me, not the relief I was expecting. "I'm so fucking envious of people with solid families because growing up, I never had that."

"What happened with your mom, Elijah?"

I shake my head. "This was supposed to be a date night, not a therapy session."

"It is a date night."

A few moments pass. "To say my life is one big mess is an understatement. It's worse."

"Were you close to her?"

"In the beginning, yes… I was born in France but moved to Seattle just before my fifth birthday. Grew up there too. When I was younger, like really fucking young, I had this wish jar."

"A wish jar?"

"Mmhmmm."

"Wow, that's really cool."

"Yeah, I used to write shit like aspirations and my wildest dreams. It was my way of escaping reality, of life how it seems. My father ran off when I was almost ten. At that stage, my older sister, Mom, and I were sleeping like a pack of sardines in this run-down share house. One day after school, she picked us up—the only day my mother ever picked me and my sister up—and she started driving in another direction. I questioned her, and she said we were going to our new home."

"Wow, just like that?"

"Just like that. I was confused because she had no money. She drove up to this house that quite frankly was worse than our own. This guy stormed out, that guy I was talking to you about in the laundromat, and introduced himself as her new boyfriend. I had nothing from the old house. Not a thing. But I didn't care for it. All I wanted was my wish jar."

I pause for a moment.

"I remember questioning her that night after dinner, and she looked me straight in the eyes and said, *this is our home now. We can't go back. Going back equals going back into the past, and none of us need that.* But I did. My soon-to-be stepdad stared me down, clenching his fists around the bottle, one he would later throw at me. Since that night, I've forced myself to forget all about it. But whenever the world gets too quiet, I think back to the last scrap of paper I wrote and placed inside of the wish jar for the last time."

"What did it say?"

"*I wish to die at the hands of my own fate.*" My heart clenches as I shut my eyes, remembering the words so vividly. "So, music isn't only my therapy from my alcoholism, it's also the reason I'm still breathing. You weren't the only one to become caged in the devil's paradise, my fallen angel, for I was there too."

"No, Lijah." Rosalia's eyes puff up, instantly a glassy mess while she struggles to keep it together. "Please don't tell me that."

Please don't cry, I want to tell her, *I crumble completely when you do.*

"It's true. I've been so fucked up since I was born that my parents forced me into therapy when I was nine to deal with my insanity. They found my songbook and confiscated it. The Dr. called me a psychopath and told me nothing would ever save me, that I'd make people like him rich… Maybe he was right."

She can't stop shaking her head. "No, of course he wasn't. You were nine, Lijah. *Nine.*"

"You didn't see those things in the songbook, Rosalia."

"I don't need to see them to know you were only hurting."

"That's exactly it, Rosalia, there was no reason for me to be hurting that young."

Rosalia raises the sheets higher, causing all the empty cannoli boxes to go flying across the bedroom, but she ignores them to push herself closer to me. My arms tighten around her waist like it's automatic, all while she cups my dark, spiky beard.

"Had anything happened?" she asks.

"No, I just…I saw the world for its darkness. Never it's light. Everything back then and up until a little while ago was just black-and-white. Nothing was vivid. Color. Stood out. Music saves me, but it's through the ears, submerged in the mind, it isn't tangible—physically real."

"What do you see now?"

I don't answer at first. Just look at her natural beauty rattling my lungs.

"I see a sad, dark world, and then the fragments of you burn the darkest shade of red."

That's when the first tear baptizes Rosalia's cheeks, rolling down like a clear pearl before plummeting in the center of the Cupid's bow. Then lower, to her heart-shaped lips that taste of wicked candy.

"That's so beautiful, baby." She sniffles, offering me the saddest smile. "But I can't be the only thing you see."

Strong words. *Brave* words. That's what they are.

My mind is tangled between those green eyes. Those that guide me back to life.

"I see speckles of green too, rolling meadows, just like in your eyes."

"Elijah."

"The pinkish hue of your lips, the darkest of scarlets coating your cheeks, bursts of roses."

More tears well in her eyes.

"The sweetest sun-kissed honey rushing down your loose waves, the lushest of dusty pinks for ballet pointe shoes. I see silk. So much silk. Wrapped in your leotard and across your skin. I see orange coating those velvet scrunchies you wear. Peaches. I see that shade everywhere, even colored outside of the lines, just how I like." My rough thumb skims over her uncontrollable tears as redness forms by her nose. "I see violet skies, baby, and cherry viper eyes whenever you're here. When I look at you, Rosalia Philips, I see color, for the first time. I. See. Color. It brings this oxygen in my lungs I once thought was toxic, but now I know it's full of life."

The sympathy rushing across my body makes vulnerability marinate, especially because it's getting harder to breathe.

Rosalia's tears turn into sobs as she holds me tight and buries her head into my neck, her entire body shaking in my touch. The warmth of my Diesel Rose hoodie she has on taints my skin. I'm so used to the cold. To the icy chill. To the comfort of lonely places.

Why do I crave her warmth?

Why do I hold Rosalia tight and bunch up the hoodie like it's my means to survive?

Why do I want to dive into a life fueled with her instead of dying right here in her arms?

It hurts, witnessing her cry so hard like this because of me. It glazes tears in my own eyes, fogging my mind and burning my gaze, but I don't dare let them slip. I don't dare make a sound. I don't dare move a fraction because I feel so unworthy of loving, and yet there's her warmth that surrounds me that finally makes me feel alive.

I want Rosalia.

I crave her like my next breath.

Why? Why? Why?

I feel so empty inside. So hallow. And while Rosalia squeezes me tighter, her hot breath hitting my neck, juxtaposed with the coldness of her dropping tears, right here, right now, during this first date of ours, this warmth spreads across my chest, and I breathe in a deeper breath, thinking I may die from the hope slipping into my heart.

The hope filled with her.

The light.

The color.

The poetry.

It oozes through my heartstrings, becomes the thing that keeps it pumping on. I finally understand all the poetry. All the classical romances. All of Brontë, Fitzgerald, and Hemingway.

Loving something so much, you almost want to let it go because you're too wild, too wicked, too crazy to be made into a home.

It happened to Rochester.

To Heathcliff.

To many more.

The morally gray villain, or perhaps not a villain at all, but none-theless, there's a scar within, a light that guides us into the color, like an 18th century cobblestone corridor, only lit up but a single wax flooded candlestick. And then, just like that, it's snuffed.

Darkness.

And even more.

The farther you walk to relight that fire, the more the wind gusts through the broken window, and right there again, *snuffed.*

Darkness.

But this time the dark thoughts pull in.

That's exactly what my life has been. An endless cycle of darkness. Of addiction. Of suicidal thoughts. But now, Rosalia is my color. My light. The woman keeping me alive.

Rosalia Philips is keeping me alive.

My heart pumping.

My air breathing.

My eyes seeing.

It's. All. Because. Of. Her.

Because she trusted me enough to run back to me when all I wanted was to end it all.

Wrapped in her arms, I understand those poets.

Those literature gods.

The tender affection.

I understand it all, and yet, I don't understand a thing.

And that's when the hot tears begin to slip, crawling down my cheeks, and Rosalia is there to kiss every single one.

"I hope you know, Elijah Diesel, that you give me the realest on-yx-colored butterflies." My Harley Quinn reincarnated in the form of an angel whispers to me, kissing away all the psychopath's pain, while he—*I*—The Joker—become addicted to her instead.

I *am* addicted.

Utterly.

To her.

Portland

Chapter
THIRTY-FIVE

Rosalia

The following day, I half expected to wake up and uncover all of it had been a dream. But as my hand slithered across the luxuriously smooth bedsheets this morning and warmth filled my body at the caress of his hand lacing in mine, I remember thinking *this is what heaven must feel like in hell.*

Those familiar gray-onyx eyes gazed into mine, brighter with the morning sun piercing through the windows, and it was so damn bittersweet the way Elijah Diesel whispered to me *good morning, baby-girl,* with a smile before kissing me slowly.

Delicately.

Sensually.

In a way that was the complete antonym of every kiss we've shared until last night.

We've played that dance all day between going to the gym together, breakfast (*and yes, something that wasn't Lucky Charms in a whiskey glass.* I don't think I can ever make him live that down now), my ballet training in which I did a few of my normal routines mixed with some weightlifting with Elijah. Dave joined in a little later on in the session, still hungover from the night before.

I didn't know if that would affect Elijah.

The hangover part.

As I questioned last night, I want to know his triggers. I don't want to accidentally set him off. I know how sensitive it is to have something consume your life so badly.

Like addiction.

I know it isn't easy. That you just can't stop. I may have only been five when my mother killed my father and then overdosed, but I still feel like it was yesterday. I remember every single pivotal moment. Not *every* moment, but just the *pivotal* ones.

Like the relapses.

The promises to change.

The fact that they were never there.

I've been through it. I'm a *product* of it.

I know with Elijah it's different. It isn't drugs, it's alcohol he's a recovering addict of, but it's still similar.

Elijah didn't comment about a single thing with Dave at the gym. In fact, he didn't even look at him. Instead, Elijah couldn't stop staring at me, stealing longing kisses, the same pecks that continued the entire day.

I've never felt this way before.

Never felt this giddy. This *happy.* This sadness twisted in my chest. A sadness due to both coming from traumas so tragic, and yet all the complicated and messy merges into beauty.

I'm not stupid, though. I'm highly aware our relationship isn't like no other. I'm fifteen years younger than him and he's never been in a committed relationship before. That combined with me working at a prestigious ballet company with ruthless hours, expectations, and policies, while he's a crazily successful sexy rock star watched by the entire world.

People talk.

They speak volumes.

But I don't want *that* to get to us.

And by the way Elijah looked at me during the private jet ride to the second last tour city when I told him to sing "Fragments of You" again, while I grinned back and swayed my head back and forth, learning every lyric lowly, I know he feels the same way too.

Elijah doesn't care about anything else.

He just cares about *us*. About *me*.

And that in itself is stoic.

Now, it's just after four o'clock in the afternoon and we just touched down with Diesel Rose's private jet in vibrantly, scenic Portland, Oregon. Maverick is driving us to the hotel to check in, and by *us* I mean Elijah and me. The other guys have other drivers. Plus, pretty sure no one wanted to deal with me and Knives's glares.

Yep, still happening.

Maverick has barely looked at me during the entirety of the drive in the same black SUV that I may or may not have lost his (my boyfriend's bodyguard/driver's) respect days ago.

So, yeah, it's reallll awkward, to say the least.

Elijah Diesel, on the other hand, is definitely not concerned at all. I don't think he even notices the tension between me and his right-hand man as we talk about everything and anything. He hasn't stopped caressing my thigh, flickering his gaze to my lips, smoldering just as my heart skips a beat.

Pretty sure Maverick is going to eject me out of my seat in a minute.

Last night was our first date and it was groundbreaking for us. It unraveled so much. Elijah opened up to me about his past and it spoke volumes. We shared such tender and emotionally beautiful moments last night that when Elijah's tears began to slip, I couldn't help but kiss them. In those moments, I knew I wanted to be his everything. We fell asleep wrapped in each other's arms, drifting into a world of reveries, and woke up still embracing.

"Are you gonna stare at me all day like that?" I giggle, crossing my legs in the back seat.

Elijah grins darkly. "I've gotta make up for those four years, *Peaches*, you know that."

He's happy today.

Feeling heat rush to my cheeks, I girlishly smile back.

Gah, my gorgeous rock star knows just what to say.

New air is sucked into me. *Hope.*

Maverick's gaze falls upon mine in the rearview mirror before narrowing.

Arching a brow back, I gulp down, awkwardly readjusting in my seat.

Damn, okay.

I get it, you don't like me.

I smile as Elijah bashfully shoots me a boyish grin. It's so raw, and there's a fire burning in his eyes. He seems the happiest he's ever been with a touch of admiration.

My heart is in ruins, good ruins when I whisper to him, "Thanks for California. I'm excited about Portland."

Elijah softly squeezes my knee, his smile so shy, and that's all I really need to know that this is huge for him. A huge step for us. And I would say yes to staying with him for the rest of the tour all over again, in a heartbeat.

Gorgeous tree-lined streets, quaint stores, huge expanses of green parks, and breathtaking views of faraway mountaintops are all I see as Portland scans past us during the drive. When we make it to the hotel, Elijah slips his hand in mine just like he always does, his other rolling both our suitcases in.

He can't stop *smiling* at the camped-out fans and taking a few pictures with bodyguards holding a few fans back, who get a little too close and touchy-feely.

Some blonde chick literally goes to grab his junk.

I shake my head.

Portland rock fans...

Before I know it, we're checking in and stepping inside the super-rich private elevator that's set to lead us straight to our apparent penthouse suite.

I finally let it out. "I'm pretty sure Maverick hates me."

Elijah looks at me in the elevator car like I'm crazy. "What? Maverick? No, he doesn't."

"Uh, yes, he does." I almost laugh. "He's planning some vendetta on me, for sure."

"Why do you say that?"

When nothing but the soft classical music of the elevator fills the space between us, Elijah steps closer, trapping me against one of the gold-plated elevator walls, coldness seeping through me as the rail presses against my ass. *An ass that is still marked with his handprint...*

Elijah raises a seductive brow, and *my gosh*, how sexy it is. I love how he's growing out his beard a bit, so now it's a little thicker. It's not only the beard but also his hair. I'm obsessed with how it licks the ends of his ears, perfect soft waves.

"Why do you think Maverick hates you, Rosalia?" he asks again, but this time much softer, raspy. "Tell me."

My lips remain shut because I like the little fire burning in his eyes. The silent game of lust we're playing as his fingers rush up my apricot-colored cropped knitted sweater, sparks lighting up all over with the way his warm fingertips caress my flat stomach like that, resting by my sparkling navel piercing.

"Rosalia?"

I clear my throat, glancing up at him through my lashes.

All of a sudden, the air is thick around us. Tense.

Filled with desire.

"*Why*, baby? You saying it 'cause I made you come three times at the back of that Volvo back in California? 'Cause he heard the moans and you screaming my name?" Elijah smirks, cocking his head to the side, taunting me. "If that's the case, *Peaches*, he better get used to it, 'cause I didn't intend on that being the last time I make you cum while he's behind the wheel."

Whoa.

I softly bite my lower lip, his words rushing heat to my cheeks.

"You seeing what I'm saying, *Peaches*?"

"Mmhmmm."

"Good girl."

Elijah's hips piston against mine, his hardening erection rubbing against me so provocatively it makes me feel things I've never felt with anybody else but him. It's been a couple days since I joined the *ex-virgin club*, but my body is still aching and marked by him.

"I'll talk to Maverick about it, so don't worry," he whispers against my lips. "I gotcha."

I nod softly against the elevator wall, my hair pulling tighter in my long, high ponytail.

It doesn't help that the lighting is so dim, or that I want him to spin me around, bend me over, and fuck all the innocence out of me. But most of all, it doesn't help that as our breaths get thicker, his hand descends lower and lower until he's right between my denim-clad thighs.

Our stare is intense and it's evident in the way his eyes darken that he feels my warmth.

Desperately craving him, I achingly lean forth to kiss him, just as the elevator doors ding open and Elijah steps back, having me kiss the air instead of him.

His sexy half-smirk couldn't be any naughtier. "Missed me."

"Asshole," I snap, playfully glaring him down.

"Hmmm." Elijah links our arms together, leading me into the posh apartment. His lips brush my ear, whispering, "I'm going to need more than just a few moments to get my fix of you. Don't you remember how wild we got, baby?"

Before I can respond, a voice clearing has our gaze snapping right ahead at Dave, who's in the industrial-looking penthouse with oak hardwood floors and coffee-colored buttoned leather couches. There he is, in nothing but a pair of white boxer briefs, practicing yoga in the middle of the open plan living room, bringing hands to heart center while standing in warrior two pose.

"Oh God," Elijah grumbles under his breath. "You've got to be joking…"

Dave lifts his gaze and smirks when he sees us. "For fuck's sake, what did I do to deserve getting stuck with the two love birds on tour?"

I can't help my grin.

We've got a roommate…

Wellll, this is going to be interesting.

And when I say *interesting*, I mean, very, *very* interesting.

I ten out of ten don't recommend living with two rockers when they're on tour, even if one of them is your boyfriend who you're crazy about and you're still having sex aftershocks.

Yeah, I know, who knew the latter was a thing? Me neither.

Elijah and Dave are the complete definition of an old married couple.

Dave leaves coffee mugs around *everywhere* without ever finishing a single one.

Elijah freaks, cleans the mess, but then proceeds to leave cigarette butts everywhere.

Dave nonstop continues drumming to the beat of their songs, on the countertop, while we're in the living room watching TV, screaming the beats at the top of his lungs in the shower.

Elijah declares a crisis meeting between them, agreeing on quieting it down, and then my onyx-eyed lover proceeds to obliviously hum every Diesel Rose song for hours on end.

Dave nearly forces us both to watch the new season of *Stranger Things* when walking in on us making out on the couch with my bare tits on full display, seconds away from fucking.

Elijah tells him to look away and that *Stranger Things* can *go suck his dick*.

So, as I said, *ten out of ten don't recommend.*

The rest of the boys came up to the penthouse during the evening and I offered to make them my specialty, *spaghetti alla puttanesca*, without the spices, of course. Elijah's all grumpy about it because all the attempts we've made to have sex in the past few hours since we touched down in Portland have been slaughtered by Dave's import walk-ins. *God bless the guy.*

Maverick drove Elijah and me to this trendy, super healthy food store so we could buy the ingredients. Elijah was so fucking broody the entire time, wearing a snapback backward with a death glare for anybody who battered an eyelash his way. The first thing he threw in the shopping cart were condoms, which had my eyes rolling but my sex fluttering. We both wanted proper *alone time*, but what I'm learning about rock bands is that there's rarely any privacy.

Now, dinner's done and Zander's helping me plate up, all while Elijah's fighting with Dave on which side is the correct side to put down the spoon and fork, while taking turns at puffing a joint. And Knives, as we can all predict, has his hoodie up, those dirty-blond waves peeking through as he scrolls through his phone by the kitchen counter, done with the world.

River had to fly out to the East Coast for a client this morning, so he's a little pissed.

Elijah sits down beside me at the grand dining table that could fit a banquette fit for a king. Of course Knives is the only guy sitting ten seats down on the secluded area of the table.

Just as Elijah's about to dive into the *spaghetti alla puttanesca*, I clear my throat and hold out my hands to the rest of the guys. "We should say grace before dinner, guys, come on."

Elijah shoves Dave's hand in mine and replaces it with his. "All right, I'll do the honors."

With a smile on my lips, I bow my head and shut my eyes, expecting the boys to follow.

I wait.

And wait.

And wait a little more.

The grace never comes. Silence. Crickets.

I side-eye Elijah, glaring over at him, only to find him staring back at me, clueless. "Do you know how to say grace, Elijah Diesel?"

"Sure, I do."

"Then go ahead, say it."

Rolling my shoulders back, I shut my eyes again.

Some more silence, and then…

"*Grace.*"

We all burst out in laughter, all while Elijah looks between us, confused as hell.

"You're such a fucker." Zander laughs, rubbing a hand over his mouth. "Come on, man."

"What? She told me to say *grace*!"

"Fucking wise guy, bro."

"And you're the lyricist?" Dave snickers. "Sheesh, somebody call my attorney."

Knives, for your information, is still glaring me down.

When the guys start digging into dinner and moan out just how good it is, I whisper in Elijah's ear. "Were you just playing that on?"

Swallowing thickly, his eyes stare down at his plate of pasta, embarrassed. "No."

Huh?

My brows knit up. "No?"

Elijah shakes his head softly. "No, I…I've never heard that term before. Growing up, my family never did…grace…or any of that stuff. We never had dinner together. It was kind of a fend for yourself environment. So, yeah, guess I just played the card of the fool just now."

My heart squeezes in sadness.

All I want to do is kiss away all his pain.

Empathy races through my veins and I lace my fingers through his underneath the table in his lap. "Sorry, I didn't know. You're not the fool, baby," I murmur against his lip. "Grace is basically saying an act of thanks to that special guy above to show gratitude over the meal."

Elijah simply nods and tucks back into his meal, but I know, from his kind eyes, that it means much more to him than just a simple nod.

Just as I'm about to take another bite of the mouthwatering pasta, Knives catches my eye. He isn't eating, just staring at the pasta with a clenched jaw like it's about to jump him.

Um, rude.

What's up with this guy?

"Everything okay, Knives?"

"I'm vegan," he blurs out fast. *Too fast.* "And gluten-free."

Elijah almost chokes on his pasta, eyeing his best friend. "The hell? Since when?"

"Since…" Knives taps his phone, smirking when he looks up. "Six forty-six."

My boyfriend glances down at his leather strap watch. *Six forty-seven.*

We share a knowing look.

This asshole…

After dinner, we're finishing up a game of pool on the huge table in the living room when my phone begins blaring.

Dad.

I cringe… *this isn't the phone call I'm looking forward to. At all.*

Elijah glances over and smirks. "Well, well, well, if it isn't my soul mate."

"Here, take my ball." I hand him my pool stick and giggle when he looks at me funny. "You know what I mean."

"Sure as fuck I do now."

"I'll only be a minute." I peck his lips before I head out the accordion doors to the balcony that's lit up with pretty fairy lights, the gorgeous skyline of Portland dazzling with so many red signs. It just finished raining, so there's this earthy scent lacing the air, and the water seeps into my socks. *Shit.*

I tap that little fated green icon just in time.

That familiar voice floods the phone, the same one that became permanently stitched in firmness four years ago when his not so little girl was found in the monster's arms.

"Rosalia, darling, how are you?"

"Dad, I'm okay, just finishing up some dinner."

"Hmmm, that's good."

"How was work today?"

"Yeah, it was all right. A neurosurgeon's work never stops. I had a microvascular decompression the second I got to the hospital, then a pituitary surgery. You know how it is…"

I nod to myself, pretending I do. "Mmhmmm, sounds impressive."

"It is." He's quiet for a little bit. "*Well,* I've seen some things. How should I say this…"

I already know what's coming, which is why I lean against the wet metal railing, rocking on my heels in anticipation. "Just say it, Dad." I sigh. "I already know what you think anyway."

"Well, okay, I read in the headlines that you're in Los Angeles…"

"Yeah, I'm in Portland now actually."

More silence.

I squeeze my eyes shut.

Shit. He is going to crucify me.

"I thought we talked about Elijah Diesel four years ago. I thought we concluded with the fact that he isn't good for you. What happened?"

"I realized I wasn't over him."

"*Not over him*? Jesus Christ, Rosalia, you were *seventeen*! Are you forgetting all the heartache *he* caused you?" My father practically growls, but the anger isn't directed at me. "You didn't eat for weeks, Rosa. *Weeks.* He's toxic and I don't see how you just don't get it."

"He's different, Dad."

"*Different*? That's what victims of toxic relationships say all the time."

I blow out a frustrated sigh. "This isn't a toxic relationship, Dad, please, just listen—"

"No, I'm not going to listen. I know you're of age and can do whatever you like, but it *is* of my concern if he breaks your heart again, and this time, even more damaging."

"That won't—"

"I mean, come on, he *serenaded* you on stage? Rosalia, all these articles… This isn't what you want. Everything you've worked so hard to maintain with ballet and every single one of your stoic Swan Lake articles are being overshadowed by this fucking rock tour and these fucking punks."

"Please don't call him tha—"

"He's only showing you what he wants you to see, Rosalia. You watch. There's more shit that hasn't come out yet. I swear to you the skeletons in this man's closet are pure carnage."

"Dad, I—"

"*Good night.*"

And then he hangs up.

I'm left staring at the phone, at my phone's lock screen, which just so happens to be a picture of that polaroid of Elijah and me. I keep on staring at it and staring at me, my chest bleeding out ocean deep, because never in these ten years has my foster dad hung up on me.

Speechless, my mind begins to spiral, and I redial his number.

He doesn't answer.

I send him a text

No response.

I call my mom.

Nothing.

But then a text comes through…

> **MOM:** He just needs some time, darling. I think we both do… We just don't want to see you hurt. He'll call you back when he's calmed down. I love you. xo
>
> **ROSALIA:** Elijah is the antonym of toxic. I just wish you both could see that. Please keep me updated with dad. Miss and love you. xx

A knife feels like it's been plunged into my chest.

I can imagine my mother's sad blue eyes already.

Deflated, I frown and scroll my contacts to the one girl who I know understands my pain.

Naomi.

She picks up within the third ring, and then… "Aye, this is Chad. Remember me?"

I have to smile at his cheery Australian accent at a time like this. "Oh, hey there. How are you? Are you treating my girl well?"

"As good as can be expected. She's a really beautiful girl."

"Inside and out. So, are you really her boss?"

"*What?*"

"Naomi told me you were the boss?"

"Ohhh, *that!*" He starts laughing. "Nah, babe, I'm just the manager in her department. You know Naomi and her games. Anyway, she's in the shower right now. We're gonna go out to the movies, so don't know when she'll get back to you, but I'll tell her you called, yeah?"

The frown on my lips deepens, but it's okay because I'm just grateful that Chad is a good guy and seems to be staying for the long haul. "Perfect. Treat her right, okay? If not, I'm kicking your ass."

"Ouch, man, I promise."

Back inside the penthouse, I kick off my wet socks, causing Dave to mockingly wolf-whistle. It instantly brightens my mood. So does Elijah as he tugs my hand close, having me straddle his waist on the toffee-colored leather buttoned couch he sits on.

Knives and Zander are nowhere to be seen… they must've left.

"Hey, is everything okay, baby?" Elijah asks, his fingers caressing soft circles on my denim thighs. "I was getting worried you were out there for so long."

"Yeah, just my dad. You know, he likes to talk."

He smiles. "What's the verdict on me?"

"Defrosting?" I half say, half ask.

"You mean *still ice-fucking-cold.*"

"Yeah." I manage to laugh, snuggling into his chest with my arms around his neck. He and his sandalwood scent are the only things keeping my heart beating. "That sounds about right."

Those warm hands of his move to my back and slither beneath my sweater to softly caress my skin. "You know you can always tell me what's really on your mind, yeah?"

For a second, I contemplate telling him what my father said, but in the end, I shut my mouth and am left smiling into his neck.

"I'm okay, Elijah," I whisper. "I promise."

I feel him nod ever so slowly, but something tells me he doesn't believe me, and that feeling is only replicated later on that night when we're in bed. The penthouse only has two bedrooms, so Elijah and I are sharing one (not that I'm complaining).

We're lying on our pillows facing each other, his fingers tangled through my blonde waves, just like he likes. There's a frown on his lips, knowingly, and there's nothing more I wish than for him to be inside me right now, but it isn't the time. I've done a shit job at hiding how much of a buzz kill my father's call actually was, and Elijah isn't stupid, he's noticed.

"I'm not gonna ask a billion questions 'cause your call with your father is your privacy, but I just want to say one thing..."

I nod.

Elijah's hand slows by my jaw as he whispers, "If I had listened to my stepdad all those years ago, Rosalia, I would have been dead, or worse, in jail. Sometimes, something's gotta give."

Something flickers through his gun-metal eyes that I can't quite understand.

I'm speechless, unable to conjure a single thought because it pains me too much.

And then, with a lingering warm kiss on my forehead, Elijah turns around in the bed, his tattooed back facing me, and that's when my heart really plunges into the deep dark sea.

Because without me uttering a single word, Elijah's figured it all out. He knows *exactly* what the call was about. In his mind, it couldn't have gone any other way.

My heart hurts just thinking that he knows my family doesn't care for him.

And that's when I finally understand it.

Seconds ago, I didn't glance into the eyes of Elijah Diesel, the thirty-five-year-old rock prodigy. I glanced into the eyes of the scared nine-year-old boy. And all he did was reach out for a lifeline. A lifeline craving to be loved, to be cared about, to give him something more than average.

Right now, when he uttered those words to me, those nine-year-old fingers were reaching out to me, clasping over my blistered hands, making a deal with the devil that I would hold on.

Hold onto him.

But I, Rosalia Philips, kept him silently begging until he turned around and in consequence...*let himself go.*

Chapter
THIRTY-SIX

Rosalia

The scattered shadows of the night project darkened monsters across the hardwood floors the further I step through the penthouse, in need of a late-night sip.

It's 3:00 a.m.

Far too early for my mind to already be spiraling in the way it does, but when I woke up, Elijah wasn't in the bed. The sheets on his side rippled a cold snap beneath my fingers, telling me everything.

He hadn't been beside me all night.

I don't like when Elijah gets like this, when he closes up so much it's hard to understand what's really going on. I know he hates my father, but I wish my thoughts of *us* were enough for him. That it didn't get to him, but that's hard to do when it's a part of your DNA.

My heart almost spams in shock when I find the hallway and Elijah's sitting with his back to me on one of the wet bar's metal bar stools. The silvery moonlight spilling through the glass accordion doors cascades across his back, outlining the tattoos with a glow and plunging deep into his toned muscles. His biceps are like wonderlands, mountains of beauty spiced with rock 'n' roll engraved in them.

Elijah's surrounded by darkness, so much so that the moonlight claws over the rich chestnut wet bar, yet blackness remains. He's only wearing a pair of sweatpants, the same gray ones he had in the bed. He has his head low, preventing me from seeing his expression, but by the half empty whiskey glass on the countertop and the way he's aggressively threading his fingers through his hair, I know it's not good.

It's almost film nourish, the way ribbons of musky white smoke lace the air around him. Whatever he's puffing isn't tobacco.

"You're up early," I whisper into the night, not expecting the shiver that rushes up his spine and the way he physically freezes up several feet away.

He thought he was alone.

"Lyrics kept me up," Elijah finally murmurs back, bringing the whiskey glass to his lips but never drinking. "Tell me, has ballet ever had you losing sleep?"

"Constantly. When doubt overrules passion."

Elijah softly nods, once, twice, puffing more of his cigarette.

"*C'est la* fucking *vie*," he mumbles and then gulps down the rest of the whiskey like a shot, the clinking of his glass slamming against the counter edges on my erratic breaths. "Can't sleep, baby?"

I stand frozen in the open space between the kitchen and where he is.

What's going on with him?

My silence has Elijah glancing over his shoulder, moonlight sashaying up and flooding his onyx-gray stare.

Whoa.

They're so expressionless my soul feels a little tattered and bruised at first. But the more puffs of the evident rolled-up joint he takes, the more they lighten up, get warmer, relish me.

"I've been banished from drinking like a fucking *ensamvarg*." He hungrily rakes his eyes up my body in a way that has my sex heating, slowing by my silk lace-trimmed sleep shorts before gesturing to the bar behind him. "So, you should join me."

"*Ensamvarg*?"

Elijah Diesel's dark chuckle is ice-cold, emulating the Joker's. "Yeah, *ensamvarg*. Means *lone wolf*. It's Swedish…and so is this whiskey."

It doesn't take long before I'm sitting right beside Elijah, his stare intoxicating. Just as he's about to pour another glass of the amber liquid I reach out and grip the neck of the bottle, tugging it to me instead. And if looks could kill, holy cow, Elijah isn't happy. At. All.

He shouldn't be drinking.

Not at the rate he's going. Not alone.

"I want another glass, Rosalia."

I ignore him completely, sliding the Swedish whiskey to the other side of the bar. "Are you going to tell me why you're drinking?"

Shaking his head, Elijah leans into me slightly, his silver rings glimmering in the light as he rubs a hand over his dark beard. "Devil's got my soul tonight, darlin', that's fucking why."

The more I glance into his eyes, the more I find they're rimmed in redness that has never been this evident before. It's the joint, his traumas, and the exhaustion of almost completing an eight-month worldwide tour with less than two weeks left. And yet, I don't like it one bit.

"Tell me the real reason you couldn't sleep," I whisper into the dark, my fingers running through the grooves of the smooth chestnut counter like they're all my confidantes. "Something on your mind?"

"Yeah. *You.*"

My heart slows. "Me?"

"Mmhmmm." Elijah takes a few puffs of his joint. "*You.*"

"Why?"

"I've been thinking about what I said before we fell asleep…"

I find myself nodding. "Me too."

"Oh." Sighing, he stares at his empty glass, his fingers ironing over the rim. "Tell me."

"Whatever it is you're thinking—*don't.* I'm with you, Elijah, I promise. My foster parents…they just don't understand it, but they'll come around. I know they will."

"They won't! This isn't a problem you can fix with a family *dinner*, Rosalia!" my melancholic rocker spits, the words meeting the air like poison. "They'll never fucking like *me* because they'll never ever give *me* a chance."

"You don't know that…"

"Give me a break, *Peaches*," Elijah scoffs, unbreakable pain in his gaze when it lifts to meet mine, our breaths a labored mess. "I've been around, okay? So, I think I fucking *know.*"

Oh. My. God.

His words lodge a bullet in my chest, and I'm left staring at him with frantic wide eyes, my jaw completely dropped.

"What the hell?" I gasp. "Listen here, bud, don't you dare talk to me like I don't know my left from my right!"

"Never intended to." Elijah sighs, obviously disappointed in himself. "I'm...*sorry*."

"Good," I hiss. "So, keep it that way."

His onyx eyes darken. "Okay. Let me ask you this. Can you swallow a fractured relationship with your parents being the consequence of you being involved with me?"

Silence.

The question is so loaded, something I can't answer with him looking at me like this.

"It's simple, *Peaches*. Yes or no?"

A fire I'm not used to shoots through my throat. "I don't know."

Elijah leans closer to me, studying me slowly, and I can practically taste his sweet whiskey on my tongue. "*This* may not even last until the end of Portland. Have you thought about that?"

I think I'm falling in love with a monster.

Stupid me.

I don't answer. I turn away toward my hands, perplexed about this entire thing. That fire in my throat turns into an ache, making it impossible to breathe.

"You should, *Peaches*," he adds, bursting the prosperity we brought into Portland. "You know why? 'Cause nothing lasts forever. You're woman enough to know that."

Elijah's words jar me so deeply that an uncontrollable, hot tear slips down my cheek.

He kisses it away with the gentlest, most vulnerable lips, his touch burning my skin.

"Don't cry. I ain't worth it. I'm just a *punk* in your father's eyes," he whispers darkly, gripping my jaw and then forcing me to meet his eyes, all while his own jaw tenses up slowly. "I'm a rock *punk*."

We exhale together. Then inhale. Then, we gradually shut our eyes, welcoming darkness.

"Isn't that right, Rosalia?"

"Why are you being like this?"

"Like *what*?"

"Being so cruel to yourself." I sniffle.

"Because…" Elijah taunts lowly with the saddest wicked smirk. "I'm just a *punk*, huh?"

I squeeze my eyes shut at the venomous word, hating that he's doing this to himself. Forcing himself to relive the trauma, the trigger, all the darkness that comes with *that* word.

Desperately needing a drink, I slip away from his grip, and he lets me. *This is all too much.* With my mind in ruins, I slip behind the wet bar's counter. "Would you like a…mocktail?"

Elijah's jaw slowly ticks in frustration.

"I may be a recovering alcoholic, but I can have alcohol, Rosa. Just in moderation."

"In *moderation*?" I question, getting myself a highballer glass from the industrial floating shelves. "Is that what you call gulping down whiskey like it's a shot glass?"

Pissed off, Elijah rushes up from his bar stool, causing it to skid. "Fuck this, I'll do it."

"*Stay.*" I hold out a hand, halting him in place. "Let me do it. What would you like?"

Need circles his eyes for a long while, alongside a touch of hurt as he retakes his seat.

"Anything but vodka."

Nodding, I resort to making him a Jack and Coke. I know he likes it, and it's evident in the way his face lights up a fraction when I slide the glass to him.

I'm halfway through putting ice and orange juice in my highballer glass because a Screwdriver is my favorite cocktail, when I stop, my fingers halting inches from the vodka bottle. I'm so close my fingertips brush against the glass.

Shit.

I pull back, my heart sinking.

Shit. Shit. Shit.

Elijah's hot stare shoots waves through me. "Have it."

"No." I shake my head, pulling back. "It's okay. I'll just have something else instead."

"Rosalia, have the vodka. It's fine."

"The way you said it before was like you have history with vodka, and I don't want to trigger you."

"Okay," he mutters. "Vodka is where it all started. I was able to fool people in social settings, you know, mixing it with other beverages so they didn't notice a thing. Did it until it became a numbed obsession. It almost killed me."

"Has it been hard since?"

"Extremely."

"How do you monitor yourself?"

Elijah pauses for a moment. "I limit myself to one glass, or if it's more, I always drink whenever there's somebody else around. To keep me accountable. It's usually Knives. I could spiral if I drank alone."

Oh.

Thoughts take over my mind. "You know my biological parents suffered from drug addiction? Well, more my biological mom."

He keeps on staring, that perfectly chiseled jaw beginning to tense up. "Yeah?"

"I never really separated the substance from the person up until you told me about you being a recovering alcoholic."

"What do you mean?"

"Well, I've kind of always blamed my parents for it. That they caused this huge void inside me, the need to go through different families in foster care, the reasons I have major trust issues, but… with *you*, I'm realizing the reasons behind the need to gravitate to substance."

A beat passes…

Two beats…

And then…

Elijah's metal bar stool brutally skids against the hardwood floors, and I can't even process what's happening before he's beside me, quickly making me a Screwdriver with a constantly clenched jaw.

The tall vodka bottle is poison in his grip—*lethal*—and when he makes it and goes to set the vodka down, his fingers linger a fraction more than they should.

"There ya go," he says all gingerly, yet never looks at me again when retaking his seat. "Go ahead, drink it. Do it."

I'm left staring at the cocktail Elijah made for me, all while he slowly sips his own.

My heart is palpitating, lodging out of my chest. I feel all the weight of the world grazing my shoulder when I wrap my fingers against the chilled glass. *Drink it, Rosalia.*

He said it's okay.

"Come on, drink it."

"But…"

"I. Said. *Drink*," Elijah angrily grits, his eyes meeting mine just as my lips kiss the edge of the rim, licking the stray drops of sweetened orange juice.

Sadness.

It's all I see pooling in those big onyx eyes as they flicker between me and the glass, or rather the vodka trapped inside. I'm doing it, tipping the glass forward, seconds away from letting the fated alcohol lace my tongue.

He said it was okay.

But no, it's not okay.

I can't do this to Elijah.

It's my own slice of Romeo's poison. But just before the cocktail meets my lips, I turn around and violently spill the alcohol into the shallow bar sink, the glass loudly rattling against the stainless steel as it slips from my grip.

Gosh.

My mind can't stop spinning, my heart aching. I couldn't do it. I'm hunched over the sink, my fists clenching the edge of the counter in a death grip, all while my back is to Elijah.

I can't drink the vodka.

Not with him sitting right here.

Silently pleading with me to save him.

Before I know it, warm hands are wrapping around my waist from behind, Elijah's bare chest against my back and every one of his hot breaths tickling my skin.

Wordlessly, I lean my head into his chest, sinking into his comfort with my eyes shut, all while aching inside.

I hate that we're like this right now. That I'm chained to the dull mood between us.

"I'm sorry. I just want you to know I'm enough for you," Elijah whispers, scattering slow kisses down my scorching hot neck, creating tingles. "More than your disapproving parents could ever be."

I remain silent.

"I'm really bad with…with communication at times. Sometimes I just shut down, don't want to speak, or if I do, I say the wrong thing."

My heartbeat is everywhere.

"Sometimes I say too much, get really intense. Maniac. I can't control how I feel, but whenever I'm with you, I… I come alive." A soft moan tangles my throat at his ravished neck kisses. "I feel free." He sucks on my sweet spots, his tongue swirling, destined to leave hickeys. "God, I *feel*."

"Elijah…"

"Believe me, baby," he says like a prayer. "*Please*."

My mind's a tangled mess, all my thoughts blurring into one as I rush a hand up to spear my fingers through his wavy hair, bringing his face deeper into my neck.

"*Please*, babygirl. I promise."

He ruins me with flowery kisses, all across my skin until the sparks turn into warmth pooling in my heart. All while his hands rush up my thighs, stretch under the tightness of my silk pajama shorts, and then further, firmly squeezing my bruised ass.

I can't stop thinking about him.

Can't stop playing around with his/my vintage silver snake ring.

Can't stop wondering if it will always be like this with him—so vulnerably intense.

"*Peaches*. You are the best part of me, little one. The *only* fucking part of me that's not tattered and bruised in recklessness."

"Do you really mean that?"

"Desperately," Elijah confesses within the same heartbeat. "Yes."

My heavy eyes shut, overtaken by his tingling kisses, and I whisper my truth, "You're the best part of me too."

Letting out a long sigh of relief, Elijah's fingers skim around to my front, and I almost lose my breath when they graze the hem of my panties. His hesitance tonight is new. He's usually so direct and dominant, but tonight, *something's different*…

Elijah's fingers glide lower.

With a heavy heart, I shake my head, my mind all over the place. Sex is the last thing I'm thinking about right now. I'm too concerned about how he openly puts himself down. Taunts himself with his trauma.

"No." Biting my inner cheek, I softly nudge him away with my elbow. "I don't feel like it right now."

His fingers instantly slip away.

That warmth disappears from behind me.

Then lights above us turn on, soft warmth.

The metal bar stool once again scrapes back.

Elijah's sitting back down again.

I can't stop staring at the vodka, my heart aching, flooded with so many questions why.

"Am I enough for you?" he whispers into the night, his voice laced in defeat. "Am I what you wan—"

"I wouldn't be here if you weren't, Elijah."

Silence takes over, and when I cast a glance behind my shoulder, those eyes my seventeen-year-old heart crushed over stare back at me. Soulless.

That response seems to be enough for Elijah...

Gradually nodding, Elijah brings the joint he left burning in the ashtray to his lips. Those wild clouds of smoke attacking the air around him like crazy.

Then why doesn't a single thing feel okay?

"Do you think I'm a monster?" Elijah asks after a while, his eyes glazed over in complete darkness.

Too choked up to speak, I shake my head.

No.

All he does is stare, like he doesn't believe me. I can't lie, it hurts a little, but I understand. He didn't grow up in a home of love and affection either. Validation is everything.

The wet bar is beginning to reek of the musky weed (okay, not *begin*, it already *is*), but I don't let it faze me. It isn't strong enough to trigger parts of my past. My parents were addicted to cocaine and other drugs, the pill-popping, nose-snorting kind. *Not this.*

Maybe this can set me free a little...make me forget the world for a little while. An escape, just how I craved doing something risky that summer of senior year and met Elijah Diesel for the first time.

"Is this the only drug you take?"

"Yeah, it's all I need."

"Can I have a puff?"

Elijah's eyes widen and he freezes up mid-smoke, his brow arching in question. "This is the good shit, Rosalia, like *get-you-high-in-a-few-puffs* kinda high."

I shrug, unfazed. "All right, I can handle it."

"You sure?"

"Yeah, it's fine. I'm not that weak, Elijah." I half-smile.

"I know, I'm just telling you you'll get high…"

"You seem okay."

He just smiles sadly. "'Cause I'm used to it, baby."

And that's what scares me.

He shouldn't need to numb the pain.

Not when I'm here, wanting to help him.

Slowly, Elijah motions the joint (that's getting smaller by the second) to me. "If it's what you want…"

Climbing up onto the wet bar counter, I hesitantly take the joint from him, glancing over it suspiciously. "It's…*safe*, yeah?"

The bastard all but rolls his eyes with that cocky smirk. *Glad to know the asshole I know and adore is back.*

"Wouldn't give my girl anything deadly."

I smirk. "Hmmm, we'll see about that."

The moment the joint meets my lips, I crunch up my nose, already foreign to everything about this.

How the fuck can he smoke this shit?

Elijah scoots me so that my legs hang off the counter between his sides. It's cute the way he holds my free hand, caressing it slowly as I take a puff of the joint, pull back, and feel…

Nothing.

I furrow my brows. *The heck?*

"Ummm, is it normal not to feel anything?"

Smoldering, he wraps his arms around my hips, pulling me close and leveling with my eyes.

"Take another two puffs and just wait," Elijah breathes against my lips, inhaling the soft smoke.

I do just that, my hand squeezing in his.

Handing the joint back to Elijah, I watch as he takes another blow, and then another, and then…

It happens.

Holy shit.

This numbness rushes over me, trapping me in like I'm comatose. It's so quick that a buzz licks down my spine, electrifying it to the core, shooting down my muscles.

Elijah's talking, but it blurs into mirrored murmurs. It doesn't feel like I'm the one breathing and *whoa*, my bloodstream is bubbling, my rapid heartbeat so deafening it mutes all else.

Thump.

Thump.

Thump.

And then just like that, I don't feel my heartbeat at all. It seems at a distance. Everything does. Like I'm in another dimension filled with wandering thoughts and...everything feels light. Like really, really light.

I tighten my grip on Elijah, convinced I'm having an allergic reaction or some shit, just as a wave rushes over me, and I just feel... *relaxed.*

Nothing hurts anymore.

Not a single thought rushes through my mind.

My gaze burns straight through those onyx-grays, and they become my only source of reason.

There's nothing inside my brain. It's all empty. Free. No bad thoughts chain me. I just feel happy, real fucking happy and...horny. Like really, really turned on. What the hell?

"Shit," I breathe, a goofy grin rolling up my lips. "I feel it, baby! Oh my freaking God! *WOWWW!*"

Elijah's warm chuckle electrifies me. "You feeling okay?"

"Yeah." I can't help my yawn. "But I feel really tired all of a sudden, but not sleepy. It's weird. I'm also, like, a little turned on..."

"Ah, yeah, that's normal."

"Really?"

"Mmhmmm."

"Well, how are you supposed to get anything done feeling like this?"

He shoots me a slow, sexy smile. "That's the point, *Peaches*, you're supposed to feel so numb to the world that you just get lost in it."

"Do you write music like this?"

"Why do you ask?"

I shrug. "I have always heard a lot about rock stars and getting high. Kurt Cobain. Jimi Hendrix. Bob Dylan."

"You mean the legends then, hmm?" There goes that sexy chuckle again as Elijah offers me the joint and I take another puff before handing it back to him. "Sometimes I write a little high, sometimes I let the real emotions of life wash over me."

"How did you write 'Fragments of You'?"

"High as fuck off this weed on a seven-hour private jet, but wanna know something, little one?"

"Mmhmm." I smile, slowly tracing over his soft lips that remind me of rich cashmere sweaters to touch and the warmth of hot cocoas in winter.

"You still took over my mind. Every single second that I was supposed to feel complete nothingness, I felt you instead."

Grinning, this giddiness gushes over me and I don't know if it's the weed or simply all the butterflies Elijah rushes out of me.

Cupping his spikey beard, I pull him close and kiss him ever so slowly, my tongue dancing ballet with his like it's my survival. I love the way his hands squeeze me tighter into him, needing me too.

"Then that's all you need to answer your question from earlier." I smile against his lips. "You're so much more than enough for me. Don't you know how damn crazy you drive me, Lijah?"

Elijah looks at me like I'm the only thing that exists, and that's really all I've ever wanted. A genuine smile carved up his lips. "Now I do."

We share the joint back and forth for a little longer as we talk, makeshift mid-'80s kinda lovers. Elijah plays music on his phone and instantly, the suite's internal speakers softly begin blaring. It's just real sensually erotic beats and scattered vocals…*really sexy.*

"I got a call just before you joined me."

"Oh yeah?" I ask.

"Mmhmm." Elijah sighs, tapping the joint against the ashtray. "My publicist backed out of our contract."

What?

My breaths slow but then…nothing. *Ugh, stuff you weed, this is serious.*

Make me feel, *goddammit!*

"Meaning?"

"Lydia, my publicist, she quit."

Oh no.

I stare at him, wide-eyed. "*Quit?*"

"Quit."

"Shit, what does that mean for you now?"

"That if I decide it's time to fuck up my life and fall into a scandal, I got no one to save my ass."

My heart aches for him because I know just how damaging something like this must be for him.

"Oh, shit, Elijah. I'm so sorry."

"You didn't do anything, baby."

"But what if I did? What… What if this is all because of me?"

"It isn't, believe me." He promises. "It's the bigger picture, not you at all."

I brush my lips against his, trying to conjure the words I need. "Will you look for a new publicist?"

Sighing, Elijah softly shakes his head. "Don't want to. Not now. My manager's calling a virtual *crisis meeting* tomorrow morning with all my team to talk it out, including Lydia, but it won't help shit. My publicist and I are both stubborn as hell."

"I'm sorry. Is there anything I can do to help?"

Elijah shoots me a tired, sexy smile, his eyes all red and glazed over, finally evident just how high he truly is. "*Pray*, little girl, your man needs a miracle."

Between the weed and the way he's currently looking at me, my heart skips so fast. I spread my thighs wider on the bar countertop, shocking him when I cup his jaw and seductively whisper against his lips, "Maybe you can find that miracle between my thighs…"

"*Fuck.*" Elijah's eyes immediately darken to an intensity that has me sensually rocking my hips to the music. "Thought you didn't want to be touched, babygirl?"

I grin. "That's right."

"What are you trying to do? Kill me?"

Biting my lip, I smile and nod through my lashes. "Just watch me. *Please.*"

"I want to do more than just watch you."

"If you're a good boy and watch me make myself come…" I taunt, my lips inches from his. "And then, maybe, I'll let you use my throat however you think I deserve later."

"*Fuckkkk.*" Elijah's jaw drops. "Is this you talking or the weed talking?"

My grin deepens. "Both… *Mostly me.*"

Nodding, Elijah Diesel darkly smirks back at me. *He loves this.*

Grinding my hips against the counter to the erotic music, I give Elijah a show. Slowly rushing a hand down my body, I dance for him as I squeeze my tits and then, while softly biting my lip, rush my hand lower. His breaths thicken, those hooded eyes dripping with hunger as desire pools on my pussy. It's aching, needing to be touched.

I need this. I need this so much.

With my hips grinding into the air, my fingers settle over the heat of my sex, starting off slowly rubbing my clit through the soft fabric, groaning at the pleasure that gives me alone.

God yes.

"Shhh, baby, Dave is just down the hall. Don't want him walking in on what's mine."

My reply is an even louder moan.

"*God.* You're making this so fucking hard for me, Rosa, almost want him to hear now."

Because my silk pajama shorts are dusty pink, the more I vigorously circle my fingers over my throbbing pussy, the more arousal seeps through, darkening the silk. I can't even breathe straight through all the satisfaction. Keeping a hand on the countertop to lean on, my right hand slowly slips into my silk pajama shorts and lace panties, my breaths scattering.

"Jesus Christ, Rosalia."

I smile at him, yet the second my icy fingertips glide down my warm, wet pussy, I'm gasping from the electrifying sensation. Cold on hot. I'm soaking, arousal coating my tensing inner thighs, and my abs clench, all while I vigorously circle my clit. *Yes. Yes. Yes.*

It's like I'm dreaming, the high from the joint making me go crazy. I'm rubbing myself so hard, so frantic as I crave reaching that bliss, all while Elijah hungrily watches my hand go crazy in the constraint of my clothes. I love how he's palming himself over his sweatpants too.

"*Peaches,*" he growls, so sexually frustrated. "Show me how you play with yourself."

God, I want that so much too, and I'm panting, wriggling all around as I stop the rubbing to slip off my shorts and panties, my hand glistening with my arousal. The same hand Elijah hungrily takes into his mouth, humming in satisfaction as he sucks on my fingers, rolling his tongue around to catch all my sweetness.

I use that same hand, coated with him, to rush back down my abs, slowing at my diamond navel piercing.

Breathe, Rosa, breathe.

My pussy is already throbbing so crazily, it has me rubbing my thighs together, almost rolling my eyes back at the smoothness. I'm even wetter. But Elijah doesn't take any of it, not wanting me to ride off my pleasure this way as he pushes my thighs open wide and I further extend them, doing a side split on the countertop.

It's a compromising position, exposes *all of me* to him. I continue grinding to the music.

"I love that you're a fucking ballerina, baby," Elijah rasps, the heat in his eyes so intense as he flickers his gaze between me and my sex constantly. "Show me how you play with your greedy, pretty pussy when I'm not around."

"Only if you touch yourself too."

We share a lazy smirk and I watch on as Elijah listens to me, tugging his gray sweatpants down and my mouth waters as his big, hard cock slaps against his abs. *Commando.* I'm fascinated with the way he sexily spits on it, then rubs it all over his length, glistening his cock before he starts to fist himself. I can feel the hot moan that ripples through him on my pussy, that's how loud it is.

I love the way Elijah roughly jerks himself back and forth, back and forth, getting tighter by his swollen light pink crown, as his cock throbs intensely in his eager grip.

It's on another level of erotic watching him fuck himself like this.

Watching those rippling washboard abs automatically tense.

Watching the way his biceps pump, his breaths deepen.

Those hooded onyx-gray eyes meet mine, all devilishly wild. "Keep going, baby. This has just begun."

I'm desperate to give us both what we crave. Slipping my hand back lower to my pussy, I stare at a grunting Elijah fisting his cock as I rush two fingers on either side of my entry.

"That's a good girl, spread yourself wide for me, Rosa."

I do, letting him see all of me just as he curses out in French. *I love how he does that.* Our gazes lock and I plunge two fingers inside my tightness, softly whimpering as I rock them in and out of me so roughly. Ever since Elijah, I want everything rough. Fast. Deep. *Hot.*

"Another one, baby."

Nodding with my eyes half shut from the ecstasy, I dive in a third finger, just how he said. Between my grinding hips and the intensity of just how hard I'm working myself, I can feel myself on the edge. The more uncontrollable moans escape me, the deeper I fuck myself. Touching myself feels so good, and especially in front of him.

My clit is pulsing, aching to be touched, so I extend my thumb, my tits bouncing together at such an intense speed that it begins to hurt. A good hurt, though, as I let my thirty-five-year-old boyfriend bear witness to how I used to cure my ache almost every single night since he left.

God.

Oh God.

Ohhh, fuck.

I can hear how wet I am, and I know Elijah does too when his curses turn into moans. "Jesus Christ, Rosalia. You don't know the things I wanna do to you right now."

"Do it." I hum through pleasure, my eyes rolling back because it's getting too much. "*Please.*"

One minute, I'm fucking myself on the wet bar's countertop. The next, I'm being roughly sprawled on the toffee-colored leather buttoned couch in the open plan living room. Elijah wastes no time picking me back up as he's the one lying down on the couch, his rock-hard erection pulsing sans hands and sweatpants halfway down his thighs. *Wow. What a sight…*

I'm grinning because he's so reckless in the way he grips my hips and pushes me farther up, so I'm straddling his broad chest. My hands fall to his shoulders to stabilize myself, all while his thumbs rub small circles on my bare hips. The low light from the bar trickles through.

Elijah glances up at me, pure desire burning up those onyx-grays and when he smirks…whoa, I just want to do this forever. He aggressively rips off my pajama top, all the buttons flying everywhere, clanging against metal, the coffee table, and God knows where.

"Elijah!"

"You said I could do whatever I was feeling."

"Yeah," I pant, unable to help my giggle. "I just didn't expect *that.*"

Smoldering, Elijah cups my ample breasts, his touch against me so scorching. "Except the unexpected with me, little one." He erotically molds them so hard I gasp in pleasure, needing a cure to how close I am to coming. "Come on, baby, don't be scared to come closer."

I look at him genuinely confused. "Come closer *where*?"

He unexpectedly spanks my ass. *Hard.* Causing my hips to jerk up higher, and apparently, by the way his smirk deepens, *right where he wants me.* Elijah urges my ass higher, his arms over my thighs and having me straddle his face, my pussy inches from his mouth. I hold myself up with my knees as they sink lower on the couch, on either side of his face.

"*Here,*" Elijah growls, meaning his mouth. "Ride out your orgasm on me right *here.*"

So hot.

I really want that.

Grinning down at him, my tits frantically rushing up and down from just how fast my heart is beating, I decide to rile him on. "I've never done that before..."

His eyes darken to pure lustful carnage.

"I would fucking hope not."

And then he's slamming my hips lower, pressing me against his mouth and diving his tongue into my dripping pussy, and I scream out in pleasure. *Scream.* The sensation is so new, so intense and raw that I feed into it, shutting my eyes while Elijah devours me with his tongue.

He's like a famished wolf, moaning and squeezing my ass as his tongue growls wild inside of me, erratic with every single movement, making my legs begin to tremble when he sucks on my swollen clit too.

"Oh my, Lijah, this feels so good."

"Mmhmmm."

I've already edged myself on so much that I know this isn't going to last long. Not as I begin to rock my hips softly, my clit hitting his nose with every move, and I feel my arousal all over him. The erotic music beats match those on my chest as I ride on his face, loving the sensation of his rough stubble grazing my thighs.

Getting lost in every minute of this, I thread my fingers through his hair, tugging so hard on the wavy ends that Elijah's eyes flicker up to me. With his tongue fucking my pussy so hard and deep, his eyes warm, and it feels like he's smirking against me before shutting his eyes again and ruining me completely. He eats me so good, like I'm his sole salvation.

I know Diesel Rose's drummer, Dave, is in this suite with us, asleep, but I can't help my screams and moans at the speed Elijah is working his jaw, burning a fire so deep inside me, I almost explode.

But I hold on, bouncing on his stroking tongue, riding his face faster with every second I'm pulling his hair, my heartbeats on the verge of overdrive as I get closer, and closer, and closer. I can't stop quivering and convulsing on his tongue, going absolutely crazy.

Elijah's nails dig deeper into my ass, and I can't even breathe anymore when his tongue works my pussy even faster. *I didn't even think that was possible.* We're both groaning messes, his noises vibrating my pulsing pussy, clenching around his tongue because I'm seconds away.

Seconds.

My legs are already trembling over him, so when Elijah spreads my ass and I feel the warmth of his finger slip down and circle around my hole before trying to edge inside, but I'm too tight, so he forces his way inside. I'm screaming, bouncing on both his tongue and his finger until the pulses in my pussy intensify, heat tensing me up, and I come crying out his name.

Elijah instantly pulls away, a panting mess with flustered cheeks as he works vigorously, rubbing my pussy so that I'm squirting out my orgasm, his fingers so wild it sprays everywhere.

"I want to taste you more. Let me taste you, baby."

Abs tense, my hips bucking forth, and my breaths are all erratic as I let him do just that. Mid-smirk, Elijah darts out his tongue, fucking me harder so that I'm spraying down his throat, my orgasm glistening all over his face, pooling and dripping down his dark stubble like honey.

"Oh my God, Lijah."

"Hmmm, yeah, baby, all for me. This is all for me."

"All for you." I grin down at him as my orgasm begins to settle, just as he attacks my pussy again, this time cleaning me up with longer strokes of his tongue, licking me so slow.

When I finally slip off him, straddling his narrow waist instead, I realize just how flustered he's gotten. His face is the deepest shade of blush, and it crawls all down his neck as he's panting, breathing properly for the first time in a few moments. His hair is all sexily tousled and messy because of me, and I can't get over just how much his face gleams in the low light with my cum.

Elijah looks at me and I look back, our shared smile something so special as we both attempt to catch our breaths. He can't stop softly caressing my thighs, giving me tender aftercare.

"I have no words for how fucking beautiful that was, my angel."

My heart is fluttering with butterflies so instead of answering, I lean down and kiss Elijah slowly, gently, in a way I never have before. It's a sensual kiss that thanks him for everything that he is, and everything that he's not. And in our high, it's the most euphoric thing.

I love tasting my sweetness on his tongue, loving just how much he loves it as my hips sink a little lower, rubbing myself against the tip of his hard cock bare, coating him with me.

"I wasn't lying about having you down my throat," I whisper by his lips. "I *crave* it."

"I know you do, babygirl. You think I don't?"

I tiredly smile at Elijah's words, resting my head against his chest for a ten-second breather. He got me so flushed that I can't even feel my limbs anymore. That orgasm was just so breathtaking, I can barely move. I'm just so happy, lying here with him while his fingers softly trail up and down my spine, comforting me, and I smile more as he kisses my forehead.

The crash from my orgasm and the joint's high as this wave of tiredness ripples through me has me exhausted, but I so desperately want to give Elijah what he deserves and what I desire. My mouth. His cock. I'm not ashamed with just how badly I want him. How much I want to prove to the world that Elijah Diesel is a good guy, and he deserves happiness, and he deserves me...

It's why I'm so pissed off with myself when the next thing I know, I'm fluttering my eyes open to his rapidly beating heart against mine, and we're...moving. Walking. Well, *he* is.

What?

My arms around his neck, I glance up at him with heavy eyes. "Huh? What happened?"

"Baby, you fell asleep on me, so I'm carrying you to our bed."

I practically groan in his chest. *Dammit.* "But I really wanted to...you know."

"It's okay. Soon, yeah," Elijah whispers.

"*Soon*," I whisper back, a promise.

And then, he smiles down at me so *lovingly*, I just want to run away with him...*forever*.

Chapter
THIRTY-SEVEN

Elijah

Crisis meetings are the bane of my existence. All they do is cause paranoia…*as if I need to add that to my growing list of fucked-up problems.*

But it's almost all over now. All done and dusted. And all I had to endure was a three-hour Skype *draining* video call between my manager, agent, and publicist, who are all back in Manhattan.

To tell you the honest truth, I was zoning out for most of the *crisis meeting*. There's only so much I can take at people telling me I'm risking everything to be with Rosalia Philip.

I'm also still kinda high, so you know…

My team thinks I'll destroy her with my lack of sanity.

That I'll cause this huge ruckus without anybody to save me.

And yet, my publicist, Lydia Fitz, refused to revive our contract.

Lydia has her blood-red lips pierced during the entire Skype call, giving me jab after jab of my own reckless past. Headlines and scandals that she's prevented from escaping the depth of my circle. My manager. My publicist. My agent. Knives. Dave. Zander. That's my professional circle at its finest. Not even my record producer knows half the shit, because if he did, Diesel Rose would be toast.

My manager and agent have left the chat, leaving just Lydia and me. Neither of us has spoken for a solid seven minutes straight. We've just been staring into the screen, and I don't know what she's looking for, but I wish she'd just tell me, so I could just give it to her.

"Lydia… You're alluding to incidents that haven't even occurred yet," I murmur into my laptop screen, the one to break the silence, at a quarter to ten in the morning. "One more chance."

My publicist is firm to shake her head, disappearing off screen for a moment and when she returns, frowns as she holds up a red manila folder with my name scribbled all over it.

Something inside me begins to shrivel up at the very sight of it… It could be my heart.

I instantly shut my eyes.

Fuck.

"I thought that was in the vault, Lids."

"It *was*, until late last night."

"Shit," I groan, rubbing my hands over my eyes, leaning against the kitchen counter because it's the only thing keeping me up now. "Put it away. *Please.* I don't want to see it."

"Neither do I, Elijah. However, it's important you see them one last night, so when the next episode like this occurs, you'll find yourself without my expertise to clean all the broken pieces. *And* you won't only lose reputation and Diesel Rose…" Lydia pauses, her next words catastrophic. "You'll also lose *yourself.* All because you didn't trust me enough to leave her."

And there my publicist goes spilling the contents of that red manila folder of gloom, holding up to the screen all the pieces of Elijah Diesel the world must never see. The parts of me that still scar me to this day. The bits of my life that I'm still spiraling in, in the shadows.

Therapist reports.

Hospital reports.

Police reports.

Pictures.

And pictures.

And more pictures.

A transcript of Knives's frantic 911 call.

The ways my publicist has deceived the world in saving my reputation.

All the reasons why I should have never involved myself with my *Peaches*.

Every single piece of evidence Lydia holds up to the screen ruins me more. It thrusts a barbaric knife in my chest, and it just keeps on fucking twisting cold. The fire rushing through my body is deadly, and maybe it is—*deadly*—because suddenly I don't feel so good anymore.

My body's weak.

It's so fucking weak.

I just need an antidote. *Again.*

Fuck, I need to make it all go away.

I'm grateful I'm alone in this Portland penthouse apartment. I don't know how I would have reacted if Rosalia walked past in that exact moment my publicist flashed those sensitive photos. Rosalia's out to ballet training, while Dave is doing an exclusive radio interview with Zander. Mine with Knives is Saturday morning, hours before our second Portland concert on this tour.

Lydia ends the call with two words that finish off the massacre in my chest, "Keep on."

Keep on.

Those were the two words she said to me when I was in that hospital bed.

The first two words I ever heard again when I came to, propelling me back to life.

And the very two words that, right now, fall short of doing what they did a year ago…

Save me.

Chapter
THIRTY-EIGHT

EXCLUSIVE:
Elijah Diesel in public relation shock!

By Beatrix Helfrich, ROCK 'N' ROLL PRESS
October 20, 2022

Elijah Diesel cuts ties with trusted publicist Lydia Fitz amid rumors the thirty-five-year-old rock star is dating twenty-one-year-old prima ballerina, Rosalia Philips.

In the major revelation, Diesel's rep responded to our request, stating, *'At this stage, Elijah Diesel refuses a public relation replacement, despite it being in his best interest. This is all Diesel's team can provide at this time, due to the pending matter.'*

It is unsure if Lydia Fitz, CEO of Fitz Public Relations, quit, or if Diesel severed ties.

This comes after Diesel serenaded Philips on stage earlier this week and fans spotted the pair attending an exclusive gourmet Los Angeles restaurant, D.A.RK. It sparks rumors as to if this could be a public relation setup gone wrong to clean up Diesel's bad boy image after battling past demons.

The gorgeous, tattooed French-American is currently in Portland, Oregon, where Diesel Rose is scheduled to perform three electrifying shows at Moda Center arena.

Diesel is set to be featured in an exclusive interview on Portland's Rad Rockstar Radio with bandmate, Knight Ives, on Saturday morning, in which sources predict fan questions will unlock the mystery regarding him and the former Swan Lake dancer.

Listen to Rad Rockstar Radio live on 669 F.M at 10:15 a.m. to catch the exclusive chat.

Chapter

THIRTY-NINE

Rosalia

Elijah is nowhere to be seen when I step inside our penthouse apartment after ballet training at the hotel's opulent gym. *And yes, I do mean* opulent. *There was a waterfall in the middle of it.*

I swear I searched every room twice and some even a third time. He didn't send me any texts, and he isn't answering any of my calls. I really wanted to ask Elijah how everything went with the crisis meeting he had with his team. He said he'll wait for me to return from the gym.

I know the likelihood of him brushing it off and wanting to talk about something else is high, which I respected, but still, I want to know he was okay.

This morning, I saw the article in *Rock 'n' Roll Press,* and it wasn't good. It can't be easy losing a publicist after a solid four years. I can imagine he put a lot of trust in her. She's responsible for his reputation in the media and keeping all publicity regarding his life as private and stable as it can be, and now he's losing that.

Elijah's losing his publicist because of me.

I can't seem to wash that thought away, no matter badly I want to. Elijah told me last night (while we were half-high) that this has nothing to do with me, and while I believe him, part of me knows it's *precisely* because of me.

Ever since I reentered the picture, my existence has caused troubles between him and his team, and I never wanted that. It's one thing for my parents not to like him. It's another for his professional team to advise him against seeing me based on the chance things could turn sour and really damage his reputation.

SIDE NOTE: And mine.

But to be honest, *just between you and me,* part of me is confused. Elijah is a rock star. An A-list celebrity. A-listers endure breakups, rumors, and trials and tribulations *all the time.*

What is going to be so diabolic if (*fingers crossed not*) Elijah and I falter?

What would be so scandalous that it destroys both of our reputations like hurricanes?

Unless…

Unless… Is Elijah hiding something?

Something from his fans?

Something from *me*?

That would make sense as to why his team is freaking out, but… what could it be?

Just as my breaths pick up speed from all the thoughts in my mind, they all soften to a normalized pace when I see *it*. A bright pink Post-it note on the fridge I missed before…

Peaches,

Going on a run to shake some thoughts.

(And that fucking weed, Jesus.)

I'll be back before 11am, babydoll.

—E.

The private elevator doors swoosh open before I can even finish reading Elijah's note, and the smile is already burning up my lip. But when I swirl around to face the elevator, said smile drops.

It isn't Elijah.

It's Knight Ives, aka *Knives*.

And the moment he sees me, it's as if he's finally meeting the darkness of death.

One glance at my sticking up sweaty hair from gym, the vintage silver ring Elijah gave me, and my workout clothes, which are slick against my skin from the intensity of my training routine, and he's doing a B-line right back inside the private elevator car.

Oh, I see how it is.

"Are you always going to ignore me like that?"

The idiot ignores me.

"I'm dating your best friend, Knives, you know, so whether you like it or not, we're going to be seeing a lot of each other," I huff out, confidence embedded in my every word. "So, we can either do a shit job at coexisting, which we currently are, *or* we can actually try to be courteous in making Elijah's life simpler and somewhat get along."

"I don't seek to *somewhat get along* with *seventeen*-year-olds, Rosalia," he practically spits, his back still to me. "So back off."

What?!

"*Seventeen?*" I almost laugh in all my brewing anger. "I'm not seventeen anymore, Knives. It's been four years! I'm twenty-one!"

"As if that's any better…"

"It's legal. It always has been."

"It's a *fifteen*-year age gap. That shit's fucked up."

"You don't know the definition of fucked up, Knight Ives."

"Whatever."

"Don't whatever me."

"Fuck me," Knives grits. "You're really startin' to piss me off, blondie."

"*Starting?*"

And then, ladies and gentlemen, the Diesel Roses bassist snaps. Because I don't only push Knives's tiny buttons, it's all the huge *do-not-touch* red buzzer buttons I clearly push too.

Knives is storming up to me like the speed of light, all tall and confident with music rippling through his blood. He's a cruel prince with the most charming light eyes, peppered in viciousness. The strides so forceful his hood flies off his head, leaving those short dirty-blond locks to sink down in waves, kissing his faded Led Zeppelin hoodie.

He was *definitely* the little kid who stole cookies from the cookie jar and then blamed the dog for it, all while casually staring up at his parents with smeared choc chip coated lips.

The elevator doors slide shut.

My breaths become one tangled mess.

Knives comes to a halt two breaths away from me, a clench is his jaw so firm and prolonged, he'd win every championship of the kind.

"Listen, blondie. I. Don't. Fucking. Like. You," he grits coldly, lowering his head to meet my gaze. "All the willing women in the world, and Diesel has to choose a fuckin' nut…"

I narrow my gaze at him, unfazed. "Could say the same about his best friend…"

"Classy."

"Thanks."

He simply glares back.

"You really care about him?"

"With all my heart."

"Like cut your arm off for him?"

"Yes."

"Like rus—"

"*Yes*," I cut in, grinding my jaw. "Elijah Diesel is the best thing that's happened to me."

Knives glares some more, and then, just like that, the darkest smirk washes over his soulless expression, and I have to be honest, the sudden mood change rushes chills down my spine. I'm not scared of him. Deep down I know he has to have some level of goodness if he's friends with Elijah, but I just don't like the way he's looking at me. Like my significance is problematic.

"*Well*," Knives scoffs, stepping away from me slightly, but close enough that his woody cedar wood laced in sage aroma lingers. "Then that just means he hasn't told you everything…"

My chest pinches at his words.

What…?

I'm left wide-eyed, staring at the rock bassist, my heart racing a million miles per second.

"What do you mean when you say *everything*?"

"I mean *everything*."

When all I do is stare a little more, Knives sighs and helps himself to the wet bar, his shoulder brushing past my head when he does. Glass slamming against something hard spikes my breaths, and I spin around, swallowing thickly at the scene folding out in front of me.

Knives rampages through the industrial floating shelves and other tucked away walnut cupboards in search of God knows what, but a tall tumbler glass is left astray on the counter.

"Where the fuck is it?" he mutters to himself, clinging expensive glass bottles together until it becomes a symphony of church bells and wind chimes wrapped together in a tight bow.

"Is it possible to know what you're searching for with all that racket?"

"Vodka."

Vodka.

Icy cold water feels like it's being dumped all over me.

I freeze up, my body tense as I stare into the back of his head. "Why the vodka?"

"'Cause I wanna tell you something."

All I can think of is Elijah's and my conversation in the early hours of this morning.

"You won't find it."

"Of course I'll find it. Every bar has vodka. This one's just being a fucker and hiding."

"You *won't* find it, Knives," I say a little sterner, taking small steps closer to him.

"Tell me one good reason why?"

I blow out a breath.

And then...

"I disposed of it early this morning."

One second, Knives is behind the bar. The next, he's right in front of me, brows furrowed. "Why the hell would you do that?"

"I didn't want it triggering Elijah."

He gives me nothing but that clenched jaw, so I explain.

"We were drinking early this morning right here, sharing a joint, and I thought—"

"What do you mean *drinking*?"

Huh?

I look at him all funny. "As in I had a...well, nothing, I didn't end up drinking anything, but I made him a Jack and Coke..."

"A Jack and Coke…" Knives repeats to himself, rushing a hand over his face. "Okay. Is that all he had?"

I shake my head. "I walked in on him drinking whiskey."

"How many glasses?"

"One."

"Are you sure?"

Panicking, I gulp down. "Well, I only saw one. Shit. Should I… have stopped him?"

"Where the fuck is he now?"

"He went out for a run, but he said he'll be back before eleven."

It's silent for a little bit, and I contemplate saying something but don't know what to. For the first time in four years, I'm seeing a glimmer of Knives I've never seen before.

Concern.

It's written all over his face and lodged inside his eyes. He practically breathes it as he begins pacing up and down, threading his fingers through his hair, giving the ends a rough tug.

"FUCK!" Knives shouts, punching the edge of the wet bar counter, only simmering down after he's shut his eyes for what feels like a lifetime, but is probably just a couple seconds.

When he reopens his eyes, they're no more the light eyes I love to hate. Something within them has shifted. I can't put my fingers on them, but they're glassier, lonelier, *fretted.*

"Rosalia," he breathes, uncontrollably shaking his head with a look that tells me it all. *This is not good. At all.* "I'm his accountability. He can't drink without me, and he knows that."

"I only found that out last night. I didn't know there were terms attached."

"Big fucking terms. If he drinks again without me in the room, you have to tell me."

"How? You won't even look me in the eye half the time."

Knives holds out an impatient hand. "Give me your phone."

"Why?"

"It doesn't matter why, just give it."

Do it, Rosalia. It's for Elijah's health.

Anxiously, I walk over to where I dropped my gym bag in the middle of the kitchen and hand him my phone. Knives is quick to type away a few things before giving it back to me.

"I put my number in. Only call me if you see Diesel drinking without my supervision."

My jaw drops.

We're making big moves today...

But I get it. This isn't about Knives and me, or our lack of friendship, it's about *him*.

"So, what? If he drinks again, I just call you? Can I text you instead?"

"You *call* me, and you tell me where you are and what the fuck he's drinking."

"Okay."

"You see him drink vodka, you slap it out of his grip like it's fuckin' venom. Got it?"

I feel my fading heartbeat all over, especially lodged in my chest with all the nervousness. I don't like how intense Knives is looking at me, as if one single drop of vodka could be deadly.

Why didn't Elijah tell me this?

Why do I feel like Knives is hiding something?

"Rosalia, you're scaring me..."

"Yes, I got it. I'll call if I see him drinking again, and as for the vodka, I do just that."

Knives nods, seemingly satisfied with my response. "Does he know you threw out the vodka this morning?"

"No, I had to get up before him for ballet training."

"So, he doesn't know?"

I shake my head, pretty sure I just answered that exact question, but whatever.

Knives steps closer to me, and when he does, his rough fingers slip under my chin, holding my face steady so his callous, pleading eyes are all I see. "Let me tell you something, blondie, just some advice, best friend to *girlfriend*, okay?"

"Okay." I keep my voice low, hoping it conveys to him just how serious I am about this.

"Diesel doesn't like playing games. I think that one is clear. The other thing is, he doesn't like other people in his business. That means people telling him what he should or shouldn't do. He doesn't want you or anybody else for that fact treating him any different just because he struggled a fuck of a lot. The vodka bottle you threw out, right, he won't like it."

Hating that I may have been the catalyst for Elijah's slip-up, I shut my eyes.

Crap.

I didn't mean to cause any drama when I gripped that vodka bottle this morning and had the porter dispose of it. I seriously just wanted to eliminate the penthouse of anything negative for Elijah. I want this place to be his happy, safe space. Vodka hindered that.

"How much has he told you about his *struggles*, Rosalia?"

"I know that he's a recovering alcoholic."

"Anything about his mom?"

"Yes," I whisper, fluttering my eyes open. "He's told me a few things."

"Like?"

"Are you testing me?"

"No, just genuinely want to know what he's told you about her."

"She destroyed him." I clear my throat. "He's told me that she didn't make the best life choices, that she placed him in an abusive home with a stepdad who emotionally tormented him."

"What else?"

"His wish jar. His numbness. He's touched on rehab, but hasn't gotten into detail."

Knives irritably gestures his hand for me to go on. "And?"

That's when it hits me… *There must be something more.*

I raise a skeptical brow, studying him carefully, seeing if he slips. "What do you mean?"

"I mean *what else did he say*?"

"About his past?"

"Yeah."

I part my lips to nothingness. My mind is spiraling, wanting to tell his best friend more, but nothing comes to mind except for the heaviness and cruelty of his stepfather's actions.

Knives keeps on staring at me.

I just keep on staring back.

He just keeps staring.

"What are you alluding to, Knives?" I say after a while, feeling my chest tight, emotion cutting through each breath. "Is there something else? Is there…something I should know?"

Knives's lack of response takes me back to just before he entered the penthouse, where I was questioning myself if there's more to the reasons why Lydia, his publicist, cut ties with Elijah. If it was because of me. If there's something in his past that he's not telling me about.

Shit.

Shit.

Shit.

My father's words from last night echo in my mind, and I hate that they do in a time like this.

He's only showing you what he wants you to see, Rosalia. You watch. There's more shit that hasn't come out yet. I swear to you the skeletons in this man's closet are pure carnage.

Knives lifts my head higher to meet his baby blues when my gaze slips away, dimming. "Just that while it may seem like I'm stopping you from being together, I'm actually trying to protect him. Diesel's been through hell, blondie, *hell*. He ain't out yet. Through all the years, *I* was the one to try and keep him afloat. Not Dave. Not Zander. Not his sister." He violently slams a finger to his chest, stabbing Led Zeppelin right in the forehead. "*Me*. Constantly. Diesel Rose, the entire world, and I cannot afford to have him spiraling into the life he had before."

"But that's just it!" I screech in protest, stepping back so his touch slips. "I'll be here too now to ensure that doesn't happen to him!"

One second…

Two seconds…

Three seconds…

Knives arrogantly scoffs right in my face. "Nah, you don't get it, kid, it's already *starting* to happen again. The publicist breaking ties, all of this other shit that's circling, it's *already starting again*, and it's all *because of you*," he spits, staring me down. "You are going to break this guy, and when you do, every single aspect of life as he knew it will massacre."

There isn't a word in the English dictionary to explain how gut-wrenching his direct words leave me. My breath is burning, and I don't care. I'm not backing down on my scowl because as much as I may have contributed to everything, I'm not being painted the villain.

"Listen here, Knives," I grit, rising on my tippy-toes the highest

I can so that we're eye level. There's a fire brewing in my eyes because of him, a devilish disgust, I just feel it. "I am not responsible for the shit that *may* happen as consequence of falling for a rock star."

"No, but you are responsible for influencing the rise and fall of one."

Our stare off is laced with malice I've never felt before.

Not even when I hated Elijah with all my heart.

"I don't know how you have a girlfriend," I spit.

"Well, neither do fucking I!" Knives growls back in the same breath. "Because River just broke up with me this morning, so there's that!"

Oh.

I can't help the way my eyes widen. "*What?*"

"You heard me. Apparently, I *have no heart.*" He scoffs and shoves past me, just as the private elevator doors ding open and I don't have to turn around to know who it is. *Elijah.*

I don't like the weight trapped on my shoulders at the very thought alone.

I don't like the way my heart feels so trapped when I do turn around, and those gorgeous onyx-grays are already on me.

I don't like the perplexity in his gaze as it skims between me and his best friend, Knives, who storms past him, giving him the cold shoulder.

"What are you doing here, man?"

Knives halts in place, fuming as he turns to my boyfriend to growl, "Oh, I'll tell you what I'm doing here. You have a fucking sip of alcohol without me present again, I'm backing."

My shocked gasp has me bringing a hand to my mouth, unaware he would be so open.

Oh, shit!

Elijah's not going to like this.

At. All.

I don't know what that's supposed to mean, but fumes slowly rush up Elijah's eyes, draining his face completely like he's seen a ghost, and it's all I need to know I stuffed this up.

In his tall frame, Elijah's stiff all over, left staring at the space Knives was, even after his best friend steps inside of the elevator car, disappearing, and it becomes just us.

Elijah's shirtless, his defined six-pack and the wonderland of inky-colored tattoos glistening with sweat from running. His black workout shorts stick to his toned thighs, the perfect amount of muscle carving them. I can't stop staring at his dark, wavy hair, buried under a baseball cap he has on backward. The ends of his hair are a little lighter because of the sun, and I really like just how long it's getting, the pure mix of fated rock star meets gorgeous biker.

That's when those melancholic grays suddenly pierce my gaze and skittered heartbeat.

Let me save you, Lijah.

Let me be your cure instead.

The icky feeling inside intensifies when Elijah does nothing but stare at me, as if he already knows what the conversation between Knives and me was about... *Him.*

In any other circumstances, I would rush up to him, slip off the backward baseball cap, and kiss him hello with a reminder of last night, but it's not the time for that right now.

It's just silence.

So much silence.

And I hate it so much.

"Baby," Elijah breathes, and for a second I'm flooded with hope. "You told him about the drinking last night?"

Boom.

And there it is. The shoe dropping.

The disappointment in his voice is like no other.

"No, it just kind of happened."

Stepping closer to me, his familiar musky cologne centers me. Elijah gestures beyond me. "What's this mess?"

"Knives was looking for..." I swallow the lump in my throat. "The vodka."

"*Fuck.*" Roaming a hand across his chin scruff over his beautifully defined jaw, his body tenses even more. "Did he... Did he mention why?"

When I don't reply...

Trepidation.

"What did he say, Rosalia?"

"In the end, nothing," I lie. "Knives just said he wanted to tell me something, but then couldn't find the vodka. I had a porter take it away this morning, so he didn't tell me anything."

"Okay, okay…" Elijah jogs backward, so obvious his mind isn't here with me right now. It's spiraling between a world of us. "Okay. I've got to go talk to him. I'll be back soon."

"Elijah?"

He stops in motion, turning back to me. "Yeah?"

I may be a fool for the sad smile that etches across my lips, but I can't help it because that would just mean I'm a fool for wanting Elijah more than I do my next breath.

"Did I do something wrong?"

Through the tension, Elijah gives me a slow, sexy smile. I feel like the luckiest and also, the craziest girl in the world when he strides up to me in his tall frame, cups my face, and plants the dreamiest kiss on my lips. It's fast. Soft. Like kissing sugary clouds. *Barely enough.*

"You didn't do a thing, babygirl," he promises with a sigh, slowly pecking my lips once more. "But throwing the vodka away won't stop me from reaching, so just don't do it again."

"Noted."

"I've gotta go."

The moment the elevator doors open and he's gone, I slump against the wet bar counter, my suspicions confirmed amid his troubling kisses still tingling my bruised lips.

Maybe my father is right…

Elijah Diesel's hiding something from the world.

Hiding something from his hardcore rock fans.

And…from me.

Chapter

FORTY

Rosalia

That night, during Diesel Rose's first Portland concert on the *Killing Me Slowly* tour, Naomi was quick to reassure me that all thoughts regarding Elijah hiding something were just in my head.

We FaceTimed in Elijah's dressing room for what was supposed to be only five minutes, but it almost ended up exceeding the entire concert. I hated that I was missing him perform, but I really needed to talk to my best friend. Truth was, I was really beginning to miss her, and even though it hasn't even been an entire week since I joined the tour, we've never been away from each other for this long.

We do everything together. *Everything.* We're literally so close that we voice message each other even if she's at our brownstone and I'm driving home from work to said brownstone.

It's why I really needed to hear her perspective on all of this. Dissect her mind.

Elijah never came back to the penthouse after walking out to talk to Knives. I showered and waited like a fool until lunch, but after pacing up and down the hotel like a loner, I said *fuck it* and spent a few hours doing some sightseeing across Portland. Just some of their iconic scenic parks, vibrant stores, and quaint little cafés.

Basically, I did anything to distract myself from my endless thoughts of Elijah.

That ended when I noticed I was being followed a few times, catching a few paparazzi circling around, asking me questions about Elijah, that infamous on-stage kiss, and my intentions. I did exactly what my foster parents always taught me to do. I smiled and ignored.

But that didn't stop the paparazzi.

Ugh.

That night, during the hour and a half that I spoke to Naomi, we came up to the conclusion that Knives is just super protective of Elijah. They've been in this band together since they were sixteen, literally almost twenty years ago, and he just doesn't want to see him crumble at their peak. It's only natural, and I, in a way, need to respect that.

Whatever Elijah is keeping, he'll tell me when he's ready. He just needs time. I need to trust that because I trust him enough to respect his boundaries. Maybe this is just one of them.

From experience, I know trust isn't always easy. Especially after traumatic experiences. There's a lot of growth that comes with it, a lot of scary steps, and Elijah's just never taken the dive with anybody else before. Sharing his truth and letting someone in is all new.

Just like it is for me.

I get it now.

Speaking out loud to Naomi definitely helped. I made it just in time to watch the last half hour of Diesel Rose's performance from the side stage, and it doesn't matter how many times I've heard the songs. They're electrifying.

Elijah caught my eyes a few times during "Fragments of You". He didn't call me out to join me that night, and neither did Dave, but in my own little way, I felt like I was right there with them as my fingers continuously skimmed over the grooves and silver detailing of the vintage snake ring he gave me.

I sang every single lyric, through every single breath, in time with him.

The screaming fans. The buzzing atmosphere. The gorgeous music all blending into one from Elijah's heavenly vocals to the perfect riffs of both guitars, to the rhythmic drums. *There's nowhere else I wanted to be than watching those four men and their dreams come true.*

After the show, the guys headed to this bar/club to meet up with Dave's friends from Portland. Elijah was so sweet in the way he asked me three times if I was sure I wanted to tag along with him. He suggested we could do something else like catch a movie or go on our own little date night, exploring the city, but I told him I was happy to join because *I was.*

Elijah didn't slip his hand out of mine all night. We didn't talk about his crisis meeting earlier on in the day, or the incident with Knives, or the fact that Elijah disappeared off the grid after that, we just simply lived life and enjoyed the night.

He couldn't stop glaring every single guy down who glanced my way, possessively wrapping his arms around my waist on the dance floor (yes, I managed to force him to dance with me), and practically growled, *fuck off*, at every guy who attempted to buy me a drink.

There were women who were eyeing him too.

Those who flirted and filmed him with the guys all night.

Ones much older than me with dresses much shorter than mine.

Elijah didn't notice them. At. All. His gaze was glued on mine all night as we grinded our sweaty bodies on the dance floor, made out in dark corners while music boomed off the walls, and he whispered in my ear just how much he missed seeing me on the side stage when I was on the FaceTime with Naomi.

Neither of us drank anything. Knives kept on showing up everywhere because of that. They didn't utter a single word to each other, and I knew that didn't signal anything good, but I decided to ignore it. I already had a big enough of a showdown with his best friend that morning. Anything else wasn't something I wanted to be a part of. Not so soon into both the tour and our relationship.

It was just after 2:00 a.m. when Elijah and I slipped into our penthouse hotel's bedsheets. He tenderly held me close with his warm lips lingering on my forehead.

His wildly beating heart pressed up against mine.

So intimate.

So sensual.

So raw.

We held on to each other like that all night, not saying a single word, but just having his warmth wrapped around me as my ears buzzed from both the concert and the club was enough.

I could have stayed like that forever, especially when he whispered so softly it hurt. "I know today was heavy, babygirl, but tomorrow will be better. I promise. I just need some time."

And Elijah was right.

It did get better.

The following day was Friday, a rest day for Diesel Rose, and Elijah surprised me from the moment I woke up.

Scattered rose petals laced the entire penthouse. Onyx and cherry brandy salmon-pink. The same kind he had sent to my dressing room during my Swan Lake season. The ones I said I adored.

Elijah seemed almost timid when I jumped on him and kissed him a million *thank you*s.

I don't think he's used to people thanking him, but I want to change all of that.

His bashfulness at times is definitely something I have to get used to.

The tension of the day melted away and in its place was him being present with me and never letting a smile go to waste. I knew Elijah must have been stressed regarding his current publicist crisis and everything to do with Knives, but he didn't show it. Not one bit.

For breakfast, we went to this cute Parisian inspired café and Elijah ordered chocolate croissants for us in French. *Gahhh*, it was unreal.

Later, Elijah surprised me with a Harley ride. *Yes*, a loudly purring, gorgeous metal monster. It was a sleek onyx Harley Davidson Dyna with chrome detailing waiting right outside of the hotel. Security had blocked off the area, causing cars to take detours and fans to be moved back. He wanted it to be simply us as he took my hand and slipped on a helmet for me.

Then Elijah gave me the prettiest pink leather jacket with white stitched roses and **Rose** written on the back in silver studs.

Breathtaking.

When Elijah turned around, his own infamous black studded leather jacket with the safety pins and cut down the left sleeve had a new alteration on the back. In the same silver studded letters as mine, was written **Diesel**.

Rose.

Diesel.

Diesel Rose.

If my stomach wasn't already flooded with butterflies, it would have been then.

The five-hour motorcycle ride to dreamy Crater Lake was beyond spectacular with the distant frosted mountaintops, scenic tall forest trees lining each side, and bending highways that mimicked slithering snakes.

I couldn't stop squeezing my hands around Elijah's waist tighter, squealing in happiness whenever he revved the Harley faster, the thundery wind tangling through my hair and slapping against my new leather jacket.

His tan leather gloved hand moved to my thighs a few times during the breathtaking ride, and I loved teasing him by grazing my fingers a little lower down his waist, rushing under the thin fabric of his blowing white T-shirt to feel his hot defined stomach.

I could practically *hear* Elijah roll his eyes once we passed *Trent*, Oregon, and started riding down Highway 58. I couldn't stop laughing about it because it could only happen to us.

At one point, my fingers trailed lower, popping the button of his jeans and sinking lower, thrills rushing down my spine at his erotically trimmed happy trail. It led down the center of his V-cut muscles. My hands slipped lower to his hardening cock, stretching in his dark blue jeans.

"What do you think you're doing, little girl?" Elijah called over the Harley's constant rumbling, and I could hear the smirk in his voice. "You wanna kill us both?"

"Maybe." I remember grinning into the crook of his neck, kissing it softly with my visor flicked up.

Elijah took the next bend in the road smoothly, but because I wasn't concentrating on the road and didn't see it, I tensed my hands around him. But because my hands were *right on his cock, it* was what I softly squeezed to secure myself on the Harley.

Elijah groaned so loudly it cut through his helmet and the wind. But I couldn't care less what the passing trucks, cars, and other fellow riders thought. I just wanted my baby happy, sans liquor.

"I think you want to die today, *Peaches.*"

"With you, yes."

It's safe to say I redid his button and wrapped my arms back around his waist after that.

Crater Lake was beyond anything I've ever seen before. Long stretches of mossy-green forest. Crystal blue lakes and rivers. Closer frosted mountaintops. *Magical.* It's how every moment felt.

Elijah stopped the Harley, and we hiked the Oregon landmark a little, hand in hand, and when I found the perfect spot between cedar trees, I snapped a photo of Elijah and me together. Me, grinning like a psycho, and him, his lips on my neck, smoldering at my phone all mysteriously gorgeous.

My heart warmed when Elijah pulled out his own phone, wanting to also take a picture. He held his phone out, the crystal-clear lake and mountains our backdrop. We took photo after photo, and eventually, they just became a collage of us kissing.

I loved every minute of our hike, how we talked about so much. We spoke about classic literature, his love of collecting metal and performing some handiworks to make bracelets and charms. I even finally confessed to him about how I used to fill scrapbooks, and how I cut him out of that *Rolling Stone* magazine all those years ago.

Elijah was so amused about it, telling me when we were back in Manhattan, I had to show him. Pretty sure my cheeks burned so bright after that, especially when he slapped my ass.

We didn't go into the heavier, deeper topics. It just wasn't the day. Besides, we were kinda avoiding those sensitive topics after the previous day.

When we reached a breathtaking observation point, Elijah suggested we should let go of all our pent-up thoughts. On a count of three, we screamed out into the lake, our shouts echoing back, releasing all our built-up frustration.

And then, one look at each other and we burst out laughing.

It helped so much to ease all our tension.

I instantly felt better. Relaxed. Myself again.

I was a giddy mess after that, all flirty and happy off the high of spending quality time with Elijah.

Which brings me to right now. It's Saturday morning, a week since I flew out of Manhattan to be with him, and we're almost finished an intense training session together at the hotel gym. Yes, *together.* We

both needed to train today, him before his show and me for work, so
we made it a little date. We've been doing that a lot lately. Going on
nice, spontaneous dates.

I did a little bit of Elijah's boxing routine and high intensity inter-
vals; he did a little bit of my barre, pilates, and conditioning techniques.
Now we're both just sweaty messes, hours away from his concert, and
I'm not gonna lie, I'm feeling very, *very* turned on with him here.

There's just something about hearing his soft grunts and heated
breaths during weightlifting and intense intervals that floods my sex
with butterflies.

*Plus, his thin black workout shorts have shriveled up so much be-
cause of the sweat that they look like briefs, and I just can't stop staring.
Swear to God I can see his piercing's outline.*

Almost finished with my training, I'm in one of the gym's glass
private rooms, revisiting my current ballet workout routine, my pointe
shoes smooth against the oak.

And Elijah hasn't stopped watching me dance...

He's sitting down, shirtless body all glistening as he leans against one
of the mirrored walls, so tall his head grazes the attached wooden bar.

Elijah's dark gaze is hot and wolfish, the kind of stare that electrifies my body one beat at a time, oozing dark poetry out of me. I
know rock music fuels his every breath, caging him in lyrical bliss,
but right now, it's like I'm his only means of surviving.

He's my gorgeous, lucid dream wrapped in darkness, a little death,
and the devil's cry. A figment of the villain in all those twisted fantasies, and my very own tall, edgy killer, sparing my soul.

In this moment, if our life were a mixtape, it would be a rendition
of Frankie Valli's "Can't Take My eyes off of You", and "Satisfaction"
by The Rolling Stones. Also, the Tchaikovsky currently playing off
my phone.

Elijah sprays some water into his mouth from the bottle, droplets gliding down his washboard abs because he's not concentrating
on drinking straight.

"You okay there?" I laugh, in the middle of a fouetté.

I love the sexy, twisted smirk that rolls up his lips. "Hardly."

The classic Tchaikovsky intensifies and so do my fluid ballet movement, seamless as I work around the floor, my gaze leveled with my
own in the mirror, yet they always seem to find his. The crescendo

builds and endless pirouettes guide my next move, over and over again, flawlessly, loving the way it fuels my body with a passionate fire.

Ballet is the only thing that when I'm doing it, I don't want to do anything else.

I finish with a grand jete, smoothly propelling myself into the air, extending my legs into a full mid-air split before gracefully meeting the floor in a steady finish, grinning.

Nailed it!

Elijah smirks, awe sparkling in his pretty eyes. "You impress me more and more every day, *Peaches.*"

Aww!

"I could say the same about you too, Mr. *Sells-Out-Shows-In-One-Second*-Rock-Star."

I don't even have time to do any stretching or conditioning before his hands are all over me, caressing my body and whispering in my ear how much of a good girl I am for being so daring.

"I think I could watch you dance like that all day, Rosalia. All. Fucking. Day."

"Well, luckily it's my job."

Elijah seductively grins down at me, those beautiful dimples sinking into his cheeks and crowfeet all deep and sexy. "It's your job to wear these tiny little booty shorts and drive me crazy while other male dancers watch you, touch your body, dance with you?"

I can't hide my grin. "Dance is a physical sport, Elijah."

He doesn't like that, at all. But I don't care. His sexy growl and the rough spank on my ass are worth it. "How the fuck am I going to deal with other men touching you on stage, hmm?"

"See it as ammunition for when you fuck me at night."

The air crackles between us.

"You mean…" His smirk darkens. "Get off on the fact other men get to hold you?"

"Yeah, that's exactly what I mean," I whisper. Biting my lower lip, I look at him through my thick lashes. "And you can be as rough as you like with me because I like that…"

"*Fuck.* Yeah, baby."

"And imagine it as you watch me in the auditorium."

Elijah trails his thumb across my lips, still a little bruised from when he sexily bit me after seeing I'd hid his love bites. I don't hide them anymore, which has gotten attention from his bandmates, but I couldn't care less.

I almost *want* to cover them up with concealer again so that Elijah can have his way with me again because I really like when he does that. It's just something about a dominant, older man who knows exactly what to do that drives me wild.

Elijah cups the back of my head so viciously a breath escapes my lips as he looks at me hungrily, as if he could devour me right here in the gym, his cock hard as steel against me.

"My girl does the prettiest splits. Nobody else should see that but me," he rasps, driving me crazy. "I wanna fuck all the jealousy out, baby, take it out on you until you're screaming."

"You and your dirty mouth…"

Just as his lips are about to crash on mine, deafening knocking has us pulling apart prematurely. We simultaneously snap our heads toward the private room's glass door, frustrated at our interruption…

Dave.

With a yoga mat in his hand… No, wait, no, *three!*

Shit. Shit. Shit.

Yeah, I can do basic math, and *ohhh no!*

By the look in his eyes and that cunning smirk, Dave knows *exactly* what he's interrupting when he barges through the door when I swear Elijah locked it.

Without words, Dave ties up his luscious hair into a high bun, the ends sticking out a bit, looking all rugged. Then he throws the three yoga mats down, clearly wanting us to join.

Elijah and I, still flustered, lock eyes and he groans every single curse word in the French and English dictionaries combined.

It actually has me laughing a little. Okay, *a lot.*

And if looks could kill…well, Diesel Rose's drummer would be very much dead.

A little before his radio interview, Elijah rented out the Harley again, and while it means we don't have Maverick or any kind of security with us, it also means *freedom* in the best way.

Zipping through the Portland lively streets at the back of a motorbike my rocker boyfriend's riding, it's heaven. I'm grinning against his shoulders, screaming as he goes faster.

The feeling only intensifies when he slows the Harley in front of a quaint antique bookstore with emerald-green detailing, reminding me of Hayes's bookstore back home. My jaw drops the moment we step inside. It's *stunning*, with vintage hot air balloons drawn all over the ceiling and fairy lights cascading down the walls.

Elijah and I walk in sync with the classic literature section. There are two full aisles of it, so I take the left and he takes the right, the bookshelf dividing us. But the more we slowly walk through the aisle, the more patches of my melancholic rocker's leather cuts through the few gaps in the shelf from missing books.

He crouches down and we stare at each other. Intensely. Slowing with every single gap until we come to a halt in the middle of Hardy and Hemingway.

Elijah's eyes are glazed over in sorrow when he outstretches his hand, scattered in his ink-colored Roman numeral, skull, and serpent tattoos.

I can't stop staring at the serpent. When we were hiking Crater Lake yesterday, Elijah told me he's always had a thing for snakes. His first pet at eighteen was a silky white and tangerine-colored python. He said it was like therapy for him, an escape.

When I told him I'm the year of the snake, his eyes lit up in glee and widened so big, I almost cried. But I didn't because it would have been embarrassing. He just looked so happy.

It's all I can think about now as my warm fingers trail up his smooth skin, outlining the detailed serpent tattoo, a gasp rushing out of me when Elijah suddenly threads his fingers through mine. He holds on to me tight, like a silent prayer, a pledge from the clouds above.

I'm sorry, Elijah's eyes beg. *I truly am.*

When our fingers do slip away, we meet at the end of the aisle, his hands finding mine again. Elijah doesn't care that there are people watching us. He simply holds me close and whispers against my lips with a tender frown, "Forgive me, *Peaches*."

I want to ask him why, but the sadness pooling in his eyes explains everything.

"Babygirl." Elijah sighs, the breath tugging at my heartstrings. "I know that it may not seem like it, but I want you to know I'm not hiding anything. Knives is, well, he's just a little…"

I fill in the blank. "Protective?"

He slowly nods, lowering his forehead to brush against mine. "Yes. *Protective.*"

I like when he does that. It's only a small little gesture, but it means the world and has my heart swirling nonstop. Affection was never Elijah's thing, but slowly, slowly, I feel him getting more comfortable with me like this.

"I'm not the most clean-cut guy in the world. I'm not the perfect guy, so I hide myself in music. And, well, you know I've been through a few…*struggles* in my life, if you will, yeah?"

"Yeah."

"Big fucking struggles that have the ability to change a man, yeah?"

With a sad smile, I nod. "I know."

"Then you can imagine the shit I've been through ain't pretty, baby," Elijah whispers lowly, his hands finding my face and cupping it so gently, the world's about to melt. "You want to know the honest truth?"

"With all my heart."

Fleeting seconds pass between us.

It's faint jazzy music, the soft chatters inside of the bookstore, and the whoosh of rushing cars outside on the street. All that noise, and yet all I can concentrate on is my rapid heartbeats and *us.*

Elijah said he needed time the night everything went to shit, and right now is that time.

Swallowing thickly, his solemn eyes softly study mine. "Rehab didn't help me, at all…it's made it worse."

My heart feels as if it's been plunged into the Atlantic, aching so deeply for him.

I can't help but cup his dark, stubbled jaw, can't help but frown against his lips and murmur, "I'm so sorry, Lijah."

"It's not your fault, Rosa. There's nothing for you to be sorry for."

"It…didn't help you?"

"No, not one bit. It's made all the monsters in my head grow wilder. The darkness intensifies. I was an alcoholic, yes, but I came out of rehab feeling even more like a psychopath than I was before."

"You're not a psychopath, Lijah."

He gives me a half-smile, not convinced. "I wrote you something, something that I… I just can't say in words. Writing is my escapism, and as I told you once, for a lyricist, I'm pretty shit at getting my feelings out. I need to write them down. That's when they truly blossom."

Elijah gives me three folded sheets of paper from his leather jacket ever so causally in the middle of this bookstore. Our fingers brush, and all I feel are sparks as I scan the beautifully cursive handwriting I could spot out in a lineup.

Looking up at him, my eyes are already a glassy mess. "Wow, Elijah, what's this?"

"A glance inside my mind. Everything I'm currently feeling. The words I should've said the day Knives stormed away from you because I should've stayed with you instead."

My smile is a reflection of my scattered heart. "You're here now."

That bashful smile of his returns.

And then, I read his words that are laced in slammed poetry…

Peaches,

I don't know where to fucking start, so let me start at the beginning. Well, kinda. There's a lot about my childhood and growing up that I'll probably never speak out loud. It's not because I don't want to tell you, because fuck, I do, but I've never told anybody before.

I'm scared to tell people. I'm scared to say it myself. So, for my own sanity, I keep it in.

All you need to know is that my mother was an alcoholic.

My grandmother was an alcoholic.

My stepfather was an alcoholic.

Yeah, Peaches, I had a brother, and he was just like me. That's why he died. Young.

So, you could say that it's laced my blood since the day I was born. That I got my practice early. That I knew, deep down, one day I would become a fragment of them...

And I became just that.

Or, perhaps...I'm worse.

As you know, my birthday is on Halloween, October 31, but the most ironic thing about this all is that my life is the freakiest, scariest, most fucked-up journey you'll ever read about. I spent my birthdays wishing I could disappear. When I was a kid, on my birthday, I used to run around the neighborhood as dusk fell with a bedsheet over my head, wishing I could be the ghost. Wishing I could just have one friend to run away with. Wishing that every and anything I did could emulate the feeling of numbness and not being alive.

I was a sad kid, Peaches.

Even sadder teenager.

Growing up, I used liquor, joints, and sex to cure me. If I were another man, I wouldn't have told you the latter antidote—sex—but I'm not like other men. I'm worse. If I'm going to be honest, if I'm going to break down my walls to fucking foolproof this relationship, then I need to be raw.

Aside from music, I've been addicted to a lot of things.

Cigarettes.

Vodka.

Sex.

Cigarettes after sex.

Vodka with cigarette.

Sex during vodka binges.

Then I met this green-eyed girl and I got addicted to something else...you.

Music saves me, yes, but you ask any fated musician and they'll tell you the same thing. Music only helps fill the void, so then when it's taken away, all that remains is space.

Empty space.

And it gets lonely.

It gets harder to breathe.

In fact, the more you think you can finally breathe on your own, without the ventilation of your fans, the more you begin to suffocate. It's called the Baader-Meinhof effect. When you think of something so constantly that your awareness of it increases, and it actually leads you to believe it's actually happening. Even if it isn't. Mind games, baby, full-blooded lies the brain feeds the rest of your body, just so you can die a little more inside.

I used to believe I was dying.

That I was caught up in a dream.

Then slowly, both those things started coming true.

I was an alcoholic before I met you, before you were even born. But something about gazing into those cherry viper eyes four years ago made me breathe you in instead. You became my kryptonite, but when I felt it coming back on—the need for numbness because I felt too much—I had to let the cherry go. So, I spent four years in hell, caged to my own precarious, troubled mind. It's been a wildfire in my heart, baby, something I don't like.

Knives was there through it all. He was the only person to keep me afloat. Since I was sixteen, this motherfucker's been keeping me afloat. That's twenty years, well, almost.

I would have died without him, babygirl, died.

I wouldn't be.

Writing this.

With you.

It's why he's so guarded when it comes to me. He may seem like he hates the entire world, but he really doesn't. I know because he constantly saves me.

I've never spoken to you about this not because I didn't want you to know these deeper parts of me, but because I know it's a lot. I never wanted to fit into the cliché, of being that liquor addicted rock star, but I am, and I'm not proud of it, but all I can do is get better.

And I am.

Getting better.

But there are people who think me being with you will destroy it. Like you're the match and I'm just here, waiting to be lit. (Okay, that part sounded better in my head). But what I mean to say is, they think I'll relapse because of us. That if something were to happen, I'll go back to how I was.

But they don't know the way my heart sped up when you got on stage with me.

They don't know the way we laugh, the way we fuck, and read classics is a remedy.

They don't fucking know that every single day with you, I'm trying. I'm trying to block out the bad, feed into the good, and that's all you need to think about, my sweet girl.

I'm trying to save myself.

Please let me.

I know you have your traumas too, your beautiful battle scars. All I want to do is save you, but I know from experience that sometimes it can be unattainable to change somebody's view. You can influence. You can help. But ultimately, one needs to be their own healer.

My mind's a fucked-up place, baby, and I know yours is too, so let's be crazy together.

Save yourself, Peaches, save yourself from the dark.

And I promise, I'll save myself, too.

Your possessive psycho,

Elijah

Oh my God.

This is everything and more.

Glassy tears coat my eyes as I look up into his beautiful on-yx-grays. Jumping into the solace of his arms, I'm certain Elijah Diesel will forever be engraved in my melting heart.

"You…you had a brother?"

He nods, defeated.

"Oh my God, Elijah, what happened? Can I ask that?"

"Overdosed at seventeen. I had just turned nine… I was the one who found him."

Eyes wide, I slap a hand over my mouth. "Shit."

"Yeah, *shit*." Elijah leans into me with a sigh. "That's when I turned to my song book."

"And that's when your parents forced you into therapy, right?"

"Well, more partially my biological father, but yes, that's right."

My heart hurts for him.

Everything hurts.

"Thank you for telling me your truth, Elijah." I sniffle, the hot tears finally spilling out, rolling down my cheek. "You deserve so much more. I hope you know that."

"Whenever I'm with you, *Peaches*, I feel it deep in my core that I do."

Silence, and then…

"Lijah, baby," I whisper by his lips, smiling through the ache. "You're my best crazy."

And by the way Elijah kisses me back, so tenderly erotic, I know he feels the same.

Which is truly everything I ever need.

Chapter

FORTY-ONE

Rosalia

O^{h.} *My.*
God.

Elijah just told the world on live radio that I—*Rosalia Philips*—am his girlfriend.

I REPEAT: The gorgeous rocker who claims he doesn't feel anything, actually *does*.

I haven't stopped smiling.

Or happily crying out.

Or both in unison.

Somebody pinch me!

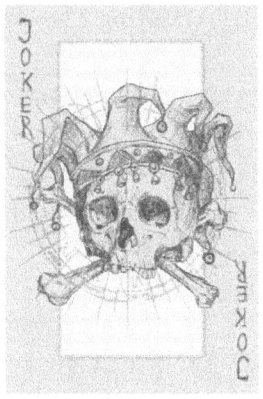

Chapter
FORTY-TWO

Elijah

It's easy to feel my heart defrost from the depths of the Antarctic every second I'm with Rosalia Philips. Never in my life did I think I would have admitted those words, but I am, *right now*, I'm telling you I'm feeling this intense tug in my chest every time I look at her and…

I don't know what to do with that feeling.

I've never *felt* before Rosalia.

This is my brave new world.

And I have to admit…

I'm scared.

Real fucking scared.

Scared I'll do something that'll make her run.

Something unforgivable that we won't recover from.

Something that'll shatter four years laced with her, and only her.

I know I can't think like that. That I need to think of the bright side. Vivid rainbows, pot of gold, and all that shit, but I wasn't made like that. I grew up on the rough side of life, and yes, although my father may have been privileged enough to pay for my childhood therapy bills, he didn't stay. When it got too much, he upped and left. Days after my brother's suicide.

Then things got even rougher, and that's when my asshole of a stepfather came in.

So, life hasn't been kind to me. Not at all. Not even a little bit. But now I have Rosalia, my muse, my *Peaches*, and suddenly, for the first time in my life, life is beautiful.

So fucking beautiful.

Because of her.

It probably explains why I wanna give her the entire world, you know, just—*probably*. It also explains why earlier on today I was lighting tealight candles, spreading them around the free-standing tub with gold vintage detailing, like I didn't see this on Pinterest.

Side note: Stop smirking at me, you stirrer, I didn't ACTUALLY go on Pinterest…

It just so happened that after fucking my girl into heaven last night, she was scrolling through her Pinterest because she wanted to show me a few pins that she had saved four years ago about imagining touring with Diesel Rose one day. I kissed the cuteness out of her and kept my eye on one of the Pinterest boards she scrolled a little too fast over.

But I saw it.

I got supersonic vision like that.

I know, be jealous, I would too.

The Pinterest board was titled **RECOVERY,** and I couldn't tell you what kind of things were in there, only that the thumbnail picture was of a fancy bathtub with scattered candles all over the ground and a record player close by.

I don't know what it meant. Any of it. But *fuck*, how I wanted to figure it out. The moment I opened my eyes this morning, I figured it out. The bathtub must have been representative of her trauma. When Rosalia tried to… *God*. When she tried to *hurt* herself, she was in the bathtub.

I know that she's told me she takes Epsom baths and all that to help with muscle recovery for ballet, but I remember her saying she only soaks her legs and feet, never being able to slip her entire body inside. It's too close to home. *Too close to the rippling darkness.*

And while I would never force her into it, I want to be the one to help her heal.

I want to be right fucking beside her.

Beside her as she sinks her body in.

And I was.

When Rosalia saw what I had set up, alongside the record player that I sneaked out to purchase because I wanted to make the moment special, there were tears in her eyes as she held me tight. Happy tears. She couldn't believe I had done all of it for her, and quite frankly, neither could I.

I was stupid enough to forget to buy a vinyl record, but luckily my tour manager saved my ass and handed me one of the Diesel Rose's limited-edition vinyls she always brings on tour as a little sentiment. Rosalia was in awe that Diesel Rose has vinyls. My girl loves vinyls. I told her it was hers. She thought I was joking, but I wasn't. I had it for her. Signed my name on the cover, right by my face, letting the sharpie marker settle for a second before adding a little love heart, because, well, as I said, my heart's fuckin' melting around this blond angel.

Rosalia didn't want to get in the bathtub. I could see it in her eyes, even though she didn't say a word. I had made it all pretty too with those girly little bath bombs and shit. I don't know what the hell I put in there, but it smelled like sweet cherries and the warm, bubbled water was a swirling pit of lighter and darker shades of pink.

"Feel whatever you're feeling, baby," I told her against her lips, unable to resist kissing her slowly, desperately longing to be everything she needed. "But just know I'm *here*. With *you*."

Rosalia took one look at me, her eyes a glassy wonderland, and then another at the bathtub. She was biting her lower lip, fastening her breaths, squeezing my hands tight.

I remember thinking to myself, *Come on, baby, I'm right here. You're safe. I promise.*

But I didn't say any of it to her because I know how trauma works. It's not easy. Not in the slightest. There isn't one quick solution. There isn't a one pill fix all. There aren't miracles. And that's the hardest thing to deal with, I think.

With grief.

With trauma.

With depression.

That at the end of the day, there's nothing to console you from the darkness. There's nothing but holding onto the pieces of your life *before* and wondering how the hell you're gonna create an *after*. Does *an after* even exist? *Does it?* And if it were to, is it even worth it?

Those questions equal sleepless nights.

Those questions haunt minds.

Those questions kill.

It's all I kept thinking as those striking green wonderlands gazed up at me, fingers threading through the wavy ends of my hair and the bravest smile pulling up her plump lips when she whispered, "You really want to help me through it?"

"No place I'd rather be, *Peaches*."

I remember the exact moment Rosalia's eyes sparkled, and I knew why.

I had never, ever, mentioned my heart *before in a single conversation.*

We took off each other's clothes at a rate that wasn't the vigorous one that comes before sex. It was so much slower, sensual, and dare I say—what I'd imagine making love to be like.

I held her hand as we stepped into the bathtub (that wasn't made for a six-three guy).

I was there with her, our gazes locked, as the warm water glistened on her skin, skimming over her flat stomach before sinking deeper, the beautiful pink shades of rouge and ballet slippers coating over her ample breasts and pebbled nipples. Over her shoulders and pretty collarbones. Over the junction of her neck, seeping up her throat. And then...

Rosalia panicked, rushing up so violently some water splattered out as she stood up in the tub, trembling, water dripping down like she was coated in tupelo honey. I could have easily mistaken the tears rushin' down her cheeks as bath water, but I didn't because *I. Know. Her.*

"I ca-can't do this," I remember her croaking out, covering up her body with her hands around her waist in a bid to stop the trembling. "I can't be in he-here and, I-I... I just ca-can't."

I stood up in the bathtub, pulled her into me, and whispered into her moistened hair, "I want you to know you're the strongest woman I've ever known. Always remember that, baby."

I meant it.

"But what if I panic again? What if it manifests into a panic attach?"

"Then I'll be right here. With you. Helping you through it. Whenever you need me, little girl, I'm here. The nightcrawler doesn't need to be nearing for you to call out my name."

And then, as even more tears flooded her eyes, we sank back into the water together, therapeutically, until it was coating almost every inch of our skin, the sweet cherry aroma lacing the air between us and being the catalyst to the way we kissed so slow. Tenderly.

I was so proud of my girl. So proud that she faced her fears that I remember kissing all of her bittersweet faded scars. Every single one. Until we were both a beautiful mess.

I told her that she's beautiful.

So fuckin' beautiful, and brave, and strong.

And that her life has meaning because she's the only one I adore.

With her in my arms in the bathtub, I asked her about her darkness, and she asked me about mine.

She told me that the flowery scissor tattoo she has a little below her cleavage is a representation of when she first stood up for herself in front of a school bully who teased her and ripped her Barbie's head off when she was little.

I told her how growing up, I was surrounded by alcoholism, how my only way of surviving it was not existing. But since I couldn't do that, I tried to hide from it. But then my stepfather changed that. He called me a punk for being so weak, for hiding, for running.

She told me that therapy helped her work through some of her issues and understand she wasn't the reason for the murder suicide, but the visions remain.

I told her I couldn't get the vision of finding my older brother— Edmond—dead either, but that unlike her, I blamed myself for not saving him, for not running away with him instead.

Rosalia kissed me sadly and told me I was only nine, that none of it was my fault.

I held tighter in my solace, telling her she was only five when her parents died.

Only fifteen when she tried to kill herself for the very first time, in a bathtub.

Only seventeen when she cut herself for the very last time.

Only twenty-one when she found the guy who saves her.

Age doesn't matter. The people you have around at that age matters.

But now I have her, and she has me, and *that's all that really matters.*

That is all I can think about as I look at Rosalia now, minutes from shooting up from below stage and performing at our very last Portland concert for this tour. How the fuck did I get so lucky with her? To score the most beautiful angel that understands the crazy tour life and all the hell that comes with dating a musician, especially a rock musician.

We're straight up crazy motherfuckers.

"I have something I want to give you!" Rosalia grins, sorting through her huge leather bag with white threaded roses as the stage crew around me work to ensure my earpiece is in and that I'm connected and ready to go.

Rosalia groans, almost as if she can't find what she's intending to as she pulls out everything from that bag. And when I mean *everything*, I mean *everything*.

Kindle.

Toothpaste.

Polaroid camera.

Shit, is that a set of playing cards?

I shoot her a *what-the-hell* look at the capsicum spray. "What's that for? Hurting me?"

She gives me that beautiful Cheshire smirk. "If you piss me off, yessiree. So, shut up."

Finally, after NASA sends three space shuttles to Mars and the Leaning Tour of Pisa straightens up, Rosalia pulls out a slightly short but wide gift wrapped up in soft apricot-colored tissue paper and a neat black velvet bow. And wait for it...*there are peaches on the tissue paper.*

That shit has me smiling. "What's this?"

Grinning, my girlfriend happily hands it over. "For you. I made you a little something to say just how proud I am of everything you've achieved in these years. It's also a thank you for putting up with me. But most of all, a dedication to you. Soooo, open it! Come on!"

I can't but simply stare at Rosalia for a couple moments, completely in awe.

She made something for me.

Nobody has ever done that before.

With my gaze locked on hers, I softly unwrap the tissue paper, and the second my fingertips smooth over cold glass, I already know what it is. *Oh my...* My heart is racing, doing a million miles per hour as I continue unwrapping it until...

Wow.

My jaw drops. "Baby, fuck me..."

It's...

Fuck, it's a...

Shit. Why am I getting all choked up?

I can't fucking breathe straight as I stare down at the wish jar. It's gorgeous and the perfect rendition of us with the peach-colored tinged glass and black folded notes inside of it.

It's a different kind of wish jar. She already wrote all of her wishes for me down inside.

Oh my God.

Rosalia Philips made me a wish jar, just like the one I was forced to leave behind as a kid. The one I was always so sentimental about. The one that laced me in nostalgia.

Now, this wish jar is laced with her.

I can't feel my heart anymore.

Nobody has ever done something this special for me.

I'm so taken aback, I don't even know what to say to Rosalia as I flicker my gaze up at her gorgeousness. But by the way she wraps her arms around me and buries her head into my chest, I already know I don't need to say anything at all. She's the emotion in my eyes, that swirling emotion that's making everything so goddamn blurry, bringing tears to my eyes.

"Thank you, baby," I manage to whisper, my voice a broken mess as I kiss her forehead.

Rosalia fondly smiles up at me, tears in her own eyes when she outstretches a hand to softly caress my spikey beard. "You don't need to thank me, Lijah, at all. *Remember?*"

I nod, her sweet words a rendition of the ones I said to her when she thanked me for buying the plane ticket to LA. Now, Rosalia just said them back to me, becoming full circle, making me wish I had never lost the four years in between our very own *before* and the *after*.

"Wish number one, Elijah Diesel, *to always know you're worth this thing we call life.*"

The devil ain't makin' it easy on me tonight.

Tonight's last concert in Portland was epic. I even had Rosalia come out on stage with me again when I got to "Fragments of You". I don't know, there's just something about it…I like singing it to her with thousands of fans watching on, filming it, getting more viral each show.

Even though, in reality, all of Diesel Rose's songs are derived from her being my muse.

Every. Single. One.

But that was hours ago, and now, we're at Ledger Evans's luxurious Portland mansion. If you rockers don't know who Ledger Evans is, he's *the* most iconic rock stars to ever exist.

Well, aside from me of course.

His heavy metal rock band—*Devil's Advocate and The Fiery Halos*—is the one that gave Diesel Rose a big break four years ago, allowing us to be their opening act of their world tour, fast-tracking the mark we have in the global rock 'n' roll world today.

Since we're all good professional friends, Ledger invited Diesel Rose to the wild early Halloween party he's hosting tonight (Sunday night). I'm not gonna lie, I kinda liked the idea and Rosalia instantly squealed out a couple's Halloween costume. *Yep, you heard that right, a couple's costume.* But I wanted it too because she was just so happy to be going out with me.

So now, we're here, dressed as *The Joker* and *Harley Quinn* (the *Suicide Squad* version), surrounded by blaring music, sex, the illicitness of liquor and drugs, and other dressed up creatures of the night.

We're looking sexy as fuck right now embodying the King and Queen of Gotham City. Because in some ways, our relationship is exactly like theirs. Complex. Twisted. Intense.

This isn't a *house Halloween party* for the super-rich. It's a fucking

Halloween rave with blue laser lights and a famed DJ prepared up on the elevated glass stage Ledger has in this multi-million-dollar mansion.

Devils. Angels. Skeletons. Freaks. You name it, and they surround us everywhere.

The lights are low, and some people have colorful glow-in-the-dark pink, yellow, and orange neon paint swirled and detailed across their faces and bodies. There were literal fire eating acrobats greeting us as we walked up the marble grand staircase to enter this mansion.

Zander didn't come because he's Skyping with his fiancée and little girl, Lola, back home. As for Dave and Knives…well, they're in here somewhere among the eight hundred people… *Knives is probably glaring everybody down, ready to call it a night after his breakup.*

But right now, the only thing in my mind is my babygirl.

Rosalia is radiating so many good vibes as we grind our bodies together on the dance floor (which is basically any inch of this ten-thousand-square-foot mansion). Inspired by Harley Quinn's costume, she has a red and white **DADDY'S LIL MONSTER** fitted crop top on, the V-neck so scooped that her perky cleavage is on full display, alongside part of that beautiful tattoo.

Rosalia wears those half-red, half-blue leather booty shorts so well. They glimmer in the soft light against the gold studded belt. The black fishnet stockings she has on underneath make me so crazy, alongside those iconic heels. I drew all of Harley's tattoos across her body, as she did Jared Leto's Joker on mine. To add to the look, Rosalia has a spiked cuff bracelet and instead of a **PUDDIN** choker, a **DIESEL** choker in thick gold letters. *I like chokers too much.*

Fuck, I want to devour her dressed like this.

From the second we walked up the grand marble staircase, I've been glaring down guys staring at my girl. And right now, as Rosalia continues grinding herself against my left thigh, her alternating black and red painted nails roaming up my ribbed unbuttoned crisp white dress shirt and silver chains, I feel the heat of her sex riding the fabric of my black Armani slacks.

Mimicking Joker, my hair is slicked back, coated in green hairspray. Gold rings. Scary fuckin' stare. I've got the devil in my gaze with my dark, smokey eyes. I don't know what's more erotic about my entire look, the fact that Rosalia seductively rolled ruby red lipstick on my lips to match Joker's, or the fact she hotly put my gold rings on my fingers with her teeth.

My gorgeous devil knows exactly what she's doing, looking up at me seductively with those smokey eyes and biting her lower lip. *Fuck, I wanna suck on those red lips, or let her suck something else of mine instead...* Her silky blonde hair is slicked back in two high pigtails, one hair sprayed pink, the other lilac in bouncy waves, only a few blonde stands framing her face. Her hairstyle exposes her ear piercings...helix, mid-helix, and triple lobe.

I *love* them.

I love how we can be so in sync with each other.

I love how every single one of my piercings matches hers.

I love how they've ironically matched since the day we met.

Tattoos, piercings, and dark, kinky sex. That's the kinda couple we are.

And I fuckin' love it.

"*Peaches*," I whisper in Rosalia's ear because of the blasting house music, a groan escaping me the longer our glistening bodies dance together. "Are you gonna play with my mind like this all night, little one?"

"Maybe."

"Don't say maybe." I smirk, bringing my arms around her waist to push her closer to me by that peachy ass of hers. "Tell me we can get outta here and back to our hotel room so I can fuck you like you deserve."

With a wicked smirk, Rosalia shakes her head. "Nope, I want to stay here."

"I can set up a rave in our hotel room."

"Shut up, baby." She laughs. "And *suck* it up."

"I'll show you *sucking*..."

It's been two hours.

Two.

And I've resisted the urge to pull her into a dark corner and have my way with her the past times, but it's too much, fuckin' me up. Her hard nipples poke the cotton, her infamous nipple piercing so damn evident as she's sans bra.

I reach for her hand, adamant to get the fuck out of here and somewhere a little less crowded because I wanna get freaky, when

Rosalia gasps. It prompts me to glance over at her, perplexed. She's frozen in place, her eyes wide at something beyond us.

"Oh my God, I freaking know that girl…"

I follow her stare, but there are literally hundreds of women, everywhere. "Which one?"

"That one… *There*." Rosalia points toward a familiar woman not too far away dressed as *Carrie*. She's with a group of men, a champagne glass in hand. "Her name is Portia."

"What? As in Ledger's Portia?"

"No, as in Portia Evans. She's a *Corps de ballet* ballerina at my work… Hates my guts."

I shake my head, making her understand. "Baby, I'm telling you that's Ledger's sister."

"No fucking way…" Rosalia's jaw drops as she stares at me. "That's *Ledger's sister*?"

"Yeah, she's… oh shit."

"What?"

"Don't look now, but she just glanced my way… She's walking over."

Rosalia's fretted eyes widen even deeper. "Are you serious? Why? Do you know her?"

"Only through Ledger. She sometimes joined the tour a couple times when we opened for Ledger's band."

Rosalia wants to say something when Portia comes to a halt right next to us, completely ignoring her colleague, her desperate eyes on me. My girlfriend glares at the back of her head.

A small smirk curves up my lips.

Well, well, well… Is somebody jealous?

Because there's no reason to be. At all.

"Hey there, Diesel! *Wow*, you're an epic Joker! Scary as hell!" Portia grins, rushing up to press a kiss on my cheek before I can even blink. "My brother said you might make it, but I didn't think you'd actually come."

"Oh, why's that?"

"You're not really one for parties…as I remember."

"Well…" I pull a fuming Rosalia pressed against my side, grip her waist, and softly caress my thumb over the smooth leather and stud belt. "My girl wanted to come and check out the extent of the parties *the* Ledger Evans throws, and I've gotta make my girl happy, you know."

Rosalia freezes up in my hold the second Portia's gaze flickers to her, darkening as cold as ice. And yet, the woman exchanges the fakest smile, pearly white displayed and all.

"It's a *pleasure* seeing you, Portia," Rosalia sneers through gritted teeth.

"I could say the exact same thing. I see you're making the headlines... I'm sure Madame Eléa would *love* that."

"Oh, and why's that? I haven't broken any rules or contracts."

"Not *yet.*"

"I'm not doing anything wrong, Portia, I'm simply *in love.*"

"*In love,*" Portia mimics, her eyes not so subtly moving back to me, roaming down my body, slowing by my cock as Rosalia grinds her fine ass to the music. "I'm sure that's the case..."

"Trust me, it *is,*" my girlfriend snaps, her hands coming around to wrap around my neck when she turns to me and seductively whispers with a zest of revenge, "Isn't that right, *amore?*"

Before I can say a word, Rosalia attaches her soft lips to mine and *damn*, if this isn't the most dominantly possessive kiss from her. She mauls me fast, having me cup the back of her head. I spear my fingers through her pigtails, roughly yanking them because I want this too. *Jesus, fuckkk.*

We're both groaning, our bodies rubbing together to the music's beats, all while her tongue grows wild with mine, swirling together at an intensity that blows my mind.

Rosalia's in control of every little second and I let her be. I let her take out her jealousy on me. Let her fingers crawl through my slicked hair, tugging on the ends. Let her cherry flavor taste consume me in ways that have my already hard cock pulsing and twitching in my slacks.

The same slacks she rushes a hand over, palming my erection with a firm grip. Rosalia must feel the twitches because she moans mid-kiss, devouring me more hungrily. I lose myself in pleasure at the way she's stroking my cock over my slacks, in front of all these people, not giving a damn. The heat crawling across my skin is unreal. *She's* unreal.

We pull back, panting, sharing a tale-telling smirk. I'm in such a haze, completely starstruck as she whips Portia's lipstick off my cheek with her thumb, and in its place, presses her lips against the exact same spot. Rosalia sexily claims me with her hot, red lipstick.

Fuck, that was so aggressive. And horny. *Possessive.*

Portia's jaw hits the ground, jealousy licking his eyes as she looks between us, stunned.

"*See?*" Rosalia is sporting a cocky grin, while I can't stop smirking at my girl, kissing and nipping her shoulder, silently praising her.

"Well, Diesel, umm…" Portia clears her throat, unable to speak straight. "I wanted to say that I'll be in Seattle tomorrow too, visiting a friend. If you're free, we should catch up."

I don't even reply. I'm so lost in those dazzling, envious green eyes that I stare at so long, eventually I feel Portia storm away in my peripheral vision.

"Little girl," I taunt against my angel's lips, my smirk never too far. "You're *jealous.*"

"I'm not jealous."

"*Liar.*" My smirk deepens. "Jealous. Envious. Invidious. There's no need to be."

And then I kiss her until she's barely breathing, proving I meant every. Single. Word.

Little did I know, her wicked game has just begun…

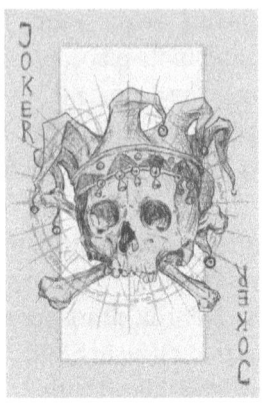

Chapter

FORTY-THREE

Elijah

Wish #2: To be the Joker to my Harley...

There she went again, rubbing a hand against my slacks over my aching cock, letting me suffer in torment as she bubbled with jealously. I know she did. It was evident in just how badly she wanted me. How desperately she palmed my dripping crown. How quickly those piercing green eyes darkened when I pulled away from her lips, menacing me.

I love this.

I love this little game of jealousy.

Because I plan to ruin her with it.

"You want me to fuck the jealously outta you?" I growl hotly. "Because I will, baby, and it won't be pretty. I'll fuck the sense right back into you, do it right in this very mansion."

Rosalia playfully rolls her eyes, yet that sexy smirk crawls up her lips as she says, "So you wouldn't be jealous if I were to just go up and randomly dance with somebody else?"

"No. Not a single bit."

Fuck, yes, I would, but two can play at this game.

Before I can even register what's happening, she's grinning, walking away backward in the crowded mansion. Just like that, she falls into this zombie doctor who looks like the definition of a player. And Rosalia plays on that. Taunts me with it.

I see red when the doctor slips his hands on Rosalia's hips, grinning into her neck as they grind together to the music, her heated gaze on mine the entire time.

What the fuck is she trying to do to me?

My Harley Quinn allows his daring touches, giggling at something he whispers in her ear and doing all this shit on purpose just to prove a point. What the point she's trying to prove is, I don't fucking know, but it's working.

I'm half pissed off that she's grinding her ass on some stranger's dick, allowing him to grope her and kiss her neck, all while her heated eyes remain on me. Then, the other part of me is fucking turned on for some reason because I know just how much I'm going to punish my girl.

I want to kill this guy. I want to fucking burn him into ash.

Rosalia's taunting me slowly, rushing a hand down her body as she sways it to the beat. But the second her fingers graze the edge of her **Daddy's Lil Monster** crop top, and she seductively bites her lip at me, I know this is going to be trouble.

What is she going to…*oh God.*

Rosalia slowly pulls her top up higher, glancing around before cheekily flashing me her beautiful, naturally perky tits. They're swollen, aching to be touched, her nipples so dark and pebbled as she pushes her tits together, her thumbs erotically flickering over her sweet nubs.

Holy fuck…

Rosalia's looking at me so sultry, squeezing her tits, that I just want to wrap those sexy fucking pink and teal pigtails around my hands and have my way with her.

That diamond nipple piercing…

Clenching my jaw, my breath thickens from the way she's exposing herself in front of all these people. It's so fucking erotic. So taboo. *So unlike the girl who has a freaking bunny waiting for her back home.*

My cock is aching in the constraints of my boxer briefs, jolting by itself. It has me losing control, aggressively palming it with a growl. Rosalia gasps at my racy movements on top of my slacks over my crown, causing pre-cum to sexily glide down my shaft, coating it with need.

Yeah, babygirl, two can play at the game.

But when zombie doctor cups my girlfriend's tits, anger floods my blood.

Fuck this.

That's it.

Show's fucking over.

Fuming, I stride up to them, shoving the asshole away from my girl and then, viciously pulling down Rosalia's top. Aggressively taking her hand in mine, I don't care how hard I'm holding it when I turn to the asshole doctor.

"Get the fuck way! You're fucking lucky you're not leaving here on a stretcher!"

I don't even wait for his reaction because anger-fueled lust has me striding away, dragging Rosalia with me. She can't stop giggling, flirting, grinning, taunting my clenched jaw and tense shoulders. She thinks this is funny. *Oh, I'll fucking show you funny, baby.*

Show her good.

I'm pushing us past people, slamming shoulders, and stepping on feet because my priority is much more important than human decency right now. And it shows as I quickly rush us down corridors and the dancing crowds, all while Rosalia asks me where we're going.

I don't tell her where. In fact, I don't say a single word until we reach a luxurious bathroom filled with gray marble and gold veins, the aroma of vanilla bourbon lacing the air. The second I slam the goddamn door shut, I'm pinning Rosalia against it, my hips rocking against her body. I let her feel just how hard she's made me, all while roughly wrapping my fingers around her neck, softly choking her in the way she likes.

"What. The. *Fuck.* Was. That. Little. Girl?" I growl, my jaw locked as I tilt my head to the side. "Wanted to make me jealous? Hmmm? Thought grinding against another man's cock while I stood there bearing witness would turn me on? Well, did you?"

Rosalia's lips part to nothingness, her cheeks flustered from the dancing and intensity of her actions. All she does is smile back, like the sweet and innocent woman she *isn't*.

What a little devil…

"Guess what, *Peaches*?"

Rosalia sexily bites her lower lip. "What?"

"We're not leaving this bathroom until I punish that peachy ass of yours and you're crying like the little girl that you are," I hiss, sucking in a heated breath and tightening my grip around her neck. "Do you understand?"

And when I say tight, *I mean fucking* tight.

"Elijah!" She gasps, not expecting it, her eyes widening a fraction, and yet, there's desire in her eyes. A fiery spark. "That's too… that's too much."

I'm so pissed off I don't let go.

"*Do you understand*, Rosalia?"

She frantically nods, the blush tinge in her cheeks deepening to a darker red.

"Use your words."

"Yes, Elijah."

"Good girl." I smile darkly, releasing her throat, and before she can say anything else, I recklessly rip her top in half with a growl. The cotton falls apart like a cardigan, spilling out her beautiful creamy tits with a slight bounce. "That's what you get for acting like a smart-ass."

"Oh my God, Lijah!"

"Take it off."

Flustered, Rosalia lets the scrap of cotton hit the marble floor. She looks at me as if I'm crazy, and yet with the devil in her eye. "Are you…are you going to give me your shirt when we get outta here?"

Mmmm.

"Babygirl." I chuckle devilishly, shaking my head. "What do you take me as?" I click my tongue. "A *gentleman*?"

And that, ladies and gents, is when Rosalia Philips decides to drive me even more wild by flashing me her iconic seductive, dirty grin. "Oh my God. Look at you! You're so jealous."

"No, I'm not."

"*So* jealous," she whispers, gripping my unbuttoned dress shirt and pulling me close. "You think I'm just going to run away with some random guy? *Never.* Of course I wouldn't. I don't want them. I just did it to prove a point. To show you that you're just as jealous as me. You enjoyed it. Admit it."

My cock twitches at her words.

I need to show her exactly what she's done to me.

The air crackles between us.

Everything gets more intense...*real.*

It's just us, muffled music, and rowdy chatter.

My heart beating furiously as I study her slowly, taking in her beauty, those plump lips.

"*Ma chérie,*" I softly growl, my smirk a devilish nightmare. "Get. On. Your. Knees."

Flustered, Rosalia blinks several times, her lips parting to a soft gape. "*What?*"

"You heard me."

Her eyes widen when she realizes I'm serious. "But...what if somebody walks in?"

My smirk darkens. "Yeah, what *if* somebody *does see,* hmm?"

Heated silence with infused sparks.

It's all that trickles between us...

Heat.

Sparks.

Heat.

Sparks.

Heat.

"Elijah, you mean you wouldn't lock the door? You'd just let them walk in on us?"

"And let them see you on your knees filled with my cock?" My lips seductively trail up her neck, blowing hot air on her skin. "*Yes,*" I whisper in her ear. "Yes, baby, I would, any day of the goddamn week."

"God, you get so freaky!" Rosalia gasps, but she's grinning soon enough. "I love it."

"Told you I was Joker obsessed, baby..." My gaze darkens. "On. Your. Knees. *Now.*"

My beautiful Harley Quinn submits, her lustful eyes remaining on me as she drops to her knees, sitting back on her heels, hands resting on her fishnet stocking thighs in anticipation.

Swallowing thickly, I cup her jaw, taking in her beauty, slowly running my thumb over her beautiful red, heart-shaped lips that are gonna be all smeared soon anyway. *'Cause of me.*

Rosalia's looking at me so intensely, and I can see just how badly she's craving me.

"You've gotta understand one thing, little one," I whisper. "The chances of me fucking you after this are high. The chances of me getting lost in you and fucking you so roughly I forget you were still a virgin just weeks ago are higher. If at any moment I get too much, tell me to *stop.*"

"Okay."

"Even if you're enjoying it, but I'm pushing your limits, you tell me. You got that?"

She softly nods. "Yeah."

"If your mouth happens to be *filled* at the time, tap me anywhere three times."

"Anywhere?"

"*Anywhere*, babygirl," I whisper, cupping my achingly hard cock. "Except *here.*"

Rosalia grins, her smile lines cutting through. "Why not your dick?"

"Because I'll only take it as an invitation to do whatever I may be doing harder."

"*Oh.*"

"Yeah, real fuckin' unfortunate, huh?" I find myself chuckling, but it all fades to frenzied desire when I unbuckle my belt with my eyes locked on her. "Remember what I said."

My leather belt drops against the dark marble floor with a slap, matching my heartbeat.

Rosalia's softly biting her lower lip, looking up at me through her thick, onyx lashes.

Dear God.

I can't wait to punish her for being so fuckin' bad.

Popping my button, I pull down the zipper of my black Armani slacks so torturously slow that the sound echoes around the bathroom, making it the only thing I hear. *Mmhmmm.* Stopping unzipping myself halfway, I motion to my cock. "Come and do the rest, baby."

Rosalia's fingers are inches from my zipper when I bat her hand away.

"With your teeth."

Seductively leaning forward, her pebbled nipples graze my thighs as she catches the zipper slider with her teeth and tugs it down, her viper green eyes never leaving mine. She's being such a good girl that I let her slip off my slacks, and then my boxer briefs too, letting them pool by my feet. My hard, big cock springs out, the crown already coated in pre-cum, my silver piercing glistening.

"Hands behind your back, *Peaches*, you don't get to touch me until I tell you to."

Rosalia watches on in awe as I fist my thick length, groans escaping me with every smooth, tight motion up and down my cock. My reddened crown is aching for her tongue, to be sucked off by her, so much so that more heat licks my spine, arousal rushing through me.

My free hand wraps around her chin as I bring my cock close, but not close enough that her lips brush it. "Open that pretty mouth for me, baby, then show me that tongue."

Rosalia parts her lips and automatically darts her tongue out, wide. It's so close that I can feel its heat inches away from where I need her most.

"Good. Stay like that for me, just like that. *Mmhmmm*."

Focusing on my cock head, I vigorously fist it in my palm, my breaths all erratic as I work myself hard until I achieve what I want. A pearl-sized drop of pre-cum pools on my slit before erotically dripping off my cock and ever so slowly, straight onto her glistening tongue.

Rosalia moans, her green eyes hooding when another two drops of my pre-cum lace over the first. I pull back, jerking my cock faster while she swallows down the salty, clear liquid.

"*Fuck*," I exhale. That was one of the hottest exchanges we've done. "You like that?"

"So much. I want more."

If it were up to me, I could come right now with the way she's on her knees for me, but I want to hold on a little longer. This is punishment after all. *Her* punishment for grinding up against another guy who wasn't me and letting him feel up her tits in the name of damn jealousy.

"Hands on my cock, baby."

I hiss at the spark Rosalia's touch brings as she works me with two hands, remembering just how I love to be jerked. Tough. Rough.

Hard into hell. She's working me so fast, her tongue gliding up and down my slit, playing with my cock piercing with every single move.

Ohhh fuck.

If my cock wasn't aching before, it's downright aching now as she fucks me with two hands, eager and grinning against my cock. But it's not enough. Her punishment is imminent. I love the way she reads my mind as she takes my cock into her mouth a little, sucking hard on my pierced head, her tongue fucking paradise, while simultaneously jacking my pulsing length.

"Good, such a good fucking girl." My hips begin to rock against her hot assault on my cock, diving in her deeper so she takes some of my length too now. "Relax that throat. *Good.*"

"*Mmhmmm.*"

With the devil in my lungs, without warning, I pull out and her tongue swirls over my head as I let her get used to the girth of just my crown again before I thrust my cock deeper into her pretty mouth with a groan. Desire urges me on, rippling through me like a damn curse.

Still jacking off my length, Rosalia's eyes meet mine, pleading me to keep going.

I do.

But I'm not even halfway inside before I feel her being to panic, closing up her mouth and trying to pull back from me. Instead of letting her go, I halt. "Breathe, baby, I've got you."

Rosalia nods the best she can but stops jerking me, so I frantically wrap a hand around hers, gliding us together up and down my length. "Keep fucking me like this as you suck me."

Oh, that's better.

Dear God. She's going to kill me.

After a few moments, I pull all the way out again, growing wild with the way some red lipstick is already smeared on my cock. *I need to fuck her damn throat right now.* My fingers tangle through her pink and teal pigtails, tugging on them hard, and just as Rosalia cries out, I recklessly thrust my pierced cock into her mouth so fast and deep, my piercing slams against the back of her throat.

Godddd.

I continuously rock my hips, and it glides my piercing around.

Rosalia makes a sound around my cock, her eyes all frantic and wide, glimmering with tears while her nails dig into my thighs in panic, not expecting my intensity. She's spluttering and gagging around me, yet she doesn't tap me three times to urge me to stop. She takes me.

I pause, allowing her hysterical breaths to calm.

"That's it, that's a good fucking girl. Stretch that throat for me. Yes, *yes*, so good, baby."

I viciously thrust my cock deeper, feeling myself fill not only her mouth but also down her entire throat, suffocating her breath. Her lips meet the base of my cock, taking me so well, and I have to let go of her teal ponytail to wrap my hand around her neck, under her **Diesel** choker, feeling the outline of my cock.

"Fuck, baby, if only you could feel this," I pant.

My moans become louder than the blasting music. My cock is burning with desire, knowing it means so much she trusts me like this. I face fuck her rougher, pulling her hair tight and closer to me, so she's trapped against me, taking every single inch of me. The feel of my cock bopping up and down her throat bringing me to a whole other level of fucking turned on.

"Fuck." I throw my head back, shutting my eyes with a gaped mouth. "*Fuck. Fuck.*"

Fueled with the need to ruin her, I watch on as the first tear slips down Rosalia's cheek from just how badly she's gagging around me. Her throat begins to tighten and just like that, she pushes away my unbuttoned dress shirt and slaps my toned abs three times.

I don't pull out all the way, just enough to return back to only hitting the back of her throat, half of my cock outside of her. Tears stain her cheeks, her mascara all smeared as she begins to fist the bottom half of my cock, all while sucking me inside her mouth so well.

"Breathe, baby, *breathe*," I instruct. "You know I'd never hurt you." I smile down at her, wiping away the tears, loving the way the tips of her lips rush up when I do. "It isn't my cock gagging you, it's your mind. You've got to win it over with your breaths, okay?"

My Harley Quinn does the best she can to nod with my pulsing cock in her mouth.

This is my fucking ecstasy.

Rosalia shuts her eyes, moaning against me now as she continues working my cock, her tongue rubbing against my cock as she jerks me harder, bringing me closer to the edge. My entire body is coated in perspiration, eager. Her sucks and slurps making me feel even dirtier.

My fingers tangle through her pink and teal pigtails, tugging on them tightly so she has nowhere else to go but suffocate on my cock.

Her red lipstick is even more all smeared around my cock, and I pull her hair tighter when I notice she's rocking her pussy against her heels, trying to satisfy just how turned on she's feeling. She immediately stops, making a sound around my cock like a fucking angel choir as I continue fucking her mouth, slamming my cock in and out of her at an uncanny velocity.

Our moans mix together louder, my chest heaving as her sounds vibrate around my cock, even more so when she cups my balls, ever so softly massaging them in a way that has me rewarding her mouth with more of my cock. We're back to that wild fucking, my cock all the way down her throat, pounding into it at an intensity that has her hands rushing to play with her tits, all while my balls tense up, telling me just how close I am so coming undone.

Rosalia allows me to use her just like I want, teaching her a lesson for allowing another man to touch her. I love just how relentless my hips work, how my ass tenses with every thrust, the way my pulsing cock disappears between her heart-shaped lips at an even faster rate.

"Next time you let another man touch your tits like that…" I threaten with a hot smirk, fucking her so hard she leans back against Ledger Evan's bathroom door. It has me cupping her reddening face as she sucks my dick between thrusts with her head pressed up against the door.

Ohhhh God.

Fuck. I'm gonna come.

"The next time you do that," I growl, trying to find my breath, "I'm going to fuck your throat in front of him exactly like this. Gonna fuck you in front of everybody, understood?"

Rosalia moans in response, those moans turning to pleasure screams the harder I get.

There's a knock on the door, but we continue going. There's a second knock.

I slam my fist against it. "OCCUPIED!"

Like a devil in lust, our groans collide, my mind everywhere as

Rosalia Philips brings me closer to ecstasy. Her hands return to my balls, urging me on, letting people outside hear.

"Such a bad fucking girl."

Rosalia gags on my dick again, but I give her recovery time, fucking her throat deeper, to selfishly chase my own orgasm. "God, look at you letting me use your throat like this. Bet you can feel my piercing colliding against you. Bet it feels so good. Look at you sucking a rock star's dick like you were born for it. Were you born for it, *Peaches*?"

A loud moan escapes my lips and when Rosalia squeezes my balls, I lose control. I'm seconds away as I groan out her name amid pants, pulling out slightly so I'm back in her mouth. I'm pulsing in her mouth. *So close.* Balls tightening, I fist her pigtails the tightest I ever have as waves of pleasure ripple through me, over and over and over, and then, *fuckkkk.*

"OHHH GOD," I scream out, my body tensing, orgasming so strongly I can barely remain standing. "Fuck me, babygirl. *FUCK. ME.*"

I feel like I'm falling from heaven, right into hell as I explode hard, ropes of my hot cum rushing down her throat to the point where my white cum drips down the sides of her full mouth, overflowing.

So.

Fucking.

Erotic.

Rosalia's eye makeup is all smeared and ruined, joy in her eyes as I pull out of her a little, so her lips are wrapped around my pierced head, pulsing in her mouth.

"Take me, baby. Ruin me. Fuck me. Taste me."

She swallows all my cum, grinning widely with a hum when she does. I continue to orgasm as she jerks me off more, long cumshots spraying all over her face and bare tits, but mostly on her widening, white-coated tongue.

I'll remember this forever, my Harley Quinn.

She milks me clean, collecting every single drop of my intense orgasm, and I can't stop moaning, adoring her cum-coated lips and the way she sucks my cock dry, the vibrations going right through me. As my orgasm settles, I let go of her hair, pick her up, and slam her against the bathroom door. She instantly wraps her legs around my waist, and there're desperate knocks on the door, but I ignore them, hitting the lock.

Rosalia sexily grips my stubbled jaw, guiding my mouth open with a smile. She's so flustered and ruined from the way I was fucking her so intently, her hair all pulled, but she doesn't care. *She wants more. And I'll always give my baby more.*

My hands rush to her ass, spanking it before massaging it good as I rush out my tongue for her. Rosalia smirks as she parts her plump lips, my thick, creamy orgasm slipping from her mouth to my tongue. It's the hottest thing I've experienced as she whispers, "*Baciami ora.*"

Kiss me now.

Italian.

Oh baby, baby.

I kiss my muse breathlessly, so fucking filthy and frantically, both of our tongues dancing with my orgasm. So salty but goddamn kinky. I have never, in my life, felt more alive.

The taste on my tongue has me squeezing her ass again, and as we pull away, I whisper, "You took me so well, baby. I'm so proud of you. Wish you could see yourself like I saw you. Now, baby, you have three seconds to get those shorts and panties off and bend over that double vanity before I do it myself. I'm taking your peachy ass here in Ledger Evans's bathroom."

Rosalia grins up at me, her entire face and throat a scarlet wonderland.

"I'm not wearing any panties, Lijah."

My jaw drops. *Don't have to tell me twice.*

A mere second later, we're in front of the luxury double vanity, and her eyes widen a fraction as she takes a first glance at herself after sucking my cock and me face fucking her.

Her swollen lips.

Her lipstick everywhere.

Her hair, a hot mess because of me.

Rosalia glances back at me, a giddiness in her soft laugh as she brushes her fingers over her mouth. "You weren't lying about the whole being really tough thing."

I smirk, catching an eye of myself and noticing the red lipstick I wore for Joker is now all smeared too. Some of the fake tattoos have sweated off, but my iconic green hair remains slicked back, looking scarier than ever. I slip off my shirt, my slacks locking my ankles.

Pinning her against the vanity, I wrap my hand around her petite waist, softly kissing her shoulder. "Unlock the door, baby."

Rosalia does and when she returns, I'm quick to bend her over the vanity, my fingers inches from her zipper slider, which is at the back of her booty shorts, when she has me pausing.

"I have a surprise for you..." she trails off, grinning at me through the mirror, her nipples kissing the marble counter, tits all pressed up while her hands are spread out on it.

I arch a brow. "A *surprise*?"

"Mmhmmm."

"Where?"

"You'll see it soon enough."

Slowly unzipping Rosalia's red and blue tight leather booty shorts, her gorgeous ass spills out, covered in her fishnet stockings, but when she bends over further...*holy shit.*

I stop breathing at the pink diamond plug between her ass cheeks. The rose-pink glimmers up at me like a goddamn masterpiece. I can't stop staring at it, caressing it, and then, when my astonished eyes meet hers in the mirror, my cock pulses, hard again. *All because of her.*

"Happy early birthday, Elijah." Rosalia bites her lip, grinning. "Do...you like it?"

"I *love* it."

Slipping off her booty shorts, I rip her fishnet stockings, leaning down and kissing every single inch of her ass, leaving the Joker's red lipstick marks as I do. Rosalia's pussy is dripping, and I give it love, dropping to my knees and swirling my tongue down it, sucking her glistening clit, my face submerged in her sweetness. Her hums and moans drown out the outside music.

When my muse quivers, I stand back up, my wet lips attacking her neck in a million kisses, unable to stop touching her as my cock piercing clangs against her diamond butt plug.

"Every day with you is a dream, Rosalia Philips," I breathe. "Please never forget that."

I don't just mean the sex.

I mean our healing.

Happiness.

Everything in between.

And the way my muse is looking at me, with a sparkle in her eye that consumes me, I want to give her the world. I *wish* I could give her the world. Because I'm so addicted to her.

Rosalia tells me she doesn't want to use a condom, that she wants me to fill her raw, and so I listen, using her dripping arousal as lube to coat my cock. With one last glance at just how gorgeous my baby looks with this pink diamond plug inside her peachy ass, getting ready for me, I give us what we both crave. A loud pant escapes her when I slip the plug out, her stretched ass quivering when in its place, I slowly rock my sensitive, glistenin' cock inside her.

It's full of grunts and groans as I break past her tightness, only managing to slip half of myself in, but that's fucking good enough as I grip her hips and plow into her. I start off slowly, urging us both on, my heart going frantic because she's got my cock in a chokehold. So tight.

"Oh God," Rosalia whispers, squeezing her eyes shut. "Faster. Please. I need more."

It's all I need to let loose, gripping her pigtails and fucking her ass hard, just like the little monster she is. *Daddy's little monster,* just like her crop top said…*before I ripped it.*

We fuck like animals, screaming and panting and grinning into the fancy vanity mirror as Ledger Evan's early Halloween party grows wild around us.

Harley Quinn and the Joker.

Harley Quinn and the fuckin' Joker are all I see, even though both of our costumes (besides the fishnets) are scattered over the floor of a luxury bathroom that doesn't belong to either of us.

It's careless. Reckless. And goddamn erotic the more I ruin her ass, one thrust at a time.

Our skin slaps together, echoing wild as she meets my pumps. Rosalia's so beautiful, all flustered and smiling through the bittersweet pain, slipping farther up the vanity each time. She doesn't once tell me to stop, she doesn't lose our gaze, she's an angel giving me all of her.

My hand comes around her waist, fingering her just as intensely as our thrusts, the double penetration her undoing. And as we simultaneously reach euphoria, moaning, she gushes around my fingers and her pretty ass clenches around me, quivering, and it offsets my second orgasm of the night.

Rosalia tells me not to pull out, so I don't, my warm, thick orgasm shooting wild inside her instead. It has us continuing passionately thrusting in rhythm, filling her ass deep with me. And the second we're falling down from our highs, we're both panting, completely sated. She's sprawled across the marble vanity, completely spent, while I pull out and *what a fuckin' sight.*

My warm cum overflows her tightness, causing most of it to ooze out of her throbbing ass, so fuckin' erotically slow I can do nothing else but stare. Rosalia moans into the countertop, pressing her thighs together, feeling the exact moment more of my orgasm drips down her pink pussy, coating it with my white orgasm.

"I could look at you all day, Princess, your beautiful ass all filled with me like this."

I know she's not on the pill because of a reaction she had during ballet years ago and we're not exactly ready for the slightest possibility, so I collect my cum with my fingers before it sinks deeper in her and spread it over her ass instead. It glosses over the red lipstick marks I placed on her peachy ass before we fucked, which are now all smudged because of our pace.

When Rosalia turns around and wraps her hands around my neck, gazing up at me like I'm worth it, I want to do nothing but hold on to her forever. I really fuckin' do. It's all I think about as my hands slip around her waist, pulling her closer to me as I kiss the hell outta her.

We pull back softly panting, smiling with Eskimo kisses. *I like that it's our thing.*

The intensity that we stepped into Ledger Evans's luxury bathroom in masks itself into the most sensual type of intimacy. Everything is much calmer now. Slower. And yet my heart is still wildly racing, palpitating, because I feel Rosalia Philips is changing me. *For the better.*

"By the way," I murmur by her lips. "You're wearing my shirt when we step out."

Rosalia seems so astonished, her green doe eyes twinkling with adoration. "Really?"

I nod. "I'd give you anything, *Peaches*, anything at all to see you this happy with me."

Chapter
FORTY-FOUR

Rosalia

Wish #3: To never forget I'll be here for you, forever, whenever you shall need it...

I'm falling deeper and deeper in love with Elijah Diesel every day, if that's even possible.

There's just something about watching Elijah in his natural element, finishing up rehearsals for his sell-out concerts with a vintage microphone, a simple gray hoodie on with the hood up, and that gorgeous, boyish smile whenever he glances my way that feels so natural.

He's a high-status rock icon.

One of the most influential lyricists since Bruce Springsteen and Keith Richards.

Millions of rock 'n' roll fanatics from all over the world worship him and Diesel Rose.

And yet, he's all mine for the taking.

The thought alone has me grinning widely as I snap pictures of my beautiful man with Zander, Knives, and Dave during their early afternoon rehearsals, even though it's their rest day. This morning, the five of us hung out together, riding Harleys up along the 101 Highway along the coast in Oregon. Newport Beach was our destination and we made it just as the sunrise was warming up the sky in embers of auburn and dreamy patches of blue.

I couldn't stop taking pictures of them all with my Polaroid camera. Pictures as they joked together, cracked smiles, had an early morning jam session sans instruments and I was there, cheering them along. With the warm sand silking my toes and the fresh, salt air flooding my lungs, I knew in that moment, as waves crashed by the shore, that my parents were wrong.

Here, with Diesel Rose, is exactly where I need to be.

Tomorrow, we're headed to Seattle, the last city on the *Killing Me Slowly* tour, for three final highly-anticipated shows. It's crazy to think it's all going too fast, but the thrill that comes with knowing I'll be going home to Manhattan and my self-acclaimed Possessive Psycho will be right here with me, brings me so much happiness.

Ever since Elijah gave me his letter of honesty at that quaint, air-balloon inspired bookstore, we've been closer than ever. Our conversations flirty yet deep, our gazes loving yet bashful. I feel like I could tell him anything and he'd just look at me with those wolfish gray-onyx eyes and the entire world would just fade around us, leaving just us.

We've also been having *a lot* of sex. Like a crazy amount of a lot. In the shower. In Maverick's SUV. Subtly at Newport Beach in Oregon when the rest of the guys took a dip in the water, but Elijah and I stayed on the shore. *And those were just this morning...*

We had a beach towel beneath us, but as the early morning beach chill mixed with the rising sunrise, Elijah spooned me from behind and covered our bodies with a thicker blanket. His fingers trailed up my inner thighs, between my denim shorts, offsetting tingling sparks as he tenderly kissed my neck.

I teased Elijah a little too long, grinding my ass on his cock until it was rock-hard. Next thing I knew, my panties and shorts were tangled by my knees. He shut my cocky grin up with a sexy one of his own, growling, "Know your place, little girl."

Then he roughly pumped inside me, all the way, making me lose my damn breath.

I was muffling my moans into the beach blanket as we fucked, praying nobody heard and arrested us. But Elijah didn't make it easy on me with the way he was blowing my mind, varying between thrusting hard into my dripping pussy from behind and then slowing whenever a beachgoer or surfer jogged down the shore beside us before heading in the water.

My gaze frantically scanned the beach for people, but it was still early, and at one point, I just didn't fucking care anymore, subtly rocking my body back to meet every rough rock of his pierced cock, bouncing on it. The blanket began slipping so many times. He kept raising it.

I couldn't get enough of him.

The feeling was so liberating and forbidden at the same time, and Elijah couldn't stop groaning in pleasure, his hot breath getting caught in my ear and all along my throat with every single spot he nibbled, sucked, and kissed.

I had come to realize that Elijah really liked marking me, and I really liked it too. The way he was claiming me so affectionately possessive, that I couldn't imagine a time when he wasn't doing it.

I was still so sore from last night, from the way we both lost our minds at that party, and then for hours when we made it back to the hotel.

I was going to good girl heaven.

Elijah couldn't stop gripping my hips under that blanket at the beach, sliding in and out of me so deeply, I almost screamed out his name. I say *almost* because the second my lips parted, his right hand, which had been resting under my head like a pillow, curled around and slapped over my mouth, shutting me up.

His reflex skills…fuck.

I moaned into his palm instead, over and over, my eyes rolling back from the pleasure so intense as he fucked me like a goddamn sinner.

We fucked wildly while watching the sunrise come up across the beautifully romantic coastline, all while I was coming undone. It was so risky, and I swear a few people noticed with their prolonged, wide-eyed stares, but they didn't say anything. And we, well, didn't care.

Elijah's hand squeezing my tits through my cropped sweater. He was going crazy because I didn't wear a bra underneath it, just like last night at the party, and I told him to fuck the anger out. He couldn't stop rocking into me deep, playing with my bare tits, and whispering in my ear all the dirty things he wanted to do with me, making me hornier by the second.

"Take a photo of us," he panted softly, moments away from coming undone together.

"What?"

"I want a Polaroid of us like this. I want to see your beautiful face as I fill you, baby."

I remember flipping the Polaroid camera around and just when I took the photo, Elijah's fingers grew wild over my swollen clit, vigorously rubbing and flicking it so intensely that I came, panting with his lips on my neck. He pulled out and orgasmed right there with me, moaning against my glistening skin, the sensation of his warm cum shooting over my inner thighs and back before rubbing it in making me smile.

Unreal.

That's what Elijah Diesel makes me feel.

Unreal. Seen. Beautiful. It's everything at once.

Elijah couldn't stop kissing me after that, spinning me around and rushing his fingers through my hair, deepening the kiss as we came down from our high.

It was definitely the most public we've been regarding sex, and I couldn't hide my flustered cheeks when the boys came back to shore, glancing between us precariously. But Elijah just pulled me to his lap and the guys started talking about something else.

I've stared at that Polaroid so many times since we returned from the beach, not helping the girlish grin on my lips. He always makes me feel this giddy.

I know Elijah once told me he wasn't the kind of guy to make love, but sometimes when our eyes lock when he's inside me, the stare we share is so intense, it's beyond just caring for each other…it's *more.*

So much more.

It's exactly what I feel right now as Elijah finished singing "Fragments of You". I teared up because of the beauty of his words. How they're always laced in such poetry. Dripping from the heart.

I blow Elijah a kiss as he finishes that song with that last line in French and he smirks, playfully rolling his eyes in the way I know he would. It has me bringing up the Polaroid camera and taking a snap.

Cute.

I can't stop smiling.

During the two-hour performance, I've attached the photos to a handmade tour photo album that I probably should have started in California, but things were too intense there.

As it seems, I've upgraded from scrapbooks, you see, but sans the diamond scissors.

The boys are all laughing at my cheering and squealing at the end of their practice, well, all except for Knives. He literally hasn't met my gaze all day.

After the rehearsals, Elijah's on his way to me when Knives pulls him aside. They disappear out of the hired-out studio and out the back, where there's a little patio with olive trees and cute cast-iron seating for two. I think it odd, but not strange, so I continue sorting through the pictures while lying on the dark carpet, smiling whenever it's with Elijah in it.

"Look at her, man, she's so fuckin' starstruck. I love it."

My gaze lifts up to a smirking Dave, who's elbowing Zander, motioning to me.

"You talkin' about me?" I laugh back, mimicking him. "Huh, man?"

"Yeah, talkin' about ya." Dave chuckles back, abandoning his drumsticks to come sit down beside me, sorting through some of the Polaroid piles from this morning at the beach. "Yo, man, Zander! Come look at these, I think blondie over here's got an eye for your ass!"

My eyes widen faster than you can say *I'm Slim Shady, yes, I'm the real Shady.*

"*What*?" I screech, reaching for the Polaroid, but he's holding it high, taunting me.

Shaking his head, Zander walks over and takes the picture. One glance and he's bursting out laughing. "Shut the fuck up, man. You know I'm the only one going places in this band."

"Yeah, the fucking penitentiary, that's where."

Zander rolls his eyes, smiling as he softly throws the picture back. "You see how this guy talks to me, Rosalia? He's so full of shit, it's actually funny."

My heartbeat finally steadies when I glance at the picture and see it's of…*the sunrise.*

I playfully glare at Dave, who's smirking back at me, playfully messing up my hair. "Now, now, Rosa, you ain't a part of the band until I stitch you up."

"You literally made me think I snapped something I shouldn't have."

Zander grins at me, just as his phone begins blaring. "Happy initiation, Rosalia."

And then he's gone, his fiancée on the other line as he walks out of the studio door, to the lobby area. When it's just Dave and me, I'm smiling while he's smoothing over my hair.

"You gotta stop messing up my hair."

"Why? So that you can make out with your boyfriend like it's *Mean Chicks*?"

If I was drinking something, I would have choked on it from the laughter. "Oh my God, it's *Mean Girls* not *Mean Chicks*."

"Yeah, whatever, I'm a rocker. I ain't supposed to know that shit." Dave pulls his hands away, and I love how comfortable I feel around him. That he accepted me with open arms since the very first day we met years ago. "I'm only messing with you, Rosa. Do you know he sang the chorus of 'Comatose' three milliseconds late 'cause he was getting lost in your eyes?"

I crack up. "Did you just say *three milliseconds*?"

"Fuck yeah." He winks. "I'm the drummer, remember? Every second counts."

"Sure it does, Jaxen Davison."

"Oooo, full name status now. I like, I like."

Just as I'm about to reply, Dave's phone begins blaring and he shoots me an apologetic look when he checks the caller ID. "Sorry, doll, I gotta get this. It's my manager calling."

Standing up, I brush off my jeans with a smile. "It's all right. I've got to use the ladies' anyway, so I'll give you some privacy. Wouldn't want to overhear anything, you know."

"Is there a female version of chivalry? Because if so, props to you for just doing that."

I'm walking down the hallway leading to the bathroom smiling. *These guys are crazy, but the best kind of crazy.* I'm finished in the restroom (which by the way has literal velvet on the walls), and just about to wash my hands, when a familiar voice breaks me out of my trance.

"Rosalia doesn't know shit about it, and I'd like to keep it that way, okay?"

It's Elijah.

And he doesn't sound the slightest bit delighted. *At all.*

His voice is rough, tense. *Spiteful.* It takes me back to the kind of way we used to speak to each other back when we hated each other's guts. It's so unlike the man I know now.

What the…hell?

Why can I hear him?

And what does he mean I don't know shit?

And then I work it out. Above the vanity and mirror there's an *open* rectangle clerestory highlight window inches from where the ceiling begins, letting in glorious sunlight.

That's when it hits me… *The patio is on the other side of the wall. Holy shit.*

"So, you're just not gonna tell her?" Knives scoffs. "Seriously?"

"You and me both know how she's going to take it."

"So?"

"The fuck do you mean, *so?* Rosalia wouldn't be with me if she knew the truth!"

My jaw drops and I have to hold a gasp from escaping.

Rosalia wouldn't be with me if she knew the truth.

What does that mean? What the hell does that mean?

I'm going into shock, not believing what I'm hearing as I continue rubbing the Italian citrus handwash across my hands until its whiteness seeps into my skin, making everything sticky. But I don't care. I just keep on rubbing because I'm too scared to turn the faucet on.

"So let me get this straight," Knives's voice cuts into the silence after a little while, and suddenly I can smell smoke seeping into the bathroom. Not tobacco. *Weed.* They must be having a joint. "You're seriously gotta go the entire relationship without telling her the truth about it? I mean, I'm not exactly you guys' greatest fan, but I also know what's *fair.*"

"You're really fucking pissing me off, Knight."

"When am I not…"

"Don't you think this is hard for me?" Elijah growls and my heart jolts at the sound of shattering glass. I don't know what the hell it is, but it emits a pregnant pause. "Don't you think that I wish I could look into her eyes and not feel like I'm fucking holding something back?"

"Never said you didn't."

"So then respect that."

"*RESPECT THAT*? YOU FUCKING *LIED* TO HER FACE IN THAT LETTER!"

No.

Please, no. No. No.

Elijah...lied to me?

He is hiding something.

It feels as if a bucket of icy water was poured over me, slaughtering every single inch of hope inside me. *What is going on?* I can't help the bubbling anxiety coating over my veins, rippling up my spine and capsizing inches from my heart. I don't know why in a moment like this, my gaze flickers down to those faded white scars on my wrists, but they do, and then...

The red flags seep in.

Every single moment Elijah promised he wasn't hiding anything.

Every single second I spent wrapped in his oasis.

Dave's right. Every single second does matter. It's what determines life. Every single second that passes in one less inside of our beating heart, and as I listen to my boyfriend and his best friend during their heated argument, I realize I haven't been looking at this correctly.

What I have with Elijah...it isn't the flowers and sweet candy kind of love. It can't be. Not if he's been lying to me about something. Toying with me into believing him when it's so obvious there's something he's hiding.

Something he's deliberately *choosing* to hide because if I knew, I may not be with him.

Elijah knows I have trust issues. He knows all about how I struggle with not getting too attached because abandonment is huge for me. He knows all this, and still...

I can't breathe.

What is Elijah hiding from me?

What did he lie about in that letter?

Is he... Is there somebody else? Another woman?

No. It can't be. It would be all over the media if there were.

Through my scattered inhales, I try doing a breathing technique, anything to help stabilize me, but nothing works. My chest is tight. My head's whirling with thoughts. Bad ones.

I shut my eyes, wishing I could just curl up into a ball and be in Manhattan right now.

Fuck! What the hell is it?

I hate that this is happening.

That it's coming off such a high.

And Elijah doesn't know I'm listening.

I wait, and wait, and wait for Elijah's response to Knives's comment about lying to my face in that handwritten letter he gave me at the bookstore days ago, but it never comes.

"DO YOU NOT CARE?" Knives shouts, and something hard clangs against iron, causing him to curse. "DO YOU NOT CARE ABOUT EVERY SINGLE FUCKING SACRIFICE?"

"Calm. Down. And. Keep. Your. Fucking. Voice. Down."

"YOU WERE DYING, ELIJAH! *DYING*! AND YOU WANT ME TO BE *CALM*?"

Silence.

Silence.

Silence.

It kills me.

I know better than to stay around and listen to their conversation, I really do, but it's about *me*. I deserve to know because at the end of the day, these guys are thick as thieves. They won't tell me. *None* of them will, not even Dave. Not if Elijah doesn't. And if he isn't prepared to disclose this part of himself—*ever*—well, then, that just means… I'll never know.

And I can't live like my life that. I refuse.

My biological parents taught me better than that.

"Elijah," Knives whispers, so low I can barely hear it, emotion coating his voice. It means something because it's the first time I've heard him call him his first name. "Please don't tell me *that* is happening again…"

"It's not happening." My boyfriend's voice is the saddest, loneliest thing. "Promise."

"Because you would tell me if it was, yeah?"

A beat.

"You know I would."

Silence.

"Rosalia was really worried about you the other day. She thinks it's just the vodka…"

"Knight, *please.*" Elijah sighs, and my heart hurts when he does. "Rosalia can't know."

Silence.

"Just. Tell. Her."

"What did I just say, man?"

"This is going to end badly, Diesel. I'm talking *real bad.* Are you prepared for that?"

Silence.

"You know what?" Knives spits. "Do whatever the fuck you want. Tell her. Don't tell her. I don't give a fuck. I'm fucking done with this conversation, man, I really am."

Metal scraps against crushed rock before heavy footsteps drill in my mind. A door creaks open in the distance, and I can hear Knives's curses all along the other side of the other wall. Loud thumps rush up the corridor, most likely to the studio, if not, through the front door.

I wait so goddamn long, my fingers trembling from everything I've just heard.

After a little while, Elijah mumbles, "*Fuck.*"

More scraping metal against crushed rock. More heavy footsteps. More door creaking.

And when all those sounds fade to a pit of nothingness, with a palpitating heart, I stare into the vanity mirror. Pearl-sized tears are softly rolling down my cheeks, *and the sad part?*

I'm so in shock right now, so numb and in denial, that I didn't even feel them escape…

Chapter
FORTY-FIVE

Rosalia

Wish #4: To let me see every single version of you...

Elijah spends the rest of the day acting like nothing happened. Like he wasn't talking about me to Knives. Like he didn't admit to hiding something from me. Like I don't know.

Because that's what he wants me to believe.

Elijah has no idea that I overheard his conversation with Knives, and I want to see how far he takes this. To say I'm pissed off is the understatement of the year. I'm so beyond pissed and more like fuming. What kills me even more is that Knives *knows* but is ignoring my ass.

I don't like these kinds of mind games.

I'm honest.

And I'm open.

I'm a say-shit-to-your-face kinda girl.

I can't hold back. Elijah knows this. He's been at the forefront of it. But what I can't understand is how he can look me in the eyes and act like everything's okay, when it ain't.

Elijah did it during the drive home back to the Portland hotel.

He did it during the movie we went to watch at this art deco theater.

He's doing it now, during late dinner, as we sit at the dining table, eating sushi.

I haven't spoken a word all dinner, and Elijah knows there's something up by the way he's constantly looking at me, trying to figure all the puzzles together.

Chaotic.

I hate that it's all that comes to mind right now.

Before our movie date, I debriefed Naomi about everything on the phone, and the first thing she did was search up Elijah's and my astrological pairing compatibility. She was never into this shit when we were just two single bachelorettes strolling around the city that never sleeps, but the guy she's dating, Chad, is into it.

Yep.

He reads the star sign section in the *New York Times* every morning.

Somehow, now, it's rubbed off on my best friend too.

"Oh my God! You're an Aries, he's a Scorpio. You guys are *fuckedddd*!" Naomi gasped through the phone. "I pulled up this online article. This is what it says. The bond you two have is unbreakable, but you are the most aggressive combination with him being a fire sign and you a water one."

"Wow, that… It makes so much sense now."

"Yeah, it says you're both jealous and possessive, which at times can be destructive, due to being complete opposites. You bring out the worst in each other and oftentimes, it can be too much to handle. You both try hard to be strong, but it only hurts one another… Rosa, why the fuck is all of this true?"

"I don't know, it's so freaky. It's literally us."

"I know, tell me about it! Aries—you—crave the simple things, wearing your heart on your sleeve, and winning over people's love, whereas the Scorpio—Elijah—craves being the only one who has ever cared, loved, and obsessed about Aries. So, because of that, he sinks into the darkness of the brain, challenging the devil himself at times."

"Oh my God, Naomi, shut up! This is getting scary!"

"You're telling me? I'm hyperventilating over here. Scorpio has a need to manipulate in order to protect his deepest, darkest ability to love. It's done to protect himself from getting hurt. Any doubts a partner may have will come out, and when it does, it can be catastrophic."

I remember the exact moment Naomi said that through the phone earlier today. I basically froze strapping up my stilettos and sat there motionless on the edge of the bed, because heck, everything about it was so accurate.

How could it be?

"*Oooo*, sex is aggressive, uninhibited, and taboo. It acts as being the gateway of unlocking vulnerability and emotion between the two signs."

"Okay, that's also true…" I said to her, playfully rolling my eyes. "Next."

"Girl, you're blushing thinking about sex with that idiot. I just know you are. Scorpio—Elijah—can be too dark and difficult, destructive qualities intensifying a love. Whereas Aries—you—are guarded by Scorpio's past and their emotional wounds and scars, but that's only because they can numb themselves from ever feeling a thing."

"ROSALIA!"

Elijah's call has me snapping out of the memory, slapping a hand over my heart as it freaking pole vaults over my head in fright.

Holy shit!

Was I out of it for that long?

Here Elijah is, frantically waving a hand in front of my face from across the table, concern circling in his eyes. When he sees me actually breathing and blinking, and you know, moving like an actual person, he groans to himself, rubbing his stubbled jaw.

"Fuck, Rosalia, you scared the shit out of me. I was calling out your name for a solid five seconds."

Don't look at him.

Don't look at him.

Don't look at him.

"Sorry." I clear my throat, going back to picking up the delicious sashimi and devouring it with a moan. "I was just thinking…"

Silence laces the air between us for a few minutes. Nothing but the echoing sound of my crazily beating heart and a clock ticking in the distance, fucking with my mind.

And then comes Elijah's voice, *soft*.

"*Thinking?*"

"Mhmmm."

"About?"

"Stuff."

"Like?"

"Nothing in particular."

"Do you want to talk about it?"

I've got to give him something for trying, but at the same time, he's still acting like nothing. Like if I didn't overhear his conversation with Knives, he would never tell me.

My head still low, I sink the chopstick in the tiny soy sauce bowl, swirling it around, the dark liquid seeping into the wood, absorbing its taste.

I shrug, deflated. "Not really."

"Okay…"

"Cool."

I can feel him stiffen up adjacent to me on the table, frozen in place, not even moving a single inch to bring the California roll to his mouth.

I don't glance up, too afraid I'll meet his broody, almost thirty-six-year-old gaze and cave.

But apparently, I don't need to because Elijah's the one to slip off his seat and round the table. He falls to his knees beside me and takes my hands in a way that I can't meet his eyes. So, when I do, *gah*, there are fireworks inside me. All colors. Glowing bright.

There's so much hope laced in his eyes, so much need and want, so much challenge to make this right, accept…*how do I know it's not all a lie? How, when he's lying to my face about something? Something he knows that may break us.*

"Babygirl, I don't like the way you're so quiet tonight," Elijah murmurs, slowly rubbing circles with his thumbs into my hands. It's a movement so subtle, but from a guy who lacked affection moving into this, it's *everything*. "Did I… Did I do something wrong?"

I shake my head, a weak smile on my lips. "No, you didn't do anything. I'm okay, just a little tired, that's all."

"Yeah, I can't blame you. We've been having some late nights and early mornings."

"Yeah."

Silence.

With that growing weak smile, I cup Elijah's face, my thumbs smoothing over the roughness of his dark beard.

He lied.

Needing to convince him, I peck his lips. Slowly.

He lied.

Just as he's about to deepen the kiss, I pull back with a whisper, "Let's finish dinner, darling."

He lied.

When I turn back to my sashimi, Elijah's still here, kneeled down beside me. He's a smart guy, I know he is, which is why I'm highly aware he senses something is wrong. Big time. And yet, I don't meet his eyes.

Not again.

Not until he returns to his seat and brings the sushi to his mouth, devouring it.

"Is there something you'd like to tell me, Elijah?"

Boom.

He slows his eating, his gaze slightly fretted, but for the most part, acts normal. "Me?"

"Yeah." I grind my jaw, my level of pissed off hitting the full-on radar. "*You.*"

"No, I… No. Why would you think that?"

Seriously?

I cock my head to the side with a mocking smile. "Just thinking out loud, that's all."

"Okay…" he mumbles, gazing at me with pleading eyes. "There's nothing, Rosalia."

Liar.

I wait, and when Elijah truly gives me nothing, I slam my napkin down and sit up a little further in my seat. I don't care that this is his tour. I don't care I'm only twenty-one. I don't give a shit about what he may think of me in a moment like this. I've fucking had it.

"Elijah?"

"Yes."

"You know how we went to the studio today, yeah?" I snap.

"Yeah."

"How you went out to the patio with Knives…?"

Elijah stiffens up, and yet, he still nods. "Mmhmmm."

"Well, I went to the bathroom at one point."

"Okay."

"Which backs onto the patio…and the window was open…"

Elijah stares and stares, and when he finally gets it, his panicked gaze widens. Severely. His eyes are the deepest shade of gray, speckles of onyx creating the prettiest rendition of him.

"*Fuck*," he groans, slamming the sushi down to run a slow hand over his face. He doesn't like this. One bit. But I'm not allowing him to get away with it. "What did you hear?"

"Enough to know you're hiding something from me."

His hands slip, and all I see is…*motionlessness*. "I'm not hiding anything from yo—"

"ARE YOU *SERIOUS*?" I shout, scoffing with crossed arms at the audacity of his statement right now. "I literally *heard you say you were*! You refused to give Knives the confidence that you'd tell me whatever it is you're hiding. You think that if I know, it'll ruin our relationship. What the *fuck* is *that*?"

"Rosalia, please, let's talk about this in a civil manner."

My heart is racing so fast that his words just rile me up even more.

"*CIVIL MANNER?*" I scoff, rushing up from my seat so fast it scrapes against the hardwood floor. "I'll tell you what's civil, Elijah, you being *honest* with me. You not *hiding* things from me. You actually *owning* your shit and *admitting* to the fact that you fucked up!"

The man I'm in love with stares at me. Yes, *stares*, because that's all he does.

Elijah has no defense.

He has no backup.

He has no words.

He simply sits across from me, broody as hell, his jaw ticking in dismay because he thought he would get away with this. He was so confident; he didn't even think this far deep.

"Because that's what you did, Elijah," I add in a trembling whisper. "You *fucked up!*"

Seconds later, he's cursing, and in a moment of anger, violently slaps his food to the side with so much force, half our dinner flies off the table, plumping to the floor in soft thumps.

"It's nothing…" Elijah rasps, the bitterness in his voice evident that he's holding on.

"It's *something*, and we both know it. What did Knives mean by *you were dying—*"

"You don't trust me, huh?" He scoffs, staring me down. "You need to sneak around to, what? Snoop?"

My jaw hits the floor.

The nerve of this guy!

"I went to the bathroom to fucking pee, Elijah! I'm not a stalker!"

"So, what now? *What*? You think I'm a monster, huh? Well, do you?"

"Yes," I growl, not caring if it stings because he deserves it. "Yes, I really freaking do!"

"I'm not a monster! I'm an alcoholic. You think I'm some beast? You think I want to be like *this*? You think I want to feel like *I can't breathe*? YOU WANNA CRUCIFY ME, HUH?" Elijah roars, rushing up to me with the devil in his reddened eyes. "WANNA FUCKING CRUCIFY ME, ROSA?"

And there it is.

I take a few steps back from the table, my chest heaving in ache the longer I look at his enraged face. The longer I look at the mess he made around him. The longer I'm in this room.

Elijah grips my jaw, lowering his head so that our foreheads almost meet. He's looking back and forth between my eyes like I'm the sinner. Like I've just stabbed him in the heart, dagger style, and now he's bleeding out cold. And his touch…it's cold as ice. *Just like him.*

"Do it," he whispers against my lips in a taunt. "Crucify me, baby, tell me I'm bad."

I can't breathe.

Why can't I breathe?

"Get. Your. Hand. Off. Me."

He does, so fast it almost hurts.

The lump in my throat throbs so intensely that I can't even look at him. With a blurry gaze, I rush away from him, darting through the hotel room and into the bedroom we share. His loud footsteps echo behind me, intensifying the harder I run, my lungs a burning, chaotic mess.

Elijah's hands slip in mine when I make it to the bedroom, eagerly pulling me to him, and just like that, he's changed again. Those onyx-grays are flooded with sorrow now. Regret.

"Baby, please, I'm sorry," Elijah begs so damn softly. "I didn't mean to yell. Just let me explain."

"Stop."

"Please, *Peaches*, please. I promise it isn't anyth—"

"I said STOP!"

His touch slips away from me, and in return, hollowness returns. I hate that we're like this, inches away in the same hotel bedroom we were devouring each other in just this morning. But I don't like the way he's looking at me, how his eyes are all glazed from the joint he smoked before dinner. I hate that he smokes it. I really do. But he says it's for the pain, that he needs it.

"Is there something you're hiding from me?" I ask, my voice defeating me, slightly cracking at the last two words, emotion cutting through.

I don't want to cry. Not because of him.

Elijah dips his head, his frown the saddest thing.

"*Baby*," I plead with everything inside me, praying to God. "Is there something?"

"Yes."

The truth. It hits me. Right in the heart.

There's something.

"Will you ever tell me?"

He can't answer. He just keeps on cursing, rubbing his neck, clenching his jaw.

I don't know when it happens. It's all a blur. But one second Elijah's standing in front of me, the next he's storming to the other side of the room, a vicious devil when he unzips his luggage, throws out a few folded clothes, and then wrapped in a hoodie is…

Oh my God.

A vodka bottle.

A *half empty* vodka bottle.

My heart aches at just how soullessly Elijah stares at me as he unscrews the bottle with his teeth, spits it across the room, and then gulps down the illicit clear liquor like it's water.

Knives.

Knives.

It's all I can think of.

Call Knives.

But my body's too fight or flight to do that first. And perhaps it's my downfall, perhaps in actuality, I should have called his best friend first for help, but my first instinct is to run over to him. I don't know how many times I attempt to knock the vodka bottle out of his grip with tears in my eyes, but every time, he just raises it higher and higher, taunting me.

In a moment like this, I can tell just how much he's not okay. And I tell it to him. I scream it to him. I scream at the top of my lungs for him to let go of the vodka bottle, for him to stop drinking it, for him to not fall back into the past that he's working so hard to see the other side of, but he's so far gone. He's not even listening to me. He's too trapped in his mind.

This isn't the Elijah Diesel I'm falling in love with.

It's another man. A fractured man. And it hurts me so much.

It hurts as I beg for him to stop, for him not to do this, but he just keeps drinking.

It hurts as *he* tells *me* that I don't trust him anymore, that I hate him, that *it's all over.*

It hurts as our fight travels from the bedroom to the hallway to back in the dining room.

"*Leave*, Rosalia," Elijah grits, finally slamming the vodka bottle on the table, but it's too late, *he's drunk too much.* "You want somebody who isn't as fucked up as me? You want a nice, proper Wall Street guy? You want a fucking gentleman? Well, there's the fucking door."

"I don't want to *leave*," I say, hot tears rushing down. "I want you to stop acting like this."

"Nah, nah," Elijah mockingly scoffs and shakes his head, halfway between being high from the joint and dizzy from the liquor. "You want to leave, baby, I see it in your eyes." Leaning against the floor-to-ceiling windows, he tips the vodka back against his lips, swallowing down the poison of his past, all while coldly staring at me with heavy eyes. "Nobody's tying you down, Rosa. I'm not having this if you don't trust me. You want to leave? I won't stop you."

More tears gush out, uncontrollable. It feels like I'm drowning in my own despair.

"No, don't cry," he rasps, abandoning his bottle on the floor before stalking up to me. Pinning me up against the table, he buries his head by my neck, his hot, alcohol breath tingling my skin. Ever so slowly, my devil kisses away the tears he prompted, a vulnerable unsteady mess. "I know you hate me."

"I don't, Elijah, that's what hurts the mos—"

"Shhhh." He brings a finger to my lips, the seductive carnage in his eyes captivating me as he slowly rushes that finger down with a sad smirk. "It's okay to hate me."

I'm shaking my head, hating that he's doing this to himself. Putting illusions in his head when he shouldn't. Taunting himself for his retuning demons. I don't hate Elijah, I just...

Oh my God. *That damn star sign thing was right.*
This is too much. Him and I right now... I can't.

"Can we at least talk about this properly? Please, Elijah."

"What is there to talk about, little one? That your boyfriend's a psycho?"

"No, that isn't true. I don't know what's going on, but...I wish you'd tell me," I whisper, wanting to slip away from him, but he doesn't let me. "You promised me you'd get better."

"I am."

"This isn't you getting better."

Elijah chuckles darkly as he nuzzles into my neck again, this time trailing bittersweet kisses over my existing love bites, killing me.

"This *is* me, baby. The real me," he whispers, his aching kisses leaving invisible scars. "Take me or leave me."

"Stop," I sob, that ache in my throat bursting in waves as I try pushing him away. "Get off me."

"Forgive me."

"Elijah, get off me."

"*Please.*"

"GET OFF ME!"

"PLEASE!"

Whimpering, I shove his shoulder back with so much force, he doesn't expect it, and just as he's tumbling back, the rage circling my heart has me doing the unthinkable. The hard slap echoes in our Portland hotel room, and Elijah surprisingly gasps, bringing a hand to his cheek.

His eyes soften.

The darkness breaks through.

And all that remains is gloom, and shock, and the man I'm in love with returns again.

Oh.

It's like he's returned to being that ten-year-old kid who was left tattered and bruised.

My.

The one who unloved life.

God.

The one who was so trapped from reality, it left a sting.

Oh my God.

I don't realize I'm shaking until my hands come over my mouth.

I just slapped him. Hard.

The air simmers between us, the tense tension exchanged with melancholy.

Elijah sadly stares at me.

I stare back. Sobbing.

What just happened? What is happening between us?

After clutching his cheek for a little while, Elijah pulls his hand back to examine it all. That's when we, in the same breath, notice a dark shade of crimson rippling across his hand.

Blood.

No. No. No. No.

Slowly, Elijah looks up at me, and I witness his eyes dilute, becoming all glassy.

There's a gash down his right cheek, oozing blood.

I glance down at my hand. The snake ring, the one he gave me, is…a bloody mess.

The intensity of my slap must've…

Oh no.

My heart… *I don't feel it.*

And then, Elijah painfully whispers four words that will forever haunt me.

"*Peaches*... You hurt me."

Peaches.

Every single piece of me shatters and burns, right in front of him.

Wiping my tears doesn't help, just like breathing the same air as him doesn't help.

I don't want to be here anymore.

I can't bear looking at him for another second.

"You hurt me too," I whisper into the oblivion. "Only this wound...you can't see."

And as I bolt to the elevator, away from purgatory, Elijah... *he doesn't even stop me.*

Chapter
FORTY-SIX

Rosalia

Wish #5: To work through all our bittersweet flaws...

I know Knives told me to call him if I needed him, but right now, I really need more than just his voice. Knight Ives is the closest person to Elijah, the only person who knows the ins and outs of his mind, and perhaps, the reasons why my heart is aching so damn much.

All I kept thinking during the brief elevator ride to Knives's hotel room was that I shouldn't have left Elijah in that state. *I never meant to hurt him.*

I should have thrown that vodka bottle out of his grip, just like his best friend said. But there was challenge brewing in his gaze and my body feels like it's capsizing into the Atlantic.

I couldn't bare breathing another breath in that room with Elijah.

It was too claustrophobic, not literally, figuratively.

Darkness coated every inch, the same darkness I've constantly worked so hard to recover from. Ballet saves me. It constantly saves me. And through loving the motions of every dance I execute, I'm learning to love myself enough to give people chances. To trust again.

I can't undo what I saw when I walked into my childhood home when I was five.

The vision will forever be engraved in me. Burnt.

But I can try to find peace with it, and I can't do that with Elijah's deafening grip.

He doesn't see the escapism.

He doesn't see that peace.

I know when I look into his eyes, sometimes they're soulless, a fraction of the man I adore. The one I'm in love with. The one I first saw in a *Rolling Stone* article and my heart flipped.

I knew loving a rock star wouldn't be easy. I'm highly aware of the statistics, the rumors, the horror stories. I once read that alternative rock, punk rock, and heavy metal had the most "accidental" deaths of any other music genre. Do you know how much that scares me?

How much it has tears burning down my cheeks?

How much that makes me want to shrivel up and die my own little death if it means saving him?

Statistics don't lie. Headlines don't lie. Depression doesn't lie.

Kurt Cobain didn't lie.

Chris Cornell didn't lie.

Michael Hutchence didn't lie.

Elijah openly told me in the letter he gave me at the bookstore that music is his savior, but when he takes it away, there's a void. Music was Cobain's, Cornell's, Hutchens's safety too, until it wasn't. That's what hurts me the most. I don't want my rock iconic boyfriend to…

It's the most dangerous field, coated with drugs, liquor, and sex. High, intense levels of stress. Anxiety. The constant buzz of needing to stay professional while the devil's knocking.

Rock and roll isn't for the faint of heart.

But I also think it's the most beautiful genre.

It speaks the truth. Solid truths. With melodies that stay with you for decades.

It's why I want to help Elijah with every single fiber in my body. Why I'm knocking on Knives's hotel door adamantly, his bodyguard who is standing outside looking at me as if I'm crazy.

After exactly fifty-nine seconds, Knives bursts the door open in only navy briefs, his blond sex hair a tousled mess. The first thing he does is glare down at me, his light eyes glazed over, and it doesn't take long for me to notice the reddening love bites all down his neck.

"What the hell do you want, blondie? I'm kinda in the middle of something…"

Oops.

My gaze wanders to a pink-haired woman sprawled on a plush couch, a white and caramel cashmere Hermes blanket barely covering her naked body. But then when I flicker up to those familiar eyes, they warm… *RIVER!*

Wow! I almost didn't recognize her with the pink hair! I do remember she regularly dyes it according to her mood.

Grinning, River subtly gives me a wave and I softly smile back.

Seems like they're resolving their issues in paradise…

I turn back to Knives, my skipped heartbeats returning. "Sorry to interrupt you lik—"

"Just get to the point, blondie, or I'm slamming the door and getting back to fucking my girl."

River rolls her eyes from the couch. "Always the *gentleman…*"

"Rosalia!" Knives groans, motioning to his evident as ever erection suffocating in the constraints of his briefs. "I'm in a life or death situation 'cause you're literally gonna give me blue balls in a second, so speak, woman."

"Elijah's drinking."

It takes an instant for the color to drain from Knives's face. "*What* did you just say?"

Emotion etches my throat, and I can't swallow it down, no matter how hard I try. "He's *drinking.*"

Knives doesn't say a word. He's just staring back at me with sad, wide eyes, frozen.

I stare right back, silently begging for him to tell me something. *Anything.* He knows so much more than he's letting on around me. I *know* he is because I *heard* him speaking with Elijah. About me. About something that Elijah is still hiding from me.

This is what got me into this mess.

Knives got me into his mess because he can't stop freaking pushing. He wants to see Elijah and me break just so he can laugh in my face. I know he does. But that doesn't mean that I don't need him right now. He may as well be the only person who can talk to Elijah when he's in this state. When he's so out of touch with reality, everything comes second to his chaotic mind.

"We got into this argument," I add, hating everything about this. "It got real heated. I told him there are times when I can't trust him. He was looking at me, Knives, looking at me right in the eyes, and yet, it was like...like he wasn't even seeing me."

"And then?"

"He pulled out this bottle from his suitcase. I have no fucking idea where he got it. I couldn't stop him. I tried knocking it out. Tried telling him that he was only killing himself, but I'm telling you, Knives, it was half empty and I just..." I pause as emotion cuts into my voice. *I'm not crying in front of him.* Rubbing my face, I go on. "Was so scared."

"Jesus Christ, Rosalia, he's *drinking*? I told you to fucking call me! Where is he?" Knives grits, rushing around the living space, a nervous wreck as he starts cursing to himself. "Where the fuck are my jeans? Where the *fuck* are my fucking jeans? Shit. Shit. Shit."

With the Hermes blanket wrapped around her, River stands up from the couch, dangling a pair of ripped black jeans from under her. "Here."

Knives can't stop hurling profanities as he slips them on in record speed. "I told him if he drank one more time without me, I was going to—*FUCK*—Why the hell is this zip broken?"

"Babe, it's not broken." River tries to calm him, reaching out to pull up his jean's zipper. "*See*? It's working. Just gotta be a little calm, that's all."

"*Calm*?" Diesel Rose's bassist spits, a fire brewing in his gaze. "My best friend is having a fucking depressive episode and you want me to be calm? *Calm*? Get off me, River."

"Knight, I'm just trying to help—"

"I. SAID. GET. THE. HELL. OFF. ME."

River does and my heart stings for her at the betrayal in her eyes. I can see there's so much fight in her, in the way she parts her lips, ready to give it back to Knives, but she stops. Those baby blues flicker to mine, and it's the saddest thing watching her blink her tears away until all that's left is complete numbness.

It's crazy how we're all adopting that exact feeling here on tour—feeling numb.

Diesel Rose may be the most iconic rock band of this century, but outside of the limelight, away from all their fans and Grammy record wins comes the truth about them…

Rock stars' lives are just as fractured as everybody else.

They have deep, bleak flaws just like you and me…

Or perhaps, worse.

Knives storms up to me, his jean zipper halfway up, phone in hand. "Where is he?"

"In our hotel room. The penthouse."

"Okay, all right, I'm heading there now. What is he drinking?"

That's when my heaviest blow comes.

Tears in my eyes, I'm too choked up to get the word out. I just begin shaking my head.

And from that alone, Knives knows.

Vodka.

Distressed, he practically shoves me out of the way, but not before turning back when he's down the hotel corridor and right in front of the elevator to softly whisper, "Thank you."

Thank you.

I don't even have time to conjure a reaction to the kindest thing Knives has ever said to me before he rushes inside the elevator car. I just keep on staring into the space he was seconds ago, praying to God that he's able to speak some sense into Elijah.

Please, God. Please.

I know I haven't been the holiest girl and church has slipped me.

But I… I really need you right now. I really need a miracle. Please.

Back inside Knives's hotel room, River is dressed in a mint green robe, that pretty silvery pink clipped up in a bun as she staggers to the kitchen, head in her hands.

"You should be with him," she says softly without ever glancing at me. "Knives may need backup."

Dead bolting the door, I ignore her words to stride over to her. She's in the modern kitchen, not a single light on, and it's there where I rush up to her, lacing my arms around her waist from behind. Resting my head on her shoulder, I snuggle her close and whisper, "Why are you thinking about me in a moment like this, Riv?"

"Because I like you and I like Elijah. I *love* you both together."

"I like you too, but Knives shouldn't have spoken to you like that."

"I know… This is the exact reason why I walked away from Knives days ago. When he gets something in his head, he's so fucking stubborn. Just like me." River's voice cracks on the next words. "But I *love* him, Rosalia." She tips her head back, keeping in the tears that the silvery moonlight glazes over. "And I'm not letting this dumb shit break us. Jesus, I'm not crying over that idiot."

When all I do is hold her tight, River turns around, her arms pulling me into the warmest embrace. She's got that brave smile on her lips that I always admired in the strongest women. I've always grown up wanting to be like them, wanting their confidence and independence.

I'd like to think I'm halfway there.

"And you shouldn't cry over your idiot either," River half-smiles, half-frowns. "I've been on tour with these monkeys for years, and let me tell you something, Elijah Diesel has never been happier. He's just going through some things, but you'll get through it, you *will*."

My caged heart sings, but then I think of how dismissive Elijah was acting before I left our hotel room to come here, and it all begins to crumble again. *But I have to give in to hope.*

It's why I nod back at River, smiling. "You're right. I just need to be here for him."

The more time goes, the more I contemplate telling her about what I overhead earlier tonight at the party, but then decide against it because I don't want to put her in a compromising position with Knives. They're only just working things out again. I don't want to be that girl.

So instead, I decide to make us some late-night coffee when she says to stay with her.

"So, what do we do now?" I sigh, falling onto the couch. "Wait until Knives returns?"

A savage smile crawls up River's lips. "*Well*, Rosa, first of all, you may not want to sit on that couch after Knight Ives and I were…"

Screaming in unimaginable horror, I practically jump out of my skin to rush off that couch, almost doing the splits when I trip on one of the fallen pillows in the process.

River throws her head back in laughter, and it's the happiest I've seen her all night, which rumbles my own little giggle up my throat. "Your face! Oh my God, Rosa, I love you!"

We settle on the fluffy chocolate rug instead, flicking through Netflix until we settle on the new season of *Selling Sunset*. I can just feel Naomi stabbing a knife in my back because it's such a her and me thing to do. But I know she forgives me. I just need a little TLC tonight.

With a soft smile, River and I clink our mugs of brewing, hot coffee together.

"To being in love with a rock star." I sadly smile back through the sting in my heart.

River nods with a wink. "And riding all the freaking waves of love with them. *Drink*."

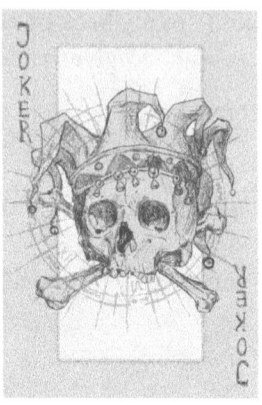

Chapter

FORTY-SEVEN

Elijah

*Wish #6: To have the courage to show me all
your beautiful scars...*

I feel like the Joker seconds before the end credits, slowly slipping into another level of insanity.

I'm alone.

All alone.

My muse ran. She's not coming back. I know she isn't.

This is all my fault.

She thinks I'm a monster.

My stepfather floods my mind, crippling my breaths, "*YOU DID THIS! YOU FUCKING DID THIS, YOU PUNK! YOU ARE THE ONE WHO MADE YOUR MOTHER LEAVE!*"

I didn't make my mother leave. I didn't. I haven't killed a soul.

The only person I've killed is myself.

Peaches is gone. She's not coming back.

It's so lonely. So lonely without her with my back slanted against the wall, the illicit liquor on my lips, fucking sashimi everywhere with the way I hurled my fist into everything in fight the moment she rushed out the door, never looking back. I didn't stop her because I…

I want to save her.

I want to save her so much.

I want to save her so much I can feel metallic blood in my mouth.

But… But what is… *What if all I'm actually doing is ruining her slowly?*

What if I'm killing my fated ballerina—Rosalia Philips—and I don't even know it?

There are heavy thumps inside the private elevator doors seconds before they rush open.

It's Knives.

Knight fuckin' Ives.

My gaze doesn't stay steady on him. He's swaying. Or maybe I'm the one swaying.

Everything blurs. Fogs up. Dims down. *Numb. Numb. Numb.*

I don't know if it's the joint's high or the vodka's deadly thrill, but I don't feel so good.

Shattering glass echoes inside my heart. The same heart with all the strings tugged undone. Because nothing makes sense without Rosalia. Not a single thing. Not anything.

The shattering glass… It was the vodka bottle. Knives must have smashed it out of my grip, but I don't feel my fingers, or my lungs, or my face. All I feel are my palpitations.

They drum in my ears.

Duh-doom.

Duh-doom.

Duh-doom. Duh-doom. Duh-doom.

Fuck, I… I think I'm dying. Or hallucinating. Or going into some toxic trance.

Knives is screaming, telling me, "*THIS IS NOT OKAY, DIESEL!*" *HOW THE FUCK CAN YOU DO THIS, DIESEL? HOW THE* FUCK *CAN YOU LOSE CONTROL LIKE THIS?*

I want to speak.

I want to tell him it's because *I'm dying.*

But I can't find my voice or the words to put anything together.

After that, I don't hear a single thing Knives is screaming at me.

Not a word.

But I sense the panic. The guilt. The fear.

Staring at the chrisom red blood staining my hand, I wish Rosalia had hit me harder. I wish she'd killed me. Perhaps then, I wouldn't be feeling like this. Perhaps then, I would feel nothing.

Because I still feel her. I do.

I feel her sensual scattered kisses down my neck.

That bittersweet sensation of being alive.

The way she's my beautiful undoing.

I thought I could change.

For her, I thought I could be a better man.

But now I know I'll always have destruction in my blood... no matter who I am.

I'm fading.

In and out.

In and out.

In and out.

One second, I'm in the dining room. The next, I'm sitting up in the shower, icy cold water cascading down my skin, piercing it through to the bones—temporarily un-numbing me.

Knives is right in front of me, throwing water in my face with agonized eyes. When he sees I've come to, he stops and with a trembling lip, rushes forth and brings me into the first embrace in almost twenty years.

It's gentle, yet it's rough, and it's everything I need right now.

"*Fuck,*" Knives croaks, his body trembling. "I thought I was losing you again, Eli."

I squeeze him tighter, and yet, I don't have a single thread of life in me. "You didn't."

A staggered breath escapes me.

Not yet.

The private jet flight to Seattle is tough. *Like real fuckin' rough.*

Rosalia isn't speaking to me, and everybody else is too scared to. They're all keeping their distance, every single one of them except

Knives. He hasn't left my side during the one-hour flight from Portland to Seattle. Not after everything that transpired last night.

Last night, I lost my mind.

Last night, I may have lost Rosalia Philips forever.

Last night, I slept alone for the first time in forever and it tainted my soul.

Rosalia is sitting at the back of our private jet, softly talking away with River, who literally did an appearing act. She must have rejoined the tour last night, when shit went down.

It's an hour flight full of tense silence, or, at times, soft muffling.

Zander attempts to lighten the air by cracking a joke. Nobody laughs.

Dave attempts to host a mid-air mediation class. We all stare at him like he's crazy.

River attempts to be the mediator by getting Rosa and me talking. Neither of us speaks.

Knives *successfully* attempts to shut everybody up, so we're flying to Seattle in silence.

Rosalia is ignoring me, as she should. *I would too.* I'm feeling myself slipping again, just like I did all those years ago when I needed to walk away from her to save us both. And I hate it. I hate it because gazing into her piercing green eyes, I don't need anything else but her.

We've locked eyes a few times, but she always looks away, while my stare lingers. It's like we're strangers. *I miss her already.* I miss her touch. I miss her smile. I miss everything.

I don't know what to do to fix this, and it's killing me.

I should have never lied to her... *Not for this long.*

Chapter

FORTY-EIGHT

Rosalia

Wish #7: To never let me flutter wild...

P art of me believes I shouldn't have ever touched down in Seattle. That I should have taken the first flight home to Manhattan instead. But if it's one thing about me, it's that I'm not a quitter. I'm not giving Elijah Diesel the satisfaction of thinking he's won the war between us.

So, ladies and gents, these are my pointers on avoiding the man you're on tour with:

1. *Request another hotel room and advocate you want to pay for it.*
2. *Hang out with his other bandmates...well, particularly Dave.*
3. *Attempt to strike up a conversation with Elijah Diesel.*
4. *If all else fails, fly back home crying the entire way.*

So far, my plan has backfired. *Immensely.* For security and privacy purpose that come with a luxury hotel hosting a globally successful rock band, there's already an allocated room block. Hence, I'm still stuck with Elijah, but thankfully there are two bedrooms.

Second, every moment with Dave simply ends with him convincing me to talk to Elijah.

Third, whenever I walk up to Elijah, he simply walks the other way = no conversation.

Forth, I'm highly considering that plane ticket. It's currently pending in my mind.

I spent most of the first day in Seattle with River. We both needed some major girl time, so we did some things that sucked the life back into us…like retail therapy. *A lot* of it.

Toward the afternoon, I called my foster sister, Maya, who currently lives in Seattle. She moved here three years ago because California life was just too much for her. She's in her fourth year of nursing school now and practically squealed when I told her I was in Seattle.

With both of us across the country, we don't see each other like we used to, so when she suggested we meet up for dinner in the city, I was so down. I was just so happy to see her again. And get some more information on how Dad's doing as he's not answering my calls.

Which leads me to right now…

Elijah is nowhere to be seen as I step out of our Seattle presidential suite overlooking the breathtaking Space Needle, but when I make it downstairs, through the blaring fans camping out, I find Maverick, who's just waiting for me beside his Volvo. *Strange as I ordered an Uber…*

But as it seems, just because Elijah and I weren't speaking, didn't mean his generosity faltered. Maverick informs me he has specific instructions to take me wherever I need, so with great hesitance I cancel the Uber and slip inside of the Volvo that holds so many memories.

During the drive, I conclude River must have told Elijah about my plans… *Ugh!*

I send two texts, the first to River…

ROSALIA: I'm going to *kick* you, traitor!

The second text is the hardest pill to swallow, because, well…
It's for Elijah.
One word.

ROSALIA: Thanks.

My phone buzzes in my grip less than two seconds later.

ELIJAH: You don't need to thank me, Rosa.

Our coined saying kept on going full circle...

I have to refrain from the glassy eyes I feel coming on. But it's hard to do when Maverick meets my gaze in the rearview mirror, as if he just *knows.*

"Ms. Philips?"

"Yes."

"I've been working for Mr. Diesel for a long while. Seen him at his worst. At his best." A small smile tips up his lips, the first he's given me since we met. "He's his best with you."

My heart pangs, but I'm not quite too sure with what.

I softly smile back, his words growing distant, but never too far from my thoughts...

"Hey there, stranger..."

My eyes widen the second I meet Maya's wide grin. She rushes up to me, squeezing me in the tightest embrace ever. Giggling, I hug back, swaying us from side to side. "Maya! Hi!"

The trendy bar we're at seems awfully familiar and the more I glance over the industrial exposed brick wall and Edison lights, the more it finally clicks.

The bar in Elijah's private recording studio back in Manhattan.

Reminders of him should fill me with joy and thrill, but tonight, after everything that's transpired in these past days, anxiety floods my stomach.

"Come with meee!" Maya smiles, her pretty blue eyes glowing under the warm Edison lights as she guides me up to the bar counter. "This is my favorite bar in town and now that you can drink, it's paradise! Plus, they whip up mean lemon pepper calamari. I know, I know, without pepper for you."

The bartender flashes us both a smile, his murky hazel eyes lingering on my sister for a little too long for me not to notice something between them. "Hey there, pretty thing."

Maya blushes.

Blushes.

I grin. *Oh, I can't wait to ask her all about it tonight.*

"I've got my sister here tonight, so play nice. Rosalia, this is Marc. Marc, Rosalia."

Marc, the bartender, tips his head, and I give him a little bit too enthusiastic wave.

"It's nice to meet you, Rosalia. Well, what can I get for you gorgeous ladies tonight?"

Maya holds up two fingers. "Well, tell the chef two LPCs, but one without pepper."

"Done, and what's my dirty work?"

"Two screwdrivers, pretty please."

Vodka.

It's all I can think about as I politely shake my head. "Umm, kindly make mine an Aperol Spritz instead. Thanks."

Maya looks at me like I'm crazy. "Girl, *what*? But you love a good screwdriver."

"I know, but I…" I swallow thickly, trying to think of the right words. "Just don't feel like it tonight."

Her gaze lingers until she shrugs with a sigh and turns back to Marc. "You heard the girl, one screwdriver and one Aperol Spritz."

"Coming right up."

As we wait by the edge of the chestnut bar counter, Maya arches a suspicious brow at me. "*You* not *feeling* like a *screwdriver*? Who are you and what have you done with my sister?"

I smile at her weakly. "It's a long story."

"Rosalia, I've got all night!"

"Maybe another time?"

"Okay, fine, but we're talking about this rock star that's about to divide the family."

"Oh, God," I groan, dreading it already. "Have you heard from Dad?"

"Mhmmm." My sister smirks at my misfortunes. "He does not like Mr. Elijah Diesel."

"And Mom?"

"Same. They think he's stealing"—she playfully cups my face—"their *little baby* away."

I can't help but laugh at *my own* misfortunes. "Oh, God! I'm twenty-one!"

"*And* have a sex glow, hmmm?" she adds, that smirk of hers deepening.

Oh my God.

My jaw drops. "Maya!"

"*What*? I'm a nursing student and the prospects of me getting married to some rich, smart, bald doctor are high. We'll probably work such intense shifts that we'll barely see each other. No sex. No vacations. No little kids running around calling out, '*MA*', and, *yes*, I'm highly aware I'm only a year older *but* right now, *your* love life is *my* love life, so TELL ME!"

See? This is what I miss being around my foster sister. She always has me smiling and cracking up, even when I'm feeling like shit inside. She's my hype girl, as is Naomi…and River.

Damn, a girl goes on tour for a couple weeks, comes back with a girl band.

"Have I told you how much I love you?" I grin over at her.

Maya winks. "I'm sure Elijah would *love* to hear that."

My smile instantly falls a fraction. I pray she doesn't notice. "It's early days, Maya."

"*Early days*? Oh, come on, *please*." She snorts, rolling her eyes. "You're literally on tour with your *boyfriend* across the West Coast, so trust me, Rosa, it's not *still early days*."

"Okay, it's…four years in the making."

"That's the spirit!"

Marc hands us our cocktails and we thank him before we sit at a nice moody leather booth in the corner of the bar. It's secluded, and I like how it's so set back from other patrons.

"So, come on, sis, I want to know all the details since we last spoke the other day!"

I take a sip of the Aperol Spritz, letting its freshness ripple down my throat. When I set the glass down, I'm left running my finger over its frosty condensation, choosing my words…

Where to start, where to start…

"Well, whenever I'm with Elijah, I feel like the luckiest girl alive…"

"But…?"

"*But…*" I sigh. "We're both so complex, sometimes we clash and it's…a lot."

"Have you guys spoken about it?"

Frowning, I shake my head. "We're currently in the *ignore each other phase*, so no."

Maya's jaw drops in complete horror. "No way!"

"Yes way."

"Ohhh, I'm so sorry. What happened, Rosa?"

"You can't tell this to anybody."

"Who am I going to tell?"

Well, here goes nothing…

"Last night we had an argument because I found out he's hiding something from me."

Maya's eyes widen, her glass halting inches from her mouth. "Hiding what from you?"

"I don't know. He won't tell me. We had this huge fight about… *things*, and at one point, he was holding on to me. I told him to let go. He didn't, so I slapped him and when I did"—I hold up my snake ring, nerves bubbling inside me—"it gashed his cheek. He bled. The way he looked at me… I feel so guilty *and* angry. I want to hate him but can't. Yet he's hiding something and…"

"*Oh*, Rosalia."

Steading my furious breaths, I rub a hand over my face. "I'm okay, babe. I just… I hate fighting with him. I really do. Because when we're together and happy, it's so perfect."

"I can't tell you what to do because you're you," Maya whispers, taking my hand. "But sister to sister, your traumas together isn't just something that can be fixed in a second. It takes years, a whole lifetime. He may be tormented forever, and while it's not his fault, and you'll have to learn to be in love with that side of him too, *at the same time*… If this relationship is constantly dragging you down, it isn't selfish to walk away, Rosa. It's you saving you."

"But I…" I squeeze her hand, tears lacing my eyes. "I *really* care about him, Maya."

"Then tell him exactly how you feel, *but* not before you get what *you* need *from him.*"

Maya doesn't have to say it for me to know what she's alluding to… *The truth.*

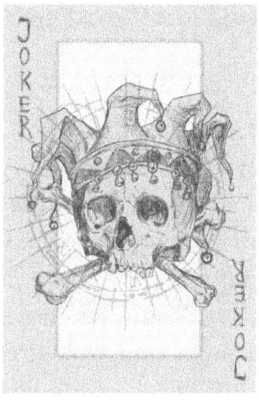

Chapter
FORTY-NINE

Elijah

*Wish #8: To unravel your demons, in the best ways
you know how, babyboy...*

The chilly midnight Seattle air kisses my skin, but really, I feel it seep through my lungs, rush across my veins, and lodge inside my palpitating heart.

I don't know how long I can hold this in.

The urge to grip my hands over the brass railing surrounding the hotel's rooftop and fist it until it snaps in half. That's the gravity of the pent-up rage circling inside me. Today hasn't been a good day.

At all.

And I can feel those demons coming through, slowly appearing like those temporary kiddie tattoos. Except nothing can make them fade. Once my demons are here, they're here to stay.

I lied to Rosalia.

I lied when I told her that I was getting better.

That I was out of the fucking pits of hell.

When I said vodka didn't still affect me.

It does.

Seeing it affects me.

Seeing anything affects me.

It's just all fucking triggers. *Triggers. Triggers. Triggers.*

My brother, Edmond, was right—*life plays cruel tricks on you—* except sometimes they're not solely tricks, sometimes it's real life. Reality is hard enough for me; I don't need this cruelness.

I observe the dazzling Seattle skyline, lit with glowing apartment windows, the epic panoramic view stretching across the heart of Seattle. There's beauty all over, overlooking the lit Seattle Great Wheel, radiant red glows of Pike Place Market's sign, and the art deco streetlight lit 4th Avenue below, and yet, I don't feel a thing.

Rosalia Philips is my only exception.

But am I selfish enough to be constantly craving her?

The question echoes in my mind on replay as I pace up and down the luxury rooftop, tightening my leather jacket closer to my chest because it's cold as fuck. I've always known Seattle as this—fucking freezing. I was a Seattleite before I was New Yorker, so I guess I follow the cold…or the cold follows me.

Despite the warmth of my joint, the midnight chill seeps into my fingers, freezing over my silver rings until I feel that spark alight me inside, and just like that, diminish. Paranoia has me glance between the exit and my phone a million times, seconds ticking away ever so slowly…

Jesus Christ.

Where the hell is she?

She said she'd be here an hour ago.

I know Rosalia would kill me if she knew what was about to go down. And before you get your panties all twisted, no, I'm not about to proposition another woman. I simply need something from her. One little thing that'll settle this train wreck in my mind, a little at a time.

Rosalia's sweet taste is still coated on my tongue from days ago. Not sure I ever want it to fade away. When we fought last night, I know I lost myself along the way. I wasn't attentive to her, I was rough. It was crazed. Diabolic. Unlike the man I want to be. I saw the murky tears in her eyes, the whimpers that escaped her with every cry, and yet, I couldn't stop myself.

It was like I was punishing myself.

Punishing her.

Punishing *us*.

And not into pleasure, it was pure pain.

I feel her distance from me already and I hate it.

I hate that I wasn't in the moment when I lost my mind.

I hate that I got like *that*. That I was so caught in my demons, I really do.

I never meant to hurt her.

They always say not to play with fire, and being with Rosalia Philips makes me do that very thing—let the flames lick my skin until I'm dying a slow death.

It's why I need *this*.

Why I crave this.

Why if I don't get a little taste of ecstasy, I may very much be found at the bottom of 4th Ave, strangled by my own crippling anxiety, and shot in the chest by a love so sugary it kills.

A creeping noise has me stilling in my spot in the middle of the rooftop. I don't need to turn around to know who it is. I told her to meet me here. Made security clear her to come.

Tick.

Tick.

Tick.

With every passing second of her heels slapping against the slate floors, the more my mind spirals inside.

Rosalia.

Rosalia.

Rosalia.

It's all I can think of as those heels come to a halt right next to me, arms crushing.

"You're late," I whisper into the night, blowing another puff of my joint, and between that and my cold breath, clouds of white frosty smoke take way. "I've been here for an hour."

"I was held back."

"Paparazzi follow you?"

"No, thank God, no. Maverick showed the service elevator into the hotel."

"So, then what held you back?"

"My brother…he was asking me all kinds of questions. Thought I was meeting up with some psycho. Laughed at that one."

But it's no laughing matter for me as I side-eye her with an uncontrollable clenched jaw. "You found that laughable? There's nothing funny about *this*. You and I both know that."

Portia stares back at me, the light in her eyes dimming the second she reads my expression. I couldn't give a shit about the fancy trench coat she has on, or her bold lips, or the way her hair is done up like she's my Grammy date. Because she's not my date. She's not my anything. And I'd like to keep it that way.

I'm not fucking stupid; I saw the way Portia and Rosalia were staring each other down at the party on Sunday night. Rosalia told me enough to know that Portia, in a way, was her rival back at New York City Ballet. That she felt Rosalia didn't earn her position as current *prima ballerina*, when she so evidently did. I hate that she's put my girl through so much.

Portia is the definition of a bully, and I know that, God how I do.

So why the fuck are you standing beside Portia Evans in the middle of the night on top of a Seattle rooftop, Elijah Diesel?

Well, thanks for asking.

I'll give you the simplified encrypted answer.

Because sometimes the hit is more important than the supplier.

Just wanting to get this over and done with, I take another puff of the joint, letting its numbness soften my tired eyes as I pull out a wad of cash from my pocket. It's all hundreds.

"You got it?" I ask her ever so casually, counting over the money. *Eight hundred.*

"Yes."

"Let me see it."

Gulping down, Portia glances around skittishly, as if there's somebody else on the rooftop when there isn't. After the all clear, she slowly pulls it out of her trench coat pocket, letting me see it.

My breath halts in my chest for a moment because all I can think about is Rosalia. What she would do if she found out. How she would probably leave me and that would kill my soul.

But I'm selfish.

And I need *this*.

To survive again, fuck, *I need it*.

You've got to understand that I'm doing this to breathe a little longer on this earth.

Rosalia Philips is my everything, my absolute everything, but we vowed to save ourselves, and I… *This* is the only way I know how. The only thing that truly works. My dependency.

I hand over Portia the money, my mind already a cloudy fog from the high I feel coming along, Ah, who am I kidding, the joint is already making me nervous with jitters. I've smoked so much weed that it doesn't fucking affect me in the way it should. It doesn't calm me; it just makes me feel numb. *Sometimes.* And I'm too insignificant to just get that sensation *sometimes.*

Just as I'm about to take *it* out of Portia's hand, she holds it back, behind her. "Are you sure you want this, Elijah? If something happens…it isn't on me."

"I get that."

"Are you sure you want this?"

Gulping down, I turn to face her, steadying my breaths. "I'm already too far gone."

"Elijah."

"Portia."

"Okay." She sighs, seeming all agitated for some reason. "You've got to promise me something."

I tip my head. "Anything."

"*This* doesn't trace back to me. Not Rosalia. Not New York City Ballet. Not my brother. If it does"—Portia takes a step forth, her eyes squaring up in challenge as she raises a hand to my chest—"I will tell the world all your fucking secrets. My brother wasn't dumb. He was *everything* on tour. He never confronted you because he's loyal, *but* if you fuck me over…"

"I get it," I grit, heat rushing up my spine that's laced in a frantic depression. "Promise."

Portia gives me one good look, and as her waves blow in the frosty Seattle air, that seems to convince her enough. And with Rosalia's face in my mind and her song in my blood, her enemy slips *it* to me, and I shut my eyes, finally breathing again.

The exchange is done in moments.

Portia counts the dough. *All eight hundred of it.*

I pretend the weight in my hand doesn't tug at my heartstrings for all the wrong reasons.

We stare at each other for a few seconds, a muted oath to keep tonight between us two.

I never intended to go to my girlfriend's enemy for *this*, but right now, I need it.

"You should go," I advise her, my gaze flickering back to the twinkling skyline that I used to grow up wondering if I'd ever see up close. "Paparazzi don't keep quiet for too long."

I feel Portia nod, or I don't know, something like that, but she doesn't leave.

She just continues staring into the side of my head, torturously, all while my jaw ticks.

"If you want to say something, say it, Porti—"

"Do you love Rosalia?"

Thump.

Thump.

Thump.

"The monster in me does, yes."

"And the man?"

"He's drowning."

Portia steps closer, her eyes pooling with darkness I'm not willing to explore. Ever.

"Don't." I hold out a hand, backing her out of my personal space. "Don't. You. Dare."

"But I thought…"

"You thought *what*? HUH?" I snap, fuming as I stare down at her with the joint smoking up her face. The more I stare at her, the more repulsed I feel. "I have a *girlfriend*, Portia."

Scoffing in my face, she rolls her eyes. "Rosalia was sucking Trent Daniels's face off during Swan Lake's season, and two seconds later, she's with you. *Wow*, some girlfriend…"

Fuck this.

I'm all up in Portia's face in seconds, taunting her with my height when I growl, "If you bad talk my girlfriend or try to ruin her flawless career one more time, *I'm coming for you*."

"I'd like to see you try!" Portia spits, tears in her eyes before storming through the exit.

I couldn't care less.

I defended my girlfriend.

That's all that fucking matters.

With weighted shoulders, I turn back to the infamous skyline, smoking my joint with my dependency clutched in my other hand. Then, at last, the depression seeps into my heart.

Sometimes I don't always see myself, and when I do, I forget who I am. And when that happens, I lose control of the man I'm supposed to be.

The rock star my fans glorify.

The lyricist my bandmates need.

The uncle my nephew simply adores.

The brother my sister is constantly there for.

The boyfriend to the most beautiful girl in the world…who after tonight, may never want to call me *hers* again.

Chapter
FIFTY

Rosalia

Wish #9: To have the courage to be honest with me, even if I won't like it...

I stayed over at Maya's Pioneer Square duplex last night, no matter how badly how intensely my heart told me otherwise. Elijah and I needed some time apart, even if it was a brief cool-off period. My mind was circling with too many thoughts I needed to dissect, each one at a time.

And I was able to do that at my foster sister's house with a little more peace and quiet.

Last night I noticed a few paparazzi when Maya and I stepped out of the bar, and she drove us to her duplex. I did my best to ignore their bright flashes and constant questions, not because I wanted to be rude, but because... I don't really feel comfortable around the press.

But now it's the afternoon and I'm heading back to *the* hotel, unsure just how to approach Elijah about everything that's conspired between us. I know the most logical thing to do is simply sit him down so we can have an honest heart-to-heart, but after his actions last night, I don't know if he's ready for that.

The vodka.

It broke my heart so much seeing that damn bottle in his grip, seeing the dependency on his lips, the chaos in his eyes. Elijah had a moment and I get that, everybody's allowed to have a moment, but the *way* in which he snapped and tortured himself really affected me.

What if this is more than just a moment?

I don't know Diesel Rose's tour schedule for the day, but what I do know is that it's Tuesday and they're not performing tonight. With this being the fifth day until the end of the tour, I should be ecstatic about having Elijah all to myself back in Manhattan soon, but right now, everything is up in the air. Including the future of us. Because Maya was right…

Before anything else, I need the *truth*, and then, the rest will come.

I feel so jittery at the back of this Uber, my fingers haven't stopped nervously picking at my denim phone case, pulling on loose threads, and constantly flickering my gaze between the driver (who thankfully isn't a serial killer) and outside the window, flashes of stunning blue tinged skyscrapers everywhere.

Should I text Elijah?

Should I text him saying I want to talk?

What if…what if he doesn't reply? I'll just look like an idiot.

Deciding this isn't going to resolve itself, I pull up my messages and tap on Elijah's.

I want to solve this civilly with him, so without hesitance, I type up a text and hit send.

> **ROSALIA:** Good afternoon. I'm in an UBER heading back to the hotel and was wondering… Can we talk when I get home?

Did I seriously just say 'at home'?

Ugh!

I almost groan at my misfortunes when I notice the error and send a second text.

> **ROSALIA:** Oops, I meant when I get to the *hotel*.

I don't expect *delivered* to flicker to *read* so fast, but it does.

My breath halts mid-inhale, nervously tapping my nails against my phone case as those three silver bubbles of death appear and disappear, and then, finally...*reappear.*

> **ELIJAH:** I'd really like to, yeah.

> **ROSALIA:** Okay.

> **ELIJAH:** I'm at the gym, almost finished up, and am gonna get some coffee when I'm done. Want me to grab you something too?

I chew on my lower lip for the longest time.
He seems to be in a better mood today...

> **ROSALIA:** No, that's all right...

> **ELIJAH:** Okay, a soy caramel ice coffee with two pumps cream it is then?

I don't know if I'm the biggest fool for the warm smile that touches my lips right now, or if I'm just the biggest fool *in love.*

> **ROSALIA:** Yeah, that would be perfect, thanks. I didn't want to hassle you because...

> **ELIJAH:** Rosa?

> **ROSALIA:** Yes?

> **ELIJAH:** You could never hassle me.

Aside from a distant soft buzzing sound, there's no sigh of Elijah when I kick off my pumps outside the private elevator doors of our luxurious presidential suite. My time with Maya really helped clear my mind because nothing comes easy when it comes to relationships.

And when you're dating a famous rock star, shit's bound to be even more complicated.

But I have my big girl panties on and I'm adamant to work things out with Elijah once and for all.

I slow by the two large takeaway coffee cups on the gray marble kitchen countertop. One double macchiato, no sugar. One ice coffee, two pumps cream.

Him and me.

I melt at the very first sip of my coffee, adoring its sweetness. *So good.*

"I thought I heard the elevator..." That sexy, raspy voice I'll never forget echoes behind me.

My fingers tense up against the plastic cup, unable to think things through. I don't know what my next move is. I stepped into this all fierce and determined, *so why do I feel so nervous now?*

It's like I've hit the jitters. Stage fright. Like it's the first time ever speaking to a guy.

I twirl around, not expecting the air to be knocked out of my lungs at the very sight of *him*. There Elijah Diesel stands, halfway between the living room and hallway leading to the massive bedroom. He looks all refreshed and scrubbed up, only a plush white towel wrapped around his waist. *Low.* So low his trimmed, happy trail dark hair leads to the base of his cock.

Holy...

Droplets of water ripple on his skin, across his broad chest, washboard abs, and all his divots, grooves, and vaunted muscles. I can't stop staring at the way his wet dark hair is sexily slicked back and all wavy around the ears, a few short stands falling over his eyes.

Johnny Depp's Crybaby, *it's what I think of every time.*

The only piece of jewelry he has on is a small, gold crucifix earring, dangling down.

If I wasn't running off the nerves of just how volatile and heated our conversation got last night, I'd be running into his arms. But Elijah's lying. To my face. I need to uncover why.

I swallow my pride and step forward. "Hi."

"Hey," Elijah murmurs softly, meeting my eyes with a little grace, not missing the way they darkly drip down my body, lingering by my right hand. *The snake ring.* "You...look so nice."

I glance down at my clothes from last night with a small smile, remembering he wasn't here when I stepped out. "Oh, thanks."

"I'm just shaving my beard a little... Want me to stop so we can have that chat now?"

"No, that's okay, continue it. I'm going to have a quick shower and change anyway."

Elijah softly nods, yet doesn't move. *He can't.* His somber gaze is locked on mine.

And I can't stop staring back at him.

At the soft mark on the gash I made.

At the redness crawling in his eyes.

At his body tensing up, cautious.

I wonder if Knives stayed with him last night or if he was alone. The questions intensify as I brush past Elijah with a heavy heart, not meeting his eyes as I stroll down the hall and into the massive bedroom suite. Just off it is the jaw-dropping en suite with an iconic wall shower, the one I strip down in front of and jump in, all steamy from him.

With the warm water rippling across my skin, I lather his vanilla tobacco bodywash, trying to scrub away our fight and the awkwardness of the chat that just transpired between us. But I can't, and especially not when Elijah steps into the en suite with another soft, fluffy towel in his hand, just as I switch off the shower's nozzle.

Elijah gave me privacy. He didn't come inside the en suite until I was finished…

Thanking him with a weak smile, I dry off before wrapping it around my body.

We're standing side by side in front of the vanity mirror. He's rushing his buzzing electric shaver over the baseline of his thick beard. I'm doing my skincare routine, anxiously fast. *It all seems so domestic.*

We keep on stealing glances of each other in the mirror.

Once.

Twice.

Three times.

The thick air between us is coated in tension… and *sensual*, even when it shouldn't be.

"*Tu m'as manqué tant,*" Elijah tenderly whispers, his onyx-grays softening to pure ache.

And it breaks my heart more.

I missed you so much.

Elijah and I have been sitting by a Pier 56 wooden picnic table overlooking the dazzling water for the past ten minutes now, not a single word spoken between us. It's just the waves of Elliot Bay softly swaying and us clutching onto our takeaway coffee cups, staring skittishly out at Seattle.

Pier 56 is located by Seattle Waterfront, surrounded by seafood restaurants, souvenir shops, and it's only a Hillclimb leading to Pike Place Market. But what I love about it most is how it captures the breathtaking views of this gorgeous city, despite the ominous gray skies blanketing the clouds. We should have brought an umbrella because I can already feel the frizz lacing around my hair, but I've never seen a rock star afraid of a little rain, so there's that.

The incredible Great Wheel literally behind us, slowly circling forty-two gondolas around. It's *huge*, and *yes, I'm literally so nervous sitting here with Elijah that I've counted every single gondola on Seattle's iconic ferries wheel—twice.*

I find it fascinating Elijah grew up here after leaving France when he was a little boy.

Seattle's cold snap ripples across my skin as I sip the last of my ice coffee. I don't expect Elijah to already be looking at me when I give him my attention. For him to be going between rubbing his forehead, to blowing warmth into his hands—his *trembling* hands—to continuously glance around us suspiciously, as if somebody is out to get him.

"Hey… You okay?"

"Yeah." He nods after a little while, sniffling in the coldness. "Just got this massive headache today, but I'll be all right."

"Oh, why didn't you tell me? I've got…" I pull out my bag of tricks, rummaging through it until I pull out the plastic bottle, shaking around the little blue liquid-gel pills. "I've got ibuprofen. Ballerina life. Want two?"

Elijah keeps his eyes on his trembling hands with a tense jaw. "Nah, it's okay. I took some painkillers just before gym. I'm not due for a few more hours, but, umm, err, thank you."

"It's okay. I've got some here if you need. Don't be afraid to ask."

He doesn't even nod, he's just staring at his hands.

"Elijah?"

He lifts his heavy eyes, barely, a war in his gaze. "Mmhmmm."

"I may be pissed off at you, but that doesn't mean I don't care about you." I shake the ibuprofen once again, the pills clanging violently against the plastic. "You want them, tell me."

"Thanks. It's probably because I'm fuckin' freezing and nocturnal too."

"You didn't sleep last night?"

"Barely. Like three hours, if that."

"Oh."

"Yeah, as you can see, tour life sleep schedule isn't the prettiest."

I just softly smile back, super tired. *I didn't sleep either.*

Silence.

"Well, umm, I guess we should talk about…" Elijah clears his throat, seeming so uncomfortable as he crosses his arms over his chest, covering his open black jean jacket and gray hoodie underneath. "The other night."

Finally.

Slipping my hands beneath my thighs against the wooden bench, I rock back and forth, trying to keep warm too because Seattle doesn't lie when the forecast is freaking freezing.

Elijah can't stop twisting his silver rings.

Clenching his lightly stubbled jaw.

Losing my gaze.

"I don't know how to start this, Rosalia, other than saying I'm… not in a good place."

As much as his words drill pain into my chest, I sit in silence, allowing him to take complete control. I want to listen to him without drawing up any conclusions. I really do.

"What do you mean by *not in a good place?*"

Silence.

I'm almost afraid to say the next words. "Are you relapsing?"

"*Fuck.*" He gulps down, staring at his hands even longer. "Rosalia, please. Don't do this."

"I need to know, Elijah. This isn't me trying to shame you or make you feel something you're not. I'm not judging you. But as your girlfriend, I have a right to understand what's going on with you."

Ever so slowly, those melancholic onyx eyes find mine.

"No, I'm not relapsing," Elijah admits, his voice a husky mess. "It's just that the demons are crawlin' back inside me, baby."

Demons are crawlin' back inside.

His words ruin me completely, vexing my soul. I don't know

what to do, what to say, other than listen to the words clustering in my brain. Those belonging to Maya from last night.

Tell him exactly how you feel, *but* not before you get what *you* need *from him*…

He lied.

Elijah *lied.*

And he still isn't addressing it.

"I wrote you a let—"

"No," I cut off, shaking my head, sprouts of anger rushing through. "No, I don't want a letter, Elijah, I want you to look into my eyes and tell me what the fuck is going on."

"But—"

"I want to understand *this*, Lijah," I cut him off, gesturing between us. "I really do. I want to help you, but you have to show me how. I can't live like this. I have boundaries. Limits. Lying is a hard limit. So if you're not willing to understand the consequences of doing it and then speaking like none of it even happened, then…"

"*Then?*"

"Then I can't"—I clear my throat, highly aware how close I am to losing it—"do *this* with you."

That's when Elijah finally starts seeing this for what it is. I can see it in the way he's looking at me, with eyes so sad and glazed over, it's lost as if he's about to break down right here. But he doesn't.

Instead, he swallows thickly, catches his breath, and extends his hand out. The moment his ice-cold fingertips wrap around mine, a chill rushes across my body so rapidly, I have to shut my eyes to survive it.

Sometimes, there's nothing pretty about us, and I just have to understand that. That sometimes we're both just pretty messes, attempting to survive.

"I never lied to you, Rosa," he whispers, brushing his thumb along that fated snake ring. "I promise to God I didn't."

"Please, Elijah." I shake my head, my throat getting all croaked up with jaded sentiments. "We're not staring this again."

Without ever letting my hands go, Elijah rounds the table until he's sitting on my side of the bench, hope in his stare.

A beautiful mess.

"I know there's nothing I can say or do to completely fix what I broke. I wish I could take it all back," Elijah begins in a murmur, so low I have to lean closer to hear clearly. "I'm so sorry, *Peaches*. I broke your trust. Your perspective of me. Your safety. I never intended to hide anything. Never wanted to be the version of myself I was gripping that vodka bottle. Never intended to feel this way."

"How do you feel?"

"No, I can't." Elijah shakes his head, backing away to rush a hand over his face, and that's when I notice just how red it's becoming. His ears the softest tinge of pink. "I can't…"

"Elijah, please," I beg, my hurried breaths all lost as I pull his hands away from his face. "Tell me."

With glassy tears in his bloodshot eyes, Elijah whispers the words that pierce my soul. "I feel so lonely inside my mind."

No.

No. No. No.

My throat throbs. "But I'm right here."

"I know." Elijah nods, scrunching his face in lucid pain. "I know you're right here, so why do I… Why do I feel like this, *Peaches*?"

He retakes my hands, squeezing them so tight I'm convinced my skin will almost burst and yet, I wouldn't care about it. All I care about is that he's suffering, in silence, and I didn't even notice.

"Why, *Peaches*?" Elijah rasps. "Why do I feel like the world would be so much better if I wasn't in it?"

A lone, slow tear rushes down Elijah's cheek, a tear of death that glistens over the scarring cut I created, pooling in its redness before curving down his Cupid's bow and baptizing his quivering, full lips.

Every part of me is ruined.

The sob that ripples through me is terrifying because it's a sound I haven't heard in years when I was at my lowest. The words Elijah just said to me grip my chest and rattle it, destined to never let go.

"That's not true, Lijah." My hands rush up to cup his chiseled jaw, softly resting my forehead against his. "The world deserves to be a part of your beauty. You're not only the lyricist, you're also the thread of Diesel Rose. You tie everyone together. Your bandmates love you, Lijah, love you so much, and don't get me started on the fans. *Millions* of them, yeah?"

Nodding against me, Elijah inhales a shaky breath. "Mmhmmm."

"Yet I'm your biggest fan. I've believed in you since I was

seventeen. *Seventeen*," I whisper through all my sniffles, a sobbing mess. "I was there *before* you went global, *before* the Grammys and broken records, *before* the world screamed out your name at concerts. You left me to clasp your dream, to make Diesel Rose legit, to have music flood your lungs for centuries. Make history. Be a legacy. You *did* that. You are *doing* that. So don't lose sight of that now. You need to remember it, recall the reasons you started, and then, when you have those reasons, don't you dare let go. The world needs you. Your band needs you. Most importantly, *I* need you."

Elijah's crying at my words, right in my hold, and for the first time in my life, I don't know how to console him other than pull him tight into the solace of my arms. He's quick to bury his head into my chest, to crush my shoulder blades, needing me, like his body is made for mine.

"I don't know what's going on," I continue, my face in his hair, the cold Seattle air hitting my skin, and a few people are staring at us, but I couldn't care less. "I don't know if you're doubting us, if you think this is too good to be true because nobody has ever wanted you this intensely before, but *I* do. Hell, I'm *in love* with you. I feel so much for you, Elijah. Fireworks. Fireflies. *Butterflies*. The bad kind, the good kind, everything in between, which is why it hurts that you're lying. All you need to do is tell me the truth. I can handle it. I promise."

Elijah's words come moments after, and when he lifts his head to mine, his eyes are bloodshot red from all the crying. His nose is the softest shade of red, and those onyx-grays…warm. So much warmth fizzles, he even gives me a small smile, still wrapped in me.

There's emotion in his gaze.

Gratefulness.

Anxiety.

Guilt.

Fear.

Joy.

It's everything at once, so intensely, and I don't know how to navigate it like I should.

Elijah's hands slither all over until they cradle the back of my head, sinking through my blonde waves, as if he's going to kiss me, but he doesn't. He knows better than that as he holds us close, our thighs brushing. I can feel his heartbeat pulse like crazy on the tips of his fingers. How wildly it beats with mine all crazed and hopelessly in love. *It's all so bittersweet.*

"*Je suis tellement désolé pour tout,*" Elijah whispers against my lips. "*Je suis tellement heureuse que tu existes.*"

I'm so sorry for everything. I'm just so happy you exist.

My heartstrings tug, all muddled up and touched because that's the nicest thing somebody's ever said to me.

"*Je déteste tellement tes parents biologiques pour toute la douleur qu'ils t'ont fait subir.*"

I hate your biological parents so much for all the pain they put you through.

"*Mais tu existes, Rosalia.*"

But you exist, Rosalia.

"*Tu es vivante, donc je les aime pour ça.*"

You're alive, so I love them for that.

Wow.

Oh my God. That was…so beautiful.

And then, just like that, all the bliss ruins at Elijah's next words.

"And I… I wish I could tell you the truth. I wish I could tell you *everything*. But I… I don't feel ready. I may never *be* ready, and that's what scares me the most."

The smile I didn't even realize laced my lips slips. *Everything* slips. The parts of me that tells me to forgive him. To give him time. To stay.

But *I can't.* I know that if I do, I'll forever be stuck in this vortex. One laced with distrust. With lies. And I can't live like that…*I just learned to heal.*

With one final glance at those eyes that'll forever be caged in my chest, I abruptly stand, losing his touch and everything that comes with it.

I don't even wait for him before throwing my cup in the recycling and start jogging away. We walked here from our hotel, and I'll run all the way back if I must.

I don't know how long I'm running, how long it's been that my chest is heaving and my lungs are burning for more reasons than just one. But I feel Elijah behind me. I feel his every step, speeding to catch up to me.

He calls out my name, screams it with a broken voice, but I just keep on running. I can't stop.

And then I do, stop that is, right by the crosswalk of a street sign that has me freezing up, hollow inside.

Oh my…

I feel Elijah slow behind me.

I know exactly why.

The street sigh above us reads: **Cherry Street.**

Cherry.

Cherry viper…

Cherry flavor is my favorite everything… And it's also what Elijah called me once.

And yet, with a shattered heart and tears in my eyes, I just keep on bolting away.

Away from everything I once believed to be true.

Away from the only man who has ever made me feel safe.

Away from the edgy, melancholic rocker who was once my everything.

And this time, no fastened footsteps follow.

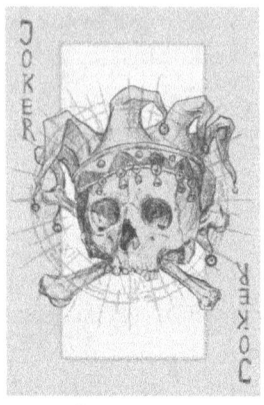

Chapter

FIFTY-ONE

Elijah

Wish #10: To be wild and free and always sing me
"Fragments of You," baby...

"**D**IESEL!" I hear the shout from several feet away, trickling through Lumen Field stadium's backstage sanctuary, and I already know it equals trouble. "Wait up, man, seriously."

It's Knives.

Of course it's *Knives*.

The past three days in Seattle have been torture, leaving me hopelessly undesiring anything. I've lost my reasons. My motivation. My *muse*. Throughout today's matinée and now, at our evening concert, my head hasn't been in it. The screams of the sold-out concerts constantly shot through my earpiece. I was there singing, moving in beat, making seventy-two thousand fans go wild, and yet, I couldn't feel...*anything*.

Not my heart.

Not my breaths.

Not the little guy in my head telling me to hold on.

Knives noticed it. He noticed just how far gone I was and just how done I am with it all. He noticed how I didn't sing the "Wonderwall" cover, so the boys did an instrumental version. He noticed the way I walked out of each show before "Fragments of You", no explanation needed.

It reminds me too much of Rosalia…

Knives noticed Knives *notices* because at times this guy knows me more than I know myself. It's why, as much as I don't want to, I slow in my step backstage and spin around with tense shoulders. Crew rush around me, apologizing for almost bumping into me as Knives nears me. Bass guitar still strapped on, he's staring, a sweaty mess from the intensity of the tour.

River's nowhere to be seen, but I know *exactly* where she is. *No. Questions. Asked.*

"We can't just end the show like this," Knives insists, panting from the vigorous run to me. "The fans are literally still out there chanting—'Fragments of You'—we can't just leave."

"I ain't singing it."

"Come on, Diesel. *Once*," he begs, and my best friend *never* pleads. "Just sing it once in Seattle and the fans will be happy. Another instrumental won't cut it. The longer we go without singing it, the more shit will spiral online that something's happened between you and Rosalia."

"Because it *has*," I grit and then sigh. *He's only trying to help.* "I didn't mean to snap. I just… I fucking ruined everything. She doesn't trust me. At all. But if I tell her the truth…"

Knives stays silent.

Swallowing thickly, I test the next words in my mind first. "Was Rosalia on side stage?"

I didn't look. I couldn't. It hurts too much knowing I am hurting her.

My dry eyes stare at Knives as if he's God, like his answer will break or make me.

"She…" His light blue eyes dim, and from that alone, I already know. "No. She wasn't."

The pounding in my head intensifies, just as everything begins to blur. *She isn't here.*

"Hey, are you okay?"

"Yeah, just need a minute." Sliding against the brick wall, I rub over my face, trying to settle the constant throbs in my head. I've still got that damn headache from yesterday.

We've got two shows left to perform in Seattle after tonight. Two more show and it'll be Saturday, October 29, the day Diesel Rose's worldwide *Killing Me Slowly* tour ends. Saturday's the night my sister and Clément will come watch us preform for the killer finale.

I don't know what to think of it. I really don't. But the fact that it's highly likely that Rosalia won't stay to watch it makes me... *I really wanted her to meet Clément.*

I feel like shit about it. About *all* of this. I never intended to be the monster who broke her. But now it's been a full day. A day since we were at that fateful Seattle pier. A day since we uttered any words to each other. A day sans the same rhythm in my chest keepin' me alive.

We've spent these hours like walking ghosts in our presidential suite. I thought Rosalia would have maybe joined River, or I don't know, even Dave, but she didn't. Her pride is still shining through, and even though I'm hurting her so much by being too scared to share my big, dark secret, I'm proud of her for digging her heels in. She isn't afraid. I don't want her to be.

Only Knives, Dave, Zander, and my sister, Elodie, know what I'm hiding. *Nobody else.*

So, we're still in the presidential suite, except I sleep on the couch as I thought it was fair.

I snap to reality as Knives swiftly sits beside me, abandoning his bass guitar. "Eli?"

"Mmhmmm?"

"What's going on, man?"

"My head is fucking killing me." I wince, feeling myself all hot and flustered. "And I feel like I can't breathe. Like I'm choking on my breath. *Fuck.* How could she not have come?"

Knives doesn't answer any of it. All he does, as our tour manager, Mindy, strides to us her heels forcefully slapping against the polished concert floors (probably wanting to slaughter my ass for hastily walking offstage for a third time), is lean over and whisper, "Do it for *him.*"

And with palpitations and shaky hands, it's all I need to rush back up on stage *and sing.*

Chapter
FIFTY-TWO

Rosalia

Wish #11: To never let go of us...

When I step into the presidential suite following a girls' night with River after missing Diesel Rose's concert for the first time on tour, I find Elijah in the main bathroom, standing in the slate terrazzo shower with his back to me. He's surrounded by misty steam, his hands pressed against the wall, his black nail polish glistening as water cascades down his rippled back muscles, kissing that faded spinal scar, and lower, over his firm, bare ass.

"Elijah?" I whisper, a tremble in my voice, because he just stands so frozen.

Nothing.

"Elijah!"

Nothing.

"ELIJAH!" I call out for the first time, my voice echoing above the falling water.

Still nothing.

Shit. Is he okay? What's going on?

Stepping forth, I reach out my fingers, brushing them against his wet shoulder and his entire body shakes. It almost scares me just how fast Elijah whips around, the devil in his eyes, as he grabs my wrist and slams it against the shower wall with so much force it aches like a bitch. I feel the pain rushing down my bones, but when he sees it's me, his eyes soften a fraction.

There's a shade of deep red circling them, something I've never seen before. And the way he's looking at me, it's manic.

Full of fury.

Rage.

And just like that, he lets go of my wrist.

His breaths are so hard, I swear to God he's about to collapse when he grips my chin with his other hand, tilting my head forward to meet his stare. "What are you doing here?"

"I called out your name three times. I thought something was wrong."

"You shouldn't be here," Elijah growls.

I can't stop staring. Can't stop smelling the ever so evident weed from a rolled-up joint, mixed with his vanilla tobacco body wash. I've never seen him like this—*so high*. It's so evident in the way his face looks so dazed, and the way he's looking at me, as if he's burning down my soul.

There's no emotion.

No sense of warmth.

No love.

It's just cold, and rebellious, and agonizingly blue.

"What, Rosalia? What are you… What are you looking at?"

I swallow thickly, my heart skittering because… *I don't want this.* I want to support him, not drag him down, but it's so hard to do that when he's suffering and not letting me in.

"I'm just… I'm just looking at you."

"*Why?*" Elijah muses, backing away, the water now rippling down his hard, broad chest. It doesn't matter that he's been naked. None of it matters. Because it's more than that.

I keep getting lost in the way water drips by the ends of his eyelashes, pooling by his full lips. Warm water oozes from the huge rain head as he slicks his wet jet-black hair back.

"Because I'm savoring you."

"How?"

"The poetic tragedy laced on your lips… The Heathcliff brewing in your eyes… The Fitzgerald igniting in your soul."

The air crackles between us.

"Why?" Elijah whispers, so fragile it kills me.

Emotion lodges deep inside me because I am savoring him. Savoring him because this could be the very last time I'm in the same room with *the* Elijah Diesel, my forever boy crush.

"Because I can't do this if you're hiding something. Everything I feel for you is real."

Time slows.

I'm losing him. I think I'm losing my Lijah tonight.

We share an intense stare, a buildup of all our tension.

"Well? Tell me, Rosalia," he hisses, cocking his head to the side, his jaw tight. "You want to see me become a monster? You want to see me at my worst, baby? You want to see me be the fucking devil? I told you to stay away from me tonight."

No, you didn't. You didn't tell me a single thing.

I step closer, not caring that the water ripples down my freshly blow-dried hair, and my clothes stick to my skin, soaking me wet. I simply cup his cheeks, shut my eyes, and in the same breath whisper against his cold-as-ice lips, "I just want to love all of you… All your forms… That's all I'm *trying* to do."

I open my eyes and when I do, his piercing onyx-gray gaze is staring right back at me.

"I just want to love all of you, Elijah."

A beat.

And then…

"You can't," Elijah murmurs. "You can't love both of me, Rosalia. You can't love the angel and the devil. Darkness and light. Death and life. You have to choose one. And quite frankly, I can never be just *one*. This is me. Elijah Diesel. The rock star. The alcoholic. The lover. The psychopath. The sinner. Leave me or love me, babygirl, but you can't love me both."

And then Elijah hits the shower nozzle shut, rushing out to quickly wrap a towel around his waist with water trickling down his skin. Disappearing out of the bathroom, he leaves glistening wet drops trailing along the Italian marble floor tiles, pooling like the Atlantic.

The same Atlantic I'm currently drowning in.

Pacified in.

Dying in.

And I know, this time, *I'm not going to make it.*

I don't know how long I remain alone in the shower, warmth transforming to a wicked, cold chill, but when I hear the private elevator doors ping open, I bolt through the suite, water spraying everywhere. I make it to the elevator in time for Elijah to freeze mid-way into the car.

He's all dressed now. Smoking a joint. Looking so devilishly sad.

"If you step into that elevator," I scream, my voice cracking mid-sentence, "it's *over.*"

Daggers sink in my heart. *Oh God.* The man I thought would be my forever blurs, forming into a kaleidoscope of heartbreak because of my stupid tears. I don't know if I hate myself or him more in this moment, but the furious foolishness I feel is diabolic. Eats me alive.

"You and I both know this was over the second we left Portland," he growls darkly.

This is worse than four years ago. This pain is agonizing. It hurts so much.

"You don't know what love is!" I spit, crazed. "Elijah Diesel, I fucking *hate you!*"

Elijah studies me slowly, jaw clenching as he strides up to me.

"Yeah, you're right, I don't know what love is," he taunts in a seductive whisper and cups my face, watching the tears roll. "That's why I'm so crazy about you? Why I know I can't live without you, hmm? 'Cause in my own fucked up way, I really do love you, little one."

My heart...it's aching. "Elijah—"

"*You said I killed you...*" Elijah whispers, quoting Brontë. Before I can react, his lips find mine in a hot, achingly slow goodbye kiss fueled with nostalgic desire. "*Haunt me, then.*"

And then, he's gone.

Chapter
FIFTY-THREE

Rosalia

Wish #12: To find yourself again...

"**A**re you sure you want to do this?"

I glance over at River from where I'm standing, surrounded by my suitcase and all the shit I'm angrily folding and shoving into it. She's sitting on the edge of the California-king-sized bed in my suite, praying hands pressed to her lips, sadly observing me.

"River." I sigh, offering her a sad smile because that's all that's left. "You know I don't have a choice right now. Elijah doesn't want to grow a pair of balls, and I'm not willing to compromise with this, so where does it leave us?"

"I know, I know," she groans, casually smoothing over the stunning black satin dress I just threw in my suitcase.

Everything reminds me of him.

In these past twenty-four hours since our goodbye kiss before he strode out the door, I've been a terrible mess and I hate it. I've been staring at the flight website all day, *wondering, wondering, wondering,* and then I finally did it...

I'll be in Manhattan when I wake up tomorrow.

There's nothing else left to do but to fly back home with a heavy heart. Elijah made it very clear that this is the end of us, and I have my boundaries, which I'm not lowering for anybody.

I've cried too many tears for this man.

Hurt too much. Accepted too much.

Now it's *my* time for healing.

I'm leaving tonight.

Elijah's finishing up the meet and greet following his second last concert on tour tonight. I have to get out of here before he comes back here.

River's been here for a little while, helping me pack and get my shit together. It breaks me that she's missing yet again another one of her boyfriend's performances after they *just* got back together. But she told me *this* is where she really needs to be, helping me, and that really warmed my soul.

"I just can't believe Diesel won't tell you whatever it is he's hiding," River pouts, catching the scrapbook I throw at her from across the room. "He just kissed you and walked out last night?"

With a heavy heart, I nod, collect the last of my items from the walk-in closet, and drop them in the middle of the bedroom. *God, how many things do I have? Jesus.* Considering I flew to LA with only one spare change of clothes, the amount of stuff I now have is crazy. I guess it's because I originally thought I was only staying for the weekend, and that turned into two weeks and two other cities, so I bought more.

After everything is packed, I feel like a part of my life is slowly caving in, moments away from vanishing because I know it is.

I join River on the edge of the bed, sharing a sad smile as her fingers lace in mine and she holds me tight.

"*Gosh.* This is so sad, Rosa." She frowns, her eyes all pretty and glassy. "I really thought you two were so fucking epic together. Believe me when I say I've never seen Diesel so happy before you."

All I can do is continue smiling because I know if I say anything else, my voice will break, and I've done my fair share of crying for that asshole. *I. Am. Done.*

"You've got to promise we'll keep in touch, babe!" River pleads. "I've gotten so used to you being on tour with us, you're like the sister I never had, and I know that sounds really strange and I've only known you for two weeks, but it feels like so much longer to me."

I pull River into a tight embrace, and through the great ache in my chest, I can't help but softly giggle as she rocks us from side to side.

"I promise"—I smile against her shoulder, meaning every word— "you're not losing me."

Because it's true. I went on this tour as the odd one out, the only person who knew everybody the least amount of time, but River, Zander, and Dave instantly made me feel welcomed. Like I've belonged. Then there's Knives… I'm still trying to digest what that soft smile and '*Thank you*' really meant. If it was for Elijah, or… if he genuinely meant it for me.

But with River, I've got a lifelong friendship, and as odd as that is to admit, I really do have to thank Elijah Diesel for at least *this* great thing.

The Uber is set to arrive in ten minutes and Elijah still isn't here.

It's better this way.

I know it is.

I specifically told River not to tell him or any of the other boys my plan. I can't risk Dave coming up to hug me goodbye because that would only make Elijah aware of what I'm doing here, and I want to leave without detection. Last night was his goodbye. Tonight it's mine.

I've been pacing our Seattle presidential suite for God knows how long, my suitcase set beside the mid-century Cowhide couch in the open plan living room, ready for my phone to buzz with that life-changing notification.

Every single thing belonging to me is packed inside my suitcase. My Polaroid camera. My belongings. Even my stupid bags of tricks. All except for one…*that Polaroid of Elijah and me.* I can't stop staring at it, staring at *us*, staring at *him*. I know it's only breaking my heart more, but my soul craves one final glance at him. He kept that beach Polaroid of us. I kept the one the owner of D.A.R.K. took of us with our hands laced together and affectionate gaze.

These are the final moments of him I'll cherish forever.

These are the *final moments.*

I still don't understand it. How volatile it all turned. How we were joyous, hopeful, starstruck, and now… *This.* Then, I set the Polaroid down on the kitchen countertop. *Forever.*

My heart jumps as my phone begins blaring in the pocket of my Levi's, wondering if it could be the Uber who's surprisingly early.

It's not.

It's my father.

Finally.

I answer on the third ring, highly aware of just how destructive this conversation will be. I haven't spoken to him since that night he hung up on me. He has no idea that Elijah and I have plummeted into the Atlantic, that there's no coming back, that I'm flying back home soon.

"Dad," I breathe into the phone before he can say anything, riddled with nerves. "Hi."

"Hey, darling," he greets, seeming awfully…composed. "I'm sorry I haven't called you back. I've just been really busy at work and, well, to be honest, I'm still trying to wrap my head around everything. How are you doing in Portland?"

"Seattle."

"Ah, right."

"I'm goo—*actually*, well, I have some *news* to tell you…"

"What kind of news?"

"*Big* news."

I go silent for a second, and all I hear is white noise in return.

Okay, maybe I go silent for more than a second trying to come up with the right words to say because all of a sudden my father's breathing hardens and he bursts. "Fuck, Rosalia Philips, I hope you're not going to say what I think you're about to say…"

Huh?

My brows knit together. "What? What do you think I'm going to say?"

"Jesus Christ," my surgeon father groans, and I can just imagine him roughly rubbing his face. "Did that fucker… Are you… I… Shit. Are you trying to tell me you're pregnant?"

My jaw hits the flaw. "OH MY GOD! DAD!"

"WHAT? WHAT JUST HAPPENED?"

"Nothing, Dad, I'm just reacting to what you just said."

"*Oh.* Jesus, Rosa, I'm about to faint over here. So it's true then? Are you pregnant?"

"NO!" I gasp, not knowing whether to laugh or cry because I'm so far from pregnant. Stress is the only thing growing inside me. "No, not pregnant. Why would you even think that?"

"Well, it didn't help that you told me you had *big news* to tell me, followed by the world-record-sized pause."

"I'm sorry for giving you a fright," I start off with a soft smile before it all fades into a frown. "Elijah and I have… The world doesn't know it yet, but we're not together anymore."

Silence.

"Dad, I said we broke up."

"Heard you the first time, Rosa. I'm just trying to collect your mom's jaw off the floor."

"You have me on *speaker*?" I squeal.

"Baby doll," my mom gasps on the other line, seeming much more affected by the news than I thought. "What did that rock star do? Come on, you know you can tell us anything."

"Because you know I will fuck him over," my father adds, all broody and shit.

I almost laugh. "Dad, he's rich, famous, *and* six-foot-three. What are you gonna do?"

"I'll rough up his head and then he'll be sorry he won't know the most successful surgeon in New York City to fix it."

A smile burns across my lips as I lean over the kitchen counter because *okay, that was pretty funny.*

"Nobody's going to be roughing up anybody. Elijah just…crossed some lines and I feel like I just can't trust him because he isn't being honest to me about something. To me, trust is everything. After what happened with my biological parents…" I suck in a heavy breath and continue, "It's been so hard for me to actually feel present. I didn't feel that with Cayden or Trent. I never felt present. Elijah's made me feel so alive, but I can't do it anymore with him like this."

"That's understandable, sweetie, you need to feel safe in a relationship."

"I do feel safe with Elijah, Mom, but he's just…hurt me so many times, you know."

"*Physically*?" My father growls. "Because I swear to God I'll—"

I shake my head. "No, no, I promise he's not like that. I meant emotionally. Mentally."

"Oh."

"Yeah." My voice cracks mid-word and I hate it. I hate feeling this emptiness inside.

"Darling, please don't cry." My dad sighs. "I tried to warn you it'll end this way."

"I know. Anyway, I'll be in Manhattan in the morning, so see you both soon, okay?"

"Okay, have a flight, Rosa."

"We'll be here waiting, sweet girl. Mama loves you."

Smiling softly, I sniffle, knowing *this* is what it feels like to be loved. "Love you. Bye."

The second I end the call, my smile vanishes, and I'm left staring motionless at the Italian marble kitchen countertop. *Why do I feel so claustrophobic? Why's Uber taking so long?*

Buzz.

I casually glance at my phone, thinking it's Uber when, *OH MY GOD!*

Gasping at the text, my eyes practically bulge out in complete shock.

…WHAT?

NAOMI: OH MY FUCKING GOD! Rosalia! Rosalia! PORTIA EVANS HAS JUST BEEN ARRESTED FOR DRUG POSSESSION. SHIT!

As in Portia my enemy at New York City Ballet.

The Corps de Ballet dancer who's always had it in for me.

The girl I basically grinded on my boyfriend's dick in front of…

Well, *ex-boyfriend now.*

"What the…"

Naomi picks up on the first dial, and it's like she's gasping for air. "OH MY GOD, ROSA! Did you see my text? Well, did you see it? I'm freaking losing my breath because this asshole guy of mine dragged my ass to the gym, but holy fuck! What the hell IS THAT?"

"I'm in such shock. Jesus, when did this happen?"

"Literally just a few minutes ago. Google it."

I do just that, keeping her on the line, my jaw dropping even further with every article with Portia's name in front. *Cocaine. Meth. Heroin.* It's all constant reminders of my childhood going through my head and leaving my mouth bitter, laced with repulsion.

CORPS DE BALLET OR DISGUISED DRUG DEALER? Reads one of the headlines, alongside pictures of her on the Lincoln Center stage, some exclusive backstage shots, some beside *me.*

"Whoa, this is so bad, Naomi. I literally can't believe it. I never in a million years would have thought she'd do anything like this!"

"Tell me about it! It's literally breaking news everywhere here, even on TVs in the gym showing NBC Nightly. Well, Portia can wave her ass goodbye to New York City Ballet."

I didn't even think of that yet.

"Didn't expect karma to be served *this* sweet…" I mumble under my breath, but my best friend hears and breaks out in laughter. "But it's so true, right? Like, I'm not a vindictive person, but the eyes she used to give me, sheesh. I guess we'll just have to wait for updates."

"Yeah, I kind of have a feeling they'll make an example of her. ANYWAY, how are you feeling, boo? I know your flight's in a little bit, but just know my juicy ass will be at JFK with open arms, waiting to pick you up. I'm gonna hug you so tight, you may just explode!"

"I love you." Laughing feels so refreshing as I playfully roll my eyes. "And I bet I will."

When a notification pops up that my Uber has arrived, Naomi and I say our goodbyes.

This is it.

I glance around the open plan kitchen, living, dining, and lobby space of the suite, a bittersweet pang in my chest as I take it all in. *But there's one more thing I need to leave here.*

I don't expect to feel so lost within myself when I slip off Elijah's vintage silver snake ring, like I'm losing a piece of myself, and yet I do, because *I am.* It's the same pull in my chest and piercing burn all over my body when I take off the handmade leather charm bracelet for one of the first times since he gave it to me in that NYC laundromat at 2:00 a.m., many weeks ago.

The history that these two pieces of jewelry hold is mammoth.

It wrecks me and then puts me all together. Constantly. Like violent waves.

And the very reason I need to let them go, no matter how hastily it destroys me.

Because just as I'm about to cling the ring and charm bracelet on the kitchen countertop for good, the private elevator doors swoosh open and I...*just freeze in motion.*

Ohhh no.

Shit. Shit. Shit.

It takes all of me to not spin around. To not look at him. To not react more than I already am. *All. Of. Me.* Without even seeing him, I feel his hot gaze burning the back of my head. I'm so used to the complexities of ballet, but *this* dance between him and me is by far the hardest.

Soft footsteps merge into fretted thumps, and then... *Nothing.*

It all stops.

Just silence.

Just silence, white noise, and a second notification from Uber on my phone.

"*Rosalia...*" whispers the famed voice my heart will never forget. "You're...leaving?"

Anticipation riddles my anguished heart and I finally spin on my pastel pink Converses.

Mistake. It's such a mistake turning around, seeing *him* like this.

Elijah.

My former melancholic addiction stands vulnerably in the middle of the living room.

Fretted onyx-grays meet mine, drinking me slowly. I remain fierce, my chin up high as his gaze dramatically widens at the jewelry in my hand, my suitcase, and then...back to me.

Everything slows so fast the longer our stare deepens, becoming something it shouldn't. He's begging me with his gaze, pleading for me not to do this, but I need to. For myself, I must.

I can see that it's finally hitting him.

Finally hitting him that he's losing me.

Losing our past four years silked together.

"Yes." I gently break the tension, clearing my throat. I hate that my plan backfired, but I need improvisation. "My ride's waiting on me. I'm probably getting charged extra for it, so..."

"*Peaches…*" Elijah whispers so softly it's haunting. "Rosa, baby, please…*don't go.*"

"Elijah—"

My words slip at the intensity of his next moves.

He rushes up to me, not an inch of space between us. Guilt brewing in those tired onyx wonderlands, our gaze locks as he falls to his knees, begging for mercy.

Oh, Lijah.

Elijah's piercing eyes pool in sadness, tears of despair caressing his cheeks so fast.

"I'll tell you *everything*. I promise," he sobs, clasping my hands, the jewelry in between. His vulnerable voice breaks in a way I've never heard. "Just please… *Please* don't leave me."

I try adamantly to hold back my tears, but it's just a glassy, crystal mess. "I need to."

"No, don't go. I can't live without you. I'm sorry. I'm sorry for *everything. Please.*"

My heart pierces at his words, at his promise, *at him*, and all that oozes out is…*us.*

"*S'il te plaît, mon ange.*" Elijah bawls, gasping for air. "*Je sais ce qu'est l'amour. L'amour est tous les fragments. L'amour signifie la guérison. L'amour est douleur.*"

Please, my angel. I know what love is.

Love is all the fragments.

Love is healing.

Love is pain.

Uncontrollable waterworks burn down my cheeks because this is… *Oh my God. Wow.*

"*Mais surtout…*" He smiles through the tears, squeezing our hands. "*L'amour c'est* toi."

But most of all… love is you.

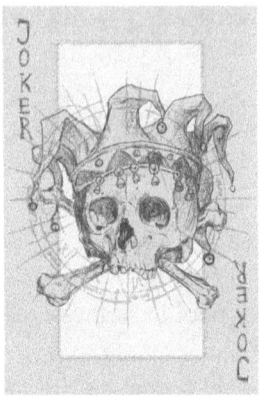

Chapter

FIFTY-FOUR

Elijah

Wish #13: To heal from the dark...with me.

S o many things went through my head the moment I walked out of the private elevator and saw Rosalia simply standing there with her luggage, waiting to vanish out of my life, just like the nostalgia we built together.

I couldn't breathe.

I couldn't do anything but rush up to her, fall on my knees, and pray for mercy.

Every single word I said to her—French, English—with my scattered heartbeats, pounding against my chest, I *meant*.

I meant every single word as she looked down at me, angelic flames in her eyes, crying.

Because all I wanted for her to do was *stay*.

In that moment I realized *everything*. Just how close I was to losing the only person in my life that truly wants me. Adores me. Cares.

And now, Rosalia's still gazing down at me.

My trembling hands are still threaded with hers.

The silver and leather jewelry between our hands have warmed, charred, clammy, but I didn't give a fuck about it. I just care about *her.*

And as her phone buzzes for another time on the marble kitchen countertop, all I want to do is stay on my knees like this, praying for forgiveness forever.

Through all her tears, through all her hate, and through all our sentiments, Rosalia sniffles. And I can see just how much she's trying to stay strong. Brave. But it's slipping.

"Five minutes," Rosalia rasps, her voice coated in emotion. "Five minutes for you to explain everything, and then I'm leaving."

Leaving.

My heart skips, plummeting. It fucking dives so deep into the Pacific that I can't reach out and grip it. Revive it. *Five minutes. I* have five minutes to change Rosalia Philips's mind and douse her with the truth before she leaves my life for good.

Rosalia slips her hands from mine and types something into her phone, leaving the vintage snake ring and leather bracelet still in my grip. I close my fist over them, feeling their beauty before slipping them into my pocket, adamant that I'll see them on her again.

This can't be the last time… It can't.

It just… *Fuck.*

It just can't.

Moments later, Rosalia's sitting on the mid-century Cowhide couch, her legs crossed and pink Converses jittering as she tries not to let it affect her, but it does, because with every single jitter, her soles brush against the edge of a suitcase. And it kills me deeply.

I can't sit down.

I can't stop pacing.

My fingers thread through my hair, wiping away my tears, sniffling away the ones that are still impending. There's so much rushing through my head.

So much commotion.

So much emotion.

So much destruction, and *yet…* And yet I feel this warmth and it pacifies me.

It captivates every single inch of my body. I know the words I murmured to her in French are still with her. She's got this look in her eyes, this moment of heat, a spark, a fraction of the fragments of us. I know those French words touched her. I want her to know I *meant* it, which is why I need to tell her *everything*.

Finally manhandling my nerves, I sit on the couch beside Rosalia, and there's a dig in my chest when she scoots back a little, giving us some more space. *Distance.* I get it. I do. I've been such a dick to her. Such a fucking jerk.

She needs her space, Elijah.

Fucking give it to her.

It prompts me to scoot back a little too and twist my body around so my back is pressing against the armrest of the couch. She's looking dead at my eyes and it's poetry. Fucking dark poetry laced in every single classic novel I know.

Four years ago, I didn't know that *The Beautiful and Damned* would be so much engraved in our story—and yet right now, looking into those green meadow eyes, sparkling in tears—*it is.*

Because I was right.

She—my *peaches*, my muse, *ma chérie*—is the beauty.

And I—Elijah Diesel, the poetically tragic rock star—am the damned.

And I am so obsessed.

Addicted.

In love.

With her.

"My Uber driver said that he'll wait five more minutes before I need to cancel the job because it's holding him up. So…." She trails off. "Elijah, please. If you want to talk, *talk*, because I have a flight to board."

I slowly nod, the knot in my throat intensifying as I play around with my rings. Vigorously. Twisting them around, feeling the grooves, doing anything to distract myself from the fact that I have never, ever, told anyone else but a few people *this* before.

So, with a heavy breath, and the lifeline to our relationship hanging above me on the thinnest fucking thread, I roll my shoulders back, compress my breaths, and lock eyes with her.

"A year ago…" I breathe.

Fuckkk.

Why is this so hard?

I feel like someone is shutting me down inside.

"A year ago…" Rosalia trails off, a little calmer than I expected. Patient.

Come on, Elijah, I tell myself. *Say it.*

You've got less than four minutes.

Say. It.

Fucking say it.

Come on, Elijah. Do it.

Don't you dare be like this.

Just open your damn mouth.

Be honest and fucking say it.

My jaw ticks.

There's so much intensity in our stare and I try again, gulping down.

"Last year, *Peaches*, on my birthday, I… I attempted and failed to…end my life."

Rosalia gasps, her glassy eyes wide with her hands moving to her mouth. "No, *Lijah.*"

Then I say the next words with a heavy heart, knowing they could break us for good.

Forever.

Rosalia

"And part of the truth I've been hiding from you, Rosalia, is that… My alcoholic mother was also an addict. A *drug* addict." Elijah sniffles. "And she wanted to abort me. She was already struggling with my two siblings. Having another kid…it was the end of the world for her. But the doctors in France said she was too far into the pregnancy. It was too late, so my mom did everything she could to get rid of me."

I have no words.

None.

Drug addict.

As I stare into his fateful gaze, I feel everything and nothing. I'm so numb, so scared, so sad for him. I know what drugs do to a person. I remember fragments of it with my parents.

"I was a NAS baby, Rosa. Know what that means?"

I shake my head.

"It stands for Neonatal Abstinence Syndrome," he whispers, smoothing a hand over his jean-clad thighs, pain in his eyes. "It's when babies get withdrawals from certain drugs exposed to the womb before birth. I was born with cocaine and opioids in my blood. So much so, my mother almost overdosed on that very hospital bed."

Oh my God.

Air knocks out of my lungs at Elijah's words.

He was only a little boy. Helpless. Defenseless.

Scooting closer to him with hot tears already slipping, I hold on to his ice-cold hands.

"With a NAS baby, as soon as the umbilical is cut, the baby is on their own, and withdrawal begins. High-pitched screams. Twitches. Convulsions. My brother, Edmond, once told me I spent eight fucking weeks in and out of hospital as a newborn. My father was going to leave my mom that very night I was born, but instead, he stuck it out for almost ten years."

"Oh."

"Yeah. By nine, I was already surrounded by the grief of my brother, finding him there… I wanted it to be me. Trauma killed me from then. The voices in my head got loud. Loud*er*. And no therapy could help me. When I was ten, my stepfather came along, and my mother's alcoholism became worse. I started having these maniac moments of complete rage, and then the next second, I'd be so calm and go through all these emotional episodes. My mother called me a psychopath. My stepfather called me a *punk*. You know the story that comes with all his torment…with the alcohol. Neither of them knew how to handle me. Nobody understood me. Nobody loved me. Everybody thought I was a burden because I should have never been born. Nobody cared, *nobody*, nobody except for my sister."

"Elodie." I manage to smile through the sorrow, my heart clenching.

"Elodie." Elijah nods, sadly smiling back. "She always used to sneak into my room late at night with a slice of chocolate cake that she got from her high school cafeteria. It wasn't always chocolate, but it was always so squished in the plastic wrap, but I loved it anyway. We were really close growing up, but I never wanted to hinder her with my demons.

"Sometimes," he adds. "My stepfather would take my sister and me to school, but because I was younger, I'd be at a different school that was farther, so he would drop me off last. But…he didn't *always* drop me off to school. Sometimes he drove me all the way back home and he locked me in my bedroom. And I would just… I would just stay there. Trapped. I couldn't tell anybody because I was scared of what he would do. I regularly had a black eye from him that I would have to fucking lie to my peers, saying I got in fist fights and things like that. My mother was always so high and intoxicated that she didn't even notice."

A heavy pause, and then…

"When I turned sixteen, I stepped into rehab for the first time because I was addicted to vodka. Got into the life of rock and roll, and slowly music became my addiction. But then I would relapse, over and over. Rosalia, those maniac episodes lasted for a long time. Fuck, I *still* have them. I can't control when they happen, how I get from hot to cold, but…"

"Yeah?"

"Things started changing the day I met Knives at this stupid fucking punk rock vegan protest. I don't even remember why I was fucking there. Little baby chicks were roaming everywhere, and I got to this barbed wire fence, needing a breather, when this blond-haired, blue-eyed guy came up to me and literally said, *cigarette?*"

I squeeze Elijah's hands, my soul warming at the chuckle that escaped his lips when talking about Knives.

"Because of the grief, I would just explode and even on normal days when I should have been happy, I wasn't. It was riddled with depression, and I didn't see the point of anything. So I stayed with Knives as much as I could. Let music fuel me. Formed Odyssey. I didn't really do well at school, as you can imagine. Sometimes…my stepfather would come home and pick a fight. Beat me all broken and bruised. Knives saw me at my worst. He *always* saw me at my worst. Well, what I *thought* to be my worst at the time anyway. I started spiraling, and I-I… I…"

"It's okay, Lijah, take your time."

Elijah nods. "My mom and stepdad held these early 2000s drug parties. Strange people in our run-down house. Syringes were everywhere. Meth. Heroin. I would go to school reeking of their weed. It was a fucking nightmare. My stepfather was her drug dealer. He was distorting my life. And then…one day, they had a big fight, and she escaped to France. She *left. Abandoned* me 'cause I was nothing to her. Not a fucking thing. My stepdad ran off soon after."

Shit.

"CPS wanted to take me, but my sister was of age, so I stayed with her instead. I was working at a record store, real cool and shit. Bought a black vintage Mustang, was sober for a couple months. Things were looking up. Then, when I walked out of work one day, my stepfather was leaning by my vintage Mustang, threateningly said, *drive.* I did. That's when I felt the knife lick my skin, right here. I ran the car off the highway. I don't remember much. I was hanging on to life, thinking I was gonna die, craved it, Rosa, wanted it. But I lived. My stepdad didn't. It was a miracle. I swear my brother was looking down at me, protecting me. The crash left me with a scar on my spine from emergency surgery to save me. Painkillers kept me alive. I was in so much pain during my recovery, it was just all…"

Elijah slips his hand from mine to slowly rub it over his stubble before blowing out an anxious sigh. "Rosalia, I… I'm so scared to tell you this next part. It'll change your perspective of me, but, if anything, please try understanding my point of view."

I asked for this.

I asked for the truth.

I want to know everything.

It's why I nod softly, not caring that it's been more than five minutes.

My heart aching from everything Elijah's endured in his life. It explains a lot already.

"After my accident, there came a point where the painkillers weren't enough. I needed more. Craved more. Knives and I began to experiment with…with *drugs.* The bad kind. Cocaine. Molly. LSD. I felt like I was becoming my brother and thought perhaps this way I could finally die like him. Drugs helped me. Made me feel numb to the grief, to the pain, to my life. There was this huge voice in my head and every time I popped one or snorted something, everything would just disappear. It was like I couldn't breathe and seconds passed, milliseconds that felt like a lifetime, then just when I thought I was fading, the *hit* would come. The high numbed my body and in its place, euphoria, that made me breathe again."

Thump.

Thump.

Thump.

My breaths all fade into one because the fear in Elijah's gaze is prevalent.

"Then, *Peaches*," Elijah whispers lowly, eyeing me slowly, "I became a drug addict."

Oh…

Oh my God…

I don't know what comes first, my petrified gasp, or the violent sting in my heart.

Oh.

My.

God.

I don't know what to say or do other than just stare into those onyx-grays. Elijah's so vulnerable sitting on the edge of the couch, he can't even look at me straight because he's breathing so hard.

It hurts me so much seeing him like this. Seeing him in such a panicked gaze, nervously playing with his hands and shaking his head to himself.

Waves of nausea rush up, laced with everything I once believed to be true. I always thought drug addicts were bad people, like my biological parents, but Elijah… he isn't bad. He's just a boy who grew up to be a man tortured by his childhood and tormented by darkness.

"Please." He cups my knee, but I'm so shocked that I pull him off. "Say something."

Elijah Diesel… was a drug addict?

I think I'm going to be sick.

I don't know how I make it to the en suite in time, but I do, and Elijah is right there, holding back my hair as all the waves of shock spill out of me.

I'm gasping for air, my throat aching from all the lactic acid as hot tears run down my cheeks. I'm sobbing and throwing up in the toilet, at the same time trying to clasp Elijah's hand to squeeze it because his pain is my pain.

I don't know what I'm feeling right now. I don't know any of it as I slump against the terrazzo-tiled wall, staring at the man I care about so much.

I'm such a mess, I know I am, and Elijah is too with the guilt lodged in his eyes. The way he rushes to me, brushes hair out of my face, and slowly presses a kiss to my forehead, his lips lingering. *He's become so affectionate.*

"I'm sorry, baby," he murmurs by my forehead. "I'm so sorry for hiding it from you. It wasn't purposely. I felt so ashamed. Invalid. Knew I would lose you."

Clasping my hand, he leads me to the vanity and pulls out toothpaste and a spare toothbrush from his toiletry bag. I reach out my hand to grip them, but instead, he softly brushes my teeth instead. He handles me so carefully, it's like I'm the most precious thing in the world.

When I'm finished, my stomach is still swirling and all the thoughts in my mind become a huge, throbbing headache. Faded glimmers of my biological parents rush over, and I just remember feeling so lonely with them. So scared. And cold. And just so freaking upset.

I should feel the same with Elijah. I should feel furious. Deflated. Hysterical.

But the longer I gaze into his gun-metal-colored eyes, the more I feel warmth. The more I breathe in his familiar vanilla tobacco scent, the more at home I feel. The more I jump up into his arms, my legs wrapping around his narrow waist as he carries me to the bedroom, the safer I feel with my head buried in his chest, his heart beating wildly with mine.

Elijah lays us on the oversized bed, coldness from the bedsheets piercing our skin, but it all comes secondary to the way he holds me tighter in his solace. We simply gaze at each other. Gingerly, our heads press against the pillows, his thumb rushing under my sweater, caressing my skin.

It must be after eleven now and the Uber driver is probably blowing up my phone, but all I care about is how the silvery moonlight cracks through the room, casting over his glossy eyes.

Reaching out a hand, I trace his full lips, his crow's feet, the soft scar on his cheek.

Sparks.

Fireworks.

Butterflies.

Still.

Elijah kisses my finger when I graze over his lips for a second time, the heat lasting.

"I want to hear more," I rasp, glancing back and forth between his eyes. "All of it."

Elijah nods.

"First, I want to confess I'm not proud of my actions. At all. I was a drug addict, but mostly, cocaine. The older I got, the more drugs helped me not feel. Became the cure to everything. Eased my episodes. From sixteen up until a little while ago, it was just liquor, drugs, and rock 'n' roll. I've been in and out of rehab all through my twenties, scattered in my thirties, because as Diesel Rose became successful, I was always worried about the press."

Then it all just clicks.

Lydia Fitz. His former publicist.

This is what they were trying to hide from the world.

"That's why you trusted your publicist so much, yeah?"

"Exactly, little one. She was my lifeline when it came to reputation. You see, everybody thinks musicians are perfect, and most of them are, but the rest, we're troubled. When you and I first met, when I was stepping off the bus in Tribeca, I came out of rehab a week prior. I already felt myself relapsing, but then I saw you, and *fuck...* I craved you instead, yet hated you for it. You became my addiction. I wanted to overdose on you every single day. I didn't touch drugs for all those months I knew you. I vowed to stay clean. I only had a few joints. When we got the call to come join *Devil's Advocate and The Fiery Halos*, I felt it coming on. I needed that rush. I needed it so fucking badly, baby. I hated I left you alone. Did you see the news tonight? About Portia?"

I frantically nod.

"Sometimes I would even buy off her. She had this huge supply that her brother never knew about. You don't need to worry, little one, she won't rat me out. But it was a huge wakeup call for me. Made me realize the impact of it all, alongside seeing your suitcase there."

My jaw drops. "Oh, I never knew…"

"Yeah, I know."

"Go on."

Elijah takes a heavy breath. "Last year, I relapsed. Badly. I didn't want to breathe anymore. Live anymore. Music wasn't enough. I had…a massive overdose in Manhattan."

My heart. It shatters because I know exactly what he must have felt in those seconds.

The seconds fluttering between life and death. It's so bittersweet that we both once stepped into the darkness, because now, right here, we're leading each other into the light.

"Oh my God," I cry, shaking my head and inching closer to him. "No, no, Elijah."

"I know, Rosa." Tears pool in his eyes. "Diesel Rose was at their highest of highs, and yet, inside, I was at my lowest of lows. I learned to mask my pain, the drugs, the alcohol so well. *So* well. It was scary. No one noticed. No one noticed I was fading."

"But how?"

"Because I didn't want them to. We'd just come off a worldwide tour, on my birthday, and Knives had found me at our studio… on the Persian rugs. He thought I was gone. So did everyone else. After they revived me, pumped my stomach, and I came to on the hospital bed, he looked me in the eye like he never had before. *Disappointment.* I could tell that it was the start of the beginning of the war. The recovery. That's the moment he became my accountability. No drinking in front of him. No drugs at all except for a few joints here and there. Lydia, my former publicist, managed to keep every single detail out of the press. *Every* single detail. That's why she didn't want me to get close with anybody because she was scared I'd all get exposed."

"I've been really fucked up, baby, but I'm trying to be better. These past few weeks, I've been spiraling. Drinking. A little coke whenever you weren't looking. When we went to Pier 56, I wasn't acting all funny because of the cold like I claimed. I was trying to deter from the fact that I was borderline high off coke, and just trying to mask it because I have been doing that for almost twenty years. Hiding it. But I don't want to be that guy anymore. Not for *you.* Not for *me.* Not for *us.*"

Elijah takes a breath, caressing my face ever so softly. "When Knives found me last year, my phone was open on your contact. I must have been seconds away from dialing you when…*it* happened. Through it all, you were the last person I wanted to hear."

"Lijah…"

"I wanted to fall asleep to your lullaby, *Peaches*, forever," he fondly adds in a whisper, a crack in his voice, lips inches from mine. "That's my truth."

Elijah's words come with a weight I've never felt before. So intense and powerful and brave. This overwhelming wave of emotion rushes over me at the severity of his past. Of his truth. Of himself.

Yet through all my heartbreak, shock, and yearning, wrapping my arms around his neck and kissing him softly is the only thing that consoles my mind. It's the only thing that forces feeling to rush down my spine. To revive my heart. To breathe again.

I kiss Elijah Diesel so passionately, our tongues salty from the tears as they ever so softly swirl together. I'm making love to his mouth. Communicating every single emotion. Devouring him. It's like the entire world could burn down, and yet, we'd still make it.

During the kiss, he flips us over on the bed so he's on top, his hips pinning me to the bed. We kiss deeper, harder, like we fucking mean it. I kiss him with deep hurt, with tears streaming down, a hand in his that I slowly bring under my sweater and between my cleavage.

Pulling back from his lips with my eyes still shut, I whisper in sniffles, "Feel my heart, Lijah?"

It takes a moment, but Elijah softly hums. "Yeah."

I push his hand deeper into my chest, letting him capture every erratic thump and vibrating ricochet. "It's beating like this because of you. It always has."

"You should be scared of me, *Peaches*."

"I know," I whimper, wrapping my legs around his narrow waist when his body sinks deeper into me. My Converses dig into his back, and I'm so conscious of not hitting his spine. "I know I should be."

"You should hate me so fucking much."

"I know."

Our eyes flutter open in the exact same second. Watercolor eyes fueled with emotion. It's all I can describe them as while Elijah Diesel studies me now.

"Maybe I've always been more comfortable in chaos, but I don't want to be anymore..." He shakes his head. "Do you hate me? Are you scared of me?"

The longer our stare lasts, the faster my heart beats beneath his warming palm.

"I'm scared of the way you tried to leave this earth," I whisper, a sob breaking through. "I'm scared of the way you've been craving love your entire life. I hate the way you didn't tell me sooner."

"I know, baby." He sighs, shaking his head to himself again. "And I'm so sorry for it. I was... I was so scared you'd look at me and all you'd see were your fucked-up parents. I'm not used to having someone who cares for me. So with you, I always thought it was too good to be true. I didn't believe it, not until tonight. When I saw you with your luggage... I felt something in my chest I'd never felt before. I don't know what happens from here, but I didn't want you leaving without knowing."

Breathe, Rosalia. Breathe.

All my life I've grown up with the stigma that drugs make you bad... But right now, the longer I'm wrapped in Elijah, his history echoing in my mind, the more I'm beginning to realize that not all people who do drugs are bad.

They craved escape. Needing that damn thrill. Addicted to feeling numb.

That was Elijah too.

My parents...they were craving the same thing. Maybe it wasn't that they didn't love me. They just didn't know how. And the drugs made them forget.

What if they died to save me?

What if... What if they knew my life was more significant than the drugs, but they just needed saving to really love me. But the drugs were too much.

But Elijah's alive. He's right here. And he's admitting his faults. He wants that saving. He wants to get better now, and I truly believe him. He wants to save himself so he can truly love someone.

Oh my... Have I been...have I been looking at my parents' death wrong my entire life?

"Did you also not tell me because you thought I'd walk away due to my parents' drug abuse?"

"Yes. I thought it would be too close to home. I saw the pain in your eyes whenever you spoke about them. How much they really hurt you. I thought… I thought you'd hate me if you knew."

"You think you deserve this pain?"

Without blinking, Elijah nods. "Yes."

"But you don't."

He seems almost stunned. "What?"

"You are so much more than my parents. You weren't responsible for the breakdown of a childhood. Your parents were. You didn't have any kids depending on you, Elijah. You were broken, and I understand the hesitance in telling me, but please, you're not my parents."

Hopeful disbelief. "Really?"

"*Really.*"

"But… Most people won't be able to handle somebody like me."

"I'm not *most* people. You're worth so much more than what they put you through. You're so much more than the drugs, the liquor, all the ache. You're more than everything you've just told me, and now I realize that about my parents too." With a heaving chest, I smile bravely. "Through all the pain, through all the pleasure, I still want you, because you're worth it. Because your scars make you real. *Human.* Deserving to heal from the dark… Just like *me.*"

Elijah smiles through his tears. "Tell me what you need to make you stay, *Peaches.*"

"Honesty. Clarity. Baby steps. I can't judge your past because you never once judged my flaws," I admit. "But make me trust you'll go to rehab and recover. That if you slip again, you'll tell me, and we work as a team through it. Make me trust *this* means something to you."

"You're more than my muse…" Elijah cups his hands around my face, looks me hard in the eyes, and breathes, "You're my *lifeline.* Because you revive me every single time, baby, just like tonight. Rehab. Trust. Baby steps. I promise I'll do it all because all I want is you."

And I believe him. I really do. Enough to give him another chance.

I believe him as we share the most tender smile all night. As we remain wrapped in each other's arms, listening to our heartbeats. I believe him as this huge void lifts, allowing me to understand my parents' death clearer and finally begin to heal from it. *Like I always wanted.*

"*Notre amour est la seule chose à laquelle je veux être dépendant,*"

Elijah whispers to me in French, nothing but love in those sparkling onyx-grays. It's everything. *"Toujours…ma pêche."*

Our love is the only thing I want to be addicted to. Forever… my peach.

"Je t'aime." Elijah brushes his hot lips against mine. "I love you, *Peaches*."

I love you. I love you, *Peaches*.

And with all my heart, through my tears, I murmur back, "I love you, Lijah. So much."

And then, he kisses me. *Wickedly.*

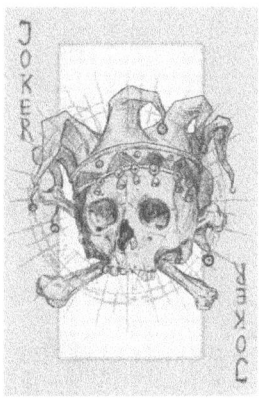

Chapter

FIFTY-FIVE

Elijah

Wish #14: To fall into a Fitzgerald kinda love...

I *love her.*
I love Rosalia Philips.
So. Fucking. Much.
I love her through our darkness.
I love her through our light.
I love her through my demons.
I love her through the healing.
I love her little quirks.
I love her endlessly.
I love her for accepting me.
Because now, she's saving me.
My muse…
My *peaches*…
My cherry viper eyes…
Is saving me.

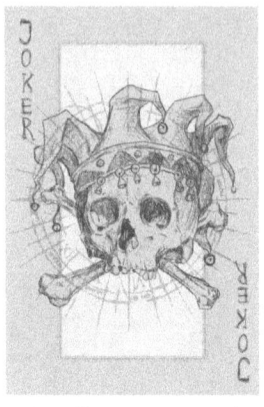

Chapter
FIFTY-SIX

Elijah

Wish #15: To fall into a Fitzgerald kinda love...
with me, of course, da.

My sister, Elodie, is already beaming and rushing down the porch the second Maverick pulls into the driveway of her stunning Seattle home. It's right between Capitol Hill and Madrona, and *Jesus Christ, who knew my sister could run this fast?*

"Oh God, she's going to embarrass the shit out of me..."

Rosalia can't stop laughing beside me in the back seat of my bodyguard/driver's SUV, and guess what? I can't stop staring at her. At the way her smile lines sink deep into her cheeks, the warmth of the laughter, at just how happy she is right now.

Last night was groundbreaking for us. I told Rosalia all my truths about my substance abuse and alcoholism and she *accepted me*. She didn't run away. She didn't abandon me like my mother. She looked me straight in the eye and told me that I was valid, so much I was crying.

After Rosalia canceled the Uber and contacted the airline, we spent the night wrapped in each other. I fell asleep to the beat of her chest racing against mine, her lips loving on mine. Never thought I could appreciate her existence more, but last night was a testament to that.

She loves me. I love her. This is love.

It just took me almost thirty-six years to feel it. To be understood. Be seen. Be loved.

And this morning, when I woke up, I made a promise to her that I'll check myself in to a detox rehabilitation center back in Manhattan, the day after my birthday. I even had a band meeting with our record producer, and we agreed to push our single's production. My thirty-sixth birthday is in exactly three days. That means I have four more days to spend every single moment with Rosalia before I go away for a little while to get better. Because that's all I want to do.

Rosalia's acceptance of my grief and my pain has given me this new zest for life.

I'm not afraid anymore. I'm not afraid of her judging me because I know she won't.

So this morning, when I asked her what she wanted to do for Diesel Rose's final rest day before the tour ends tomorrow and she said she wanted to meet Elodie and Clément, I almost died from happiness. From nerves. From every single fucking emotion because… *Wow.*

Rosalia wants to meet my family. My only *family.*

Do you know how special that is to me?

The void in my chest is gone, and it's all become just her inside. Only her. *Forever.*

Which leads me to this exact moment. Forgot? Let me remind you. My sister's rushing down her porch steps like a damn hurricane. I'm sweating balls because I just know she's going to shit-stir me sooo bad about making her meet my first ever girlfriend and grin while doing it.

Side note: I told Elodie that I was coming, but I'm surprising her with Rosalia.

And then there's Rosalia…

"But I'm *looking forward* to her embarrassing the shit out of you, baby." She grins.

I shoot her a playful glare. "Whose side are you on, blondie?"

"Yours," she sweetly murmurs before pecking my stubbled cheek. "*Always* yours."

The lyrics pouring out of me are poetry.

Always yours too, little one.

Maverick parks.

Rosalia reaches for the door, but I quickly clasp a hand over hers, stopping her.

"I'm pulling out the gentleman moves today. Don't stop it. I'll come around."

Rosalia gazes back at me all dreamy and roses, biting her lower lip. "Lucky me."

Our stare lingers.

We've been doing that a lot since last night.

Perhaps because every time I look into her eyes, there's this pang in my chest, three words on the tip of my tongue that I'm dying to tell her because for the first time in my life, I feel it.

My sister Elodie's screaming her head off the second I step out of the SUV and shut it behind me, practically jumping into my arms as sobs escape her. "*Oh mon Dieu! Oh mon Dieu! Oh mon Dieu!* You're here, Elijah! Holy fudge, I missed you so much!"

"Wow, what a welcome…" I chuckle into her soft brunette waves, squeezing her tight.

"Shut up, idiot, and tell me you missed me too!"

I smile deeper because *fuck*, I have. "I missed you too, Lodie. Eight months."

"Eight months," she whispers when she finally gets off me, bringing her hands to my chiseled jaw in complete horror. "Never. Again. Fuck the tours, you need your sister."

"I'm sure my fans would love that…"

"You're such a cocky bastard. You know that, yeah? *Look at me, I have a fan club.*"

I can't help smirking. "But I *do.*"

Groaning, Elodie rolls her onyx eyes. "Cock-y."

As I said, I missed her. Immensely.

"Anyway, while you roll those eyes into the next century, I…" I clear my throat, feeling a little timid as I rub the back of my neck. "There's somebody I'd like for you to meet…"

"Who?" Elodie glances up and down her driveway with a

narrowed gaze. "I don't see anybody! Shit! Is this an episode of *Candid Camera*? Is Opera surprising me with a new car?"

For fuck's sake, this woman.

Someone give me a wall. I want to slam my head against it.

"No." I shake my head, gesturing behind me to the tinted windows. "*In the car*, Lodie."

"Shut up!"

Rounding the other side of the car, Elodie follows me, stopping inches away when I brush my fingers over the car handle. *This is it. This is the moment* my *life becomes* ours.

I pop the door open to a nervously smiling Rosalia, and it has me chuckling as I help her out of the car. "You have nothing to worry about. My sister doesn't bite. *Well*, not today anyway."

"*Comforting*."

"Very." I peck my babygirl's lips with a little growl, subtly squeezing her ass for emphasis when I whisper in her ear, "She's gonna adore you, Rosa, I promise. Just watch."

Shocked, Elodie gasps so loud, her gaze flickers between me and my girlfriend.

Told you she'd be surprised.

"Rosalia," my sister suddenly growls, glaring my girlfriend down. "Rosalia Philips!"

Wait, what?

My heart and jaw drop at the same time. *The hell?*

Rosalia's frantic eyes widen, panic circling them like crazy.

"Rosalia Philips…" Elodie's glare slips and transforms into the brightest grin I've ever seen in the midst of bursting out in laughter. "WELCOME TO THE FAMILY, *PEACHES*!"

And here starts the shit-stirring…

Relieved, I flap a hand over my heart and my sister pulls Rosalia into *the* embrace of their lives, all while hysterically laughing. *She's the class clown who never really grew up.*

"Oh my, I thought you hated me!" Rosalia smiles as they pull away. "Swear to God."

"I could never!"

"Good." My girlfriend's smile deepens. "Because I really adore your brother."

Elodie smirks, not so subtly giving me a side-eye. "I bet you do."

My cheeks heat. Yep. Like actual bashfully-blush-heat.

Stupid heart.

And of course Rosalia notices and elbows my sister with a smolder. "Look at him!"

"He likes you so freaking much. Oh my God, look at the way he's looking at you!"

"Elodie," I groan.

"Sorry, I'm just talking to my future sister-in-law, so can you just shut up? Thanks."

Rosalia laughs and returns to my side, surprising me when she rushes up on her tippy toes and softly kisses the corner of my mouth. "You're so cute, Lijah baby."

From a psychopath to being cute…sometimes life really does change you *for the better.*

A gust of cold Seattle wind breaks through, kissing my skin and dancing through her wavy hair. Rosalia's phone begins blaring, but she ignores it. It rings for a second time, and she apologizes and puts it on silent. Her phone rings once again, vibrating in her jean jacket pocket.

One glance at the contact and her eyes widen a fraction, "Shit, sorry, I've got to take this. It's the HR division of New York City Ballet. It's probably about Portia. I'll take the call in the car."

Yeahhh, about that…

Portia got sentenced to one-year imprisonment this morning. She didn't retaliate because she was caught red-handed. Thankfully, for some odd reason, she also didn't drag my name in the mud for my past. Rosalia's ballet company probably want to talk to her about it.

"Take your time, *Peaches.*"

Rosalia blows me a kiss before slipping back into the Volvo. *Well,* not before driving me crazy. The SUV is high, and while it's a good height for me, she has to bounce up to get in. Because of that, she unintentionally gives a whole fucking show with just how high her short, yellow tweed skirt rides up, baring more of her gorgeous ballerina legs, white fishnet stockings, and *fuck,* almost exposing her lace panties.

Dear God.

The car door softly shuts, yet I keep staring…*until* Elodie dramatically clears her throat.

"What?"

"I'm just proud of my little bro, that's all." Elodie gets all serious for a minute, stepping closer to me to speak lower. "I'm not going to lie, when you first told me about Rosalia, I was a little skeptical. About the age gap, about everything, but seeing her today... She's *perfect*."

I offer a lopsided grin. "Yeah, the best thing that's ever happened to me."

"I see that in the way you look at her, the way she looks back at me."

Slipping my hands into my jean pocket, I lower my voice, "I... I told her."

Elodie looks at me all confused. "You told her...?"

I arch a brow.

"OHHH!" She gasps, slapping her hands over her mouth. "Really? When?"

"Yes. Last night."

"*Everything*?"

All I can do is nod.

It's instant the way tears pool in her dark eyes, bittersweet tears, I know. We've both been through so much. Elodie knows how hard this has all been for me, the judgment I chain myself to, but last night something broke free inside me when Rosalia told me those words that changed my life forever. For the first time since I was nine, I can breathe. Not hide from myself.

"I'm so proud of you." My sister sniffles. "I love you. I hope you always know that."

My heart squeezes.

Kissing her forehead, I smile and tell her something I never have. "I love you too."

I've been Seattle dreaming with Rosalia all day. It's been a perfect oasis after the roller-coaster ride of life we've been on, but right now, as I glance at her in the back seat of my sister's Porsche, I couldn't be happier. By the way she's grinning back at me, I know she couldn't too.

"I can't wait to see Clément's face when he sees you guys!" Elodie beams from the driver's seat. "He's going to *freak*."

We're currently parked in the parking lot of my nephew's school, waiting for him. Because of the tour, I haven't seen him in eight months and it's killing me, especially because the last time I saw him, my mind was spiraling from recovery after the overdose.

His parents and I agreed that it was best we didn't tell him the truth. They didn't want to approach the subject just yet, and I was so ashamed by my recklessness, I didn't want my nephew to look at me any different. So they told Clément that his uncle just needed to get better.

"What's he like? Still his larrikin self?" Rosalia murmurs into my ear. "Any pointers?"

"Just be yourself, that's all, and I promise he'll catch onto you like a house on fire."

Rosalia softly gasps.

"What?"

"Nothing. I just realize I'm only ten years older than him…" And then she giggles.

Shaking my head, I spank her knee. "I'll show you funny, baby, show you *real* good."

Rosalia's eyes dirtily darken.

Ohhh yeah, that's my girl.

The click of the front passenger seat averts our gaze there, my entire soul singing at the first glimpse of those dark, luscious curls. But he isn't looking anywhere but his hands as he slides into the car with a slight groan, stuffing his schoolbag by his feet. He. Is. Not. Happy.

Elodie subtly winks at us and then turns to her son with a frown. "*Mon petit garçon*, what's wrong?"

"Mommm!" Clément groans. *Again.* "Please don't call me *a little boy*, I'm not seven!"

"No, you're eleven, and still *mon petit garçon*."

Staying as quiet as we can, Rosalia and I exchange a look, biting our lips to stop from bursting out laughing at just how much my sister likes to tease my…*mon petit neveu.*

My little nephew.

"Okay, okay, in all seriousness, what's going on?" Elodie sighs, concern picking her brow. "Did somebody at school pick a fight with you? Did you tell him your dad's a cop?"

"No, I didn't get into a fight."

"Then what's going on?"

"It's nothing. I just…" Clément is quiet for a bit. "I just really miss JahJah."

JahJah.

I'm JahJah.

"That's real ironic, Léme," I say. "'Cause *JahJah* really fuckin' misses you too."

"LANGUAGE!" Elodie gasps.

Clément almost snaps his neck at just how fast he turns around and glances between the car seats. The second he sees me, his eyes light up and happiness floods me so deeply.

"JAHJAH!" he happily screams, rushing over the console, ignoring his mother, who's groaning over the fact she just cleaned the car this morning, but homeboy doesn't care.

"Léme!"

I don't even have time to unbuckle my seat belt before my nephew is toppling over, trampling over me as he holds me tight, shaking around in joy like a damn automatic rifle.

"YOU'RE HERE! OH MY GOD, JAHJAH! I MISSED YOU SO FUDGING MUCH!"

"Missed you more, bud," I whisper, playfully wrestling him, laughing when he does.

This is what eight months do.

So lost in the moment, I glance over at Rosalia, only to find there are tears in her eyes. Happy tears by the way she shoots me a beautiful smile, wiping them away with her sleeve.

I turn back to Clément with fire in my belly. "I've got someone I want you to meet…"

My nephew follows my gaze, gasping the second he sees my girlfriend.

I love how shy Rosalia can be sometimes, bashfully waving at him. "Hi, Clément, I—"

Rosalia doesn't stand a chance as Clément practically jumps on her too, accidentally kneeing her in the stomach as he does, but she just laughs it off. "I KNOW WHO YOU ARE!"

"Clément, kindly turn the volume down." Elodie smiles from the front. "Your uncle is a rock star and literally has people screaming his name every night, so save him the hearing aids?"

My cheeky nephew rolls his eyes.

Yep, basically a carbon copy of yours truly.

Clément eyes me suspiciously. "Can I sit between you guys?"

"Um, you can sit on the other side of me. Your uncle wants to sit next to his girl."

"But I wanna sit between you guys."

"Well, buddy." I smirk. "I'm the one with the belt already on, so…"

He unclips my belt in two seconds with a growing smirk.

This little shit…

Groaning, I slide to the window seat, and Clément happily sits between us. Once he's all clipped in, he starts talking, and when I say *talking*, I mean nonstop questions.

It goes like this…

Soooo, you're that Swan Lake ballerina, huh?

What does Swan Lake really mean?

Is it about a swan?

Is it about a lake?

Is it about both? Probably is or else it wouldn't be called that…

JahJah talked to me on the phone about you once. Said he really liked you.

Do you like him? Like really like like him? Or just like him? Or, is it loooove?

Has he ever bought you flowers? I gave some girls flowers once, didn't end well…

JahJah, she's real beautiful. Are you gonna marry her? Gonna have babies?

If you marry her, can I be your best man? Stuff your band. Where's your band?

Also, can you help me with my music homework later? My teacher is a nightmare.

Oh! Speaking of nightmares, I had one last night… I was a fly and cried 'cause I couldn't eat all my favorite meals. You know, corn on the cob, spaghetti, ice cream. Real sad, right? That's why I was crying. You know, like boo-hoo, poor me. Can flies eat ice cream?

MOM! CAN WE STOP AT THE STORE AND BUY SOME PEACHES?

A box full of peaches, a headache, and a hearing problem later, we're back at Elodie's.

Of course Clément sneaks Rosalia into his Star Wars themed

bedroom as soon as we step through the door because he wants to have a *boy-to-woman chat about JahJah.*

Lucccccccky me.

But they don't call me the devil of rock and roll for nothing. It's why after a couple minutes, I slowly make my way down the hall and lean against the wall of his slightly ajar bedroom door, wanting to hear what Mr. Clément is talking to my girl about.

And the second I hear, a smile rushes up my lips.

Gah.

"Wow, JahJah made you a charm bracelet? That's so girly."

"Well," I hear Rosalia softly chuckle. "It's a little fitting seeing as I'm a woman."

"Ohhh, right. Can I look at the charms?"

"Aha."

It's silent for a little bit, aside from the casual clinking of silver.

"JahJah made me something similar the first time he went on tour... *Here.*"

Silently sliding down the wall, I squeeze my eyes shut because I already know what it is. *A silver shark tooth on a leather necklace chain.* I made that for Clément because he loves sharks and whenever I was in Seattle, I'd always drive him down to California and we'd go to a beach for a sharks' stakeout.

We even made a bucket list together. We never saw any sharks, but I always spoiled him later, telling him I'd buy him anything he wants. He would always choose bucket hats. He has about fifty of those now, okay, maybe even close to a hundred.

The point of this, though, is that I felt so bad during Diesel Rose's first worldwide tour, that I made him that silver charm of a shark tooth and then braided the leather, giving it to him before I left. The thing is, I was high during that entire exchange, and he didn't even know it because I was hiding it so well. I felt like I wanted to die, and yet, out of the glimmer of warmth in my heart that I'll always have for Clément, I made him something to remember me by. *Remember me by* because I didn't know if I would make it to the end of the tour.

I did, though.

I continue to.

And I'm right here. Breathing. Alive. Happy. That's all I've got to think about now.

So lost in my own thoughts, I missed half of Rosalia and Clément's conversation about the silver shark tooth necklace, but what I do catch…*God*, it makes it all worth it.

"Wanna know why JahJah made us these pieces of jewelry for us?" Clément asks.

"Of course," Rosalia replies, and I can hear the smile in her voice. "Why did he?"

A beat.

A pause.

A breath.

And then…

My nephew's voice cuts through the quiet. "JahJah made us these 'cause he loves us."

Rosalia and I are roasting s'mores over the glowing firepit in my sister's backyard when we finally get some alone time. Elodie made us stay for dinner and it worked out perfectly because Rosalia got to meet my brother-in-law, who finished his shift. We all cooked dinner together and my beautiful girl couldn't stop catching my gaze as we made peach cobbler for dessert. *The irony…*

Rosalia's just gazing at me, her smile so wide as shadows of amber flames flicker in her eyes from the firepit. She's been looking at me like that all day. After Clément and I hugged in the car. While making that peach cobbler. Constantly across the table at dinner.

"What are you looking at, babygirl?"

Her grin deepens. "You."

"*Fuck yeah*, you're looking at me." I smirk, and with one hand holding the damn s'more, I cup her face, not caring I'm at my sister's place as I—

"Elijah, what if somebody sees?"

"Ooooo, is kissing your girlfriend illegal?"

Rosalia smirks. "How should I know? I don't have a girlfriend."

"You're such a smart-ass," I growl hotly. "*My* smart-ass."

I crash my lips on hers, and we both moan at the same time,

relishing the heated kiss. It's been hours since I've kissed my girl. Her sweet, peach taste is ecstasy on my tongue.

"Thank you," I break the kiss to whisper. "For today. For being here. For *everything*."

And I don't know if it's the reflecting embers in her eyes from the fire, or just her natural beauty glowing, but she looks so *happy* wrapping her arms around my neck.

"There's nowhere else I'd rather be, Elijah Diesel."

"You mean that?"

"With all my heart."

My own heart swells. It actually *swells*. Fuck. My muse gives me butterflies.

"Got something I want to say. I know you said baby steps, so you don't have to answer, but…" I swallow thickly, brewing my next words. "When we return to Manhattan and after I go to rehab, I'd really like for you to move in with me, or we can get a new place together—"

"God, I love you." Rosalia grins. "Yes, I want that so much, but baby steps, okay?"

"Baby steps. Got it." I chuckle, just so damn in love. "*Fuck*. I love you too, baby."

And just as I'm about to show her how much I love her…

"JAHJAH! ARE YOU BURNING MY S'MORE?"

With the moment ruined, I groan, pulling away from her lips. She can't stop laughing.

Ahh, shit. I totally burned the poor kid's fuckin' s'more.

Chapter

FIFTY-SEVEN

Rosalia

Wish #16: To realize you are loved...

As Elijah, Knives, Dave, and Zander rush into a rock 'n' roll kinda group hug in front of seventy-two thousand fans, piercing screams, and their wildest dreams, it marks the end of Diesel Rose's *Killing Me Slow* tour. And I'm just so freaking grateful to be witnessing it.

The concert was epic, full of their stunning array of showstoppers like fire and moody lights. The fans were buzzing, chanting out the boys' names, and screaming out their gratitude.

Elijah didn't only have me up onstage for "Fragments of You", he had me up on stage for the *entire* show, even had one of his people bring out a comfortable chair out so I could sit. It felt like a dream, watching my boyfriend thrive in his element, knowing all the things I know about him now.

Happier.

I sang along to every lyric, laughed whenever he would throw a wink at me, get up and dance with him. It had the screams intensifying to a whole new level. My hair is probably looking so wild with all the hair flips I did, but hey, I'll happily look like a hot (rock chick) mess if it means telling the world that I love Elijah Diesel. Because I do. Endlessly.

I'm willing to accept his past and be here to support him through every single trauma, grief, and pain. I want us both to thrive in healing. I want the world to see the Elijah I see.

The man who opens doors for me.

The man who adores the classics like me.

The man who tells me he loves me in French.

The most tragically beautiful Diesel Rose rock icon who now takes my hand and kisses me in front of all of his devoted fans in Lumen Field stadium, just as a vivid ensemble of red, yellow, and green booming fireworks explode above the stadium, crackling in a dazzling show.

I'm in a wonderland.

I'm in wonderland every time I glance into those onyx-grays.

"I'm so proud of you, Lijah. In another world, deep down, your parents would be too."

And the way he looks at me, so lovingly tender, *God*, I just want to give him forever.

When the show's finally over and River's grinning over at me because I'm convinced she's the one who gave Elijah the heads-up to come up to the presidential suite before I was leaving that night, Dave playfully shoves both my boyfriend and new girlfriend away from me.

What the…

And then Knives is next to me.

And Zander.

They're all huddled around me as we stride down the long, polished concrete backstage hallway with people with earpieces and **DIESEL ROSE CREW** shirts guiding us to the dressing rooms and hangout space.

"All right, I don't know what you fuckin' did to the coldest motherfucker in Diesel Rose, but he's turned into a puppy." Dave smirks, slinging an arm around my shoulders as we walk. "I'm not joking. He's literally turned all gooey and lovey-dovey and shit. Totally not on-brand."

"Not on-brand at fuckin' all," Knives teasingly agrees with a nod on the other side of me, and *holy shit, is he smiling?* "Let's be honest, blondie, it's no secret I hated your guts—"

"*Hated?*" Zander chuckles, a little ahead of us. "More like *obliterated.*"

"Shut up, Oxford."

Grinning, Zander flips him off and keeps walking.

"Soooo." Dave smiles down at me. "You joining all of our tours? Because let me tell you, I wouldn't mind seeing your beautiful face every day for eight months straight, Rosa."

The longer our stare continues, the more I burst into giggles like a schoolgirl.

Ah, good ol' Dave, always being the perfect drummer gentleman...

"Dude! Hands off my girl!" Elijah growls from behind. "This band ain't doing groupies."

"Yo, man, imagine if we did. I'd be *Dave-no-dick,* 'cause I'd always win over the girls."

Knives and I lock eyes and share a soft chuckle.

Gosh. He's like a changed man tonight...

Elijah practically trips Dave over so he can be on my left side instead. Possessive Elijah Diesel is out to play when he snakes his hands around my hips as we walk. I smile, loving when he's like this. It floods me in his sandalwood cologne, still lingering after an intense two hours.

When Dave tries to match our strides, my boyfriend smirks over at his close friend and bandmate, jokily saying, "Don't you dare. How'd you like some broken wrists, drummer?"

"Yeah, not tonight, I've got things to do..."

"Oh yeah? *What?*"

"Sleep, man." Dave fake yawns. "I'm fucking sleeping for eight months straight. None of you motherfuckers annoy me."

Zander snickers. "Well, I'll be getting married to my lady, so just get up that day."

"Ahh, all right, I guess you're worth it just a little bit, Z."

"Just *a little?*"

"Just *a little.*"

"*Skittles,*" River calls from behind while typing away on her phone. "What's our plan?"

Knives full-on groans beside me. "Well, first, for you not to call me *Skittles*."

"Never!"

"Second, I don't know." He shrugs. "Get you to finally meet my porn star parents, I guess."

River's excited gasps echo throughout the entire hallway. "BABY! Are you serious?"

Again, Knives just shrugs, but there's a genuine grin crawling up his lips.

"I love youuuuu!"

Her phone begins blaring, so she says she'll meet us in the dressing room/hangout area.

I glance at Elijah, a little confused, only to see he's already smiling down at me.

"Oh… Are his parents really…?" I whisper.

"Porn stars?" he mouths. "Are they really porn stars?"

My cheeks heat. "Yeah."

Elijah slowly nods. "Ye—"

"Yep." Knives sighs, butting in. "My conception went fucking viral, for fuck's sake."

I don't know whether to laugh or be sorry for him. Somehow, I manage both.

Dave begins to walk backward in front of us, flickering his gaze between all three while whistling. "Yep. You guys finally did it. You finally depressed me. I'm feelin' *real* fucking lonely, you loved up shits. Diesel, you break my wrists now. I want in on that groupie. *Pronto*."

We all burst out laughing. *Poor Dave.*

"*Psst*, blondie?"

It's *Knives*.

Huh? I stare at him all confused as we turn a corner, leading down another hallway.

He steps closer to my right, and I almost stop walking when his gravelly voice lowly mumbles, "So as it turns out… I think I was wrong about you."

"Yeah?"

"Yeah."

We're talking so low, plus, the other boys and River are having a conversation.

Knives tugs on the ends of his loose blond curls before returning his hands to the safety of his strapped bass guitar with a harsh swallow. "What I want to say is… You're actually pretty cool, like part of me hates myself for saying this, but I actually kinda like you now."

Wowsers. Am I hearing him right?

My jaw drops. "But…but what changes your mind so much?"

He seems almost timid for a second as he subtly nods beyond me. *To Elijah.* Knives can't quite meet my eyes after that, but when he does, they're glazed in the same thing they were that night when I told him that Elijah was drinking vodka and thanked me before rushing to him. I can't quite describe it, but the longer Knives gazes at me, the more I get it…

Gratitude.

There's gratitude swirling in those piercing baby blue eyes. So much of it.

"You saved his life," Knives whispers in my ear, for me only. "Sorry for judging you."

"I'm sorry for judging you too."

"It's okay. I'm… I'm happy for you guys, and I really do mean it."

And just like that, as he backs away, a stray tear glides down his cheek and he's quick to wipe it away. But I see it. I *continue* to see it. And it has my own little tear slipping as I reach out and squeeze his coarse hand.

"Promise I'll take of him, Knives." I softly smile. "I know how special he is to you."

Love.

There's freaking love in Knight Ives's gaze as chokes out. "*Thank you*, Rosa."

Chapter
FIFTY-EIGHT

Rosalia

Wish #17: To love every single part of me...

Never have I seen more paparazzi in my life the second Elijah and I exited our Seattle hotel for the last time the following day. I know it must be nothing compared to the Grammys and other award ceremonies like that, but for a girl who solely craved ballet and only has to encounter a handful of press, it's overwhelming, but not a deal breaker.

It's just something I have to work through. *You know, with time, of course.*

Alongside Elijah's advice after attending to all the fans, but the paparazzi won't stop.

Tinted sunglasses.

Keep your head down.

Run into the Volvo full speed.

The second we touch down in New York City… *We're going viral all over the internet.*

Him and me and Diesel Rose. *And I love it.*

The moment Naomi Ryder's eyes meet mine, we're suffocating ourselves in cuddles.

I. MISS. MY. BEST. FRIEND.

"Oh my goodness, girl." She beams. "I thought I'd never see you again!"

"I would never!"

"You better not."

After we pull away, Elijah clears his throat awkwardly by the front door of my brownstone. He's just standing there cutely, one hand in his pocket, the other holding my suitcase.

"Well, well," Naomi huffs, giving him a poker face. "If it isn't the man of the hour…"

Offering a hand to shake, Elijah looks genuinely scared of her. "Hi there… Naomi."

My best friend glares him down. "You think that's going to cut it?"

"Ummm, *huh*?"

"Get on your knees."

My boyfriend's eyes bulge and I laugh as he looks at me helplessly. "She wants me to do *what*?"

"Aye, lover boy, no distractions." Naomi snaps her fingers together. "On your knees."

Elijah submits.

Oh my God.

This is just too good.

"Good. Now lean down and kiss my slippers."

"But I—"

"Do you love my best friend?"

"Dearly."

"Do you want to change?"

"Immensely."

"Completely?"

"Yes."

"Kiss. My. Slippers."

Clenching my jaw, I watch my rock 'n' roll boyfriend kiss her fluffy pink slippers, his hot stare on me the entire time. *Yeah, he's definitely never going to hear the end of this one…* The second it's over, Elijah bolts up so fast that he hits his head on the top of the front door doorframe, because he's *that* tall. The funniest thing is he doesn't even react.

"*Now*," Naomi warns. "If you ever fuck over my bestie again, remember this moment. And remember when I say I will use these very same slippers to smother and kill you, got it?"

Elijah swallows thickly, and right now, it's hard to imagine him as a rock star.

He genuinely looks so scared.

"Boy, are you listening?"

"Loud and clear. I understand. I promise."

"Good." She grins, pinching his cheeks, just like a grandma would. "Now that we understand each other, Rosalia?"

"Mmhmmm." I grin at her.

"I approve."

And with one final embrace, Naomi's out of the house to work, considering it's already late, just after nine.

Elijah remains shell-shocked, completely dazed like he's entered another dimension. "I just…I just kissed a grown-ass woman's slippers."

"Welcome to my world, *lover boy*."

And then, out of the corner of my eye, I see that familiar white natural cotton teepee bed with Pom Poms and rush up to my bunny. *My baby.* There Mr. HotLips is, a fluffy velvet gray cutie, chewing away on a crunchy piece of lettuce.

Picking him up, I rock him in my arms as he finishes the last of his breakfast.

"Hello, babyboy, gosh, I've missed you so much. Yes, I have. Mama's missed you so much. *Gahhh*, you're *so cute!*" I scratch behind his soft ears. "Guess what? I've got someone I'd like for you to meet…"

Mr. HotLips twitches his nose suspiciously.

I cradle the bunny to my chest, smiling as Elijah shuts the front door and walks to us.

"Mr. Rubin Tommy HotLips, meet my boyfriend, Lijah," I whisper close to my bunny's ear, kissing his soft fur. "He's this scary rock star. I know, I know, *such a diva*, I *knowww*."

Elijah's smirking so deep, his dimples sink through. "Shhh, don't shit talk to our son."

Mr. HotLips can't stop side-eyeing him.

"I know, I know, HotLips." I grin. "He's pretty darn fine. You want to go to daddy?"

Elijah's eyes darken devilishly. "Yeah, give him to daddy."

Seeing Elijah hold Mr. HotLips is the equivalent of baby fever. He's so attentive, holding the fluffy bunny to his chest, patting him softly. Mr. HotLips is so happy, eyes shut in glee.

"Wow, you're a natural! I've never seen him so comfortable with a first-timer before."

"Because I ain't a first-timer, *Peaches*. I plan to do this forever."

Aww.

"He's my therapy bunny."

Elijah smiles, and I just love how perfectly he fits in my life. "I understand the effect."

And I, Rosalia Philips, understand the Elijah Diesel effect.

I've missed New York. There's just something about being home that feels so refreshing.

After our hilarious welcoming by Naomi, Elijah and I spend our first day back in Manhattan, visiting the places we love most. It's Elijah's birthday/Halloween tomorrow, and the day after, he'll be going away to detox rehab. It's why we want to do everything before. Vintage stores. Central Park. And right now, we're stepping into a bookshop emitting nostalgia.

Hayes's Bookstore.

We want to spend the day getting lost in the classic romance section and sugary poetry.

The moment Mr. Hayes sees Elijah and me together—holding hands—he excuses himself for a moment from a customer and rushes out from behind the counter, toward us.

I love that he's still staying true to tradition and wearing an iconic chestnut corduroy suit with a new fancy tie. Pink and white polka dots.

One look at us and Mr. Hayes is grinning.

"*You'll ache,*" he begins softly, quoting Hemingway. "*And you're going to love it. It will crush you. And you're still going to love all of it.*"

Elijah squeezes my hand and my heart's the fullest it's ever been. Because the words Mr. Hayes just spoke are so perfectly *us*.

My foster parents had no idea I was bringing Elijah to dinner.

When Mom called me just after we exited Hayes's Bookstore saying she had made one of my favorites and invited me over to welcome me back home, I didn't mention my boyfriend. Not once. And she didn't mention him, but I was adamant, determined. I want him to be a part of my life forever, so…*I did the unexpected.*

Elijah was more than happy to stay at his industrial loft apartment. For me to have some one-on-one time with them, but I didn't want that. I wanted more. He had mellowed down since the last time we had spoken about my parents, and the digs about my father had stopped. He was being respectful, meaning, it was finally time…

Which explains my father's horror the second I stepped into their Park Avenue apartment, holding hands with the one man he detested. His mouth literally hung open, all the way to the expensive white Italian marble floors.

He must have just come home from work because he was still wearing his blue scrubs. But the second he locked eyes with Elijah, I knew it wasn't good.

It had been four years.

Four.

Four years since they were in the room together. And considering last time wasn't exactly…well, friendly, nervousness bubbled in my stomach, but tonight was important for me.

For us.

I wanted my parents to accept my boyfriend so bad, so, if I had to add a little for shock value, here it goes.

Which leads me to right now…

Elijah Diesel looks gorgeous as hell in that black, custom-tailored suit of his. I've never seen him in a suit before, and so I can't stop staring at those expensive slacks, structured black blazer, and crisp white dress shirt, a few buttons undone. And oh, let's not forget the shiny, fancy leather Italian derby shoes.

But there are still core aspects of the Elijah I know and love with it. Like the silver chain detail attached to the belt loops of his slacks. The way his dark hair is perfectly jelled back, slicked, like a '50s movie star. How he was leaning against his new sleek black vintage Mustang when I opened my brownstone door, cigarette in mouth, smiling at me.

But now that we're here, inside my parents' Park Avenue apartment with panoramic views capturing Central Park and dazzling skylines with twinkling stars, and yet, I hear crickets because my father hasn't moved a muscle. He stands frozen by the lobby area, jaw tense, constantly flickering his gaze between Elijah and me.

"Rosalia, what kind of sick joke is this?" My father finally spits, staring my boyfriend down some further. "Didn't invite *you* to dinner, *punk*. Get the hell outta my house."

My chest aches at the word.

Punk.

Shit.

I don't know how long I'm squeezing my eyes shut, trying to digest it all, waiting for something to happen, but when I see Elijah, I'm shocked. He seems...totally *composed.*

His jaw isn't ticking.

He isn't fuming.

He's controlling his breaths, not an inch of hatred licking those beautiful onyx eyes.

He's trying.

Oh my God.

He's trying *for me.*

And then, *it* happens.

Elijah steps forth, a modern bad rock star Brando as he holds out his hand to my father, a soft smile tracing his lips. "Hello, Mr. Philips, my name is Elijah Diesel and I'm not the enemy. I'm your daughter's boyfriend, and I love her dearly."

"*Love?*"

"Yes—*love.* I may not be perfect, and I get that. I'm not a corporate guy. Couldn't give a shit about crypto. Don't even understand the definition of Wall Street. And no, my career doesn't include saving lives, well, maybe it does, depending on how you look at it. But what I'm trying to tell you is that I'm not a perfect man. I never claimed to be. But I can try to be. For you. For your wife. For your daughter. It's why I'm going into rehab on Monday. I'll be away for a little while, trying to clasp that perfect."

"*Rehab?*"

"Yes, Mr. Philips, as I stated, I'm not perfect, but all I can pledge is to try to be better. I know you hate me. I know you hate me for being so untraditional. I would too in your position, but I'm sure, as I would have imagined, that aching pang in your chest the first time you saw Rosalia is the same aching pang in my chest the first time I saw her. I think a part of me loved her from the first moment I saw her. I think you noticed that. I think you were scared of that. But I'm here, right now, telling you I adore Rosalia Philips. I love every single thing about her, and you know what that means?"

Stunned, my father softly shakes his head.

"It means I have to love her parents too. That's what you're scared of. You're scared I'll steal her away, brainwash her, condition her to believe you're a bad person, you, and your wife too, right?"

"Well, yes, I am."

"I'm here telling you, hand on my heart, that it isn't my intention. I love your daughter, Mr. Philips. I love her, and that means growing to love you and your wife too. I respect you. I understand you. I apologize to you for my actions years ago. I would love to spend the rest of my life with your daughter, unconditionally, if you let me."

Wow.

My heart is beating like crazy in my chest, butterflies everywhere as I gaze at my boyfriend, in awe of everything he just said. There are tears in my eyes. Happy tears. Because I never expected this. I never expected for him to speak to my father like this.

My father is in such shock, his light eyes haven't moved from my boyfriend. He just stares, and stares, and stares, rubbing a hand over his salt-and-pepper stubble.

Please, Dad, please say something…

"Elijah?"

It isn't Dad, it's *Mom.*

My head snaps across the room to my mother, who's standing right by the curve that leads to the kitchen. She must have watched the entire ordeal because tears brim in her eyes with every slap her Valentinos make across the marble floor at her approach. She holds me right before turning to my boyfriend, offering her hand.

"Elijah, I'm Jessie Philips. I can speak for my husband when I say we didn't expect you to come, nor did we expect *that*. But during that entire pledge, I was looking between you and Rosalia. Noticed the adoration in your eyes. The empathy. The depth. And for me, I know that's enough."

The most beautiful smile breaks out on Elijah's lips as he takes my mom's hand and instead of shaking it, softly kisses her hand.

Mom blushes.

Like full-on blushes.

"I am utterly devoted to Rosa, Mrs. Philips."

Mom flashes him a grin. "Call me Jessie."

My father hasn't spoken a single word all dinner. He can't even look anybody in the eyes straight. He changed into a three-piece suit just before dinner, and now, he can't stop vigorously tugging at the tightness of his tie.

And then there's Mom, who hasn't stopped asking Elijah about tour life, Diesel Rose, and what it truly means to be a musician. They share a few smiles, some laughs even.

I couldn't be prouder of Elijah, of the way he's handling everything. Like a real man. His hand's been under the table and on my knee all night, squeezing it affectionately every time our hopeful eyes meet.

After the delicious Italian dinner and gourmet dessert, my father stands up and walks straight to his wet bar. We all watch on in anticipation as he clings two crystal low ball glasses and pours stiffly into them.

Oh no.

My father's swirling the amber liquid upon his approach and outstretches a glass to Elijah. "Let's go into my study. We need to talk."

I don't miss the way Elijah freezes up for a second, a rich fragrance of the sweetness of honey tones lacing the air around us.

"I would prefer not to drink, Mr. Philips."

My father isn't buying it. "You want to have a proper conversation, you take this glass and follow me into my office."

"I, umm, I..."

This is too painful to match.

Elijah can't even look him in the eye. His gaze is all over, scattered, mainly by his hands.

"Dad," I murmur, offering him a slight smile. "Elijah is in recovery. He's an alcohol and drug abuse survivor. He's going into rehab on Monday. The press don't know anything, so please don't tell anybody."

A shaky breath escapes Elijah.

"Thank you, baby," he mouths.

I smile back.

Teamwork.

After the stare down of the century, my father sets both glasses down on the table. "Okay, I've got some cigars in my office as a substitute. Follow me, Elijah."

My boyfriend submits, but not before softly kissing me, right in front of them, a lopsided smile burning up his lips before he disappears with my father.

"Rosalia, okay, I was wrong…" Mom beams across the table, leaning against her hand. "I think I really like him."

I grin back, my heart doing summersaults, pirouettes, and everything in between. "I really like him too, Mom."

"He's perfect for you, sweetie."

A weight lifts when the two men return a little while later, and my father's soft gaze meets mine. I don't know what was said between Elijah and him. I may never know. But all that I do know is that it was something big.

Why?

Because my father's light eyes are brewing with the unexpected, with everything I've ever craved of him…

Everything I've ever tirelessly worked hard on…

Everything I've strived to impress him with after finding me inches from death…

Acceptance.

Elijah didn't want to do anything for his birthday/Halloween, not even get a cake. I tried my best to convince him, even a little get-together with his bandmates, but those wolfish gray eyes met mine and he told me all he really wanted to do was spend his birthday with me.

I couldn't complain about that. After all, today is Elijah's last day in Manhattan before he goes to Rochester for his detox rehab program. He'll be gone for a month and a half. *Fifty days, to be exact.* I still haven't quite wrapped my head around it.

I don't know if I want to.

I want him so desperately to get the help that he deserves, but I'm going to miss him so freaking much. Being on tour with Diesel Rose, I got so used to being with Elijah almost 24/7, it's going to feel so strange now without him. But he's going to come out a better man after this, and I, a better woman for understanding him better.

Last night, after Elijah met my parents, he asked if I wanted to stay over at his for the night. I could tell by the look in his eyes that he was wondering if this was baby steps too much. As much as my head told me I should sleep at my brownstone, I listened to my heart instead.

The second we stepped inside his warm, industrial loft apartment, he pinned me against the exposed brick wall. Between a hanging collector's guitar and a giant vintage movie poster of James Dean's *Rebel Without A Cause*, we hotly made out until our lips bruised.

Because of the baby steps we were hanging onto, we still didn't have sex, and instead, cuddled as we watched the television from Elijah's bed. But I was really just gazing up at him the entire time, my nails caressing over his chest, admiring just how beautiful it is that he exists.

This morning, I managed to sneak out real early to grab a few things for his birthday. He was still asleep, softly snoring when I returned. I woke up Elijah with the sugary aroma of the fluffy pancakes I was making in his kitchen, humming some of Diesel Rose's greatest hits.

(Side note: they're all great in my option)

Elijah melted as I walked to his bed singing him *Happy Birthday* with two musical candles that read 3 and 6 on top of the heart-shaped pancakes. Tears glazed his eyes as he blew them out and I said he didn't want a cake, so I gave him pancakes instead. Elijah kissed me and told me this was his first birthday cake ever, and that I was his greatest wish.

Then I was the one crying and melting from joy like a hot mess.

I understand why today is so bittersweet for Elijah. Yes, it's his birthday and Halloween, but it's also four years to the day where he left for the *Devil's Advocate and The Fiery Halos*'s tour and one year since the overdose.

The rest of the day, I tried to give Elijah the best birthday and goodbye party all at once.

I hate just thinking about it.

Just after dinner at Sogni D'oro (our first official non-official date), I surprised him when I walked us to a tattoo parlor in the middle of the city. Elijah was perplexed, yet intrigued. I couldn't hide my smile and I urged him closer to the parlor. I only had one tattoo—the scissors—little did he know that by the end of the night, my count would be three.

(Amateur still, I know, I know.)

Night had fallen at this stage, and because it had rained while we were at the restaurant, the air was tinged with this earthy scent. I loved the way the cool red neon sign of the tattoo parlor skimmed across puddles, glowing and scattering life into the reflections.

Elijah never let go of my hand when we finally stepped inside of **HÄVËN**. I had booked an appointment when we were still in Seattle because from the moment Elijah opened up to me, I knew the perfect birthday present.

Something to thank him by.

Forever.

A tall, edgy-looking guy dressed as a risqué vampire with a fierce buzz cut, tattooed sleeves, and nose ring greets me with a broad smile.

"Hey, gorgeous, we don't usually take walk-ins, so unles—" His gaze casually trails to Elijah, and then… "HOLY SHIT! ELIJAH DIESEL!"

A few heads snap our way in the parlor and chatter reaches an all-time high.

Elijah simply tips his head.

"*Wow*, man, I respect you, brother, been to every New York show."

"Respect you, brother, thanks."

The guy turns back to me and again, his eyes widen. "Shit, and you're his girl. Fuck, this must be my lucky night… Well, welcome to HÄVËN. What can I do for you?"

"Hi." I smile, leaning closer to my boyfriend. "I have an online booking under Rosalia for 8:35 p.m. I received a confirmation, if you'd like to see it."

"Oh yes, Rosalia! I remember seeing your name on the system. You're with me. I'm Creed, by the way. It's nice meeting you both. Follow me."

We do just that, but before we enter the private tattoo room, Elijah whispers in my ear, "What have you done, little one?"

"Giving you your birthday present."

"But, baby, I said I didn't want a present. You're enough for me."

Grinning, I throw him a wink. "Well, I guess you'll have to wait and see then…"

Just over an hour and a half later, the butterflies across my chest flutter wild when Elijah's eyes light up in awe at the two completed tattoos running across both my inner wrists.

He looks so happy.

So touched by emotion.

Exactly how I hoped he'd react.

On my inner left wrist, in a thin cursive black ink, alongside music notes, reads:

Your words
Your love
Your flaws are still here, undressed
But not loving nothing else but…
The fragments of you

The cursive tattoo on my right inner wrist reads:

My only wonder.
My only cure.
Is you.

They're both lyrics from Diesel Rose's "Fragments of You".

First, they cover over all of my faded white scars from when I used to cut. Now, instead of jagged reminders of darkness, there's light—*his* light merged with mine. It sets me free.

And second, I know they're on my skin, but these tattoos are his lyrics, his heart, for him. He poured his skin and bones into every single lyric beauty, and I wanted to praise him by having the words that speak to me more inked into my skin.

Forever.

Elijah can't take his poignant eyes off me as he takes my slightly reddened wrists in his hands, analyzing the beautiful tattoos. Doesn't lose my gaze as he kisses them over the plastic wraps. As he tells me just how much he loves them and how beautiful I am.

"You did this for me," Elijah breathes against my lips, emotion trapped in his throat, but it isn't a question, it's a statement. "Nobody has ever made me feel this special before."

"Baby, you're special. And you're loved. And you're mine." I smile, softly biting my lower lip. "And I really wanted to give you a birthday you'll never forget before…"

I don't have to finish my sentence. By the way Elijah's eyes slowly shut, he knows.

Before you go away, babyboy.

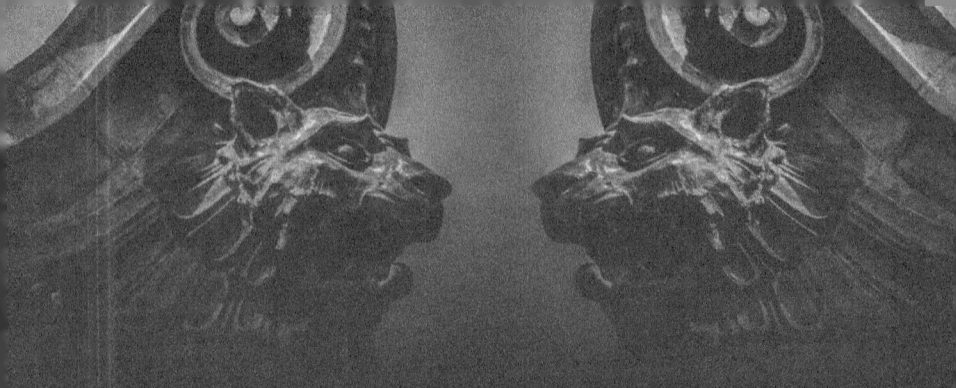

Chapter
FIFTY-NINE

Elijah

Wish #18: To love every single part of me...just as I promise to forever love all of you.

I *don't want to let her go.*

I know it'll only be for fifty days. Time will fly. I know it will. And yet, it'll be fifty days...

Without seeing her smile.

Without hearing her voice.

Without supporting her grief.

Fifty days without her I'll never get back.

But I need to do this. I'm going to get better. This time around, I have an anchor to keep me afloat. I'll never drown with Rosalia here, supporting my every step.

I've never had detox rehab before.

I've had both individually, numerous times, but never a combination of the two.

It's a strict, reputable facility that my manager was able to sweet-talk into another intake in just days. It's in Rochester, New York, just over a five-hour drive from Manhattan. For maximum concentration, the facility has a stern no-phone and no-visitor rule. And while it's jarring, it'll really help me confront the fact that I'm in desperate need of being clean and sober for life. Just like I want to be.

NDAs are signed. My bags are packed. Everything's good to go… expect me.

This will be the best thing for us. I know it will. I've never had a reason before. Never had someone significant waiting for me. *Now I do.*

She's in love with me. She's enough for me.

And right now, even as Rosalia falls asleep on me halfway through *Corpse Bride*, I can't help but smile. *Fuck.* I'm going to miss her so deeply. I'm going to miss everything. As I scoop Rosalia into my arms, my lips lingering on her forehead while I carry her to bed, I know I'm going to miss *this* too.

All the tender seconds.

All the little things.

All those moments in between.

After I slip us under the bedsheets, Rosalia stirs in my solace, stretching a little before fluttering her tired eyes open.

A slow, beautiful smile shoots up her lips. "Sorry, did I fall asleep?"

"Mmhmmm." I smile back.

"Aren't you tired?"

I shake my head. "I just want to admire you all night…engrave you in my mind."

"*Lijah*…" Rosalia moans, biting her lower lip tiredly. That's so sweet."

My warm lips graze over her forehead, kissing it for one of the last times in a little while. "Sleep, my angel, for I'm gonna be right here when you wake up."

I promise.

Standing outside of the rehab facility's cast iron gates in Rochester, I've finished saying goodbye to all of the Diesel Rose boys and River. Even

Naomi came for moral support. As did Lydia Fitz. *Yep, my publicist...*
We had a heart-to-heart and after she saw all my positive progres-
sion had a change of heart. We're resigning contracts when I get out.

Now, there's only one more person to say goodbye to...

It's the hardest one.

My cherry viper.

I spent all night wondering how the hell I was going to do it. I
hated goodbyes, I really did. All my life I'd been cursed by them, but
Rosalia changes that all for me.

She's been trying to keep it together all morning, but as our eyes
meet, the first pearl-sized tear slips.

Baby.

"Please don't cry, *Peaches*." I try smiling through the pain, but it
pierces me deep as I kiss away her salty tears. "I promise I'll be back
before you know. Then I'll never leave again."

"I know. It's just..."

"I get it." I nod slowly, lowering my head so our foreheads touch.
"Stay strong for me, babygirl, okay?"

"Always." Rosalia sniffles, just as the first pelts of rain pour down
on us. The heavens above rumble, a dark gloomy storm set to reel
havoc, and she rushes in my arms at the first devilish bolt of thunder.
"Just hold me a little while longer."

And I do just that, my face buried in her neck, breathing in that
honeyed scent I'll never forget. I slip my vintage Mustang car key
and my house keys into her back jean pocket. My phone's already at
home. "Take care of these while I'm here, little one."

"Of course."

I'm doing this. I'm going to detox rehab with only clothes and a
Polaroid of Rosalia.

It's just us, the wild storm soaking our skin, and the people who
have become family to us, a few feet away.

When it comes time that I need to enter the detox facility, my
heart hurts when I sink my fingers through Rosalia's damp honey-blonde waves, cupping her head. I'm glancing down at her, studying her slowly, just like I have all night.

God. She's so beautiful.

"What did I do to deserve you, hmm?" I whisper darkly against her lips, craving her so badly the sensation is eating me alive. "Tell me, Rosalia Philips, what did I do?"

"You kept breathing."

The overwhelming urge to run away with her dazzles every spark I'm feeling as I kiss Rosalia so passionately intense, in ways I know we'll never forget. The hot, emotional kiss gets even more desperate in the rain. *Wild.* With my heart exploding, our tongues dance in a way that screams *forever.* I can't stop kissing her, feeling her.

After numerous attempts, we pull away panting, sharing a bittersweet smile.

"See you on the other side," I rasp, savoring the moment for all the days I'll be gone.

I turn to my bandmates, Knives in particular. "Take care of my girl for me."

Knives nods, and when he does. I know he means it.

He's a real good guy. I should give him more credit. I really do love him.

The wheels of my luggage crush against the gravel path, lined with flowers, leading to the gates. Just as I reach the security guard, awaiting to be allowed in, it's my muse who brings me back, calling out my name like the sweetest of poetry.

"Elijah!"

I glance over my shoulder, my throat tight with emotion, but then I see Rosalia grinning at me, and hope floods my lungs. "Yes, babygirl?"

Her smile deepens. "Make me proud."

With all my heart, Peaches, with all my heart I'll make you proud. I promise.

Chapter

SIXTY

Rosalia

Wish #19: To heal...forever with me. I love you, Lijah, all your beautiful and damned.

Fifty days later...

The first few days without Elijah were the hardest. Getting back into the rhythm of Manhattan life without him was tough, and it felt odd stepping into his industrial loft apartment and him not being there. For the past fifty days, I've been finding myself going there, seeking solace in the lingering musky scent of him, and adding a few things to his apartment.

You know, normal things people have like little knickknacks, candles, and cute tiny plants.

I can't wait to see Elijah's face when he sees them all.

Gahhh.

Some nights when Naomi has Chad sleeping over, I come to Elijah's loft instead and fall asleep smiling, trailing my fingers over my new tattoos, thinking of him. I've been going to training and ballet rehearsal (*new season begins soon*—Giselle) a lot in his vintage Mustang.

Rock 'n' Roll Press loved that one.

Another thing I've been doing a lot of is reading, and I don't mean classic literature romances (even though I adore them), I mean books that outline the route to recovery after substance and alcohol abuse of loved ones. I wanted to absorb as much information as I could to be the best support system for Elijah when he returns.

So, I listened to bestselling audiobooks during my morning runs, absorbed podcasts between errands, and read a hundred pages every night before bed while cuddling Mr. HotLips.

I've been dedicated.

Determined.

Driven.

It's five days from Christmas now and my greatest gift is that fifty days have passed, and as I wait for Elijah now, leaning against his vintage Mustang, I couldn't be happier.

Also, I'm proud of myself for driving all the way to Rochester without any detection from the press… Or totaling Elijah's vintage car. That would have been a disaster and a half.

I jump out of my skin at the violent bolts of lighting, brightening up the gloomy, darkening New York stormy sky. Winter ain't kidding nobody this year with blanketing snow as harsh pitter-patters of rain pour down on me, having me clutch my umbrella tighter. Sleet.

My fingers are cold from the icy chill of the falling snow. It's pooling by my Dr. Martens, sinking my soles in as coldness ripples through my bones, menacing my soul. But it's all worth it because I'm seconds away from seeing my favorite person in the whole world after almost two months.

The security guard pacing by the closed cast iron gates (with the don't-you-dare-talk-to-me vibes) hasn't stopped pacing up and down for the past half hour, his hands casually behind his back. Yet the second the iron fence buzzes unlocked behind him, it diverts both our attention behind the gate, and…

Oh my God.

There *he* is.

My onyx-eyed dream with not a glimmer of melancholy in him.

My gorgeous Elijah Diesel is wearing the same Dr. Martens and iconic studded leather jacket with the safety pins that he was wearing the first day we met. Heavy rain pelts down on them, smoothly gliding off the leather, while the storm soaks his charcoal sweater, blue jeans, and defining the curls of his dark, sexily tousled hair that almost kisses his shoulders now, rocker style. But he doesn't seem to mind as he strolls his suitcase through the crushed pebble path.

My heart skips a beat the second Elijah's eyes meet mine, the most beautiful grin sprawling over his face, his dimples deepening, and *oh my God*, he sexily bites his lower lip.

I'm grinning like crazy, waving at him like a weirdo as he comes to a slow on his side of the gate, speaking to the security guard for a moment before the guard swings them open. The second Elijah steps through, I run to him with happy tears glassing my eyes, throwing the umbrella as I jump into his open arms, my lungs relishing that familiar tobacco vanilla I love.

My Lijah.

He's right *here.*

Right here with me. Again.

He holds me so tight in the solace of his embrace, I may just explode, but I don't care. I *want* to because I'm squeezing him just as tight, one arm around his neck, the other cupping his stubbled jaw, so much darker and longer than the last time we were here fifty days ago.

Elijah's warm lips are on mine before I can say anything, kissing me hard, his tongue passionately dancing with mine until I can barely breathe. I'm smiling through the kiss, sobbing, feeling every single emotion at once and it's everything. *All the healing. The love. Our forever.*

Our sizzling *hello* kiss is fueled with both desire and emotion at the same time. I can't get enough of him. Can't stop touching him. It's a beautiful new rendition of us as we devour each other in the rain as he tastes the sweet Cherry Cola I had on my way here on my tongue.

"*Peaches!*" Elijah breathes against my lips, and it feels so good to hear it again.

"Oh my God! Lijah!" I sob, resting my forehead on his. "I missed you so much!"

"Missed you so much fuckin' more, babygirl. What am I without you? *Nothing.*"

I wish I weren't crying this hard, but I'm just so overwhelmed and happy he's *right here*. He kisses away my tears, his lips scorching against my cheeks as rain pelts down on us, soaking my hair and the tartan Carrie Bradshaw inspired coat I'm wearing, but I don't give a damn.

And when Elijah pulls back to look at me, like *really* look at me with those onyx-grays I'll always love, we share the most tender smile. It's life-changing. *This man saved my life.*

There's just so much love in his eyes.

So much warmth.

So much *life*.

There's hope. A lot of it. And a changed man before me. I know this is the beginning. Just like the very start of permanent recovery, but I am going to be here every single day for the rest of my life if I'm lucky enough, supporting and being the best accountability he's ever had.

(No offence to Knives, of course.)

"How are you, baby?" I sniffle. "How did everything go? I've got so much to tell you!"

"Life's looking up, baby. I'm feeling really good, the best I have ever felt."

"I'm here for you. Whatever you need. I'm here because we're a team."

"The greatest team the world has ever seen, huh?"

"Precisely. Gosh, I've got so much to tell you!"

"I want to know everything, *Peaches*."

"I got the star role in *Giselle*!" I beam, and then get so excited I basically blab out all the rest in fast motion. "And Naomi and Chad are still together. Knives has called me every night since you left. Did you hear that? *Every. Night.* Sometimes our conversations were so short they were only thirteen seconds, but *he called*. I think he likes me now. God bless his heart! Dave always checks in too. He got a tattoo of you, by the way. Zander's in Australia, trying to escape this weather. I've been sleeping at your loft apartment, and sometimes I bring Mr. HotLips too. Once, he hopped up to one of our Polaroid pictures, sniffled the hell out of you and he actually cried! Like can you believe it? Cried!"

Elijah's eyes widen, looking so damn mortified. "That little fluffy thing can *cry*?"

"*Cried*! But he's not the only one who missed you… I read a lot of information outlining recovery because I want to be your right-hand man through all of this…okay, right-hand *woman*. OH! I bought us a Christmas tree. Yes, for *us*, because, in a way, I've already moved in! You should see the place. Plants *everywhere*! And I wasn't going to decorate it, but I got major FOMO, so I kinda did it all except for the star. It's too high to reach and I thought that when my gorgeous, smart, musical, literate, sexy, *did I say gorgeous?* boyfriend returns home from getting better, he could help this short-ass girl out."

"You done?" Elijah smirks, chuckling when I playfully shove him. "I'm only kiddin', angel, all that makes me so happy. I'm glad I can finally be a part of all the updates now. I'll be honored to put the star up… I've never had a Christmas tree before, so my heart's beating like crazy now. Butterflies and shit, the good kind you know, the ones laced with all that's us."

It's laced with all that's us.

Pouting softly, I ask, "You've never had a Christmas tree before?"

"No, never," Elijah whispers, but he isn't sad, he's hopeful. "It'll be my first ever."

Smiling, we Eskimo kiss and it's the cutest thing because it's been so long.

"I'll happily give you all of my firsts, Elijah Diesel."

"I like the sound of that."

With one final passionate peck, I slip off him, a drenched mess from the rumbling storm and lightning. We're walking toward his vintage Mustang hand-in-hand when he slows.

"*Peaches*?"

"Yeah?" I ask, arching a brow when he just stands beside me, looking hella nervous.

"I made you something…" Elijah bashfully smiles. "Oddly enough, they had a silver jewelry program in there. Well, it was kind of laced with therapy, but you know what I mean. I was gonna give it to you when we returned to Manhattan, but… I can't wait any longer."

Oh?

Several lightning bolts light up the sky.

I stay frozen, watching him in such anticipation.

Eyes locked on mine, Elijah Diesel drops to one knee.

Oh my Godddd!

Gasping, I slap a hand over my mouth at the beautiful piece of jewelry Elijah pulls out of his leather jacket pocket. It's a stunning, detailed silver ring with pretty rose grooves engraved in it. It's lined with so much craftsmanship, doused with adoration in every single petal.

It looks like a…

"It's a promise ring, *Peaches*," Elijah explains, rain gliding down his long, pretty lashes, dripping across his dazzling, boyish grin. "Represents everything I promise to do. From today forth, I promise to be the best version of myself. I promise to love you until my very last breath. I promise to spend every single day of my life *with* you, healing *with* you, finding beauty in every moment *with* you. I hope you stay for all the crazy, but if you leave, I'll find you again. In every life after this, I'll find you, just like I did in this life, and in all the ones before." Elijah squeezes my hand, romantic tears falling as he whispers, "I *promise* you, Rosalia Philips."

Oh.

My.

God.

Oh my God.

Oh my God.

Oh my God.

"Do you promise me too, *Peaches*?"

Grinning, I uncontrollably nod, tears in my eyes. "With all my heart, I promise too."

Elijah slips the gorgeous rose silver ring on my left hand and my heart floods with a warmth I never imagined could exist. Even more love pours out of me when he softly kisses the ring, and then, when he stands to his full height and cups my face, I know it's forever.

"Wow, Lijah, I didn't know you were going to do that!" I sob, holding up my new ring to the sky. "*This* is so beautiful! I don't know why I'm crying. I just love you so much!"

"Happy tears." He grins, holding me close. "I love you more, babygirl. *Forever*."

Forever.

He'll love me forever.

"A. F. Scott Fitzgerald's quote reads, *I wish I had done everything on Earth with you*," Elijah rasps. "I'm telling you, *Peaches*, that from this very second until the day I die, I promise you I will do just that. I'm going to do everything on this Earth. *Everything*. With you."

And if I could go back to my five-year-old self, I'd hold her tight, wipe away her tears, and tell her everything will be all right because one day, all the fragments of her will be loved. She'll be loved by the wicked monster who transformed into her greatest gift—*life*.

Life is the greatest gift Lijah has given me as I kiss him hard, until my air is consumed by his, and he kisses back, so damn fondly. Because we made it. We're alive. Breathing.

I'm so glad Elijah Diesel is mine.

I'm so glad this new life is ours—*together*.

I'm so glad I saw that fated Rolling Stone *article and fell in love with Diesel Rose.*

Epilogue

Elijah

Wish #20: Write your own Wish for us...

Two months later...
FEBRUARY 2023

Peaches,

I know I'm right beside you in bed right now and you probably think I'm a weirdo for writing down this shit instead of simply telling you it (and let's face it, baby. I am that weirdo), but I wanted the words I tell you right now to be tangible.

Want you to remember it like this.

Want this wish to forever be ours. Rosalia, babygirl, you saved my life.

You.

Saved.

My.

Life.

And I'm not just saying it to be all sappy and poetic. I'm saying it 'cause I genuinely feel it in my wildly beating heart. Yes, feel. You saved my life, and you continue to save it every single day since.

With you, I'm not scared of the dark.

Of the demons.

Of the scars.

Because every single day, I feel them fade.

And I'm learning they're all beautiful parts of me.

Just like yours are all beautiful parts of you, Peaches.

This is recovery.

You and me.

Together.

You're my everything. I fuckin' love you so much. I know this letter was supposed to be about that new wish I had to create, but fuccck, I can't resist you, baby. I'd never want to either. Not now that you gave me life.

Not when I named my rock band, Diesel Rose, after you—after us.

Not after I asked you to marry me last weekend and you said spending forever with me is all you want to do.

Baby, I want it too. I want it so badly. Soon you're gonna by Mrs. Rosalia Diesel, and I'll be vowing to love you forever. But I already love you forever, and you know that.

It's why I proposed to you in a crowded Time Square with our faces plastered on the biggest billboard, lighting up the darkened Manhattan skies with our iconic Rolling Stone magazine front cover. I didn't give a shit it went viral, that the entire world was watching on. All I cared about was you. You, and me, and us.

I love how that pretty peach-colored diamond ring fits you so perfectly. How it's laced with all that we are. (And hold on a sec... Can we talk about how epic that Rolling Stone magazine front cover billboard you and I are on is? Talk about life going full circle, hmm?)

So, what's my wish for us, my darlin' fiancée?

My wish is that we make it.

That you love me in this life, and into the next life, and then into the next.

Because I know I will, Peaches, I'll rattle the caged gates of heaven to be with you forever.

I'm never leaving you, Rosa. Not now. Not ever.

I promise, my cherry viper.

I do.

Je t'aime tellement que je peux te le promettre.

I love you so much that I can promise it.

Forever.

Always,

Your Lijah <3

*P.S Okay, fine, below are the lyrics of "Cherry Viper Eyes". I know I've been secretive about them for so long and I wanted you to hear it for the first time when Diesel Rose record the single in the studio next week, but as I said before, I can't resist you. So, here it is...

*P. P. S If this song gets leaked, I'll know who did it... HAHA! Joking, I love ya. xo

They say not to adore sin,
But she's my cure
A ballerina in a green-eyed disguise
I ain't just a saint to be so cruel

Baby, you've got the melancholy in your eyes
Cherrrry viper,
I'd like to meet you, againnn
Again

Cherry viper eyes, ah-ah
Cherrrry viper, mm-hmmm
Cherry viper eyes, ah-ah
Cherrrry viper, won't you marry me?
(Yeahhh)

* *NOTE: Knives and Zander's riffs go super crazy and melodic here, Peaches*

Baby?
And here
(Yeah)
And here
Darlin'?
And here too
(Yeahhh)

Cherry viper eyes
Pleeeease forgive me
For what I'm about to do, aye

* *Dave goes fuckin' crazy here, like beats the shit out of those drumsticks*
For what I'm about to do, aye

For what I'm about to do, aye
For what I'm about to do, aye
* *Progressively gets louder here, mimics the onyx
butterflies growing wilder for you*

Cherry viper eyes, ah, hey
I looove you, oh-ahh
Didn't mean to leave, but I ah-ah
Loved the cherry most, (mmm-yeah)

You tas-ted divine, ah-ah
Could have kissed ya all night, ah-ah
Now I've made up my mind, ah-ah
It's a won-derful life but I, ah-ah
So twisted with you

* *It's a Dave solo right here, beats continue with
the next lyrics*

So twisted wi-th you
(Ohhh yeah)
Twisted with you
So twisted with—now I don't know what I'm gonna
fuckin' do

* *Crazy riffs and crescendos*

Cherry viper eyes, ah-ah
Cherrrry viper, mm-hmmm

Cherry viper eyes, ah-ah
Cherrrry viper, yeah

Cherry viper eyes, ah-ah
Cherrrry viper, mm-hmmm
Kept me up all night, ah-ah
(Cherrrry viper, mm-hmmm)
Make me lose my mind, ah-ah
(Cherrrry viper, mm-hmmm)
Won't you take my soul now
(Ah-ah)

Need another hit, yea-h, of you

(Of you)
Of you
(Of you)
Of you, of you, of yo-u
Of you, of you, of yo-u
Of you, of you, of...

Cherry
(Cherry viper)
Cherry
(Cherry viper)
Cherry viper eyes
(mm-hmmm)
Your cherry viper eyesss
(mm-hmmm)
Cherry viper eyes
(mm-hmmm)
Your cherry viper eyesss, yeahhh

Read on for the first few chapters of Vanessa Luisa's angsty age gap, emotionally gripping, dad's best friend forbidden romance standalone, *Oceans of Us.*

Available to buy now on Amazon & FREE in KINDLE UNLIMITED!

Oceans of Us: An Age Gap Forbidden Romance Standalone

He's Italian, older, a gorgeous tattooed Harley lover… and the one man I can never have.

From the moment Saint Lisconti moved in next door and recklessly stepped all over my favorite rare tiger lilies, it's been war between us. Now, three years after our first encounter, hate simmers down, giving way to heated stolen glances that leave me drowning in his piercing ocean blue eyes.

Our attraction blooms. Sparks I crave to unravel fly.
Everything changes.

Saint becomes my savior. The reason I find poetic beauty in life. He's thirty-six, burdened by the scars from his past I so desperately want to heal. I'm eighteen, a good girl, but no matter how many times Saint warns me away, I find myself breaking all the rules for a taste of the forbidden.

Because Saint isn't just a guarded bad boy... he's also my father's best friend.

And when he agrees to wanting more, all bets are off.

But as I fall deeper, our love may be the very thing that breaks us when fate twists with our plans...

Or will it?

Preface

Paisley

PRESENT DAY…

In a perfect world, it could be him and me until the very end. But this isn't a perfect world…

It's far from it.

After all, he's whiskey, tobacco, and speeding Harleys. I'm green tea, poetry, and twirling flowers. To the naked eye, we would be beautifully incomplete if up until this point life had gone our way. But we were never that—*beautifully incomplete*—we're the opposite.

Saint Lisconti is wholeheartedly the best thing that ever happened to me.

Our newfound spark…

Our emotional connection…

The heated stolen glances we share…

It's all like a fairy tale and he's my very own forbidden desire. But Saint isn't a prince. He could never be. And although I'm a good girl, one to follow the rules, he's always enticed me. Halfway through hate

I fell in love, and now we're two broken souls mending each other's flaws, but love isn't supposed to hurt this deep.

Saint was never supposed to be anything more than the bad boy next door. My father's best friend. A man eighteen years older than me. Someone I can *never* have. Instead, as the years progressed, he's become my entire life…

My every single thought.

My every single second.

My every single breath.

They are his. *All his.*

Until I'm drowning in the oceans of us…

Chapter
ONE

Paisley

Three Years Prior...
Paisley is 15. Saint is 33.

"He did it again! He put his big ol' feet all over my lilies!" I grit, stepping closer to my house's front-facing window to witness the devil at work. My fists clench until my nails threaten to puncture the thick skin. *Damn him!*

"Just let it go, Paisley." My father sighs from the couch. He's typing away on his phone with zero to no interest in my preoccupation. "Besides, you can barely see that the lilies are there."

"But they're in bloom! They'll never grow now!"

"Let it go, sweetheart."

Let it go.

Let it go.

Let it go.

No, I can't *let it go*! I can't just stand here and do nothing! I need to do something. Run out and tell him to be a little more careful at least. *Nana would want me to say something...*

Yes, that's it.

Nana. I'm going to go outside and do this for her.

I stare through the shutters a little longer, observing the three men unloading various furniture items from a white hire truck. Due to the shiny black metal Harley Davidson parked in front of the new house next door, the truck is parked in front of mine.

The men bypass one another with little conversation, each effortlessly carrying items diagonally across the parking strip into the house on my left. My heart thumps to the untuned rhythm of their leather boots violently stomping all over my rare blue tiger lilies, crushing them to get through.

How RUDE!

Two of the men work around the delicate flowers, but not this one particular guy. He's the tallest and most handsomely mysterious of them all. It's almost as if he's doing it on purpose. *Darn it!* My gaze stays on his six-foot-two frame, taking in his beautifully tousled dark hair and perfectly chiseled jaw. He's easily the most attractive man I've seen in my fifteen years of living. But there's something about him—almost a glowing dangerous aura—that has me staring longer, deeper, harder. And that lethal crooked smirk he flashes one of the men he bypasses after saying something only confirms it.

He sports a leather jacket, except he's shirtless underneath, wearing nothing but black jeans and a fancy chestnut belt. As he pulls a walnut bookshelf from the truck—not that he looks like someone who would read—the hot summer Californian sun illumines his naturally tanned olive skin, bronzing his glistering washboard abdominal muscles and vaunted V-line. I'm almost certain that leather jacket is hiding some ink.

I'm so blinded by the godly sight, my cheeks flush, and for a moment I forget about the lilies... until he sets the bookshelf right on top of them and finishes massacring them all!

It's as if he doesn't notice or care. I hear shouting from a blind spot to the left and he looks up, nods, and proceeds to leave the bookshelf right there on the parking strip. Then, he jogs out of sight.

"Oh my God! Dad, come look at this!"

"It's your summer break, sweetie, enjoy it instead of stalking the new neighbors!"

"It's not stalking if it's looking out for what's mine."

"Yeah, that's what Ted Bundy said, and we all know how that ended up."

Dramatically rolling my eyes, I ignore my father completely and hurry to the hallway. I don't bother announcing my plans or kicking off my fluffy pink slippers before I rush to unlock the front door.

I'm out of the house in seconds, bolting to the parking strip in an attempt to pull the bookshelf away. But after countless efforts, it's no use. I don't have muscles, not like *him*.

"Hands off what's not yours, kiddo."

My body tenses at the harsh voice and I glance up, raising a hand to my brow to shield the sun's glare, but find myself squinting just the same. There's a man standing beside the truck with his arms crossed over his chest. Cocking his head to the side, his brows rise in challenge at my lack of response.

While the other two men looked in their early to mid-thirties, this man seems older but intimidating just the same with a lethal stare, perfectly styled hair, and a white scar just above his upper lip.

"Lost something, kiddo?"

"No." I gulp, taking a step back when the corners of his lips rise in a cold, sly smirk.

"Then get outta here. This ain't the place for little kids."

"But I live right next door and saw that my lilies are getting ruined!"

The man scoffs and gestures toward the house to my left—*the new house.* "From now on, that's where my good friend lives. Don't like something he does? Learn to live with it."

And then, just like that, the man rounds the truck, gets in the driver's side, and takes off down the street. My mouth remains hung open, left to simply witness the truck get smaller and smaller until it transforms into a distant shape of white nothingness.

"So rude!" I utter under my breath, glaring at the ultra-modern home beside mine. Its exterior slaughters every chance of brightness with its dark color palettes of black, Pietra gray, and midnight blue... the devil's colors.

That's it. I'm not giving up.

I'm doing this.

The house was only listed for a few weeks before it was sold. Mr. and Mrs. Jenkins were the best kind of neighbors. Always remembering birthdays with apple pies, treating the lilies with kindness, and after Nana June passed always looked out for me while my father worked shifts at the hospital as a doctor.

My mom left my dad and me when I was one. It's crazy... the fact that I haven't seen her since and don't even know what she looks like. My father ripped up every single photograph of her in a fit of rage one night when I was too young to comprehend what was happening. He doesn't like to talk about her, so I never push it. I know he's been hurt by her—*deeply*—and I don't want to cause any more pain. My mother wasn't happy with us—that's what she apparently told him. She hated routine. Hated Sacramento. Hated the prospect of revolving her entire life around me, especially because my parents were only twenty-two when I was born.

There's a gaping hole in my heart, an unfilled void from missing out on what most people are too fortunate to realize. I don't blame my mother for leaving. I blame her for the cracks she left behind. I blame her for my inability to contact her because it's as if she's vanished without a trace. I blame her for the darkness clouding me, that same darkness that remains with me no matter where I go after my father spilled what exactly she thought of me.

My mom doesn't care for me. I'm convinced she never will, and I'll never know her face. I can be the perfect daughter for however long I like. She isn't coming back to Sacramento. Her story with my father and me is done. It was a long time ago when I was too young to both remember and understand what it felt like to be held by her. I've come to accept it, but it still hurts to comprehend I've seen Mr. and Mrs. Jenkins more times than my actual mother.

Mr. and Mrs. Jenkins' house has always comforted me... *Now it's home to hell.*

My Nana always used to say, *those who fear the devil's home fear freedom itself.* The words are a metaphor to life, a testament to follow your gut, no matter how daunting or risky, which is why I'm going to go ahead with my plan.

Gravel crushes loudly underneath my feet as I power walk past the neighbor's gate and through the short maze of vibrant green short hedges, before climbing up the wooden porch steps. Two knocks on the black heritage door—the only vintage element—and it swings open ajar on its own.

"Hello?" My voice lowers, giving up on me as the whisper escapes my lips.

No answer.

"Hello?"

Nothing.

Curiosity gets the better of me as I peer my head through the large gap between the door and the doorframe but see nobody.

Do it.

As I step inside, a mixture of leather, tobacco, and musky sandalwood flood my lungs. Massaging the nape of my neck, I step through the gap and glance down the never-ending hallway. While the plain entryway in my house is straight and leads to the living room—so you can see exactly who's stepping in—this one is different. It has a huge floor-to-ceiling mirrored wall on the right-hand side, which ends just before the hallway curls to the right, leading to the kitchen, living room and beyond.

The silence accompanying my every step has me thinking that perhaps the men are in the backyard. It would be the only logical answer as to why they haven't heard me. And then I hear it, the sound of the backyard door sliding open, followed by a few heavy foot thuds before the crashing of glass. Men exchange streams of curse words.

"I said they're *fragile*, you bastard!"

"Do you think I *meant* to break them? Plates are the least of your problems now, Saint."

Saint?

I halt in my position in the hall, my back pressed against the wall. *Maybe this isn't the best idea.* I don't know who these men are, but I've come too far to back out now.

Think of Nana. Save her lilies.

"You walked straight into the fucking glass door. I was right behind you," Saint grits.

"Yeah, okay, fine, I wasn't thinking. That any better?"

"Much better."

"*Jesus.* Focus on your final fight tonight instead, will you?"

Fight?

"Already am." Saint chuckles, his voice a hot, gravelly tone.

"Yeah, you'll have the fucker knocked out in the first round for a three-time streak, you watch. I've learned that from... well, let's say *experience.*"

"Didn't mean to knock you out that time, man."

"Bullshit."

The previous bickering turns into full-blown laughter.

The back of the house. They're in the back of the house near the kitchen. Slowly, I walk closer along the hall to hear them clearer, my hands pressing against the cold wall to steady myself from making a sound. My heart pounds wildly at every step. I have no game plan from here. I didn't think any of this through, *but I can't leave now...*

I settle by the edge of the hallway, inches from where the wall curves, and listen on.

"All right, I'm going to head out and see if Nico is still there or went for another load."

Oh no.

Just like a moth drawn to a flame, my mind begins to burn at how my curiosity triumphed over any minimal thought of an escape plan before I stepped inside. Because now as heavy footsteps speed toward me, my body freezes up when I finally process what Saint said; *I'm going to head out and see if Nico is still there.*

Crap.

He's going to see me!

All of a sudden, my confidence from a few moments ago falls down a never-ending rabbit hole. I glance toward the front door to my left, knowing that if I make a run for it down the hallway now, someone is bound to hear me. My only option is to crouch down into a little ball and pray Saint changes his mind or passes without seeing me.

What false hope considering I'm adjacent to a mirrored wall... but I do it anyway.

The thumps get louder.

My palms begin to sweat.

My heart rate exceeds normality.

I shove my head into my knees and hug them to my chest. *Please don't see me.*

Please don't see me.

Please don't see me.

Please. Please. Please.

Black leather boots round the hallway and the supply of air to my lungs cuts short.

He hasn't seen me yet. Thank God.

I've never held my breath for this long before and while I may die in this very spot from it, at least it's better to go out this way rather than him seeing me first. Yes, I'll still be their problem, sure, but at least I'll already be their *dead* problem. And besides, they can't bring me back to life just to kill me again… *right?*

Oh, God. Where did my young woman pride go?

"Owww, my feet!" I scream out as the man's heavy boots step on me, crushing my toes in my flimsy slippers. "Ow! Ow! Ow!"

"Shit. Where the fuck did you come from, kid?"

Oh no!

I squeeze my eyes shut and let out a frustrated breath at myself for getting caught so easily. It was going so well until I stuffed it all up for myself and screamed. Now it's all going to blow up in my face. *Just great.*

I remain quiet, not glancing up a single inch as I clutch my throbbing feet in agony.

"Kid, I asked you a damn question."

"Don't you ever look *down*?" I murmur to myself.

"If you're going to act all smart and talk into your knees, you and I are going to have a problem, not that we don't already."

Slowly, I lift my gaze up and my eyes widen in shock. *Him.* My lips part to no words. It all just stockpiles in my brain. *It's him*—the mystery man I saw outside who crushed all my lilies. I also recognized the man's voice as… *Saint.* How ironic that the most devilish man on my street has a name that kisses the gates of heaven.

Damn this guy and his habit of stepping on every damn thing in his way without looking down for one split second. *First my lilies and now ME.*

Saint stares down at me, his piercing ocean blue eyes narrowing at my every breath. He's even more attractive up close, but it all doesn't matter after everything he's done today.

"I said, don't *you* ever *look down*?" I hiss, balling my fists as I rise to my aching feet.

Saint's extended stare is beyond intimidating, but I give in to the fading sensation in my heart and stare right back. My five-foot-three frame beside his tall one gives him the upper hand. *Well… it's not just that.* He's taller, sure, but he's perfectly built with just the right amount of toned muscle, and not only do his broad shoulders and narrow waist reveal God's unexpected favoritism in sweet sin, but I'm one thousand percent sure he's strong enough to throw me out of his house with his pinkie finger.

Not today.

Yes, I'm fearful, but I'm not leaving without an apology from him.

"What did you just say to me?" he growls.

Sure, let me repeat this to you for the third time, why don't I…

"I said don't *you* ever *look down?*"

"What on earth are you on about, kid?" Saint hisses, stepping so close into my personal space that my back hits the wall. My jaw ticks at the whiff of his masculine, musky cologne. *So hot.*

"The flowers!" I explain. "You stepped on my *flowers* outside and then proceeded to put a bookshelf on top of them! There's even a sign I made out there that clearly says, '*no walking*' for a reason!"

"Rules suck, kid."

My nose scrunches up in fury. "No, *you* suck! They were rare. My nana gave them to me to grow before she passed away last year."

"Still don't know what you're talking about, kid, and guess what? I don't *want* to know." Saint confidently snarls. He continues to look at me for the longest time, so long those light eyes burn deep into my soul, destined to steal anything he likes. He dusts off his leather jacket before crouching down to my level and wags his pointer finger at me. "Get the hell out of here, kid. Don't know how your parents raised you, but entering a stranger's house unannounced is a big no in my book."

My eyes narrow. "But my lilies—"

"Forget the damn flowers, kid. Nobody cares."

"*I* care!"

"And who exactly are you?" He smirks, rising to his full height, and begins to take smooth, long strides toward the front door. He oozes dominance in his fierce walk, as if he's some type of supermodel with that head held up so high and those relaxed shoulders pulled down and back at every step.

"I bet if my father were the one to tell you all this, you'd listen!"

Saint pauses in his stance and I witness those shoulders tense up, a tall devil ready for the burning flames.

"No, kid. That's where you're wrong," he says without turning back. "I don't listen to anybody. I do everything on my own terms."

"Fine, but how'd you feel if somebody ripped out your flowers?"

"Never ask that to a man whose heart has been ripped out of their fuckin' chest."

"Makes sense. No wonder I couldn't find it."

That has Saint turning around and lowering his gaze on me. Although I take a step back, I keep my head high and poised just like his moments ago. This man… he scares and frustrates me all at the same time. He's wrapped in fury, a fury begging to be unraveled and challenged, and that's exactly what I plan to do whether he likes it or not.

"Say that again," Saint deadpans. "I. Dare. You."

My lips press shut.

"No, don't lose that mouth of yours now." He clicks his tongue with a mocking chuckle, his dimples the most perfect I've ever seen. So deep and long, even under all his stubble. "You definitely said something. Spill it. I don't like being lied to."

"I alluded you have no heart."

"*No heart*?" Saint scoffs at my comment, shaking his head as his hands rest by his waist. It draws my attention there for a little too long. I've never seen a man so perfectly up close like this before, but the scarlet flush on my cheeks and pitter-patter of my heart don't come close to my disdain for him. *Such a coldhearted, cruel, rebellious outlaw.*

"Yeah, *no heart*," I confidently nod.

Ha!

"Get the fuck out of my house!" he roars. "And while you're at it, that sign of yours—wherever it may be—I want it removed too. Never wanna see your face again, kid. If I do, so God help you for what will happen, got it?"

"But the lilies—"

"I said fucking run, kid." Saint widens his hands on his waist to reveal a red Swiss Army Knife tucked into the right side of his waistband. "This isn't the place for you. Wanna know why?"

I bolt past Saint, darting out of the house before getting to know the reason. Outside his gate, I give in to my blurry vision and tears burn down my cheeks. Standing up for myself has never burned this badly. Any second now and my heart will beat out of my chest, never to be found.

I hate him.

Hate him.

Hate him.

Crouching down beside the patch of my damaged lilies, in all my anger, I manage to finally push the bookshelf away. The damage is already done. The flowers are flattened, dead.

My nana wouldn't want this.

More tears fall as I work to get rid of the sign, trying my best to repatch all the dirt, but again it's no use. *They're all gone. Just like Nana June.*

I feel a presence beside me and turn to my left to find Saint feet away, leaning against a sidewalk tree. His soul-piercing stare remains on me all while he locks his ankles, pulls out a cigarette from his back pocket, and lights it. The burning orange tip distracts me for a second before the toxic nicotine smell has me scrunching up my nose.

"Smoking is bad for you," I whisper under my breath and wipe away my tears with the back of my hand. But this man must have some super-hearing because he seems to hear my every breath.

Saint smirks, pulling out the death stick for a moment to blow out a large cloud of white smoke. It obstructs his entire face before clearing up again. "Concerned about me, kid?"

"No. Just saying it kills over eight million people each year. That's one every five seconds and equals just under five hundred thousand people here in America."

Saint looks at me as if I've lost my mind. "Where'd you come up with that statistic?"

"The news."

"The fuckin' *news*. Doesn't faze me that you watch that shit."

The second he continues smoking with that big smug smirk, something inside me snaps. My young woman pride can't have it any longer. I stand up, brush the dirt from my knees, and storm up to him. It takes rising on my tippy toes to reach for the death stick and crush it underneath my slippers to finally feel satisfied.

I don't think I'll ever forget the switch to coldness in Saint's expression or how his narrowed eyes darken in havoc as he towers over me like roaring thunder. His jaw clenches so tightly I think it may explode right here on our tree-lined street, Portola Way.

"Why did you do that, kid?" Saint growls.

"I gave you five extra seconds." I smirk for the first time today. "You should be thanking me."

"*Thanking you?*" he spits. "One day you'll grow up, kid, and you'll learn that life isn't always about listening to the statistics or following the fixed rules all the damn time—it's about *surviving*. It's about constantly getting knocked down and instead of getting back up on your feet again, crawling your way to the finish line. We all need little releases in life, and you, kid, you just slaughtered mine."

And then he's off, collecting the bookshelf so effortlessly before storming toward his house.

My smirk drops.

Oh.

I stand there frozen, unsure of everything around me. *What just happened?*

I stare at the back of Saint's head, at the speckles of allusive flames wrapped around the man next door, all the while he climbs up his porch steps. I gulp down as he glances over his shoulder just as he reaches his front door. Saint's blue-eyed gaze meets mine and narrows. It's as if there's this unspoken havoc between us, a vow that this is unfinished business.

Rushed footsteps come from behind me. It's my father. I just feel it.

"You okay, Paisley?"

I turn to him. "I will be."

Silence laces the air for a moment as my father's dark brown eyes travel beyond me. "Who is he? Our new neighbor?"

I don't even have to ask who he's talking about. I just *know*.

"He's the devil of Sacramento… and he's just getting started."

And just like that, Saint's front door slams shut, confirming he heard every single word.

Great. Just great.

My heart thumps wildly in my chest.

Game on, neighbor dearest.

Chapter
TWO

Paisley
PAST

Two Years Prior...
Paisley is 16. Saint is 34.

I told my father not to apologize to Saint on my behalf after the flower incident a year ago... *Because I wasn't sorry!* People like Saint never learn. Besides, what was I even apologizing for? Apart from a minor privacy breach, I did nothing wrong. *He's* the one who crushed my lilies and young woman pride!

Saint could have simply apologized, and we could have moved on. Instead, now, a year later, I'm still thinking about the heat of the fire that rumbled inside me when his gorgeous blue eyes landed on me in his fateful hallway.

That one conversation between my father and Saint, one I wasn't involved in, was all it took for my life to become ten thousand times worse. Ever since that day, they've become close friends and it's an instant *boom* backfiring in my face. I knew it was a possibility with my father only being four years older than Saint, but I guess I just didn't expect it to happen so soon…

After being a professional boxer for the past ten years, Saint Lisconti retired at the end of last year. Now at thirty-four, Saint is a personal trainer at Fearless Fitness. It's a respected and successful fitness studio he cofounded with his close friend and ex-coach, Nico Quivez. Nico's also the man who was by the moving truck and told me to mind my own business when Saint moved in last summer.

For the better half of a year, there hasn't been a week where I didn't see the Devil of Sacramento at my house with my father… *okay,* the *hot devil,* but *still,* looks are nothing when you have the attitude of a fly on the wall. So, no matter how attractively beautiful Saint may be, *and gosh how much he is,* it doesn't change the way I feel about him—utter hatred.

Whenever I see him, I rush into my room to study or out the door to attend to my flowers. Saint always has that conniving smirk on his face that I'd love to wipe off with my bare hands. It's as if he's winning this invisible race between us, but there isn't any and even if there were and Saint was my prize at the end of the race, I'd start running backward.

So, okay, perhaps I shouldn't be doing this right now, but somebody has to be a good citizen and look out for danger in the neighborhood, *right*? I swear that's all I was ever doing. I didn't intend to witness a scene between Saint and two other men out of *The Godfather.*

Because I adore the warm, sultry breeze, I usually do my homework on the balcony outside my bedroom and while today should be just like any other afternoon after school while my father is at work, it isn't because of one single aspect…

Saint.

My balcony partially overlooks some of his backyard and I was in the middle of a math equation when a shout had my eyes wander there. My pen fell from my grip, and I sat up on my heels to see better, and now five minutes later my gaze still hasn't been able to return to my page. In fact, the math book is long forgotten, spread out on the terracotta-tiled ground.

Saint and Leo—the other man I saw moving a few furniture items the day Saint moved in—have another man cornered in the backyard, a few feet away from the crystal clear in-ground pool. From where

I'm standing, I can't see the victim's face, but his hands rise in surrender as pleas escape him.

"You don't have to do this! I'll make sure it doesn't happen again! Please!"

"It isn't the first time you've said that, Anderson," Saint hisses, crossing his toned arms over his black short-sleeved V-neck. "And to be fair, I'm getting a little sick and tired of all the running around to make sure you have your head in the fucking game. It ain't my job, understand?"

"I know, Saint, I know it's not your job. But lately my whole life has gone to shit. My job is the only thing I have, and yes, I slipped up, more than once, but there won't be a third."

"I don't know, Nico told me to finish you off good, and seeing as I own half of the business…" Saint shakes his head, veering his gaze off to the distance before glancing toward Leo. "What do you say, Leo? Should we believe a word that comes out of his mouth, because I already have my answer."

Leo laughs mockingly and begins shaking his head. In a domineering stance, Leo rakes a hand through his dirty-blond hair and slowly rubs his clean-shaven jaw as if in thought. "I say do what Nico asked and what you called him over to do."

Anderson's hands lower and he makes a run for it, rushing past Saint and around the pool in a flash, but he doesn't get far. Leo bolts after him and the thuds of his feet over the grass section by the shed violently echo in my chest. Anderson is seconds from reaching the pocket doors before Leo takes him down from behind and slams him to the ground.

Still stationed by the perimeter fence dividing our homes, Saint slowly shakes his head. "You know not to run from us, Anderson," he says, striding toward them. "When are you going to listen, huh?"

Leo has Anderson pinned down and that seems to be the only security Saint needs before his big fist collides with the poor man's jaw. He doesn't stop there. He keeps going and going until the man's light skin turns all bloody and crimson stains Saint's hand. Loud groans come from the man, who attempts to fight back, only for Leo to restrict his hands from moving.

Anderson's body weakens as he spits out blood into the grass, his eyes still widening in fear as Saint seems to settle down… *for now.* "Please, please don't do this. I have a son."

Saint lets out a cold chuckle while pulling out something from inside his jacket. I cover my mouth, desperate to mute my gasp as the shiny blades of his Swiss Army Knife catch the sun, blinding me for a split moment.

Oh no! Holy sunflowers!

He's going to kill him!

Saint's going to kill this man. Right here, right now.

"You have a son? And what did you think that was going to change after you fucked with my business, huh? Thinking you can do some dirty work under the table and steal money and then pledge my name like you want to drag me down with you. Sorry to break it, man, but that's fucking low."

"Saint, please."

"I SAID WHAT IS THAT GOING TO CHANGE?" Saint roars, lifting the knife for a beat, but when Anderson does nothing but thrash his arms in Leo's grip, he lunges the knife down toward him and my heart aches in disbelief.

"NO! DON'T DO IT!" I scream, my throat burning, just in time for the tip of the knife to halt an inch from Anderson's chest.

It takes one breath, two at the maximum, for Saint's head to snap over his shoulder in the direction of the scream… *my* scream. *Holy…* Saint eyes my house and his gaze quickly lands on me, widening for a split second before darkening back to his signature style.

Heated fear rushes around my heart.

Oh no.

Trembling, I let go of my sweaty grip on the metal railing and feel my body begin to shake. I don't like the look in Saint's eyes. The look of death. It's lethal and sickening. As if he was actually capable of digging that knife into that man's heart with no regrets or second thoughts.

I know Saint and I are from completely different worlds. I understand from the conversation that Anderson was stealing money from Fearless Fitness, but what Anderson did… could it really merit death?

Saint hands Leo the knife and stands to his feet. Leo glances toward me, narrowing his gaze before Saint screams at Anderson to run, which he does, bolting through the side gate and down the street, away from the property.

I want to move. I want to go back inside and lock the door, but a devious numbness has overtaken my entire body, immobilizing me from taking a single step. My eyes snap from Saint's clenched jaw to the speckles of blood on his face and clothes as he walks toward me.

I stare down at him from the balcony, nervous about what exactly Saint is capable of. And just like that... I *learn*. He climbs the dividing fence between us, despite my pleas to stay away. But he doesn't care. It's as if this is our own version of Romeo and Juliet, except we are not fateful lovers and the poison comes from his stare, not a little toxic bottle.

From the fence, Saint latches onto the metal railing of the balcony and pulls himself up with his toned arms. It's there where adrenalin kicks in and I rush backward, only to trip on my math book and fall on my ass. Meanwhile, Saint casually perches himself on the edge, swings his legs over, and jumps into the balcony, always with those same speckles of chaos clouding his big blue eyes.

He brings a finger to the center of his lips, signaling *silence*.

I scurry to get myself up, using the outdoor wooden chair to steady myself, but there's barely enough space between us on this tiny balcony. Saint inches away, ready to pounce... I'm in trouble.

Locking his jaw, Saint gestures toward the door behind me. "You go inside. I go back down."

"You let him run... Were you going to kill him?"

"Get. Inside. *Now*."

I shake my head at the sensory overload of the metallic smell of blood. It's even worse up close, worse to see the fresh crimson sprayed and smeared all over his beautiful face like he's some wolf disturbed while going in for the kill.

"Were you going to kill him or was it a warning?"

"Inside, kid."

"I—"

Saint cuts me off. "Paisley, I'm going to say it one more time."

"I don't trust my back to you. I don't know if you have any other weapons on you... like a gun."

Saint lets out a frustrated breath. "I don't own a gun."

"Prove it."

Saint glances off to the side and lets out a deeply irritated sigh. His chest must be pounding, beating so fast because it rises and falls beneath his top out of control. I'm so caught up in the moment that I don't realize the blood-stained T-shirt gets closer until a hand covers my mouth and the other lifts me up against his chest.

I let out a muted scream, kicking and screaming for him to let me go, but he doesn't. My cheek grazes against his stubble as he whispers in my ear to calm down.

Calm down?

How can I *calm down*?

No matter how many times or how hard I slam my fists into his chest, it doesn't faze him. The only thing it does is transfer some of the blood to my hands. Tears burn down my cheeks as Saint walks us inside from the balcony, through my bedroom, and out into the hallway.

Another hallway.

Saint's eyes meet mine and my whimpers soften, but my throat already begins to ache from my restricted screams. "If I set you down here, promise me you won't scream. Nod if you won't scream, kid."

It takes a full moment, but I eventually slowly nod.

Saint continues staring for what feels like years before he must see something in my eyes he's willing to surrender to and puts me down. *Finally.* His hands instantly move inside the pockets of his jeans, while mine rub my tender cheeks from just how tight his grip was.

"You didn't have to do that," I grumble, staring at the smeared blood on my hands.

"You saw nothing, Paisley, understood? You saw *nothing.*"

"But I did! I saw you and Leo—"

"You saw NOTHING."

"Okay." I blink away the harshness of his tone, my voice a bare whisper when I say, "Just promise me you won't kill him."

Saint's eyes roll and he blows out another impatient sigh. "Yeah, yeah, I won't kill him. Promise."

"No, you're just saying that!"

"No, I'm not. I promise we were just giving him a warning."

"Really?"

"Yes. I made a promise to you, kid. A promise is a promise."

"Except I don't know you and it seems as though you hate rules."

"Fuck." Saint pinches the bridge of his nose. "Okay, fine, listen to this. You don't say a word to your father about what you saw, even though it was just a warning, and I'll pay for some new lilies out the front, deal?"

"Mmmm…" I ponder the thought.

This could be a good deal… Maybe.

"And you won't step on them this time?" I ask out of curiosity.

Clenching his jaw, Saint shakes his head. "No, I won't step on them this time. One hundred dollars. I'll give it to you right now, deal?"

"And I can put my sign back up too?"

"Yes, kid. That too. You can put that damn sign of yours back up too. Now, is there anything else?"

"Yes."

"God help me…"

"You have to promise to be nicer."

"I don't do nice, kid. If you really knew me, you would know that."

My brows furrow. "But you're nice to my dad and I met you first!"

"Look, kid, I'm busy. One hundred dollars for the damn lilies and we'll both go back to our lives as we know them. The altercation outside and this deal right here never happened."

"One hundred and fifty dollars and we'll be even."

"One hundred."

"One fifty."

Saint's jaw ticks. "One hundred."

I cross my arms over my chest and narrow my gaze up at him. "Okay, two hundred."

"One-*fucking*-hundred."

"Two-*freaking*-hundred."

"One fifty."

"Two fifty."

"Two hundred. Shit, I mean—"

"SOLD!" I grin as Saint recoils, raking a hand through his hair as a curse word spills.

Eventually, Saint reaches inside his back pocket, pulls out his wallet, and fishes through his bills. *All hundreds.* I eye a photo of him and an adorable little girl who can't be more than three or four in the photograph section. It seems like the photo was taken a few years back as he seems younger and she's cutely kissing his cheek and hugging him, while he's grinning at the camera with his piercing ocean eyes and hugging her back. I step closer to see it better, but he notices and slams his wallet shut with a grunt before I can take in anything else.

"Who is she?"

Ignoring the question completely, Saint hands me the money and I take it. "This never happened, okay?"

"Okay."

And then just like Saint entered, he leaves, walking through my room and smoothly maneuvering himself down from the balcony like it's an Olympic sport. Only when I know he's truly gone, do I step into the bathroom and almost lose my footing at the brush of blood on my face from where he held me.

As I wipe it away and stare down at the red blotches on my damn face towel, I can't help but cringe and whisper to myself, "But it did. It did all happen."

Chapter
THREE

Saint

PAST

One Year Prior...
Paisley is 17. Saint is 35.

"My dad's not home," Paisley softly murmurs by the front door, her small fists gripping the doorframe so tightly, blotches of white smooth over her creamy skin. "He should be back any minute, though. He just went to the store."

My brows furrow down at Alaric's seventeen-year-old daughter, the same woman who thought she could rip a fucking cigarette out of my mouth and I'd just let it go. The same one who had the audacity to stop me while I was showing Anderson what happens when you mess with my business. But in this case, I'm forced to freaking let go. Paisley's my best friend's daughter. *Innocent to this world of mine.*

"I'll wait inside then."

"No," she squeals when I proceed to take a step forward, shutting the door slightly ajar. Fortunately for me, my Italian leather biker boots are caught in the door. "No, you can't come in."

"Why?"

"Because Dad said I can't allow anybody in unless he's home. I know he said you're an exception, but…"

"Don't you remember what I always say about rules, kid?" I ask, taking this as the perfect moment to pull out my stash. I slip a cigarette into the center of my lips and pull out my lighter to get it going. "Rules fuckin' suck. They're illusions."

Paisley seems almost mesmerized by the burning orange light whenever I take a drag. It's as if her dark eyes glitter with rebellion, at the same time the flame brings her intrigue to life.

"Rules don't suck, they are placed for a reason," she says after the longest pause.

"Finally found your voice again, huh?" I smirk, a low rumble echoing in my throat when she crosses her arms over her chest as if *that's* going to intimidate me. *Nice try, kid. I'm gonna need a little more than that.* "Took you a while, didn't it?"

"Stop mocking me."

"All right, all right. Listen, I'll stop pissing you the fuck off if you let me in. I'll wait for him inside. I gotta talk to him."

"But Dad said—"

"Rules suck, kid."

Paisley lets out a huff, glaring up at me before she opens the door to reveal her entire face. Sun-kissed skin, light freckles on her cheeks, dark waves wrapped in a messy bun like she doesn't give a shit and I like it better that way. Paisley's not a girl to swear. At least her hair can do it for her. She's grown up so much in these past couple of years but is still the freaking strictest person I know.

I tell myself I better start freaking concentrating because all of a sudden Paisley has a notebook and a pen in her hands and is busy scribbling something down. My brows uptick in amusement as she bites her tongue, head down in concentration until she halts, pulls back the page to see it clearer, and nods to herself. Then, she thrusts the notepad up, inches to my chest. "Please sign at the bottom."

Yep, this one's going to be a Harvard fucking scholarship graduate.

"Sign at the bottom?" I ask.

"Mhmm."

"What the hell am I signing?"

"A contract that states if you want to come inside, you need to promise you'll be on your best behavior first. That means no smoking, no cursing and… no saying rules suck."

"So basically, you want my three signature traits to fuck off, yeah?" My gaze flickers between the paper with her large cursive handwriting to her *I'm not-backing-down* expression between my drags. "Can't sign something I don't agree with, kid."

"Then you can't come inside."

"Aren't you supposed to be at school anyway?"

"No, student-free day. Aren't you supposed to be at work?"

A slow, crooked smirk rises on my lips. "I *am* working. I'm just currently on break."

Paisley rolls her eyes. "Going around on your Harley all day with a death stick and beating people up is your *job*?"

"No. Fitness, maintaining both grit and resilience, and training people to be their best self is my job. Cigarettes, my Harley, and whiskey are just added bonuses… alongside iron fists. Sure, I'm suited to fight in the ring, but I can also protect people like you. Seeing you all in one piece has me thinking I'm doing a pretty good job of keeping people like you safe from a city full of corruption, guns, and false alibies. Which has me thinking, I haven't heard one thank you."

Paisley huffs and pushes the notebook into my chest. I chuckle and for a split second decide to give her the benefit of the doubt. Even though that doesn't relate to nor define the kind of man I am at all. I don't forgive. I don't forget. And I certainly don't give in to seventeen-year-old women.

I hand the notebook back to her. "Said I ain't gonna sign it. Take it and draw on the back instead. Save the trees, help climate change, or wherever the fuck the world is heading toward nowadays."

"*Please*." Her deep-set gaze follows mine, a silent plea alongside her parted plump lips.

Paisley Reign's a different type of girl from the rest. For some reason, she isn't afraid to speak her mind with me, yet at the same time I get the feeling she recognizes when she oversteps. It's evident in the way the paper shakes in her grip, and yet she attempts to have a poised, composed face. Tight jaw. Steady eyes. And now pierced-shut mouth…

But Paisley isn't fooling me. I've been around people like her for too long not to call them out on their shit. Every single time I see

Paisley, she evokes the devil in me, pissing me off beyond repair. This time is no different and this little contract she wrote up, it can go right back where she found it… *hell*.

In the midst of my thoughts, I flicker on my cigarette lighter and catch the edge of the paper with the allusive orange flame. Paisley's eyes widen and she gasps out a large breath, covering her mouth as we witness the contact burning into a charcoal mess.

I can't wipe the smirk off my face when she grumbles something under her breath and swings the door entirely open. I follow her in, but she bolts away down the hallway and stomps up the stairs in fury.

"Pointless rules get you nowhere, kid. Running doesn't get you anywhere either. Remember that—" The thud of her bedroom door slamming shut cuts me off. I shake my head with a soft chuckle and settle onto the living room couch. "Remember that for next time."

"What are we gonna do about this girl next door?" Nico asks beside me on my porch steps, blowing out a cloud of smoke. "What's her name again? Ainsley?"

"No, Paisley." I take a drag of my cigarette, burning my vision into the house next door and Paisley, who's been by the parking strip digging up dirt with a pink shovel and planting seeds for the past half hour. "Paisley Reign. And I don't fuckin' know. All I do know is I don't trust her to stay tight-lipped about last year. She's already seen too much. Alaric would kill me if he knew his daughter witnessed me beating the shit out of Anderson last year."

"Exactly. I'm not placing my fate in the hands of some sixteen-year-old who's already got her own hands three feet into soil."

Of course Nico Quivez—my ex-boxing-coach and co-partner at Fearless Fitness—is getting hotheaded about it. That's the type of guy a man training boxing beasts like myself and MMA fighters in a thirty-square cage for the past twenty years becomes. One wrong word out of someone's mouth and he's ready to ruthlessly pounce. A man whose mind never stops ticking. A man whose good judgment and coaching were a major asset in my fighting career years ago.

"Paisley's seventeen, Nico."

"Sixteen, seventeen, same shit. She has no reason not to run to the police because you listened to me and warned Anderson of what happens when you fuck around with business. Who knows if she opens her mouth to her father, or worse, the police. We don't need that shit."

"She's got a reason to stay quiet, trust me."

"What is it?"

Alaric's dark Jeep turns into the drive next door and Paisley glances up, waving at him.

Grinning, I crush the cigarette under my foot and nod toward the car. "We're looking at it."

"Gonna talk to Alaric about his daughter? Yeah, good fuckin' luck."

"None needed, Nico."

On my way to her, my hands slide into my jean pockets. Paisley glances up when I pass her by the parking strip. The way her jaw ticks has me halting. I guess I can spend a couple of minutes with *Miss Door-slammer.*

Crouching down over Paisley's array of garden tools, I pull out a light pink frilly blossom from the flower cluster already in bloom and twirl it between my thumb and pointer. Drawing it to my nose, I take in its sweet floral scent of… well, I have no freaking clue. I'm not a flower guy. Never have been, never can be, never will be. *Fucking sue me.*

"Great, just great!" Paisley glares up at me and lets out an agitated groan. "You've really done it this time!"

"What? I thought the whole thing about planting flowers was to pick them, no?"

"If you want them to die, yes. If you want to preserve their beauty, you stand back and *watch.*"

I smirk, continuing to swirl the pinkish flower around. "What are these flowers called?"

"Geraniums. Why?"

"Was gonna say they look like a pain in the ass to maintain to me."

"You're terrible, you know that, right?"

"Sure do."

"Good," Paisley grumbles and goes back to planting new seeds. I nod over her work. "Yeah, keep digging, kid."

I turn around and look over at Nico, who nods toward the girl with knitted brows. I raise my hands up with a shrug before jogging up Alaric's driveway and throw the flower I've already forgotten the name of aside.

Sporting a white polo shirt and dark slacks, Alaric's in the midst of taking out two bags of groceries from his car's trunk when he glances my way. Smirking, his brows rise in amusement. "What you looking at, Sainty boy?"

"Nothing." I laugh, shrugging casually. "I just love how you switch from doctor to *'let's go to Vegas'* in two-point-five seconds."

My best friend grins. "It's called Clark Kent-ing the shit out of life. Don't worry, I don't expect you to understand."

"Oh, I'm already there, man. Guess you just gotta catch up to be in the race."

"Fucker." Alaric shakes his head in laughter. "God, I love how you're acting all smart now, but we'll just forget last year after the Sawyer versus Jenson match in Vegas where you drank the whole liquor store and I had to freaking carry you home like you were a newborn. The way I was running to prevent my back from breaking and you know—dying—*that's* being in the race."

"Thanks for having my back and *not* reopening the Vegas vault."

"Welcome. We say the same shit every year, and then right about this time, fly back to Vegas to get our asses kicked. Have I mentioned that I *love* being your best friend?"

"Many times." I laugh. "Good thing we actually don't live in Vegas."

"Yeah, I thank God every day for that one."

"Sure you do."

"I really do." Alaric chuckles as he gets the last of the grocery bags and sets them down on the concrete garage floor. "Oh, while you're here, I was going to ask if you wanted to stick around for dinner. Paisley's making her signature chicken and rice. I know how much you like it. What do you say?"

"Would love to, but I have Nico back at mine. Promised the fucker I'll go to one of the matches he's coaching tonight. Somebody had the audacity to say MMA is for the big dogs, while boxing is for the Chihuahuas."

"Did you tell him to fuck off?"

"*Fuck off*? I was going to show him the mark *chihuahuas* make."

"Why didn't you?"

"His niece is watching the game. That was his defense. Didn't want her to worry about a black eye."

"Shit. Where the fuck did Nico's balls go?"

I smirk. "Was wondering the same thing. Apparently big dogs get neutered first."

Alaric throws his head back in laugher, resting a hand on his chest. "Fuck, that was a good one. I love it, man."

My own chuckle rumbles up my throat. "Shame I didn't tell him that one yet."

"Real shame. Anyway, I'll catch you later then. When you pass by Paisley, can you tell her to come in soon so we can start dinner 'cause I'm getting a beer the second I walk in, yeah?"

"Sure thing." Glancing over my shoulder, I don't expect Paisley to be staring at me. She's a good ten feet away and I mockingly wave at her. She rolls her eyes at my smirk and turns back to the flowers unamused, yet I keep on staring. "So, what college degree is she interested in? Journalism? Landscape architect? Flower arranging? Professional eye roller?"

Alaric bursts out in laughter. "I have no clue, but she still fucking hates you, man."

"Well aware of that fact. I learned today that you're apparently not supposed to pull out flowers. They're purely there for *observation*. Who knew?"

"God, I think my daughter's going to be the death of you."

"She already is."

"Trust me when I say it's better this way. She doesn't need to be around guys like you. God forbid she wants to be when she's older. I'd kill any guy who looks at her for a second too long."

Nico's voice comes ringing in my ear. I need to make sure what Paisley witnessed last year wasn't repeated to anyone. If she's spreading any word that I'm exacting my own type of revenge to men who double-cross me… well, I'm fucked.

"Does Paisley talk to you much?" I ask.

"Rarely."

Good.

"Nothing out of the ordinary lately?"

Alaric shakes his head with a slight shrug. "No, she's not the type of girl who speaks a lot. She keeps to herself and out of trouble. Total opposite to me, right?"

"She doesn't keep to herself around me."

"True. She speaks her mind with you. I think her mom not being around a lot affects her. Paisley never vocalizes it, but I see it. You know how it is. Everybody at school probably talks about theirs, whether it be good or bad memories… and instead, she doesn't have any of those stories of her own. After the divorce, Faye told me she was fucking off to Spain to be with some rich bastard and hasn't contacted Paisley and me since."

"Shit, I didn't know that part. I'm sorry, man."

"Yeah, it's fucked up. I mean, I don't give a shit about it, but it's not fair on Paisley. She never hears from her mother. No birthday messages. No Christmas cards. No nothing. It's as if she doesn't exist, and I know that's bound to hurt at some point. But what can I do? Paisley was close to my mom, her nana June, so when she passed three years ago, she really needed family to rely on. There wasn't any. Her mother, Faye, was long gone, and I was busy working overtime to distract myself."

"Does she have a couple friends at least?"

"No, doesn't have any close cousins or friends. So Paisley started with these flowers and poetry and hasn't spent a single day without them. It's a good habit, but I can't help but think she's wasting available time where she could be out socializing, you know."

I knew about Alaric's dramas with his former girlfriend and Paisley's mom in the past, but never to this depth, especially never spoken about the long-term effects it has on Paisley. From the day we met, Alaric and I have been super tight. I'm an only child, so he's like the brother I've never had. I can tell him anything and he'll keep it safe, just like all the shit I've told him about my past. I know he has a lot on his plate and that being a single father isn't easy. I just think sometimes he doesn't give himself enough credit. He's doing incredible. Far much more incredible than I would be in his position.

Glancing back over at Paisley, I watch as she drops a few seeds into another dug-up hole. But then I look at her, like *really* look at her, and notice the frown on her lips. How she reaches up with her dirty glove and sweeps underneath her eye, almost as if she's stopping tears from flowing.

Swallowing down, I pull Alaric into a brief side hug. "You've both been through a lot, man. But at least Paisley has you. You're taking care of her and you're *here* for her. Continue being there for her. Even when she says she doesn't need you and pushes you away, be there."

"I will, but I just feel at times what I do is not enough," he admits, his voice breaking at the last word. "I feel like Paisley suffers in silence and doesn't let me in. I'm the closest person to her and yet... I can't help her. You get what I mean?"

Alaric doesn't know how close he's hit home. I massage the lump in my throat and nod. We're silent for a few moments and I shift my eyes to the sky outside the garage on this clear, sunny day.

I clear my throat. "I don't know how it would help, seeing as Paisley hates my guts, but anything I can do to help, you know I'm just one house away."

"That means more than you know, Saint. Thank you for that and for listening."

"Anytime. I better go now, or else Nico will bust my balls. See you tomorrow, yeah?"

Alaric smiles softly, playfully slapping my back. "Yeah, see you then, man."

I squeeze his shoulders and smile back. "You've got this, brother. Be brave for her."

"I will."

I give him a curt nod and jog down his driveway, knowing that somewhere deep inside me I'll remember the words he told me. Those of himself. Those of Paisley. They came from a place of raw emotion and hurt, and who am I to challenge Paisley now that I know the truth about why she's so uptight, yet vulnerably timid?

Who the fuck am I to do that?

Paisley doesn't have anybody, and on the outside looking in, it could appear like I'm losing my damn mind and someone's unscrewed my balls, but I... *I feel sorry for her.* I really do. I need to leave her the fuck alone. The bickering and constant back and forth tension-filled conversation—it needs to stop. It's not fair for us to venture any deeper into spiraling hate.

We're neighbors, I'm her father's best friend, she's eighteen years younger. I need to tone this shit down. Because now that I know Paisley's hurting, I won't be able to deal with myself if she got caught in the crossfire of the scorching war in my mind. I can't let anything happen to innocent people who deserve more than the path life has callously given them.

Paisley catches my gaze as I pass her by the parking strip. "Dad said dinner's soon."

"Okay, thanks. What were you and my dad talking about?"

"Nothing you haven't heard before."

"You seem pensive. What are you thinking about?"

"Just that if you get stuck on the past too much, you drown in a pit of burning flames."

Paisley's gaze narrows and she places her hand by her brows, blocking the sunlight as those honey-brown eyes dive deep into my soul. "Thought you didn't have a heart to begin with…"

"True. I don't." Slowly, my smirk turns into a frown. "But the heat hurts just the same."

I should leave.

I should continue walking back to my house, but I don't. Something stops me. Something beyond my control. I turn toward Paisley's father's garage just as it begins to close. I catch a glimpse of Alaric stepping into the house through the garage access, head in his hands.

Glancing at my own home, it seems as though Nico has ventured back inside. My gaze flickers down to Paisley on the ground, who's working her magic with the flowers, but I don't need to make my presence further known as Paisley's eyes haven't left me once.

"Are you coming over for dinner again?"

"Not tonight, no." I nod toward the pink flowers again, avoiding her stare because I know it's bound to unlock another question if I don't change the topic soon. "What are those flowers called again?"

"Geraniums."

"Right, geraniums. Well, I didn't mean to pull it out, kid. Those flowers must mean something special to you. Didn't mean to disrespect what you stand for."

Paisley's brows rise a fraction. "Are you… are you *apologizing*?"

Her comment draws a smile to my lips. "Maybe."

"Wow." She genuinely gasps. "And to respond to your previous comment about maintaining geraniums being a pain in the… well, *you know*, geraniums are perfectly easy to maintain. You just need to water them accordantly, speak to them, and not *unnecessarily rip them out.*"

"What the fuck, did you just say speak to them?"

"Yes, speak to them. Stop swearing."

I can't help but chuckle. "Do you *read* to your flowers too?"

Paisley rolls her eyes and turns back to her work, but not before a small hint of a smile crawls its way up her lips. She may never admit it, perhaps didn't even notice she did it at all or that I would pick up on it, but I did. I've seen it all, but this is something I thought I'd never see. Witnessing a smile come out of Paisley Reign, the one girl in this city I was beginning to think was born with the defect to smile. I mean, yeah, I'm one to talk, but Paisley smiling because of me? So fuckin' rare that if I hadn't seen it, I would have pinned the world ending before I saw a fraction of her upturned lips.

"Hold up. You actually do read to them, don't you?" I smirk.

"No... well, not novels anyway."

"What do you read to them then?"

She's silent for a second before she says, "Poetry."

"Don't worry," I murmur. "Your secret's safe with me, kid."

Paisley looks up at me with flushed cheeks. "What secret?" She bites down on her lip, squinting as the sun moves into her eyeline, illuminating her honey browns. "I don't have any secrets."

"Yeah, you do. You're a flower nerd and you know it."

Paisley laughs brightly, a cute snort escaping her, and I can't help but smile. "Am not!"

"Don't get so defensive, the government hasn't made it illegal... *yet.*"

"Go away, Saint," she says with the biggest grin I've ever seen on her lips.

I smile. "Not until you read me a stanza from your favorite poem."

"Never."

"Come on, Pais. One stanza and I'll leave you to keep on diggin.'"

Paisley looks away and begins to shake her head before halting. The beautiful smile on her lips transforms into a slight frown as she pulls off her grimy, vibrant pink gloves and sets them to the side, one on top of the other. If it were me, I would have thrown them to the side, but not Paisley—she's precise, organized, and my greatest nightmare living right next door.

Paisley dusts down her floral print yellow sundress and muddy knees before standing up before me. The distant sounds of rumbling car engines and children laughing in nearby front yards drown out at the look in her eyes. At how they're such perfect almonds and look into mine so deeply she has me gripped. It's like I'm the only one who can save her from a stare so potently rich of tales nobody ever dared to unravel or hear from her.

Standing before me isn't Paisley Reign the cigarette snatcher, crime stopper, or wildflower… it's simply *her*.

The depths of her pain will be laid out in the next word she speaks, in the poetic rhythm of her voice, in the very poet she chooses. You learn a lot about a person by their favorite line of poetry… and Paisley has unraveled me from the first day. How she shifts from timid to sweet to fierce. How she's so mature for her age. How she managed to seep through all the cracks in my soul and somehow, we've gone from flowers to poetry.

Nobody knows this. The boys would give me shit about it and to be honest, I've never needed to bring it up, but I know a thing or two about poets. The best of them turn madly insane by the time they reach thirty, with every stain of ink a representation of all the tears burning inside them like a lethal flame.

They keep their agony inside.

Slow river their anger across the page until they're drowning in a sea of nothingness.

Some of them don't make it to publish their work. The audience— the protagonists of their own destiny—seeps in the pain of the words and translates them to relate in their life. It's funny how people collect poetry like little pockets of hope and have faith in pulling somebody up from the deep end, but little do they know they've been refusing the anchor the entire time.

"Do you want me to…" Paisley swallows thickly in a fit of nerves. *Nerves.* This is what I don't understand about her, the push and pull of who she really is. "Do you want me to tell you who it's by first?"

"No, let me guess who after you say it."

"You know poetry?"

"I know a thing or two."

"Oh… I didn't know that." She clears her throat as if she's

preparing herself for the performance of her life. Her eyes are all over the place, from my boots to her hands to my eyes. "Okay. Ready?"

"Ready."

Paisley nods softly, keeping her head on my worn-out bikie boots, her voice even lower as she begins. "I've… I've looked for…" She shakes her head and turns away from me, her long, rich chocolate waves covering her face. "I'm sorry," she chokes out, her voice so low I barely catch her words. "I can't say it. Not today."

I furrow my brows. "Everything okay?"

"Mmhmmm."

"You know when somebody responds *mmhmmm*, it usually means yes, but I don't think that's the case here."

"Promise I'm okay, Saint," she whispers, but her tone gives it all away.

She's *not* okay.

"Paisley?"

"You can go. I'll be okay."

Go, Lisconti. She told you to go.

Turn the fuck around and get inside your house.

NOW.

I shake my head with a sigh and curse at the small fucking part of me that wants to help her. I don't know why. I don't know how. But I feel like I owe her something. I was the one to bring up the poetry and it seems as though it's exactly what set her off… *but why?*

Reaching out my hand, my fingers wrap around the soft cotton of her left wrist that's covered by her long-sleeved sundress. Paisley jerks her head to my hand at the action and just as I anticipated, I fall witness to the big tears rolling down her cheeks. It's crazy how the stiff tension between us for two years straight breaks away right in this moment.

I don't know for how long, or even the true reason why it does, but I know it's the right thing to do. It's as if our past fights, our past misunderstandings, our past troubles don't matter anymore.

Nothing else matters when my hand slips from her wrist.

Nothing else matters as my thumb slowly wipes her tears away.

Nothing else matters but those anguished doe eyes that find their way back up to mine.

Paisley isn't my opponent. She's a seventeen-year-old with no-where to go and no one to call home.

"Geraniums!" she blurts out suddenly, her glassy eyes snapping to mine as my thumb falls from her face. "Geraniums are one of the most popular greenhouse plants. They were first discovered in 1576 in Southern Europe. Versatile. They're a very versatile flower and can be utilized for cakes, teas, and other things like compresses. They love the sun and prefer damp but well-draining soil."

I arch a brow at the outburst of information. *Huh?*

"Something tells me that wasn't the poem."

"No, not the poem. Whenever I'm stressed, I say as much as I know about a flower. You… probably think it's weird."

"No, not weird at all," I assure with a genuine smile. "Just wasn't expecting it, that's all."

"Why are you being nice?"

"I'm being nice?"

Paisley gives me a side-eye and shoots me a small grin. "Yeah, nice."

"Guess I woke up on the right side of the bed, kid."

"You didn't. You pulled out one of the flowers from the root. That's definitely not waking up on the right side of the bed."

"Ah, *right*. All right, I just feel like it then."

"Well, it feels… strange."

I can't help but laugh. "Thanks for having faith in me, kid."

"Is your real name Saint?" she asks after the longest time.

A warm smile breaks on my lips because out of all the things she could have asked me, *this* is what she aspires to unravel. "No, well, technically yes, but my real name… it's…" I clear my throat, yet the burning knot remains. "It's Santo."

"Why Saint then?"

"Fighters are typically susceptible to nicknames. Mine was Saint, and it just stuck. Santo is also Saint in Italian."

Paisley nods twice as if she gets it. Sniffling, she wipes away her tears. "But you're no saint."

Anyone else who said that to me would already be six feet under, but with her, I find myself laughing. "Ironic, isn't it? Don't want to get into too much, but they call me that because I'm the opposite. But it's better the devil you know than the devil you don't, right?"

Again, Paisley nods. But this time, I'm not too sure she understands it.

"Sorry I couldn't say the poem. Tomorrow just isn't a good day for me and so today... it's hard. The poem... it's mine and I wrote it about somebody I loved." She shakes her head to herself with a deep sigh. "*Still* love. Tomorrow... it'll be three years since my nana died."

And just like that I find out my why.

Fuck. Paisley has it freaking hard.

"Sorry to hear that. I know what it feels like to lose somebody you love. Keep that poem to yourself, kid. Maybe one day I'll be mad enough to want to hear it."

"I don't think it's any good. Haven't performed it to anybody, not even my father."

"The flowers listened."

"And what good does that do?" She shrugs, as if it all doesn't matter, *but it does.*

"Well, they're still alive, aren't they?" I chuckle and when silence greets me, my expression falls. I turn to leave but just like before, something stops me in my tracks. I come back, rubbing my stubbled jaw twice over. "You know, Paisley, sometimes it's not about having a lot of people around. Sometimes it's just having that one person who makes everything feel okay and them filling the void of what a hundred people would."

"I like that, but there's only one problem."

"Go on."

"What do you do when that one person goes away?"

I know what she means and what she's opposing, but I give her another response anyway. "They'll come back eventually."

Paisley shakes her head adamantly. "No," she whispers and gestures up to the clouds up above. "What do you do when the only person you have leaves you?"

"I think it's about keeping their memory alive in all that you do."

"Yes, but there must be more than that."

I frown and look down. "Don't know, Pais. Haven't figured that part out yet myself."

"Neither have I."

I smile softly at those sad eyes and turn around, prepared to return home, when I hear the faintest call.

"Santo?"

I spin around, acknowledging how Paisley called me by my first name, but don't dare show what it does to me. I smooth my clenched jaw and let go of the tension in my broad shoulders, as well as my fists that have balled in my pockets.

After everything that happened, only two people call me by my real name.

Two.

"Yeah?"

Paisley looks up at me and a painfully hopeful smile rises on her lips. "Just let me know when you've figured it out, okay? I could really use the answer."

I stare at her for the longest time, wondering when the hell we got on civil ground. Something tells me it won't be like this again, always this peaceful, that soon we'll return to the fighting, but for now, right in this moment, understanding paves its way to acceptance.

I give Paisley a curt nod, keeping my eyes on her five-foot-three frame as I walk backward. At my gate, I shoot her the faintest smile before turning around into my front porch and losing sight of her, but never of the promise I vow to make her.

I will, I tell myself. *At whatever costs, I'll find it out for the both of us, kid.*

Chapter
FOUR

Paisley

PRESENT DAY
Paisley is 18. Saint is 35.

G*reat. Just great.*
    I can't believe I locked myself out of the house on a night like tonight. Not only is it my eighteenth birthday—not that I care much about it—but my father hasn't showed up yet, even though he should have finished work at the hospital by now... *this isn't like him.*

After all, he was the one to book dinner reservations at this new rustic Italian restaurant in the heart of Sacramento to encourage us to do something different when it comes to celebrations. But now, as I glance down at my watch and it veers onto seven o'clock, hope fades. I've been sitting on my wooden porch steps for an hour in this sweltering humidity of a day with no luck of getting the door unlocked as I left my phone, my purse, and house key inside.

Yeah, today is definitely not my day.

Earlier on, I thought I heard my father hoot his car horn and so I rushed outside in my floral satin robe to tell him I need a few more minutes as I was having trouble picking an outfit, only to find it was just a passing car and I had locked myself out in the hurry.

My only hope is that my dad returns home soon, but as time goes on, I'm not so sure. I can't even get up and render assistance in my half-naked state. With all limited options exhausted, I run my hands over my face and through my wavy, dark hair.

How can you do this to yourself, Paisley?

I shake my head at just how unlucky one person can be. *This could only happen to me.*

Just when I think I may die in here… I hear *it,* the engine roar of road thunder. I know that sound. I've heard it during all hours of the day and night for the past three years… a Harley's rumble. It's loud and clear in the middle of my despair.

A dark, shiny Harley Davidson turns into my street here on Portola Way, alongside three other similar bikes that follow close behind in a V-type formation. The vibrating engines grip at my chest, trembling my entire soul. *I can only hope it's Saint.*

Although I'm not too sure what Saint can do to help seeing as he gave me back the only spare key he had for my house at the start of the year when I began working part-time at Maralyn's Florist. It's senior year and I needed a key to enter after walking home from my shifts. My father said he was going to copy another spare for Saint because it's always good for him to have in case of an emergency, but with work being so hectic he hasn't had the chance to do it yet.

But… maybe just maybe Saint can help me out of this mess.

Or, maybe he can tell me what's keeping Dad seeing as my phone is inside my house.

The four motorbikes kill their engines in front of Saint's house, striking down their kickstands almost synchronously. It almost seems like a scene out of an outlaw movie, a gang of tattered-up men, leather jackets their tough uniform, three with full-face helmets and another younger-looking man I don't recognize with a black bandana with skulls and crossbones and a buzz cut.

I lower my legs and cross them over the porch steps, well aware I only have hipster panties on and a bra that's too small for me underneath this satin robe. The frilly white lace bra exposes way more cleavage than I would ever show, and the robe doesn't do too good of a job hiding it.

I gulp down hard at the sight of Saint pulling off his full-face helmet. *Whoa.* After resting his black helmet on the handlebars of his Harley, Saint rakes a hand through his beautiful dark hair, giving it that sexy bad boy tousled look. His vibrant blue eyes entice me from feet away and he isn't even looking my way. Just then, he laughs at something inaudible Leo says, and those deep, long dimples come to play over his short, stubbled beard.

Aside from Leo, Nico's also present, but as they all swing off their sleek bikes, Saint speaks to the unfamiliar younger-looking man.

I don't know what to do. Don't know if I should approach him or let it go and wait it out a little longer for my father. My decision chooses for itself when the four men begin to approach the gate of Saint's house and I launch up from the wooden porch, unexpectedly catching the attention of the younger man.

He nudges Leo and nods toward me with a sly smirk. "Look at that fuckin' hot babe," he says, his voice booming. "Hey, baby! I'm sure there's a spot open at the new strip joint that just opened downtown if you want to give your incredible tits a run for their money."

Oh.

My.

God.

My eyes widen in shock. *What the hell?*

The nerve of this guy!

The man roars in laugher, capturing the attention of all the other men… including Saint, but he isn't laughing, he's livid. I've never seen eyes like his turn to stone-cold black so quickly as his attention snaps to the younger man.

Loud thuds in my chest trail up my body like burning waves of electricity. Lethal electricity. I simply stand here on my porch steps, gaping and incapable of saying a single word.

"Saint, I didn't know Alaric's little girl grew up that fast. Oh, she's looking at me now. Hey, baby, want me to put that gorgeous mouth of yours to work?" The young man winks, a full-blown smirk on his lips as he suggestively clutches his crotch. "Time of your fuckin' life. Believe me."

I cringe. *For the love of God, can I just punch this guy in the nose already?*

Just as I'm about to tell him to shove his comment up his ass, Saint has him in a headlock faster than I can blink. Saint's muscular, toned right arm wraps around the guy's neck, restricting him firmly. *Whoa.*

"Shut the fuck up and listen to me, you bastard," Saint grits near the man's ear. "Don't you dare fuckin' speak to Paisley or any damn woman like that. She's not yours to fucking comment on, so keep your damn hands and eyes off her before I mess you the hell up. Understood?"

Oh my God.

The young man simply chuckles, redness crawling up his face. "Come on, man, I was just teasing. She's hot, that's all." His hands grip onto Saint's muscles to loosen the strain, but Saint doesn't allow it and instead tightens it. It takes seconds for the man to gulp down and begin coughing, slapping on Saint's arms to let go, but he doesn't do a thing. "Okay, okay, okay, I understand. This won't happen again. Promise."

"She's Alaric's daughter. She doesn't need to hear the shit that comes out of your mouth, got it?"

"Yes, got it. You can let go of me."

"I let go of you whenever I fucking feel like it, got it, Jason?"

"Yes, got it." Jason nods, gasping for air.

Saint's jaw tightens when his eyes meet mine in a lingering gaze. It's as if he's staring straight through me. Jason struggles in Saint's grip, tensing in the chokehold. Nico and Leo simply watch on as if this is a normal Friday night. Leo even pulls out a cigarette to his lips and leans against the fence, his leather boot up against it. *Normal.*

But it isn't to me.

This isn't *normal.*

Not even in the slightest.

Scarlet blotches rise on Jason's face as his hands fall away from Saint's bicep when Saint lets go. Jason falls to his knees, massaging his neck in a fit of coughs. "Fuck. *Fuck!*"

"Talk to Paisley like that again and you'll wake up in a hospital or perhaps not even at all, you piece of shit." Saint kicks him hard in the groin and Jason lets out a howl, gripping his crotch with a hand, his head to the concrete ground. My neighbor dusts off his leather jacket and turns to the other men. "Get him inside. All of you."

Oh my…

What the hell just happened?

My eyes lock with Saint until it's just us around. The back of my throat has never felt this dry, and it only worsens as Saint walks up to me, his jaw clenched. I see tension in every single part of him, and yet he's still the most beautiful man I have ever laid eyes on. Yes, he's a little older than me, well, *a lot* older... eighteen years older to be exact—but that never stopped a woman from looking before... *or ahem, gawking.*

I can't peel my eyes away from how damn sexy and reckless Saint looks. He's getting closer and I love the way his white T-shirt hugs his solid pecs and biceps and how his jeans are that perfect shade of worn-out baby blue. His light outfit complements his beautiful Italian olive skin and the stunning dark ink that laces down his left sleeves, stopping short of his wrist.

For the first time since we met, Saint stood up for me.

He was there for me.

Protected me.

The first thing Saint does when he's in front of me is grip the edges of my robe and inch them closer together, hiding away my breasts. My eyes shut at the warmth of his calloused knuckles brushing against my cleavage. I know it's by accident. A quick accidental motion as he closes my robe up and pulls away, but I still feel sparks I know I shouldn't feel about him.

We live in completely different worlds. He's the bad boy. I'm the good girl. He shouldn't come to my rescue like this. I shouldn't have these sparks spreading across my entire body. It's the same odd sensation that grips me when I reopen my eyes to his ocean eyes and instantly shut them again.

Stop feeling like this.

Stop making something out of nothing, Paisley.

Saint's touch lingers and he raises his hand to softly caress my jaw. In one sweep motion, he pushes back a loose wave behind my ear and rests his thumb against my chin to lift my head to him. Every inch of his warm touch electrifies me. "You okay, kid?"

I meet his eyes and manage to nod. "I am now. Do you know where my father is?"

"Work emergency at the hospital. He told me to let you know he's going to be a little late as he couldn't get through to you."

Makes sense.

"Oh," I whisper, gulping down.

Fumbling with my hands, my gaze meets my shoes and I let out a heavy breath.

At least Dad's okay.

The air crackles as silence takes over between us. I try to concentrate on the warm Sacramento breeze… on the sidewalk trees as they rustle in the air, leaves swaying… on anything, but with my wildly beating heart, it isn't so easy.

"Paisley, what's going on?" Saint raises my chin higher until his eyes are all I see. "Why were you out here when I arrived?"

"Well… I kind of locked myself out."

"Then let me help you get back in." He pauses for a moment. "Let me also apologize on behalf of Jason for what happened. He's a newbie Nico is training. What he said was beyond unacceptable and disrespectful. Don't know why Nico didn't say anything. But don't worry, it won't happen again. You can trust me on that."

I smile. "Thank you, Saint. I really appreciate it."

Inside, my eyes are widening in pure shock because this is such a different man from when we first met. I don't expect Saint to be here for me, protecting me. We don't matter to each other like that. For the past three years, it's been tense conversation and glares, but for some reason, that isn't tonight.

In the past year, my disdain for Saint turned into having a crush on my father's best friend. I don't know when exactly *everything* changed but I feel as though *something* changed the day I attempted to perform to him the lines of poetry I've kept buried inside me.

Now, I feel my walls slowly coming down and that the dynamic between us is shifting.

I'm not sure into what, but it's *shifting*.

"Also, thanks for standing up for me." I casually wrap my arms around my waist. "It means a lot."

"Anytime." Saint's eyes flicker down to my cleavage, and he instantly snaps his attention away from me, pinching the bridge of his nose. "Jesus Christ, Paisley," he groans.

I glance down and gasp. "Shit! I knew I shouldn't have put this bra on. I freaking hate it!"

"Yeah, I didn't need to hear that." Clearing his throat, Saint grips the back collar of his white T-shirt and peels it over his body. *Oh, wow.* He simply hands it to me to wear while he stands there looking like some shirtless sex god. "Here, put this on."

I'm left gaping and not so subtly eyeing Saint's beautifully sculpted abs, narrow waist, and that vaunted V-cut for a little too long... *but I can't help it.* It's hot and tempting and laced in undeniable desire. Arousal heats my blood as I fixate a little too long on the sexy, short trail of dark hair beneath his navel that runs down the center of his V-cut and disappears into the waistband of his jeans. *Oh my good God... so sexy.*

Being a former professional boxer and current personal trainer, there's no denying how much Saint's body screams grit and endless resilience from maintained fitness. I love all the ridges, grooves, divots along his body. Love the devotion and thrill that must come from not only *being* your best self, but *feeling* your best and also putting that into a career.

I've admired the tattoos across Saint's body too many times to count in this past year alone. I've been in his pool countless times, subtly absorbing every detail of his left arm sleeve and astonishing back tattoos whenever he and my dad are working the barbeque and not looking.

God, get yourself together, girl.

Gulping down, I know I need to snap myself out of it... *for now.*

Thanking Saint, I pull his shirt over my robe, his warmth and that alluring, masculine scent of musky sandalwood flooding my every breath. The T-shirt is extremely oversized on me and reaches my mid-thigh, but I guess it's better than flashing unwanted cleavage at my father's best friend... *a man so off-limits.*

"All right, come with me, I have some tools in my shed to get this door opened up."

I follow suit behind Saint, entering his front yard and turning left alongside the side of his house. As we enter the already open side gate that leads to his backyard, my eyes snap to the huge epic work of art on his back. A thick, black-gray outlined cross runs down his spine, stopping at his mid-back, almost as if it's 3D. Vines of shadowed roses, thorns, and leaves wrap around the cross. It's beautiful, almost as if it's a tribute to somebody special as breathtakingly rendered wide angel wings lace underneath the top half of the cross, expanding up his back and broad shoulders. Then, at the bottom of the cross, a few inches above the two perfect dimples of Venus on his lower back, is a name written in a thin cursive script…

Lea.

It's as if his back tattoo tells a story of its own. Such beautiful ink.

Who's Lea?

Saint enters the shed, a little far from the pool, while I wait by the grass. Staring into the glass pocket doors on the adjacent side of his backyard that open to his living room, I eye his friends inside. The three men are all huddled in the living room; Nico cracks open beers, while Leo is deep into a conversation with him on the leather couch. Jason, on the other hand, is limping toward them. My gaze narrows on him, softening as I turn back to Saint.

"Where did you all come from?" I ask.

"The fitness studio." Saint's voice comes from inside the shed.

"*Oh.*"

"Why? What did you think I was gonna say? Church?"

My eyes widen. "*Church?*"

Saint emerges from the shed chuckling as he holds up a black leather tool bag. "Good reaction. You won't see me in there. I wouldn't be allowed into the Jesus type of church, only the devil's kind."

A few moments pass.

"Just wondering, why don't you fight anymore? I asked my father once, but he didn't give me much. What secrets are you hiding?"

"No secrets." Saint clears his throat, avoiding my gaze. "There comes a stage when you need to let go and not overdo it after your peak."

"That's true. I can imagine that personal training is incredible, don't get me wrong, but I guess with you being so much in the industry you could have ventured into being a boxing coach instead, no?"

"Yeah, I could've but… let's just say at times life fucks with you and you can't always obtain what you love. So, I switched careers and focused on personal training. I teach self-defense, boot camps, and all that shit instead. It's better for my headspace."

"Were any of your fights televised?"

"All." Saint arches a playful brow. "Why? What are you scheming against me, Paisley Reign?"

"Nothing at all."

"I don't believe you…"

"I promise!" I find myself laughing, softly biting down on my lip when he shoots me a slow, beautiful smile. "I just… want to see one of the boxing fights you were in, but I guess it just feels weird searching you up online when I know you personally, you know?"

Saint's smile instantly falls.

Oh…

His eyes fall away from mine. "Don't look me up. I don't want you to see that side of me, Paisley."

"Why not? Want to keep the reputation of being my knight in shining armor for five minutes out of the three years I've known you?" I tease.

"You know I'm anything but that."

"Okay, I'm sorry. I just wanted to see you in your element. Understand you more."

That has his ocean eyes snap to mine. "There's nothing more to understand about me, Paisley. I shouldn't…" He shakes his head, blowing out a sigh. "I shouldn't intrigue you or be somebody you want to know. You're my best friend's daughter. We live next door. We're amicable now. That's it. Don't try and find me, or watch me, or anything. Just concentrate on senior year. On yourself. On your future. You shouldn't give a fuck about me."

It feels as though my heart has taken a hit and I don't even know why. Yes, I have feelings for him, a big, reckless crush, but I'm curious. I want to know more, everything there is to know about Saint Lisconti if that's possible. But he doesn't want me in. He doesn't want me to see that side of him. He leaves me no choice but to just accept it.

"I'm sorry. I just thought…" Not even knowing what point I wanted to make, I remain tight-lipped. Glancing down at the grass beneath my feet, I feel Saint's hot gaze on me. "I just thought we could get to know each other better if we want to be amicable like you said."

"There's nothing good about me, Paisley."

"Well, a part of me is inclined to believe that, but what I really feel like saying is *yeah, right*," I murmur and clasp my hands together. "I'm sure your girlfriend wouldn't say that."

"I don't have a girlfriend. I'm not seeing anybody."

"I know… I'm just saying in the future. Your future girlfriend or fiancée or wife will love you for you, with all the bad parts included.

That doesn't mean there's nothing good about you. Just that you have faults and flaws, just like every other human on this planet."

"But that's just the thing, Paisley, I don't do love or real relationships in that case. Not now. Not in the future. It isn't me, so you can forget about the lovin' part."

"Why only casual relationships?"

Yes, you really did just say that out loud, Paisley.

Saint stares at me long and hard. "Because in a world like mine, love isn't forever, and in my case, not even for a flash of a second."

It takes a split second to fully grasp what he said. A question brews in my mind, one I wanted to know ever since I set eyes on him returning home tonight. I'm eighteen now, and to be honest, ever since last year something changed for me whenever he looked my way. When he asked me about saying a line of poetry and wiped away my tears, his touch was electric. I wanted more of him, just like I crave more of him now, even though I know I'm nothing to him. *Nothing.*

"Does that mean you've *fucked* but have never actually *made love* before?" I blurt out.

Oh. My. God.

Holy sunflowers, does my mouth not know when to just shut it?

You're a fool, Paisley. Fool. Fool. Fool.

Saint's shoulders tense, but he gives me nothing more. Absolutely nothing. Not a hint of a smile. Nothing in his eyes. He remains completely motionless as the bright sun casts over his face.

I groan, feeling my cheeks flush. "I'm so sorry. I didn't mean to overstep by asking—"

"I don't deserve love. I haven't deserved it for a long time. Does that answer your question?"

Why doesn't he deserve it?

Does it have to do with Lea?

"Yes," I whisper, gulping down. "Yes, it does."

It's just like I suspected it to be. Saint is the type of man to fuck hard and fast, not sensually slow and passionate with somebody he truly loves and would go to the end of the earth for… *but why?* It shouldn't concern me so much. I know it shouldn't, especially considering I've never had either and he's eighteen years older, so forbidden… and yet right now it's *just us* and that has me thinking wild things. *Very* bad, wild things.

What is Saint hiding?

He doesn't want me to see his past fights.

Doesn't do love.

Doesn't want me to call him by his real first name.

He's hurting. But from what?

Does my father know? *They're super close. He must know.* But asking my father about his close friend... I can't do it. It's too risky. My father can't know the slightest bit about this fascination I have with his friend. How I just want Saint to see me as something more than the little girl with lilies.

I'm not little anymore. I'm a woman and I know what I want. And that something is Saint. I want to feel his strong arms wrapped around me, his warm lips pressed on mine. I want to feel his rough stubble graze my inner thighs as he takes me to pure ecstasy, pure bliss.

Hmmm. A woman can dream. Just like I did last night when I imagined my vibrator was his tongue and came so damn intensely at the mere thought of that alone. *God. So incredible.*

"Stay in the house while I get your door open."

I snap out of my thoughts at Saint's call as he ventures past me. *Huh?* I'm breathing heavy and only register what he said moments later. Getting his attention, I gesture toward the glass pocket doors. "You mean you want me to go in there with your friends?"

"That's what I said, didn't I?"

"Honestly, I..." I swallow the lump in my throat. "I don't really feel comfortable going in there with them after what Jason said."

"He'll behave himself this time, trust me. Just knock on the pocket doors and one of the guys will open it for you. I'll come around when I'm done with your front door, all right?"

Saint doesn't even give me a chance to answer before he strolls away from me, rolling his shoulders back. *Damn. Is he pissed at me?*

Have I ruined everything?

I'm left standing in the middle of his yard, numb and completely frozen as I eye the pocket doors. *I don't want to go in there.* I've never been in a room with men like those before and I don't want today to be the day I find out. I want to follow Saint. *Wow, 'follow Saint'...* how the tables have turned.

And yet it's exactly what I do as my slippers crush the fresh green grass with every jog toward him. I catch up to Saint, only for him to stop in his tracks, and I crash right into his hard, muscular back. *Shit.* I stumble back with a squeal and land right on my ass in the gravel.

Ouch!

Saint turns to me, arching an amused brow as he eyes me on the ground. "You losing it, kid?"

"You still call me that. I'm not a kid anymore. I prefer Paisley."

Saint stares at my breasts through the T-shirt and I feel my nipples harden. My heart is pounding, my entire body throbbing in anticipation of the thoughts clouding my mind. But Saint doesn't give me much. He simply nods and rubs his stubbled jaw with his free hand, as if he's relieving some tension. "Yeah…" He clears his throat. "Clearly not a kid anymore."

The air crackles between us.

Say something, Paisley.

ANYTHING!

"I'd rather stay with you and wait by my porch while you open my front door, Saint."

Saint glances at me for the longest time, as if he's considering it, then at the last minute averts his gaze to the tool bag he's holding. "But I may take a little while as I have to go through this shit and figure out how to unlock the door. You and I both know I'm not calling a locksmith. You'll probably be waiting on your porch with me for a little while…"

"Yeah, that's fine with me."

"Well, it's not with me. I'm not giving into you, Paisley." Saint sighs, pinching the bridge of his nose before slightly crouching down to take my hand in his. His grip is strong, electric, confident… everything I'm not as he helps me back to my feet.

His hand slips away from mine the second we turn back to his backyard, and he knocks on the pocket glass doors. Leo slides them open, smiling kindly at the both of us as we peek our heads inside. I bite my lip and offer a shy smile back while brushing myself off. The other two men snap their attention our way and Jason instantly rolls his eyes at me.

"As you're all aware by now, this is Paisley. She's Alaric's daughter," Saint announces, so tall and confident. "Paisley will be here for a few moments until I unlock her front door. Leave her the fuck alone or you'll deal with me, got it?"

All the men nod.

Saint turns to me. "Feeling okay?"

I swallow thickly and let go of a heavy breath. "Sure."

Yet deep down I feel uncomfortable, and somehow, Saint must manage to see that because next thing I know he curses and says, "Fine, come with me, Paisley."

Back at my front porch steps, I watch him work his magic on my front door. The grin hasn't left my lips since we walked back. I love how he was able to understand me.

"I thought a guy like you could kick front doors open." I smirk.

Saint chuckles. "If I did that, I'd break it off the hinges. You and your father would both kill me if that happened."

We share a brief warm smile before he turns back to the door in silence, unscrewing a part and jiggling a few things around. It's as if he's an expert at this, as if everything he touches turns to gold.

Biting my lip, I lean back against the wooden railing, eyeing the gorgeous beast in front of me. This definitely feels like one of those moments where I should have my phone to film him in his element on YouTube or TikTok and the video goes viral with millions of views. Saint lets out a rough groan as the screwdriver slips from his grip and he picks it back up, but the groan comes out all breathy. So damn sexy.

Yeah, this is definitely one of those viral moments.

I try to concentrate on something else.

The tense silence.

Birds chirping in the distance.

Cars rushing down our street.

An instant replay in my mind of the 'making love' question I asked him.

I shake my head to myself. *Oh God. I can't believe I actually said that to him.*

"Saint?"

"Mhmmm."

"I'm sorry if I made things awkward back then. I didn't mean to mak—"

"It's already forgotten."

"Thank you," I whisper in relief. "Also, thank you for before. For making me feel comfortable."

"It's all right."

More silence, and then…

"Where were you heading tonight?" he asks.

"Out to dinner with Dad, but as I now know he'll be a little late… it's my eighteenth."

"Nothing from your mom again this year?"

"Nothing."

"So, for now you'll be alon—"

"Alone? Yep," I sniffle, unshed tears coating my eyes. "I'm sorry. I don't mean to get this emotional about it or play the role of the victim. That's not what this is at all. I'm just thinking about my mom and how different life would have been if I had known her."

"But you *are* the victim, Paisley. There's constantly victimizing, but then there's also not seeing ourselves as the victim enough, so we eventually cave from the inside in, and the latter is what you are doing and it's going to end up killing you inside if you don't feel those emotions. If you feel hurt, allow yourself to feel it. Don't make excuses for it when you're the unfortunate victim in this story with your mom." Saint jerks his head over his shoulder but never completes the full turn to actually look at me. A sob escapes my mouth and I cover it just as his sharp jaw clenches. "Maybe it's not my place to talk, Paisley… but you deserve so much more than how she treated you by abandoning you and your father. You really do."

His words engrave deep into my soul.

You deserve so much more.

"Thank you. In a way it's all I know, seeing as she left before I could even remember, but it still hurts."

"You have every right to be hurt. Every single fucking one."

Something crosses my mind. "Any leads in figuring out what to do when the only person you have leaves you?"

"Working on it, Pais."

"Okay," I whisper, just as he unlocks the door and swings it open. "Oh, thank you!"

A desperate relief rushes over me as we stand up. Saint has his head down, hands in his jean pockets as I pull off his T-shirt and wordlessly hand it to him. He takes it with a soft nod and slides it back on. For a moment, I ruminate over the idea of my jasmine scent now mixed with his.

"You can come in if you like…" I offer.

The corner of Saint's mouth twitches into a smirk. "No permission this time from your father or with your signed paper and contract?" "Oh my God, no!" I laugh. "None of that. Plus, that was ages ago!" Saint grins, dimples and all, and it's one of the first times I've seen one last more than a few seconds. He shakes his head softly. "I should get back to the boys. I'm heading out to a fight soon but seeing as your father will be late... if you need me for whatever reason, I'll come back for you."

My heart squeezes. All I feel is warmth. "Oh, you don't have to do that!"

Saint smiles sadly, "Yeah, I do. Nobody deserves to be alone on their birthday. Even girls who are overprotective over lilies."

Fresh tears well in my eyes and without thinking, I run up to him at full speed. Saint responds instantly, catching me as my legs wrap around his waist and he laces his big arms around me in a bear hug. Arms around his neck, I bury my head in his collar, taking in his cologne as he simply holds me through the trembling tears.

He doesn't know how much this moment means to me.

Saint's fingers softly lace through my hair, relaxing me with every touch as he massages the back of my head. I never imagined a man like Saint could hug so well, so tight with no roughness, to be so responsive to me, to witness my vulnerability without judgment.

We don't have to say a word. It just feels right. *He* makes me feel right. It's as if he understands it all and I've never had that. Never had somebody I could silently vent to. Not even my father. He would cut me off, tell me to think of other things, but the insecurity and pain remain, burning me deep, and that's something nobody else seems to understand... *except Saint.*

"I'm sorry," I sniffle after a while. "I don't know why I'm crying."

Still wrapped in him, Saint lifts my chin higher, so his eyes are the anchors to my rising tides. "Don't you ever apologize for feeling emotion, Paisley. *Ever.*"

Our embrace turns so much more intimate. We're so close as I rest my forehead against his. I feel the sparks envelop my entire body as his hot breath lands on my lips, our eyes shutting as he holds me even tighter to him. I swear if Saint were to rest his hand by my chest right this minute, he'd feel just how crazily it beats... *for him.*

"Promise me," he murmurs against my lips. "Promise me you'll never apologize for it."

"I promise," I whisper back, giving into temptation and blindly cupping his stubbled jaw. "I promise I won't, Saint."

"Good."

My cheeks heat as he sets me down and my feet hit the ground. I leave the door open and step inside, shaking my head to myself at my phone and purse that are right there by the hall table. When I step back out onto the porch, I hand Saint my phone to write his number in my contacts. I don't know why we haven't done this sooner, perhaps because he's just one house away, but it's good to have his number, especially in a case of an emergency with my father.

Excuses, excuses, excuses.

Saint saves his number, calls himself so he has mine too, and once he's done slips his phone back inside his pocket. Smiling, he hands me my phone. "Anything you need, just call me, okay?"

"Okay. Thank you, Saint. I really appreciate it."

"No trouble. Even if you need a ride to work after school or on the weekends, I'm here."

"Why are you helping me?"

Saint parts his lips, pausing for a moment. "Because maybe I got you all wrong, Pais."

Maybe I got you all wrong.

I blink up at him, astonished. "What's that supposed to mean?"

Saint simply shrugs, but there's so much in his clouded eyes he doesn't allow me time to analyze as he says, "Nothing." And then he's gone.

Once inside my house, I shut the door and head to my bedroom. Stripping down, I put on my favorite floral pajamas and make my own dinner—chicken and rice. Just when I'm about to strain the rice, my phone buzzes, and I rush to it, thinking that perhaps it could be Saint, but my thoughts come crashing down when I read the text.

It isn't Saint, it's from my father.

DAD: Sorry, sweetheart, I have to cancel our plans for tonight. Work emergency. Don't think I'll finish until 10 p.m. or so. I'll make it up to you, Paisley. Promise.

I spend the rest of my night browsing the net for new flowers and writing poetry. At a quarter to ten, just as I'm about to slip into bed, the doorbell buzzes. I hurry downstairs and swing the front door open, only to find there's nobody there.

Weird.

I'm just about to shut the door when something on the faded 'welcome' mat catches my attention. A white box with a yellow satin bow.

What's this?

Collecting it, I step inside and press my back against the oak front door. There's a little envelope attached to the bow, but my curiosity has me opening the box first. A gasp escapes me at what's inside. A huge cupcake with buttercream frosting shaped in a flawless pink rose. It's the most beautiful design I've ever seen in my entire life!

Ecstatic, I pull out the card and my jaw drops right there and then.

Finally, a flower I won't step on...
Happy Birthday, wildflower.

There's no sign-off, but there doesn't have to be. Not after a night like tonight and not for a man like him. *Saint. This is from Saint.* He was so raw and compassionate with me tonight, it was like a dream the way he defended me, clasped my hand, held me through my tears.

Maybe he was right…

Maybe I've gotten you all wrong too, Saint.

My mind can't stop racing. *He called me wildflower.*

Back inside my bedroom, I devour the sweet red velvet cupcake in a flash and send him a text.

Paisley: Wow, what a surprise! Thanks for making everything better, Saint. xx

My heart clenches as I hold my breath and await his response. I feel all these butterflies in the pit of my stomach, threatening to unravel and let go.

The '*delivered*' under my text message instantly changes to '*read*'. Saint sees my text within seconds but never replies.

Want to continue reading *Oceans of Us*?

Read Saint and Paisley's age gap, father's best friend forbidden romance today! *Oceans of Us* is available and FREE on Kindle Unlimited!

Acknowlegments

Elijah and Rosalia abruptly emerged into my head at 2:30a.m., and by dawn, I had already written the first 7,000-words of their story. Their voices echoed loudly, getting more vivid with every second. Their love unfolded just as messy and complex as the people they are.

Rosalia Philips and Elijah Diesel are my favorite couple I've written, for they challenged me a lot. The angst, classic romance, music… I loved writing every aspect of their story, sinking into the core of Diesel Rose and writing every lyric. Those were special too.

Writing their story was addicting, and at times, not even I knew what was coming next because they took on a mind of their own. It felt like their healing journey, and I was happy to be witness to it all. *Onyx colored butterflies…* I felt that while writing this rockstar romance. **Remember I'm Yours** and **Diesel Rose** shows we're not, nor can we ever be, perfectly perfect, and that is *okay*. Flaws are *okay*. Just be kind to yourself. And your heart. That matters too.

Elijah challenged me at times. He was that sweet spot between psychopath and morally gray. His complexities were deep, his hurt deeper, but I truly believe he needed Rosalia to survive and escape the ominous darkness. He needed his muse. Just like she needed her Lijah.

Ellie and Emily, thank you for polishing the manuscripts and making them so perfect!

Gemma, you're always my cheerleader. Thank you for proofing and loving these two!

Stacey, you're beautiful. Thank you for the gorgeous formatting & making me smile!

Lori and Kim, thank you so much for the BEAUTIFUL covers & your dedication!

Daniel, thank you for the stunning Remember I'm Yours picture. Appreciate you!

Mamma, I love you more than words exists. *Grazie di cuore. Ti amo per sempre.*

Nonno and Nonna, *vi amo entrambi per sempre. Grazie.*

My author and blogger friends for always being by my side, for showing my work so much love. My wonderful babes over in my

Facebook Reader Group: *Vanessa Luisa's Lovelies*—I adore all of you too. ARC readers & PR team, thank you, I'm so grateful!

And last but not least, big thank you to all my beautiful readers, because without you all this wouldn't be possible. Thank you for adoring my words and all your love. Love you!

Vanessa Luisa xo

Also by
VANESSA LUISA

The Giannotti World:
An interconnected series of bittersweet romance standalones set in Seattle.

Merciful Vows (#1)

DIESEL ROSE:
The poetically tragic rock star and his muse…

Remember I'm Yours (#0.5)

Diesel Rose (#1)

STANDALONES:

Oceans of Us

Kisses in Heartache

Happy reading!
Vanessa Luisa xo

About the
AUTHOR

Vanessa Luisa is a contemporary romance author. She resides in Melbourne, Australia, with her army of current reads, sassy cat, and Tom Hardy…the latter is purely all in her mind, but shh don't tell her!

She loves writing angsty, emotionally gripping, sexy romance with passionate alphas and strong-willed women. Her love of reading and writing have always been with her, and while she has a background in certified personal styling, nowadays she's turning her dream of being an author into reality.

She adores all things from the Golden Age of Hollywood, Seinfeld and believes tea is a writing essential. When she isn't writing, she's busy running her own business and spending time with loved ones.

Vanessa loves interacting with readers so please feel free to reach out to her via socials, subscribe to her newsletter, and/or contact her at vanessaluisaauthor@gmail.com for any questions or comments.

Connect With
VANESSA LUISA

Join my Facebook Reader's Group: www.facebook.com/groups/
vanessaluisaslovelies

**Subscribe to my MAILING LIST/NEWSLETTER to be notified
of new releases, behind the scenes, and receive exclusive bonus
material:** www.vanessaluisa.com/contact

Instagram: @thevanessaluisa
www.instagram.com/thevanessaluisa

Facebook: www.facebook.com/vanessaluisaauthor/

TikTok: @thevanessaluisa
www.tiktok.com/@thevanessaluisa

Twitter: @thevanessaluisa
www.twitter.com/thevanessaluisa

Follow me on Goodreads:
www.goodreads.com/author/show/21142369.Vanessa_Luisa

Follow me on Amazon:
www.amazon.com/Vanessa-Luisa/e/B08W1V47PC

Follow me on Pinterest:
www.pinterest.com.au/thevanessaluisa/

Follow me on Spotify:
open.spotify.com/user/itisnessa

Follow me on Bookbub:
www.bookbub.com/authors/vanessa-luisa

Website/Blog: vanessaluisa.com